IRON
PRINCE

IRON PRINCE

BRYCE O'CONNOR
LUKE CHMILENKO

For the developers, designers, artists, staff and every other mind and talent behind the incredible games that inspired a passion for characters like Reidon Ward.

PROLOGUE

EARLY DECEMBER, 2461

ASTRA SYSTEM – ASTRA-2 – SECTOR 22

"Progress in CAD technology over the last two centuries has proven itself the single most valuable advancement humanity has made in our war efforts. When firearms and the largest portion of our other ballistic weaponry lost all value against the enemy's reactive fielding and adaptive armor capabilities, all that remained to mankind was to chase after the same sort of armaments. It took decades, but from the moment Devices and their Users start heading for the front lines, we found a foothold once again in what had long been thought a lost battle."

Essentials of Simulated Combat in Military Training
Lieutenant Colonel Hana von Geil, Ph.D.

And THERE IT *IS*, ladies and gentlemen!" the match announcer shouted with what could only be described as genuine glee, his voice crackling over the worn speakers of the Matron Kast's ancient pad. "The Iron Bishop's Repulsion has sent Alex Rightor flying! Will she—*YES*! Valera Dent is chasing, following up with a *vicious* barrage of strikes. The Defense spec of Captain Rightor's Carnus is no joke, but the Bishop is peerless in finding vulnerable attack points with her Kestrel. Two blades are always better than one and—*OH*! Rightor lands a heavy kick, and it's the chief warrant officer's turn be sent sailing! I must say, this is a fight for the ages!"

In the small hands of an 11-year-old boy, the borrowed pad vibrated lightly with every exclamation the announcer provided. It didn't bother the child. It made the fight that much more enrapturing, and even if he hadn't been able to see the two S-Rank CAD-Users going at it he thought he might have managed to imagine the details of the bout just from the descriptions.

Fortunately, the Matron kept the clear smart-glass tablet in good condition, and so it was with wide eyes in a dark room that the boy watched Valera Dent and Alex

Rightor break against each other like titans made of flashing light and carbonized steel.

As an exhibition match in commemoration of Valera Dent's retiring from the professional SCT circuit, the field had been randomly selected. The two Users fought in 30 yards of open grassland—the standard size of any competitive Dueling ring—their movements completely uninhibited by obstacles or deterrents that were commonplace in other zones. No trees. No buildings. No scattered stockpiles or crates. It allowed for a truly unfettered view of the fight, and the child who had snuck into Kast's office to watch didn't think for a second he was the only one pleased with the choice.

Captain Alex Rightor's Carnus was a breathtaking Device. As an S-Rank, his CAD covered every inch of his body, forming an intricate battle suit whose interlocking plating shimmered and shifted with each movement the man made. The standard tricolor, it was mostly gold and green steel with accents of light blue vysetrium, and it complimented its User's stellar Strength and Defense specs with its bulk. Rightor was a Mauler-Type, the initial form Carnus had manifested as undoubtedly having been some basic design of the massive two-handed hammer the man was now whirling at his smaller, lighter enemy. As the Device and its User had grown in ability, though, so too had Carnus upgraded and evolved. To the boy taking in the captain now, Rightor reminded him of a lion, powerful and graceful despite his massive size.

On the other hand, when it came to grace, Alex Rightor was outmatched twice over by his opponent.

Chief Warrant Officer Valera Dent moved with the speed and elegance of some great raptor of war. Kestrel's externals—suspended over both her shoulders—completed the illusion almost too well, the eight angular modules floating like the broad, red feathers of metallic wings. They served a purpose, of course, allowing Dent to channel her CAD's electromagnetic energy freely, granting her the ability to skate over the twisting grass of the plains without so much as a hint of effort. Her Device was the antithesis of Rightor's. It was spare and dignified, a mirage of minimal red plating over a skin-tight blue under-layer, detailed in glowing white. All of Dent's vitals were armored, but Kestrel sacrificed S-Rank Defense for the Speed and Offense that had made short work of so many of the Iron Bishop's opponents in her years on the circuit. Even the woman's weapons could not have been more different, a pair of identical, narrow sabers whose handles and blades matched the colors of her armor, ivory vysetrium forming long, florid edges.

"Oh!" The announcer's narration came through again loudly. "Captain Rightor has thrown his hammer in an attempt to bring Dent down! This can only mean one thing—YES! Magnetic Hunt! An Ability both of these fearsome opponents share! As you can see, ladies and gentlemen, Carnus will hound the Bishop across the field until it takes her out or Rightor recalls it! Magnetic Hunt is a high-level Ability, and cannot be maintained long by your average combatant, but then the captain is anything but average!"

"No! Go! Run!"

The boy didn't even hear himself shout, too mesmerized he was with watching Valera Dent hurtling a foot above the ground around the edge of the simulated grassland, attempting to shake the massive hammer that was now careening after her as though attached by an invisible chain. She was skating backwards, trying to keep an eye on both the weapon and Rightor himself, the glowing white eyes in the red plating of her helm flicking between the pair at an astounding rate. All the same, Rightor saw his moment coming, and when the time was right he bent low—not unlike the crouch of the lion he so embodied—preparing to pounce.

Then, with the *crunch* of shifting ground, the captain lunged.

There was no Ability triggered, no trick to the move. Alex Rightor's Strength and Speed specs were simply so significant that the man was able to clear 15 yards of distance in a blink, catching Valera Dent in the moment she looked away from him. His heavy gold-and-green form collided with the lighter User, slamming her into the invisible perimeter wall of the Dueling field with a *crunch* that made the simulation shiver and flicker for a moment before stabilizing. From the pad the boy heard the "*Ooooh!*" of the audience lucky enough to be watching the match in person, but the excited shouting of the announcer was lost as Rightor reached out with one armor-clad hand, the other pinning Dent to the wall by her throat. To her credit, the chief warrant officer didn't so much as struggle, not even when the massive hammer that had been chasing her flew into its User's waiting grasp with a satisfying *clunk*. Instead, she calmly brought a sword up in a thrust at Rightor's faceplate. A flick of the captain's head kept him from being run through the eye by the glowing blade, Carnus already lifting, ready to come down on the Bishop.

Unfortunately for him, even that brief dodge cost him his focus long enough for his opponent to turn the tides.

The second sword slashed in an upward arc that only someone of Valera Dent's caliber and skill could have achieved from the awkward position of being pinned to an intangible wall. The bright blade caught the arm that held her in place under the elbow, between the gold plates of Rightor's armor, passing clean through. The limb remained intact, of course—CADs in simulated combat matches were always phantom-called—but the wrist went immediately limp, along with the hand and fingers around the chief warrant officer's neck. At once she took advantage, and with a lateral blast of electromagnetic energy skated sideways around the solid boundary just as the hammer impacted where she'd been a moment before with another static jolt in the physical projection.

"And Valera Dent strikes the first true blow of the match, severing her superior officer's neural connection to the better part of his left arm!" The announcer's voice came back to the boy as relief at Dent's escape washed over him. "Fear not, new viewers! The captain will regain full function not long after this Duel is over, but for now he's down a limb! Not a good place to be for a Mauler!"

It was true, of course. Rightor wasn't among the exceedingly rare Users who could manipulate their CAD's weapon configuration using Arsenal Shift. Unfortunately for him, that meant wielding Carnus to the Device's optimal function was going to be difficult, now. With its evolution over the years had undoubtedly come an increase in the two-handed hammer's weight to improve the CAD's Offensive spec, so the captain was likely to have difficulty even lifting his weapon with only one hand, much less swinging it.

Unless…

There was a flash, and the blue accents in Rightor's armor blazed. Ion fire of the same color flickered between the plates of his CAD, and when he whirled the azure eyes in his red-and-gold helm were glowing almost-blindingly.

"OVERCLOCK!" the announcer bellowed across the excited roar of the audience. "A common Ability shared among many Users, but in the hands of someone with the captain's skill, a truly terrifying turn of events!"

Sure enough, Valera Dent—who'd changed course to come at an angle for her opponent's flank—was suddenly withdrawing with all speed. It was fortunate she had, too, because Rightor spun in a blink, the hammer ripping through the air exactly where the woman had been not a heartbeat before. She continued to retreat, but the captain crouched once more, armor still glowing, his massive weapon held stoutly in one hand.

Then he lunged again, and the Iron Bishop was suddenly dancing between raining blows that came so fast, Carnus's colors became a mirage of gold, green, and blue.

It was breathtaking, and the child sitting in a chair that was too tall for his feet to touch the floor couldn't help but gape. Rightor was a terror, and as long as he could maintain the Overclock he was likely among the most dangerous Users in the Astra System, if not the entirety of the ISC. With one hand he brought the hammer down again and again, and before long the field—pristine at the start of the match not 3 minutes prior—was cratered and pocked from a score of impacts and glancing blows.

But it wasn't the captain and his Carnus that the boy watched with such awe.

Valera Dent moved with such liquid poise, he couldn't help but wonder if the announcer had missed the triggering of her own Overclock. Kestrel's visual energy output hadn't changed, though, and a quick glance and scroll through the live combat log in the top right of the feed showed no Abilities activated since Rightor's last-ditch effort to secure himself a win.

The Iron Bishop was just that fast.

Dent's motions were so clean, so calculated, they could have been choreographed. Her top-tier Speed and Cognition specs showed themselves off in all their glory as her entire form became a red-blue blur streaked with white to match Carnus' constant hammer blows. Here and there the child with the pad barely 2 inches from his face could catch a clear moment of her stepping to the side or deflecting a descending strike with a heavy flick of both blades, but as a whole the two combatants didn't allow their spectators much more than glimpses of clean action in the furious exchange.

And then, abruptly, it was done.

The boy thought he saw the moment, though he caught the opportunity, but Valera Dent moved with such speed he would never figure out if he'd seen the same thing she had, or if he was just trying to convince himself of that in retrospect. To his eyes, Alex Rightor had overdrawn, had brought the weight of the hammer a fraction too far back in an attempt to build up as much momentum as possible. The difference was a matter of inches, barely pixels in the feed of the glass tablet, but it had been enough. The strike came, horizontally in a thundering sweep meant to cover every foot of space Dent and her Device could possibly escape to. The chief warrant officer, though, dropped under the attack, possibly even onto all-fours—it would be impossible to tell until a frame-by-frame replay was released. The hammer sailed over her head, colliding with several of the floating externals that made up Kestrel's red wings, crushing and sending them flying with an ear-splitting *crunch* as their phantom-forms processed having been destroyed.

Their sacrifice was well worth it.

The moment the hammer cleared her overhead space, Dent was lunging upwards, both swords leading the way. Rightor jerked back, seeing his fatal mistake, but even his own high Cognition and Overclocked reflexes could do nothing for him. The ivory-edged blades found their mark together, slipping under the captain's gold faceplate in which his eyes still glowed blue, puncturing with all the power Dent could manage in her upward thrust. There was a *cracking* sound, and the swords broke through the top of Rightor's helmet, having skewered him jaw-to-skull. There was a moment, almost a full second in which the hammer in the captain's hands held, the Device kept grasped in an armored hand by the lingering will of its User.

Then the weapon fell to the broken grass with a *thud*, and Captain Alex Rightor went limp on the lengths of the Bishop's swords.

"Fatal Damage Accrued," the light, mechanical voice of the Arena announced. "Winner: Valera Dent."

"YES!"

The exclamation came threefold, once from the crowd, once from the announcer, and once from the boy sitting in the too-tall chair several planets away from the fight. In his excitement he punched a fist into the air with another yell, then cried out as his bandaged shoulder screamed in pain at the motion.

"It. Is. OVER!" the announcer's voice came from the pad as the boy slid it up onto the Matron's desk in favor of clutching the offended joint, shutting his eyes tight against the stabbing ache. "Ladies and gentlemen, Chief Warrant Officer Valera Dent—the Iron Bishop herself!—walks away with her head held high, finishing her circuit in our System SCTs with an *astounding* 54 to 6 record! We will have interviews for you with *both* our combatants once Captain Rightor has recovered, and stay tuned for a return to our regularly scheduled tournament matches starting shortly! For the time being, however, let us all take a moment to applaud the chief warrant officer, and let her know that our thoughts and hopes go with her as she heads for the front line!"

There was another roar of approval from the crowd, which the boy managed to join in with again after his shoulder settled. He was just reaching for the tablet, intent on turning it off and heading back to his room, when he made out the sound of hurried footsteps not seconds before the door along the far left wall burst open.

"What in the MIND's name is going on in here?!"

Matron Avalyn Kast of the Estoran Center for Children stormed into her office with a fury. A flash of the NOED in her right eye had the line lights of the space flicking on, and at a glance the boy noted that not only had the aging woman

So when the punch came, Rei was ready for it.

He dodged to the side, keeping his right hand up to shield his face as he jabbed with his left. The blue frame lines of the NOED in Kent's eye were obvious too, though, so Rei wasn't shocked when the testing blow was smacked away. A leg followed next, and he ducked, attempting to sweep at his opponent's ankle, but the boy planted and twisted, and Rei earned himself nothing more than a painful slamming of shins. Turning his momentum into something valuable, he shifted and flipped back over his hands in an upward kick. He felt his toes catch Kosh a glancing blow under the chin, and by the time he'd rolled onto his feet again the boy had stumbled back several paces, almost outside the marked lines.

Damn, Rei thought, realizing that might have been his chance to knock his opponent out of the ring.

A few of his teammates were shouting encouragement behind him, and he made out Viv's voice in the drone, but tuned it all out. He had to. His right elbow was killing him after taking the weight of that flip, and Ansley Kosh had murder in his eyes as he shook off his moment of surprise and approached the center of the mat again.

Red highlights.

Rei ducked, then dodged once more, Kent's one-two combo turning half his vision crimson as the NOED only barely registered it. Rei kicked low again, this time straight on, and managed to catch Kosh in the ankle, sending his front foot sliding back. The boy caught himself on his other leg, though, and brought a chopping blow jetting down at Rei's head. Rei got both arms up in time to block, bracing for his elbow to scream in protest.

The strike never came.

WHAM!

The impact of Kent's knee catching him square in the face would have broken Rei's nose if it weren't for the thin layer of reactive energy shielding his head from potential trauma, transmitted by the mandatory combat collar around his neck. Just the same, the barrier was only designed to *reduce* the force of a blow, so Rei wasn't surprised to smell blood as he was thrown onto his back. He lay there for a bit, stunned, and was unsurprised when he heard the shout of "Match win! Carter's School for the Gifted!" from the referee.

Dazed, Rei only barely managed to sit up. The ref was beside him a second later, the man's plain whites almost painful to his swimming vision.

"Easy, kid. That was a hell of a hit. Can you stand?"

It *was* a hell of a hit. Rei grunted and closed his eyes, pretending to consider the question. In reality, with a series of quick eye commands he had his NOED pull the footage from the mat-side cameras, then watched the last few seconds of the fight from the spectator's angle. He had to admit that Kosh played him well. Instead of bringing the blow down on his head, the move had been a feint to get him to defend up and open himself for a knee-strike.

Block with one *hand next time, idiot*, Rei berated himself, already hearing Coach Kat's criticism ringing through his ears.

"I can stand," he told the referee, opening his eyes again and pushing himself up. As he did, he tasted metal, prompting him to bring a hand up to his nose. His fingers came away bloody, soaking the wraps that looped over most of his exposed limbs to cover up as much of the scarring as possible, or at least what wasn't hidden under his black combat suit already. He looked up, offering Ansley Kosh a grin. "Good match. Hope you don't mind if we don't shake hands." He held up the reddened hand in explanation.

Kosh, for his part, grimaced. It made his designed, handsome features take on an ugly quality that even reached his orangish eyes. He addressed the ref. "Can I go?" He asked, looking like he distinctly preferred to be anywhere but sharing a mat with Rei.

The ref frowned, but nodded, having no reason to keep the victor from his cheering teammates. The Carter's fighters, in their red robes, were all smiles and shouts as Kosh turned on his bare heels and stepped out of the ring. There were laughs as well, but Rei chose to assume those were hoots of excitement rather than anything else.

He didn't have the energy to believe anything else, in that moment.

"I'm okay," he told the ref with a nod of thanks. "I can walk off on my own."

The man patted him on the shoulder, offering a look of forced encouragement. "Good fight."

It made Rei feel sick.

He turned and approached his own bench. Coach Kat was standing at the edge of the mat, arms crossed and looking bored. She offered Rei a cursory once-over, lacking anything more than apathy, eyes lingering on his bloody face.

"Block with one hand next time, idiot," she muttered by way of feedback, then waved him by with an unenthusiastic wave. "Go get cleaned up."

Having expected nothing less, Rei moved on without another word.

There were no more shouts of encouragement from the combat team, now, much less cheers or smiles. On the contrary, the majority of the boys and girls of the squad didn't meet his eyes as he stepped off the mat, or even move out of his way to make it easier to reach the bench. He still got there, though, and had already sat down to start looking for a clean towel before discovering his punishment wasn't half over.

"What the hell, Ward? Do you have *any* useful function, other than acting like a living training dummy?"

With an internal sigh, Rei looked up in time to find a broad-shouldered boy standing over him, his black hair striped with artfully designed slashes of red, his clear blue eyes burning in his perfect features.

"I just got kneed in the head, Lee. Hard." A few strands of Rei's own bone-white hair had fallen out of the tail he'd gather it in behind his head, and he blew them out of his face before waving at his bloody nose for emphasis. "Are you going to cut me some slack, or just keep up the trend of being a monumental dick?"

Lee Jackson's expression hardened, and he put his hands on his knees so he could bend down to be closer to eye-level with Rei. "You'd think three losses in a *row* would have taught you to shut your damn mouth, freak. If you cost us the lead in this tournament, I'm—"

"Lee, it's the 25th century. If you've got a thing for Rei, you can just *tell* him. No one's gonna judge."

Rei wasn't proud of the breath of relief he involuntarily took at the sound of Viv's voice, but it was worth Lee snapping up and away from him, cheeks flushed. From his left, a tall girl with brown hair—twisted into artful curls that had *no* business lasting the length of a day-long school combat tournament—slid into view from out of the rest of the gathered team.

"What?" Lee seethed. "I'm not—"

"Oh, you're *not* into him? Weird." Viv cocked her head in feigned confusion as she approached the two of them, people moving aside for her without hesitating. "You have a tendency to get in his face so much, I figured a burning desire for some make-out action was the only plausible explanation."

There was a roll of healthy laughter from the other members of the squad, and Lee's cheeks turned almost the color of the streaks in his hair.

"Screw you, Arada. Ward just gave up three *consecutive* matches. If he loses us this tournament—"

"It'll have about as much to do with you as with him, jackass. His day's record is 2 and 3. What's yours again? Oh right. 3 and 2. And you've got what? 6 inches and 40 pounds on him? If Rei had your height and weight, you'd probably make a better barbell than opponent for him."

More laughter, louder this time. To top it all off, Lee wasn't quick on the come-back, giving Viv enough of an opening to lift a hand and make a shooing motion in his direction. "Walk away, loser. Go play with your boytoys."

Rei couldn't decide if Lee looked more ready to explode or melt into a puddle, but at that moment one of the boy's friends decided to save him some face by taking him by the shoulder and pulling him into the gathered bodies of the others. When he was gone, Viv turned to Rei, holding out a clean white towel he hadn't seen hanging from her other hand.

"Asshole," she muttered under her breath.

Rei grinned up at her, accepting the cloth and starting to wipe off his face as he answered. "That's rude. I kinda thought I was in the right, there."

The girl snorted in answer, turning to plop down in the empty space to his left, earning her a sidelong eye from Rei.

Viviana Arada was, it could be argued, his only real friend at Grandcrest Prepara-tory Academy, which technically made her his only friend period. It had taken him a while—and then some—to come to term with her interest in spending time with him, but a mutual distaste for the politics of the Grandcrest cliques and a shared passion for CAD-combat and the SCT circuits had proven enough to make them fast friends—to the displeasure of more than just the students of the Academy. In a lot of ways, having Viv as a companion had made life a lot harder for Rei in a school he'd known he was never going to fit into. She was gorgeous, she was smart, and she was popular—or would have been, if she'd spent less time around him—and he'd taken more than one punch from some jealous suitor of *both* sexes.

On the other hand, Viv was also the only reason Rei had made it through all 4 years at Grandcrest at all.

"How's the pain today?"

The question caught him off guard, but only for a moment. Viv wasn't looking at him, pretending to watch a match he knew she couldn't see through the black-clad bodies of their teammates. If anyone else had asked him that, he would have lied through his teeth, like he did every time Coach Kat or the school doctor did, or even Matron Kast in their occasional NOED calls.

But Viv wasn't anyone else.

"Not great," he admitted, setting aside the now-bloody towel to start undoing the wraps of his right arm. "It was acting up during the fight."

"I could tell. You're supposed to be taking it easy, Rei."

He shrugged, trying for a grin as the last of the bindings fell away, revealing a thin forearm marked with a score of identical, round scars. "Since when have I been good at taking it easy?"

"Since you have surgery *tomorrow*, and the CAD-Assignment Exam is in a *week*, jerk."

Rei shrugged again, a little more stoically this time, flexing his arm and feeling relieved when his elbow only mildly protested. "I'll be fine. It's just another laser correction. A couple days in a sling, and I'll be good to go." He turned, raising both eyebrows at Viv and pretending to flex for her. "Not like I have much to worry about in this form of epic manliness, right?"

It was Viv's turn to look at him sidelong, but after a moment she couldn't seem to help herself, and she cracked a smile at the image he cut, thin chest out and scrawny arms up. "Maybe not, but get your CAD and the girls will be all *over* you in a year or two."

Rei laughed then, loud enough that not a few among the squad turned to glare at him. He grinned in their direction, earning further glowers until they all gave their attention back to the matches.

Once they had, though, he felt the amusement slide away a little bit.

"A little bulk would be a nice bonus. But you know that's not what I'm going for."

Viv nodded once, staring ahead again. "I know," she affirmed. "But you've got a cute face. Some muscle and a little catching up in the height department, and you might just be a cert-if-ied *hunk*." She drew out the last two word for emphasis, and Rei knew she was trying not to laugh herself.

"Uh-huh," Rei answered, not looking at her as he started to undo the wraps of his left arm. "You'll forgive me if I don't take your positive assessment of my facial features to heart. I haven't kept track, but I'm pretty sure you've stolen away more girlfriends at this school then every boy in our grade combined."

"Don't go putting me in a box, Reidon Ward." Rei didn't have to look up to know Viv was smirking with what might have been pride. "Just because I *tend* to prefer the female form doesn't mean I can't handle a decent slab of man-meat when it comes along."

Rei stopped his unwrapping, turning his head slowly to face her. "Please—for the love of the MIND and all that is good in decent in this world—*never* use the term 'man-meat' in my presence ever again."

Viv's smile was almost evil now, and she shrugged. Then her eyes moved to Rei's arms again, following a longer scar than the others that traced the back of his left elbow. "Just… take it easy, okay? It's only for the next week. Weird as you are, I wouldn't want to get into Galens without you."

Before Rei could respond, an intercom call pitched over the thrum of the combat and cheering happening all around them.

"Our top-scorers bout will begin in fifteen minutes in the center ring. Second seed: William Errie of KLM Schools. Six-foot-four. 232 pounds. First seed: Viviana Arada of Grandcrest Preparatory Academy. Five-eleven. 165 pounds."

Viv sucked her lip at the ceiling, having tilted her head back to listen. "Tsch. I told them to knock twenty pounds off my weight for that announcement." She glanced at Rei one last time. "You hanging around to watch?"

He shook his head sadly, looping his now-lose wraps about one hand again and starting to stand up. "No. I wish. I've got to get to work."

Viv rolled her eyes and pushed herself to her feet too, tugging down the knee-cuts of her skin-tight combat suit that had ridden up from sitting. "So much for taking it easy, then?"

Rei winked at her. "Gotta make sure this 'weirdo' doesn't have his diploma held by Grandcrest for unpaid dues." He brought up a hand, imitating her shooing motion from early. "Go on. Get. It sounds like there's a mountain of 'man-meat' waiting for you to 'handle' him."

There was a moment of silence.

Then Viv frowned, looking a little green.

"Okay. You were right. I'll never say it again, if you promise to do the same."

CHAPTER 2

EARLY MAY - *ONE WEEK LATER*

ASTRA SYSTEM – ASTRA-3 – LOW ORBIT

"With the successful implementation of the MIND, the hope was for a system of governance ruled outside of politics. This was eventually achieved—though not without some initial rebellion from Presidents and Ministers of the more strictly governed worlds—but mankind finds a way to corrupt all things, given enough time. It wasn't more than a few years before the parliamentary and diplomatic capering that once plagued our systems was replaced by a more subtle, but no less corrosive, dance: that of social supremacy."

The Influence of the MIND,
TL Latham, MD, Psy. D
Distributed by Central Command, Earth

There is something both infinitely terrifying and absolutely centering about taking in one's own reflection against the vast backdrop of empty space. In static orbit over Astra-3, the Laurent satellite estate was designed and positioned deliberately to offer four breathtaking views at any time of the day: Solar-4 in an endless state of rising over the planet below, Astra-3 itself rotating steadily like a carpet of land, ocean, and clouds, the edge of the world against space, and the blank emptiness of the universe, dotted with nothing more than other stars, the systems of the ISC, and far-distant galaxies.

It was this last scene that Aria Laurent often found herself taking in whenever she was home from school. She couldn't put it into easy words, but there was something about the black that calmed her nerves, that made breathing easier in the grand emptiness of the orbiting mansion. It shouldn't have been hard to breathe in the first place, of course—the estate had more redundant life-support systems than the massive five-thousand-man battlecruisers that dropped ordinance into conflict zones—but Aria's anxiety when home had nothing to do with the dangers of 0 degrees Kelvin and an empty vacuum.

There was a *click* as the handle to the door of the study she'd secluded herself to was lifted, and a moment later a tall, graceful figure in a blue business suit swept into the room, casting about. Aria didn't look around as her mother caught sight of her, watching the woman's reflection in the massive, 10-foot-tall glass pane that was the center of three windows taking up the room's back wall. It was her father's office, but Carmen Laurent was hardly home more than any of his children these days, if that were possible.

War tended to trump family, after all.

"Aria, there you are. Come along. The evaluators have arrived."

Her mother's voice was easy, but Aria had spent enough time around the woman to detect the edge of impatience lingering there.

"I already told you, I'm not interested in an individual test," she answered stiffly, watching the passing lights of a different satellite trail by in higher orbit. "The public examination is fine by me."

"And *I* already told you that wasn't happening," her mother said from the door, crossing her arms and bringing herself to her full height, as was her fashion whenever presented with a disagreement. Any opportunity to talk down, she would take, even if it was at nothing more than her own daughter's back. "We don't have time for this. Do you know the strings your father and uncle had to pull to get an evaluator to visit us privately? Stop being childish and come with me."

Aria didn't move, but she met the woman's eyes—yellow-gold to her own emerald-green—in the reflection of the glass. "What's the issue with letting me take the public exam?"

She knew the answer, of course. *Both* answers, in fact. The truth, and the one she was about to get.

Her mother didn't so much as blink as she lied to her face.

"I've told you. Kalus and Amina were both nearly C-Rank Users by the time their first terms started. Every trainer you have thinks you have the ability to match them, if not surpass them. A public exam would have your User Rank entered immediately into the ISCM database. That means everyone would have access to it. If you *do* end up with the same potential as your siblings, this family does not need that kind of attention before we can get ahead of it."

Siblings who haven't been home in years just to get away from you and Father, Aria thought bitterly. Indeed, Kalus was busy making a name for himself in the pro circuits, while Amina had voluntarily deployed to the front line to put as much room between herself and the family's influence in the Astra System as possible.

"You just don't want the embarrassment of my not meeting the public expectations if I *don't* match them," Aria muttered.

She'd intended for the words to be said under her breath, but the darkening of her mother's expression told her she'd been overheard.

"Enough. This is not a negotiation, Aria. You *will* see the evaluators, and you will do so *now*, rather than wasting more of anyone's time."

The impatience had finally seeped into the woman's voice in truth, and it was this fact that had Aria at last whirling away from the window, fists clenched at her side. She faced her mother, her own anger rising.

Salista Ethalees Laurent stared her daughter down with golden eyes, framed in auburn hair she, Aria, and Amina had all been engineered to possess. Whereas Aria liked to think her expressions had some range, however, her mother's face was carefully composed in an almost-statuesque placidity, absent even of the frustration that had inadvertently infected her last words.

This was expected, of course. Aria had never known Salista Laurent to be capable of anything but calm, cold calculation.

"I attended the preparatory school you wanted me to, despite my wanting to go somewhere else." Her voice shook as she spoke, and her nails bit into her palms by her sides. "I stayed away from people I could have been friends with, just because you told me the 'Laurent' name shouldn't be associated with their families. I even agreed not to apply to anywhere but Galens, despite the fact I told you I wanted to attend a military academy in the inner systems. Could you—just *once*—let me do what *I* want to do?!"

Her last question came out as half a yell, and yet her mother didn't so much as blink.

When she spoke, however, the woman's words surprised Aria enough that her mouth dropped open.

"If you agree to the private exam, I'll allow you to attend the Galens' summer training session."

The offer was like a bolt of electricity up Aria's spine, and she was fully aware that more than a few seconds passed before she could speak again.

"The... A summer training session?" she asked, not completely understanding.

Her mother nodded curtly, the hint of a frown on the corners of her lips speaking to the fact that she wasn't pleased with having her hand forced in this way. "You'll have to qualify, but neither your uncle nor your trainers expect that to be any issue. The sixteen top-ranked incoming cadets are offered the opportunity to attend a 2-month early practical training course, starting in June."

Abruptly, Aria understood.

"The favorites," she clarified with a frown.

"If by that you mean the favorites to qualify for the Sectional SCTs, then yes. 'The favorites'."

Aria contemplated this news. She wasn't thrilled at the prospect of starting the school year already marked by her potential, but the reality was that a summer session like the one her mother was describing meant she would be free and clear of the estate a full *2 months* earlier than expected. There was another week of school left at Carleson's Military College—she'd come home for the Sunday leave at her mother's behest—but after that Aria had been under the impression she would be back on the satellite, studying under the same tutors and combat instructors she'd been working with since she'd turned old enough hold a training weapon.

"Two months…" she whispered, not even realizing she was saying it out loud, nor noticing her mother's frown deepening.

She would have to qualify. That wasn't a given, per se, but if Aria was honest with herself she was under the same impression as her trainers. She'd known her siblings' numbers growing up, and knew just as well that she had surpassed both of them in most scoreable areas. She knew the specs of their CADs on assignment as well, and could only believe that even getting *close* to either Kalus' or Amina's starting potential would be enough to qualify her for the top sixteen incoming. The Galens Institute was arguably the best military academy on Astra-3, maybe even the system, so unless *every* top-ranker from every neighbor planet applied and made it in…

"I'll do it."

Aria said the words before she knew she'd even made the decision. She realized she'd been staring at her mother with what could only have been a dumbfounded expression, and closed her mouth with a *snap* before standing straight.

"I'll do it," she said again. "If it means even a shot getting out of this place 2 months early, I'll do it."

Her mother stared at her for a second, something inscrutable playing in her stony, beautiful features. Was that… sadness, maybe? No. More likely it was just disappointment.

At last the woman shrugged, turning and leaving through the door as she waved for her daughter to follow over her shoulder.

"Then come along. Like I said, they're waiting."

CHAPTER 3

"The advantages of being assigned a CAD are not innumerable, but they are great. Setting aside the gain of measurable specs for the Device and its User, there are also the benefits such technology have on the body. In order for its assignee to apply its full potential with any measure of safety, maintaining the health of the User is a top priority for every CAD. Muscular cross-density optimization. Oxygen de-dependency. Osteoformic integrity. Genetic correction. These are just a few of the wonders advancement in this technology offer those fortunate—and brave enough—to bear one."

CAD and User Relationships
Lieutenant Colonel Hana von Geil, Ph.D.
Distributed by Central Command, Earth

Ugh…"

Rei allowed himself to reach up and massage his temples with both hands, closing his eyes for a moment against the headache building behind them. His right arm protested the slightest bit at the flexion, but he ignored it, focusing instead on trying to wake himself up.

"If you're making that noise because your elbow is hurting, I swear you're the first person I'm going to stab once I get my Device. Right before I say I told you so."

Rei opened his eyes and looked up. He'd been waiting—along with about a hundred other people—in the lobby outside the east entrance of Grandcrest's combat gymnasium. The space was wide and large enough to fit its current occupancy five times over, but still Rei disliked the sterile white of the curved plasteel plating and arching windows showing a bright spring day outside. It all felt about as welcoming as a the school's 6-by-6 disciplinary cubicles he'd… uh… "visited" more than once in his time at the Academy.

Fortunately for him, the view had improved somewhat since he'd last glanced up from his feet.

"Took you long enough," he told Viv, who had appeared as though out of thin air to drop herself down in one of the stark-blue couches opposite the wall he was leaning against. "I was getting worried you wouldn't make it."

"I've still got 15 minutes, Mom, so stop worrying." His best friend gave a group of boys from some other school a charming smile and a wave as they stared at her, her brown hair bouncing against the front of the grey-green dress she'd chosen for the day. When they blushed and spun away in embarrassment, she turned back to Rei again, her expression sliding into serious. "Don't change the subject. I asked if your elbow was hurting. You were just groaning."

Ignoring the temptation to comment on her funny way of "asking", Rei shook his head, starting to roll up the long sleeve of his black shirt. "No, don't worry." He showed her the inside of his right arm, where a new, circular scar about half-an-inch across marked his skin, indistinguishable from the others all along the limb aside from it being a few shades redder. Viv, seeing it, got up from her couch, leaving behind the fashionable satchel he hadn't seen her put down as she moved to examine the mark.

"Grandcrest's docs have been dealing with me for four years, now," Rei continued, letting the girl take his arm to poke and prod at the joint in question. "I told you it barely took an hour, and I even kept my sling on the whole week, just like you badgered me to. Made cleaning the gym a pain in the ass, I might add. Hence my groaning. I was up till 0100 last night wiping down the second year locker rooms, given I only had one hand to work with."

Viv continued to scrutinize the laser scar for a little longer before she appeared satisfied.

"Sleep deprivation can be fixed," she said, turning and moving back to the couch to pick up her bag, rummaging through it as she kept on. "An elbow you can't bend for an exam that includes *physical testing* can't." She found what she was looking for, pulling out two capped cups. Offering him one of them, she grinned. "Besides. I've got your back."

Rei let out a moan of thanks as he took the coffee in both hands, tapping the lid so that the auto-seal retracted, leaving an opening just wide enough to drink from. The smell made his skin tingle, and he gave Viv the best doe-eyed look he could manage. "I take back what I said. You can be late to any potentially life-changing test you want if it means you bring me caffeine."

She chuckled, but didn't answer as she unsealed her own cup and joined him on the wall to drink.

As lighthearted as their banter had been to that point, the silence that hung between the two of them then as they shared each other's company spelled out nerves neither wanted to speak of out loud. It seemed a common stress, too, because despite sharing the lobby with scores of other graduating students, the hum of conversation was more akin to that of a library than the minutes preceding what would possibly be the most important moments of any of their lives. Thinking about it, Rei found himself looking around, studying the hopefuls as they clumped together in quiet discussion, or sat alone with their NOEDs bright in one or both eyes, getting some last-minute studying in.

One in twelve. That was the average rate of CAD-assignment compared to test participants. Including the other lobbies, there would be some 500 applicants at this testing site alone, with a dozen other venues scattered throughout Sector 6 of Astra-3, and in twelve sectors across the planet as a whole. He, Viv, and the scattering of other classmates Rei could see among the crowd were lucky their graduation had landed on a year Grandcrest was one of the exam hosts, but that fortune seemed small when he considered that less than 10% of the students murmuring around him would achieve their dream today. They would be allowed to try again the following year, he knew, but passing the CAD-Assignment Exam after failing it was astronomically rare.

Doesn't matter, he told himself, taking a drag at his coffee and staring at nothing. *Doesn't matter how many tries it takes.*

He hadn't told Viv his thoughts on his likelihood of passing that day. She would have smacked him outside the head for "being a pessimist", and her shared enthusiasm was a big part of the reason he'd worked so hard in the last half-year in particular to prepare. He'd been blessed with more fortune than he could credit himself ever deserving for having her by his side, and he sure as hell hadn't been about to dampen her spirits in the days leading up to the test.

Still… That didn't mean he held any high hopes.

The written examination was one thing. Rei had known more about CAD tech, history, and combat theory *entering* Grandcrest Prep than most of the students around him now had probably absorbed after months of studying. He couldn't put a finger on when he'd become obsessed with the Simulated Combat Tournaments, by Matron Kast and the other staff of the Estoran Center had sworn up and down he'd been swinging at invisible opponents from the moment the major surgeries had started when he was 3, allowing him free use of his arms and legs for the first time in his life. To call the SCTs a passion would have been an understatement, and the day Rei had learned *anyone* could apply to join the Intersystem Collective Military as a CAD-User …

Yeah… The written exam wasn't a concern.

The problem was the second portion of the test: the physical analysis. Rei didn't think he would be expected to actually *fight* as part of the process—all his research into the feeds and forums had mentioned nothing of the like—but that was, if anything, a downside. At 5' 5" and barely scraping 130 pounds, Rei wasn't much more than a bony runt for his 18 years. Even Viv towered over him—not to mention *outweighed* him—but that had never been enough of a reason to stop Rei. His two wins at the combat tournament the weekend before had been against boys half-again his weight, and even if he was at the bottom of the barrel, the fact that he'd made it onto the team *at all* was something given his stature.

But that was the problem. If he *was* allowed to fight, maybe the examiners would be more willing to give him a shot at assignment…

Rei looked around again, taking in the crowd of students.

One in twelve…

Of course, even if by some miracle he *didn't* fail the physical assessment, there would still be the mysterious final evaluation to overcome…

"Attention, if you please."

The voice, steady and easy as it was, had such an intense effect on the room you could immediately hear the rapid breathing of some poor soul trying desperately to calm themselves in the back of the lobby. All heads turned inward, towards the stairs that led up to a pair of closed sliding doors blocking the floor of the combat gym from view. On the steps, a figure had appeared, flickering a moment until the simulation stabilized into the form of a tall, thin man with sharp eyes and a cropped, greying beard. He wore the black-and-gold regulars of the ISCM uniform, complete with the flat-topped cap, and stood at ease with his hands behind his back, looking over the heads of everyone in the lobby.

"My name is Major Albert Connelly," the projection continued, "and I have the honor of being your lead evaluator today as you pursue your Combat Assistance Device Assignment Exam. I want to first thank every one of you for applying. I am aware that a military lifestyle has its own appeal—particularly for those of you seeking merit in the circuits—but it also takes an element of bravery and self-understanding to know the path of becoming a CAD-User is the one you seek to walk." Major Connelly held out a hand then, lifting it almost to the level of his eyes. Rei just caught the glimpse of a purple-and-grey band of metal around his wrist when electric pixilation disrupted the officer's simulation, causing a few of the hopefuls in the crowd to yelp. An instant later, however, the hologram stabilized, and Connelly was left standing as he had been, his raised hand now wrapped about the black steel handle of a massive sword whose broad, iron-grey blade was edged with glowing purple vysetrium. His eyes, too, had changed, taking on the faint brightness of a similar shade of violet, irises alight as he looked around again.

"Saber-Type," Rei muttered, low enough that only Viv could hear beside him. "Probably a high B-Rank at least, judging by the complexity of that call."

In the corner of his vision he saw Viv nod, but she said nothing as the major continued speaking.

"This is a partial-call of my Device, Calysta. As all of you are *hopefully* aware, the form she has taken classifies me as a Saber-Type User." His eyes swept the room a little too-high—he was likely addressing all the lobbies at once—as if to discourage anyone who hadn't made this assessment from proceeding. "*This* is what you are all seeking, though even those of you assigned a Saber-Type CAD will have many years of training before you can achieve this call-level." Abruptly the massive sword vanished in a whirling mess of grey-black steel and purple light, vanishing in hardly a second.

"Of course," the major kept on, clasping hands behind his back again, "I am sure all here are equally aware that very few of you will be assigned a Device today. No matter how deserving you feel you may be, no matter how true you think your desire is, the fact remains that the parameters of difficulty you are about to be put through are not barriers everyone can overcome. Failing the written exam implies a lack of understanding in the core concepts of essential military, CAD, and combat theory, putting you at risk of becoming a danger to yourself and others on the field or the front lines alike. Failing the physical evaluation implies an absence of a person's true likelihood of being able to handle the physiological toll of being assigned a Device, which can be great. Failing the final portion of this exam… well…" The major frowned, almost in commiseration. "It takes a certain kind of mind to properly wield a developing CAD, much less excel in its use."

There was a pause in which Connelly looked to be considering his next words carefully.

"For those of you who do not manage to achieve your goal on this day, you are of course welcome to try again in the future. That being said, I would also encourage you to consider other careers within the structure of the ISCM, including assignments in piloting, ship combat, command management—"

"He's trying to shake us."

It was Viv who spoke, and Rei nodded in agreement at once, having come to the same conclusion. As the major rattled on about the merit and value of other paths those who failed could take, it was possible to see a myriad of reactions in the faces all around them. Some, like he and Viv, watched the speech impassively, waiting for an explanation on how to proceed. Others, however, responded differently, a number of people paling as the possibility of their not passing was so strongly harped on, others cheering up when they realized failing wasn't the end of their hopes of a career in the military.

One by one, Rei watched people fail before the testing even began.

No… That wasn't right…

If anything, the test had clearly already started.

"Now, regarding today's proceedings." Major Connelly's return to the pertinent subject had Rei giving him his full attention again. "There are a total of 521 applicants at this venue today, all of whom will be taking the written, physical, and final parts of the exam in tandem, assuming you pass each portion. We will—as stated—begin with the written evaluation. As you pass through the doors behind me—" as the simulation spoke, the double entrance to the gym floor slid open behind him "—you will be assigned a seat number. Please find the correlating desk. You may keep all items you have in your possession, including neuro-optics, pads, and any other devices. I will say that it is not recommended you use any of these in an attempt to search for answers to the written questions, but my warnings don't tend to have much of an impact, I've discovered over the years." There was, then, the subtle flash of a grim smile on the aging man's face. "Now, without further delay: best of luck."

With a blip of light, the simulation winked out.

"What? We're allowed to keep our NOEDs?"

The question came as a whisper from a dozen different places, and Rei frowned, watching the brave souls closest to the gym doors start to make their way up the stairs.

"How many do you think will go in the first 5 minutes?" Viv asked him quietly, sounding a little too excited.

"Too many," he answered, watching people pulling pads from bags and pocketing them, or fiddling with their neuro-optic settings. He gave Viv a glance, eyeing her as she played with her hair for a moment. Despite her amusement, she was still nervous. "I don't need to remind *you* not to cheat, do I?"

She scoffed, hitching her bag a little higher over her shoulder and motioning with her head that they should join the crowd as it started to move. "After what you told me you'd found out researching the test? As if." She brought a finger to her temple, and the bilateral glow of her display blared an off-grey, different from its standard red or green or blue. "Locked it this morning. Set to unlock in three hours, around the end of the written time limit."

Rei stared at her for a moment as they walked. "Huh." Pretending to finish his coffee, he looked away and locked his own unilateral NOED for an hour and a half.

By his side, Viv laughed, then the two of them were in the throng, passing into the gym together, the number 221 and 222 popping across their vision as they did.

As expected, more than twenty people failed within the first 5 minutes of the written test starting. Major Connelly—in the flesh—walked up and down the aisles of plasteel desks that took up half of the gym floor, joined in his circuit by a some dozen other evaluators in their own black-and-gold regulars. At first the interventions were frequent, one or more of the military officers pausing in their pacing as information flit across the frame of their NOEDs, then converging on the unfortunately involved applicants. There were protests, initially, shouts from the guilty parties that they weren't doing anything wrong, but after the first score were escorted out, people smartened up.

"Idiots," Rei muttered to himself, bent over his test, and he thought he saw Viv fail to hide a grin on his right.

Sure, he'd had the sense to look up as much about the exam as possible in the weeks prior to it, but to have discovered that anyone trying to cheat on the exam were the first to fail had hardly surprised him. One in twelve passing meant the military was satisfied only with the *best* making it through to actual assignment of CADs, and one could hardly imagine someone willing to cut corners for information would qualify.

Still, even Rei had been taken aback by the level of entrapment opportunities offered. Aside from being allowed to keep their devices, Rei realized that his and Viv's proximity had been more deliberate than chance when several of the students pulled left in pairs, sometimes even trios. Friends and acquaintances had been grouped to encourage temptation, which couldn't have been hard to succumb to given one final astounding fact:

The written test had been provided to them on paper.

This was such an odd event that Rei was only one of hundreds, he suspected, to have run his hand across the top sheet of his exam in amazement upon sitting down. Paper was worthless in a modern age of neuro-optics and pads, sure, but it was also exceedingly rare, and this was the first time he—and likely most people in the room—had ever seen any. They'd been offered "pens"—not unlike the styluses used for writing on tablets when taking notes in class or at lectures—and Rei hadn't been able to stop himself from running the tip of the fascinating apparatus down the center of his left palm, marveling at the line of black it left behind on his skin.

Then, though, major Connelly had called a beginning to the exam, and Rei had been forced to focus.

It started simple enough, of course:

In order of highest to lowest, list the 7 tiers of CAD-Rankings, and all relevant sub-rankings.

It had taken him a moment to get used to the pressure he needed to apply to the paper to get the answer to come out clearly, but eventually Rei managed it.

S
A
B
C
D
E
F

The values of 9 to 0 are applied as sub-rankings to the Ranks of A through F, with an A9-Ranked individual being the highest-level User before achieving S-Rank, and F0 being the weakest. In the S-Ranks, however, sub-rankings are applied using a Class system derived from the game of chess. In descending order, these Classes are: King/Queen (depending on the gender identity of the User), then Rook, Bishop, Knight, and Pawn.

Moving to the next question, Rei felt his confidence begin to grow a little.

List all Specifications relevant to CAD-combatants, separated appropriately, as well as their broad definitions.

The middle directions made him smile, and he wondered if the other examinees would be tripped up by not reading the questions fully.

User-specific specs include:

1) Strength - measures a User's physical ability to push, pull, lift, carry, and throw weight.

2) Endurance - measures a User's physical ability to perform strenuous activity without fatiguing.

3) Speed - measures a User's physical movement and reaction speed.

4) Cognition - measures a User's speed of cognitive information processing, and amount of information able to be processed at once. Due to concerns over long-term cerebral damage, Cognition is only active when deliberately applied, most commonly during a CAD-call..

CAD-specific specs include:

1) Offense - measurement of a CAD's direct offensive power.

2) Defense - measurement of a CAD's total defensive ability.

4) Growth - measurement of a CAD's ability to adapt and upgrade itself and its User over time with input of combat information.

These measurements are Ranked in the same fashion as CAD Rankings, though standard 0 to 9 values are applied in the S-Ranks as well, rather than titling. In these measurements, a Ranking of F0 is akin to the ability of an average 30-year-old male citizen of the Inter-system Collective.

Rei second-guessed himself after writing the last line, given that it wasn't exactly relevant to the question, but discovered in searching for a method of removing it that his pen wrote in what appeared to be permanent markings. Sighing, he decided to move on, resolving to keep to the questions.

List the 7 CAD-Types.

Brawler

Mauler

Lancer

Saber

Duelist

Phalanx

A-Type

It was in this fashion that the test continued for several pages, Rei ripping through the more basic questions in the span of a quarter-hour. After that the exam steadily grew in difficulty, and before long he found himself gnawing at the end of his pen as the inquiries shifted from asking for the abbreviations of the likes of Simulated Combat Tournament and Combat Assistance Device to requesting a detailed molecular breakdown of carbonized steel, what the recommended Type matchup would be against a three-man team consisting for a Mauler, Saber, and Phalanx, and what the electrical input difference between a phantom-call and a true-call was, as well as the partial calls of each.

An hour later, Rei reached the final page, letting out a breath of relief as he saw that only two questions remained to him. Inadvertently, he looked them both over at once, and found himself staring at the last for several seconds. He read it again, then twice more before understanding the question was, in fact, apparently asking for an opinion rather than a fact.

Eventually, Rei forced himself back to the top question.

CADs offer their User a variety of physical advantages over non-Users, all of which improve over time with a Device's progress and evolutions. List as many as you can, and their broad definitions.

Another few seconds he sat there, staring at the question, then at the follow up. It seemed so… odd. Odd, to pair these two specifically, and at the end to the test. For a second, he almost looked to his right to glance at Viv's exam, wondering if she'd reached the last page and was puzzling over the same thing.

Catching himself—and suspecting she was probably a ways behind him—he started to write.

1) Neuroline - synthetic axonal growth in the white and grey matter of the brain and spinal column, allowing for significant improvements in mental faculties while a User's Cognition spec is applied.

2) Synaptic override - artificial synaptic replacement in the limbs and core muscle groups, reducing delay between thought and action.

3) Cross-density optimization - reassignment of trained muscular and tendon growth for strength and speed, allowing for significantly improved levels of physical power and agility.

4) Oxygen de-dependency - reduced dependency on blood-supplied oxygen, sharply increasing muscular and mental endurance.

5) Osteopathic integrity maintenance - increased density and size of skeletal tissue, allowing the body to bear the stress of CAD use and combat.

6) Genetic correction - a repairing of individual DNA imperfections, resulting in varied positive physiologic changes over time.

Finishing, Rei lifted his pen and moved to the final question, already knowing what his answer would be.

Of the physical advantages listed above, which is most important to you?

CHAPTER 4

Ma'am? I was told I deliver my test to you?"

The woman seated at the single table facing the examinees stared at him in surprise. A warrant officer—judging by the insignia on her left breast pocket of her uniform—she'd watched Rei approach warily from the moment he'd stood up and asked what to do with his papers from one of the other soldiers patrolling the rows. Clearly this question was not what she'd anticipated—maybe she'd thought he was coming to complain about the unfairness of some part of the exam?—and it took her a second to look from him to the holographic display of a running timer hovering a few feet over their heads, clear for all test-takers to see.

"Are you... Did you complete all the questions?" she asked, trying to regain her composure as she stood up, holding out a hand for his carefully ordered papers. He nodded, passing them over as requested, and she flipped through them quickly to make sure he hadn't skipped any pages and wasted her time. Her eyes widened just a little as she saw that every answer was indeed there, and she moved at once to a small, rectangular machine at the edge of the table he hadn't even given a second look. Sliding the test into a slot on her side of the device, there was a quiet whirring of sound, like the sheets being scanned and processed, and not two breaths later a display Rei couldn't see illuminated for the warrant officer to peer at. She did so, and there was no hiding it this time.

Her eyes *definitely* widened.

"Uh... yes. I can consider this a passing grade. You'll move on to the physical assessment next." She paused to look him up and down—some of the surprise leaving her face in favor of what could only have been doubt—then stepped around the table and motioned him to follow her. "I don't know if they expected anyone to finish so quickly, so I'll escort you and check."

Rei fell in smartly behind the woman, a little warm in the face, though he couldn't decide if it was because he was pleased at her disbelief at his speed and obviously decent grade, or downcast from her obvious qualms regarding his stature. Whatever it was, she led him out of the combat gym through a smaller entrance between the south and east lobby doors he knew well.

"They've set up in the medical facilities, then?" Rei asked once they were out of earshot of those still taking the exam.

The warrant officer looked around at him curiously.

"I'm a student at the school here," he explained the unanswered question. "Part of the combat team, actually." He tried for a grin, but thought it likely came out tense. "I've spent my fair share of time in a recovery bed."

The soldier relaxed, letting out a polite laugh before answering as they took a short set of stairs and turned left along one of the narrow back halls under the amphitheater seating. "They have. It's a smaller space than we'd like, but the written exam is where we'll lose the most applicants, so it shouldn't be a problem."

"Am I allowed to ask what my grade was?"

She gave him a warning look, and Rei brought both hands up in surrender. He was about to apologize for pushing when they reached the door to the medical facilities, and the warrant officer pressed her palm to the plasteel. It opened sideways silently, and she stepped inside, motioning for him to follow.

Whereas the chamber usually consisted of nothing more than several exam spaces and beds separated by automatic privacy curtains that could change from clear to opaque on a whim, the space Rei walked into now looked more like something out of an army base camp. Medical officers and attendees were bustling around, and six black tents, about 10'-by-10' each, were lined up in two rows along either wall, leaving only a modest walkway of space between them to allow for passage. As Rei and his escort walked in, one of the workers caught sight of them, frowned, and hurried over.

"Is there a problem, warrant officer?" the man asked. He was clean-shaven with thick black hair, and had on a white lab coat with a surgical mask pulled down around his neck. "Has someone taken ill?"

"No, lieutenant," the woman answered sharply, saluting the man. Rei looked closer, and the worker indeed had the insignia of a lieutenant in silver over the pocket of his coat. "I've brought your first passing grade from the written portion." She motioned Rei forward. "This is Reidon Ward. He completed his first section ahead of our expected schedule, so I thought I'd make sure you were ready for him rather than sending him along on his own."

The lieutenant did a better job of hiding his surprise than she had, reaching into the pocket of his coat and pulling out a small pad to peruse.

"Hmm… Yes. We can take him." He nodded, waving down another individual in similar vestments, who approached at once. "We typically try to get at least one assessment suite up quickly in case of situations like this. Ward, Sergeant Valenti will be your examiner, if you'll follow him." The lieutenant glanced back at Rei. "Good luck, son."

Rei nodded, then turned to thank the warrant officer. She beat him to the punch, though, leaning in as her superior walked away, leaving the sergeant waiting expectantly.

"About your test. Let's just say you did just fine, okay?"

The way she said it made Rei believe he had done better than "fine", and he stammered out a thanks. The smile he got in return was a little *too* encouraging—like a mother pretending to be proud of a child's finger painting—but he appreciated the gesture nonetheless. As the woman left, the sergeant stepped forward to introduce himself at once.

"Valenti," he repeated, holding out a hand in greeting and motioning over his shoulder with the pad he had in the other as Rei shook. "We're in the back corner, if you'll follow me."

Navigating through the bustle of teams still setting up their own spaces, Valenti led the way. He was a younger man, maybe mid-20s, with a streak of blue hair down the middle of his head that gave him the look of one of the orbital racing pilots whose sport was the only one that still held any weight against the SCT feeds. Reaching the last tent, the officer pulled the flap open to gesture Rei inside, then let it drop behind him as he followed. Almost all excess sound ceased the moment the entrance was sealed again, and Rei whistled.

"Dampening cloth. You guys aren't messing around."

Valenti chuckled, moving to a small lift-desk docked in its station in the corner and tossing his pad down on it with familiar casualness. The desk spun into its active mode at once, floating up out of its dock and drifting over to follow the examiner within arm's reach as he approached Rei again. "Not for these exams, no. Results are confidential until released. They even keep things blind between the first two test portions, just to avoid influencing our results."

Rei nodded absently, looking around the space, impressed at the equipment packed into the relatively tight area.

An examination table stood off-center from the middle of the suite, with a zero-grav treadmill mirroring it. All kinds of tubes sprouted from a mask hanging off a hook on the arm of the running machine, and a complex-looking computer with several ports and windows for what could only have been samples had been set up against the back wall. A series of solar lights hung overhead, giving the entire space a warm, welcoming orange glow that was definitely deliberate, but just the same Rei could feel his pulse quicken as he studied the contents of the tent.

One in twelve… he thought yet again.

"So. Straight to it." Sergeant Valenti's matter-of-fact voice interrupted Rei's trepidations, and he was grateful for the distraction as he looked around. The examiner was studying the pad before him with interest, having taken a seat on an adjustable stool that had slid to him from the corner with a flash of his NOED. "Room sensors have your estimated height and weight as reported—five-foot-five and 132 pounds—but I'll need you to remove your shoes and everything but your underwear for an accurate measurement. Do you have a concept of what we're getting done today?"

Rei nodded. "Vitals and reflexes. Lung volume. Lactic acid buildup. Red and white blood cell count. Pathologic and neuropathy testing, too, among other things."

Though he never glanced up from the tablet, Valenti's eyebrows lifted. "You've done your research. That's always good. Makes things easier." He paused in his scanning of what had to have been Rei's submitted profile and other collected data. "This is a pretty extensive medical history, kid… And a *lot* of surgery… What—?" He cut his own question off, apparently finding the answer he was looking for. The officer read for a long moment, undoubtedly taking in the layered explanation written within, and said nothing for a while after finishing. Rei started to get worried again, and when the sergeant looked up his face was set.

"Roll up your sleeves, please."

Rei's heart fell. He hesitated, then did as he was asked, pulling up the sleeves of his black shirt to reveal the scars he knew Valenti wanted to see. The officer stared for a moment, eyes tracing up both limbs, his gaze lingering a little while on the new, redder mark on the inside of Rei's right elbow.

When he finally spoke, however, it was measured, and lacking any of the pity or disappointment Rei had been afraid of hearing.

"It's not up to me to ask questions. I'll leave that to the final portion of the exam, if you pass my assessment." The sergeant paused, studying Rei's face intensely. "You ready for this, kid?"

Feeling not a small amount of gratitude, Rei managed a real smile.

"Absolutely."

In the end, it took him less than an hour to fail.

Sergeant Valenti was—to all his credit—encouraging till the end. He pushed Rei through the endurance and lung volume assessment, and took his reflexes three different times. The man even drew his blood twice when his cellular counts came up sub-optimal. Valenti didn't *tell* Rei his numbers were less than ideal, of course, but some of the readings were easy to make out on the medical computer at the back of the tent, and Rei had memorized the minimum thresholds of expectation front and back in the weeks approaching the exam.

It turned out he just wasn't *physically* good enough.

The last of the tests—a simple flexibility measurement—was done in a subdued tone. Rei still worked for his best, thinking he might at least be able to make a request for his results to see what could be improved on for next year's exam, but Valenti's words of encouragement came less-heartily. Once they finished, the sergeant motioned to the final corner of the tent, where an ion shower rose and lifted as soon as Rei approached it. Within a minute he was clean, the varied particle waves first drying him off, then scrubbing the stickiness of the salt sweat left on the skin, and finally he was told to put his clothes back on.

"Come sit, kid." The sergeant told him after he was dressed, motioning that he should hop back up on the exam table. Rei did so, feeling a lump build in his throat as the officer refused to meet his gaze, instead scratching at the back of his blue strip of hair while perusing the pad, as though looking for an easy way out.

Eventually the man sighed, gesturing for his stool with one hand as his neuro-optic flashed. It rolled over to him on command again, lifting to its max height so Valenti could sit eye-to-eye across from Rei.

"There's no easy way to say this, but… I can't pass you. Not today. Most of your tests meet the absolute minimal criteria, and a lot of the ones that didn't can be improved on with time and training. But…"

"You can't pass me," Rei repeated quietly, finding himself rather abruptly looking at the floor. Try as he might, he couldn't lift his head, the lump shifting down to settle first in his heart, then his stomach.

"No," Valenti confirmed gently. "No. I can't." He sighed, lingering there for moment before continuing. "This is the part where I'm supposed to tell you about all the other opportunities you could still have in the military, but I get the distinct feeling whatever I say is gonna wash off of you like water." Rei could practically feel the man's eyes pass over his shirt and pants, hiding the scars again, including the longer ones from his several more-major surgeries. "It's clear as day on a world with no night that you're a fighter. I can *get* why a CAD-assignment is important to you. If I had the ability to, I'd shove you through to the next stage, and I could get fired for saying that, so don't take it lightly."

Rei could only nod. The lump was spreading, and he could feel numbness start to take over him. It angered him, for some reason. Hadn't he been ready? Hadn't he been prepared? He might not have told Viv as much, but he thought *he'd* at least been set in mind and heart to face down this truth he suspected very well to be coming down the line.

"Listen, kid. You finished your writing test up in what's got to be record time, which gives us a while before anyone pokes their head in here wondering why we haven't wrapped up. I need to submit your results, but after that let's go over your numbers and talk about what you can do to—"

Valenti paused suddenly, and when he spoke again it clearly wasn't in address of Rei.

"What the hell…?"

The abrupt change in the sergeant's demeanor finally pulled Rei out of the spiral of his dark thoughts long enough to lift his gaze, and he found the officer staring in confusion at the pad he must have grabbed from the lift-desk. Rei couldn't see whatever was being displayed—the tablets were clear smart-glass, but data only showed one way for obvious privacy reasons—but he could see a weird orange glow reflecting on and off in the man's eyes, like the blinking of some large notification.

"What is it?" Rei asked him, worried something had happened to the data. At the very least he couldn't walk away from this kind of day with *nothing* to show for it. "What's going on?"

"I just submitted the results and…" Valenti trailed off as the reflection shifted, the display clearly changing to something new. The sergeant read whatever was written quickly, mouth falling open ever so slightly.

Then, abruptly, he stood up.

"Wait here. Do not move. Do not leave this tent. Is that understood?"

The brusqueness of the order took Rei so aback, he could only nod. Without another word Valenti dropped the pad back onto the desk and swept from the assessment suite, the sounds of bustling activity sneaking in for a breath as the flap opened, then disappearing again when it fell shut once more. Rei was left confused, not understanding what was going on, staring after the examiner with a clenching in his gut he didn't understand. What had happened? If it was only that his data had been wiped, would Valenti have acted like that? Was it something else? Maybe the examiners suspected foul play because of the speed at which he'd finished the test…?

That thought made Rei angry, and he clung to it for no reason, needing an outlet for the daze the officer's departure had left him in. How was *that* fair? He'd *known* he would have to make top marks on the writing to balance out his abysmal physical scoring even *if* he passed the evaluation. He'd had to grind out every spare moment of study he could between school, combat team practice, and his job at the Academy! If they were going to hound him for *that*, then what the hell was he doing here in the first—?

A light had Rei stop, then, and he looked slowly around. In his hurry, Valenti had knocked the lift-desk a little too hard, because despite its suspension stabilizers the floating table was rotating steadily in the air. As it did, the pad came into view, the orange light of the data bright even in the well-lit confines of the tent.

There, the last message the sergeant had seen blazed against the glass.

CANDIDATE REJECTION: OVERRULED

CHAPTER 5

Based on a *very* impressive written test score, Mr. Ward, I'm going to make the assumption that you are attentive enough to already know my name and who I am. Is that fair?"

Rei, who had snapped up from the table the moment the man had entered the tent, answered at once. "Yes, major."

The quick response seemed to please Major Albert Connelly, because the aging man nodded. "Good. Then I'm also going to pretend that—despite Sergeant Valenti's careless abandonment of his pad when he rushed off to get me—that you also have no idea why I am here."

To this, Rei could give no good answer, so he chose instead to stay silent. From over the major's shoulder, Valenti broke attention to give Rei a quick thumbs-up and mouth the word "thanks" behind his commanding officer's back.

"Excellent," Connelly said after a moment, moving to take a seat in the very stool the sergeant had vacated not 3 minutes before and motioning Rei back up onto the table. "Sometimes silence is the best response. You're going to keep pretending you have no concept of what is going on, and I'm going to act like I believe you. Understood?"

"Yes, major," Rei replied as he pushed himself back up to sit.

Connelly waited for him to settle before speaking again. "Sergeant Valenti would have me believe he has already informed you that you did not pass the physical examination." The shadow cast over the higher officer's face by the short brim of his military cap shifted as someone accidentally bumped into the outside of the tent, sending the solar lights above them to swinging briefly. "I'm here to inform you that is not actually the case, and to apologize for the miscommunication on behalf of the ISCM."

He paused, giving Rei a moment to speak, and catching him off guard.

"N-No apology necessary, sir," he stammered, not sure what else to say. His heart was hammering in his chest. So it was true... The rejection had been overruled. By whom, though? By the major? That seemed unlikely.

"It is, and it is not easily given. I do have to clarify, however, that this does not mean you have passed the *exam*. You are merely being qualified for the third portion, which you will have to take along with every other student given the opportunity. Do you understand?"

"Yes, major."

"Good." Connelly paused again, but this time not seeming for any reason other than to look Rei up and down carefully. When he opened his mouth again, his tone was less formal. "I'm going to speak freely, son, so listen up. You're approaching the start of an exceedingly difficult path at a very fast pace. That has its own value, but you also need to take care not to trip on your own feet." He stopped, considering, and his NOED lit up his eyes briefly. "You took this exam alongside a 'Viviana Arada'. Is that correct?"

Rei didn't ask how the man could know that. "Yes, sir."

"I see... While I'm not at liberty to share the information of applicants, I have a *strong* feeling that Ms. Arada is going to end this day a very happy young lady. Do you understand my meaning?"

"Yes, sir." Rei barely managed to hide a smile. So Viv was crushing her portions. No surprise there, but it was heartening to hear the confirmation.

"Good. My profile on the two of you shows you've both applied to the Galens Institute. That's a hell of a swing, but if you make it, remember that good friends can be hard to find in the world you're about to share. Got it?"

"Yes, sir."

The major made a satisfied grunt, watched Rei a moment more, then stood up.

"There's an officer waiting at the entrance of the medical facilities. You're in the system as having passed, so they'll direct you to where you need to go. Dismissed."

The release was abrupt, but Rei hopped off the table at once. For a second he stood in front of Connelly, considering attempting a salute, then thought better of it. Instead, he managed to get out a shaking "Thank you, sir." before hurrying out of the tent as instructed.

Even after the short, scarred boy was gone, Albert Connelly couldn't help but frown at the flap of the assessment suite through which Ward had disappeared.

He considered the situation several seconds longer, then turned on his heels and made for the still-floating lift-desk he'd had Sergeant Valenti pull out of the way when they'd arrived. Reaching it, he picked up the pad still laying across its angled surface in both hands, taking in the message with narrowed eyes.

"Sir…?" The sergeant started from behind him. "Permission to speak freely?"

Connelly gave a grunt, which the officer took as liberty.

"Sir… What's going on? I've never heard of an… an 'Overrule'? I assumed you had something to do with it, but…?"

Valenti trailed off, leaving Connelly to chew on the question for a while, looking over the message on the pad for the tenth time and seeing nothing different yet again.

"No… Not me," he acknowledged. "As for what's going on, sergeant, I can only venture a guess. Not in twenty years of evaluation have I seen something like this." He gave up searching for answers in the tablet's simple notice, lifting his gaze instead to the northeast corner of the suite above his head where a small, almost-imperceptible camera was set up to record.

No… Not to record… To *observe*.

"Small, weak, and with a medical history a mile long…" he muttered under his breath. "What the *hell* is it thinking?"

Aside from the lobbies, medical facilities, and several restrooms for participants, staff, and spectators, the space under the amphitheater seating of Grandcrest's combat gym also housed multiple classrooms for lectures by the school's coaches, trainers, and instructors on a regular basis. It was to one of these that Rei was directed, and it didn't take him long to find the place, having attended more than one of Coach Kat's heated speeches—though they were usually for the benefit of the members of her team she had greater faith in.

Arriving, Rei was greeted by yet another evaluator—this time a young corporal—who only scanned his NOED for identification before motioning towards the classroom door. Opening it, Rei had stepped all the way inside before realizing the space looked nothing like he was used to.

He'd been expecting a change, of course. He didn't know exactly what to presume from this third portion—it was the only part of the test kept relatively under wraps even on the feeds—but he somehow couldn't imagine the final portion of such an important event taking place among shuffled desks, disorganized combat modules, and old holo-projectors.

Still… Rei had even *less* expected to walk onto a massive, oblong floor of dark steel that had absolutely *no* business fitting inside the confines of a common classroom, complete with sweeping stands rising up all round him and an open-air roof high above, over which the words "Match Start" had been projected in shimmering black-and-red lettering.

He knew, of course, where he was. At least broadly. He'd known the moment he had seen the silver lines on the black, plated floor. The floor he was sure would extend 150 yards long and 70 wide, with an additional 5-yard minimum buffer around the extent of the space for movement, on-field viewing, media, and medical staff standby. Within that broadest Wargames loop, six other circles were marked as well, two 70-yard Team Battle fields, and four 30-yard Dueling fields.

Rei was standing, for the first time in his life—real or otherwise—on the floor of an SCT Arena…

"Please watch your step as you enter, Mr. Ward. As I'm sure you're aware, no extent of advances in simulation technology can remove solid walls from a room."

The voice came simultaneously from everywhere and nowhere. Rei started, casting around for a moment, then jumped again when a shimmering pixilation began to take form not 5 feet in front of him. A second later a person was standing before him, though not any kind of person Rei had ever known. A single shared surface of white from head to toe, it was faceless and without distinct gender. It was clothed in nothing, but at the same time requiring no coverage given all absence of anything that might demand modesty.

"My apologies," the voice said with a laugh now coming from the figure itself, waving him closer. "I can't help myself doing that. The look of astonishment amuses me every time."

Rei hesitated, distinctly unsure of himself, but approached when he considered that this could only be part of the exam.

"Closer, boy. I don't bite. See?" The figure vanished in a blink, only to appear inches from Rei's right side. This time he actually *yelped,* which drew another chuckle from the bizarre character.

"Very well, very well. I'll end my games now." It stood still, waiting for Rei to recover a little before speaking again. "You did quite well on your written exam, Mr. Ward. I have you at a 98.7%. It might have been higher, but I can't abide smudging on the papers."

Rei smiled weakly at that, lifting a hand to show the dark stain the pen writing had left on the side of his palm in places, intending to attempt an explanation before realizing the ion shower had scrubbed him clean of the evidence. Letting his arm drop again, he struggled to find something to say.

"I… I don't know whether to ask you who you are, or ask if you're allowed to give me my results before the exam is complete…?"

A shifting in the blank face of the figure *might* have been amusement, confirmed by yet another laugh.

"Usually the former is the first question everyone asks, and the second never comes up. I confess I'm breaking protocol a bit, but you caught my interest. And—since it is *my* exam—I'm quite confident no one is going to try to fire me for doing so."

Rei frowned. "… *Your* exam?"

"Yes," the figure answered plainly, bobbing its head as though this was enough of an explanation. "Well… mostly. I admit there's a small amount of input from the ISCM's higher ups, but rarely do they provide me with any insight I'm not already processing."

Rei understood, then.

"You're an AI."

He stated it as a fact, completely sure of himself. Artificial intelligence was hardly a foreign concept—the Intersystem Collective was *run* by such a program, after all—but he didn't know of any other, nor fathom the military's exclusive application of one to the CAD-Assignment Exam…

"Hmm, yyyees…" the figure answered slowly, like it wasn't sure how exactly to word the correct response. "Technically, though I like to think that's an understatement." It "smiled" at him again. "To be blunt: you would likely know me most commonly as the Massive Intellect Networked Database."

Rei *gaped*.

"You're the *MIND*?!"

He hadn't meant to shout, but the demand came out with such disbelief, he couldn't help it. If that was true, this wasn't an exclusive AI at all.

It was the *exact* AI that ran the ISC!

"Yes, and please don't shout," the AI implored of him, having brought its white hands up to where its ears would have been. "These rooms aren't as well sound-proofed as the assessment suites from your medical exam, and I would hate to have the nice corporal who let you in here come rushing in in a panic." It waited, watching Rei for a bit, then dropped its hands again when it was sure he wasn't about to yell a second time. "That's better. Yes. As you have deduced, I am the MIND, or at least an extension of it."

"But… But how?" Rei asked, not comprehending. "How are you… Why are you *here*?"

The MIND chuckled at that. "My dear boy, you may have piqued my curiosity, but I can't have you thinking that I am *only* here. At this very moment I am interviewing 176,592 CAD-assignment candidates across all seven systems and their collected forty-two colonized planets. That is, of course, only the part of me currently monitoring and administering the testing, which I'm pleased to say is less than a thousandth of a percent of my—"

"Oh," Rei interrupted, and only much later would he realize he had cut across the single most powerful entity in the history of humankind. "The cheaters. In the written exam. I was wondering how they kept getting caught so fast…"

The MIND perked up, apparently not at all bothered at being butt-in on when it came to what it clearly perceived as an entertaining topic. "Oh that *is* fun, yes! One of the very suggestions provided by the ISCM generals I mentioned earlier. Of course, even such creative entrapment is something I could have come up with on my own given the application of enough processing power, but I'm always happy to hear a good idea from somewhere else first." It lifted a finger to tap the side of its head. "When it comes to our future Users, neither I nor the military are looking for the kind of person willing to take the short way out of a problem, you see."

Rei nodded. He'd guessed as much even before the exam, but certainly hadn't deduced *this* level of involvement in the ploy.

"So…" he began after a moment of silence, looking about at the projection of the Arena around them. "What are we doing here? You mentioned an interview?"

The MIND clapped its hands together as though in delight. "Yes! Precisely. This, Mr. Ward, is your assignment interview!"

There was another flash and the figure vanished, appearing again some 5 yards ahead of Rei, along the edge of the Wargame field, directly in the center of what he would have guessed was the true space of the classroom they had.

"Come join me, if you would?"

With a wave, a stark white table and two chairs appeared beside the MIND, shimmering into view from the ground up. Rei did as he was told, grabbing at the back of the nearest chair and being unsurprised to find it solid. It was possible it was an actual seat being overlaid into the projection, but just as likely was it a solid-form simulation.

Either way, he pulled it out and sat down, the AI doing the same across from him.

"There are a few thing to clarify first," it began, leaning over the table and intertwining its fingers before it like one of the lawyers on the drama shows Matron Kast would sometimes let them watch as children. "First—and this is important—under *no circumstance* are you to deliberately reveal, discuss, or record any part of this portion of the exam, under penalty of law, the minimum being the stripping of your CAD should I choose to assign you one after this conversation. You have already deduced the level of monitoring my systems are capable of, so I would ask you not to test me on this. Understood?"

Rei nodded, feeling a bead of sweat form on his forehead. So *that* was why information was so sparse on this portion of the test…

"Second—and this is a condition for you exclusively—similarly are you banned from revealing to anyone the method by which you were passed through the physical evaluation. You are the first to have been assigned such treatment, and I do not foresee the news being well-received, particularly among others who have failed that specific section of the exam."

"The first?" Rei spoke up finally, surprised. "Ever?"

"Ever." The MIND nodded. "Given your written score, I'm going to assume you know a bit about the archons, Mr. Ward?"

"Artificial entities," Rei recited practically from memory. "Encountered by settlers more than two hundred years ago when humanity tried to extend into the Sirius System."

The MIND waited, clearly anticipating more, and Rei thought he knew what the AI was waiting for.

"Our enemy on the frontier."

"Nearly full marks," the MIND said, leaning away from him to settle more comfortably in its chair, "but lacking one crucial detail you have no way of being aware of: the archons are also the primary source of our Combat Assistance Device technology."

Rei felt his jaw drop, and the hint of a smirk on the mostly featureless face said this was the anticipated response.

"Yes. That tends to be the reaction your kind make when this information is shared with them. The basis of our frontline defenses. The centerpiece of our greatest form of entertainment *and* military training. Largely adapted from pillaged archon tech."

"But… Isn't that dangerous?" Rei hissed, unable to keep himself from questioning the sense of this. "The archons are a networked being. You're not… afraid of that?"

It was a lot to take in—a *lot*—but it wasn't wholly shocking. While the public information about Devices claimed they were merely a complex technology invented by the military and being constantly improved on, there were more than a few rumors circulating the feeds that CADs were too far beyond anything else humanity had created for itself.

"If you're asking whether I'm concerned that the archon hive-system is capable of tapping into our Devices, therefore either spying on us or using them or their Users to enemy advantage… No. I am not." The MIND smoothly waved the question away as though it were a trivial matter. "I said CAD technology was *largely* adapted from archon machinations, not *entirely*. Along with a thousand of mankind's brightest minds over some centuries, yours truly has seen to that. Our Users are safe, and our Devices are not 'hackable', as you would put it."

The assurance made Rei feel a little better, but it still unsettled him.

"My point in telling you all this—" the MIND pressed on before he could question anything else "—is not to concern you about the nuances of CAD implementation, but to make you understand *why* you have been given a rather unique privilege, at least as of this moment." The AI leaned forward again. "Archons adapt. Did you know that?"

Rei nodded. "Yes. It's the reason why Users are so important. CAD evolution and the various Types allow mankind to maintain a foothold in the war. Otherwise we would be overrun by the enemy's transient nature."

"All true, but with one caveat: archons adapt faster than Users should be able to respond to."

Rei blinked, not understanding. If that were true, then the war that had raged for over a century at the edges of the ISC should have reached the systems a long time ago…

Then what the MIND had *actually* said registered.

"…Should? They adapt faster than we *should* be able to respond to?"

The MIND smiled. "I'm not one to stutter, Mr. Ward. Now… With that in mind—and the knowledge I've otherwise imparted on you—I would like you to tell me what it is, exactly, that keeps our fine planets from being overrun in a matter of years."

The request hung in the air for a moment, and Rei realized abruptly that—though it hadn't been phrased as a question—the third part of the exam was already underway. Allowing himself a breath, he leaned back in his chair and crossed his arms, dropping his gaze to the sheen of the table's surface as he thought.

At a glance there *was* no good reason. If the archons could adapt faster than Users could train, evolve their CADs, and be deployed, logic dictated that the war would have been over a long, long time ago, with mankind on the losing side. But that wasn't the case. In fact, while humanity hadn't made *great* progress in the last decades, it was generally understood knowledge that the war effort was going well, with the archons steadily being pushed deeper and deeper into space. Sirius had actually been colonized some 50 years after the start of the war, having been claimed as the seventh of the ISC's galaxies, and thrived.

Stranger still… There were the SCTs…

The Simulated Combat Tournaments *were* the military's sole source of revenue, which wasn't surprising given the popularity of the events. The slower-than-light orbital ship races still managed to hold a measure of viewership on the feeds, but the SCTs were watched some 68% of the ISC populace with access to NOEDs or pads. They were the reason the military had thousands of schools across the different systems, mostly for training in various careers on the frontline, but hundreds still designed exclusively for the CAD-Users.

But… The SCTs were also the reason combat wasn't a requirement for Users who managed *any* decent kind of reputation in even just the collegiate tournament circuits…

That was where Rei found himself tripping up as he considered the MIND's request. It was a fact that popular Users had a massive impact on military recruitment and credit intake, but around one in five combatants were never required to head to the front lines, to see live combat, and those one in five were typically the *best* Users the Systems had to offer. Some of them—like the famed A-Type user Valera Dent, the Iron Bishop—had *chosen* to fight after retirement, but most ran the course of the circuits until they fell out of favor or stepped away on their own terms.

For the strongest 20% of the military's most effective measure against the archons to be allowed not to take part in active—

And then it clicked.

"They *are* taking part." Rei said the words aloud, and the MIND—who had somehow been playing an accurate game of thumb-wrestling with itself—looked up expectantly.

"Oh-ho..." the AI started. "It sounds like you've come to an interesting conclusion..."

Rei didn't speak for a moment more, trying to ensure he had the right words for his explanation. At last, he managed what he thought was a fair articulation of his assessment.

"I was struggling to understand why—if the archons adapt at a rate faster than we can deploy—one in five CAD-Users are allowed to exclusively participate in the tournament circuits. No live combat. Just entertainment. Then I realized: it's not *just* entertainment, is it? I mean obviously it assists with recruitment and military funding—everyone knows that—but there's more to it, isn't there?" Rei narrowed his eyes at the MIND, wondering if he had deduced correctly. "The fighting... The evolution of Devices *built* from archon tech, and the way Users adapt to each other and problem-solve both in combat and out of it..." He chewed on his final words a moment. "We—*you're*—learning, aren't you?"

For several seconds the AI stared at him—or managed the best equivalent to staring it could, given the figure had no eyes. Whether Rei had actually challenged this offshoot of the system enough to delay its process, or the MIND was just pausing for emphasis, he couldn't guess.

Finally, the AI sat up abruptly straight clapping its hands in delight.

"Bravo!" it exclaimed, sounding genuinely thrilled. "I've asked that question 12,176 times in the last hour, and no one has come up with that answer quite as substantially." The figure settled, growing almost sober. "Indeed, I am learning, though you had it right the first time. *We* are learning. User data has been an essential part of the ISCM's measures against the enemy, and that information is nearly as valuable coming from battles between Users—as well as their growth over time—as the intelligence we gather from live combat. Couple that with the recruitment and finance advantages you mentioned, and you have your answer as to why we have not been overrun by the archons." The AI cocked its head. "Now... Can you explain to me why, then, I chose to overrule your physical assessment rejection by Sergeant Gregor Valenti?"

Rei didn't look away from the strange white face this time, the answer coming much more easily now. "You need variables."

The MIND nodded slowly. "Precisely. And hence my interest in you, Mr. Ward." The figure leaned forward again, and for once Rei got the impression the action was actually inadvertent, as though the AI couldn't help itself from peering at him more closely. "I don't think I will surprise you when I say that you have nearly *all* the essentials required in the making of an excellent CAD-User. Your gathered history tells me you've spent the last decade of an impressively short life striving to that goal, and I am pleased to say you have achieved it. It… and much more." The white face was yet closer, and Rei realized the MIND's neck was extending so it could approach even after its "body" could no longer bend further over the table. "You are—for lack of a more modest term—a rather perfect specimen of 'outside the norm' when it comes to typical User candidates, particularly top-notch ones such as your friend 'Viv'." It smiled a little as Rei blinked in surprise at the name, but made no other commentary on the subject. Instead, it brought one hand up to point at Rei's arm and the black sleeve that covered his scarred skin once more. "Your physical condition is—if anything—an opportunity. A chance to try something new."

"Put more simply: you want me to be your guinea pig."

There was no malice in Rei's voice as he said it, nor did he feel any. He just didn't want the matter to be beat around.

Instantly the MIND retracted, pulling back into its original form and crossing one leg over the other as it draped a casual arm across the back of its chair. "Does that bother you?"

"Does it mean I'd be assigned a CAD?"

The MIND's formless face scrutinized him for a moment more.

Then it nodded. "Most certainly."

"Then no. It doesn't bother me.

The MIND smiled then, in truth, the formless surface of its face shifting into something uncomfortable, like it was going to very much enjoy seeing where the world went after that moment.

"Excellent. Now, then, with that matter settled… I would like to start querying as to the nature of your diagnosis, and its relevance in your abandonment by your parents…"

CHAPTER 6

By the time Viv found him—seated once more at the number 221 desk in the main floor of the combat gym—a good hour had passed, and Rei had managed to regain a little bit of his composure. He still trembled if he didn't consciously focus on keeping his hands steady, but he was no longer sweating, and most of the anger, fear, and nervousness had faded away. He jumped as the chair at his right was pulled out, feeling his heart skip a beat when Viv eased down beside him, looking about as shaken as he felt.

"So… How about that third part, huh?" she asked weakly, looking nowhere but straight ahead, her blue eyes a little puffy. Rei, deciding imitating her was for the best, nodded slowly, but said nothing more. For almost a minute they sat in silence, two of only a half-dozen applicants to have completed the exam, but eventually he decided talking—about *anything*—was better than dwelling on the psychologic upheaval he was sure the MIND had put them *all* through.

"Did you get your results?" he managed to get out faintly. He held up the single sheet of paper that had been handed to him as he'd entered the gymnasium a good half hour before anyone else finished. "They gave this to me on my way in…?"

Viv didn't answer immediately, her gaze still far away. After a few seconds, though, Rei's question appeared to reach her, because she started and looked around.

"I-I did!" she answered, a little too enthusiastically, clearly as eager as he was for any distraction from the dark places her thoughts had likely been dunked into. Reaching for the bag she was still carrying around, she pulled out her own—slightly-crumpled—sheet and held it up. "97th percentile in the physical assessment!" Viv's voice regained a little of its usual energy as she pointed out the line, which was sub-marked with a dozen different measurements and the broken-down percentiles of each. "99th in flexibility and red blood cell count!"

"Whoa!" Rei said, genuinely impressed, reaching to tug the paper from her. "Bad*ass*, Viv!" His eyes trailed the lines. "Only 93rd in bone density, though. I *told* you that you should have been doing more high-impact training."

"Yeah, yeah," Viv waved the comment away with one hand as she plucked the page back before he could read any of her other numbers, folding it in half to leave on the table. "What about you? Let me see!"

Sheepishly, Rei handed over his printout. Viv snatched it up like a starving man offered bread, eagerly looking it over.

"98.7% on the written?! Holy *shit*, Rei! I scored a 94.5 and I thought *that* was good."

Rei laughed nervously, waiting for her eyes to drop, knowing what she would see next. They did, and he felt his stomach lurch.

On the line for "Physical Assessment", all that had been printed was a single word: "Passed". No percentile ranking. No sub-markings. Just the word.

"'Passed'." Viv read it out loud, quietly at first. Then she read it again, then again, louder each time. "Passed? Passed! Rei! YOU PASSED!"

She practically screamed the last bit, and Rei was suddenly being lunged at, Viv's long arms wrapping around his neck as she laughed and danced in her seat. He found himself smiling even as he tried to fight her off, the final dregs of the darkness the MIND had left his thoughts in trailing away.

There was an echoing cough, and Viv stopped moving abruptly. Together they looked around, towards the front of the line of tables, where an evaluator in his black and gold uniform was standing at ease even as he stared at them very, *very* pointedly.

"Sorry," Viv said in a stage whisper to the officer, releasing Rei but not letting go of his result. "But he passed. He *passed*!"

A hint of a smile crossed the man's face, but then he was looking dead ahead once more, pretending he hadn't seen anything.

"Rei. This is *amazing*!" Viv was breathless as she looked down at his sheet again. "Not gonna lie, I was really, *really* worried."

"Ha," Rei managed to squeak out, wondering how many of the MIND's eyes and ears were trained on their conversation right then. "Yeah… Me too…"

"But you *passed*," she hissed again. "It's weird that they didn't grade or sub-mark you, but maybe they only do that for the upper echelons. And that writing score…" Her eyes were afire when she turned on him. "Rei, if you get a CAD with a decent Rank, Galens might just take you! We can do it! We can do this!"

"You're assuming I get one," Rei corrected her softly. "That we *both* get one. They didn't mark the third portion on this printout." He tapped the blank white under his

"Physical Assessment" line for emphasis. "Nothing's for sure until they call our names."

Viv, however, was apparently in no mood to be deterred.

"That third part was awful, but I nailed it. Knowing you, I don't think for a *second* you didn't too, if we had a remotely similar test." She grinned, the flame in her blue eyes growing all the brighter. "We've got this. We've *got* this!"

Rei couldn't help it, then, seeing his best friend's enthusiasm on their behalf. He smiled back.

"Yeah," he managed to get out more confidently than he felt, recalling his conversation with the MIND. "Yeah. We've got this."

Even if it's as a guinea pig.

O ver the next two hours the other finalists slowly trickled into the gym, taking to their seats one at a time. Finally, after what seemed like forever—and more warning looks from a few of the evaluators when their whispered conversations got too animated—Rei and Viv watched what had to be the last candidate to have passed the first and second portions of the exam enter, because the officer who handed the boy his results at the entrance closed the sliding door behind him.

Sure enough, the moment the examinee had found his seat again, Major Albert Connelly made his appearance once more, striding out from one of the lobbies at what must have been some digital summoning, his flat-top military cap in perfect order atop his head, a wide pad in one hand. Seeing him again, Rei felt a buzz of nerves and excitement.

Reaching the front and center of the tables, the major turned to face the scattered hopefuls who had managed to serve the day's trials.

"Applicants," the man barked, "this marks the end of your CAD-Assignment Exam. First of all, a congratulations to all 112 of you who have made it this far. Of the 521 in this gymnasium at the start of the day, *you* are the only to have weathered the tests without cause for disqualification. Regardless of what happens from this moment onward, that is commendable, and worthy of praise."

Rei might have imagined it, but he thought he saw the major's eyes flick to him from under the brim of his cap.

"*However*," Connelly continued, and a tingle of anxious fear crawled up Rei's spine, "while the exam is complete, the selection process is not. I have here—" he held up the pad he'd carried with him into the room, and as he spoke the light of blue text appearing on the tablets surface shined off the gold buttons of his uniform "—the names of thirty-four individuals who have been deemed appropriate for Device-assignment over the course of the third portion of the exam you all undertook."

Despite the reduced, scattered number of people left in the room, there was a hum of mumbled noise at this announcement. Rei couldn't blame them.

"Thirty-four?" Viv hissed quietly from beside him. "Only *thirty-four*? That's *way* less than one in twelve…!"

Rei didn't answer, feeling her nervousness, but also clinging to the major's every word as Connelly continued.

"Yes, that *is* below the average pass rate, but it is called an 'average' for a reason. If you are on this list—" he waved the pad briefly "—then you *earned* your place there, as you have all certainly experienced today. If you are not, then consider what elements may have caused you to fail the third evaluation and try again next year."

At that, the major flicked his other hand, and several things happened at once. First a rumbling sound from their left had all heads turning towards the south lobby door, where four or five men and women in uniform were escorting a floating white platform with a large, awkward shape atop it hidden from view by a black drape. Second, the lights in the combat gym went out, tossing everyone into the dark for a moment before color blazed to life over them again. There were gasps and shouts of amazement as the projection cast itself over what had been a plain synthetic floor, old tables and chairs, and amphitheater seating. In their place, a ballroom out of some science-fiction epic built itself into being around them in rapid order, pixilated blocks forming and sliding into place from the ground up. Within a handful of seconds a dozen stone pillars of intricately-cut marble towered up on either side of the still-seated examinees, reaching for the ceiling where they arched and formed a webbed lattice whose empty in-betweens were left unfilled. This space extended to the floor, and beyond these intricate—if meager—walls, a view unlike anything Rei thought *any* of them had had the opportunity to witness hung in slow rotation.

"Whoa…" Viv breathed from Rei's right.

Gaseous clouds of every color were suspended in a sea of black and stars, with narrow points of brighter light marking the largest or hottest of distant suns. Like dyed silks the nebulas overlaid each other, bathing them all in a faint, handsome glow.

"Deeeefinitely a hologram," Rei whispered sidelong to Viv. "That's the Crab Nebula, projected right next to the Eagle."

"Shut up," she hissed back, eyes fixed on the endlessness of the heavens that were turning slowly all around them. "It's pretty."

Rei chuckled, forcing himself to bring his own attention earthward again. The tables they'd all been seated at were still present, but hidden under simulations of heavy wood covered by black cloth. In the center of each of these, the seven stars and crossed swords of the ISCM had been stitched in gold, and Rei was pondering at the impressive quality of the projection when a motion at the front of the room caught his eyes. He looked up in time to see that the floating platform the evaluators had been bringing into the space had finally reached its resting point at the front and center of the room, and was being settled down atop a raised dais of stone behind which hung nothing but more of the wondrous heavens. Two of the evaluators were in the process of pulling the black cloth free of whatever it was that was atop the platform, and as they slid the covering loose, Rei swallowed.

A surgical table.

No. That wasn't exactly right. It *was* similar to a surgical table, but not formed from the clean titanium or sterilized steel Rei was accustomed to feeling as the drugs dragged him under. Rather, this table looked to be made of several different sections of a dark, matte sheen, the seams of which were outlined in glowing purple lines which appeared illuminated from within, faint shafts of light swimming upward, like something was moving beneath the metal.

Carbonized steel. Stryon particle-powered vysetrium.

CAD materials.

Archon technology... Rei couldn't help but think.

Whispers started breaking out all about the room as others noticed the device, and Rei elbowed Viv in the ribs to make her bring her eyes down from the nebulas swirling around them. She grunted in pain and was very likely about to curse at him when she, too, saw the table.

"Thaaaat's not freaky at *all*," she muttered.

"Everyone, if you would please turn your attentions to your NOEDs." The major was standing patiently to the side as the officers under his command finished setting up the strange object that would clearly be key in the assignment of those who would be granted their Devices that day. "You are about to receive an essential contract of military service. *All* are required to review this, and sign before we can proceed with distribution of CADs. For those of you who are being assigned to duty, this will serve as your bond of service to the Intersystem Collective Military. For those of you who do not receive a Device, this contract acts as an agreement of non-disclosure regarding anything you might see or hear from this point forward. It is also an implied letter of recommendation from the evaluators of this test for any other employment you may or may not seek within the ISCM, given the fortitude and ability it takes to reach this point in the Assignment Exam."

As he finished, a notification indeed flashed into view in the frame of Rei's neuro-optic, and he selected the message—sent directly from the ISCM—with a quick eye command. It opened, and text started streaming across his vision.

It wasn't, in the end, an overly complicated contract, with most of the details citing to known documents anyone who had passed the written portion of the exam would have memorized by heart already. The ISCM's "Oath of Duty". The military pay-structure, generous especially to CAD-Users, SCT circuit successes in particular. There were even addresses to the intersystem civil codes, adding mostly that the responsibility of Device wielders rested mainly on the banning of calling on a CAD outside of sanctioned areas without valid reason, in any form, phantom of true. Rei read it through carefully—answering a few whispered questions from Viv as others directed theirs to the major—before finally reaching the bottom.

In agreeing to this document, I Pledge myself to the Responsibilities listed above, as well as the charges of Good Faith and Sense in the undertaking, training, and application of my Combat Assistance Device, should I receive one on this day.

AGREE / DISAGREE

Rei smirked a little, reading over the simplicity of the sign-off. It seemed wanting, somehow, compared to the weight of the moment. He even hesitated, staring at the "*AGREE*" for a time, feeling the burden he was—potentially—about to bring down on his shoulders.

Then, with a quick flick and blink, he signed his consent, and the contract vanished.

"And so I grant thee my life and soul, oh cruel mistress of battle," he quoted dramatically, earning a snigger from Viv as she, too, agreed to the terms.

It was another couple of minutes before the others had read through the document to their satisfaction, in which the pair of them sat in silence, feeling the tension in the room grow. By the time the major cleared his throat and began to speak again, both Rei and Viv had knees bouncing nervously beneath the table.

"With that done, we shall proceed." Connelly held up the pad again. "Names will be read out in alphabetical order. If you are called, please stand, and join me here—" he indicated the spot beside him, in front of the dais and its raised table "—and I and the other evaluators will instruct you further. If your name is *not* on the list, I respectfully request that you stay seated until all CAD recipients have been assigned their Devices."

He paused then, letting the distinctly non-optional "request" sink in. Beside Rei, Viv made a jerking motion, and he felt her take his hand under the heavy wood of the table, gripping it hard. He didn't look around, but returned the pressure, understanding her anxiety. If they were indeed going alphabetically, then there was a decent chance that—

"Arada, Viviana."

The trembling inhalation Viv took then was something between relief and absolute, sheer terror. She didn't stand immediately, staring at the major as though not believing her ears, but with an encouraging squeeze of her fingers Rei spoke to her quietly.

"Viv. Go."

After a seconds more hesitation, she finally got up, shaking and releasing his hand to move unsteadily down the aisle. For all her strength, for all her height and designed beauty, Rei's best friend looked then like a newborn fawn trying to stand on unsteady legs. No one laughed, though, as she half-walked, half-stumbled to the end of the row, then around to the front of the hall to come to a halt beside the major. No one did anything more than stare, watching the proceedings with an anticipation that roiled in the atmosphere of the room despite its silence.

Connelly bent down when Viv reached him, instructing her quietly and motioning to the table. She nodded, and as she moved towards it two of the evaluators—a man and a woman—fell in beside her. As a trio they climbed the dais, then the platform, then the officers helped Viv slide onto the table and lie down. The light of the purple vysetrium pulsed a little as she let her head down on the flat, hard surface, and Rei could practically *hear* her breaths coming harder and faster while the evaluators shifted her position a little this way and that, paying particularly close attention to the placement of her hands. One of them appeared to ask her if she was ready, because she swallowed hard even as she gave a quivering nod. The officer who'd asked the question—the man—in turn gave an affirming gesture to his female partner, then stepped smartly off the platform. The woman, meanwhile, had moved to the back of the table, and looked to be inputting some sort of command into a master panel Rei couldn't see.

For a little while, nothing happened. The Crab and Eagle nebulas spun around them in drifting silence, the quiet of the room so absolute they might have all been *actually* adrift in space. The absence of sound and action extended so long, in fact, that Rei started to worry something had gone wrong.

Then, with a pulsing *woomph* of sound like pressurized atmosphere being released from an airlock, the table blazed into life in a brilliant plume of violet light.

Beneath Viv the dark plates of carbonized steel around the outline of her body began to shift, lifting and moving into a complex array that bent steadily upwards around the girl in their center. Before long a half-dozen ribs of broken, angular black shapes had curved over Viv's body like a distorted cage. The light flared brighter, so much so Rei was forced to bring a hand up to cover his eyes as a few cries of surprise and discomfort came from the other examinees around him, and Viv's form was completely lost to the glow. There was a building whine of machinery, like the ramping whir of a neutron-collider engine, rising in pitch until it hurt the ears.

And then, with a flash and a down-spinning calming of all sound, it was over.

Rei had to squeeze his eyes shut a few times to clear his vision, and by the time he managed it Viv was being helped off the table by the two evaluators who'd seen her initially settled. For a moment she teetered, like the process had drained her, but then she stood... tall? Too tall, almost. Viv too, looked surprised by her own composure, her mouth hanging slightly open as she looked down at something on her arm.

That was when Rei saw the CAD.

It sat, just tight enough not to slip off her hands, around both wrists. Nothing more from the outside than matching plain, thin bands of the same carbonized steel that made up the table behind Viv—now still and returned to its original configuration—Rei thought he could make out a faint silvery glow in a clash of dark purple and yellow. The colors fit her, somehow. Firm, and yet bright in the same space and time.

"*Nice*, Viv." Rei whispered under his breath.

On legs now much steadier than they had been when she'd first approached him, Viv strode down the steps towards Connelly. Despite it being only an initial form, her CAD was already making improvements to her physiological base. It would be a few weeks of slow changes before her body adjusted completely, but even the immediate adjustment was noticeable.

Reaching the major, Viv listened as Connelly said something quietly to her again, then brought up her right arm. He held the pad over the purple-and-yellow Device there for a moment, then motioned for her to face the room with him once text began scrawling itself across the screen.

"Calling on your Combat Assistance Device for the first time is an experience I will have the honor of sharing with all of you," the major said to the infinitely attentive watchers. "Eventually, it will be as easy as breathing, requiring nothing more than a thought, but for new cadets, vocal command is the simplest way to get used to the process. Arada—" he looked to Viv, who was watching him carefully "—please focus on the weight of your Device on your wrists, and say 'Call'."

Viv did as instructed, lifting both hands before her.

"Call."

The CAD responded immediately.

With a shimmer of shifting silver light and expanding metal, the bands transitioned in a rippling flash. One moment Viv was standing there, showing off a pair of shiny new bracelets to a crowd of a hundred-and-something envious onlookers.

The next, she was holding a pair of glowing, rippling blades.

In her right hand, a weapon roughly the size and breadth of a shortsword had materialized, the handle and pommel comprised of different shades of the purple carbonized steel, the inside of the blade itself a solid length of yellow. The double-edge, on the other hand, shone a vibrant silver, the Stryon particles in the vysetrium made the alien element glow and flicker. There was no crossguard—not for now, at least—and in Viv's left a single-edged dagger of a similar design now shown.

"CAD Name: Gemela," Major Connelly began reading in a formal tone from his pad as Viv stared in wonder at the weapons, bringing them nearer her face for closer inspection, her NOED coming alive in her eyes. "Type: Duelist. Rank... D6."

Finally, at the announcement of the new Device's Rank, the silence from the examinees broke.

There were several *whoops* of excitement, along with not a few grumbles of jealousy. Rei was happy to join in the former, barely suppressing an exited banging on the table and a shouted "YEAH!" D6... D6 wasn't just a *good* starting rank. It was two levels higher than the average first year inductees at the Galens Institute! With her written score and a CAD of that ability, Viv had just signed herself her dream ticket to the best military school on the planet!

"As Arada is currently demonstrating—" the major was speaking again, motioning to Viv as she continued to scrutinize her weapons. "Anyone assigned today will be able to scan their CAD specs at any time. This is called a 'Specifications Request'. To recall your Device, merely focus on them again, and say 'Recall'." He looked at Viv pointedly, and she had the nerve to hesitate for a moment before closing her NOED and doing as was clearly being suggested.

Holding the two blades away from her, she enunciated clearly. "Recall."

With a flash, the weapons collapsed once more into the twin bands of purple-yellow detailed in silver around her wrist.

This done, the major put the pad behind his back and held out a hand to Viv. When she took it, Connelly offered what had to have been the first real smile Rei had seen him give.

"Congratulations, cadet. Welcome to the ISCM."

CHAPTER 7

After the fourth or fifth assignment, the novelty of the event began to wear off. By the time the tenth new cadet had been welcomed to the military by the major, Rei and Viv had spent most of the wait with their heads together, gaping over her Device's specs and talking in hushed squeals of excitement.

Viv was positively vibrating with happiness, for which Rei could hardly blame her. Aside from the adrenaline and physiological changes that probably made her feel not-unlike a brand-new person, her CAD was a *D6* rank. The moment she'd sat down—and after an obligatory repeat of the excited hug-dance from earlier—Viv had shared Gemela's information with him without pause.

20 minutes later, they were still fawning over the stats.

"Holy *hell*, Viv!" Rei breathed, reading the numbers for the hundredth time. "I still can't believe this… Your Defense is trash right now, and your Strength and Endurance aren't far ahead, but what the *hell* is up with these Speed and Offense stats?! D8?! D9?! With enough training you could *absolutely* qualify for Sectionals with starting specs like these!"

"I *know*!" Viv squealed, barely able to reign in her enthusiasm—much less keep her voice to a reasonable pitch. "Do you think it will get me into Galens?!"

"Definitely," Rei answered without hesitation, frowning just a little. "Your Growth could be better—D4 is above-average, but barely compared to your other specs—but if you work hard enough with this there's no reason you couldn't became a *terror* in the collegiate circuit starting as a second year, and once Gemela evolves a bit." He closed his frame, putting away the numbers and looked around at her directly. "You're into Galens. Definitely. You're in."

Her half-shriek of excitement was fortunately drowned out by the building whine of the assignment table as the eleventh new cadet received his device, and Viv was glowing and talking to herself for the next quarter-hour, sometimes pulling up her specs to look them over again, sometimes listing another person she had to call the moment they were excused from the exam space. Rei smiled all the while, basking in her positive energy, up until the twentieth person was summoned to the table, then the twenty-fifth. In that time, only a single cadet was assigned a CAD with a higher Rank that Viv's Gemela—a Lancer who managed to earn himself a D7 Device—but even this announcement Rei hardly heard.

Internally, the nerves began to take hold again.

Every time a new name was called more cries of denial and frustration rang out from the snubbed all around them, fueling his fear. Logically Rei knew his name would be close to the end if it was on the list—probably even the last given—but it was the *if* that started to eat at him. His written score was superb, and the MIND had overridden his physical assessment personally. After that, hadn't there been a measure of assurance from the AI that he would receive his CAD today? Abruptly Rei doubted, painstakingly going over each moment of the conversation that had followed those words, picking and prodding at every answer he'd made and every statement he'd given over the course of the MIND's brutal "interview."

It's not happening, the fear began to say. *No way. It's not happening.*

The thirty-second assignee returned to their seat, and the thirty-third was called.

"Vessena, Alexandra."

A thin girl with blue-grey hair stood up from a table a few rows ahead of Rei and Viv, and he watched her approach the major, watched her get led up to the table and placed upon it. He didn't even have the mind to look away when the light and the whining came, his thoughts elsewhere and his mouth going dry even as the process finished.

It's not happening. It's not happening. It's not—

"You're next, Rei."

Viv's firm words cut through his spiral, and he looked around at her shakily. She wasn't actually watching him, her chin held high and her eyes set forward, taking in Alexandra Vessena being announced as a Mauler-Type, but the utter confidence in her bearing sparked a little warmth in his chest. She repeated the words, sounding as convinced of them as she might have been of gravity or air or the solidity of the table and seats beneath them.

"You're next."

Silently, Rei managed to nod, watching Vessena shake hands with the major, then start back for her seat. Then his eyes shifted to Connelly, who was looking down at his pad again, searching for the next name.

The moment the major paused, the smallest hint of surprise showing in the widening of his eyes under the brim of his cap, Rei knew.

"Ward, Reidon."

L ieutenants Espen and O'Flynn will get you set up on the table. Once they have you situated, you are *not to move*, even when things get bright and loud. Is that understood?"

Rei only heard the major's words from a distant place, but had sense enough to nod as expected. He watched Connelly give him a final testing look, then the commanding officer lifted his gaze to where the lieutenants waited expectantly, gesturing for them to proceed with a flick of his head. A touch had Rei turning around numbly, and he found himself staring into the smiling face of one of the two officers, the man.

"Come on, cadet. I promise it's not half as bad as it looks from the outside."

Rei said nothing, allowing himself to be led towards the dais, then up onto the platform. He was faintly aware that he was receiving more assistance then any of the other assignees before him, but he couldn't tell if he didn't care or was simply unable to, in that moment. He stood, gazing down at the carbonized steel table, watching the purple light dance from the vysetrium seams between the plates. On approaching, the intricacies of the Device were nothing short of entrancing, the lines forming a symmetrical pattern up the length, including a few clear markers that shaped the vaguest tracings of a person. He stared, incapable of believing that he was so close, *this* close.

His name. They had called his name…

A voice reached him, muffled.

"Cadet… *Cadet.*"

Rei jumped, rousing himself from his trance. The officer who'd helped him towards the table was watching him with some measure of concern.

"Do you need a moment? It's all right. It can be overwhelming for some people."

"N-no, sir." Rei shook his head, turning his attention back to the device. "I just… I didn't expect this…"

The lieutenant gave a knowing laugh. His counterpart, meanwhile, was already on the other side of the table from them, watching Rei expectantly with her hands hovering over the data panel Rei could see, now. "Most of the people who *do* expect it don't end up standing where you are." He lifted one arm so that the sleeve of his black and gold uniform slipped a little, revealing the edge of a white-green CAD. "Believe me, I know the feeling. But if you're here, then you earned it. So buck up, and on you go."

The words were the push he needed, and with tentative hands Rei stepped forward and slid himself unto the table. The carbonized steel was pleasantly warm—nothing like the hard surfaces of the surgical benches the contraption had first reminded him of—and though his heart still thundered in his chest Rei found himself breathing a little easier as he settled down.

"Bring yourself towards me and a bit to your right," the lieutenant at the panel said, not looking away from whatever data was showing up for her. Rei did as instructed, and after a few more minor adjustments the woman gave the okay. Her partner bent over the edge of the table to look Rei in the eye.

"Remember: no moving. Understood?"

Rei took a shaking breath, then nodded. The officer stepped away, and for a while the world went silent again, empty and still but for space turning high above, patchworked by the decorative stone lattice of walls and ceiling. Watching the simulated nebulas pass by without a sound, Rei finally calmed in truth, the understanding settling at last.

They had called his name…

And then his vision was completely obscured by the quick build of blinding purple light.

He tried to keep his eyes open, tried to watch the proceedings, but from within the illumination it all was too bright. He only managed to hold out long enough to see the black plates begin to shift and move, begin to curve over him in the same organization of strange, alien arches. After that, he shut his eyes tight, but even through closed lids the violet light danced and streamed. Soon the growing whir of the machine had begun, and Rei had to grit his teeth to keep from yelling out as it reached a pitching scream in his ears. There was no pain. No prodding and poking or physical sensation of any kind. Instead, what Rei felt was… deeper. The shriek of the device and the light felt like it was burrowing into him, implanting itself into his flesh. Into his bones. Into his mind. It started first in his head, then crawled down his neck into his shoulders, trailing the length of his form until it faded over his fingers, then his hips, then his toes.

Finally, some true sensation *did* reach him, and Rei had to consciously focus on not moving as he felt hard, warm metal come into being seemingly from nothing, lifting his wrist slightly off the table as it shaped around them.

Then it was done, the brightness fading to black, the wheeling of the machine winding down.

Rei opened his eyes and had to blink a few times before the world came back into focus. At first everything was blurred, the shapes of the evaluators a little unclear as they bustled around him, but slowly his vision returned.

"Good job, cadet," the man said, bending over his face once again. "Get yourself up easy. You'll probably feel some differences, but don't push it."

As instructed, Rei sat up carefully, sliding one leg off the table, then the other. Finding himself a little light-headed, he waited, then pushed himself down to the platform. As he did, there was the *clink* of metal on metal, and he froze, feeling his breath catch in his chest.

At last convincing himself to look down, Rei had to force away a lump in his throat that might have threatened tears.

In the form of twin rings fit snuggly at the edge of his shirt sleeves, the CAD was a calm combination of black loops interrupted by a white section that made up a third of the bands. Set between these two parts, ice-blue vysetrium separated the colored steels, narrow partitions of glowing, azure stone. More of the shimmering element decorated the outer surfaces of the white portion, forming a trio of matching, clean diamonds.

The Device was—there was no other way to put it—beautiful.

"Ward. Front and center, if you would."

Ward blinked and looked up from the CAD, finding Major Connelly watching him expectantly. Promptly he stood up off the table, intending to make his way tall and proud to the officer's side. He started forward down the step of the platform.

And immediately collapsed as his leg gave out beneath him when it attempted to take his weight.

Rei fell so suddenly, he didn't even have time to yell out before he hit the projected stone of the dais. There was a shout, and as he struggled to figure out what had happened he felt two sets of hands grab him under each arm.

"Up you get, cadet. Up you get." The male lieutenant's voice was gentle in his ear. "No worries. It happens. Just means your starting Strength and Endurance specs aren't high enough to counteract the toll of the process."

"Y-yeah," Rei go out, as they helped him to his feet. "Assignment fatigue... I know it..."

A stone began to grow in his stomach. Assignment fatigue was rare, and for good reason. For even initial CAD specs to be that low…

No, Rei told himself firmly, not looking up from the ground. *No. No need to panic. It just means my other specs are probably a lot higher to balance things out.*

With that self-encouragement, he steadied himself, then thanked the evaluators on either side for their help. They stepped away, but didn't move out of reach, clearly ready for him to stumble again.

This time, when he took the 8 inches down from the dais to the floor, Rei didn't *allow* himself to fall.

His leg accepted his weight—if barely—and it was with careful steps that he approached Major Connelly, who had watched his collapse without a word. Reaching the man, he held out his CAD as expected. Connelly considered him a moment, then passed the pad over the Device.

"Cadet, you may call your—" he started as data began to appear in quick lines on the tablet screen, but stopped abruptly. He stared at the numbers only he could see, and Rei felt the weight in his gut redouble.

At last, with a cough to cover up his pause, Connelly started again.

"Cadet, you may call your Device."

This was it. This was the moment. Rei had been waiting for this chance the better part of his entire life. Lifting both hands up before him, he took in the twin bands with every ounce of focus he could muster, vowing to never forget whatever happened next.

"Call."

A blur of motion from his right wrist. As he watched, the ring there dissolved, repositioned to his hand, and reformed in the space of a heartbeat. Black steel wrapped around his fingers, forming a grip that pulled them into a loose curl, and a white strike-plate assembled itself over the resulting fist, split by three equal lines of the blue vysetrium. In the end, Rei found himself staring at a contraption not unlike the weighted gloves they sometimes used in combat team training, only instead of pads to cushion the blow, the outer portion was flat metal.

He didn't even notice, in that moment, that the other band of his CAD hadn't so much as shivered around his left wrist.

"CAD Name: Shido," Major Connelly started to read off the pad in his formal tone. "Type: A-Type. Rank… F8."

Rei's heart plummeted.

F-Rank… Forget not being near the D4 mark that was the average of incoming first years at the Galens Institute. F8 was more than a full *tier* lower than the average CAD *assignee* Rank of D0. With an initial Device of this level, Rei would be lucky to get into *any* designated combat academy, much less *Galens*. He might even end up at one of the ISCM's common military schools who focused on the non-User career paths…

Feeling his face growing red, Rei finally tore his eyes from his one-handed CAD—"Shido", the major had called it—and looked out over the tables and the faces of the other examinees. A majority of them—the ones who hadn't received *any* Device—were watching him sullenly, while among the actual assignees more than one smirk or laugh was being hidden behind a lifted hand. Rei trailed them, searching, until he found Viv, who was looking at him with her mouth hanging open, face pale. There was no hope there, this time. No words of encouragement. She seemed stricken, and could do nothing more than stare in that moment, sharing in his heartbreak.

"Cadet Ward… Have you checked your Device specs?"

The major's question, oddly, was subdued, voiced quietly enough that only Rei could hear him. Using the excuse to turn his gaze from Viv's wet eyes, Rei turned to Connelly, who himself was still facing the tables.

"N-No, sir," he got out unevenly, his mind still on the cracked dreams falling to his feet before him.

"Do so. *Silently*, if you please."

Rei's brow creased, not understanding the man, but he looked to Shido as instructed and pulled up his NOED to make the Specifications Request. Why would the major ask him to be quiet? What did he expect? That Rei would whoop for joy over stats which averaged out to an abysmal Rank like the one he'd been—?

And then Rei almost choked, seeing the numbers slide up the frame of his neuro-optic.

Specifications Request acknowledged.

…

Combat Assistance Device: Shido. User identification… Accepted.

Type: A-TYPE

Rank: F8

…

User Attributes:

- Strength: F0

- Endurance: F0

- Speed: F0

-Cognition: F0

. . .

CAD Specifications:

- Offense: F1

- Defense: F0

- Growth: S

Rei *gaped.* With an emotional war covering the mélange of confusion, awe, and disbelief, he stared at the final line of the Request.

Growth: S

How was that possible? How was that *remotely* possible?! He'd heard of initial CADs presenting with individual specification as high as the B-Ranks, but an A-Rank spec was unheard of, much less an *S*. And in *Growth*?! The one attribute that tended not to evolve greatly over the evolution of a CAD's life?! For it to be maxed-out from the go...

Rei couldn't fathom it, couldn't wrap his head around it. His other specs were believable in comparison, which irritated him, because who had ever heard of a Device that offered almost *no* boost to its User's abilities, even an initial one. His Offense value of F1 meant that his attack capabilities were very, *very* slightly above that of an average man's, but his Ranks of F0 in all the other categories marked him as having seen no change over the process of the assignment. For a moment Rei felt anger building, felt betrayed by a dream and a system that had allowed him to have it.

But then his eyes slid down again, and read once more the final line of the Specification Request.

Growth: S

You want me to be your guinea pig.

The statement he had made to the MIND came back to him, as did some clarity. He understood, suddenly. He understood what the AI—humanity's single greatest protector—had been after in seeking its "variables". It wanted something different. Something completely outside the box of anything any previous User had experienced.

It wanted to see what evolution from nothing looked like…

"Major, with all due respect… What is this bullshit?"

A voice cut across Rei's thoughts, and he rose from his internal considerations to find a boy—another one of the examinees—standing up from the right center of the tables before them. He was tall and well-dressed, with lightning-orange hair patterned with black, and eyes designed into the same color. He wasn't looking at Connelly as he addressed him, and was instead glaring at Rei with what could only have been disgust.

"This guy looks like he *might* weigh as much a wet bath towel, and his specs aren't even high enough to counter assignment fatigue! Now you tell us his Rank is in the *F*s?" he put his fists on the table and bent over them. "This is ridiculous! I ended the written section with more than a 91% score, got full marks on my physical assessment, and *know* I passed the third portion of the exam without issue! How the hell did *this* asshole get assigned when *I* didn't?! He's an *F*!"

There was a muttering of agreement from several of the other exam-takers who hadn't gotten their CADs that day, and Rei saw Viv whirl in fury and start to stand, ready to come to his defense.

Fortunately, before she could get a word out, Major Connelly was already responding.

"The CAD-Assignment Exam measures more than statistical merit," he said steadily, his voice even, as though he'd just been asked a polite question. "If you were not chosen as a recipient by the system, then I encourage you to consider what areas you could improve on should you decided to make another attempt next year."

"'What areas I can improve on'?" the boy repeated sourly, grimacing. "Bull! I ripped through every portion of that test, just like I bet a lot of the others sitting here disappointed did." He lifted one hand to wave at some of the other stony faces among the tables around him. "This is ridiculous. It's *theft*, if anything. Someone else should have gotten that CAD, and would have put it to higher use. My aunt is a general at Central Command, and I demand that—"

"I am *well*-acquainted with your aunt, Mr. Abel," the major cut him off now in a rumbling tone that thundered across the exam space. "Just as I am well-acquainted with the fact that the general will be woefully disappointed—not to mention *embarrassed*—when word reaches her that her oldest nephew chose a public platform in

front of more than a dozen officers of the ISCM to make a whining fool of himself."
At his table, the boy called Abel blanched, but the major didn't let him get a word in
edgewise. "With that in mind, I suggest you *cease* your complaining, accept the fact
that there may be areas the military has found you lacking in that Cadet Ward was
not, and consider how best to explain yourself to your aunt when you receive your
next call from her."

Silence took hold again, echoing in the emptiness of the endless space still turning all around them. After a few seconds Abel eased himself back down to his seat,
his cheeks devoid of any color. When he had, the major looked to Rei.

"Recall your Device, cadet."

Grateful he hadn't been dragged into the exchange, Rei looked down at the
blue-streaked punching glove of white-and-black steel looping his right hand.

"Recall," he said, focusing on Shido's weight. The CAD flickered into itself,
reforming into the ring about his wrist. The moment the transformation was done,
Major Connelly put the pad behind his back as he had thirty-three other times that
day already, and extended his hand in formal greeting. Rei took it, blinking at the
officer's own purple-and-grey Device as the band slipped out from under the sleeve
of his uniform.

"Be careful who you share those specs with, son. I don't know what that damn
AI is thinking, but it's safe to assume you're in for a difficult climb."

The words were quiet, again meant only for Rei, and he lifted his gaze to see the
major watching him almost-imploringly. Connelly said nothing more, and waited
for the small nod of understanding Rei finally gave.

Then the officer smiled.

"Congratulations, cadet. Welcome to the ISCM."

By the time Rei took his seat again, the major was already speaking once more,
explaining the final details the new cadets would have to take to apply to the
ISC's combat schools, if they chose to do so. Though familiar with the process—they'd
been dreaming of the Galens Institute together for 3 years now, after all—Rei and
Viv sat quietly listening, not looking at each, though Viv did take his hand again
under the table.

This time, he knew the pressure applied there was for his sake, rather than hers.

"That will be all. This concludes this year's CAD-Assignment Exam. For those of you who received your Devices: congratulations, and I hope to hear your names in the circuit feeds soon. For those that didn't: best of luck, and perhaps we will see a few of you again next year."

With the major's final statement, the projection of the ceremonial hall flickered and vanished, leaving them all in blackness only as long as it took for the lights of the Grandcrest combat gym to come back on again. Finding themselves once more in the familiar space with its plain floor and amphitheater seating, Rei watched as the black-and-purple assignment table was lowered on its platform back to the ground, then covered with the dark cloth to hide it from view once more.

"Rei… You ready?"

Viv was watching him carefully, her expression somber. He nodded, standing up again as she gathered her bag and did the same. Seeing her new CAD bands shift over her wrists as she tossed the straps over her shoulder, Rei made his decision.

"Viv. Come with me."

Not waiting for an answer, he turned away from her and started through the tables, heading for the same smaller door that led into the back corridors they'd been directed through to the medical facilities for the physical assessment. Hearing her surprised call for him to wait up, he slowed down until her hurried footsteps were on his heels, then slipped into the hall, leading the way. He knew where they were going by heart, having taken the path more times than he cared to think about almost every day for the duration at his time at Grandcrest.

Reaching the door he was looking for, Rei put a hand on the plasteel surface. It read his allowance to enter, and slid open at once. Stepping back, he turned to find a flushed Viv right behind him.

"Inside," he said, motioning into the long room beyond the opening, its length lined on either side with 10-foot-high, multi-layered shelves on which various appliances, solutions, drones, and tools sat. "I need to show you something."

Viv raised an eyebrow at him. "And you need to show it to me in the custodial closet because…?"

"Just get in, Viv. *Please*."

Rei hadn't meant to sound desperate, but he didn't think his imploring could have come off any other way. Still, it did the trick, because Viv's face went from skeptically confused to concerned, and she stepped smartly by him into the room. Following her, Rei let the door slide shut behind them before opening his mouth to speak.

Viv, though, beat him to it.

"Are you okay?"

He stuttered to a halt. She'd turned to face him, and was clutching at her bag straps like they were a lifeline. Her face had fallen again, and the sadness there pulled at Rei's heart. His best friend in this or any other system had just been assigned a CAD that would change her life. She was walking the path they'd been talking about since the day they'd realized they both wanted to be Users.

And yet here she was, worried about him…

Good friends can be hard to find in the world you're about to share.

Major Connelly's words—spoken plainly in the warm light of the assessment suite not two hours ago—came back to him then, and any reservations Rei had had about showing Viv what he'd dragged her to the custodial closet for vanished.

Taking a breath, he lifted his right wrist—presenting Shido to her to look more closely at—pulling up the Specification Request again to grant her permission to examine his specs with a few quick commands in his NOED.

"You tell me," he answered breathlessly.

Viv frowned at that, not understanding. After a moment she let go of her bag and took his arm with one hand, holding the Device steady with the other. Her bilateral neuro-optic flared, and Rei saw the tiny lines of script scroll upward across her retinas as she, too, made a request.

The reaction was predictable. At first Viv's expression grew more and more crestfallen. Rei could see her heart breaking, could see her watching their paths diverge so absolutely, there was no hiding her sadness and disappointment. His User-specs of universal F0s slipped by her vision first, followed by starting lines of Shido's CAD-specs.

Then, at last, he saw the script stop in her frame, and Viv stared.

For a good ten seconds she didn't budge, eyes only barely moving as she read the last line of the Request again, then again, then again. After going over it what must have been twenty times Viv dismissed the display, her vision clearing so that she could meet his gaze. They stood like that for a little while, Rei waiting, Viv processing.

Then she opened her mouth.

"REI, WHAT THE FU—?!"

"SHH!" Rei got a hand over her mouth in time to cut off the tirade of expletives he had no doubt was coming. Whereas once he might have knocked Viv back a step as he half-collided with her in his desperation to shut her up, she didn't so much as flinch now, her new CAD specs holding her as firm as a wall.

Ignoring a flair of jealousy as he realized that Viv—already an ace of the Grand-crest combat team—was probably exponentially faster and stronger now than she had been even an hour ago, Rei held his hand tightly in place.

"SHH, Viv!" he hissed. "I dragged you in here so I could share this *quietly*, not for you to bring half the damn building running!"

In his grasp Viv went rigid, blue eyes wide as she took him in with a disbelief that had nothing to do with him clapping five fingers around her mouth.

Eventually, she finally relaxed a little, and Rei pulled his hand away, stepping back again.

"Rei…" she began in a loud hiss, still not looking away from him. "An S… An *S*?!"

"I know," Rei answered with a sigh, his back finding the support beam of one of the shelves behind him, and he let himself slide to the ground. "I *know*, Viv!"

"But… *how*?! I've never heard of a CAD being assigned with anything higher than a *B*-Ranked spec! And in *Growth*! This can't be normal."

"No way." Rei agreed with a shake of his head, gazing across the aisle at the clear containers of cleaning solvent on the bottom shelf opposite him, like an explanation might magically appear somewhere in the text of their labels. "I haven't even heard of an A-Rank spec being handed out like this, much less an S…"

They were quite for a while, neither looking at each other, involved in their own churning disbelief…

"How do you… What do you *do* with that?" Viv at last asked out loud. "F1-Offense…" She finally dropped her eyes to him. "Can I see Shido again? Up close this time."

Without a word, Rei lifting his right hand.

"Call."

The band around his wrist shimmered, then the black steel grip capped by white plating and blue vysetrium lines materialized in and over his fist. Viv stepped towards him, taking the Device in both hands, studying it closely.

"A-Type?" she asked of herself. "Isn't this a Brawler weapon?"

Rei frowned, considering. In the excitement—or shock, more like—of his Growth spec, he'd completely forgotten that other odd detail about the CAD.

"Yeah…" he answered slowly, taking the punching-glove in carefully for the second time. "That's not completely unheard of, though. Lots of Atypicals start off looking like something out of the other Types, or develop adaptive Abilities. But still…" He lifted his left hand to his face. The other half of his Device hung from his wrist, limp and innocent, as useless as common jewelry. "Maybe it's got something to do with getting this one to activate?"

"Maybe…" Viv let his right hand go, kneeling down before him to reach for his left. She, too, took in the unchanged band. "I'm not completely surprised, though… You're other specs are so trash you should be glad you're not going to be made to bang your opponents over the head with just this." She shook the wrist for emphasis.

"Thanks for the encouragement," Rei muttered, tugging his arm free from her grip. Viv almost smiled then, one corner of her mouth twisting upward.

Then even that hint of amusement vanished.

"Do you have a plan?"

It was a question Rei should have expected. Probably even had an answer to. But given the scramble he was already in to get any kind of solid footing on his situation, he had nothing and less to respond with.

His silence, apparently, said as much.

"You should still apply to Galens."

The statement was so unexpected, Rei was sure for a moment he'd misheard. When his mind caught up to the words, assuring him he'd made them out right, he squinted in concern at Viv.

"Is your new neuroline frying your head already? You should definitely have that checked by the evaluators before we get out of here."

Viv, though, wasn't in a joking mood. "I'm serious, Rei. Your overall specs suck— there's no denying it—but this is *huge*. An S-Rank spec out the gate? In *Growth*? If anything, you might be *more* interesting to the Institute's board of admissions then just another person with decent test scores and a strong CAD."

Rei shook his head. "Don't tease me, Viv. I'm an F8. An *F. 8*. Galens has never accepted anyone lower than a D-Rank, and even the D0s and 1s they take in are always exceptional in some other way."

"Sure. But they've never accepted someone with an S-Ranked spec either, and in the one CAD attribute that measure how fast and how far your Device can improve."

Rei had no response to that. He wasn't sold on the idea of making a fool of himself, but he couldn't help but concede that there was a *fraction* of logic in Viv's argument. Maybe.

"Just apply with me," Viv pressed him, taking advantage of the crack in his certainty. "Please. I don't even care if you put your application in to other schools. Just apply to Galens with me."

Rei snorted. "What other schools? With an F8, I'd be lucky if the ISCM doesn't just have me pretend I never got a CAD and make me go into tactics or combat theory."

"Then you have nothing to lose, do you?"

It was, of course, the base truth of the matter.

Rei sighed, leaning his head back to rest it with a dull *thunk* against the beam behind him. "Fine. I'll still apply. But when I end up a cargo pilot delivering supplies to the developing colonies, you're gonna owe me tickets to your SCT fights."

Viv, at last, grinned.

"Deal," she answered, standing up and brushing the knees of her dress off. "Even if you make it in, I'll probably still have to get you tickets. Can't imagine you're going to get near the tournaments any other way."

Rei appreciated her attempt to stroke his competitive streak, but in the situation he was in, he just couldn't manage it.

"Recall," he muttered, and Shido pulled itself back into the band around his right wrist again. He studied the clean black-and-white steel and blue vysetrium for a moment, possibly hoping to lose himself in the Stryon particle flickers.

It didn't work.

"What do I do now?" he asked quietly, more to himself then any intended audience.

Viv, though was the one to answer, crossing her arms so that Gemela's bands *clinked* against each other. "Rei, step away from this for a minute." She gave him a stern frown. "You have Device stats and mathematics memorized better than anyone I know. Better than anyone on this damn planet, probably. Pulling yourself away from *your* situation for a second: if a new CAD assignee popped up and told you they had an S-Ranked spec and shit on everything else… What would you tell them?"

"That their NOED had gone haywire, and they should have it checked." Rei snorted. "Maybe that's what's going on! Maybe—"

"Shut up and take this seriously. New User. New CAD. S-Ranked spec and trash stats in all other attributes." Viv stared him down. "What would you tell them?"

Rei sobered up, settling and contemplating her question a moment.

"Low stats means fast advancement," he answered eventually, staring blankly at the jugs of cleaner across from him again. "At least initially. Even with a terrible Growth Rank, F-Ranked stats can ramp quickly with enough work and training put into them."

A spark flared in Rei, then, hearing his own words. He knew, too, what Viv was going to ask him next.

"And what if their Growth spec *wasn't* tanked?" the question came. "What if—just theoretically—it happened to be the S-Ranked attribute?"

Still from his place on the floor, Rei felt a weird sensation in his cheeks. It took him a moment to place it, took him a moment to deduce what his face was trying to do.

After the turmoil of the last hour, it felt strange to find himself smiling.

"That's what I thought," Viv said, offering him her own crooked smile. "Now get your ass up, Mr. S-Rank. We've got more than two months before commencement ceremonies start, and I happen to know someone with unfettered admittance to a combat gym and brand-new access to the ISCM's virtual training protocols."

CHAPTER 8

*In the case of child abandonment, separation by the state from any and all poten-
tially claiming parties, orphaning, or related relevant causes, the state shall take
full and complete responsibility for said child until they should achieve the age of
18 or request emancipation from the state with due cause and evidence.*

*Children under such responsibility who have not received a surname shall be as-
signed a common surname for the purposes of governmental identification and
benefits claiming.*

Said surname shall identify the involved child as a ward of the state.

Bill C.P. 1077 of 2334

aka: *"Minor's Protection Act"*

Section 42

Now: applicant number… Where are we again? Oh yes. Number 1489." From
her seat a couple places to the man's right, Captain Valera Dent watched
Colonel Rama Guest swipe steadily through the files on the wide pad in his
large hands. "Ah. A familiar name. Logan Grant, eighteen, from the Kanhurst School
on Centauri-4. Mauler-Type and… an assigned Rank of D7? Very impressive." The
colonel looked up from his tablet to a narrow-shouldered man along the circular table
to his left. "I believe he was on the list of likely candidates for our summer training
course you sent out, correct, Major Reese?"

Across the table from Valera, Major Dyrk Reese—coordinator and principle
arbiter of the Galens Institute's Intra-School and public SCTs—nodded on cue,
the stubble of his shaved head a dark crown above heavy-set eyes and loose cheeks.

"Of all our applicants thus far, Grant's ranking places him as a top five potential
to qualify for Sectionals as a first year student. His written test scores are decent,

his physical assessment was top-tier, and—" the man tapped his own pad to expand some portion of the boy's profile, his grey-and-green CAD shining on his wrist below the gold-trimmed sleeve of his regulars as he did "—he earned a 'HIGH' recommendation for recruitment from his final interview with the Mass Intellect." Reese looked up from the tablet. "I would ask for his immediate acceptance. He would be an excellent addition to the school as a whole, with the potential of claiming our three first year squad-leader positions come Sectionals."

"Agreed," the colonel said without preamble, reading for a moment more before continuing. "All in favor of acceptance, please show by a vote of hands."

Unanimously each of the eleven individuals around the table raised an arm in favor. Even Valera complied, not voicing some of the qualms she had about a few of the notes on temperament and family history the MIND had buried in the Logan Grant's interview assessment. She'd been picking her battles carefully all day, keeping her mouth shut more than once in preparation.

But now—with the afternoon coming to a close, dusk reflecting off the rising faces of Castalon in the distance to bathe the meeting room in dim shades of orange and red through the window that made up the west wall—Valera's fight was up next.

"Accepted." Colonel Guest glanced over his shoulder at a slender woman with blonde hair, hazel eyes, and fair skin. Maddison Kent, his chief assistant, nodded in affirmation before marking Grant for approval.

"Good." Guest returned his attention to his tablet, swiping over to the next profile. "Now: applicant number 1503. Reidon Ward, 18, from Grandcrest Preparatory here on Astra-3. A-Type, and—" the colonel frowned suddenly, the silvering brown of his beard twitching in disappointment "—F8? That can't be right…"

There were several good-natured chuckles from a few of the committee members, as well as a snort from Dyrk Reese.

"Brave of him to have put in his application," wheezed old Lieutenant Colonel Willem Mayd, Galens' head doctor and chief medical officer. He was squinting at his pad through the glasses that supplemented the repeated corrective ocular surgeries that just hadn't been able to keep up with his failing eyesight. "He did well on his written exams, I must say…"

"That he did…" the colonel acknowledged, eyeing Reidon Ward's written results with a modicum of genuine interest. Then he made to swipe the profile aside as well. "Regardless, I'm surprised his application made it this far with a Rank like—"

"Just a moment, colonel. I'd like to recommend Cadet Ward for acceptance."

Guest wasn't the only one to pause at Valera's words as she seized her chance. All around the table, every face turned to her, some curious—like Willem Mayd's— others annoyed—like Reese's.

Unpleasantly, it was the latter of the two who spoke up before anyone else.

"The boy is an F-Rank, Bishop," the major said evenly, as though this was more than enough to settle the matter. "Galens is not a good fit for him."

"This isn't the circuits, major," Valera answered with a fake smile, the synthetic skin over her artificial jaw ever a little too tight around her cheeks. "Address me by rank or name, if you please. As for getting stuck on Ward being an F... I think that just means Galens has an unhealthy attachment to assignment rank."

She could practically *see* Reese's hackles rising at the comment, but before he could quip back, Colonel Guest raised a broad palm to stop him.

"I did think you'd been unusually subdued today, captain." Guest addressed Valera with a steady gaze. "I'm assuming this application—" he tilted the pad in his hand slightly in indication "—is the reason?"

Valera turned her smile on the school's commanding officer. "It would appear you've seen right through me, sir." She let the smile drop. "Yes. Reidon Ward is an interest of mine. I personally requested his profile be added to today's consider- ations." She looked around at the rest of the table. "I'm not surprised anyone but me took note of him in the initial intake of applicants. I set a parameter-check for all incoming A-Types, so his name came across my desk nearly a week ago."

"Being an A-Type is hardly a reason to consider an F-Ranked cadet for accep- tance." Captain Elean Samsus, head of Combat Theory Department, leaned over the table from Valera's right. "Likely the opposite, in fact. I would expect you to know that you are one the few successful Users of that Type, captain. It takes a very particular wielder to effectively use a Device like that."

"I am aware, captain, yes," Valera acknowledged, picking her pad up from where it had spent most of the afternoon blank and ignored in front of her. With a tap she woke it up, Reidon Ward's profile already pulled up at the ready. "His CAD-Type, however, is only what drew my initial eye. The reasons I am recommending him for acceptance—" with a swipe, she called the resume up to project over the center of the table before them "—are quite different, you'll find."

A few seconds passed as the other members of the committee humored her, studying the hologram as it spun slowly in place for them all to see. A half-sized simulation of the boy's body scanned in the second portion of his CAD exam, it rotated alongside a list of values, including his height, weight, and the sub-markings of his physical assessment. Several lips pursed in annoyance as they took in these statistics, only then moving on to the other side of the body projection.

Reidon Ward's CAD specifications.

"S? *S*-Rank?!"

Lieutenant Major John Markus's chair scraped against the floor as he stood up so suddenly it was shoved backwards. Head of Galens' Device Evolution Department, Valera had suspected he might be among the first to see reason in her presentation. At his exclamation, however, the others around the table looked for the source of his excitement, and eyes started to go wide as they found the data line.

"Yes," she asserted, leaning back to cross one leg over the other, watching Reidon Ward's metrics cycle before her. "Cadet Ward was assigned a CAD with S-Ranked Growth, something completely unheard of. That, though, is only the foundation of my recommendation." She swept a hand across herself, and the information in the center of the table changed. "As some of you have noticed, Ward also scored a 99.5% on the written portion of the CAD exam—though notes from his final results say he was informed otherwise for testing purposes at the time. Out of more than two *million* applicants this year, he is one of less than a thousand to score in that percentile range."

"So he's a genius of theory," Dyrk Reese said with a disgruntled grumble across from her, shrugging in an unconvinced manner. "I admit a CAD with an S-Rank is something rather unique, but the Galens Institute is founded on quality, not risk. Let him make a name for himself as a tactician. Maybe even a commander on the front lines, like Carmen Laurent."

"What you mean to say, I believe, major, is that your Institute is founded on monotony, rather than potential."

Valera hadn't meant it as a barb—all right, maybe a *little*—but Reese's pale complexion turned pink rather quickly, threatening at red.

Holding up a subduing hand before the man lashed out, however, she pressed on. "I do not mean to imply that Galens has suffered from that approach. It hasn't, obviously. But nor has this Academy made a great progress in the advancement of User and CAD applications, despite considering itself a top military school within the Intersystem Collective." She shifted her gaze to Rama Guest. "You're aware of this, colonel. It's the very reason you requested me for the post of chief combat instructor. To 'shake things up', if I might use your own words from my interview."

In answer, the colonel nodded carefully. "True enough, captain, but my intention with those words was for you to find me a way to challenge this Institute's approach to Users, not have us rebuild it from the ground up." He gestured to the still rotating profile or Reidon Ward. "Can you give me a reason why this isn't anything more than a testing shot into blind space?"

Valera almost smiled again. "I can. The Galens Institute's incoming class sizes are limited to 128 cadets, a *fourth* of the average class size for military school across the ISCM. Is that correct?"

The colonel nodded.

"The reason for this is obvious," Valera kept on. "It is this Institute's intention to supply the ISCM and the SCT circuits—both collegiate and profession—with the *best* Users it can develop. It does this first by limiting its class sizes to only the most impressive applying cadets, and then using those small sizes to create focused programs. Limited curriculums, designed for the individual Users to maximize their growth and the evolution of their CADs over their three years at this school. Is that fair?"

Another nod.

"Keep that in mind, if you please," Valera urged not only the colonel, but the other committee members, looking to each of them in turn while she spoke. When she had all of their attention, she waved at the projection of Reidon Ward's specifications again. "These numbers are the values provided to us by the evaluators at Grandcrest, where Cadet Ward took his examination eight days ago."

"F0s almost across the *board*," Major Reese muttered in annoyance under his breath.

Valera, however, only nodded. "Indeed, major. However… You might be less dismissive if I told you that Reidon Ward has—in those eight days—evolved *every one* of his specs, with the obvious exception of Growth."

"*What?*"

John Markus managed—barely—to maintain a bit more of his composure this time, keeping to his chair in favor of staring at Valera in disbelief.

"It's the truth." Valera waved at the tablet in front of the department head. "You can look it up yourself on the ISCM database. In just over a week, Cadet Ward has not only evolved each of his specifications to F1, but raised both his Speed and Cognition to F2." She indicated the stats floating over the table. "Even his CAD-Rank is out of date. Reidon Ward is now an E0 User."

"It's true."

All eyes turned to Major Hadish Barnes. An absolute bear of a man, the man's black-and-gold uniform stretched and flexed over his muscular frame, as did the band of white stitched with the school emblem: a red griffin holding onto the four edges of tilted square border, wings outstretched beyond its outline. It labeled him as a staff of the Galens Institute—as did the identical markers each of the others around the table wore about their own arms—but the symbol of the school was at the moment half-creased as the chief of campus security bent over his pad, slowly scrolling through script.

"It's true," the man repeated after a second, and with a flick of his finger he sent the updated data out to float alongside the old. "These are Reidon Ward's specs as of this afternoon, according to our systems."

All around the table, more than a few whispered conversations started up as the new numbers were compared. Indeed, Cadet Ward was now an E0-Rank CAD-User, with all of his specs at F1 or higher.

Unfortunately, not every committee member was moved by this.

"Is this really so impressive?" Captain Sarah Takeshi, Head of the Tactical Studies Department, spoke up. "He's starting essentially from nothing. With proper teaching and adequate training time, it's hardly strange he would move through the lowest F-Ranks quickly."

"And what, may I ask—" Valera *did* smile this time, witnessing her trap close "—would you consider 'proper teaching and adequate training', captain?"

Takeshi seemed to sense that something was amiss, because she hesitated in answering.

Fortunately for all but himself, Major Reese wasn't so quick to let go of an opportunity to get his point across.

"With the right instructors and enough time devoted to conditioning, most any User—even of this cadet's level—" he indicated Reidon Ward's profile dismissively "—would be able to manage pushing from F0 into a few higher Ranks. As Captain Takeshi just stated, I would not qualify this as impressive."

Valera, for her part, only nodded with mock somberness, having listened to Reese while searching through the ISCM database. "I completely agree, major. With the right instructors and enough time, anyone could do it. Are you familiar, however," another flick, and Ward's profile disappeared, replaced by an altogether different series of projections, "with the nature of this boy's last name?"

Video logs and projection selections settled into place, overlaying one another to show off a variety of options for combat technique learning, from offensive and defensive posturing to footwork and movement strategies.

"This is a basic simulation program," Colonel Guest said with a frown, studying the scripts and item descriptions. "Why are you showing us this, captain?"

Valera crossed her arms and tilted her head towards the projections. "Ladies and gentlemen… meet Reidon Ward's 'instructors'."

There was a moment of quiet, then, a *true* silence as all present processed what she had just said.

It was Guest who spoke again first.

"He's learning through this?" he asked, his stoic composure finally cracking a little as what might have been astonishment crept through the slightest bit. "Through basic combat simulation?"

"These, and a dozen other similar programs we made accessible to him after his assignment." Using her NOED, Valera had the table projection snap through several other selections in quick succession. "Hand to hand. Boxing. Martial arts of all kinds. He is aware that the ISCM bans simulated combat or sparring without an accredited supervisor present. Keeps our new Users from developing bad habits and forms we have to break them of later. In Ward's case, however, he has no access to certified trainers. So—" she stopped on the final example, a simulation focused solely on disarming and disabling sword-wielding opponents "—he uses these."

"No access?" Hadish Barnes asked, apparently not comprehending. "He attends a private preparatory school. Surely his family can afford to see him properly instructed?"

"Reidon Ward has no family. He was abandoned by his parents before they even granted him their last name, and became a dependent of the state until he emancipated himself from the ISC at age fifteen. Hence his surname. He attends Grandcrest Preparatory Institute partially through well-earned scholarships, and partially through his own income working part-time as a custodial staff at the school." Valera's gaze fell on Sarah Takeshi again. "What was the other part of your theory, captain? Adequate training time?" Another eye command, and the projection changed to an outline of a student's weekly schedule, a small portion in each day's late afternoon highlighted in red. "Reidon Ward has barely two hours a day to train following classes before his cleaning shifts start five days out of each week. Even that time he carved out for himself by quitting the Grandcrest combat team, where he has been an active participant for the last two years despite measuring at more than five inches shorter and thirty-five pounds lighter than the average fighter. *Including* the female combatants."

More muttering, now, with even the colonel leaning over as Maddison Kosh approached to show him something she'd pulled up on her tablet.

Perfect timing, Valera thought, catching the woman's eyes subtly and giving her the smallest of winks.

She would have to thank her later for her tactfulness.

"His family," Guest rumbled over the conversations, still reading off his assistant's pad. "Ward's birth records list only 'medical abandonment' as the cause for their relinquishing him to the state. Do you have an explanation?"

Valera nodded, a little of her excitement ebbing. She was confident in her argument, but it didn't make the subject any easier. "Reidon Ward was diagnosed at birth with a condition called 'fibrodysplasia ossificans progressiva'. It is an exceedingly rare genetic disorder that steadily replaces his skeletal tissues—muscles, tendons, ligaments—with bone." She frowned. "The disease has no pharmaceutical solution—it's not common enough to warrant one, even in an age of 250 billion humans—and I can only imagine his parents were unwilling to take on the toll such a disorder would place on them, either financially or emotionally, or both."

"So he's *crippled*?" Reese demanded angrily, staring at Valera through the projection like he couldn't believe his ears. "You asking us to take on a *crippled* boy into one of the most prestigious military programs in the ISC?"

"He's anything but." Valera found herself having a hard time keeping the distaste out of her voice as she snapped back, the synthetic skin stretching uncomfortably along her jaw again when she sneered at the man. "There may be no *medicine* for Cadet Ward's condition, but there *is* treatment."

"Surgery."

It was Lieutenant Colonel Mayd who interrupted the threat of an argument. He had removed his glasses, and was reading large-printed script off the frame of his NOED.

"The only current treatment for fibrodysplasia is extensive and frequent surgery," the old man explained, summarizing whatever medical source he was scanning through. "Typically minor, but invasive in severe cases, or if growth isn't caught early enough in the process. They remove the excess bone, stimulating replacement tissue, and do so over and over and over." It was the chief medical officer's turn to frown, and his NOED winked out. "Captain Dent, pull up Cadet Ward's body scan again, if you would."

Valera did as instructed, and a moment later Reidon Ward's mostly-naked form was rotating before them once more.

Mayd replaced his glasses, squinting at the projection. "Now focus in on his arm, please."

"Which one, sir?"

"Either. It makes no difference."

Valera complied, deliberately zooming in around Ward's left elbow, thinking she knew what the doctor was after.

There were more than a couple of gasps from the other committee members, then.

Harder to see in the glow of the hologram when the figure had been half-sized, the markings that carved an ugly pattern into Reidon Ward's skin were suddenly brought into keen relief. Even Valera—who hadn't examined the boy's body in this detail—felt her stomach clench when the image rotated to show the longer scar along the back of the Cadet's elbow. Involuntarily she lifted a hand to her cheek, fingers tracing the visible line of her full-frame prosthetic jaw. Realizing her slip, she forced herself to cross her arms again.

She had no desire to recall a time when the agony had nearly driven her mad.

"Reidon Ward has had more than 165 surgeries over the course of his life." Willem Mayd spoke for her, fortunately. "Some twenty of those have been invasive, hence his larger scars." The chief medical officer waved at the projection, indicating the line behind Ward's elbow. "Otherwise, he is seen almost every month for minor laser removal and tissue regrowth." He paused, eyebrows pinching together in consternation. "This child has likely lived in constant pain his entire life…"

"And despite that, he has risen above every obstacle, every unlikely scenario." Valera was finally able to speak again, looking to the colonel, now. "He's been through hell—a hell so profound it turned his damn hair *white*—and he survived, then got himself into a preparatory school on the planet of the military academy he wanted to attend. He paid his own way through for four years, made the combat team in his third after failing to do so in his first and second, and is set to graduate with top marks, not unlike the astounding written score of his Assignment Exam. Now, not only has he been appointed an actual Device, but he is applying the only advantage he has—an S-Rank Growth spec—as best he can to get as strong as he can as fast as he can." She set her face. "Colonel… If we let this boy go, I swear on my *name* that the Galens Institute will regret it…"

Rama Guest said nothing, contemplating her words as he watched the damaged arm of Reidon Ward turn slowly over the center of his table.

"What about the scars...?"

It was, strangely, Maddison Kent who asked the question, and when Valera looked at her the woman was staring at the projected limb with a painful sadness that hollowed out her dark eyes.

It made Valera's heart ache to witness.

"The ISC covers the cost of surgery for debilitating or life-threatening illnesses," she said quietly. "It does not, however, shoulder the responsibility for ectodermal restoration, deeming it an 'elective' intervention."

"The Collective will not pay for them to be removed, and he has likely never been able to afford the procedures himself," Colonel Guest translated heavily.

The quiet that took hold of the room then carried a different weight than any previous moment.

Until, that is, Dyrk Reese decided to break it.

"Reidon Ward's condition is truly terrible," he said, sounding genuinely subdued, "but if anything it is all the *more* reason why Galens is not a good fit for him. Aside from the irresponsibility I would feel participating in putting a deteriorating body through the rigor of CAD-training—even our initial parameter testing is demanding—we need also consider the toll of taking on the surgeries and care Cadet Ward would require. It cannot seem reasonable to everyone at this table that we expect Lieutenant Colonel Mayd and his team to assume responsibility for that level of—"

"I thank you for your concern, major, but you needn't bother yourself on my count."

Willem Mayd's wheeze cut across Reese smoothly. The chief medical officer was on his pad again, reading even as he spoke. "Cadet Ward's diagnosis is typically secondary to a genetic mutation. A malformation in the ACVR1 gene, to be specific. Now that he has been assigned a CAD, his Device will have already started making adjustment to that code." The lieutenant colonel's eyes stopped moving as he focused on something separate from their conversation. "By my estimation, Reidon Ward is likely to be symptomless by the beginning of the next calendar year, and completely disease free soon after that. If the Device's genetic correction can additionally *reverse* any ossification already in progress, it is quite possible the Cadet will never need another surgery related to his fibrodysplasia again."

It was at that point, apparently, that Dyrk Reese seemed to realize that he was going to lose this battle. He started to look around, his desperation only subtly apparent as he sought support from the others seated about the table, but even Sarah Takeshi didn't meet his gaze despite her earlier reservations.

"But Galens has *never* accepted an individual below a D0 Rank," the man said with a touch of anger as his looming defeat began to weigh on him. "To change that now—"

"To change that now would be to adapt to a situation of greater potential than merely judging a possible student on their starting specifications," Valera interrupted him. "I asked you before to remember that this Institute's goal has always been to provide the military with the *best* Users it can develop, doing so by focusing its energy on only those it believes have an extraordinary ability to achieve greatness in the world of CAD-combat and military potential. I'm not asking you to change that mentality in the least. I'm not asking you to abandon your ideals or your methods. On the contrary, all I'm asking is that you expand your concept of 'extraordinary'." She looked around, meeting Rama Guest's even gaze. "I'm *challenging* you to consider something outside the norm."

The colonel took in her words for a long moment, contemplating them without breaking eye contact. After what seemed like an eternity he sat back in his chair with a sigh, entwining his fingers on the desk before him before holding his tongue a few seconds longer.

Finally, when he spoke, Valera felt her heart leap.

"All in favor of acceptance, please show by a vote of hands."

As arms began to lift around the table, one after the other, Valera closed her NOED and joined with enthusiasm. The script across the frame winked out, hiding the final push she'd been ready to give, but hadn't been forced to use.

CAD-Assignment Exam - Test 3 Interview Results:

Institutional Recruitment Recommendation Level:
TOP PRIORITY

CHAPTER 9

LateMay - *One Week Later*

Astra System – Astra-3 – Sector 6

"When it comes to the best of the best, there always seems to be a story behind them, a tale of need, desire, or both that pushes those Users to a level beyond those of us lacking such a driver. You see it across the centuries, from old favorites like the Gatecrasher to newer celebrities like the Lasher, or Aria of Flames. Even Storm-weaver. It's a strange thing to contemplate, honestly. There's jealousy. Jealousy at the fact that there are fighters out there who have something that pushes them in a way I lack.

At the same time, though… I can't imagine what life must have been like for them—what struggles they each must have gone through in their own way—to need to outrun their old lives with such absolute desperation…"

Razielle "Monster" Arroh
Post-Match Interview, c. 2480

Rei's NOED flashed red, and he brought Shido up to shield the right side of his head just as his simulated opponent sent an arching kick at his temple. The CAD offered little additional protection given it wasn't more yet than a flashy steel plate with a grip, but the minimal reactive shielding provided by its new F2 Defense helped stabilize his closed fist as he accepted the blow. His arm strained under the impact, but held, the minor improvement to his Strength spec Rei had managed to pull out of the Device over the last two weeks working wonders. Taking the opening his block offered, he punched at his opponent's face, but the figure—a pre-rendering of a generic male in a plain combat uniform—ducked under the strike. Immediately it responded, driving its own fist into Rei's gut, the physical projection landing with the same simulated impact the phantom-call of a CAD was supposed to feel like. Rei very much experienced the hit, and he grit his teeth against the blooming mix of real and imitated pain.

A warning line appeared in the top corner of his neuro-optic, read out loud for him by the training simulation.

Organ damage registered.
Internal bleeding in process.
Applying appropriate physiological restrictions.

"Yeah, yeah," Rei grumbled, ignoring the notification even as he felt the projection bind him, slowing down his movements and limiting his abdominal flexibility. His opponent, meanwhile, had retreated a safe ways away, bouncing on its toes as it eyed Rei's "wounded" torso, then the rest of his body, looking for openings.

Thus far, of all the simulations the ISCM granted new cadets access to, these mixed martial arts trainings had felt the most realistic.

Another flash of red, and Rei dodged back in time to avoid a front kick to the chest, chased by a punch at his face. He caught and redirected the fist that had been aiming for his nose, just managing to snag hold of the projection's bare wrist with one hand, twisting it and bringing his elbow down on the extended back of his opponent's. The blow hit with a heavy *crunch*, and Rei knew with a thrill he'd done good damage, but refused to allow himself to be distracted just as he finally had the advantage. Keeping a hold of the wrist, he wrenched on it, trying to get the projection's whole injured arm behind its back to pin it. The figure, though, flipped with the twist, landing on its feet again, and Rei was suddenly on the receiving end of a cutting chop at his exposed neck. He dropped the arm in time to dodge, then lunged forward again, bringing Shido up for a heavy blow.

For another minute the pair of them battled it out like this. Rei had indeed "broken" his opponent's elbow, so between that and the pain and restriction of his own simulated internal injuries, they found themselves fairly evenly matched again. Ducking and darting about became steadily harder as time passed, Rei's F1 Endurance Rank little more than theoretically better than that of the average person's. Blows came weaker, kicks slower, until the pair of them were pulling apart more and more often to catch their respective breaths, him realistically, his opponent only well-simulated. They would collide again, though, over and over, until finally the projection overextended, its pseudo-exhaustion causing a slip in focus, resulting in a too-heavy swing at Rei's head. Rei ducked under the blow, then brought Shido up into the underside of the opened shoulder, dislocating it instantly. Seeing his victory at hand, Rei didn't stop, taking the figure about the torso with a looped arm and sweeping the back of its legs out from under it with his own. His opponent fell heavily, hitting the ground with a *thud*, and Rei followed it down with a driving punch from his CAD that caught the simulation full in the face.

"Fatal Damage Accrued," the training program announced in the smooth mechanical voice of an Arena. "Winner: Reidon Ward."

Rei let himself fall back to sit with his arms extended behind him, holding him up as he gasped in an attempt to catch his breath. The program hadn't rendered any sort of environment—only his opponent and the notifications of damage—so he sat there gulping on the same sweaty combat mat he'd just actually fought on as the physical hologram of the still man glitched and disappeared. He waited, hoping against hope, his chest heaving. That opponent had been the strongest martial art's simulation he'd managed to bring down thus far, and it had taken him more than a dozen attempts over the last three days to do so.

He was rewarded a moment later as his NOED flared to life of its own accord.

...

Processing combat information.

...

Calculating.

...

Results:

Strength: Adequate

Endurance: Lacking

Speed: Adequate

Cognition: Adequate

Offense: Adequate

Defense: Lacking

Growth: Not Applicable

...

Checking combat data acquisition.

...

Adequate data acquirement met.

Device initiating adjustments to:
Endurance.

…

Adjustment complete.
Endurance has been upgraded from Rank F1 to F2.

"*Yyyyes!*" Rei exclaimed, punching Shido into the air in victory as the notification blink out of his vision. F2 in Endurance wasn't any great leap overall, but it was the last of his specs to have been left stubbornly clinging to its F1 Rank after two weeks of training in the simulations every spare second he could grab out of the day. Grinning, Rei focused on his CAD and made a Specifications Request, the data pulling up at once as the application was acknowledged.

Combat Assistance Device: Shido. User identification… Accepted.
Type: A-TYPE
Rank: E1
…
User Attributes:
- Strength: F2
- Endurance: F2
- Speed: F4
- Cognition: F3
…
CAD Specifications:
- Offense: F2
- Defense: F2
- Growth: S

Finally feeling himself start to catch his breath, Rei dismissed the request with a blink, falling back onto the mat to smile at the ceiling. "Recall," he told the air, and he felt Shido shift away from his right hand to return to his wrist.

E1… He was still a far cry behind even the average assignee rank of D0, but he'd managed to pull his CAD-Rank up *three whole levels* in less than the same number of weeks. His specs were climbing steadily, and he could feel his body adjusting little by little to the new neuroline the Device would be laying down in his brain and spine, along with all the other changes going on. He bent his right leg—feeling the ache that had been developing in his hip slowly for the last couple of weeks, and was pleased to note that the discomfort hadn't gotten any worse since the day before.

"Oh shit. Viv."

Rei rolled back up to sit with one arm draped over his bent knee, pulling up his NOED again. Usually the girl would have been there by his side—she'd quit the combat team the same day as him to allow for a couple hours additional training in the evenings—but one of the two Duelist specialists the Arada family had hired for her instruction had had to reschedule their session that day. As a result, Rei was on his own, but he'd promised Viv he would let her know if he managed to break through on Endurance.

Got it! he spelled out with one hand over the projected keyboard the neuro-optic pulled up for him on request. *I'll be caught up with you by next Friday, at this rate!*

He sent it with a chuckle, and only a few seconds later received a reply back in the form of a digital cut-out of an extended middle finger next to a face that looked to be laughing so hard it was crying. It was immediately followed up with a thumbs up, and Rei smirked.

He was about to pull up the combat simulations again—considering pushing his martial arts opponent up another level to see what kind of challenge he was expected to overcome next—when he happened to glance at the timestamp of Viv's last communication.

19... *1920?!*

Swearing, Rei leapt up and sprinted for the door of the classroom he'd dragged the mat into. The main gym had been in use by the combat team, like every week-day evening, but he and Viv had never had trouble finding an empty corner to get a couple hours of conditioning in. Now, though, Rei's enthusiasm and chasing of that elusive F2 Endurance had caused him to be more than a quarter-hour late to clocking in for his work shift.

"Damn, damn, damn, damn, damn, damn, damn," he muttered over and over again as he bolted down the hall, his bare feet almost slipping when he rounded a corner and took the stairs leading down two at a time. As he did, he clocked in on his NOED, fully expecting a notification from his supervisor—Mr. Alib—asking what the hell he had been doing to be so late.

Fortunately, by the time Rei reached the custodial closet, no such condemnation had pinged him. He opened the door with a quick slap of his palm, rushing for the tiny locker at the back of the long room. In seconds he was out of the sweaty workout clothes that had doubled as his "combat suit" since quitting the team. Deciding that a run to the team locker room for even a quick ion shower wasn't worth the risk of incurring additional ire, Rei started pulling on the custodial uniform. It wasn't like he was known for tardiness or anything, but he still had to work the next 2 months through Grandcrest's summer school programs to make sure his tuition was paid off. The headmaster had already done him a favor of promising his diploma when they graduated at the end of the week—and even then only after Rei had been logged as a CAD-User in the ISCM database—but he doubted the old bastard would be forgiving of unpaid dues by the time the new term started.

Rei needed this job. More than 20 minutes of extra training, he *definitely* needed this job.

Once the clean brown of the jumpsuit was zipped up around his neck—complete with "Grandcrest Preparatory Staff" stitched over his left breast—Rei wrenched on his shoes and finally breathed easier. He was late, but if he got everything done before calling it a night, Mr. Alib might be content with warning him to keep an eye on the clock next time. Satisfied with committing to a little extra effort for the evening, Rei grabbed a couple of clean towels and the fullest bottle of sanitizer he could find, slapping several sterilization drones waiting in sleep mode on the closet shelves into activity as he hurried out of the room.

While a lot of the cleaning process of a space as large as the combat gym could be handled through automation, there were still some aspects that required a human touch. Letting the drones zip around for a time—treating every surface with heavy doses of intense UV-light—Rei set about wiping down the mats that had been left out, spraying particularly sweaty—and occasionally bloody—spaces when needed, then pulling all the padding into the storage room off the main gym. This done, he started to repeat the whole process with the floor, letting his mind wander as he watched the machines buzz about, completing their sweeps of the circular building with mechanical efficiency. Some 15 days prior, this room had been made into a ceremonial assignment hall, suspended in the wonders of space. Unbidden, Rei's eyes drifted to the place Major Albert Connelly had shaken his hand, welcoming him to the Intersytem Collective Military.

It seemed… a dream. Not the CAD around his wrist. Shido's weight had steadily become a comfortable presence, the blue vystetrium against black-and-white steel a familiar glow he had taken to falling asleep staring at every night. More so, it was the time *since* that felt like it had passed in half a daze, the last weeks of Rei's final months at the Academy sometimes trickling by, sometimes vanishing in a rush.

E1… In 2 weeks he hadn't just managed to pull himself out of the F-Ranks, but climbed a *whole level* more than that. It blew his mind even then, considering it for the hundredth time since passing out of E0 the day before yesterday with a jump to F4 in his Speed spec. It hadn't been easy, of course—Rei had given up more than a few nights of good sleep and solid studying for a late evening or early morning of training—but it was still astonishing. He knew Viv's specs had started significantly higher than his, but despite the conditioning she did with him being only in *addition* to the two sessions a day she had with professional trainers, the girl had only managed to bump her Defense, Offense, and Endurance specs a level, and her overall Rank not at all. To be fair it had only been 2 weeks, but Viv had always been something of a prodigy at pretty much anything she set her mind to, so Rei couldn't help but feel like even those meager changes were probably impressive in their own right.

He knew, of course, what the variable was.

A day hadn't gone by since Shido had been assigned to him that Rei hadn't spent at least *some* time staring at the letter "S" beside his CAD's Growth spec. He had yet to wrap his mind around it—and got the feeling he probably never would—but the disbelief and confusion had slowly started to shift into a sort of resigned understanding that he very likely wasn't *meant* to know anything more. It was his job to be a good little test subject, he knew, and every time one of the school security cameras flashed in his direction, or someone passed him on a NOED-call, he was reminded that the party in charge of this experiment was not only everywhere, but very, *very* watchful.

He shivered at the thought as the sterilization drones finished their loop of the gym floor and started moving into the stands. That the MIND was all around was the sort of understood fact everyone knew and no one talked about, but to know he was *specifically* being monitored was somehow… disquieting. And yet—despite that discomfort—the ISC's AI was also the only reason he had been given a chance, an opportunity—thin as it was—to climb the mountain Rei had been eyeing for as long as he could remember.

With a sigh he picked up his bottle and rags again, heading for the center of the floor to check for anything the bots hadn't managed to clean up.

"Ward."

Rei nearly jumped out of his uniform, his combined distraction and the fact that he'd been very much under the assumption he was the only living soul left in the building lending themselves to his surprise. He turned around, expecting to find Mr. Alib thundering towards him in a mood, ready to chew him out for being late to his shift.

He had to stop himself making a face, therefore, when he found four figures he knew all too well approaching him from under the overhang of the south lobby entrance.

Lee Jackson and his teammates—Mason, Suresh, and Silva, the only girl of the group—hadn't changed out of their grey training suits, leading Rei to believe they'd probably been waiting for him after practice, which meant they'd been watching him for some time. While Lee approached him with a cocky sort of swagger, the other three seemed less certain, Mason and Suresh even eyeing Rei warily.

"Gotta say, man, that uniform fits you a lot better than this one." Lee stopped some 5 feet away, taking in the brown custodial jumpsuit with mock approval. "Wish I'd taken the time to see it before now."

With his towels in one hand and the spray bottle in the other, Rei watched the others move to surround him *too* casually. He let them, seeing no easy way of getting out of the situation other than making a run for it.

And he'd never been much good at running.

Ding. Rei's NOED notified him that "Viviana Arada" was attempting to call him. He declined it, suspecting now wasn't the time to talk about the day's progress.

"Someone told me the team colors didn't make my eyes pop," Rei finally answered sarcastically, looking slowly around at each of the fighters in turn. "What do you want, Lee?"

The taller boy smirked. "Just to see the famous new 'User' on campus. Can't say I really believe it." He glanced down at Shido's two bands peeking out from beneath the brown sleeves. "The military giving a scarred-up freak like you a Device? I'll bet a hundred credits those are fake."

"If that's all you wanted to know, you could have just searched my name on the feeds. I'm registered in the ISCM database, along with most of my general CAD info." Rei cocked his head to the side. "But you knew that already."

Lee's grin broadened a little. "Maybe. Maybe I did check. Maybe I checked, and saw that you were a nothing F-Rank assigned what basically amounts to a pair of shiny bracelets."

So you checked as soon as you found out weeks ago, and haven't bothered to since, Rei translated in his head.

In reply, though, he shrugged. "Then you've got all the data *I'm* about to tell you. So I ask again: what do you want?"

Lee's expression faltered, shifting into a scowl for a moment before he managed to plaster the smirk back on his face. "Actually, I'm just here to lend a hand, man! Word on the mats is you and Arada quit so you could have more time training. Given your… uh… situation—" he stared pointedly at the "Grandcrest Preparatory Staff" stitching on Rei's uniform "—I figured you might be lacking in decent sparring partners." He waved around at himself and the three others now pinning Rei in on every side. "We talked it over, and thought it was the least we could do for our school's new *military* man."

Rei didn't take the bait. "Sparring? Sure. I can pull the weighted gloves out of storage, but I should warn you: my Device comes with a full-body reactive field now. Not just the neck-up shield the combat collars would give you. Might be a little one-sided."

That made them sweat a bit. To Rei's right and left Mason and Silva glanced nervously at Lee, who—to his credit—didn't even blink.

"No," he said slowly, his smile fading as his patience obviously started to fail him. "Not with gloves, Ward. We want to see what your trash 'Device' can do. As for your energy field… Might be interesting to make a study of how much punishment it can take before it gives out."

DING. Viv tried calling him again.

Not. Now. Rei thought privately, declining a second time.

"Calling a CAD on non-Users is a criminal infringement outside of self-defense." Rei grit his teeth, feeling some of the confidence come back to the others at Lee's lack of hesitation. "But again, you knew that. I'm not going to play this stupid game, Lee. You want me to call, so you can say I threw the first punch. I don't know what your damn problem is, but either get this shit over with, or get out of my way and let me do my job."

He took a step forward, and this time Lee moved back, away from him. The retreat had obviously been reflexive, because the boys face flushed with embarrassment beneath his dark hair, and he closed the distance between them again in an instant, bringing himself nose-to-nose with Rei—or as close as was possible with their 7 inches of height differentiation.

"Even if you don't bring it out first, I doubt anyone is gonna care. You think you're hot stuff, huh, 'User'? With your F-Rank garbage jewelry? I've beaten your ass enough times in practice. Maybe you'll actually make me break a sweat this time."

Rei glared up at the boy, thinking fast. There was a time where he and Lee *would* have made an off match. He was the more skilled fighter—Rei doubted even Coach Kat would have argued that—but Lee's significant advantage in size had almost always been too much of a gap to close. Rei had lost nearly every pairing they'd had in practice, and usually quickly.

Now, though... Even ignoring calling on Shido, Rei's F2-and-above specs probably made him close to a fairer rival. He was pretty sure he could bring Lee down, in fact. The problem would be the other three... If they managed to pin him, Rei didn't have the Strength numbers to fight them all off. They probably wouldn't have too much trouble holding him down, and while Shido's energy shield would help a lot, an F2 spec in Defense didn't lend itself to a lasting barrier...

He decided, then. He would have to take Lee out, and fast. Lean into his best spec, his F4 Speed Rank. If he could down the ringleader, Mason, Suresh, and Silva had all already shown they weren't as keen on kicking his teeth in as the asshat who'd obviously talked them into it.

Rei set his feet, feeling the muscles of his legs knot in preparation as Lee continued to stare down at him from bare inches away, daring him to make the first move.

"Reidon Ward?"

Immediately there was a scrambling of surprised movement as all five of them started, Lee whirling around. From the south lobby—the same entrance the group had approached Rei from—a lithe woman was crossing the empty floor of the gym quickly. Rei blinked, taking her in, at first confused by the figure's presence in the middle of the mess he had found himself in.

Then he registered the uniform.

Black trimmed with gold, the unmistakable colors of ISCM regulars gleamed in the gym lights suspended high above them. Her leather boots *clicked* as she neared, and her hair—brown and cropped shorter on one side than the other—was mostly hidden under the iconic, brimmed military cap. As she got closer, Rei made out bright eyes undercut by narrow lips that were almost too red, set against oddly tanned skin. He had just a moment to think that something was a little off about her face, but the consideration was barreled aside in a heartbeat when he took note of two other facts:

The first: she was holding a smaller, rectangular envelope in one hand.

The second: around her left arm, a white band of cloth was emblazoned with the distinct shape of a red griffin holding onto the four sides of a tilted square.

"Galens," Rei choked out, not hearing himself. He couldn't believe it. He *couldn't*. It wasn't possible.

But the woman—a captain, he saw from her insignia once she was close enough—kept moving towards them with a purpose. When she was 5 feet away she finally came to a halt, eyeing the four uniformed fighters with a level of such complete disinterest, Rei was convinced any person subject to a similar look would shrivel into themselves in shame.

At last, her pale eyes fell on him.

"Are you Cadet Reidon Ward?"

Numbly, Rei nodded, unable to form the words to respond.

A twitch at the corner of her lip might have been the hint of a smile, but it vanished in a strange way.

There was *definitely* something odd about her face…

"Your supervisor informed me you would be here." The woman's quick words swept the notion away again. "My name is Captain Kana Loren. I'm an A-Type combat instructor at the Galens Institute, where you applied for enrollment thirteen days ago."

No way. No *way*.

"I'm pleased to inform you, cadet, that your application has been approved by our board of admissions." She brought up the envelop she'd been holding, presenting it to him formally with both hands. "I'm here to welcome you to the Institute, should it still be your intention to attend."

For a long time Rei could only look down at the object in Loren's hands with such dumb fascination, he suspected later to have appeared nothing short of a star-struck idiot. From an empty void of sheer astonishment he took in the pale paper fold-over of the envelope, sealed by hand in the ancient fashion of melted red wax pressed with the symbol of the school. After a solid 5 seconds of silence, Rei was finally able to bring his hands up to accept it, only to discover he still held the towels and spray bottle.

They fell to the ground together.

"I… I got in?" he asked quietly, not looking up from the winged griffin in its square as he finally took the envelop.

"You did." The captain's voice was a little gentler, now, clearly registering his shock. "Congratulations."

Rei was just able to lift his eyes to meet hers.

"How did I… I mean… How could I have…?" He trailed off, not sure if he wanted to open that line of questioning for *any* present party to pursue.

Fortunately, Loren seemed to follow his train of thought.

"If Galens accepts you, then you earned it somehow, even if you don't think you deserved it." Her face grew suddenly hard. "Am I to assume, then, that you intend to enroll in the Institute, cadet?"

Rei—who had looked down at the wax seal once more—started to nod again, then caught himself.

"Yes!" he said quickly. "I-I mean—Yes, ma'am!" He gave the captain a stiff salute, right hand opened and fingers brought to his brow with palm out, hoping the small amount of time he and Viv had put into practicing the movement paid off.

The bob of approval told him it had.

"Excellent. In that case…"

In a blur of motion Rei barely followed with his naked eye, Captain Loren stood in front of Lee Jackson, her height—though still a few inches short of the boy's—much more of an even match compared to Rei's, particularly with her cap on. She came up so close to Lee's face that he yelped and leapt back, almost tripping over himself.

"As an intended student of the Galens Institute, Cadet Reidon Ward is officially under the purview of the school's teachers, instructors, and staff. He is correct to inform you that calling a Device on civilians without just cause is *highly* illegal, but you should also be aware that as ranking officer of the ISCM, those limitations are a bit more… lenient, for me." Loren took a step towards Lee, who again retreated. "I witnessed enough of your exchange to know the intention of your presence here tonight, Mr.—" she paused a brief moment as her NOED undoubtedly pulled the boy's information up "—Jackson. Do you mean to pursue this matter any further?"

"We were just messing with him!" Lee half-wheezed, half-squealed, his expression one of absolute terror as he continued to backpedal. "Honestly, miss, were just going to—"

"Do not *lie* to me, boy." Loren snapped, and for a second time she blurred as she closed the growing gap between them again in a flash. "A high-level CAD can read your pulse and breathing as easily as you might a picture book. Now—" she brought one hand up to point at the nearest exit "—get out of my sight, and if I find out you've distracted *any* military cadet from their preparation for Commencement again, you'll have the opportunity to see a Device in action up close and personal, just as you wished." She looked over her shoulder, and Rei almost gasped aloud as he took her in, watching the captain glare at each of the other three combat team members in turn.

Kana Loren's eyes were *glowing*. Not the faint reflection you might catch in a flash of sunlight or the like. Actually *glowing*. Her irises blazed a deep, dangerous white, much brighter and more vibrant than the fainter purple Major Connelly's had gleamed when he'd shown off his "Calysta" at the start of the CAD exam. At the time, Rei had judged the head evaluator to have been a high B-Rank at least, too, and yet the outward indications of this subtle partial-call indicated there was no comparing that man's ability to the woman before him. She was a top-level A at the very least, and if Rei had been a betting man, he would have assumed himself in the presence of a Pawn- or Bishop-Class S-Ranked CAD-User, maybe even a Knight…

"That goes for every one of you," the captain said coolly, the burning of her eyes not fading as they held the group stricken in their grasp. "Is that *understood?*"

With affirming answers coming as an assortment of nods, yells of confirmation, and half-intelligible whimpers, Loren grunted, satisfied. With a dismissing jerk of her hand the power behind her gaze faded, her irises returning to their typical pale coloring.

Or were they… just for a moment… brown?

Regardless, Lee and his seconds needed no other release. In record time they'd bolted from the gym, so desperate to put as much space between themselves and the terrifying captain that Silva actually tripped over Suresh's feet, tangling them both up and bringing the pair to the floor before they were halfway to the lobby. They were back up in an instant, though, hounding the others' heels like the group was fleeing an active fire.

Once they were gone, the captain let out a snort.

"Well that was fun," she muttered to herself. Turning around, she caught Rei staring at her, and seemed to remember her position. Coughing into a fist in what was obviously an attempt to steal a moment and collect her thoughts, Loren brought her hands behind her back to take an at ease stand in front of him, continuing their conversation like nothing out of the ordinary had happened.

"Your notice of acceptance, along with instructions on how to confirm your enrollment, is in there." She dipped the brim of her cap towards the envelope still held—somehow momentarily forgotten—in Rei's hand. "Once you complete the process, your NOED will register the data, but you *are* encouraged to memorize your ID number yourself. Your cadet regulars will be delivered to your provided address of residence within three weeks of school Commencement in August, where you are expected to present yourself for assignment in dress." She met Rei's eyes. "Do you have any questions for me?"

Rei blinked, reeling for a moment at the torrent of information. Once he'd caught himself up, he hesitated, then spoke.

"Uh… As far as I know, there's no registered CAD Ability that would let the User know if someone is lying…?"

Loren, in answer, stared at him.

Then she laughed.

"I was told you were an odd one, Ward…" She smirked. "Sometimes embellishment resolves unnecessary situations a bit quicker than fact, if you understand what I mean."

Rei nodded at once. "Of-of course," he stammered before pausing again, considering. "You said you're an A-Type instructor? Would we… Would I be training under you? At the Institute?"

Hearing himself say "the Institute" almost had Rei swooning once more. He still couldn't believe it. There was just no way they would let an F—no, *E*-Rank, now, he had to remind himself—into Galens.

And yet here a staff captain of the academy stood, having handed him the very acceptance letter that said otherwise.

"The school employs a good number of instructors and sub-instructors, so chances are you'll be working with a lot of trainers." Loren dodged the question masterfully, eyes dropping to Shido's bands. "My understanding is that your Device is currently presenting as a Brawler weapon. I would assume your conditioning and lessons will start there, and adapt as your CAD evolves."

Again, Rei nodded.

"Any other questions?" Loren asked, checking the time pointedly in her NOED. "I have a few more notices to hand out in different time zones of Astra-3 before my day is over."

"Oh! N-no! I'm sorry, I just…" Rei couldn't help but look down at the envelope again, distantly hearing the buzz of the drones still making their sweeps of the gym galleries. "I didn't expect this…" he finally finished.

He was too busy studying the griffin of the Galens Institute to see Loren smile her approval.

"The best of us rarely do, cadet."

Then she clicked her heels, turned, and left the gym in the same direction she had come, leaving Rei to stare after her until the captain vanished down the lobby stairs and around the corner of the entrance.

Only then, as he stood there alone in his brown jumpsuit, with his acceptance letter in one hand, did it sink in.

"YYYYEEEEEESSSSS!" he yelled to the empty stand, punching the air with both hands, the envelope highlighted as a rectangle against the lights high above. "Yes! *YES!*"

A notice caught his attention, then, a small marker in the corner of his vision, and as he opened it he started when the recording of Viv's squealing voice nearly blew out his eardrums.

"Jerk! Pick up! Pick UP! I got in! I got IN, Rei!"

Recalling her missed calls, Rei rang her back immediately. Almost at once Viv's blue eyes and brown curls popped into his frame as she picked up in video-mode.

"Look! *Look!*" She was still squealing, and the camera view was suddenly filled with a red blur. After it corrected itself, the shape of the griffin came into focus, the wax seal of Viv's envelope already cracked. "Some lady officer stopped by my training session twenty minutes ago! I would have called you immediately, but my instructor was being a jerk and made me wait till we were done! I'm in, Rei! I'm in!"

"That's great, Viv!" Rei answered enthusiastically, thinking fast. "What did you think of Captain Loren? She seems kinda badass, doesn't she?"

"Totally!" Viv agreed, her face popping back into view as she pulled the envelope out of frame again. "The instructor was pretty sure she was an S-Rank, though he'd never heard of her. I hope I get to train under her! She seemed totally—!"

Viv froze, Rei's words finally hitting her. She stared at the camera, still as a statue except for the understanding slowly dawning across her face.

"Wait… Rei… How did you know what her name—?"

And then she shrieked, her excitement and glee making Rei smile so hard his cheeks hurt as he showed her his own—still-sealed—envelope.

From around the corner outside the combat gym, Valera Dent listened with a grin as Reidon Ward and Viviana Arada celebrated together with yells and screams. When she was satisfied, she eased herself off the wall she'd been leaning against, making her way from the building exit in truth this time. The doors opened for her automatically, and stepping outside she looked around. Evening was turning into night, and there looked to be nobody around.

Perfect.

Valera slid a hand between the buttons of her uniform to turn off the projection unit hung around her neck like a necklace. Her vision shimmered for a moment as the skin-tight hologram that had shifted the details of her face faded, then cleared, and she looked up into the clean, rapidly darkening sky of Astra-3.

She hadn't been able to stop herself from requesting she be the one to hand Reidon Ward his letter. She'd had her sub-instructors—Michael Bretz in particular—research him heavily in the days before the board of admissions had met, but there was only so much one could glean from data on a page. She'd needed to see him with her own eyes, to take him in in person, before she could feel satisfied she'd made the right choice.

As though on cue, a line of script wrote itself out, unbidden, across her NOED.

"Why didn't I intervene earlier?" she asked the empty air, turning and moving down the paved path that would lead her to the flyer waiting to take her to the nearest space port. "Isn't it obvious? I wanted to see what he would do."

Another line.

"What do you mean, 'why'?" Valera snorted, pulling her cap a little further over her eyes as a few students heading back to their dorms crossed the way some distance ahead of her. She hated using the projection unit, but she also didn't want to risk getting spotted by a fan or CAD enthusiast who might otherwise recognize her. "Because you give someone a taste of power who's never had it before, and there's always the risk they're too keen to use it. I wanted to make sure that wasn't the case."

A pause in the conversation, then, and Valera watched a shooting star—common enough a sight in the Astra system—flash in a sweeping arc across the dusk sky.

Then, eventually, a final script.

"Yeah, Kes," Valera answered quietly, not looking away from the coming darkness that expanded infinitely beyond them as she kept walking. "Yeah. I think we picked a good one."

CHAPTER 10

"It is no uninvolved trick, triggering mental commands. It's like trying to teach yourself to use a muscle you've not only never employed before, but had no idea you possessed in the first place. It takes diligence, discipline, and an enormous amount of frustration to learn even the basics, but mastering the ability to instruct your Device in silence is a minimal essential for any higher-level combatant. Face off with a User who has experience in the ring, and shouting your commands is as good as handing them a detailed playbook on how to feed you your own steel."

Captain Sarah Takeshi

Head of Tactical Studies, the Galens Institute

Aria Laurent caught the neon-grey blade of the halberd sweeping down on her head with the edge of her shield, deflecting the weapon aside. In her right hand Hippolyta's spear flicked forward in a flash of red, gold, and green, going for her opponent's exposed thigh. The blade was knocked away at the last moment, and Aria wrenched it back into position, retreating a step and setting herself into a defensive posture, her plated greaves adjusting with her legs helping to support her weight.

"Good!" her uncle shouted as he pressed her again, his "Taj" thundering down from above for a second time. "Excellent foot movement! Perfect Phalanx retreat."

Aria didn't have a breath to appreciate the compliment, applying her D8 Speed spec into a lunging side-roll out of the way of the descending blow. She successfully dodged it, and the blade of the halberd bit into the floor of the empty, all-white Neutral Zone variation field they typically used for their morning exercises. Finding her feet, Aria lunged, pulling her shield to the side as her spear led the attack.

Again it was deflected, and again she found herself tactfully withdrawing to a more defensible distance.

"Good!" Uncle Ram said again, drawing Taj back and bringing the glowing halberd to bear before him. "Quick shifting like that will take most opponents by surprise. A Phalanx is a blade that happens to be made of stone. Not stone that happens to be carved into the shape of a blade."

Aria almost laughed, but kept her composure.

"Wise words from a wise man," she teased, inching forward, lifting her spear over her head to rest it atop the red-and-gold steel of her shield. Standing in the middle of the field a few yards in front of her, her uncle waited, Taj still held at the ready. He was sparring with a partial-call—the only manifested part of his device apart from his weapon being the metallic orange-green and grey-lined armor that encased his hands and forearms—but that was more than fine with Aria. She might have been the star of Galens' summer training program, but an S-Ranker bringing his full ability to bear against her would likely have resulted in Aria's rapid exiting from this plane of existence, regardless of if they were just practicing or not.

"Watch it, brat," Uncle Ram warned her with a chuckle, eyeing her footing carefully. "This 'wise man' can have you running laps around the Institute grounds until graduation, don't forget. Now keep track of your steps. Spreading your legs too wide in a defensive crouch makes you easy to bowl over."

With a *whoomph* of shifting air, he demonstrated this fact promptly, closing the distance between them in a blink to put a boot on the surface of Aria's shield. She yelped as the older man gave her a good shove, immediately falling backwards to land on her rear.

"Owwwe!" she complained, pouting up at her uncle, Hippolyta's shield and spear limp in either hand. "I *know* I need to watch my stance, but how many of my opponents any time soon are going to be rushing me with S-Rank Speed?!"

"A8," Uncle Ram corrected her, reaching down to offer her help up. She accepted, letting herself get pulled back up to her feet. "And maybe not any time soon, but you're on the shortlist for Sectionals, don't forget. I doubt there will be any A-Rankers in the first years' brackets, but *anyone* with the right specs could manage what I just did a little slower, if they timed it right. Third Eye won't help you in that kind of situation either."

Aria grumbled, not disagreeing, but not finding the will to admit the man was right either, even regarding her Ability. In answer her uncle laughed and tousled her hair playfully. "Muttering under your breath and being bad at taking advice? It's like

I'm trading blows with your father all over again."

Aria gave a grunt of acknowledgement at that, having no desire to speak of her parents as she reached up to try to flatten her red hair back down while she eyed him hopefully. "One more round?"

Uncle Ram's eyes tilted up and to the right as he checked the time in the corner of his frame, and he shook his head. "Not today, unfortunately. I need to start getting ready." He looked at her critically for a moment. "As should you. Are you prepared for this afternoon?"

Aria shrugged in faked nonchalance. "If the likes of Grant and Vademe weren't able to put much of a scratch on me all summer, I'm not too worried about some random with a lower Rank and even less training. Bring it on."

Her uncle nodded slowly, reading a communication off his NOED that must have been sent while they practiced. When he finished typing out a quick reply one-hand on a keyboard Aria couldn't see, he finally answered. "Probably fair, but don't let your guard down completely. The sixteen of you are only the *favorites* for Sectional qualification. There hasn't been a year I've been at this school that a good few 'randoms' from outside the summer courses got the individual slots instead."

Aria's stomach clenched unpleasantly. She still wasn't too worried, but if she made a fool of herself in front of the other first years…

"But you're right, it's not anything to worry about." Uncle Ram grinned down at her, putting a finger on her forehead. She looked at it cross-eyed, a little confused, until the man continued.

"Just remember—" he hooked the heel of her weight-bearing leg with an ankle before she could stop him "—to watch your footing."

And then, with the tiniest of shoves through her head, she was on her ass again.

"Owwwe!" Aria repeated, recalling Hippolyta with a word so she could rub her rear. The CAD's reactive shield hadn't bothered triggering for *either* impact. "Uncle Ram, have I ever mentioned how much I am *not* going to miss these mornings sessions with you?"

The man recalled his own CAD silently, the Neutral Zone around them disappearing at the same time. They were left to float gently down the 2 feet of empty space to the projection plating of the training chamber floor, coming to rest near the middle of the 30-yard Dueling ring that took up their favorite East Center room. Reaching the ground, her uncle turned and made for the door, beside which his black-and-gold jacket and cap were waiting for him on a hook.

The old man hadn't even broken enough of a sweat to bother showering, Aria realized with a groan.

"You have, my dear, several times." He flashed her a smile as he pulled on his uniform and tucked the top of his grey-black ponytail under the cap. "Now go get yourself cleaned up and ready. It would be bad form to show up late to your own Commencement Ceremony."

Aria grumbled an acknowledgement in return, letting herself fall onto her back as her body registered the beating of the last hour.

"Oh, and Aria…"

She lifted her head again, seeing that her uncle had paused as he opened the door.

"Remember that it's 'colonel' when we're at school," Rama Guest, commanding officer of the Galens Institute, told his niece with a raised eyebrow.

CHAPTER 11

And so I grant thee my life and soul, oh cruel mistress of battle…"

The Collected Poetries of Adison Gimble
Major General Adison Gimble

Specifications Request acknowledged.

…

Combat Assistance Device: Shido. User identification… Accepted.

Type: A-TYPE

Rank: E3

…

User Attributes:

- Strength: F5

- Endurance: F3

- Speed: F6

- Cognition: F5

…

CAD Specifications:

- Offense: F4

- Defense: F4

- Growth: S

With a sigh Rei closed the Request, feeling a strange combination of pleased and dejected. The low-atmosphere tram swayed gently around him, and he shut his eyes as the thrum of the orbital turbines beneath his seat hummed.

E3… In the 2 months since he and Viv had received their acceptance letters, Rei had only managed to eke out an additional two level in his CAD-Rank. He wasn't *disappointed*, per se—jumping four levels in Rank over the space of 10 weeks was practically unheard of, even for someone starting with specs as low as his—but he couldn't pretend it wasn't a little disheartening. After leaping out of the Fs and almost straight to E1 in what had essentially been a matter of days, he had to admit he'd expected to see a more substantial improvement over the duration of the summer. Courses had ended—with him not-unexpectedly finishing in the top of the graduating class—and, with nothing left but his job, he'd been able to spend several times as many hours a day training as he had in the last weeks of school.

Unfortunately, while Rei had certainly not served himself short on *commitment* to his conditioning, it was the tools of his education that appeared to have failed him.

The ISCM simulations available to new cadets had only lasted him another week after he'd finally managed to break through to F2 Endurance. He'd made good progress even in that time, seeing steady boosting across the board, but the basic instructional projections were well... basic. They weren't designed to teach anything more than essentials of various combat, with the military preferring to entrust more complex direction to their combat schools, or at the very least to the sanctioned trainers many User's families—like Viv's—tended to hire for the gap months before term started. As a result Rei had found himself hitting a wall pretty quickly, and—if he was being honest with himself—was actually decently pleased with the progress he'd managed to make in the meantime repeating and reusing simulations, trying to challenge himself on beating every projection level a little faster and a little more cleanly dozens of times over.

Frustration leaked into his thoughts, and Rei absently lifted a hand from where it had been resting on the top of the flat military cap settled in his lap, running his scarred fingers through his newly trimmed hair. The ISCM had long since done away with most aesthetic regulations for their servicemen and women. Mankind had always staked much on the value of their outward appearance, but with the now-common practice of designer genes coming along around the same time as the rising popularity of the SCTs, having distinguishing characteristics among Users who were popular in the circuits was important. Still, Viv had downright *refused* to let Rei attend the Commencement with his regular wash of disorganized white, so he found himself rubbing at the shaved sides of his head, the clean trim fading up to a healthier three or four inches running along the top and back. He liked the cut—Viv had paid for it from her own pocket as a congratulations for breaking into E3 only a few days before they'd been set to depart—but it was definitely a change.

Everything was a change...

Rei opened his eyes and glanced to his left. As expected, Viv hadn't so much as twitched from her place facing the wide tram window, looking out at the split horizon of a white-blue planet and the unmoving darkness of space above. He could see her reflection in the glass, her own black-and-gold regulars matching his against the glow of Astra-3 below them, and he watched her stare at nothing in particular for a while before deciding she looked like she needed interrupting.

"Credit for your thoughts, space cadet?"

Viv blinked, then met his eyes in the reflection.

"Oh you know," she answered in a deadpan after a moment. "Just thinking of all the new hotties I get to meet today."

Rei chuckled. "Don't go making a name for yourself on day one. Leave some ladies for the rest of us."

Viv huffed and sat back in her seat, looking around at him with narrowed eyes. "You always get fixated on the *girls*. I've had my fair share of dates with some handsome gentleman too, you know."

Rei smiled, lifting his cap from his lap to pull it low over his eyes before leaning back against his headrest, like he were going to take a nap. "Uh-huh. I remember. Mikael Dorsey. In our first year. You dated him for a month after he beat the shit out of me behind the physics lab for not letting him copy my paper on planetary magnetics."

"Yes." Viv snatched the hat off his head, tossing it back onto his knee and sticking her tongue out at him. "And you know damn well I led him on for that whole month before breaking his heart for messing with you."

"My hero," Rei sniggered.

Viv just managed to hide a smirk. "My *point*—" she said with intention, crossing her legs and settling back again "—is that you should worry about me stealing all of Galens' best looking girls *and* boys. Give me some credit."

Rei made a noncommittal grunt, but said nothing more. After a little silence, though, he realized that Viv was eyeing him sidelong.

"What?"

She hesitated for a moment, like she didn't know how to broach whatever subject was on her mind, her attention lingering on the golden cuffs around his wrist. "Well... Speaking of looks. I noticed today, when I saw you in the uniform... When were you gonna tell me you're getting taller?"

Some of the levity left their conversation abruptly, and Rei tensed a little. He twitched his hands a bit, trying without success to hide the ring of bare skin between his CAD bands and the edge of the cuffs.

"How much?" Viv pushed.

Rei sighed, giving in. His best friend had never been one to let go of a subject once she latched onto it. "Just over half an inch," he admitted. "Some muscle mass gained too, if Shido's readings of my metrics are right." He lifted one arm, letting the blue on black-and-white shine in the reflection of the planet through the window. "A lot of the latter probably has more to do with our training than any genetic correction, though."

"Not bad," Viv murmured. "At that rate, you might only have another year or so of being legally considered a toddler."

"You're hilarious, for an over-sized flagpole," Rei answered dryly.

Viv grinned, but her amusement didn't last long.

"And your pain? Any symptoms?"

Rei shrugged. "Fine, actually. I was a little surprised. I was starting to have an issue with my right hip at the beginning of the summer, but it didn't get any worse, and even started feeling a bit better about a week ago."

Viv was beaming, then. "That's great!" she exclaimed quietly while the tram took a bump over some turbulence. "That's even better than you'd hoped, isn't it?"

"Yeah," Rei acknowledged, a little more readily this time. As always, Viv's excitement could be infectious, even when it came to subjects he didn't love talking about. "I'd read that the correcting *might* be able to address active symptoms of some diseases, but the research was spotty, and nothing on fibro directly. No Users had it before me, apparently."

"Whoa. *Such* a shocker." Viv rolled her eyes so hard it looked painful. "Probably because most people with *bone needles* stabbing them in the joints and organs every couple weeks might have had the sense to take life a little easier."

"Are you saying I don't know when to quit?" Rei asked, raising an eyebrow at her in mock displeasure.

"Rei, I'm saying you're the damn *king* of 'not knowing when to quit'," Viv huffed, throwing her hands up in surrender. She let them hang there for a second, though, grinning at him.

"Then again... That *did* get you into Galens, didn't it?"

For the thousandth time in 2 months Rei felt his heart skip a beat at the thought. It still hadn't really processed. Not really. Not when he and Viv had accepted their enrollment together the very night Kana Loren had handed them their letters. Not when he'd signed his vacuum-sealed uniform, dispensed to him by a delivery drone through his dorm room window. Even now, swaying along in a car of a tram moving 1000 miles an hour as it hurtled him towards the very epicenter of his disbelief, it hadn't processed.

He'd made it in…

Of course, he wasn't about to let *Viv* know just how much he still couldn't wrap his head around the fact that he, like her, wore a grey band stitched with the red griffin and square, marking him as a first year cadet at the Institute.

"I like to think it had more to do with my grades and work ethic then my *pain tolerance*, thanks very much."

Viv scrunched her nose at him and dropped her arms, obviously displeased he wasn't humoring her games that morning.

Then her blue eyes took on a mischievous gleam.

"Uh-huh. Well it definitely had to do with something, cause there's no other way the board of admissions would have let in a guy the average height and weight of a pre-teen with an eating dis—*Owe!*" She laughed when Rei smacked her in the arm to shut her up.

Masking his own smile, Rei let his head fall back again, actually planning to sleep a little if he could manage it, given they were traveling twelve time zones away.

"Shut your trap, flagpole. Just wake me up when we get there."

Given that Astra-3 had four times the surface area of the Sol System's Earth—the ISC's origin planet—it wasn't much later than mid-morning locally by the time the tram finally came to a halt at the Sector 9 orbital station. Disembarking, Rei and Viv were told by arrival notification to their NOEDs that an auto-flyer was waiting for them off the platform, and so it wasn't long before they were out of the station and loading what pads, spare clothes, and other belongings they'd brought with them into the oblong vehicle's rear storage compartment. All around them people were on- and off-boarding, leaving and finding their own flyers, and more than once Rei had to keep Viv focused as she noticed other cadets in uniform obviously heading to the Institute. After reminding her some half-dozen times that they would have *ample* opportunity to meet their school- and classmates that same day *without* putting the two of them at risk of being late for their scheduled time of arrival, the pair finally tucked themselves into the vehicle and were soon zipping back down towards the planet at breakneck speeds. Rei watched the clouds whip by them with a small measure of awe, having rarely had the chance to leave Astra-3's surface other than his very infrequent trips back to see Matron Kast and the other staff of the Estoran Center on Astra-2. It was an awesome sight every time, only mildly distracted from by Viv's nervous bouncing in the seat beside him.

Finally entering the troposphere, Castalon—the city the Galens Institute was set practically in the middle of—came into distinct relief, and the flyer's momentum shifted steadily from vertical to horizontal until Rei and Viv where zipping along an upper air-lane through a brilliant plethora of glimmering, towering skyscrapers. The "ground" seemed a foreign concept to the metropolis, Rei realized, feeling their vehicle rise and fall as theirs and other lanes apparently adjusted to accommodate a seemingly infinite number of walkways and closed bridges that interconnect the buildings until the place felt more like a hive of steel and glass than a city.

"The shortest of these must be four hundred floors high," Viv hissed, and Rei glanced around to see her looking out her own window in awe. It made him feel better for staring. The Aradas were a well-off family—this was the first summer Viv hadn't joined them on their annual vacation to the resorts of Venus, in fact—and she'd seen a good bit more of the humanity's expansion than he had. If *she* was impressed by Castalon, therefore, it stood to reason he was allowed to gape.

"Apparently most of this sprawl has been in the last seventy-five years or so," he told her, returning his attention to the behemoths of twisted and spiraling metal, watching neon signs of every shape and scripting whip by them in barely legible streaks of a thousand different colors. "The city's built itself up around Galens' reputation."

"*What*?" Viv sputtered. "There's only like four hundred cadets at the Institute at any given time!"

"384," Rei corrected automatically. "But the top finishers in the Collegiate Intersystems consistently include a couple of Galens grads every year, and there's a few well-known S-Rankers who are still in the pro circuit. They even have a *pro* IS Champion to their credit, from back in the 30s: Dalek O'Rourke."

"The Gatecrasher." Viv identified the man by his circuit name. "Yeah, I know. My mother met him once. Told me she'd never known another person filthy rich enough to buy his own terraformed *asteroid* as a second home."

"The pros of getting crowned a King," Rei agreed, following a massive sign for the "Easthold Mall" that encompassed three different buildings as it passed them by. "With names like that attached to theirs, though, it's not surprising Galens is a civil hub."

"Aaaah that doesn't help my stomach," Viv moaned, and Rei could practically hear the nerves in her words.

"You'll be fine, Ms. D7," he assured her, emphasizing Viv's breakthrough from the week before. After two and a half hard months of training and instruction, she'd earned herself her first CAD-Rank improvement. "You can leave all the anxiety to the *E-Ranker* sharing your ride."

"Why do you think we're friends?" Viv groaned. "I need someone to make me look good by comparison."

Rei rolled his own eyes with a chuckle.

They talked and joked the rest of the short ride, their humor strained and their laughter a little forced while they approached their final destination. When the flyer started to descend sharply, Rei knew they had to be getting close, and the pair of them grew quite. Taking a corner in the wide throughway between the skyscrapers they'd be following, a massive, open space expanded outward before them like a crater in the middle of the city, and Rei blinked as he saw green for the first time.

They'd both seen pictures of the Institute before, he knew. Rei had done personal searches on the feeds for them occasionally before meeting Viv, and a hundred times together since. Still, despite that, there was no comparing the awesomeness of the grounds as taken directly from the sky.

Despite housing only 384 students and some quarter that many members of staff and security, Galens was a sprawling institution with dozens of buildings of as many different shapes as uses that encompassed a full square half-mile of space. A massive wall formed an imposing 4-sided barrier around the edge of the campus itself, beyond which a band of verdant forestland 100 yards wide separated the Institute from the ground floors of Castalon's nearest structures. This greenery was in turn divided and interspersed with a careful system of paved paths leading to and from the four cardinal entrances to the school. *Inside* the wall the actual buildings formed a balanced pattern of symmetry, centering around the very heart of the Institute where a single colossal, oblong building stood out like a black-and-grey gem in a complex setting of metal and earth.

Even as he looked at it, the angular roofing plates of the Arena caught in the sunlight of the day, glimmering in Rei's eyes.

"Holy. Shit," he muttered, so low that even Viv didn't hear him as she shamelessly pressed her nose to her own window to ooh at the spectacle of their approach.

Too soon, their flyer had dipped below the canopy of the tree line, and the Arena disappeared from view. The vehicle came to rest lightly in a wide, semi-circular court-yard of synthetic marble outside the south entrance, joining a half-ring of identical vehicles from which other students were ducking out of in ones and two, some with the grey armbands of first years, others with the green and blue of second and third years. The flyer door opened with a faint *hiss* on Viv's side, and she led the way out, gazing with an open mouth up the wall that extended an easy 100 feet above their heads. Only the wide entrance that cut a massive wedge through the old-fashioned mortared stone gapped it, accented on either side by massive, hanging black cloths. These banners were emblazed in gold with the seven stars and crossed swords of the ISCM, below which a smaller section of white showed off the red griffin of the school itself. Rei, standing up next to Viv, would have called the sight ostentatious, but the sheer weight it exuded to anyone beneath its heights made it easy to forget the uselessness of such a defense in an age of flying transports, wormhole drives, and a scattered percentage of high-level Users who could have cleared the top of the wall if they got a running start.

"You two. Keep moving. There's more flyers inbound."

Together Rei and Viv looked around as a Sergeant with the red-on-white arm-band of a school staffer addressed them sharply from where he stood in the center of the courtyard. Hurrying to gather their bags from the storage compartment, they didn't bother watching the pod fly away to be replaced almost immediately by an-other, instead moving together to approach the officer. The sergeant had a wide pad in one hand and looked to be checking off arrivals and instructing them on where they should go from there.

"Eyes up," the man said when they came to stand before him. Rei and Viv met his gaze one after the other, his bilateral NOED blazing for a moment as it obviously scanned their own for identification.

"Cadet Arada and Cadet… Ward. Good. You came together. You're quartered on the third floor of the Kanes, the first year dorm. Suite 304. Do you need a map of the campus?"

By his side, Viv looked surprised, but Rei answered before she could ask any questions. "No, sir. Got one here." He reached up to tap under his eye.

"Good. Thinking ahead. You're making my job easier already." The sergeant frowned down at his pad. "Arada, your NOED meets specifications for course use, but you're going to need an upgrade, Ward. Quartermaster will want to handle it before classes start tomorrow." He looked the pair of them up and down again, doing a good job of covering up his uncertainty at Rei's height and weight by respectively eyeing the visible skin and socks around his CAD bands and military-issued boots instead. "He'll want to address your uniform measurements as well. Sorry about that. We use the specs from your CAD-Assignment Exams, but genetic correction occasionally makes those obsolete."

"No problem, sir," Rei assured the man. "I'll make sure it's all taken care of."

After telling them where they could find the Quartermaster's stock depot and explaining they were at leisure to explore the Institute until Commencement began at 1400 in the Arena, the sergeant dismissed them. Together they started for the massive opening that was the entrance to the grounds, noting as they did the steel teeth on either side of them that looked like foot-thick metal doors retracted into the wall. Viv followed Ray's lead as he pulled up the map of the Institute he'd indeed downloaded earlier, requesting the first year dorm be highlighted.

"Are we rooming together?" she asked him once they were definitely out of earshot of the sergeant.

"Sounds like it," Rei answered, finding Kanes outlined in the top north-east corner of the grounds and shifting their course slightly.

"That doesn't surprise you?"

Rei shrugged. They passed a small group of other first years clearly already walking the campus, and he ignored them when they slowed down to watch him and Viv pass with confusion printed clearly on their faces. "Not really. Should it? I can't imagine we'll be the *only* ones in the room, so Galens is probably trying to make sure it can maintain what few relationships incoming students are arriving with. Good friends can be hard to find."

Major Connelly's words to him during the exam slipped out without meaning to, surprising Rei so much he stopped paying attention as he took a corner in the path and almost slammed into the chest of a uniformed figure so tall, it probably wouldn't have been unlikely running face-first into the Institute wall.

"Sorry!" Rei exclaimed stepping back quickly and craning his head up to look the cadet in the face. "That's my bad. I didn't see you."

The boy frowned down at him. His eyes were so dark they were almost black, designed with a distinct hint of red in them, and the long, straight hair spilling out from under his military cap was similarly jet. He looked first at Rei, then at Arada, studying her a good bit longer before turning his attention back to Rei.

"You lost, kid? I didn't realize they allowed twelve-year-olds on tour here."

Rei's felt his cheeks flush a bit.

"Judging by your sense of humor, I'd say they obviously do."

The boy's dark eyebrows twitched up in what was the barest hint of surprise, clearly not having expected the quick response. He had a handsome face, but it was made ugly by the curl of a sneer that looked to be almost permanently holding over his upper lip. Around his left arm the grey-and-red band of a new cadet was tight over what must have been well-formed muscle, and the white-and-red rings of his CAD hung from his wrists.

Before either of them could say another word, however, Viv had taken Rei by the elbow and was pulling him around the towering figure.

"Come on," she told him, though she took the time to glare at the boy as they passed. Rei tried to protest, attempting to wrench his arm free from hers, but Viv's Strength spec was several times greater than his own, so it felt like trying to pull his elbow from of an iron manacle.

In the end, all he could do to satisfy his irritation was lean into profanity, as he thought was duly appropriate.

"What the shit was *his* baggage?!" he demanded furiously, looking over his shoulder to where the tall cadet had turned to watch them go, following them with his black-red eyes.

"Don't know, don't care." Viv said, face now set resolutely forward under the brim of her cap, hitching her bags higher over her other shoulder as she continued to pull him along. "All I know is that I'm not about to let some pretty-boy dickwad mess with our first day on campus. Come on." She tugged on him a little more firmly, and Rei finally stopped fighting, letting himself be dragged along the path into an alley between two identical four-story buildings with walls of solid glass. Inside, several older cadets who had to be third years were practicing unarmed grappling on rubbered flooring, all of them in matching, skin-tight red-on-blue combat uniforms that left only their heads, arms, and from the knees down bare. Watching the sparring through the windows as they moved by, Rei managed to shake a little of his anger at the encounter in favor of taking in their surroundings again.

Whereas Grandcrest Preparatory had been built with a mind to imitate an ancient history of stone, slate, and diamond-paned windows, Galens had left the nod to the past to its perimeter wall. Inside the grounds, every building was sheer glass and clean construction steel, not unlike the towering skyscrapers of Castalon that still rose up to the heavens in a staggered ring on all sides of them. The Institute's structures were smaller, of course, and far less imposing, with none extending higher than a dozen floors, and most not even half of that. Since they'd be cutting through the center of campus later to get to the Arena for Commencement, Rei and Viv decided to take a round-about route, him reading off his neuro-optic as they walked while she listened in rapt excitement. Rei hadn't forgotten the asshat with black hair, but taking in the grounds did a lot to alleviate his irritation.

"That's the Device Evolution Department over there." He pointed to a long, squat building whose flat walls leaned inward, giving it the shape of an elongated pyramid that had had its upper half removed. "I think we'll have classes there on adapting to our CAD changes? And that—" he indicated a series of three tall, narrow structures interconnected by skyways "—is the Combat Theory Department. *Most* of our lectures are probably going to be in there, at least initially."

They kept moving, Rei prattling on, pointing out Vellus, the third year dormi-tory—the second years', Elberts, was on the other side of campus—the Institute Security Center, the school mess hall, and one of two 24-hour combat training facilities which housed dozens of Dueling-sized fields for sparring and small-scale tactics practice any time of the day. After a good 15 minutes of walking, a simple, boxy structure appeared around a bend in the path, and Rei let Viv know they'd ar-rived. Making for the building, the name "KANES" flashed into projection over a pair of long clear doors that slid open for them as they stepped inside.

"Whoa," Rei muttered, stopping short.

The inside of the first year dorms reminded him of pictures Viv had brought back of the resorts from some of her family vacations. The open lobby was spacious, with strip lights illuminating a crimson carpet over which a large number of varied seats, couches, and tables were artfully assorted. The building, it turned out, was also not half as plain as it might have seemed from its exterior, because the inside wall of the space was absent, leading out into an open-air courtyard centered around a massive, gnarled tree whose leaves were a pretty red-orange color.

It felt like the lobby of the system's grandest hotel, and had Rei gaping around in wonder for longer than he realized.

"Rei."

Viv—clearly more accustomed to this sort of sight—nudged him, indicating a figure waiting patiently near the inside of the doors when he looked around. Another sergeant, the officer stood watching them expectantly, a knowing smile on her face.

"Pretty great, isn't it?" the woman asked as they approached. "You guys have it good. The staff quarters aren't *close* to this well put together."

"We'll do our best to not drool then, ma'am," Viv responded humorously before indicating herself, then Rei. "Cadets Arada and Ward. The sergeant at the south gate told us we're in 304?"

"And he had it right." The officer's NOED flicked as she checked the info. "Third floor, northeast corner. Elevators are behind me," she threw a thumb over her shoulder. "Stairs on the other side of the building. I have you two as the last of your suitemates to arrive. Make sure to get along."

"Yes, ma'am," Rei and Viv said together, waiting until the woman dismissed them with a jerk of her head. They made for the elevators as indicated, finding them near the entrance to a hall-space labeled "101-105". The car reached them shortly, the clear door to the circular pod opening in silence to welcome them in. Rei gazed out the back window, letting Viv punch in their destination, and within seconds they were moving down the third-floor hall. They found 304 easily enough, and with a knock and an announcement that they were coming in Viv opened the door and stepped inside.

This time, Rei stopped himself from voicing his awe. Basically a miniature version of the downstairs lobby, the entrance to the living quarters opened up from a short hallway into a decently sized common space with the same reddish carpet. It was even complete with two matching couches centered around a handsome cement coffee table, the seating set at an angle to the transparent rear wall of the room. Beyond it, the Institute's perimeter "defenses" rose up in the distance, but a hedging of trees could be made out over the stone, with the facade of Castalon's northern skyscrapers towering several thousand feet over that. There was a kitchen space, too, on their left as they walked in, but before either of them could explore further a boy with short-cropped blond hair poked his head out from one of the six doors that led off the common area.

"Oh! Hey!" He stepped out of what must have been his room, approaching them genially. He wore his Institute regulars, but his cap was nowhere to be seen. "You guys Arada and Ward?"

"Arada," Viv confirmed for him, dropping one bag to stick her hand out to shake. "Call me Viv. And the munchkin behind me is Rei."

Rei rolled his eyes, but took the boy's hand without complaint when it was offered to him next.

"Nice. Layton Catchwick, but everyone calls me Catcher. Need help with the luggage?"

"Nah." Rei shook his head, stepping around the other two to take a closer look about the suite. "We packed light. At least after I nixed Viv's collection of stiletto heels and nail extension."

Viv gave a strangled choke of denial, but Catcher laughed, looking between them. "Gonna guess you guys already knew each other? Seem pretty chummy for a pair who just happened to share a flyer..."

"We graduated from the same prep school," Viv said, and Rei could practically feel her glaring at his back as he moved to examine the clear rear wall. As he'd suspected, it was smart-glass, meaning they'd be able to pull feeds, draw up schematics, and work out problems on it just like a pad. "Although right now I'm thinking I should have booted his ass off the tram station when I had the chance..."

"The same school..." Catcher repeated, sounding impressed, and Rei turned away from the glass to find the blond boy sizing them up one after the other. He had yellowish eyes that had obviously been designed to match his hair, and they were sparklingly with interest. "That's gotta be pretty rare."

"Probably," Rei dodged the subtle query, taking in the other doors around the space and noting they were assigned with engraved metal plaques that had their names on them. "Chancery Cashe... Jack Benaly. Are they here?"

Catcher's expression darkened a little, and he nodded before answering in a lowered tone of voice. "Yeah, but they don't seem much of the social types. Cashe shut herself in the room the moment she got here, saying she wanted to prep for Commencement, and Benaly's apparently been at Galens the entire summer already. Some special training course."

That piqued Rei's curiosity. He'd heard that the Institute had an exclusive camp for its top recruits, and if that was true it meant their suitemate was likely one of the highest Ranking intakes among the new cadets.

"Nice," he said under his breath, his hands twitching a little as his excitement started to boil over. Between that, the circumstance of their housing, and just the base fact that he was standing *inside* the grounds of *the* Galens Institute, Rei could feel himself starting to get jittery.

"So what Type are you guys?" Catcher asked enthusiastically, watching as Viv found her room and peeked in with interest. "I'm a Saber. D5." He said it proudly, clearly aware of the fact that his Rank had him seeded above the average first year ability.

"Duelist," Viv answered over her shoulder as she entered her quarters, raising her voice so that she could be heard from inside. "D7. Oh, nice! I got a window!"

"It's a corner suite. I think we *all* got windows," Rei called to her with a snort, moving to open the door labeled with his own plaque. Within, he was pleased to find what looked like a strip of more smart-glass horizontally bisecting the left wall to look out over the grounds, complimented by a work desk, and double-wide bed, and a sizable closet. It was spartan, but it would more than do the trick.

"D7?" Catcher asked, clearly taken aback. "*Damn…* Between you and Benaly's D8, the rest of our Rankings are gonna be small fry."

"Wouldn't worry about that, man." Rei said, dropping his bags down on the inside of the door before shutting it again. As little as he'd brought with him, he'd sort them out later. "In terms of Ranking, I've definitely got you beat in the 'small fry' department." He smirked at Catcher. "Not to mention I'm an A-Type."

"Ooooh no shit?" Catcher's yellow eyes suddenly fixed him with genuine fascination. "So you're either gonna sweep the floor with us, or flunk out fast, huh?"

Had most people asked the same question, Rei might have bit his tongue to keep from snapping back. Their enthusiastic suitemate, though, had managed to come off as nothing more than captivated by the predicament of his CAD-Type, so Rei just nodded as he answered.

"Hopefully the former, but the latter's definitely not out of the realm of possibility."

"Oh shut up, you'll be fine." Viv had apparently dropped off her own things and was closing the door to her room to join them again. "Some of the best SCT Users out there are A-Type."

Rei was about to explain, but was pleasantly surprised when Catcher beat him to it.

"That's kind of the nature of it." The boy plopped down on the nearest couch as he watched Viv move to explore the kitchen. "Atypicals generally have really decent versatility compared to the more streamlined Types, but that also makes them a real pain to master." He looked back to Rei, who'd returned to the smart-glass wall, intending to start messing around with it. "Are you hoping to develop Arsenal Shift, or going for an abnormal manifestation? What's your Device presenting as right now?"

Rei froze, momentarily taken aback.

Then he whirled.

"You know about Arsenal Shift?" he demanded excitedly, hurrying over to sit across from Catcher.

"Hell yeah!" their suitemate exclaimed, feeding off Rei's sudden eagerness. "The Red Tank and Valkyria each used it for their ISSCT Championship runs!"

"Rigo Voss and Lenora James-May," Rei affirmed, leaning over the coffee table earnestly, feeling his giddiness rising again. "The 2398 and 2425 circuits. You know your stuff, man!"

"I would hope so!" Catcher scooted forward on his couch, obviously sharing in Rei's excitement. "My mom was a Luhman System champ. Back in the 2453 circuit. She's been grilling me on this stuff since I was old enough to talk. Not that I minded." His eyes gleamed. "Who's your favorite current fighter? Have you been to any of the championship matches recently?!"

"No," Rei groaned, hanging his head and almost losing his cap in the process. "I've never had the chance, actually. But—" he looked up again "—I *did* catch the Intersystem Championship match on the feeds last year. The Heaven's Blade versus Kalvanos. Epic fight. I'd say Cassandra Adams is probably my favorite current User. She trounced Kalvanos pretty handily, so I'm hoping she has another decent run this season."

"*Ooooh* that was so good!" Catcher almost squealed in agreement. "The Blade's one of my favorites too, *especially* after I got assigned a Saber-Type like her." He pulled the sleeve of his uniform back to reveal a yellow-and-white CAD accented in purple on his wrist. "My summer instructor actually had me watch some of her last year's matches as part of our training. I might try to style my fighting a little after—"

"*Great*," Viv interrupted with a teasing huff, dropping down to sit beside Rei, a glass of water in one hand. "*Another* dork. I'm as much an enthusiast of the tournaments as any User, but listening to you two makes me feel like I'd have to sit my ass in front of the SCT feeds for a decade straight before I caught up with you fanboys."

"You could have asked if we wanted something to drink." Rei eyed her water hopefully.

Without looking at him, Viv pointed over his shoulder. "Kitchen's over there. More importantly… What's 'Arsenal Shift'?"

With a grunt Rei got up, letting Catcher take over the explanation.

"It's a really rare Ability. A few standard Users have registered as having it in the past, but it's more 'common' in A-Types. It allows for extreme manipulation of your Device's weapon call, completely shifting the shape of it." He waved around an invisible sword, then brought his hands together for a fake, heavy swing. "It's usually limited to one or two variances, but that's honestly enough. The Red Tank—Igor Voss—could shift between a Saber-like weapon and a massive Mauler axe pretty much at will. It won him the IS Championship in 2398, like Rei said. He lost in the next years, but only because the other S-Rank Kings and Queens started coming up with tactics designed *specifically* to counteract Arsenal Shift."

"The *hell?*!" Viv exclaimed, and Rei saw her head turn towards him as he finally found the glasses in one of the kitchen's plasteel cabinets. "You didn't tell me *that* was something you might be able to do!"

"I didn't tell you because it's not gonna happen," Rei answered, setting the sink's temperature to "COLD" with his NOED before filling two cups one after the other. "At least not anytime soon. It's the kind of Ability most CADs wouldn't register till A-Rank. B at the earliest."

"That's still insane!" Viv insisted as he moved back to the couch and offered Catcher a drink, which the Saber accepted with a word of thanks. "I don't know of any Abilities exclusive to Duelists that have that sort of versatility."

"I'm gonna make you wash your ears out," Rei told her with a snort as he sat down again. "Apparently you can't hear well. It's not exclusive. Just more common in Atypicals."

"Which, if it's that hard to come by, makes it basically exclusive." Viv dismissed his correction with a wave. "I'd be happy enough with Break Step and a few other speed-focused Abilities." She jabbed at an invisible enemy a little too enthusiastically. "Gemela can do a lot of damage if I can get around my opponent's defenses and specs."

"Same with my Arthus," Catcher agreed with a nod. Then he seemed to recall something, looking to Rei. "Did you say what your A-Type is presenting as right now?"

Rei grimaced. "Brawler," he answered with a sigh. "I'm seeing decent numbers in my Speed, Cognition, and Strength values, but everything else is lagging. I've been training with simulations all summer, but hit a wall. Hoping to see better growth once classes start."

Catcher skated right over the subtle admission that he hadn't had any private instructors over the break, leading Rei to decide that he did indeed think he could like this energetic suitemate of theirs.

"I'm sure you will, especially if you're in the lower values like you said. Even the difference in low to high Ds can close fast with the right training, and any Es you might have will definitely jump." The blond boy grinned. "Apparently we get our class assignments at Commencement. Hopefully we're in the same section. Would be nice to have some people I—"

The *click* of a door interrupted him, and all three of them looked around to find a squat, broad-shouldered youth stepping out of his room in uniform, pulling on his cap as he did. Jack Benaly, it transpired, wasn't tall for a User—maybe 5' 10" at most—but he was heavy-set and thick around the arms and limbs, with hands so big they looked like he could have punched through a solid steel wall without breaking a sweat.

Which—if his Strength was high enough—wasn't entirely out of the realm of possibility, Rei considered.

Benaly didn't pause as he stepped away from his room and made toward the suite door, though he did nod politely as he passed their group. They watched him go silently, waiting for the front entrance to shut behind him again, before Catcher spoke up once more.

"Speaking of Brawler-Types, apparently Benaly's one. Maybe he could help you out, Rei? Especially if your A-Type sticks to its form for a bit."

"Maybe," Rei said half-heartedly. He hadn't gotten a *bad* impression from the massive cadet, but he also hadn't read any interest to interacting much either.

Benaly's appearance and exit, though, had reminded him that he still had things to do before the Commencement ceremony, and luckily Viv seemed to have recalled the same thing.

"We should get going." She plucked Rei's half-filled glass from his hands, then got up to move to the kitchen and set both their drinks in the sink. Immediately an automated sterilizing system kicked in, leaving the cups empty and clean before she even stepped into the hall again. "Catcher, we've got to find the Quartermaster. Any interest in coming along?"

"Thanks, but I'll have to pass." The Saber gave Viv a mock salute from the couch as Rei pushed himself up across from him. "I need to finish unpacking anyway, and my mother will have my head if I don't call her to let her know I made it. We live in the Luhman System, and she's not keen on hole-drives."

"Fair enough," Viv said with a shrug, heading towards the door.

"Catch you at the ceremony?" Rei asked the boy as he stood up and made to follow her.

"Definitely," Catcher smiled after them. "I might head over a little early, so I'll save you guys a couple spots if I can."

"Deal. See you then."

With that, Rei followed Viv out of the suite, heading for the elevator again at the end of the hall. As the door closed behind them, they didn't see Catcher's grin slide slowly off his face, nor the blaze of his NOED as he pulled up the ISCM database. It only took a quick search to find what he was looking for, and the blond boy's jaw dropped as he took in the data lining out before him.

"What the *hell*...?"

CHAPTER 12

"Name?" the Quartermaster behind the clean steel counter of the Institute stock depot—a major named Bashir Sattar, according to the plaque by his right elbow—asked without looking at Rei after he was called up. The officer was already typing into a pad suspended on a lift-desk floating beside him, drawing out a small, circular metal ball from a dispensary set up next to the table.

"Reidon Ward, sir," Rei answered.

The major nodded in response, pulling up Rei's profile, where he finally paused.

"Ah," he muttered, as though recognizing the data. "Right. Uniform measurements, too. Dent did tell me there would be a new cadet looking to give me a headache this year."

"A-a headache, sir?" Rei asked hesitantly. Sattar ignored the question, instead finally turning in his chair to face Rei and motioning for him to present his arm. "Let me see your CAD. I can pull up your current metrics and see if we have something in your actual size."

Rei did as he was told, and the major picked up his pad from the lift-desk to hold it over Shido's right band. It only took a moment, but apparently sifting through the stocks of first year uniforms was more intensive, so Rei instead chose to brave a glance over his shoulder at the line behind him.

As expected, almost every eye in the room was trained on his back, though a good number of the cadets looked away quickly as he caught them staring.

Having no reason to enter, Viv had been stopped at the depot door, where she'd assured him she would wait until his NOED upgrade and uniform corrections were finished. As a result, for the last 10 minutes Rei had had little distraction to deter him from feeling the stares while he waited in what had ended up being a long—if quick—line. More than a few first years turned out to need upgrades to their neuro-optics, and for a little while Rei had been able to focus on that, excited to consider what sort of specs the hardware had to have to require so many students to trade in their old ones. He'd tried thinking about all the kinds of tinkering he could do with the coding—assuming he managed to get into an ISCM encrypted device, of course—but by that point the repeated glances and low whispers from the others in line had become too much to ignore. Rei's face had grown hot, but he'd kept his chin up, deliberately trying to meet the gaze of anyone brazen enough to eye him a little too long. It had happened before, when he'd been at away-tournaments with the Grandcrest combat team.

But here, at Galens, among what generally seemed to be nothing but peerless physical specimens of the human condition, Rei got the sense he was going to have to brace himself for a whole lot more such scrutiny.

He shrugged the disgruntled feeling off. He'd grown more than a half-inch in 2 months, and gained a fair bit of weight to boot. He might never catch up to some of the monstrous examples of the boys in the line behind him, but he had no doubt it was only a matter of a year or so before he was tall enough not to attract any more awkward looks.

Couple that with the fact that his hip had barely bothered him on the walk to and from Kanes, and Rei suddenly felt like he could handle all the smirks and sniggers in the world.

"Got something," Major Sattar announced at last, bringing Rei back to the task at hand. The man punched a few numbers into the pad that was now returned to the floating desk, and a few seconds later Rei saw a drone whirring towards them from the back of the cages behind the Quartermaster's counter. Reaching them, it deposited a square box beside the officer, then flew off again.

"There's a locker room in the back you can change into when we're done," the major said, now peering at Rei's face as his NOED flared in his eyes. "Unilateral, huh? Is your module right or left?"

"Right, sir," Rei answered, motioning the relevant side of his head.

"Pull your hardware."

Reaching up, Rei brought the top of his index finger to his temple, feeling for the tiny patch of firmness in his otherwise malleable skin. Finding it, he pressed on the point for 5 full seconds, the standard security length to avoid accidental ejection.

There was the faintest *click* Rei knew only he could hear, and when he pulled his finger away a tiny circle of fused metal, boarding, and wires surgically glued to a layer of synthetic skin came away with it, about a third of an inch in diameter and half that deep. His frame hadn't been live when he'd ejected the device, so nothing more that the military micro-clock set in the corner of his immediate vision vanished.

Still, he felt somewhat vulnerable knowing he *couldn't* pull up the neuro-optic even in the few minutes it would take to upgrade.

"On the counter, here." Sattar tapped on a small cutout in the steel before him, and Rei complied, peeling the NOED off his finger and setting it down in the center of the square. The officer held the ball of metal he'd been holding onto over the device for a few seconds, watching his pad as he did, but as soon as the tablet flashed a notification he handed it to Rei. "All your logged data should be transferred, but check it thoroughly when you can. We'll keep your old module for two weeks in case there are any issues." As he spoke, the cutout retracted with the hardware, returning empty almost at once. "Are you comfortable installing it yourself?"

"Yes, sir," Rei said too quickly, swallowing when the major gave him a look. No need for Galens to know how much he was hoping to play with their software scripting.

In the end, the Quartermaster just grunted.

"Locker room is in the back. Leave your current regulars hanging by the door. Someone will gather them later. Dismissed, cadet."

Grabbing the box that contained his new uniform, Rei stepped smartly out of line, making for the hall that led to the rear of the building. It didn't take him long to find the locker room, nor to pull himself out of his ill-fitting jacket and pants and hang them as indicated. He kept his original cap—for no reason other than nostalgia—but a couple minutes later was standing in front of a pane of smart-glass he'd requested a reflection out of.

Better, he thought to himself, feeling the fit fall around his wrists and ankles more cleanly. Satisfied, he opened the silver sphere by twisting it apart, fawning for a moment over the NOED disk that even an untrained eye could tell was probably a decade newer tech than the old neuro-optic Grandcrest had given him. Peeling it off carefully, he didn't bother with the mirror, finding the empty space of the port in his right temple with well-practiced ease and installing the hardware with another tiny *click*.

Facing his reflection again, he smiled at the pale splotch of color that even before his eyes was transitioning to the exact gradient and texture of his actual skin.

This is wild! *This* is what you guys have had on me this entire time?! If I'd known that, I would have totally asked to borrow your NOED for our combat tournaments!"

Viv scoffed at Rei's exclamation, walking side by side with him as they passed through what she'd just identified as the Institute hospital and the Tactical Studies Department. "And let you browse my feed history when I wasn't paying attention? Not likely."

Rei grinned, but otherwise ignored her, enjoying the crisp clarity of his new frame. It was his first time with a bilateral module, and he had to admit that access to both his optical nerves made the experience distinctly better. The interface responded faster, too, and he'd stopped them more than once to test how quickly he could bring up information on some particular part of the campus as they passed.

They'd been finishing their tour of the grounds for the last little while, taking their time and finding most of the major teaching departments along with a variety of other places of interest. Now, however, with the anticipated hour finally nearing, they were heading for the center of the campus, making for the massive grey-black walls that were visible from nearly half the windows and every foot of open ground in the Institute.

Approaching the Arena felt not unlike creeping towards some sleeping gargantuan, some dragon whose scales were made of darkened steel. It exuded a presence even from a quarter mile away, and with every moment Rei could feel his heart thrumming a little faster. So long. So *long* he'd waited for this. The projection from the third portion of their CAD Exam had been picture-accurate, he suspected, but he didn't for a second think that that experience could compare to living and breathing such a place. There were scores of Arenas across most planets—more than a hundred on Astra-3 alone—but each was unique in its own fashion, designed in homage to the grand sporting and entertainment stadiums of an era of mankind long past. The Institute's was no exception, and while most venues shared the ability to open their great ceilings to the sky for fair weather, Galens' Arena did so by pressing a dozen massive triangular plates up and away from the roof. The result from the inside was astounding—Rei had seen it happen more than once on the feeds when the school had hosted the System tournament a few years back—but never before had he had the chance to take in the display from *outside* the building. A crown atop the slumbering beast, the points of the slats extended skyward, their flat surfaces catching the sunlight and gleaming like clean-cut jewels to tempt passersby into approaching.

Tempt them, and then consume them whole with the frenzy and violence and magnificence promised within.

Clearing the other campus buildings, the pale stone path beneath Rei and Viv's feet turned to white marble fairly abruptly, cut into uneven rectangular designs that complimented the artistic chaos of the Arena's walls. There were only two public entrances to the interior—to the west and east, along the broader lengths of the structure—and it was into the shadow of the former of these that the pair of them let themselves be swallowed. A semicircular cut 20 feet tall, it tapered like a gullet towards a set of wide stairs, at the base of which two staff in uniform were checking identification. Joining a scattered crowd of other arrivals, Rei and Viv were scanned, then waved through, and with electric anticipation Rei eagerly led the way, taking the steps two at a time.

Bursting out into the sun again, he caught his breath.

In an enormous oval amphitheater that could seat some 150,000 people, the stands extended to the north and south of him, then bent around the loop of the Arena's ends only to come together on the opposite side. Far above, the curve of the black ceiling shaded most of the white, carved stone seats, the raised slats making it feel like Rei was looking up from inside the mouth of the dragon at its massive teeth. Dark paths of black granite stairs cut crafted lines through the galleries, and—hovering suspended in the middle of it all—a trio of diamond-shaped apparatuses floated equidistant from each other along the length of the open air. These networked scanners were for the audience's benefit, supplying a close-up of any part of any fight for the NOEDs of viewers not near enough to see the action in detail for themselves.

And there, 10 feet below the bottom edge of the lowest amphitheater walkway, the Arena floor's silver lines gleamed against the black projection plating they were set into.

If Rei had been confident enough in his specs, he might at that moment have vaulted the rail he'd at some point found himself leaning over, like an elated child trying his best to get close to the captive animals in a zoo. He took in the shining base of the combat fields, tracing with his eyes the great length of the Wargames area, then the pair of smaller Team Battle zones, followed by the four Dueling fields. He would have gone looking for a way down regardless, perhaps, if Viv hadn't taken him by the sleeve of his uniform with a sigh, muttering about "fanboys" again as she led him to the right, towards the south end of the Arena stands. He might have protested, but he saw then the large projection that had been cast over the loop in the stands she was pulling him towards, the red griffin on grey, just like the bands they had about their arms.

Against a stage that could hold tens of thousands of spectators, the meager collection of Galens' new cadets seemed almost disappointing. They had gathered from the lowest point in the seating upward, finding places in the very middle section of the south loop as several more uniformed officers directed the incomers, but despite this building wedge of bodies—gold against black interspersed with a vibrant array of colored hair under caps—the showing was sad. As they neared, though, Rei considered that this was likely by design.

It impressed on the gathered students the weight of the curriculum they were about to take, and the eyes of the world they might—just might—one day be taking on.

Reaching the loop, Rei and Viv took the stairs one of the staffers had indicated to them, keeping their eyes on the cadets. Fortunately Catcher looked to have been watching out for them as well, because they found him waving them down near the middle of the third row, sitting between a pair of seats he'd managed to hold. Begging pardon to the dozen or so boys and girls they had to awkwardly slide by, the two of them reached their suitemate as he shifted over to let them sit next to one another.

"Did we miss anything?" Rei asked as he and Viv eased themselves down beside the blond Saber. The Arena seating *looked* like nothing more than cut lines of oversized marbled stairs with white cushions, but as they sat some hidden simulation unit in the stone projected a faint, curved support up to their shoulders, allowing them to lean back as though in a regular chair.

"Not yet," Catcher answered, briefly waving hello to some other cadet he must have known. Gesturing towards the Arena he indicated the concentric rings of the Team Battle and Dueling fields set inside the south loop of the Wargames space. "My bet is a light show will tell us when things are about to start."

Rei and Viv nodded together, watching the other first years trickle in. For a while they sat, chatting about the grounds and the surrounding city—Catcher had spent some time in Castalon before, apparently—Rei taking the time to show off his new NOED, though their suitemate was more intrigued that he had suffered a unilateral frame for as long as he had. Eventually Catcher greeted a third cadet, and Viv's curiosity seemed to get the better of her.

"How do you know so many of these people?" she asked once the girl Catcher had exchanged a few polite words with moved on to find a seat.

"The combat circuits," he answered, looking around as though in search of more familiar face. "My parents made me go to a ISCM-funded preparatory college. The tournaments for those schools are partitioned from the regular institutions, so it's a *much* tighter knit group than your circuit teams, probably, even across systems. A lot of the kids who go to a military prep tend to attempt the CAD-Assignment Exam, and since a portion of the best of those end up at Galens…" He waved at the surrounded rows of cadets to finish his statement, then indicated at a boy climbing the stairs to their right, his flat-topped cap under one arm. "Like that guy. Kadness… Something Kadness.. I can't remember his last name. He's was just shy of a top sixteen finisher at the Wolf System's championships last year. And that—" he pointed to a girl with a black tail of hair and narrow eyes "—is Lena Jiang. She's actually from the Luhmnan too, so we've had a few bouts, none of which I won. Apparently she's a Saber-Type like me, but got assigned a D8-Rank."

"She might have been one of those invited to the summer training, then," Rei said, recalling Jack Benaly had also been given a D8-Rank as he watched the slender girl peer around before settling on a seat higher up. "I wonder what kind of edge they're going to have. two months of instruction before the rest of us is going to seriously make it tough for anyone hoping to qualify for the Sectionals to—"

"Rei."

Viv's muttered interruption cut him off, and he glanced around to find her dipping her head to draw his eyes to her left. Following the line of sight, it only took a moment for Rei to locate who she'd caught sight of. Only a few cadets were still arriving, reaching their seating in the nick of time.

Among them, a towering figure with dark hair and black-red eyes was climbing the steps with frightening grace.

"Catcher." Rei caught Catcher's attention, indicating the cadet—who fortunately hadn't seen them—with his own subtle jerk of his head. "The tall guy with black hair. Any chance you know who that is?"

It took a second for Catcher to find who Rei meant as the boy climbed the stairs to a higher row, but when he did his face grew stony.

"I'm not a hundred percent positive, but I think so. Hair and eyes like that… That might be Logan Grant. Supposedly he competed on the Centauri team at the Intersystems last year."

"The *Intersystems?*" Viv demanded, astonished as she leaned around Rei to gape at Catcher. "Seriously?!"

"Seriously." Catcher nodded gravely, still peering back and up after the boy. "I've heard he's bad news."

"It's him," Rei confirmed with a groan. His new NOED hadn't taken more than a few seconds to smoothly tap into the ISCM's User registry to find the name "Logan Grant". With a wave, Rei shared the profile with the two on either side of him. "And if he was bad news on the preparatory combat teams, he's a hell of a handful now."

Viv and Catcher frowned together, but it was the former that caught what Rei was stressing about.

"D*9*?!" she hissed, half-incredulous. "*And* a Mauler-Type! *Dammit*, Rei! You had to go and pick a fight with a guy who could probably rip our heads off with his bare hands!"

"You picked a fight with Logan Grant?" Catcher demanded before Rei could get a word in edgewise. "Dude…"

"It wasn't my fault!" Rei whispered back. "I apologized! *He* was the one who—!"

"OFFICER ON THE FIELD!"

The shouted announcement cut across the mumbling conversation of the gathered cadets, and the response—at least from part of the group—was instantaneous. Just under half of the first years were on their feet in an instant, Catcher included, snapping up as a collected unit to assume a rigid salute. A handful of others—Rei and Viv among them—caught on to the expectation quickly, leaping up and assuming their best imitation of the others' strict postures. From the rest of the new Users a roll of laughter rose, along with scattered whispers and questions about what they were supposed to be doing.

The two officers who'd been guiding them to their seats were standing at attention at the base of the stairs on either side of their small section, and it was from one of these men that the shout had come. Along the Arena floor below and beyond them, a procession of people in uniform were pacing quickly into view from an entrance the cadets couldn't see. It didn't take this group of some score of men and women—most of them bearing the red-on-white armband of Institute staff—to reach the 30 yards of the Dueling field set front and center, kissing the southern edge of the wider Team Battle ring. Spreading out across the space, the procession turned to face the cadets, a myriad of different colored eyes suddenly sweeping over the new students with sharp scrutiny. It took all of 20 seconds from start to finish, but in that time barely any of the saluting cadets so much as twitched, with the likes of Rei and Viv alone exchanging the occasional anxious glance.

Then the field under the feet of the officers below began to glow.

In a slow rise the projection built up from under the Galens Institute higher-ups, lifting them gracefully from the ground on a foot-thick disk of solid white light.

The red griffin of the school appeared beneath them as the group rose, expanding in unison with their gaining altitude so that the tips of the emblem's wings had barely touched the edges of the circle once it stopped at level with the gallery. When the physical projection was still, a black chair pixilated into being behind each of the officers, allowing them to sit together in practiced fashion.

All of them, that is, except one stiff, broad-shouldered figure with light-brown skin and a grey-black beard that matched the long tail of hair falling out the back of his cap.

"Those of you still sitting, take a look around you." The man's augmented voice rumbled like thunder as he stepped forward to claim a front-and-center position on the disk. "The students currently saluting myself and the officers seated behind me are the boys and girls who have spent the last four years in a ISCM college, or were smart enough to imitate the peers who clearly knew better than them in the moment." His dark eyes, visible even under the brim of his cap, swept the stands. "Despite your laughter, despite what you might think of them, *these* are the cadets who you will be envious of in the coming weeks. *No.* Do not attempt to correct yourselves now." His sharp words sent several individuals who had started to stand back down to their seats quickly. "You are not expected to know these requirements and duties upon arrival at this school. You are not here to *know* things, after all. You are here to *learn* them, indeed far better even than those still at attention do now. Despite what many of you think—despite that most of you here likely believe you have come to Galens for a life of entertaining the masses—you are now a part of the Intersystem Collective Military. You are part of an organization who prides itself on order and rule, an organization who—though much of mankind is happy to perpetually forget—is at war with a constant enemy ever lingering at the edges of our furthest system."

The man paused, letting his words weave their way into the silence a moment before saying anything more.

"Take your seats, cadets."

Rei and Viv did a better job of matching their repose to the others' this time, taking to sitting again almost at the same time as Catcher did beside them. Still, not a sound was made by the first years, every fiber of attention now trained on the single standing officer below.

"My name—" the man continued at last "—is Colonel Rama Guest. I am the commanding officer of the Galens Institute, and therefore in charge of both the broad and minute runnings of this school. While I understand that an illustrious career in the SCTs is the goal of most of you seated before me, the reality is that the majority of you will have a brief showing in the feeds, then spend the rest of your careers as Users on the front lines beyond the Sirius System. My task—and that of the department heads behind me—is to train you for the former, but prepare you for the latter. You, every one of you, are exceptional. You are among the best CAD-assignees this year has brought into the ISCM. You are among the most talented and capable, and the same drive, work-ethic, and will that allowed you entry into this institution will be that which carries you forward through the next three years and into whatever path you find yourself walking as a User. You should take pride in the fact that you are sitting here, but you should also prepare yourselves. There is a reason why enrollment at the Galens Institute is so sought after. There is a reason why nearly a tenth of *all* new assignees apply to this school each year, apply to be in the seat you are currently taking up. Of every one of those requests, one in a 500 make it to the desk of any member of our board of admissions. Of *those* thousands, 128 alone of you are now here."

Without looking away from the stands, the colonel half-turned, casting an arm out to indicate the Arena that extended, empty and vast, behind him and the seated officers.

"Here, in this place, you will be given every opportunity to grow, to thrive. You will be given every chance to better yourselves, to become Users at the head of your generation. With that, however, comes a price. An expectation. This is only the starting line. This is only the place you have earned for yourself thus far. We of the Institute will build you a ladder to the heavens, cadets, but it will be *your* task to climb it, *your* responsibility to seek a higher rung every moment of every day of every year you spend with us. By being here today, you have already proven yourselves the carriers of a rare potential even among the limited numbers of those assigned a CAD. But starting tomorrow, it will be time to prove—additionally—that you have what it takes to bring that potential to fruition."

Rama Guest paused stepped aside, making a smaller gesture towards the gathered officers on the disk with him.

"With that in mind, I would like to introduce you to the person who will be most directly involved in hammering you all into the combatants you have the ability to become. Having recently accepted a post here, she spent two very successful seasons in the SCT circuits before voluntarily joining the front lines, where she has been for the last seven years." An individual stood up from the forward row of seated officers, stepping forward to join the colonel. "Cadets, meet your chief combat instructor: Captain Valera Dent."

Rei felt his legs go cold beneath him.

"Wha... What did he just say?" Catcher wheezed from his right.

All around them, the rapt silence that held through the commanding officer's speech shattered like a hammer taken to ice. Rei knew Catcher, too, would be gaping at the woman who was formally shaking hands with the colonel, while on his left Viv was probably trying to place where she'd heard the name before. He didn't have time to look at either of them, so busy was he watching the exchange below with frozen disbelief.

Then the whispers started to reach them.

"Dent? *Valera* Dent?"

"Wait... The Bishop?"

"The Iron Bishop!"

The Iron Bishop... There it was. There was the name, the confirmation, and Rei's thoughts fell into a tumbling drone of senselessness.

"Wait. Who is she?" The buzz of excitement had finally gotten to Viv, because she bent to look between Rei and Catcher. Their suitemate apparently couldn't make a sound, however, so Rei took it upon himself to drag his mind out of its stunned limbo to answer.

"She's a Knight-Class S-Rank," he answered quietly. "Nowadays, anyway. One of the best to ever fight in the Astra professional circuit. She never earned a championship, but it was only a matter of time, especially since she has one of the highest win-loss ratios of any SCT User *ever*."

"Ever." Catcher managed to echo him numbly.

"She only fought in the circuits for two years. She was Bishop-Class, then, known for being impossible to take down. She was too fast, and even when she took a hit she usually just pushed past it despite her CAD not being designed for defense. People started calling her the Iron Bishop, and it eventually became her field name."

"She would have pushed into the Intersystems given time. For *sure*." Catcher appeared to have finally found his tongue just as the colonel stepped away from Valera Dent below them to take a seat in a chair that materialized for him as he approached the other officers. "But she retired from the fights to volunteer for the front lines. That's where she earned her Knight-Class. And apparently—" the NOED blazed to life in his eyes "—had half her face blown off by the archons."

That information was new to Rei, and he copied Catcher at once, focusing his frame on the captain's features so that a sub-window of an up-close image—curtesy of the Arena—popped into the top corner of his vision. Studying the woman's face, he swore under his breath.

Valera Dent had narrow, handsome proportions and pale skin, with a hawkish nose set between two vibrant brown eyes. Her easy smile was soothing, plain aside from the perfect balance of her complexion that was the eventual blessing of any CAD's genetic correcting. At a glance, the woman's face might have been considered unremarkable.

Unremarkable, that is, except for the thin, clean line of black that started at her right temple, trailing down just outside her eye before cutting vertically across her cheek, over the bridge of her nose, and all the way to her left ear.

A full-frame prosthetic, used only on the most devastating of injuries, ones where augmented tissue regeneration and all the other heights of modern medicine just couldn't keep up with the damage.

"Cadets, welcome." Dent's voice was familiar to him, and Rei flushed a little as he considered just *how many* of the Iron Bishop's interviews he must have seen over the years for that to happen. "As Colonel Guest has stated, I am Captain Valera Dent, formally of the 87th Combat Contingent outside of the Sirius System. I will not feign modesty—particularly after such a clear reaction." She smiled brighter. "I am aware that many of you likely know of me, and I am honored by your enthusiasm. My time in the circuits is long past, but I can't say I'm not pleased to be reminded that I left an impact."

The smile fell away, and her brown eyes were scanning the stands slowly. "I find myself, standing before you, in need of repeating the colonel's words. I am here to train you for success in the Simulated Combat Tournaments, but I am likewise here to prepare you for something altogether different, something altogether more fearsome and brutal than any Wargame you can imagine. As I'm sure many NOEDs have confirmed among you, I am an example of what can happen on the front lines. It is the reason I am no longer there, truth be told. After my… uh… inadvertent makeover—" she gestured to her face humorously, earning a few nervous laughs from the stands "—I was awakened to the fact that my place was no longer battling the enemy directly. I was fortunate, not long after, to be accepted to the position of chief combat instructor here at Galens, and have been anticipating your arrival every moment since." Her expression grew harder, and suddenly the kind, bright woman stood as rigid as the iron that was her namesake. "I do not wish to belittle the value those of you with a future spent in the circuits hold for the military. You will be essential—likely even more than I was on the front lines. *But*... While the SCTs will certainly be the means by which you prove yourself in the coming years, I will not be teaching you the skills necessary to beat your opponents. I will be teaching you to kill them. I will not be instructing you on the best tactics for outlasting an enemy. I will be instructing you how to survive their relentlessness. A foe who is stronger, or faster, or holds out longer in battle... Here, in the safety of the Intersystems, that means nothing more than a loss and a lesson to be learned. Out there, however..." She gestured up at the edged cutout of the sunny sky above them, framed by the Arena's open roof. "Out there, there is no 'loss'. Out there, there is no opportunity to seek the lesson of defeat, much less learn it. Here, at this school, I have a chance to turn you into the best fighters you can possibly be. I can only hope that for many of you, this will result in nothing more than a life of excitement and luxury. For some, however—for most, even—being the best you can be may one day be nothing less than the difference between your life... and your end."

The silence that followed this was so absolute, time itself might have been holding its breath. The dark words weighed heavy, and Rei found himself suddenly considering the path he was walking on with a bit more scrutiny than ever before.

Which was—he imagined—precisely the point.

"With all of that in mind—" Captain Dent's voice cut through the quiet again "—it is important for each and every one of you to realize that some among your number are stronger than the others. I do not say this to discourage anyone, but rather to urge you to watch those cadets in your class who are excelling, who are closer to chasing down that which you all desire. It is from your instructors that you will learn your lessons, but it is from those standing over you that you should seek your drive to improve, to climb higher. Considering this, the other heads and I have put together a demonstration, partially to celebrate your Commencement, and partially to open your eyes to what is expected of you in the coming weeks. Of the 128 first years, sixteen were invited to Galens two months early, to participate in a special training program designed specifically to give them an edge in the coming months."

There were a few cries of surprise—as well as protests—from the cadets, followed by a buzzing of angry conversation, but the captain silenced them all with a raised hand.

"You're disapproval is noted, but it is also not unexpected. You will be *pushed* at this Institute. More than physically. More than mentally. Those with greater ability will—by that nature—earn themselves greater opportunity, while those with less will be pressed to make themselves better, to make themselves stronger, and gain those advantages as their own. The sixteen who partook in the summer program were selected from this year's CAD-assignees with the highest Device Rankings, and were therefore granted the highest opportunity to prove themselves." She dropped her hand, glaring up into the stands as though daring anyone to contradict her. "You will learn that I will not be a 'fair' instructor. I will not be gentle, nor kind, nor giving. My responsibility is not to spare your feelings or address your desires. It is to ensure that you leave these next three years as the best CAD-Users you can be. On that note—" she looked over her shoulder, gesturing towards one of the figures seated behind her "—let me present to you the first example of what it is you should be chasing down."

As the person stood, Rei realized that she was not, in fact, an officer. Indeed, as the girl strode silently forward to stand beside Valera Dent, he saw the grey on the band of her left arm, distinct to the captain's white.

"This is Aria Laurent," Dent announced, indicating the cadet. "She is a first year, like you all. A Phalanx-Type User." The woman paused, and Rei wondered if the hint of the smile he'd seen was an illusion in the line of her prosthetic. "She is also the only C-Ranked assignee among you."

That caught the gathered attention of the audience, and in dramatic fashion. More than one "*What?*!" of surprise called out from the stands, and in the rows before him Rei saw several people exchange astounded glances.

He didn't remotely blame them, staring as he was himself at Aria Laurent.

A C-Ranked first year?! By the end of their first term there should certainly have been a few among their number, but to be *entering* the semester as a *C*-Rank?! It was astounding. Jack Benaly and Lena Jiang's D8s had already been more than impressive, with Logan Grant's D9 being downright staggering, but a C-Rank? There couldn't have been more than a handful of first year cadets in the whole of the ISC at that level. The Galens Institute was a premier institution, but it was still incredible that they'd managed to recruit one of probably a score of new Users with that sort of potential in the entirety of the settled systems.

Willing the focused window of his NOED to shift focus to the girl, Rei took her in initially with energetic curiosity, then with more... acute... interest. She had a slender build—athletic and supple—with long arms and legs that could only do wonders for her reach, especially if her Phalanx-Type was presenting with a spear rather than a sword. Under the brim of her cap Aria Laurent's eyes were a brilliant shade of green that sparkled like the shifting glass shards inside of a kaleidoscope. Her hair was designed as well, a deep, vibrant red that—while obviously not genetically organic—was still not so far gone from the standard spectrum as to be jarring. Her skin was clear, with a number of attractive freckles crowning each cheek, and Rei didn't miss the flush of color despite the girl's rigid, well-rehearsed posture.

She might have been a C-Rank User, but she looked about as pleased to be standing there on display as Rei might have been to be tossed naked into a public fountain.

Something scratched at his thoughts, then, and at first he had trouble placing it. There, at attention in the sun beside a legend of the SCT world, Aria Laurent looked… out of place. He found himself wanting to see the girl in a different sort of light, one where her ability spoke more than her specs. He wondered how *he* would feel standing there being gawked at, with empty accomplishments being touted before having the chance to prove one's worth.

Abruptly, Rei could feel the pressure of Shido's weight on his wrists, and it hit him then.

Some part of him, some deep—possibly masochistic—part of him, wanted to *fight* Aria Laurent. Not to best her. Not to challenge her, or put her to the test.

No. Rei wanted to fight her so that he could witness first-hand what a User like her was capable of, and find out just how far he still had to go.

"Whoa…" Viv mumbled, so quiet Rei wondered if she'd meant to speak aloud. "She is *gorgeous*…"

Catcher, on his other side, seemed to be thinking the same thing, because his yellow eyes were far away even behind the bilateral frame of his neuro-optics. Rei, suddenly feeling embarrassed by his level of scrutiny, snapped his focused window back to Valera Dent, though he couldn't help his natural gaze from flitting to Laurent several times before the captain started to speak again.

"As I mentioned, a demonstration has been prepared in order for you all to start developing an understanding of what is going to be expected of you in the coming months. Of the sixteen who spent the summer training here at Galens, fifteen of them will be splitting into three groups of five for a Team Battle match. You'll have the opportunity to observe them, to study what the strongest currently among you have already spent much time learning, and perhaps approach your courses tomorrow with a bit more fervor and intent."

Dent smiled again, and there was something like a wicked sort of amusement playing across that grin.

"Before that, however, one of *you* will be taking the field against Aria Laurent."

Rei was on his feet like lightning, hand in the air before any other person in the crowd around him could so much as think to beat him.

"HERE!" he yelled, the word echoing a dozen times back in the stunned silence that followed.

CHAPTER 13

adet!" the nearest of the two supervising officers snapped in Rei's direction. "Sit down! The captain will—"

"It's fine, warrant officer." Valera Dent's words were quiet, but still carried over the augmentation provided by the Arena.

The man's words cut off, and his eyes flashed away from Rei as he resumed his silent attention at the base of the stairs.

Dent was looking at Rei with an odd expression. Her NOED had flared across her brown eyes, and when she'd caught sight of him she seemed almost… satisfied.

"I said those of you who sought advantage would earn them. I won't be made a liar." The script in her frame shifted, and she started reading from his profile. "Ward, Reidon, of Grandcrest Preparatory Academy. User-Type: Atypical. Rank—" she paused, but where Rei expected her to look surprised, the woman appeared distinctly pleased "—E3."

"*What*?!"

Immediately the whispers started around Rei as he brought his arm down from where it had still be flung in the air like a signal flag.

"She said E3, right? *E3*?"

"No way. She must have misspoken. Someone look it up."

"What the hell? It's true! This guy's a friggin' E-Ranker!"

All around Rei neuro-optics were blazing into life as the other cadets who had turned to face him pulled up the ISCM database. There were snorts, along with some outright laughter, but he only had eyes for Dent and Aria Laurent. The captain might have been looking smug about something, but even without focusing his frame on her he could see a frown marring the C-Ranker's face.

"You're stealing a little of my thunder, Cadet Ward." The Iron Bishop addressing him by name sent a tingle down Rei's fingers, particularly when Dent graced him with a crooked smile. "Not that I mind. If you want to fight, get down here. The warrant officer will show you the way."

"Yes, ma'am!" Rei shouted back, an electrical excitement rushing through him as he started to make for the stairs.

"Rei, are you sure—?" Catcher hissed as he passed, but his question was cut short when Viv, smirking, put a hand on the Saber's arm and shook her head.

She could do nothing, however, about the others.

"Wait, he's seriously going to fight her?"

"An E3 versus a C-Ranker? Is he suicidal?!"

"He's an *E*! What the hell is he even doing here?!"

It wasn't just the students, either. As he reached the steps and started for the waiting warrant officer, a figure got up from his chair on the floating projection to approach Captain Dent. Rei couldn't hear their conversation, but it was obvious that the exchange was heated, if brief. In the end the man—an older staffer with a shaved head and deep-set eyes—apparently walked away defeated, returning to his chair stiffly where he proceeded to glare at Rei with distinct displeasure.

"Follow me, cadet," the warrant officer said curtly, and Rei fell in at the man's back as he was led along the railing, leaving the mutterings and confusions of the other first years behind.

The way down to the Arena floor, it transpired, was simple enough. A number of small passages Rei hadn't taken note of when he and Viv had first arrived were set here and there into the slant of the stands, leading down into a series of looping underworks. The walls were of some white, polished stone, but sheeted with what was obviously more smart-glass, because images flicked into life in the panels as the warrant officer led Rei south again along the tunnel. Some were announcements, old postings from the summer session that hadn't been updated yet, but most were moving frames of Galens graduates who'd gained fame in the highest levels of the SCTs. Rei assumed this second part, basing the guess on the fact that he recognized several of the names—and the A- or S-Rank Devices—of many of the Users.

Serena von Bor, "the Ivory Shield", slashed at invisible opponents with her curved sword, her Phalanx-Type CAD a rare solid white except for lines of brilliant yellow at the intricate joints. James Wicky, who had fought under his real name, flicked twin, slender blades in complex patterns only a Duelist could master, his Flechet a blur of black and silver in both hands. The famed Dalek O'Rourke was next, Galens' Intersystem Champion, Cerebyx taking the form of two red pistons of solid carbonized steel about his forearms, rams that "the Gatebreaker" had used with his Brawler's speed and power to devastating victories. There were more, too, dozens more, but Rei wasn't given a chance to fawn over the history of the Institute as his escort turned right, leading to a set of grey doors that slid open quickly after the man put his palm on a reader beside the frame. A short ramp extended slightly upward, then the pair of them were out in the sunlight again.

The warrant officer stepped smartly aside, letting Rei proceed, which fortunately required no explanation. The projected platform had been lowered and recalled, and the gathered heads of the Galens Institute were in process of clearing the field, leaving only two figures in the perimeter of the Dueling space. As soon as the rest were beyond the silver line, one of them—the taller of the pair—approached him calmly, and Rei had to remember to breath as Valera Dent came to a stop in front of him, just outside the field markers, the cut of her brown hair falling over one side of her face.

"You've got balls, cadet," she told him with a smirk. From up close, the synthetic skin that formed most her jaw and nose was flawless, marred only by the black line of the full-frame that had probably saved her ability to speak. "You sure you want to do this?"

Beyond her, on the far side of the field, the other figure waited silently, having already stripped out of her regulars until she stood barefooted in nothing but her white shirt and black slacks. Aria Laurent had bound and looped her red hair into a bun at the back of her head, and her green eyes bore into him like jeweled daggers.

Rei swallowed at the intensity of that gaze, but nodded. "Yes, ma'am," he breathed. "It's like you said: I want to know what I'm chasing."

Once more that strange look of satisfaction passed across the captain's face, but she offered no explanation.

"Are you familiar with SCT Dueling rules, or do I need to brief you?"

"Thirty-yard field with a hard perimeter." Rei answered promptly this time. "Phantom calls only. Fight ends when one or both fighters get marked as Fatal Damage Accrued, are otherwise incapacitated, or either yields. Excessive combat avoidances as judged by the arbiter earns a penalty. Two penalties and it's a match loss."

Dent nodded. "Textbook. Good. You can leave your cap and jacket with me, then step into the field whenever you're—"

"May I keep them, ma'am?"

The captain blinked, apparently not used to being interrupted.

"What?" she asked, like she wasn't sure she'd understood the question.

"May I keep them?" Rei asked again, though he did start unbuttoning the front of his uniform. "The cap and jacket?"

The captain continued to stare at him for a moment.

Then she chuckled dryly. Without telling him otherwise, she waved at the silver lining that was the border of the field. "Go."

Throwing her a quick salute, Rei stepped quickly into the perimeter—leaving his own boots on, given no cause to remove them—joining Aria Laurent within the boundary as he finished undoing the front of his jacket.

5 yards from the other side of the Dueling field, the girl was still watching him, the frown from earlier having not fallen from her face. She stood empty-handed, but the even confidence in her bearing was enough to give Rei a thrill.

Whether it was anticipation or terror, he wasn't sure he knew.

Along the north side of the field a man stepped out of the crowd of presenting officers—a major, judging by the insignia on his breast. Glancing at him, Rei realized it was the same officer who'd clearly not been thrilled about his volunteering to take on the new class' prized C-Ranker, likely thinking whatever Rei could bring to bear wasn't worth the demonstration. The shaved sides of his head gleaned in the sun under the edges of his cap, and his deep eyes moved between the two combatants steadily, lingering on Rei a little longer than was comfortable.

Still, when the major spoke, no hint of his annoyance was distinguishable in his voice.

"Combatants, take position."

A body-length to Rei's right, a glowing red circle about 3 feet wide appeared, and he moved to step inside as indicated. Across from him, Laurent hadn't had to move, having knowingly already placed herself exactly within the starting boundary.

"This will be treated as an official Duel," the major stated clearly. "It will therefore be subject to regulation ruling. Once the field is formed, you will be ordered to call, then engage. Premature Device manifestation will result in a penalty. Premature approach, attack, or the like will result in a match loss. Is that understood?"

Rei nodded, watching Laurent do the same. She *still* hadn't looked away from him, and he couldn't get a read on whether she was impressed by his gall, annoyed at his recklessness, or just a bit too comfortable with staring.

Any further consideration of the matter was interrupted as the Dueling field came to life around them.

Projections were typically instantaneous. They were, after all, solidified con-glomerations of light, and therefore could be summoned up at the speed of their atomic parts. For the purposes of CAD-fighting, however, the process was a little more drawn out, largely for the theatrical value of letting the audience watch the battleground piece itself together for them in dramatic fashion.

The floor came into being first, dusty concrete rising up beneath Rei and Laurent's feet as the simulation started to lift them off the ground. By the time old steel crates marked as "Supplies" began to shimmer into being, stacking on top of each other as obstacles, the two of them had been lifted 5 feet of the standard 10. A ceiling formed overhead, rusted tin sheeting that dripped dirty water, holding up several worn-out cranes suspending grimy chains to hang some few yards above them. The walls came last, the same corroded paneling as the roof, and barely a dozen seconds after the projection had begun to form Rei found himself coming to a halt to stand on one end of a warehouse that looked like it had seen better days some years before.

"Field: Abandoned Depot."

The Arena's voice was smooth and mechanical. Rei felt his hands shaking, and hadn't realized how unsteady his breathing had become.

"Cadet Aria Laurent versus Cadet Reidon Ward. Combatants... Call."

"Call," Rei echoed, focusing on Shido's bands. With a glimmer of light the black steel grip with its white-and-blue strike-plating was in his right hand. At the same moment, he brought up his NOED, pleasantly surprised when a notification flared for him immediately.

Field presence detected. CAD-call detected.
Reprioritizing all processing to combat functionalities.

Well that's useful, Rei thought. *One less thing to mess around with.*

Then his eyes fell on Aria Laurent, and his mouth went dry.

He *had* heard Dent list the girl as a Phalanx-Type, but the base awareness of that information did not register a fraction as strictly as witnessing the C-Ranker in all the glory of her Device. In her right hand a spear some 6 feet in length shimmered, a simple head of gold joined to a red shaft by a patterned loop of green vysetrium. On her left arm, an irregular shield of the same colors hung, mostly flat at the top, but tapering to a blunt point along its bottom edge. Plated greaves covered Laurent from the knees down, the pattern of the Device simple and fluid, but imposing nonetheless. The armor shifted and gleamed as the girl brought herself low, lifting her shield to the bridge of her nose and bringing the spear overhead like the striking tail of some mythical beast.

That was when Rei finally found himself. In the moment before the storm, in the instant before the drop of the blade. Abruptly his head and heart calmed, and a steadying breath later he was taking in Aria Laurent not as a wonder of archon technology and human potential, but as an enemy.

This was what he had been waiting for.

"Combatants…" the Arena's voice rang out again. "Fight."

Despite being built for defense, in that moment Laurent proved her Speed spec was nothing to be scoffed at. With a *crunch* of scraping cement as her steel boots tore into the ground as she flashed forward, hurtling at Rei, closing the 20-yard gap between them with terrifying quickness. Rei watched her come, knowing better than to try to match a C-Ranked User for head-on dexterity, doing his best instead to count the time. His neuro-optic proved itself invaluable, displaying a shrinking number of inches between himself and the coming Phalanx, and when he judged the moment right he, too, lanced forward, his empty left hand lifting to his head.

His cap, thrown with as much precision as could be mustered when facing down a charging force of spear and steel, caught Laurent squarely in the face.

The girl gave a sound of surprise, her focus broken. The reactive shielding of her Device was unlikely to have triggered under the minute pressure of the odd attack, meaning she'd probably take the hat in the nose, but Rei hadn't been going for damage. All he'd needed was the moment, the instant of possibility. Laurent had still kept her defenses up, but her charge had faltered, her eyes breaking from his for the span of a heartbeat.

It was all he needed to slam himself bodily against her shield.

Despite her Strength value no doubt being several times his own, the girl's feet had not been braced for an impact. She staggered a step, finding her balance again quickly, but not before Rei took advantage of the opening to power a swing with Shido at her face. She ducked, the strike clearing her hair, and with him too close to bring the spear to bear she instead kicked forward as she straightened again, catching Rei in the chest with an armored boot and sending him clear off his feet. He flew through the air, slamming into a stacked pile of supplies several yards back, the boxes tumbling off one another. His own energy shield had taken most of the impact, but he didn't miss the notifications flashing across his frame.

Posterior torso contusion registered.
Fracturing of anterior ribs registered.
Applying appropriate physiological restrictions.

Pain to compliment that of the original kick flared in Rei's chest, and he felt a sudden difficulty breathing. Pain, though, he could deal with, and so ignoring it all he scrambled to get back on his feet, managing to free himself of the tangle of boxes just in time to leap away, narrowly avoiding a sweeping cut from the spear that would have gutted him. Laurent had closed the distance between them in a blink and was pressing the assault, using her regained reach to strike even as she kept him at bay.

The attacks came in arcing blurs, but what edge the girl's range gave her meant Rei had an instant to react before each descended, his NOED flaring in warning time and time again. He kept dodging—only occasionally completely success-fully—half-stumbling, half-dancing backwards. His frame registering several small wounds across his chest and thighs that fortunately didn't restrain him any further, Rei quickly ran out of room, running up against another pile of supplies. With a shout Laurent lunged, shield held before her like a battering ram. Rei threw himself out of the way, rolling free of the blow that would have crushed him against the metal as the girl collided with the heavy boxes, sending them scattering. Coming up on his feet, he watched the Phalanx working quickly to extricate herself from the mess, and saw his opportunity.

Turning tail, he ran.

The projection blocked out all external sounds, but just the same he could almost *hear* the laughter of his fellow first years as he sprinted away, making for a third pile of supplies very close to the east wall of the Depot. He didn't care. He couldn't. All he could do was fight—was *survive*—and to do that he had to use every chance he could give himself. With all the speed he could pour into his legs he dodged behind the boxes, hearing Laurent thundering up on him from behind.

When her uncle had informed her a few days prior she'd be taking part in a combat demonstration during the Commencement Ceremony, Aria hadn't been much bothered. She wasn't concerned she would lose—not even the fearsome strength of Logan Grant or reach of Kastro Vademe had been able to best her all summer—and she supposed it was probably a good thing that the other first years see what she was capable of. If she could make it clear she wasn't a User to be trifled with, she'd likely have the other students less keen on pestering her for sparring matches in an attempt to prove their own abilities. She'd agreed without much fanfare, and—despite Uncle Ram's concerns otherwise—*had* spent the last half-week preparing diligently for every kind of opponent she thought she might encounter.

For that reason, Aria couldn't decide what was more confusing about the situation she'd found herself in.

For one thing, Valera Dent—the famed "Iron Bishop"—had allowed an *E-Ranked* Cadet to volunteer as her opponent. What such a low-level User was even *doing* at Galens Aria would have to take up with her uncle later, but she'd regardless felt somewhat cheated of the hope at a half-decent match as the short, thin boy had walked onto the Dueling field.

For another, within 5 seconds of the fight starting, Aria had been hit in the face by what she was pretty sure was her opponent's *uniform cap*, then put briefly on the defensive when the Atypical had thrown himself bodily in her direction.

Lastly—and perhaps most confusing of all—Aria was having *fun*.

She hadn't expected it. Not before her opponent had been selected, and certainly not after. What an E-Ranker had been supposed to do against her she wasn't sure, and even going a little easy on the guy she'd anticipated the fight likely ending with her first charge. The boy, though, had proven quick-thinking and thick-skinned, brushing off what had to have been at least a few cracked ribs to roughly dance his way out of her slashes and thrusts by keeping at the very edge of her range, where his Speed and Cognition skills were apparently just enough to survive by paying with only a few scrapes. His open uniform flapping about himself, he hadn't even bothered trying to block with the odd, one-handed punching weapon his Device had manifested as, likely anticipating that the blue-on-white over black plating wouldn't hold up to Aria's Strength. Eventually, though, the boy had found himself drawn up against some of the supply boxes projected as elements in the field, and Aria saw her chance, powering forward with a shout as she shouldered her shield, intending to crush him under a pinning strike. With a martial artist's grace, though, her opponent had once more dodged defeat by a hair, flinging himself sideways and rolling to his feet a couple yards to her left.

Then, unexpectedly, the short cadet had turned on his heel and bolted for another pile of crates, stacked up near the closest field wall.

Oh no you don't! Aria thought with a rush, wrenching herself free of the mess her failed attack had made. She dashed after him, only 20 feet between her and the E-Ranker as he dodged behind the supplies. Careening after him, she came around the same corner only a few seconds after, shield held up in case of a surprise attack. Instead, Aria's NOED picked up the flap of black and the glint of gold facing away from her, and with a shout of victory she lunged, spear leading the way, driving deep.

And catching nothing but empty air.

Despite her D9 Cognition, it took Aria a moment to make sense of the lack of impact, to parse out the blade of her phantom-call sinking into the black fabric of the uniform only to pass through the cloth without resistance. The unexpected lack of resistance carried her forward, pulling her off-balance, and it was in the moment of catching herself that she saw the truth, that she gaped at the trick.

The jacket hung empty from a rusted edge in the wall. Clearly tossed in passing, it still hadn't settled completely, giving it the illusion of motion.

A trap.

Too late Aria made the connection, heard the scraping of sound overhead. Too late she saw the shadow of a body vaulting over the top of the boxes to her left, dropping down towards her with its right fist drawn for a devastating blow. Her back was to her opponent, her shield at her knees. Even with her decent Speed Aria had no way of turning in time to get her defenses up.

Had she had the chance, she would have smiled, then, realizing she was enjoying herself more in that moment than any time during the months of rigid training with the pompous grouping of the other top sixteen rankers.

Instead, Aria focused, drawing on the single mental command she'd managed to master, the only silent order she could yet give Hippolyta.

Third Eye!

Rei leapt with everything he had.

Having pulled around the other side of the piled boxes as soon as he'd freed himself of his jacket and tossed it at a promising bend of rusted metal in the east wall, he put every ounce of his will into the jump, hoping against hope he had timed his ploy right. He launched into the air, dragging himself up and over the steel crates with his left hand, Shido rising high in his right. With a jolt he saw Laurent retracting her spear from the back of his empty uniform, saw the rigidity of her body as she realized she'd been tricked. Her shield was at her thighs, her back to him. For the instant that he started to fall, started to plunge down on his defenseless opponent, Rei wondered if he might pull off a miracle. Shido drove down, aiming for the nape of Laurent's neck. She would fall. She would fall, and Rei would hear the Arena shout his name as the match winner.

And then, in a blink, the red and gold shield stood between him and his one shot at victory.

Shido's strike-plate smashed into the layered steel. With all Rei's weight and strength behind the blow, it brought Laurent to one knee, bearing her down as the force of the impact rammed through her back.

Wait… Her *back*?

Rei himself slammed into the shield an instant later, rolling off the metal to land on his feet and leap away, wanting to avoid a blind slash of the spear. Sure enough, with stunned disbelief he watched Aria pick herself up, standing straight to face him, pulling her left arm and the shield attached to it from over her head, where she'd *just* managed to get it in time to defend herself from the fatal blow.

No… No. That wasn't possible. Even for a C-Ranker. The level of Speed and Cognition required for that kind of quick-thinking…

And then it hit him.

"You have *Third Eye*?!" he half-screamed, half-squealed, not sure if he was more intensely jealous, annoyed, or fascinated at the prospect.

Laurent, for her part, stared at him in surprise. After a second she opened her mouth to speak, then thought better of it.

In the end, she just nodded.

Rei simultaneously wanted to jump for joy and stamp his foot in exasperation.

"That's so *cool*!" he groaned. "I mean it's bull, too, but *so* cool!"

Then he blinked, remembering himself.

"Oh, right. We're fighting."

And so, with no other tricks up his sleeve, he lunged.

Taken aback by the sudden shift, her Ability was likely all that got Laurent's shield up in time to stop Shido catching her in the throat. Steel met steel again with a grinding *clang*, but before Rei could retreat the girl answered his momentum with a shove forward, closing the gap between them in a flash. He slammed into the curved surface of the defense's plating—anything but deliberately this time—then was lifted off his feet with a yell as the C-Ranker bent down suddenly, then up again, rolling him up and over the shield like he weighed nothing more than a rag doll. He fell, slamming onto his back on the cement, his NOED greeting him with more notifications of further contusions, but he shoved himself up to whirl and face Laurent.

Face her, and promptly cough in surprise as the Phalanx's spear impaled him through the gut.

Schlunk!

Immediately Rei's NOAD blazed red, but he hardly needed a notification to tell him that the simulation had registered his spine as having been severed. Losing all feeling in his legs, the limbs collapsed beneath him, bringing him down to an awkward half-kneeling sprawl, his weight still supported by the haft of Laurent's weapon. Pain bloomed in his abdomen, and if Shido's neuroline hadn't negated the response, Rei knew he would have vomited. Still, the CAD couldn't stop him from retching, his abdominal muscles spasming to bring him forward, his free hand taking hold of the spear haft reflexively for balance.

He clung to the weapon, though, when he started to feel it being pulled away.

Tightening his grip about the steel with all the strength he had left, Rei forced himself to look up, forced himself to set aside the pain. He'd had worse. He'd had *much* worse. He met his opponent's green eyes unsteadily, watched her try again to retract her Device with a tug, only to have him hold more tightly to it.

Then, shaking, Rei lifted Shido, drew the CAD back, and struck.

It was no use, of course. Even had she not had the reflexes for it, Laurent's Third Eye protected her, snapping her shield into position without need of conscious thought. Shido met the plated metal with another *clang,* then another, then another. Over and over again Rei punched at the girl's defenses, trying to break through, trying to overcome. Steadily, little by little, his blows came weaker, the strength draining from his arms as the pain in his gut continued to build. Finally he found himself unable to pull Shido back from a punch, the Device scraping down off the shield to hang limply at his side.

Once more he saw Laurent's eyes, and had he been in any sort of right mind to tell, Rei might have thought there was a different sort of look about them than there'd been at the start of their fight.

Instead, however, the world started to go black, and he felt himself falling forward as somewhere a mechanical voice announced "Fatal Damage Accrued. Winner:

Aria Laurent."

As the world dimmed, Rei could have sworn someone caught him, sworn he felt slender, warm hands take him by the shoulders, and a presence kneeling in front of him. In the end, though, he couldn't be sure, and as he slipped away all he could make out were soft words spoken as though from a long, long distance away.

"Thanks for the fight… I had fun."

CHAPTER 14

Processing combat information.

...

   Calculating.

...

Results:

Strength: Lacking

Endurance: Lacking

Speed: Lacking

Cognition: Lacking

Offense: Severely Lacking

Defense: Severely Lacking

Growth: Not Applicable

...

Checking combat data acquisition.

...

Adequate data acquirement met.

Device initiating adjustments to:

Strength. Endurance. Speed. Cognition. Offense. Defense.

...

Adjustment complete.

Strength has been upgraded from Rank F5 to F6.

Endurance has been upgraded from Rank F3 to F4.

Speed has been upgraded from Rank F6 to F7.

Cognition has been upgraded from Rank F5 to F6.

Offense has been upgraded from Rank F4 to F7.

Defense has been upgraded from Rank F4 to F7.

...

Calculating.

…

CAD "Shido" has been upgraded from Rank E3 to E4.

…

Checking combat data acquisition.

…

Adequate data acquirement met.
Prioritizing reasonable evolution parameters.

…

Selected Prioritization:
Defense. Offense.

…

Recategorizing for future parameters.

…

Processing.

…

Evolving.

…

Evolution complete.

U p you get, cadet. Come on now."

Someone was tapping Rei on the cheek, gently but firmly. It took him a moment, but slowly he came to with a groan, rising from a fitful state of unconsciousness riddled with words and numbers he couldn't recall clearly. Trying to open his eyes, he had to squint against the brightness of a strip light set in the ceiling overhead.

"Up you come," a wheezing voice spoke to him again. "Up now."

In a blur, the world came back into focus.

"Wah!" Rei yelped, sitting bolt upright and nearly slamming his forehead into the face of the bespectacled man who'd been bent over him, patting his cheek. "Wha…? What? How…?"

His recollection returned, and he reflexively reached for his stomach with both hands, padding at his shirt and abdomen. Logically he knew he would find nothing amiss, but all modern science and CAD technology had never quite been able to separate the mind from its survival instincts.

"Calm down, Ward. You're fine. You just took a good bit more sensory input than you should have, after Cadet Laurent ran you through."

Finally registering that he was, indeed, whole and well, Rei's pulse settled a little, and lifted his face to look around.

He was, he realized, back in the underworks of the Arena, now seated upright on some kind of gurney suspended off the ground with lift technology. At his left the man who'd been tending to him was watching him expectantly over a pair of wide-rimmed glasses, a rare sight indeed when corrective surgery could usually accommodate most any vision issue. He was older, likely in mid to late 60s, with thinning white hair the same color as his heavy beard, and the insignia on his black-and-gold uniform marked him as a lieutenant colonel of the ISCM.

"S-Sir!" Rei started, trying to throw his legs off the side of the gurney and salute at the same time, resulting in an awkward mess of motion. "I'm sorry! I didn't know you were—"

"Calm *down*, cadet," the officer repeated with a chuckle, putting a hand out to stop Rei's attempt of sliding off the floating plasteel platform as he finally managed sit himself at its edge. "You've just been through what I'm told is likely your first Fatal Damage Accrual, and a prolonged one at that. I will excuse some lack of decorum for the time being."

Rei swallowed, then nodded, settling back after a moment to sit straighter before the man.

"Better. Now... Hold still, if you please."

The officer's NOED came to light in his eyes, and he looked Rei up and down as a vertical line descended over his retinal, obviously scanning for abnormalities.

"My name is Lieutenant Colonel Willem Mayd," he spoke as he worked, his voice weak and breathy, his gaze moving first along Rei's torso and head, then over to each of his arms and legs in turn. "I'm the chief medical officer here at the Galens Institute. It had been my intention to summon you to the school hospital sometime in the coming week, but Captain Dent was kind enough to offer me this opportunity to expedite our meeting." Apparently satisfied with whatever information the examination had provided him with, Mayd gave a sound of approval and closed his frame. "I assume you will understand I am not *just* referring to your recent skewering when I ask you how you are feeling?"

"Ah. Yes, sir. I-I mean no, sir." Rei flushed, cleared his throat, and tried again. "I do understand, sir. I've had some mild symptoms since my CAD-assignment, but nothing severe. The pain actually seems to have started improving this last week."

At this the lieutenant colonel exhaled in what could only have been quiet relief. "That is excellent news. I admit that when your condition was brought to my attention I did not know what to expect of your Device's genetic correction. But if your active symptoms are improving, that's good. Very good…" His gaze dropped to take in Rei's arms again, this time eyeing the hint of the scars on his fingers and those peeking out from under his cuffs beneath Shido's steel. "Any other changes? Anything you can tell me? You'll understand that I'll be keeping a careful eye on you until we have a better sense of how your genome adjustments progress."

"Yes, sir," Rei said again. "I've grown a little more than half an inch in ten weeks. Also gained around seven pounds of weight."

"More than that in muscle, yes. Your body fat percentage has reduced since your physical examination, and it was already respectable. To be expected, given your history with the combat team." A roar of sound interrupted Mayd, and the old man glanced up at the ceiling with a flash of consternation. All of a sudden Rei was aware he could make out the distinct clashing of steel on steel, and what sounded like the Arena's automated voice once again.

The Team Battle, he recalled suddenly.

"I need to be getting back to the Commencement," the lieutenant colonel said. "You stay here. Recovering from neural interruption should only take a short while, but you pushed your luck back there."

"S-sir!" Rei started quickly as the officer began to step away. "Can I—I'd like to see the match, if I—?"

"No," Willem Mayd cut him off kindly, but firmly, offering him a small smile. "You've been out of it for a good quarter-hour, so I imagine they're about to wrap up soon anyway. Consider it disciplinary action for pushing your body further than you should have." He paused, his gaze shifting past Rei. "And besides… I do believe you will be shortly otherwise preoccupied."

Then he was leaving, stepping smartly down the corridor with a pace that belied his wheezing, and Rei was turning to see what it was that had drawn the man's attention over his shoulder.

He nearly jumped off the gurney when he found a tall woman with short-cut hair falling across one side of her head standing not 4 feet from him, watching him with piercing brown eyes.

"Captain!" he wheezed. "I didn't hear you approach."

In answer, Valera Dent chuckled. Slung over one arm was the jacket Rei had left on the Dueling field, his cap tucked under the other. Offering them both over for him to take, the woman looked him up and down before speaking.

"That was a hell of a fight, cadet. I think you gave some of your classmates the surprise of their lives."

Rei grimaced, accepting the articles and pulling the cap back over his white hair before sliding an arm into a jacket sleeve. "Thank you, ma'am, but I doubt it. I can't imagine I lasted more than a minute out there, not to mention the end hardly left me looking good."

"I wouldn't say that. If anything that finish was rather spectacular. Though next time I'd recommend trying to punch something *other* than her shield."

She grinned slyly, and after a moment's hesitation Rei managed a strained smile back. "I didn't have a chance against her defenses, in the end. It's not that I had high hopes of winning, but..." He sighed. "Maybe if I could have at least gotten a *hit* in?"

"Ward, you took on a User almost two full tiers higher than you—one of the most promising cadets this institution has seen in decades, by the way—and made her work for the win." The captain's eyes bore into him, clearly intolerant of his self-doubt. "That's not even mentioning the fact you forced Laurent's hand. I guarantee you she would have preferred to keep Third Eye quiet for as long as possible, but you gave her no choice with that last trick of yours. Had she not had the ace up her sleeve, I put the odds in your favor that you would have had that bout."

Hearing Valera Dent—the Iron Bishop herself—praise him after speaking his name was such a bizarre experience that Rei could only blink at the woman for a time. Fortunately his mind caught up to the shock fast, and he could almost *see* Viv's nod of approval as he decided then was not the moment to squeal in delight.

Instead, he snatched at the opportunity Dent had offered him.

"I was right, then?" he asked, having to fight not to sound too eager. "She *does* have Third Eye?"

"Fairly sure Laurent affirmed that for you herself, but yes. She does. Hippolyta—her Device—developed the Ability sometime in her first month here, and she's been working on the mental command for it consistently since."

Rei mouthed at the air in disbelief.

Six weeks... Aria Laurent had gained her first Ability within *six weeks* of being assigned her CAD. That wasn't unheard of, but it was incredible, nonetheless. What's more, Third Eye was about as potent as they came, and rare to boot. The Ability tapped into the minute information frequencies of opponents' Devices, allowing a User's CAD to bypass cognitive procedures and react separately from the mind's intake, processing, and response pathways. It "read" any incoming attack—similar to the fashion the NOEDs could warn of the same—but required no visual, auditory, or other cues to act. It was typically used by higher-level SCT combatants lucky enough to possess it to allow one arm to move freely while the other engaged separately, often letting the most-talented Users take on two or three opponents at once so long as their neuroline could manage the load—which, to be fair, was substantial. In Aria Laurent's case, she had used it to let her Device—Hippolyta, apparently—handle blocking Rei's punch at the back of her neck, in her blind spot, giving her a chance to regain control of the fight.

In retrospect, it might have been an unfair matchup from the start, but the C-Ranker's quick thinking was still mesmerizing.

"Speaking of Devices, cadet… I'd like you to confirm something for me."

As Rei had been pondering, the captain had stepped to the other side of the corridor and taken to crossing her arms and leaning up against the smart-glass where a recording of Helman Werkers, the "Stone Giant", was swinging around a massive two-headed axe like it weighed little more than a broomstick.

"I'd heard an interesting rumor regarding your CAD specifications."

The suggestion sent a tingle up Rei's spine, but he didn't respond, watching Dent carefully. When nothing was said between them for almost 10 seconds, the captain's eyes narrowed.

"Not answering an officer is punishable by time in the school brig, cadet."

Rei swallowed. "Apologies, ma'am. I just didn't hear a question in that statement."

Dent glared at him for a moment.

Then, to his surprise, she gave a dry laugh and relaxed. "Fair enough… Word around the staffroom is you have a particularly potent specification among your numbers. I'd like to see it."

Rei frowned. "Are my live stats not accessible to Institute staff? I would have assumed they would be."

"To some," the captain offered him a half-shrug. "Myself included. But I think there's much to be said to witnessing something like that with your own two eyes, don't you?"

Rei nodded slowly, but hesitated. He wasn't sure why he was apprehensive—

the woman had just affirmed that she could pull his specification up anytime she wanted—but sharing them directly still felt... poignant. He was reminded, not for the first time, of Major Connelly's words at the end of the exam.

Be careful.

In that moment, however, there was nothing to be lost. Pulling up his NOED, Rei made a Specifications Request, and an instant later the list of stats was scripting across his frame. He granted viewing privileges and lifted a hand, about to send it to the captain, when he froze.

"What the...?" he muttered, confused as he read.

Specifications Request acknowledged.

...

Combat Assistance Device: Shido. User identification... Accepted.

Type: A-TYPE

Rank: E4

...

User Attributes:

- Strength: F5

- Endurance: F4

- Speed: F7

- Cognition: F6

...

CAD Specifications:

- Offense: F7

- Defense: F7

- Growth: S

Were these... Were these *his* numbers? It wasn't possible. It seemed so unlikely, in fact, that Rei went to the top of the list to read the identification information, double checking. Confirming that he was looking at the right Device's specs, he read over the list again, then again, then finally a third time, not understanding any better each time.

E4? *4*? How was that possible? In ten weeks of training Rei had managed to jump five ranks total, breaking out of the Fs all the way to E3. But now, suddenly, Shido was reading as an E*4* not four days after his last jump?

And what in the MIND's name was up with his specs?! Everything was up at *least* a rank from when he'd checked on the tram that morning—even his stubbornly lagging Endurance—and his Offense and Defense values had somehow made an *insane* 3-point leap each from F4 to F7! They were matched with his Speed, now! What the hell was going on?

No matter how long he stared, however, Rei could make no sense of it. He had quite forgotten Valera Dent was standing in front of him, right up until she spoke in light, almost-amused tone.

"What's the holdup, cadet?"

Rei—even then unable to look away from the list—started and tried to speak once, then again. Finally, on the third attempt, he managed to form a few distinct words.

"My... My specs... I think somethings wrong with the Request I just made..."

"Oh? Let me see."

After another blank moment, Rei finally gathered the wherewithal to send the numbers across the corridor, seeing them pop into being on the captain's eyes.

"Oh-ho... Well that's interesting." Dent scanned the list a couple times, then pulled up another window. After a few moments she shook her head. "Nope. No problem that I can detect. These are the same numbers I have access to in the directory. The ISCM has you officially registered as an E4 User."

"B-but how?" Rei hissed, not believing his ears. "You announced it yourself! At the start of the match! I was an E3 before the Duel, so how—?"

He stopped himself, his words catching in his throat. Across from him, Dent had something of a knowing smile pulling at the synthetic skin of her face.

"The Duel..." Rei repeated slowly. "Could that...? No. No way. I've had dozens of fights, and even when I first started my specs didn't jump *this* fast."

"Sure," Dent shrugged again, pulling up a hand to study her fingernails as though what he was saying was hardly of any interest to her. "Of course I'm certain all those *dozens* of fights were against a fellow CAD-User, and obviously one several times stronger then you."

Rei stared at her in silence. Despite the sarcasm, it struck him that the captain was onto something. *Definitely* onto something. Hadn't he just been thinking that morning about how the military's basic simulations had run dry on him? About how he'd hoped to start seeing faster improvement again once with proper combat training and instruction? Of course he had.

But still...

S-Rank. The words—the realization—rang across his thoughts.

"I told you that those who seek advantage will find them."

Valera Dent was looking at him again—intensely, this time—like she could tell he had understood something.

"I told you that I would make you all chase the strongest among you, that I would make you seek out the opportunities those top rankers are already receiving. Every one of the cadets seated in those stands right now is special, Ward. Every one of them is talented. Able. But you…" Her arms still crossed, she stepped closer again, leaning down to peer into one of his eyes, then the other, as though trying to discern what might be hiding behind their grey hue. "*You* are something else, aren't you? Something entirely different. Do you know there's never—*never*—been an assigned CAD with an S-Rank in any area, and certainly not Growth? There *have* been a handful of As over the course of history—pretty carefully guarded secrets even you won't find out about digging around in the feeds—but never an *S*. And then, out of nowhere—" she brought her synthetic lips together to make a *popping* sound "—*you* show up. Any idea what we're supposed to make of that, cadet?"

Rei's whole body had gone stiff. The Iron Bishop—one of the most acclaimed Users in the history of the Astra System—was staring him in the face, asking him what she was supposed to think of him.

"Fail to answer me again, Ward, and I *will* have you brigged."

Rei started, realizing he'd been sitting tense and silent, eyes wide as he listened.

"N-no, ma'am," he spluttered. Then he gathered himself, a memory of a white, featureless face flashing across his thoughts. "I'm sorry. I've got nothing for you. I have no more idea than anyone else how things turned out like this." He brought up one hand, letting Shido's blue on black-and-white glimmer between their two faces. "I've wanted this. For as long as I can remember. Not *this* specifically—if you think you're confused by my specs, consider how *I* feel—but a CAD. A Device. I've wanted it more than anything. I think that might have been a part of all this, in the end."

It pained him not to tell her of how sure of that fact he was.

Valera watched him a moment more, as though trying to read a lie in his words.

Then, apparently satisfied, she stood straight again. "Out of curiosity… Have you checked your call, yet?"

Rei frowned, not understanding.

"Your Device," the woman clarified. "Have you checked its manifestation since getting these spec upgrades?"

"Oh. N-no. The lieutenant colonel was here when I came to, and then you were—"

"Do it."

Rei blinked. "Ma'am?"

"Do it," Valera Dent repeated, stepping back further, like someone opening the cage as she released some wild animal. "I'm curious. Call your CAD."

Still confused, Rei paused, then brought both arms up.

"Call."

Even in the moment before the manifestation was complete, he knew something was different. At his word, not only did Shido's right band shift out of being, but so did the left. Rei's breath caught in his chest, seeing the blurred twist of steel and glowing vysetrium, but before he could voice his confusion the call was done.

And Rei could only mouth at the air in astonishment.

Instead of a simple steel grip and flat strike-point, around his right hand the Device had manifested as a sort of plated glove, black steel forming multiple distinct joints about each of his fingers, linking atop a skin-tight underlay of white, flexible fabric. It extended to just above his wrist, overlapping itself like scales, but the most significant change had happened to the white metal over his knuckles, where three lines of ice-blue vysetrium had originally dissected the steel into even sections. The splits were still present, but had shifted slightly, coming to rest atop the knuckles of his index and pinky finger, and between those of his middle and ring. From the vysetrium, three wide, subtly curved claws of carbonized black steel now extended, tapering to wicked points, the outside two some 4 inches long while the middle was half again that length. Even at a glance Rei could tell the weapons were horrifically sharp, and would probably punch through most armor with relative ease once his Strength spec was up to the task.

Shido, though, was hardly done with the surprises.

Around Rei's entire left forearm and hand, from just below his elbow to his fingertips, the same white underlay encased his skin. Black studs capped his knuckles, but the larger change came in the form of the four dark plates, lapping over one another starting at the rear of his hand, then moving upward to cover the back half of the forelimb. Lifting the arm in wonder, Rei made a fist, then released it, flexing and twisting his wrist this way and that way. Despite a lack of vysetrium jointing, he still had free movement, and he could already imagine the value of the heavy steel when it came to defending himself in the future.

"Shit…" he breathed, unable to take his eyes off Shido, going between the new defensive plating and the curved claws.

Then he remembered who has standing not feet from him, and he flushed.

"Apologies!" he said quickly, straightening as best he could, which was made awkward by the fact that he was still seated on the gurney. He hadn't exactly dived deep into military etiquette over the summer —being assigned a CAD had left him with enough reading and research to do in what little spare time he hadn't spent training—but he was fairly sure profanity in the presence of an officer *wasn't* on the list of allowances.

Valera Dent, though, waved his regret away with a face.

"I just spent seven years on the front line of a war, cadet. Your cursing isn't about to light my fuse." She paused, taking in the CAD Rei still hadn't recalled. "Besides, I think I can forgive you a little excitement. Congratulations on your first evolution."

Evolution.

There it was. The greatest offering Devices could grant their Users. Change. Correction. Adaptation. As a wielder got stronger, so did their CAD, adjusting themselves to best fit the User's combat style and needs. Rei had spent 10 weeks fighting with nothing but a glorified punching glove, and his lack of defense and attack had shown through against Aria Laurent. He'd been able to do nothing against her spear's sweeping strikes but dip and dodge, and throwing his own *body* against her defenses had proven better results than actually swinging Shido at her shield.

Now, though… Now things would never be so one-sided again.

"As far as I know, you and Laurent are the only students in your class to have achieved an evolution. You're a ways back from the starting line, to be fair—particularly compared to her—but that's no reason not to celebrate it." Dent was eyeing the three claws protruding from Rei's right knuckles. "You won't be able to hide it, either. Everyone's seen what your CAD looked like as of twenty minutes ago, so prepare yourself for the attention, both good and bad." She chewed on her words before continuing. "Honestly, you should probably work on getting used to it… Do you know what the name of your CAD means, Ward?"

A little of Rei's enthusiasm faded away. He *was* aware of Shido's meaning, as it happened. It had been a curiosity—or a suspicion, rather—from the moment he'd heard the Device's name announced after his assignment. It was Japanese—one of the old languages they still used on Earth, in the regions the culture still thrived—which upon discovering had weighed on Rei's mind for some days, and not in a pleasant way. His own name, after all, was variation of another word in the same tongue, and an ironic one at that.

His parents, in giving him that name, had ended up making a mockery of the ancient god of lightning he had obviously been meant to take after.

"'Seed'," Rei finally answered roughly. "'Shido' means 'seed'."

Before him, the captain nodded. "It does. And don't look so damn disappointed. Instead, consider it. Consider its meaning. Whoever gave you that CAD—or *what-ever*, rather—" Dent clarified pointedly, eyeing Rei "—did so with a purpose in mind. You seemed impressed to learn that Aria Laurent had developed an Ability in six weeks, and you should be. But since assignment, Laurent has also only upgraded two ranks, from D8 to C0. *You*, meanwhile, have now seen an improvement of *six* ranks without the resources she had access to, and have just gone through your first evolution. Your Growth spec is not for show, Ward. You need to remember that moving forward. I think 'Seed' is going to prove itself an apt name for your Device, if you give it half the chance."

Rei took in her words, forcing himself to swallow them. She was, right of course. In 10 weeks he *had* seen magnitudes of improvement. From almost exclusively F0, all of his specs were all *at least* pushing on halfway to the E-Rank, with his Speed, Offense, and Defense now only three points away. If he continued to see that level of development, or even anything marginally of the like…

All of a sudden the image of a sprouting tree etched itself across Rei's thoughts, its branches spreading and rising, its leaves reaching for the heavens and beyond…

"Sounds like they just finished up."

The Iron Bishop was looking to the ceiling, from which Rei, too, could hear the roar of his classmates as the Team Battle match they'd been treated to sounded to have come to a spectacular end, the Arena voice announcing "Blue Team" as the victors. There was much shouting and fanfare, and Rei's disappointment at missing out on the excitement would have been extreme were it not for the fact that he was still holding Shido's new evolution before him, the improvements unbelievable every time he took them in.

"They'll be wanting me back up there for the ceremony wrapping, so here's this." Dent's NOED flared up again, and a moment later a window opened in Rei's own frame. A picture of his face, it was set beside his updated public User info, along with a new designation.

"Class… 1-A?" he asked.

The captain nodded. "Your class-block assignment. They were allocated after your fight, when you were still out of it. Five classes, each with around twenty-five students, randomly allotted. That being said, I happen to have it on good authority that your friend Arada is in your section, so be grateful for that."

Rei *was* grateful, and it must have shown in his expression, because the captain snorted.

"To have your enthusiasm, kid…" she muttered, turning and starting to walk away. "Stay down here until they call for a dismissal upstairs. You might be feeling good with those new specs, but neural interruption of the entire spine is no joke."

"C-Captain!"

Rei cursed himself, but there was no helping it. As the woman had started to leave, the 11-year-old who had once gotten in trouble for breaking into the Matron's office took over.

Valera Dent stopped, looked around at him curiously.

"I…uh…" Rei struggled to get the admission out. "I saw you retirement bout. The exhibition match at the '61 Intersystems…"

Dent didn't reply, but watched like she expected him to continue. When the silence began to stretch, she finally opened her mouth.

"And?"

Rei swallowed nervously. "I just… You finished 54 and 6, right? I… I want that. *That's* what I'm chasing. That's why I'm looking for those advantages you spoke of. I know I'm not that strong now, but—"

"Did you see the matches I lost?"

The captain's interruption took Rei so aback, it was a moment before he found his words again.

"N-no," he finally managed. "I didn't really have easy access to the feeds, as a kid."

Dent nodded, but didn't seem to be paying attention to him anymore. Her eyes were flicking under her live frame, which had popped up again as soon as he'd started answering her. A few seconds of commands, then the woman waved a hand in his direction, and several recordings layered over themselves in his own vision one after the other.

"Watch them," the captain said, turning and starting to walk away again. As she left, however, she kept talking over her shoulder. "Don't aspire to be like *me*, Ward. Aspire the be like the ones who *beat* me. And I'm serious about taking it easy. You don't want to be jello for your parameter testing tomorrow."

Rei—who had already started playing one of the videos on mute, watching intently—opened his mouth to thank the officer. Before he could, though, he registered what she'd said.

"Wait... Testing? What testing?!"

CHAPTER 15

By the time Rei made out Colonel Guest wrapping a brief closing welcome to the first years and found his way once more into the stands, most of the cadets had already left the Arena. Hurrying after a trailing few, he reached the east stairs they'd originally entered by, descending back down to the white marble pathways to step into the sun again. He'd just started looking around, wondering if Viv and Catcher were heading back towards Kanes, when Viv's familiar voice called out to him.

"There he is. Rei! Over here!"

They were waiting from him not far from the mouth of the Arena, standing together and looking like they'd been searching the exiting trails of students for him.

Jogging over, he was all smiles as he reached them. "I have to show you guys something!" He didn't care that he could hear the glee in his own voice. "You seriously won't believe this. After the fight, my CAD—"

"Shh!" Viv shushed him quickly, glancing pointedly around. More than a few other first years had paused in their passings and conversations to ogle Rei when they noticed he was back among their number. Jerking her head to the north, in the general direction of the dorm, Viv motion that they should start walking. "We'll take a long way. Less eyes."

Rei opened his mouth to argue, but realized she was probably right. Catcher, meanwhile, was watching him with an oddly stressed expression, like he was biting back something he, too, was dying to say. Still, the pair of them fell in behind Viv as she led the way, first around the northern bend of the Arena, then east, towards the Institute's perimeter wall.

The moment they crossed into the moderately secluded garden courtyard in the center of the Combat Theory Department's three entwined building, it was Catcher who broke first, whirling on Rei and grabbing him by the collar of his uniform. At first Rei feared their suitemate was going to scream at him for being stupid or suicidal, but then he caught the shine in the boy's yellow eyes.

"That. Was. *Awesome!*" Catcher exclaimed in something between a shout and a groan. "Did you plan all that beforehand, or was it on the fly? A C-Ranker. A friggin' *C*-Ranker, and you had her twisting in circles and bending backwards to pin you down. Man!" He shook his head in what appeared to be genuine awe. "When you first shot up out of your seat, I thought you were insane. An E3 going up against a *C*? But then the hat, and the *jacket*." He laughed out loud, letting go to grab his own cap and uniform with a hand each as he remembered. "It was great! That story's gonna get told for years, I'll bet you anything!"

"I take it you knew Rei was an E before Dent announced it, then?" Viv asked evenly, giving Catcher a firm look.

"Ah." Catcher froze, still holding onto his brim and collar. After a moment he met her eyes, then Rei's, then back again.

And then he seemed to deflate.

"I did," he admitted, sounding regretful. "Sorry." He looked at Rei with a strained, apologetic smile. "It was pretty obvious you were dodging talking about your rank back at the dorm, so after you guys left I pulled your ISCM profile. Not gonna lie, I was a little shocked, but…" He shrugged. "If you're here, there's a reason, right?"

Rei and Viv exchanged a look of surprise.

"I… I guess…?" Rei agreed hesitantly. "Gotta say, that's not the reaction I expected to get from the first student who found me out…"

Catcher gave a grunt of understanding. "And probably won't be what you get from most. But the reality is that CAD-Rank is only a measure of a User's physiological potential. My mother was pretty clear about drilling that into my head, after I told her I wanted to be an SCT combatant. Her opponent for her System Championship title was a Pawn-Class S-Rank, and she was an A7 at the time. She said it was hands-down the hardest fight of her life, but she won." He grinned at Rei. "She told me that if you *really* want to get a feel for an opponent's threat level, you gotta watch them have it out with someone stronger than them. So… Seeing you almost knock out our resident C-Ranker was pretty badass, in that regard."

Rei grinned back. He really *could* like this overly-enthusiastic classmate, he decided.

Then a thought struck him.

"Maybe that's why they're putting us through additional testing?" he mumbled, considering it. It seemed feasible enough. After all, if CAD-Ranking *was* the only determinate of greater ability, there would be no point to the SCTs.

"Additional testing? What are you talking about?"

Viv was watching him with a grimace, and Rei realized he'd spoke aloud.

"They're putting us through 'parameter testing' tomorrow," he explained. "Mind you, I have no idea what that entails."

"Parameter testing?" she repeated incredulously. "Didn't we go through a lot of that in the Assignment Exam?"

"That was all just physical assessment." Catcher was the one to answer her. "Not that much different from our Device specs, if you consider it." He looked to Rei. "I've heard there's some kind of regular testing done over the course of our years here. Supposedly it's to help track our progress in a more functional way than our specs, but more standardized then our combat results."

"Any idea what we're expected to do?"

Catcher shook his head. "Not at all. My mother has some old friends from the circuits who graduated from Galens years ago, but they were pretty tight lipped when I asked them about it."

"Probably didn't feel right giving you an advantage, if they're standardized…" Rei considered, watching a bee—one of hundreds of animal species essential to the terramorphing that had allowed for the expansion of humanity into the stars—buzz about an intricate hedge of rose bushes in the center of the courtyard.

"Well that's bull," Viv huffed, putting her hands on her hips and looking distinctly peeved. "I'm sure the majority of us will be fine, but Rei—" her blue eyes were fire when she looked at him "—assuming they allow CAD-usage for these tests, you're gonna be at a hell of a disadvantage. You know I love you dearly, but your Device is next to useless right now, and if the expected starting line is the typical D4 average of Galens first years…"

She let the implication hang.

Rei, though, only grinned. He didn't argue that his CAD-Rank was still going to have him miles behind the others, but as far as Shido being next to useless…

"About that… Remember that I wanted to show you something?" He looked around briefly. Then—sure that there was no one in the immediate vicinity of their little huddle—he brought both hands up. "Call."

Shido shimmered, and an instant later took the form the paired gloves, the right boasting its new claws from the white steel of his knuckles, the left gleaming as the black defensive plating along his forearms caught the sun above. For practical purposes the entirety of the Institute grounds was approved territory for manifestation, though actual combat was to be kept to the training centers.

So long as Rei didn't punch anyone with the Device, none would blink at a group of first years ogling each other's CADs.

"Whoa. *Whoa.*"

Catcher was the first to react, largely because Viv looked to have been struck utterly speechless. The boy bent low, hands reaching up and fingers twitching in obvious desire, but he was smart enough to pause and glance at Rei. "Can I touch them?"

"Go for it," Rei laughed, making twin fists and holding the black-and-white device out, the blue detailing of the vysetrium brilliant even in the daylight. "Make me feel better. Tell me I'm not dreaming."

Catcher needed no other approval, taking hold of Rei's right hand and bringing it up to study the three 4- and 6-inch claws from a *much* closer vantage point than might have been advisable.

Viv, meanwhile, had found her voice.

"Rei… Shido evolved?"

Rei nodding, turning his hand over at Catcher's request so he could peer at the intricate joints of the black finger plating. "After the match. I don't remember clearly, but I'm pretty sure the protocol happened while I was still passed out. I woke up and… well…" He nodded towards his left hand in indication.

Viv gaped at the Device a moment more. Then, with the hint of a frown, her NOED blazed, and a few seconds later a message appeared in Rei's frame.

Spec changes?

He answered quickly, electing to type with his eyes as he let Catcher move enthusiastically from the claws to the defensive plating along his opposite forearm.

Yeah. Big ones. I'll show you later.

It was a testament to their friendship that Viv accepted this with nothing but a short nod, as was the fact that she'd known better than to ask the question out loud. Rei hoped Catcher would stick around, but for the time being trying to explain his rapid stat improvement and S-Ranked Growth spec was too much of a risk. Word would probably leak out eventually, of course. Specification details weren't public information, so his classmates wouldn't just be able to pull up his stats—and vice versa—but if even only *some* of the staff at Galens could access his numbers… well…

But… That didn't mean there wasn't some value in delaying the inevitable. A single intense match with Aria Laurent had given him enough of a rank boost to evolve Shido. If he could repeat that a few more times, his specs would hopefully all be in or nearing the E range, his CAD-Rank rising with them. If he could get himself to the D before news got out of his Growth stat…

With that hope in mind, Rei looked between Viv and Catcher.

"Can you guys keep this quiet for now?" he asked. "What with the parameter testing I know I probably won't make it past tomorrow before everyone finds out Shido has evolved, but after that fight… Captain Dent wanted me to be careful of the kind of attention I might bring down on myself."

Viv tensed at the request, while Catcher—who had been trying to manipulate the black plates of Rei's left arm by hand while muttering to himself—froze, then slowly turned to him with wide eyes.

"Captain Dent?" he asked breathlessly. "*Valera* Dent? You spoke to her? Directly?"

Rei nodded. "Trust me, I was shocked enough for all three of us when it happened. She's the one who told me to check my manifestation." He waved his free hand, the claws flashing. "She's also the one who told me about our parameter testing."

"That explains where she got off to…" Viv mumbled, exchanging a look with Catcher, who finally let Rei's arm drop. "We were wondering where she went, after the old man with glasses had you taken off the field on a gurney."

"Careful. That old man is a lieutenant colonel."

Viv blinked at him in surprise.

"Yeah," Rei affirmed with a laugh. "Lieutenant Colonel Willem Mayd. The chief medical officer for the school."

"Look at you, Mr. Popular," Catcher chuckled, giving Rei an approving nod. "Not strange though, I suppose. You had to have surprised some of the higher-ups as much as you did the other first years."

Rei felt some color come to his cheeks, and he had a hard time not grinning. "Recall," he said, shifting Shido back into its bands before pressing Catcher. "I surprised the cadets?"

Viv snorted, giving him an "are you serious?" look, but Catcher appeared thrilled.

"Oh you have *no* idea. I mean there was obviously a lot of muttering and skepticism when you were heading down to the field, but the moment you threw that hat, man… And then the body check! A lot of people changed their tune pretty quick. And then, when you—!"

After some encouragement from Viv that they should get moving again, Rei spent the rest of the walk back to the dorms listening to Catcher give a blow-by-blow playback of his fight as seen from the stands. He suspected the boy of embellishing a lot of the details—he certainly hadn't thought he looked *remotely* as badass as he was being made out to be in the retelling—but every time he would glance at Viv for confirmation she would just shrug and nod, as if to say "that's how it went." As it turned out, he *had* been laughed at and booed when he'd run away from Laurent near the end of the match, but Catcher assured him most of his harassers had shut up quick when they realized the trick he'd almost pulled off, and the rest had gone quiet after he'd been gutted by the spear only to keep punching at the C-Ranker's shield like he still had a prayer of getting through.

Feeling pretty good about himself, Rei had then asked after the Team Battle, and this time Viv joined in the recounting with enthusiasm. She and Catcher both spilled the details they remembered of the class' other top rankers, and told him about the fight, which had been set in the massive "Cargo Bay" field that emulated the cavernous storage bay of an intersystem transport craft. Apparently it had been a decently well-balance matchup, but the Blue Team—the other two designations having been Red and Green—eked out victory when Logan Grant had bested a Lancer named Kastro Vademe. It had been a pretty vicious fight—every other combatant already FDA—but Grant, a Mauler-Type, had ended up taking Vademe's head off, accruing instant Fatal Damage.

"It happened so fast!" Catcher's voice was tinged with glee as the doors to Kanes opened for them, bringing his hands around together to slash horizontally at the air. "They were going at it, and then *wham*. Vademe didn't duck in time. If it had been a true call, I think we would have seen part of him go flying into the seating."

"Good thing SCT stands for *Simulated* Combat Tournament for a reason," Viv said blandly, though she couldn't hide her own enthusiasm completely. "And keep your voice down."

Catcher blinked, looking around, and seemed surprised to find himself in the lobby of the first year dorms, as well as the point of attention for many of the dozens of eyes lingering in the space.

Fortunately for him—and *less* fortunately for Rei—the interest was quick to move from Catcher when people realized who the blond boy was standing with.

Contrary to the empty quiet of the space when he and Viv first arrived at the dorm that morning, there were now maybe forty or so cadets taking up many of the seats, couches, and chairs arranged over the chamber's crimson carpet. Even beyond them, in the open courtyard, a half-dozen people were seated along the top of the knee-high stone wall that surrounded the bent, red-orange tree at its center. While many were still in their regulars—perhaps having loosened a button or two—most had doffed their caps, or even shed their jackets, with a scattered few apparently having already taken the time to change into casuals now that they were at leisure with the end of the day's scheduled events.

Almost exclusively, though—regardless of the state of dress—every gaze that had looked in their direction as they arrived was now trained on Rei.

Whispers started up, and soon more people were turning. From the group a few people raised friendly hands in welcome, but the larger part of the attention was subdued at best, and less than amicable at worst. Even in the few seconds he had to take it all in before Viv pushed him towards the elevators, Rei saw dozens of frowns, and even a frequent open glare. As he was rather firmly guided away from the center of the lobby—he *really* needed to ask what her newest Strength spec was—a few voices did rise up to shout after him, telling him they'd "enjoyed the fight" or were "impressed he held out so long." These encouragements, unfortunately, were immediately drowned out by the buzz of intense conversation as Viv pushed him into the elevator car that had mercifully already been on the first floor, Catcher stepping in right on their heels.

Dent had a point about the attention, Rei thought with a bit of a grimace once they started rising.

Unfortunately, the unpleasantries proved themselves far from over.

Reaching the third floor in silence, the three of them didn't comment on the mutual hurry in their step as they made for 304. Rushing inside together, Rei shut the door behind them a little *too* quickly, breathing a private sigh of relief.

"Well that was… interesting," Viv said uncertainly.

"Putting it mildly." Rei stepped between them, pulling his cap off with the intent of heading for his room before figuring out the shower in the shared bathroom he assumed was the sixth door off the common space. "Was I imagining it, or were some of them looking at me like I was fresh meat in a buffet line at—oh, sorry."

He stopped short as he stepped into the living area, his jacket halfway undone. A dark-skinned girl with long, platinum-silver hair was seated on one of the two couches in the room, her attention fixed on the smart-glass wall, where several varied screens depicting as many different SCT fight recordings where playing all at once. He'd been afraid he'd disturbed her entertainment—*Or study?* he thought, noting the pad and stylus in her hands as he walked around the couches to see her face—but she hadn't so much as glanced back at him as he came in.

"Oh! Chancery!" Catcher said with his trademark spirit, coming up behind Rei and noticing the girl for the first time. "Nice! You haven't met Rei and Viv yet. These are our—"

"Roommates, yes." The girl's voice was flat, and she didn't look away from the wall as the stylus moved steadily over the pad's surface. "I'm capable of reading, Catchwick. And I'd prefer you addressed me by my surname, if you please."

Raising an eyebrow, Rei looked to Catcher—who rolled his eyes—then Viv—who shrugged even as she frowned at the back of the girl who had to be Chancery Cashe.

Deciding to try and take another approach, he moved to ease himself down opposite this newest suitemate, tossing his cap on the coffee table between them before looking over the fights she was indeed very obviously studying.

"The Cutter versus… Oh! Gobta Rimuru!" It didn't take him more than a moment to get excited. "And that's Cameron Athens versus Lancela, isn't it? These are all some of the best Lancers in the last twenty years!" He turned to Cashe with a grin, hoping to extend an olive branch. "Is that your Type?"

The girl *did* glance at him, then, but her purplish-green eyes were anything but friendly even in the brief moment he had her attention. She looked—there was no other description for it—like he had just forcefully shoved something rather unpleasant under her nose.

"Yes, that's them, and yes, that is my Type. Any other questions, or can I get back to work?"

Bewildered, Rei looked around at Catcher and Viv again. The Saber threw his arms up behind Cashe as though in annoyed surrender, while Viv sported the expression of someone wondering how best to get rid of a corpse on campus.

"Cha—I mean *Cashe*." Catcher corrected himself quickly when the silver-haired girl twitched irritably at the slip up. "It's our first night here. Maybe we can hang out? Get to know each other? We're going to be living together for the next year…"

Apparently, this was *not* the correct thing to say.

Rei saw Cashe's neuro-optic flare in her eyes, and the smart-glass wall went blank, then clear, flooding the room with late-afternoon sunlight. She whirled on Catcher, glaring at him even as she tapped out of whatever notes she'd been taking on her pad.

"No, we can't 'hang out.' I don't know what you three are expecting from this Institute, but if you're already spending time worrying about making friends more than our purpose here, then I'm pretty sure I won't need to worry about you crowding the suite for very long. What's more—" her strikingly-colored eyes slid to Rei's before snapping back to Catcher, like she hadn't meant to look in his direction "—I've been here less than ten hours, and have already been given reason to believe the Galens reputation won't be worth as much as I'd hoped upon graduation. I'm clearly going to need to work *twice* as hard as I planned to if I want to leave this school in good standing with the front line officers, and would therefore *appreciate it* if you wouldn't go out of your way to distract me."

"What the hell is that supposed to mean?"

Viv made the demand through clenched teeth, hands in fists by her sides, her obvious anger speaking to the fact that she—like Rei, and very likely Catcher—knew all too well what the girl was about.

Any possibility of the contrary was cast aside as Cashe, without so much as looking at him, pointed right at Rei's face.

"Why is *he* here?" she seethed. "I heard Captain Dent—we *all* did—and even after that I checked his ISCM records. What's an *E-Ranker* doing at the Galens Institute?"

"The same thing you are, I imagine." Viv had unlocked her jaw, speaking a little more clearly, but the look on her face could have murdered. "Working to become the best User he can be. And if the board of admissions accepted him, then maybe you should trust that there's a reason."

"Ha!" Cashe scoffed, standing up prissily. She still hadn't looked at Rei again. "I very much *doubt* that. More like someone's family didn't like the idea of their son going to some nameless military academy, or the favorite nephew of a board member somehow ended up in the 'accepted' pile." At last the girl turned on him, her anger like a brewing storm in her dark face. "Some of us actually *worked* for our place here. Did you know that? Some of us worked very, *very* hard."

"You shut the fu—!"

"Viv. Don't."

Rei cut across Viv's fury sharply, holding up a hand to stop her. She whirled on him, undoubtedly ready to argue that she had *every* right to tongue-lash the pompous girl into a thousand flayed pieces, but came up short when she caught the look in his eyes.

Rei had gone cold inside. He had expected hesitation, expected bullying and backlash. But this… This was not something he had prepared for. It occurred to him, then, for the first time, that he bore more than the weight of his own hopes on his shoulders. He was a *risk*, he realized. An outlier. A recruit so far outside the norm of the Institute's usual crop that already there were people questioning the means by which he'd gotten himself admitted to the prestigious school. He wanted to kick himself, wanted to curse his own idiocy for not realizing it.

In that moment, though, he more than anything wanted to slam his first into someone's face.

Forcing himself to take a breath, he met Chancery Cashe's gaze steadily. "I'm sorry we disturbed your studying," he told her as calmly as he could. "We'll be more considerate, next time, if you're working."

He got nothing but a sneer in return, and with a huff Cashe strode out from around the couches, shoved open the door to her room, and slammed it again behind her. A few seconds later the muffled sounds of the feeds she'd been watching picked up again as the girl must have brought them up on the private smart-glass of her own window.

There was the shuffling of feet, and a second later Rei felt the cushion he was seated on shift, and he knew Catcher had taken a seat next to him.

"Catcher…" he started after a moment. "Do *you* know what my last name typically means?"

In the corner of his eye he saw the boy nod, pulling off his cap as he did to set it beside Rei's.

"Wasn't gonna make any assumptions, but I will if you're asking me that. You didn't want to tell her?"

Rei considered, then shook his head. Across from them, Viv was taking her own seat, still vibrating with anger. "I don't get the impression she's had the easiest time getting here. I don't think embarrassing her would have been a step in the right direction."

"A step in the right direction would have been me stepping my foot right up her—*gah*!" Viv made a face, punching a fist into the cushion by her thigh so hard there was a distinct *creak* of bending metal.

Together they all froze, staring at Viv's hand, still sunk into the couch.

Then, finally, Rei managed to laugh.

"I'm *definitely* going to need to get stronger. If your Strength spec gets any higher, they're gonna have to start replacing the entire floor anytime you overhear someone giving me shit."

Beside him, Catcher started to chuckle at that. After a few seconds more of scowling, so did Viv, retracting her fist and doing her best to smooth out the wide dimple left in the cushion.

There was the *click* of the suite door opening, and all of them looked around in time to see the broad form of Jack Benaly stride into the common area. The big Brawler froze when he saw them, apparently taken aback at their presence.

"Yo," Catcher attempted a greeting, raising a hand in welcome. Viv did the same from the other couch, as did Rei, and it was on him that Benaly's beady eyes fixed. There was a tense moment as one of the first year's top rankers stared at Rei, a pause that extend into 3 seconds, then 5. Then, like he'd never hesitated to begin with, Benaly made a line straight for his room, and Rei's heart sank.

Great, he thought privately. *Two out of three roommates hate me before classes even—*

"How did you keep going? After Laurent speared you?"

Rei started, then turned. Benaly had stopped with his palm on the handle of the door, and was looking around to face him again.

"S-sorry?" Rei stuttered, too surprised to process the question.

"After Laurent speared you through the gut," the Brawler repeated, his voice even, but earnest. "How did you keep hitting her? I've been going over it nonstop in my head, and I can't figure it out."

"Oh," Rei scrambled for a good answer. "Uh… She probably just missed all my vitals, right? Otherwise it would have been a pretty quick end."

He tried at a smile, hoping Benaly would buy the lie.

He didn't.

"It was a clean thrust," the boy said, eyes narrowing. "Through and through, stomach to spine. Your legs even gave out—*both* of them—which would only happen with *complete* bilateral interruption of all voluntary motor control. Cord dissection. So don't try to tell me she missed your vitals."

The smile slipped from Rei's lips. He hesitated a second more, trying and failing to come up with a good excuse, *anything* that would sound like the truth.

In the end, though, the truth was all that was left to him.

"I have… I've got a pretty high pain tolerance," he admitted slowly, watching Benaly carefully. "It helped me keep my head on straight. At least for a while."

Another pause, the top ranker peering at him in the same way Valera Dent had not an hour before, like he were trying to read for the lie in his words.

And then—like the captain—Benaly seemed to choose to believe him.

"Pain tolerance," he muttered to himself, as if taking some mental note as he turned the handle to his room and started to step inside. Before he closed the door behind himself, however, Benaly paused, glancing over his shoulder.

"Good fight, by the way."

And then the door shut with a click, and Rei was left to stare in disbelief after the boy with Catcher and Viv doing the same right alongside him.

CHAPTER 16

"We are not machines. We are not machinations of war. There is too often a mis-conception within the broader society of mankind that Users are little more than tools to be selected and wielded as needed. I add my voice to this idea of public tournaments and demonstration not for the entertainment value and potential revenue many of my colleagues have cited, but rather because it is an opportunity for us to press upon the populace the fact that—though we may be military men and women—we are yet men and women."

Major General Daniel Weber
Central Command, Earth
Committee for Simulated Combat Establishment
6th meeting, c. 2275

Aria, you're the first cadet in nearly a decade to start your years at Galens as a C-Ranked User. You're the first in two to already have an Ability. And you're the first since *before I was born* to enter the term with *both*." Rama Guest shook his head at his niece from behind his wide, lacquered desk, clearly not comprehending. "So—with all of that in mind—why are you choosing to spend your time asking me about an E-Ranked outlier we admitted *on a whim?*"

If Aria had thought it an appropriate time to roll her eyes, she most certainly would have.

"The Galens Institute is possibly the best school in our system, and counts itself amongst the best in the ISC," she replied flatly, not looking away from her uncle. "You will not be able to convince me for *even a moment* that the admission committee let anyone in 'on a whim'."

"And yet that's exactly what happened," the colonel told her with a sigh, leaning back in his broad chair and closing his eyes as the light of sun setting over Castalon's skyscrapers washed across his face from the west window. "I won't pretend there weren't some circumstances to the decision—you're smart enough to know that, as

I hope the majority of your classmates are—but the details of them are not for me or any other staff of this school to share."

"It's *because* I know that there must be circumstances that I am asking," Aria pressed, crossing her arms in a disgruntled fashion as she stood across from her uncle in the center of his office. "First I'm made to fight a boy six inches shorter than me and almost two full tiers under my rank, then he very nearly *beats* me. How could I not be curious? And what was up with those *scars?*"

The colonel cocked his head at her with a look of amusement.

"I was under the impression you were going fairly easy on the boy…"

Aria didn't miss for a beat that her question had been deftly dodged, but decided to pick her battles carefully, for the time being. "I *was*. At least at first. How much of a bully would that have made me look like if I'd cut him down within ten seconds of the fight starting?" She frowned. "But it was a mistake. I almost lost because I didn't take him seriously. If it hadn't been for Third Eye, I probably would have. He was… capable. He took advantage of the margin I offered him without hesitating, and it almost cost me."

But it was fun.

She didn't voice this last thought, of course. There was no reason to give her uncle cause to suspect she had any cause for her questions other than curiosity at the anomaly that was Reidon Ward's presence at the Galens Institute.

"I did warn you," the man offered with a slow exhale. "I warned you this morning you needed to be ready. There is a reason *every one* of the students in your class—in this school as a whole—are within these walls. Cadet Ward is hardly an exception." The colonel paused, chuckling and casting her with a fond eye. "You're reminding me of your father, with these badgering questions. He used to assault me in the same way if he ever thought I was keeping anything from him."

Aria bristled. "My parents care about nothing but perception and the value of their family name." She only barely managed to keep the snarl out of her voice. "It's cost them Kalus and Amina already, even if they refuse to acknowledge it. I am *nothing* like them."

"You forget yourself, cadet."

The rumble of Rama Guest's words brought Aria up short, and the man stood slowly from his chair.

"I will not pretend your mother and I are any kind of close, but your father is my greatest friend. I was the best man at your parents' wedding, and present at the birth of each of the Laurent children, *yours* included. You will not speak ill of Carmen in my presence. Is that clear?"

Aria brought herself to attention before the desk, fixing her gaze at a spot in the window over the commanding officer's right shoulder. "Yes, Unc—Yes, colonel." She just managed to correct herself as her uncle cocked an eyebrow in warning at her. "I apologize for speaking out of turn."

The colonel gave a curt nod, and when he spoke again his voice was subdued, familiar once more. "I'm aware of the pressure you and your siblings have been put under, Aria. I have my own opinions regarding it, believe it or not. But I am also sure that your mother and father want nothing but the best for you and your brother and sister. They just... They have a hard time conveying it in a language you all speak."

Vapidity and manipulation from one, uninterested silence from the other, Aria considered saying out loud. *Yes. Those are certainly two ways to show concern for your children's wellbeing.*

Instead, she held her tongue, hoping her mutiny on the topic was clear in her averted eyes.

Her uncle sighed, moving around the desk until he was leaning back to sit on it directly in front of her. "At ease, cadet."

Aria relaxed, bringing her hands to clasp behind her and spreading her feet a little more comfortably as she met the colonel's eyes again.

"Regarding your curiosity involving Ward," he started, apparently eager to bring the conversation out of dangerous waters. "As I said, I won't be sharing the details of his acceptance to Galens with you or anyone else who asks—including the calls I've so far fielded only today from no less than *eleven* families demanding why an *E-Ranker* has been allowed into the same prestigious program as their talented children." He met her gaze evenly. "That being said, I'm comfortable encouraging you to consider paying attention to what information you already have on your classmate. I suspect the reason for the board of admissions' 'whim', as I called it, will become apparent fairly quickly." He gave her an affectionate smile, then dipped his head towards the door of his office, set among the dark-stained bookshelves that encircled every wall of the room that wasn't glass. "Now if you'll excuse me, I do have a school to run."

Aria hesitated, her uncle's cryptic suggestion only adding to her questions. When his steady gaze said that he wouldn't be hearing more on the subject that evening, though, she caved, throwing up a firm salute. "Thank you, colonel. Good night."

"Good night, cadet."

Turning on her heel, Aria left the office swiftly, easing the door shut again behind her. She paused there, in the narrow corridor that led from the Chief Assitant's office and waiting room, considering the man's final words.

Information I already have?

With the answer not immediately presenting itself, Aria muttered her disappointment under her breath and turned to make down the hall. In the waiting room, her uncle's chief assistant had apparently stayed late, and was behind her desk in the process of packing a bag for the night, back to Aria. The young woman looked as though she'd spent some time in the bathroom doing her hair up, and that was *definitely* not the top she'd been wearing 20 minutes earlier…

Coming to the edge of the counter as quietly as she could, Aria leaned over it with a grin. "So where's the date, Maddie?"

Maddison Kent nearly upturned her bag as she jumped, letting out a squeak of surprise. Whirling, her hazel eyes the size of dinner plates, she sagged when she realized who stood behind her, putting a hand on her chest in an obvious attempt to calm a franticly beating heart.

"*Aria!*" she gasped under her breath, shaking her head. "You scared the life out of me!"

Aria snickered, hardly feeling apologetic as she bent even further over the counter. "Worth it. And no dodging the question. Where's the captain taking you?"

Maddison shook her head with a faint grin. "Brat…" she mumbled humorously before smoothing out her clean top—a pretty black blouse with silver frilling along its shoulders. Then she stuck her tongue out at Aria. "If you *must* know: we're going to Sapata's, in the shopping district."

Aria groaned, resting her chin in both hands and putting on her best pout. "Jealoooooouuus… Take me with you? I haven't been outside the grounds since *June*."

"I'm aware," Maddison said with a laugh, gathering her bag up. "But no. You're too old to be tagging along, but too young for us not to get weird looks." She hitched the straps over one shoulder, then spread her arms a little. "How do I look, though? It's only been a couple months. I'm still trying to impress."

"Gorgeous," Aria answered earnestly, leaning away again to take the woman in more deliberately. "Your hair, too. You'll be knocking them all dead, I promise."

Maddison laughed, moving out from around the desk. "I only need to knock *one* dead, thanks. Now come on, cadet. If you're done with your uncle for the night, you can escort me out."

"My uncle?" Aria feigned confusion, stepping in beside the older woman. "Oooh you must mean the colonel. Sorry. He's gotten so uptight since the end of the summer program you'd almost forget the old man's knew my name before I was born."

"Hush, you," Maddison said with a giggle, motioning for Aria to keep her voice down until they were out of the waiting room and into the hall proper, making for the staircase halfway along the brightly-lit corridor. "It's well-meaning and you know it. You might be a tough cookie, Ms. C-Ranker, but some of your classmates could be quick to forget your merits if they found out you're related to the *commanding officer* of the Institute."

"Well we're not, technically. If that helps."

The woman waved the correction away as they turned into the staircase and started down, making for the ground floor. "Like it matters. Every year it gets a little worse, I swear. Like with that poor boy I heard you had a match with earlier."

Aria, trailing behind, almost tripped down the last three steps before the first landing. Recovering, she glanced at her friend, hoping she sounded only casually interested as she spoke. "Yeah… The colonel mentioned that. Apparently he's gotten like eleven calls about it?"

Maddison snorted. "Those were only from the families of the incoming cadets. He took that many again from parents from the other years who heard the news, and another two from a couple superior officers. Doesn't even count the preparatory academies of some of your classmates reaching out, trying to ensure they haven't attached their names to a 'falling program'." She gave Aria a sharp look. "Not that I told you any of this, mind."

Aria nodded, but frowned, turning off the last landing before the bottom. Where her classmates had failed, Maddison Kent had been the one steady source of companionship over the course of the summer months, even more so than her uncle. She wasn't about to let slip anything that might get the assistant in hot water. "Sure. But why the concern from everyone? All because of one new student's rank?"

"A rank nearly a full tier lower than any previously accepted student in the history of the Institute." Maddison sighed as they reached ground level and stepped into the clean, open atrium of the administrative building. "I must say, I do hope it all ends up being worth the gamble…"

Aria bit her lip, trying her damnedest not to come off to keen on the subject. Only after they'd passed through the sliding doors out into the dusk light—the highest of Castalon skyscrapers bearing the shadows of the night over the grounds an hour earlier than true sunset—did she think it safe to try speaking again.

"It does seem a little odd…" she tried tentatively. "I was pretty surprised when I got matched up with an E-Ranker…"

She glanced at Maddison hopefully, but the woman only gave an "Mhm" through her nose, taking in the pink and oranges of the sky visible through the branches of the oaks and maples that hung over either side of the path.

Aria decided to push her luck.

"You don't happen to know *why* he got in, do you? I mean it's pretty bizarre. And you should have seen our fight. I think the guy threw a single punch with his CAD the whole time, *maybe* two."

"If your uncle didn't tell you why Cadet Ward was accepted to Galens, I certainly hope you don't expect *me* to."

This time, Aria *did* trip, catching the toe of her boot against a protruding edge of the path's synthetic stone. She caught herself quickly, her Speed spec getting a leg under her before she could really stumble, but she was still blushing when she came up.

"How did you know?" she mumbled, embarrassed at having been called out.

The young woman giggled. "Because your face is an open book, sweetheart." When Aria clearly didn't take this as funny, Maddison smiled and took her by the arm to walk alongside her beneath the trees. "I know the colonel's schedule better than he does. I know you had your practice bout this morning, so for you to come for a late visit like you did tonight could only have meant something came up between now and then you wanted to discuss. I knew about your fight, and who it was against. Aside from that…" Her smile turned roguish. "You seem a liiiitle eager. What was it? Was Ward handsome? Tell me he was handsome."

"What?! No! I mean… Maybe? I don't know!" Aria could feel her face warming further by the second. "I wasn't really paying attention to his jawline, you know? I was more worried about not getting my head punched off."

"Oh? And were you still worried about your head when you caught him to keep him from falling on his face at the end of the match?"

Aria thought her ears would catch fire.

"You saw it!" she squeaked, mortified. "You *saw* the fight!"

"Oh of course I did. I had the file pulled from the Arena's recordings the moment I heard it was you two." She reached up, tapping Aria's nose in the fashion of a doting older sister. "I. Saw. Everything."

"You're the worst," Aria muttered, turning away in an attempt to cool her cheeks a little. When she finally felt like her face wasn't the color of her hair, she looked straight again.

"I just…" She started as they passed by the Institute hospital, the lights within illuminating them in the fading light. "He surprised me, that's all… I wasn't expecting him to put up that kind of fight. It was… It was fun, honestly." She frowned. "And those scars… What the hell was with those scars on his hands? I noticed them when he was punching at Hippolyta, at the end. It looked like he'd been branded…"

In the corner of her vision, Aria saw distinctly the downturn of Maddison's mouth. She turned to try and meet her eye, but the woman didn't look at her, and spoke only after a few seconds of silence.

"What did the colonel tell you about Reidon Ward, Aria? Did he tell you to stay away from him? Or anything of the sort?"

"What? No. Nothing like that…" Aria considered again the words her uncle had left her with. "He said… He told me that if I wanted to figure out what Ward is doing at Galens, I should pay attention to 'the information I already have'. Whatever that means."

Maddison's face softened, and turning a corner in the path the south gate of the school—the only entrance to the grounds left open at all times for the comings and goings of staff and visitors—came into view.

"Good. That's good. I was worried that… But it doesn't matter." She slid her arm from Aria's to take her by the elbow and stop her, pulling her about so they faced each other. "Have you figured out what he meant?"

Aria shook her head.

"You will," Maddison assured her. "Just… Think literally, okay?"

Aria stared at her, not comprehending, and the older woman laughed. "That's the only hint I'm giving you. Now get off to your dorm. You've got new roommates to meet, and I'm going to be late for my date."

Aria opened her mouth to protest, but Maddison had already turned away.

"'Literally'?" Aria called after her. "What do you mean, 'literally'?"

Maddison only raised a hand over her head in farewell, an auto-flyer in the process of dropping down from the traffic high above them to descend towards the outer courtyard beyond the school entrance.

Watching her go, Aria couldn't decide if she was more confused or annoyed. She understood the school staff weren't about to outright *give away* information, but did they have to beat around the damn bush so thoroughly it probably left a nice worn track in the dirt? With a sigh she gave up, turning north to start the long walk back to Kanes on her own.

After the heat of the late summer day, the fading of the sun left a chill in the air that had Aria glad for her jacket and hat. Tucking her hands into the pockets of her slacks, she followed the path for a time, trying to distract herself by watching the reflection of the dying evening to the west reflect in a wash of colors off the glass and steel of the skyscrapers east of the Institute. It was her favorite time of day, and had fortunately largely fallen within the limited hours of leisure she and the other top sixteen had had over the summer program. The cooling temperatures and the dimming light had always helped her relax, helped her gather herself after rigorous—and sometimes frustrating—mornings and afternoons spent in near-constant combat.

She didn't *regret* the summer, of course. It had gotten her away from the Laurent estate and her mother, and any circle of hell at the hands of Valera Dent and her merciless sub-instructors was worth the escape of that particular torment. Still, it hadn't been without its downsides. Aside from an exhaustingly intense training regimen, the other Users from her class—all high D-Ranks, like she'd been starting off—had proven themselves a fairly cold-shouldered lot. She couldn't count any one among them a 'friend', per se, even if a couple—like Jack Benaly and Kay Sandree—had been pleasant enough. It didn't surprise her, though. Of all 128 new students, the sixteen of them weren't only the top in terms of Rank, they were also the favorites to make it through the Intra-School SCT and qualify for Sectionals. As incoming cadets that was as high as they could go in the collegiate circuit, but they also had their own bracket, which made the first years' pairing a sort of exclusive, separate event even within the other tournaments. To add to that, the Galens Institute's presence in Sector 9 meant *their* Sectionals was often times the most-watched feed of the entire series across all five of the Astra System planets.

With that amount of pressure, of course it wasn't easy to make nice with the very people you were directly competing against.

Aria sighed sadly, turning her attention to the sky above, where several interweaving air-lanes thick with flyers and larger transport vehicles cut patterns across the orange clouds. She was more than proud of her CAD-Rank. Salista Laurent's manipulations hadn't driven her so far as to reject her own potential. Aria had been ecstatic to receive her D8-Ranking at assignment, and doubly so when she'd broken through to C0 not 2 weeks back.

And yet...

And yet, as she had stood there beside Valera Dent on the projected platform in front of the other 127 students she would be spending the next 3 years of her life with, Aria had been jealous of the heads she'd seen leaning together to whisper quietly, jealous of the excited looks exchanged and smiles traded. She wouldn't have given her rank—or the effort she had already put in to attain it—for the world, but there had been a distinct part of herself in that moment that had wished she wasn't the *highest* level in the class, that wished she'd been sitting with the rest of them, watching some poor other soul standing alone while everyone else talked and made friends and—

Aria stopped short, her head still upturned, a sudden suspicion electric in her mind.

Her rank. Her… rank?

No. It couldn't be that simple.

… Could it?

Training her attention back to the deepening shadows of the ground, Aria decided there was no harm in checking. With a flick of her eyes she brought up her NOED, the frame adjusting automatically to the dimming light. Entering a half-dozen quick commands, she accessed the ISCM User database.

The *first thing* she had done after the Commencement ceremony had come to an end was pull up Reidon Ward's profile, trying to find anything of interest in his publicly available information that would help sate her curiosity about the boy. Nothing she'd found was unsurprising. Not his birth world—Astra-2—not his previous school—a local preparatory institute in Sector 6—not even his age—18—the lattermost of which Aria had been a little ashamed to question initially, given Ward's height and size.

Still… Her uncle and Maddison had both implied she already had access to all the information she needed to figure out what was going on.

Literally.

And so with a final order, Aria pulled up Ward's User registration again, going over with more deliberate care this time.

USER: Ward, Reidon

CAD-NAME: Shido

CAD-TYPE: A-Type

CAD-RANK: E4

BIRTH YEAR: 2450
BIRTH SYSTEM: Astra System
BIRTH PLANET: Astra-2

PRIMARY SCHOOLING: N/A
SECONDARY SCHOOLING: N/A
TERTIARY SCHOOLING: Grandcrest Preparatory Academy
MILITARY EDUCATION: The Galens Institute

It was all there, undoubtedly unchanged from when Aria had checked it only a few hours earlier.

But this time, she didn't get past the fourth line.

For almost half a minute she stared, not quiet believing her eyes. It was so surprising, in fact, that for a bit she convinced herself she must have misheard Valera Dent at the Commencement, that she hadn't caught the announcement of her challenger's specs correctly.

But no… There was definitely no mistaking it. The captain had *absolutely* said "E3" when Reidon Ward had gotten himself enthusiastically selected as her opponent. The *E* of the rank is what had been so distinct though, so bizarre, resulting in Aria's eyes having tracked right over the *new* number when she'd first pulled up the Cadet's profile.

"CAD-Rank… E*4*?" she asked the evening.

It was possible, of course. It *was* plausible that Ward had been on the cusp of a rank-up before their match, and the fight had just pushed him over the edge, but also too much of a coincidence to stop Aria rereading the line several times just to make sure she wasn't mistaken. When she was positive her eyes weren't deceiving her, she had a thought, and scrolled to the bottom of the profile, selecting the "Additional Information" option hovering there, causing a secondary window to pop into view. While the ISCM didn't provide the public history of a User's ranking—just like they didn't provide details on a Device's individual specs—it *was* possible for a member of the ISCM to access a person's baseline, if a pain in the ass. Aria hadn't had the opportunity earlier, but she did so now, becoming more irritated every time she was required *once again* to provide her name, CAD-name, school, and school identification number to prove she *was* a registered cadet. After almost 5 minutes of strained patience she was allowed access to the "Assignment Details" database page, and without a second to lose she typed in Reidon Ward's name, bringing up his information.

ASSIGNMENT YEAR: 2468

ASSIGNMENT LOCATION: Astra - Astra-3 - Sector 6 - Grandcrest Preparatory Academy

ASSIGNMENT RANK: F8

F8?! Aria considered in silent alarm.

Things were getting closer to impossible. Pushing from the high Fs into the mid-Es *might* have been feasible in 10 weeks, but only with the correct trainers and *complete* commitment to conditioning. For starters, there weren't that many capable A-Type instructors to be had in the Intersystem Collective—even Aria's parents had had trouble finding a competent few for her brother—but for another, Reidon Ward was... well... a "Ward". She doubted very much there were any families left who voluntarily kept that surname, so long after the ISC had requisitioned it when the war had started to leave hundreds of thousands of orphans without parents across the systems. What's more, didn't Ward's lack of information regarding his primary and secondary schooling point to his education having been handled even out of the public paths?

So... Assuming the E-Ranker had no family to support him, how would he have managed a training regimen intense enough to leap *seven* ranks in a summer?

The answer, of course, was that there was no way he had...

And then, slowly, understanding began to dawn on Aria, and a few seconds later several passing second years were treated to the sight of a beautiful, red-headed girl in her full military regulars launching into a tirade of unexplainable expletives so colorful as to have made the average drill sergeant blush.

CHAPTER 17

"You will be pushed at this Institute. More than physically. More than mentally. Those with greater ability will—by that nature—earn themselves greater opportunity, while those with less will be pressed to make themselves better, to make themselves stronger, and gain those advantages as their own."

Captain Valera "Iron Bishop" Dent
The Galens Institute
First year Commencement Ceremony, 2468

The morning of the following day started off rather tediously for Rei. Aside from having an awkward—though mercifully silent—encounter with Chancery Cashe as he exited the bathroom, it transpired that their kitchen space was not stocked, and breakfast would have to be had at the campus mess hall. This in and of itself wasn't awful—the mess turned out to be more arboretum than food court, with what had to have been half a rain forest rising up around the provided tables and chairs the first years had mostly taken over—but Rei had to again suffer the stares and murmurings of the other cadets all throughout his meal. Viv and Catcher made the experience tolerable—and apparently provided enough of a deterrent to keep people from approaching outright—but Rei could still feel the eyes on him as he ate his eggs and toast, and thought some of the second and third years had started looking his way, too, as they made for other parts of the hall.

After breakfast things got only momentarily less awkward. He and Viv had indeed been assigned to the same "1-A" class-block, so after eating they said farewell to Catcher—who was unfortunately in the "1-C" section—and headed for a classroom in one of the Combat Theory buildings. Their week's schedule had been sent to them the evening before, and all three had shared a groan when they'd noted how the full mornings of the 6 instructional days were taken up. It was less than enthusiastically, therefore, that Rei and Viv climbed the stairs of Building B to the third floor, then followed signs that projected themselves for their NOEDs to the designated room.

Through the open door the buzz of conversation could be heard, and Rei steeled himself, letting Viv take the lead as they entered.

The space proved to be a modest amphitheater, with enough rising seating to host some fifty or so students. A massive smart-glass wall faced the rising desks, currently clear to show off a sunny view of the school's east grounds. About fifteen first years had already convened, scattering themselves among the seats, and most were chatting pleasantly, contributing to the drone of conversation. There were, however, a few exceptions, two of which stopped Rei dead in his tracks at the entrance of the class.

The first was a boy so tall he still looked of a height even sitting at the peak of the amphitheater along the very back of the room. His jet hair would have been enough, easily recognizable beneath his military cap, but Rei had the misfortune of catching sight of him just as the figure looked in his direction. Logan Grant's black-red eyes locked on him for a moment, then shifted to Viv, then back to Rei. If it hadn't been clear before that the boy wasn't a fan of him, his contemptuous glare spoke volumes to the fact. A couple of other cadets had gathered around to sit with him, talking amongst themselves, but stopped at a word from Grant. They turned as one, all smirking together in Rei's direction, and the leering was enough to make him look away with clenched teeth.

Fortunately, the next anomaly was far less unpleasant a surprise.

At the opposite end of the room, seated halfway up the theater, a girl with brilliant green eyes and red hair now plaited over one shoulder was scrolling across a wide tab set at an angle between her lap and the edge of the desk in front of her. Aria Laurent sat alone, and hadn't looked up when they had entered, nor did she when Viv motioned to one of the lower rows—closer to the front of the room—getting a nod of agreement from Rei. As the rest of the gathered students steadily took note of the presence, the talking died quickly, and whereas newcomers apparently weren't enough to peek Laurent's interest, this growing silence appeared to let the C-Ranker know something was amiss. She lifted her gaze just in time to meet Rei's as he and Viv started along the empty row a couple below hers, aiming for the center seating. He considered waving, maybe even trying a "Hello" in an attempt to assure her there were no hard feelings for the beatdown she'd given him the previous day, but before he could lift a hand or open his mouth Laurent had quickly looked away again, so focused on whatever script was streaming across her tablet that she appeared almost to be deliberately avoiding his eye…

"That was weird," he muttered as Viv pulled out a chair for herself.

"What was?" she asked distractedly, sitting down and tugging her own pad out of her bag to kill the time.

Rei, though—glancing back towards Laurent after he'd settled and finding her still intently scrolling—decided he must have been imagining it.

"Nothing," he whispered after a second. "Did you see who's in the back?"

"Yup," Viv grunted, a look flashing across her face that might have fit better on someone who'd just gotten a brief whiff of rancid meat. "Looks like we're in for a fun year."

"*I'm* in, you mean. Don't worry about me. You can't keep getting tangled in every mess I end up in."

Opening her pad to the week's schedule, Viv smirked. "Uh-huh. Sure. Whatever you say, honey."

Rei snorted, and was about to reach into his bag for his own—significantly smaller—tablet, when the shadow of several people loomed over the two of them from behind.

"Hey man, caught the fight yesterday. It was… something."

As one Rei and Viv turned in their seats. A trio of cadets—two boys and a girl—had come to stand along the row above them. The one who'd spoken had a mane of greyish hair frosted with orange at the tips, his eyes matching the colors perfectly.

"Thanks…" Rei answered tentatively, taking in the three of them one after the other. "I can assure you it was a lot more interesting from my point of view."

The other boy, his head shaved to a clean sheen, cracked half a smile at that, but the first was the one to speak again.

"I'm sure it was. Listen…." His tone suddenly cooled. "What's your deal, man?"

Here we go, Rei sighed internally.

"My deal?" he feigned ignorance.

"Come on. Don't play dumb. I'm not trying to be nosey. We're all just wondering how someone like…" The boy hesitated, clearly making an attempt to be tactful for a moment before giving up. "Well… Like *you* ended up… here."

"Lottery system," Viv answered, turning away from the group again, clearly having lost interest. "Started this year. Galens puts all the Fs and Es in the Astra System together in a hat and pulls one out at random for a free ride." She gave Rei a feigned, fawning look. "Lucky you."

Rei almost chuckled at the confusion on the others' faces, but decided to try and save the situation.

"She's kidding, ignore her. I don't really have a good answer for you, but if I had to guess I'd say my written portion of the Assignment Exam probably had something to do with it all. I know I'm not at the level of you guys Rank-wise, but maybe the higher officers are hoping I've got the chops to catch up…?"

It was the best answer to this exact question he'd been able to come up with the night before, laying in his new bed and staring into the darkness of the room around him, unable to sleep. There was a healthy dose of truth to it. He couldn't imagine his score had *hurt* his chances of enrollment after all, and it was obvious the Institute staff *were* anticipating he'd catch up. It had seemed the sort of explanation at least a few people looking for a reason to accept his presence might grab onto.

"No way," the girl said, sounding more impressed than doubtful. She had long, blueish hair with a stylish streak of red tucked behind one ear from under the brim of her cap. "What was your score?"

"Just under ninety-nine percent," Rei admitted awkwardly. He'd never been the type to enjoy boasting about his grades—not to mention Viv had always done enough of that for him at Grandcrest—but he'd decided this was a necessary moment.

"*Damn*," the bald boy said under his breath. "I was at ninety-five, and I thought *that* was good."

Viv gave a snort behind Rei—undoubtedly recalling her own reaction when he'd told her what the MIND had scored him at—but it only earned her a shared scowl at the back of her head from the trio.

"She didn't mean it that way," Rei tried to clarify quickly, taking the chance to attempt and change the subject. "She just said basically the exact same thing at the test. We went to the same school—Grandcrest Prep, in Sector 6 here on Astra-3." He stuck out a hand even as he pointed over his shoulder at his best friend. "This is Viv, and I'm Rei. We're looking forward to—"

"Hold on," the grey-haired boy cut in as each of his companions started to reach for Rei's offered hand. "I don't buy it. That can't be. There has to have been *loads* of people over the years who got comparable scores, and I've never heard of any other E-Ranker getting in." He put his hands on the desk in front of him, leaning closer to eye Rei suspiciously. "There's got to be more to it."

With the ruined opportunity to make nice, Rei's patience ran its course. He stared coolly at the boy, not flinching away. "I don't know what you're looking for me to tell you, man. Believe it or not, I wasn't sitting in when the board of admissions met to review my file. Maybe I got lucky. Or maybe someone thought my face was pretty."

"Oh no!" Viv chimed in on cue, feigning a crestfallen look. "We should've sent them an updated pic with the new haircut!"

From the other side of the room, someone stifled a laugh. As one they all looked around, but if Aria Laurent was still paying any attention to their interaction, she was doing an excellent job of hiding it now.

"Leron, come on," the girl told the boy with grey-orange hair. "It's not worth getting in his face about. Maybe it *was* the written score. You don't know."

"The hell it was his score, Kay!" Leron snapped, glaring at Rei again. "They wouldn't let someone in who got one hundred percent *and* topped every other part of the test if their CAD-Rank wasn't up to snuff, and I have a hard time believing *this guy* passed his physical." He frowned. "How tall *are you*, man? Five-five? Five-*six*? They just wouldn't do that. It's too likely the weak link will drag everyone else down."

Behind him Rei heard Viv start to turn around again, and he could almost feel her beginning to get angry.

"What's so special about you, *E*?" Leron pressed, obviously starting to lose his cool and shaking off the girl named Kay when she put a hand on his arm to try and pull him away. "The hell makes you good enough to suddenly make an entire school change the way it—?"

"OFFICER PRESENT!"

The bellowed announcement rang so sharp and so near, Leron actually collided with Kay as he leapt sideways, nearly knocking the poor girl over. The second, bald boy caught her by the shoulder, and together the trio stared at the newcomer who'd approached them unnoticed from the classroom door, now closed. Rei, meanwhile, had learned along with Viv from Catcher's quick reactions at the Commencement Ceremony, and the two of them had leapt from their chairs the moment the words had been spoken, drawing themselves into the best salute they could manage.

All around them it appeared the rest of the class had arrived and found their seats while Rei and Leron had been exchanging words. In front of them now, a squat woman stood rigidly, watching them with dark eyes from beneath bangs of mousey grey hair, the red-on-white armband marking her very likely as the instructor of the course.

"TOO SLOW!" the woman shouted as many of the other students were still scrambling to stand and salute, her carrying voice making all those nearest too her—Rei included—flinch in surprise. "AT EASE!"

They all relaxed, and those who knew to spread their stance and clasped their hands behind their backs.

"If I can see your CAD bands right now, you are wrong!" the instructor snapped, moving along the row and glaring up into the theater seating. "If your cap is not on your head, you are wrong! If you are looking me in the eye miss-with-the-black-braid-and-her-freckled-friend, you are WRONG!" She stopped her pacing. "Sit down, cadets!"

There was the clatter of chairs, and behind him Rei heard Leron, Kay, and their bald friend start to head back to their seats.

"DID I SAY FEEL FREE TO WALK AROUND THE ROOM?" the woman barked, staring at the three of them with wide eyes. "NO! I SAID *SIT. DOWN!*"

Rei didn't think he would ever hear rears planted into the nearest available chairs so fast again.

"My name—" the woman started, even her normal voice carrying an angry sort of pitch "—is Lieutenant Candice Voss! My job—" she began walking up the row again "—is to work some manners into you lot! About half your number look to know what you're doing, with a scattered few hopefuls who might just make the cut by the time we're done. The rest of you—" Rei swore the woman's glare could have broken glass "—will likely learn the hard way! I have one week to instill into you the basics of military etiquette! After that, those of you who haven't grasped the *very simple* concepts we are going to be reviewing will probably be finding yourselves spending a *lot* of time in the Institute brig making friends with four cement walls! Now... Let's try this again... OFFICER PRESENT!"

The response, this time, was much faster.

For the next 4 hours class 1-A was drilled in the minutia of military decorum, from proper salutes to correct marching to appropriate addressing of higher officers. Before the first hour had gone by, Rei was tired of the tedium, and by the time Lieutenant Voss dismissed them for their lunch leisure hour he was sure those among them who'd already been familiar with everything she'd had to teach were likely to have been falling asleep standing up. This was confirmed 10 minutes later by Catcher when they met him at the mess hall again, the boy somehow having developed bags under his eyes in the short period since they'd last seen him.

"That bad for every class all around, huh?" Viv asked drearily, kicking a chair out to sit down next to Catcher with her tray of food, collected from the automatically distributing buffet line in the middle of the hall.

"I think I have more of the chief warrant officer's spit in my mouth than my own," the boy confirmed with a groan. "And it was bullshit, too. There was *nothing* wrong with my salute. The asshole just didn't like that he couldn't find something about me to correct."

"You guys from the ISCM preps are about to have a dull first week," Rei agreed, taking a seat on his other side. "I was almost glad for Voss' volume by the end. Kept me awake, at least."

"Careful what you wish for," Viv muttered, cutting into her roasted chicken half-heartedly. "I get the feeling she didn't like the fact we were preoccupied when she got there. What the hell was up with that guy, getting in your face like that?"

Catcher's brow furrowed over his salad, and he looked around at Rei. "Someone got in your face?"

"Kinda," Rei acknowledged with an unenthusiastic shrug. "Guy who didn't like that I couldn't explain what someone with my Rank—"

"Or height," Viv added with muttered venom.

"—is doing here." Rei finished.

"Yeah… I actually got the same," Catcher sighed, sounding exhausted as he gave up on the food, dropping the fork with a *clink* to lean back in his chair.

The other two exchanged a look, then frowned at him.

"You did?" Viv asked. "Didn't you say you're a D5? Why would someone take issue with an above-average rank?"

"I don't mean about *me*," Catcher corrected with a dark laugh, eyes on the sky through the curved, clear ceiling of the arboretum they could see through the palm trees, a massive dome comprised of what had to have been several hundred large, triangular glass panels. "I mean about Rei."

"Oh," Rei caught on. "Shit… I'm sorry, man."

Another thing he'd failed to consider. There was no way people hadn't noticed where he'd been sitting during the Commencement, and others had seen the three of them returning to Kanes together after the festivities had ended.

"Eh. Don't sweat it. I wasn't ostracized or whatever." Catcher smirked, sitting forward again to look at Rei. "If anything you made me more popular. Had three different girls come up to me and ask me if I knew what was going on with your rank. All really pretty, too."

Viv rolled her eyes, not waiting to finish chewing her bite of chicken to speak. "Smooth. You're officially famous enough to get your friends dates, Rei."

Rei managed a bare smile at that, but kept pressing Catcher. "What did they want to know?"

Catcher made a face, picking up his fork again to attempt another go at the salad. "Probably nothing more than you'd expect. 'Who is he?' 'What's his deal?' 'Is he really an E-Ranker?' For someone who said yesterday you're not keen on attention, you sure porked that pig wrong, man."

"Ugh," Rei groaned, shoving a potato into his mouth more to have something to do than anything else. "And this afternoon sure as hell isn't gonna help that," he grumbled after he'd swallowed, spearing another roasted spud.

Still, despite the over-interest of his classmates, he couldn't help but feel his usual eagerness spark in his gut again, snuffed out until then between Leron's badgering and 4 hours stuck in a room learning how to stand properly.

Parameter testing was next.

Rei had no idea what to expect, and even the feeds had been sparse on information when he, Viv, and Catcher had spent a good hour scouring them the night before. Apparently there were three tests, and each cadet would have multiple chances to attempt them, but as to the specific nature of the exams… Nothing. Zilch. Their schedules told them they would all be heading to one of the several subbasements Rei hadn't realized were beneath the Arena—he and Viv immediately after lunch, with Catcher 3 hours later—and that alone spoke in some sense to what they could expect, but offered nothing specific.

"I don't know…" Viv answered Rei's anxiety hopefully. "Maybe you're just a flash in the pan. We've got Aria Laurent and Logan Grant *both* in our class. I'll bet a lot of eyes are gonna be on them after the excitement dies down over your new knuckle-duster toothpicks."

Ignoring her amicable jab, Rei considered her point as Catcher spoke up.

"Whoa. Laurent *and* Grant? That's a powerhouse class… Benaly is in mine, as well as another guy—Aadhik Khatri—who was pretty loud about also having been invited to the summer training course. I thought they might be friendly already, given they spent the last 2 months together, but they actually didn't really seem keen on each other…"

"Huh." Viv sounded like she'd realized something. "Laurent and Grant were the same, actually. Sat pretty far from one another." She grimaced. "Then again, not sure who would want to be friends with a waste of good looks like that dick."

"Quite a few people, apparently."

Rei wasn't looking at either of them as he spoke, instead having tossed one arm over the back of his chair to turn his attention on something nearer the center of the mess. Following his eyes, Catcher and Viv both grimaced when they caught sight of Logan Grant sitting with his feet up on the table, smirking as a group of no less than half a dozen other cadets sat and stood around him, talking animatedly. On a whim Rei glanced around the massive room for Aria Laurent, but no flash of red hair was visible in the crowded tables he could make out through the trees.

"Whatever," Viv grumbled, turning back to her lunch. "My point is you shouldn't worry as much, Rei. I'll bet anything Grant will be happy to hoard the attention, and Laurent may not have any choice."

Silently, Rei nodded, hoping against hope she was right.

Once they'd finished and handed their trays to a passing service bot, the three of them parted ways again. Catcher wished them good luck, saying he was headed back to the dorm to review an Instrasystem pro fight of some Saber he'd apparently set his NOED to record. When he was gone, Rei and Viv made for the center of campus, theorizing what the parameter testing could consist of as they made for the great black shape of the Arena. By the time they reached the entrance—where more projected signs had them taking the stairs up into the stands beside several other members of their class—Viv was convinced they were going to be doing timed sprints and miles, along with counted pushups, pull-ups, and the like. Rei was less sure of that, arguing that those sorts of measurements could hardly offer them anything more than their CAD specs already did, but Viv stuck to her guns.

"It's logical," she insisted as they crested the landing. "They want to be able to see where we start at and how much we improve over the years, right? Baseline testing is the easiest way to do that."

"I will bet you a hundred credits the Galens Institute will *not* be testing us in the same way Coach Kat used to baseline the combat team," Rei chuckled, pointing to the right, where an indicator in his frame told him they should be headed. "It's got to be more comprehensive than that."

"What's more comprehensive?!" Viv argued, trailing behind.

Rei shrugged, noting a couple cadets ahead turning down one of the smaller entrances that led into the underworks. "I don't know... Combat ability? Or the like? And there's supposed to be only three tests, right? Would pushups, pull-ups, and a mile run be enough?"

"Oh..." Viv muttered, following his point. "Right. Maybe..."

They kept theorizing as they descended into the Arena underbelly, following a growing group of the other 1-A first years ahead of them. Eventually they reached a small chamber that must have sat under the southern loop of the stands, joining a dozen other cadets to watch the clean glass doors of the elevators set into each wall. Huddling in with three or four of their classmates in the second car to arrive, Rei ignored the sidelong glances he was getting, instead watching a thin girl with orange-yellow hair select the symbol "SB2" from a projection in the surface of the right wall. A few seconds later they were spilling out into another lobby identical to the one they'd just left.

"Pick up your suits here. Locker room is down the hall."

On their right, a pair of officers in sleeveless red-on-white skin-tight combat suits were greeting the students as they arrived, checking identifications and handing out vacuum-sealed bags. Rei and Viv joined the lines, reaching the staffers together.

"Ward... Reidon," the rightmost of the two—a young woman with short-cropped, ping hair—handled Rei while the other addressed Viv. "Confirmed. Here's your suit. It has some minimal automatic adjustment, but if you need any major changes done over the course of the year you'll have to take it to the Quartermaster." The officer handed the black airtight bag to Rei. "Locker room is around the bend behind me. Lockers will tune to your NOED. Next!"

As the next person in line was waved forward, Rei waited briefly for Viv before they set off quickly down the hall together. They found the locker room as directed— a set of double-doors that opened for them as they approached, and stepped into a wide, clean chamber with rows of rectangular steel storage compartments extending from the white floor to black ceiling. Rei saw privacy stalls in the back of the space for those who desired them—not much more than two plasteel barriers and a heavy curtain—but most of the cadets already getting ready were stripping down in the aisles, putting their uniforms and belongings away before pulling their new combat suits over their undergarments.

Viv nudged Rei, motioning towards the far end the room, and the two found a mostly empty aisle along the north wall, occupied only by a single boy and girl neither of them recognized. Nodding politely to the pair, they chose their lockers with a command of their frames, Rei tossing his cap inside and kicking off his boots before unsealing the black bag.

The uniform was exactly as he'd expected, the same solid shade of gray as their armbands, with the red griffin of the academy standing in its square across their chest. More red trailed in lines down the uniform's shoulders, torso, and legs, ending at the armless seams and the cut-offs just above the knee. Pulling off his jacket and slacks, Rei hung them carefully in the locker, noting gratefully a slight reduction in gravity inside the storage space that would help reduce creasing. This done, he pulled off his shirt and did the same.

Almost on cue, there was a gasp from behind him.

Rei didn't turn around, letting the two cadets sharing the aisle with him and Viv make what they wanted of his scars. He knew what he looked like, knew how he must have appeared with the countless laser burns and the longer markings of the more involved surgeries that traced his spine, shoulders, knees, and peeked above the lining of his underwear. He didn't say a word, stepping into the open back of the combat suit and sliding his arms through the holes provided for them, pulling the uniform up all at once. The moment it was comfortably adjusted, Rei felt fabric close itself up automatically at his back.

Neat.

"Show's over. Keep gawking and I'm gonna charge you for tickets."

Viv's voice was steady as she spoke, but Rei could imagine her glaring daggers down the aisle. There was a squawk of surprise and the sounds of a couple quiet apologies being hastily made, then the closing of two lockers before the patter of bare feet over the white flooring told Rei he and Viv were alone.

"*Those* whispers will be fun to hear later," he said as nonchalantly as he could, still not turning around.

Viv only muttered in answer, her annoyance lost to the chatter and slamming doors all around them.

It didn't take them long to figure out where they were supposed to be headed after leaving the locker room. They needed no signs to follow the hall north, away from the elevators, and before long a massive opening in the left wall could be made out, reaching clear to the ceiling some 20 or 30 yards overhead. Stepping through, Rei could absolutely understand Viv's awed hiss, as well as the gaping expressions hanging from the faces of the other students.

He didn't imagine he looked any more composed.

There, undoubtedly directly underneath the true Arena floor above their heads, a *second* Wargames field covered the massive, oblong chamber. 15 feet separated the shear wall for the 150-by-70-yard match space, outlined in its silver perimeter against the black projection plating. Whereas a traditional Wargames area was further subdivided into two Team Battle zones and four Dueling rings, *this* floor had clearly been specially designed, because in the absence of the former, no fewer than *six* 30-yard circles formed three lines of two in the wider field.

"There," Viv was the first to speak, pointing across the way from them. About half the class was already gathered around the far middle Dueling circle, most standing around talking, a few looking to be warming up in anticipation of whatever ordeal they were about to face. Among this second group, Rei didn't miss Aria Laurent bending side to side, her hair back up in the bun he'd seen yesterday in their match. They didn't meet eyes this time—the girl seemed attentively focused on something inside the perimeter of the field she was standing by—and as Rei and Viv approached with some other scattered stragglers he saw exactly what had her attention.

Near the middle of the ring, Valera Dent was talking intently with a group of six men and women who stood in front of her in a half-circle. While the captain wore regulars, the other staffers were in the red-on-white combat suits, and among them, Rei recognized the two who'd greeted them at the elevator, having obviously finished meeting the incoming 1-A students. Joining the other cadets around the ring, Rei tried to catch a word of what was being exchanged between Dent and what had to be her sub-instructors, but they were too far away to make out anything.

"At least they're leaving you alone this time."

Glancing around, Rei found Viv glaring in the direction of a small group, noticing the grey-orange hair of Leron, as well as the girl named Kay and their other, bald friend. This last boy actually saw the pair of them watching, and Rei was surprised when he got a brief nod of acknowledgment, which Leron or the others fortunately didn't take note of.

"Well… Looks like not everyone's a bad apple in the class, at least," Viv grunted, clearly having seen the gesture as well. Looking around, she studied the others somewhat apathetically. "So much *color.* Did no one's parents question whether yellow crimps with purple bleaching might even remotely be a bad idea, or do you think they just went with whatever the geneticists told them was going to be 'in' by the time their kids grew up?"

"Speak for yourself, blue-eyes-for-days." Rei gave her a sidelong look. "And you might have your natural shade, but don't tell me you believe your curls just stay perpetually perfect like that by magic."

Viv sniggered. Her hair was in a tail behind her head, and she *still* managed to look like a model in her two-tone outfit. "Talking to the kettle much, *pot?* I guess you think human eyes are just naturally slate-grey then, huh?"

Rei looked away pointedly. "You can't prove anything."

"Oh *bull*. We've had this fight before. You're as much a designer product as the rest of us freak shows."

Rei reached up to run a scarred hand through his white locks, thumbing the shaved sides of his head as he did. "I don't know about that. If that were the case, I feel like my sperm and egg donors would have wanted to give me some cool grey stripes or something. Even when my hair was black."

Viv looked at him blankly. "Would have made you look like an old man."

"The term you're looking for is 'silver fox', I believe."

"Are you *seventy*? No. So don't go getting ideas about dyeing your hair or—" Viv paused, frowning. After a moment, she spoke again in a low voice. "Can you give me any good reason why our class C-Ranker would be staring at the back of your head?"

Immediately Rei started to turn, and Viv only just barely caught him by the shoulder to stop him.

"Don't *look*, dummy!" She glanced past him instead, and seemed to relax. "She saw me catch her. She's turned away."

Rei made to look around again, and this time Viv let him. Whereas a minute ago Aria Laurent had been intent on Valera Dent and her entourage, it appeared that she'd now developed a sudden fascination with the sheer curve of the north wall as she shook her arms out, loosening her shoulders.

"She was looking at me earlier today, too," Rei finally said. "Before etiquette class this morning. That's why I said something was weird. She saw me for a second, but then was pretty obviously avoiding my eyes."

Viv considered this for a moment, mulling the information over.

Then her features broke out in a vapid, toothy grin. "Maybe she thinks your scars are hot."

"Oh shut up," Rei snorted, giving her a shove that barely budged her. Viv was all titters, but before she could tease him any more her face stilled, then settled into a glower. Rei, feeling his heart sink, turned around only to find his nose inches away from the body of a griffin. He had to tilt his head back to meet Logan Grant's eyes, and when he did he set his expression into as neutral a composition as his annoyance would allow.

"Can I help you?" he asked steadily.

Grant grunted, staring him down. "You're not a big fan of personal space, are you, Ward?" At his back the small group of other cadets he'd apparently spent the last 24 hours cultivating stood by, either smirking at Rei or watching him carefully.

"That's rich, coming from the guy who just walked up so close to my ass I could have confused you for part of my suit." Rei stepped away, easing the wrenching on his neck to meet the boy's eye. Grant really was *stupidly* tall, with what had to be almost a foot on his own stunted growth. "Do you want an autograph or something? Sorry, I left my pad in the locker."

Grant's lips twitched, and his gaze lifted first to Arada, then moved as he turned his head to peer over his shoulder.

"Between eyeing Laurent and shoving your girlfriend here around, you're giving me a seriously creepy vibe, friend," he said, finally looking back to Rei. "You're already well into the process of painting our class-block with a bad name just by being here, so I thought I could come over and have a chat while we wait for things to kick off."

"Oh. Cool. Then good chat."

Rei turned around, intending to grab Viv by the arm and pull her further along the edge of the Dueling field. Before he could take a step, though, Grant's question brought him up short.

"What's up with the scars?" the boy's voice carried, and suddenly a lot of heads were turning in their direction that had until-that-point been minding their own business. "You look like your mom had a one-and-done with a meat grinder."

Rei took a breath. Viv was shaking with indignation in front of him, but he gave her a minute shake of his head.

This was a battle he needed to start handing on his own.

"How many of your posse's names do you actually remember?" he responded, half-turning to look around at Grant again. When the boy's mouth tightened, Rei smirked. "See? Feels weird getting asked awkward questions, doesn't it?"

"What you think is awkward, others might consider valid." Grant's eyes were narrowed, apparently not used to being put on the defensive. "You're small, you're weak, and you're stupid. You proved all that yesterday the moment you volunteered to go up against a C-Ranker you had no business sharing a field with. If we're stuck with you for a year, Ward, then that means *someone* is always going to be wasting time and energy lugging your weight around. Some of us—" he spoke pointedly, making it very clearly who he was speaking of "—are gunning for heights you can't even dream of. Having to worry about carrying your ass through the next months is a burden we can't afford to shoulder. So if there's a reason you've shown up here looking like a messed-up scarecrow, we've got a right to know, don't you think?"

"Did I ask any of you to carry me?" Rei felt like spitting, the bitter taste in his mouth building up like he'd been forced to swallow something sour. "No. In fact, I haven't spoken a word to most any one of you, cause you're too busy staring, whispering, and breathing down my neck to have a conversation."

"We're having a conversation now, aren't we?" Grant said with a smirk.

"No. We're having an interrogation. A conversation would have involved you coming up to me and introducing yourself, instead of breathing down my neck like a dog in heat. Here, I'll demonstrate, since apparently *your* mom's fling was with some pretty-boy mannequin with shitty manners." He faced the boy, sticking out a hand. "Rei Ward. I heard you're a badass on the mats. Hope we can have a match sometime."

His aim had been to throw Grant off his game, and in that he'd definitely succeeded, at least for a moment. The boy blinked as he stared at the offered hand, obviously taken completely aback. A brief flurry of confusion crossed his face, and Rei could almost see the wheels turning in Grant's mind, trying to find the best way out of the situation he'd been presented with.

In the end, he chose the predictable path.

"You and me? In a match?" He sneered, crossing his arms to show he had no interest in shaking. "Get real, *E*. Laurent went easy on you yesterday because she's soft. I'm not." The curling of his lip was an ugly marring against his handsome features. "Tell you what: anytime you want to fight, just say the word. I'll show you every reason you shouldn't be here weighing us down that Laurent was too nice to."

Rei let his arm drop. "Sounds good to me. I'll take you up on that sometime. Maybe if I grind your face into the field hard enough you'll wake up less of a dick."

And with that he spun on his heels, taking Viv by the arm and dragging her away. Grant made a strangled sound behind them, obviously finally losing his cool, but Rei didn't look back as a few of the cadets who'd been standing by watching stepped smartly aside to let them by.

"'If I grind your face into the field hard enough'?" Viv repeated with a snigger when they reached the end of the gathered group, separating themselves a little from the others. "Nice line, drama queen."

"Shut up," Rei grumbled, feeling his cheeks go red at the thought. "He pissed me off. It slipped out."

"Yeah, well… Guess now you really do need to put the pedal to the metal on that Growth rank of yours, huh? Pretty sure sexy gorilla-boy back there is gonna be gunning for your skin any chance he gets." She looked over her shoulder mournfully.

"It's too bad. He's *seriously* hot."

"Hey. No repeats of Mikael Dorsey. You got it?"

Viv snorted. "Hell no. Dorsey had buck teeth and never heard of a comb. There's no *way* I'd be able to keep my hands off Grant for a whole month."

"Encouraging," Rei muttered, rolling his eyes.

It was at that moment, fortunately, that a pulse of light caught everyone's attention, turning their focus to the field whose eastern edge they'd scattered around. Valera Dent and the other instructors were striding towards them even as a white platform started to rise beneath their feet, much like the one that had brought the officers of the Commencement Ceremony up to the height of the viewing galleries. This one only lifted some 3 feet off the ground, however, and so by the time the captain reached the end she was just high enough above the students to address everyone at once.

"Good afternoon, cadets!" The woman spoke clearly, her voice echoing a little in the vastness of the subbasement as the six officers in combat suits jumped down lightly from the platform to stand before her, facing the first years. "Given everyone arrived on time, I'm going to get things started. As the only reminder I will offer you: I am Captain Valera Dent, your chief combat instructor. I will be overseeing the majority of your practical training and conditioning over the course of the next three years, as well as the application of parameter testing and coordination of Galens' traveling SCT team."

There was a murmur of interest at that, and the captain looked visibly amused.

"Thought that would get a few of you excited, yes. As I'm sure most of you are aware, the collegiate tournaments extend to the Interstellar level, just like the professional circuits. While Major Dyrk Reese will oversee all Intra-School combat, any individual or team who qualifies for Sectionals and above will be under my purview, so I hope you're all willing to bleed to get there."

Several people voiced their assertion, but the captain was already moving on.

"Obviously we are not here for practical training or SCT prep, however. As your week's schedule dictates, today you will be partaking in your initial parameters testing. These officers—" she indicated the six in red-on-white standing at ease at her feet "—are your Type-instructors. They will be administering the assessment, which involves three distinct parts." She held up a finger. "The first is designed to measure your speed and agility. The second—" a second finger came up "—will quantify your endurance and offensive ability. The third—" a final finger, and the hint of a smile on the woman's synthetic lips "—your fortitude. Some of you—" she dropped her hands as grumbling could be heard from the first years "—are now complaining to your friends that there doesn't seem much point to such testing. After all, your CAD-Rank generally measures those exact parameters, do they not?" She shook her head. "Incorrect, and you are best served separating yourself from that concept as soon as possible. CAD-Ranking and specifications are nothing more than measurement of what you *could* do. Not what you *can*. This assessment is designed not to gauge what you and your Device are theoretically capable of, but rather the limit of your true, current capabilities." She lifted an arm, showing off the blue-red with white band of her A-Type Device, the famous "Kestrel". "Today, you are establishing a baseline of how well you wield your own potential, as well as that of your CAD. This testing will be reapplied every quarter, and I encourage you to strive for improvements in every way, every time."

As she dropped her hand again, the light of her neuro-optic blazed across Dent's eyes. A moment later a massive "3" shimmered into being behind and above her, floating over the Dueling field. All around them, the other fields were labeled in the same fashion.

"Find your instructors, and follow their direction." Dent's NOED vanished with a blink. "Every cadet will have three opportunities to attempt each test. Do not let them go to waste."

Before anyone realized they had been dismissed to their orders, the sub-instructors were yelling over their gathered numbers.

"Sabers! To me!"

"Lancers! Here on Field 3!"

"Maulers—!"

Steadily the crowd dispersed, and Viv gave Rei a brief wave of farewell as the Duelists were called to Field 4. Soon Rei was left standing on his own, watching Valera Dent expectantly.

It didn't take her long to catch his eye.

"Ward, you're with the Brawlers for the time being. Field 1."

Snapping the woman a quick salute of acknowledgement, Rei hurried off to the most southwest of the six smaller circles.

There were four others in his group, he saw as he reached the field. Evenly split with two girls and two boys, he didn't know how to react when he realized the bald cadet who'd been shadowing Leron was among the Brawlers. No one saw him coming up from behind, however, so Rei had no opportunity to deduce anyone's reaction before the sub-instructor caught sight of him lagging.

"You're late, Ward," the man growled. He was younger, with shoulders so broad he likely had to turn to make it through a typical door, and he was eyeing Rei over a trimmed brown beard. "I'm not a fan of repeating myself, least of all an introduction."

"Sorry, sir," Rei apologized the moment he'd fallen in beside a short girl with cropped hair the color of fresh brick. He considered making an excuse about his delayed assignment, but thought better of it.

The instructor nodded curtly, eyeing him—and his stature specifically—for a second more before returning his attention again to the group as a whole.

"As I was saying, my name is Chief Warrant Officer Michael Bretz. I will be your primary instructor for the foreseeable future. I'm a Brawler-Type, A8." He smirked as several jaws fell open, but didn't address their astonishment. "As the captain already said, you'll be participating in a trio of different assessments today, with all of you having the right to three attempts at each." He indicated the ring behind him with a wave. "The first is Speed & Agility, and will encompass all thirty yards of your standard Dueling field. You will receive an explanation once the projection is in place, but are there any question for the moment?"

"How will we be scored, sir?" the other girl, dark-skinned and orange-eyed, asked smartly from the other end of the line.

"Different for every test, but that will be explained as well. Any other questions?"

When everyone was silent for a few seconds, the warrant officer nodded his approval. "Good, then moving right along. I need a volunteer to go first."

Silence answered him, all five of their group tensing at once. Rei knew well what was going through everyone's heads. It had crossed his in the same moment. Assuming they were all going to be allowed to watch the test being administered, there was a distinct advantage to avoiding being the first participant. At the end of the day, after all, every cadet at Galens was in competition first and foremost with the other students if they wanted a shot at getting beyond the Intra-School SCT…

Everyone except Rei, who could only hope whatever abysmal score he would ring up today would one day be nothing but a bad memory…

"I will, sir," he spoke up after almost 10 seconds of silence, raising a hand.

Bretz looked briefly impressed, as though he hadn't expected anyone to volunteer, much less Rei.

"I like not having to pick someone out of the crowd, Ward. Points for balls."

The sub-instructor's NOED came to life, and a moment later a circle of red light—identical to the starting ring of a true match—was glowing against the black plating beside him, a few feet inside the silver ring of the field. He pointed at it. "Stand here. The rest of you—" he waved a hand towards the others, and five other rings formed outside the perimeter, 10 feet apart "—take a seat. You are allowed to watch, but not to discuss what you see or share information until *all* of you have taken part in all three attempts. Is that understood?"

Four nods, and four rears planted firmly on the plating in all but one of the circles a few moments later.

Bretz, meanwhile, was still giving orders to his neuro-optic. When he was finished, a disk of light about 2 yards wide appeared under his feet, lifting him a short ways off the ground.

"The Speed & Agility test," he started simply, and as he spoke what had to be the assessment field began to materialize all around them. "After a five second countdown, you will have fifteen seconds to hit as many disks as possible. You can use any means at your disposal, but *must* touch the disk with some striking part of your body, be it hands, feet, head, knees, whatever. Any questions?"

Rei would have shaken his head, but he was too busy staring in wonder.

The projection, which had lifted him off the gym floor about 3 feet as it manifested, looked to be a variation of the "Neutral Zone" field that was actually one of the more popular SCT fighting spaces among fans. Whereas that simulation was nothing but an empty white void with a flat floor and cylindrical walls, *this* space had more detail applied to it. For starters, the ground was anything but level. Hexagonal pillars each 2 feet in diameter made up the flooring, sunken and elevated alike, with most on the same plane as Rei, but some extending as high as 10 feet above his head in intricate waves and a staircase of altitudes.

More distracting, however, were the "discs" Bretz had made clear were the singular goal of the test.

About half a foot in diameter and a fraction of an inch thick, some hundred black circles floated above the field at various heights. It would have been bad enough that a few hung less than a few yards from the subbasement ceiling high above them,, but the fact that they were all *moving* made the sight all the more intimidating. In an endless frequency of patterns the black shapes dipped and darted, circling and flipping and rising in as many directions and at as many speeds as there were actual discs. It only took a glance for Rei to realize that those closest to him were the most stable, low to the ground and hardly dancing about at all in comparison, but the further and higher he looked from the starting point the more the circles became a blur of movement, like a swarm of dark insects buzzing about in an utter, eerie silence.

"Cadet. Call."

The warrant officer's platform had lifted him some 20 feet almost straight up in the air, well out of the way, and the formality of his order told Rei he'd lost any opportunity he might have had to voice any potential questions. With a pang of apprehension he brought his arms up to just below his face, feeling most natural in assuming the loose combat stance that had been drilled into him by a 1000 repetitions of fighting simulations over the last 10 weeks.

For a little while, he'd forgotten about this part…

Taking a breath and focusing, Rei opened his mouth just as the number "5" flashed into being a foot in front of his face.

"Call."

4.

Shido whirled into being, encasing his hands in its still-alien black plating, the carbon steel claws protruding from his right knuckles glinting as they caught the light.

3.

There were gasps from behind him, and someone swore.

2.

Blocking out all distraction, Rei brought up his NOED, letting the display register the situation.

1.

In an instant his frame highlighted the pattern of the moving disks in curving red lines, and he locked onto his first target.

0.

CHAPTER 18

Rei launched himself from the starting circle, hurling towards his chosen disk. Shido's claw took it through the middle, and it vanished with a pixilated *bzzt* of sound. Already moving on, Rei planted a foot on a raised pillar and shoved up as hard as he could into the air, aiming for two higher discs in the process of swinging towards each other as they followed the red lines provided by his NOED. He caught one with his left hand but missed the other, landing and rolling again to come up running. A third he swiped when it flashed by him as he passed, and a fourth that darted low to a ground, almost between his legs. Vaulting over a chest-high wall of the hexagonal prisms and kicking deftly through a fifth as he did, Rei threw himself in the direction of a descending pair he hoped would be his sixth and seventh.

Just as his fingers were about to touch them, though, the disks vanished, and he stumbled to an awkward halt.

"Time!" Bretz bellowed. "Total: 5 discs. Ward, recall and take a seat. Gisham, you're up next!"

Straightening up, Rei did as he was told, Shido dematerializing to bands as he made for the empty fifth ring outside the perimeter of the field. He caught the eye of the second test-taker—the girl with buzzed, reddish-orange hair—and would have tried to wish her a silent good luck had it not been for her expression. She wasn't… angry, per se. More so, the cadet looked confused, her attention flicking briefly to his CAD before they passed each other as she took up a starting position. Rei had been expecting it, but he still groaned internally when he saw the wide eyes of the others taking him in too, a mixture of shock and disbelief scattered across their faces.

Reaching his ring, Rei sat down without looking around at anyone, choosing instead to commit himself to watching and learning.

The disks had reappeared, the ones he had touched replaced in identical locations. They moved in the same dizzying pattern, and above the mess of flashing black circles Chief Warrant Officer Bretz still stood on his floating platform, observing carefully.

"Cadet. Call."

With a word from Gisham, a pair of red-and-green gauntlets encased the girl's forearms, matching the colors of the jointed-steel boots that shimmered into being around her lower legs and feet. Rei took the Device in with interest as the countdown began to flash, noting the hint of dark blue vysetrium between the plates not unlike his own.

Then the marker hit 0, and Gisham was moving.

She chose an identical starting angle as he had, her neuro-optics likely presenting her with similar variables if the system started the test at the exact same moment in the discs' patterns each time. With impressive speed she barreled through the first, then leapt into the air for the second and third. From there, however, she changed direction, pounding up a simulated staircase formed by the flat tops of the hexagon before throwing herself off one side, arms and legs flashing. Four-five-six. The girl landed and came up lunging, diving at another grouping, smashing through them before jumping for yet another pair.

"Time!" Bretz shouted, and the discs winked out again, leaving Gisham to pull herself up as she caught her breath. "Total: 11 discs. Not bad, cadet. Recall and exit the field. Emble! On deck!"

It was in such a fashion the next three took their exam, claiming 10, then 13, then 14 discs each. By the time the bald boy Rei knew now to be "Senson" proved himself a particularly quick mover, a lot had been shown and a lot had been learned.

"Ward! Round two!"

Getting to his feet, Rei entered the ring with his NOED already live this time. The others had all ended up taking a slightly different approach to their test, but everyone started the same, which told him he definitely had that part right. Memorizing his plan of attack quickly, he stepped into the ring as Senson exited, catching the boy's glance at him from the corner of his eye.

No. Focus.

He summoned Shido. The countdown started once more. He waited for the 0, watching the movement of the discs.

Then he launched himself forward again.

"Time!" Bretz announced 15 seconds later. "Total: 8 discs. Good improvement, Ward. Gisham, up you get!"

The Brawlers of 1-A proved themselves a clever lot over the course of the next two rounds, clearly observing and learning from each other's success and failures. When Bretz called an end to Senson's last attempt, Rei had managed to up his count to 9 discs, which he might have been proud of had that not been *half* of the second lowest scorer's, and almost a full third of Senson's top count of 24.

"Good effort, all of you." Bretz's stern expression didn't change, but he sounded pleased as his platform came down to sink into the field floor, now returned to black plating. "Next up is Offense & Endurance, but take a five-minute reprieve while I set up the program. You are now free to discuss your Speed & Agility test, if you'd like, but stay here. No disturbing the other instructional groups."

At once everyone stood from the relatively uncomfortable flooring, the other four converging on each other as the other Type-groups continued their identical testing on their respective fields around them. After a few seconds hesitation, Rei moved to join the Brawlers.

"It evolved," he heard the dark-skinned girl named Warren whispering as he approached. "I know it has."

"No way," the other boy, Emble, breathed, his rows of natural brown hair glistening with sweat from the exertion. "Not possible."

"Totally possible," Rei cut in, stepping into the ring of the group and looking around in resignation. "And if you wanted to know about it, why not just ask?"

All four of the others drew back from him, and a few faces flushed at being caught. Eventually, though, Senson cracked what looked like it might have been an actual smile.

"Fair enough," he conceded, eyes sliding down to Shido's bands. "Put us out of our misery, then, Ward. Your Device evolved, didn't it?"

Rei considered a snarky answer, but decided to give the group the benefit of the doubt. Take a breath, he nodded. "Yeah. Happened after the match against Laurent yesterday. You guys really shouldn't be surprised, though. I'm an E-Ranker, while most of you are probably mid-D's I'm guessing? All of you already have multiple components to your Devices." He lifted a hand to shake Shido indicatively. "You all saw my CAD during the fight, right? Pretty bare bones."

"To put it mildly," Warren said with a snort, but a glare from Senson shut her up.

"So you're just… What…? Catching up?" Gisham asked tentatively.

Rei gave a laugh. "I don't know about 'catching up'. I'm pretty far behind you guys. I mean, just look at our agility scores. But climbing from low-Es is *bound* to happen faster than ranking up in the Ds, isn't it? Especially at a place like Galens."

It was only half a lie. If he could steadily ensure even a fraction of the kind of improvement he'd seen after duking it out with Laurent, Rei was on a course to catch up and then some. As it stood, however, there was no need for anyone other than him and Viv to know that. CAD-Rank was public knowledge, so it was only a matter of time before someone made the realization. If Rei could settle some of the animosity his enrollment was obviously causing in the meantime, though, things would probably be easier when that time came.

"Makes sense…" the boy named Emble agreed after a brief silence as all of them contemplated. "I was a D0 on assignment. I'm surprised I made it in, honestly. But I'm a D2 now, whereas I bet most of you guys—" he glanced around at the other three "—got maybe a Rank, right?"

"Not even," Senson admitted with a barely-repressed scowl. "Parents couldn't afford a trainer, so I've been a D5 since passing the exam."

"Same," Gisham echoed with a sigh. "D4 since the day I got Feron." She lifted her own CAD to clarify.

"See? So don't be surprised. And *don't*—" he cut across Warren quickly when the girl opened her mouth as she stared at him suspiciously "—ask me what I'm doing here with all of you. I've been grilled on that twice today already, in case you didn't notice, and I've got no more answers now than fifteen minutes ago."

"One minute, cadets!" Bretz's voice rang out from the field. "Return to you places."

With a last curious look at Rei, Gisham, Emble, and Warren all did as they were instructed. Intending to do the same, Rei himself turned to go back, but a hand on his arm held him up for a second.

"Hey, listen man…" Senson seemed a little uncomfortable as Rei looked around again in surprise. "About Leron, this morning… I'm sorry about that. He's my room-mate, and honestly doesn't seem like a bad guy. I didn't think he was gonna take things that far when he said he wanted to talk to you…"

Rei searched the boy's face for a hint of deception, but found nothing. As far as he could tell, the cadet genuinely felt bad.

"Don't worry about it," he said with a shrug. "I get the feeling I'm gonna have to get used to it for a while. At least until I crawl out of the E-Ranks, or they realize there's been a mistake and finally kick me out of here." He offered Senson a crooked smile that was only a little rigid. "But I appreciate the apology."

Senson answered with the start of his own grin, but before he could say another word Bretz's bellow caught across their conversation.

"WARD! SENSON! Do I have to repeat how much I DO NOT LIKE TO REPEAT MYSELF?!"

With mutual looks of horrified realization the pair of them whirled together to face the warrant officer, snapping to attention. "No, sir! Sorry, sir!" they exclaimed together, then split to hurry back to their rings as the others watched.

Bretz glared after them for a long moment, even once they'd both taken a seat, but eventually either gave them the grace of it being their first day or just couldn't be bothered with chewing them out further. Instead he pointed at the field behind him, which was not a solid surface of projected white.

"As I said, next is your Offense & Endurance test. You will take position in the center of the field." Behind him, a red circle manifested as indicated. "Alternating in these two points—" two more circles, black this time, appeared about 5 yards each due north and south of the starting position "—an opponent will appear. These projections will imitate an adversary with uniform CAD-specs, starting at F0, and moving up five ranks at a time. You're task is deal Fatal Damage Accrued as quickly as possible. You will have two opponents at each rank—F0, F5, E0, E5, et cetera—and they will not attack you, nor make any significant attempt to move away from their starting positions unless you force them to. They will, however, defend themselves, and dodge attacks. The test ends when any opponent has lasted more than thirty seconds before FDA." The warrant officer scanned his Brawlers critically. "This test actually quantifies two areas that can be improved on. Can anyone tell me what they are?"

Unsurprisingly, all five hands went up.

"Emble." Bretz addressed the boy with rowed brown hair.

"Number of opponents dealt FDA, and how quickly FDA is dealt per rank, sir."

"Precisely." The warrant officer nodded shortly. "It goes without saying that no two Users are exactly the same. That means that their skillsets will never be identical either. One of you might be able to overpower an opponent quickly, but be outclassed by more-capable enemies, whereas another might outlast bigger and stronger adversaries, but struggle in actually *ending* a fight. These are hugely important factors to consider, *particularly* when deciding on tactics, squad composition, and positioning for Team Battle and Wargame formats. Follow?"

All together the five of them nodded, and Rei studied Bretz in a little bit of a new light. Nothing the man had said would be news to most tournament enthusiasts, but the fact that he was already taking the time to drill them on combat tactics had Rei considering that Valera Dent was probably pretty particular when it came to her sub-instructors.

"Good." The warrant officer turned his attention on Senson. "Since you apparently have enough free-time to laze around chatting after I've given you a directive, you can go first, cadet."

Senson nodded without a word of argument, pushing himself up to step onto the field and move to take up a position in the red starting ring.

"First opponent will project at the north point. The next will appear to the south immediately after FDA is announced, then back again. Any questions?"

Senson shook his head, shifting around to face the black circle Bretz had indicated.

"Cadet. Call."

Senson's Device manifested in a blur, an emerald sheen atop a dark underlay and white vysetrium. His fingers had no individual plating, making dexterous movement difficult, but the heavy steel of his bracers extended over his wrists and knuckles into two lethal punch daggers. Like Gisham, Senson's CAD had started to extend to his legs, but his boots came higher than the girl's had, encapsulating his knees as Aria Laurent's red-and-gold greaves had the day before.

The 5 second countdown initiated, and Rei held his breath as it ticked away. At 3 a shape manifested at the north circle, a modestly rendered figure of a tall woman, entirely monotone grey down to her skin-tight combat suit. At 1 the projection's hands were up, ready to defend, and Rei noticed that it had the digits "F0" marked in clean black on its back.

Then 0 hit, and Senson rocketed forward with a shout.

The poor projection didn't have a hope in the world. The Cadet's right first broke through its guard—no stronger that the average human's—and Rei doubted the head of the punch dagger plowing into the F0's chest had been necessary. Indeed, 4 seconds after the start of the match the automated voice of the Arena rang out.

"Fatal Damage Accrued."

On the field Senson whirled. A second opponent had appeared—this one taking the shape of a man colored in identical grey. A similar "F0" labeled its chest, however, and so it lasted no longer than the first, collapsing in the same fashion the moment the cadet crossed the 10 yards to reach it.

"Fatal Damage Accrued."

The woman reappeared, on this occasion marked with "F5." It took only momentarily longer to down, managing to deflect Senson's right fist only to take a follow-up blow from his left squarely in the face. The man manifested, and this time the Brawler was even quicker, anticipating the initial deflection to bring an end the projection a full second faster with a similar one-two combo. The E0s appeared after that, followed by the E5, all four projected opponents proving only moderately more difficult to handle.

Finally, when the first D0 presented itself, there came the barest semblances of a real fight.

Senson's opening strike was deflected, as was his follow-up, then his third. The cadet tried for a heavy side kick, which his opponent promptly ducked under, but Senson managed to halt the momentum of his leg to bring the steel heel of his boot straight down on the crown of the woman's head. She fell to all fours, and a ripping punch to its temple announced FDA again.

The second D0 manifested, and this time Senson was a little faster. He feigned a thrust with his right, the projection adjusting to block his left when it came around, but leaving itself open for two quick jabs to the side. Before it could recover, Senson swept the feet out from under his opponent, following the falling body down to stab a punch dagger deep into its chest.

Unfortunately, it was the first D5 that finally bested the boy's time limit.

The woman's projection moved nearly as fast as he did, deftly blocking, redirecting, and dodging the heavy blows as they came in. A kick caught her crossed arms, sending her staggering back over the white floor three full paces, but she kept her balance well enough to drop under a following windmill punch at her head. For a few more exchanges they battled it out like that, Senson trying to break her guard, the projection managing just to keep it.

"Time!" Chief Warrant Officer Bretz called. He hadn't taken to the air for this test, instead watching the fight from a safe distance across the field floor. "First D5 reached. Total time: 3:06.34. Excellent start, Senson. Off you get."

The cadet only nodded his thanks, too winded to get a word in, and it was as he left the center of the ring that Rei really understood the second measure being tested with this assessment: Endurance.

He was already cursing his misfortune when the warrant officer's eyes fell on him.

"Ordinarily I would have had you go last, Ward, but maybe next time you and Senson will be quicker on the draw when it comes to following orders. You're up."

Rei had seen it coming, but still felt a weight of anxiety plummet from his throat into his gut as he got to his feet. Stepping onto the field, he approached the red starting ring at its center with no small measure of apprehension. He forced himself to take a calming breath, forced himself to focus. Senson was several times faster and stronger, but his fighting was heavier. If Rei could beat even one of the D0s, too, maybe he could earn himself a little credit with the class, or even just the Brawlers...

Reaching the starting ring, he turned to face north.

"Cadet. Call."

Shido slipped over Rei's hands, and the countdown began. He watched it tick by, bringing his arms up and planting his feet. The grey woman shimmered into being on the other side of the numbers.

Then the clock ran out.

Rei was slower than the others by far, but his speed was still one of his greatest assets. He was across the 5 yards in a heartbeat, punching just as Senson had. He hadn't had an opportunity to spend any time testing out Shido's evolution, so he stuck to his form, trusting the claws of his right hand could only make even his basic abilities more lethal. Indeed, his punch caught against the woman's blocking arms, but the razored steel ripped through, skewering a wrist before burying multiple inches of metal into the projection's skull.

"Fata Damage Accrued."

Wrenching Shido free, Rei spun and launched himself across the white floor of the Arena. The F0 man was ready and waiting for him, and Rei decided to try a feint with his left. His opponent turned reflexively, opening up the side of its head for a clean blow from the claws.

"Fatal Damage Accrued."

The F5 appeared, and Rei sprinted back again, steeling himself. He opened with a forward kick, leading with all of his momentum, but the move was apparently telegraphed because the woman side-stepped. He managed to catch himself barely, stopping from careening by, and he turned on the projection with a vengeance, punching at its torso, head, and sides. The F5 dodged a few of his blows, even deflecting one or two others, but it slipped up by dropping its hands to stave off a second frontal kick. The moment its guard was down, Rei's left fist clocked it in the side of the head, sending it staggering sideways. With a yell he lunged, razored metal going for the woman's throat.

"Time!"

The projection vanished, and with a choking sound Rei dove through nothing, managing to tuck himself into a roll before bouncing to his feet.

"First F5 reached. Total time: 0:52.34. Step off the field, Ward. Warren!"

Feeling distinctly let down by his own performance, Rei recalled Shido and walked out of the ring. Reaching his designated circle, he sat down heavily, trying to force himself to pay attention as Warren began her fight. Both F0s were down in 15 seconds, and the F5s took her only a little longer than Senson's attempt. The girl slowed down a lot at the D0s, but passed, only to also get completely locked out by the first D5.

"Time! First D5 reached. Total time: 3:37.62. Emble! On deck!"

Emble reached the second D0 before his Endurance seemed to end him, but Gisham ended up with the fastest time reaching the D5s, breaking the 3-minute mark. Senson stood up again when called, but Rei tuned out of the fight, contemplating his own next attempt.

What could he do differently…? That had actually been a fairly good showing for himself, though he'd remember not to open with all his impetus behind a kick if he wasn't *absolutely* sure it would land. Aside from that mistake, his fighting had been fairly clean, so he wasn't clear on what adjustments he could make in order to clock a better performance this time around, much less during his third shot at the test. He considered, eyes only distantly on the battle before him.

He *did* have one chance, but he was loath to attempt such a major change in his style without having been able to so much as put Shido's new form through a test run…

"Time! Second D5 reached. Total time: 3:19.09. Good improvement, Senson. Ward! Second attempt!"

Making his choice, Rei took to his feet once more. By the time he was in the starting circle, he'd planned out his assaults, hoping he wasn't overestimating the value of his CAD's evolution.

Shido formed in his hands, and the countdown hit 0.

His first two opponents, Rei took as before, feeling the hits come a little cleaner now. When the F5 that had bested him materialized, he sprinted at the woman again, making a firm fist of his right hand to cut diagonally down at the projection, hoping he'd judged the distance accurately. His opponent brought an arm out to block the blow, but instead of wrist it caught sharped steel, and with a thrill Rei felt the claws cleave through the F5's defense. The woman's hand went lip, but the swing carried through, carving into one side of her chest. FDA wasn't announced, but the projection sagged and fell to one knee, looking up at him with colorless eyes in time to catch a large amount of black-and-white metal in the face.

"Fatal Damage Accrued."

YES! Rei celebrated internally, but he otherwise kept his focus as he whirled. He had a little more trouble with the man—the projection's thicker arms kept most of the damage away from its torso following the same opening slash—but he managed it all the same. The second F5 fell, and Rei turned again to take on the E0 with her arms already at the ready. Shido worked its cruel magic much the same, and it was the *E5* woman, this time, than bested him.

30 seconds into the blitz of a fight with the projection, Bretz's shout cut the match off.

"Time! First E5 reached. Total time: 2:31:14. Excellent adjustment, Ward. Next!"

Panting, Rei took to his spot, rather pleased with himself. He didn't think he had a shot in a hundred for beating the E5 in only 30 seconds in a straight on fight—not yet, at least—but even Bretz's simple praise was enough to tell him he was thinking in the right direction.

The second attempts wrapped, then the third. Rei focused only on shaving time off his completions, managing to reach the first E5 again a full 4.5 seconds faster. Trading places with Warren—*seriously* winded this time—a pleasant surprise greeted him not long after he half-sat, half-collapsed into his ring, arriving in the form of text scrawling across his NOED.

...

Processing combat information.

...

Calculating.

...

Results:
Strength: Lacking
Endurance: Severely Lacking
Speed: Lacking
Cognition: Lacking

Offense: Lacking

Defense: Lacking

Growth: Not Applicable

…

Checking combat data acquisition.

…

Adequate data acquirement met.

Device initiating adjustments to:

Endurance.

…

Adjustment complete.

Endurance has been upgraded from Rank F4 to F5.

Hiding his delight, Rei accepted a bottle of chilled water from one of several buzzing service drones who had appeared from the hall sometime in the last 10 minutes. Covering his grin by chugging half the drink's contents down immediately, he realized he shouldn't have been so surprised. He *was* participating in training, and one of a fashion not unlike the simulated instruction he'd been following all summer. If anything, he was a bit disappointed fighting projections brought him so little *despite* his S-Ranked Growth. Abruptly, Rei recalled the itch he'd experienced when he'd taken in Aria Laurent for the first time, when he'd seen past her attractive features and form to the C-Ranked beast that lay beneath.

All of a sudden, Rei realized he wanted to fight again.

Not Laurent specifically, he deduced after a moment's more ponder, sipping on the rest of his water. Anyone. Anyone who could challenge him. He itched to see what would happen after his next match, itched to see what would happen *in* the match. His specs might be abysmal, but they had all made a significant jump just from the Commencement Ceremony.

He wanted to see what he could do, and continue to get a sense of where he and Shido could go together…

"Time! Second D5 reached. Total time: 3:12.41. Good wrap, Gisham." With a wave of his hand, Bretz dismissed the field, the projection vanishing to leave short-haired cadet on all fours, gasping for breath atop the cleared plating. The chief warrant officer waited for her to recover, and once she'd staggered back out of the Dueling perimeter he addressed them all again.

"Excellent work, all. Some of you have a ways more to go than others, but everyone saw improvement across all three attempts. I commend you for that. Take another five while I set up the final assessment."

This time Rei and the other Brawlers made no move to gather. Even Senson, who'd completed the test first some 10 minutes ago, was still sweating, though he'd looked to have caught his breath fairly quickly. In a contented silence the five of them kept to their rings this time, chugging each from their own waters and distracting themselves by finally turning to watch the activities around them.

Fields 2, 3, and 4 penned them in to the east, north, and north-east respectively, and only the Duelists in the lattermost had finished the second test quicker than Rei's group. He caught sight of Viv among them, but she now sat with her back to the Brawlers, breathing hard after what must have been a recent attempt. At 2 the Sabers looked to be wrapping up, while at 3 the Lancers clearly had several rounds to go. It was fascinating watching the different Types' approach to the unarmed opponents, and Rei noticed that both group's delay appeared to be because they were getting further in the test than the Brawlers had.

"Must be nice to have a sword."

There was a *thump*, and Rei looked around to find that Senson had ended up getting to his feet after all, for some reason electing to join him in observing the other groups.

Not one to ignore an olive branch, Rei nodded. "The other Types will have an advantage in the earlier ranks when it comes to Offense, since their Devices give them more reach than Brawler weaponry. But look—" he lifted a scarred finger to point out the Lancer group, where a girl with a vibrant green-blue and black spear was trying to break through the guard of a C0 "—I don't see anyone other than Aria Laurent showing any lower extremity armor, apart from you guys."

"Yeah I noticed that too." The bald boy looked at Rei sidelong. "Is that normal?"

Rei shrugged. "Not sure, but I would assume so. If Brawlers lack in Offense initially, it would make sense there would be a compensation in Speed or the like. If they post the results of the exams, I'll bet you four are in the top for the first test, maybe only behind the Duelists, and at the bottom for the second."

"Huh." Senson watched him a moment longer. "You *actually* scored a ninety-nine percent on the written exam, didn't you?"

"Almost," Rei corrected him with a laugh. "98.7, if you want to be specific."

"Damn…" the boy muttered, obviously impressed. "Then what about the third test? Where are we gonna be there?"

"No idea," Rei admitted. "Depends on what *exactly* they're testing us on."

"Didn't Dent say fortitude?"

"Yeah, she did…" Rei frowned. "That's kinda what bothers me, though…"

"Because Defense can't be a fun thing to have tested."

Rei looked around, and it was his turned to be impressed. "You read my mind."

"I told you this morning when Loren was being a dick, I scored a ninety-five on the written myself." Senson chuckled. "We're fortunate enough to be in a school where no one's going to be an idiot."

"Depends on your definition…" Rei grumbled, conjuring up—unbidden—the face a certain black-haired behemoth.

"Fair," the boy grinned, then grew serious again. "But yeah, I was thinking the same thing myself. If we break down the specs we've already been tested on, leaving out Growth we can count Speed and Cognition in the first test, then Strength, Endurance, and Offense in the second. Which leaves us with…"

"Defense," Rei finished with a sigh. "Yeah. Exactly."

There was another silence as both of them took in this understanding.

"This last one is probably gonna suck, isn't it?" Senson grumbled finally.

Rei smirked. "For sure."

The bald cadet nodded. Then, with a deep, tight breath like he was steeling himself to jump off a cliff, he shoved himself up. "Should get back to my spot before Bretz has an excuse to skin us." He looked down at Rei, looking like he were considering something.

Then, tentatively, he held out a hand.

"You tried introducing yourself this morning. I'm sorry again that Leron was an ass about it. I can't say I know what the hell you're doing here, man, but you seem okay, so I'll believe you if you say you don't know." Senson smirked good-naturedly. "Or at least I'll believe you've got a decent reason not to explain yourself."

Rei managed a tight laugh, but reached up to accept the hand. "I appreciate that. Rei Ward. But you already knew that."

"Bandt Senson," the boy answered, shaking. Even controlling himself, his grip indeed hinted at an impressive Strength spec. "Everyone calls me 'Sense', though." They let go. "Good luck on the third test, man."

"You too, Sense." Rei replied with a nod, which the cadet returned before heading back towards his spot. As he left, Rei felt a little of the tension leave his shoulders, the anxiety of the constant eyes and whispers of the others all day had placed upon him.

Catcher first. Now Sense.

Maybe—just maybe—he actually had a shot of carving out some small place for himself in the first year class, and possibly even make himself and Viv a few friends along the way.

"Eyes forward, cadets."

At once Rei spun himself back around to face Field 1. Chief Warrant Officer Bretz had approached their end of the ring again, having obviously finished his setup. Under his feet, the Dueling space was a brilliant white once again, but this time the projected pattern upon it couldn't have been more different. It was flat, just like during their second test, but instead of a single ring in the center of the space, a balanced arrangement of five large red circles contoured the outer field, each about 5 yards across, with a smaller 1-yard ring in the middle of each.

Despite the benign design, Rei felt his stomach clench as he took in the simulation.

"Your final exam, Fortitude, will test your physical and mental mettle," Bretz began, meeting the five student's eyes one after the other. "As a couple of you may have already figured out, however, this assessment tests a different kind of perseverance than how many jumping jacks you can do before breaking a sweat. It is the nature of your chosen paths as Users to deliver violence, but it also therefore your curse to bear it. There is no person in the world—not even among the Kings and Queens and Rooks of the last 200 years—who can claim to have emerged unscathed from every match they have ever taken part in. There are, however, more Device wielders than I can count who have turned the tides of a fight on nothing more than willpower and focus." The instructor indicated the field behind him. "This assessment is one you will all be taking together, and I encourage you to compete, to draw strength from each other's hardiness, and seek to chase after those who prove themselves stronger, here. As Cadet Ward demonstrated yesterday at the Commencement—" Rei blinked in surprise at his name "—pain and injury do not necessarily amount to defeat, at least not immediately. Just because you are hurt does not mean you are done. Just because you are at a disadvantage does not mean you have to lose. Challenge yourself to conquer that which might otherwise end you on the field, and push yourselves to stand up a little longer against it." Bretz paused for a moment, leaving the words to settle across the group before continuing more deliberately. "This third test will assess your ability to overcome injury and fatigue. It will test your fortitude in the face of pain, exhaustion, and overwhelming pressure. You will each take your place in the center of one of the rings behind me. Once the exam begins, you will find yourself in some… discomfort. This will increase steadily over the course of several minutes, and your CAD's reactive fielding will not help you. You will hear me announce rankings as the pressure increases. These will mark the point at which the average Galens cadet of that Device-Rank usually tolerates the test until. I encourage you strive for your own level at the *least*, and do your utmost to push yourself further. As time goes on, the changes your CADs will have on your bodies will improve your ability to outlast pain, to outlast injury, but physical ability is only a portion of grit." He looked around at them individually again. "Are there any questions?"

At Rei's left, Warren raised a tentative hand, and Bretz nodded in her direction. "How do… How do we end the test, sir…?"

She had done her best to hide the apprehension in her voice, but to little avail.

In front of them, Bretz's expression didn't so much as flinch as he answered.

"Most people scream."

CHAPTER 19

They took their positions at the chief warrant officer's command, spreading out around the edge of the Dueling field to each claim the middle of their own set of two circles in quick succession. When they were ready, Bretz took to the center of the space, where he could keep an eye on them all equally. Making sure they were each prepared, facing him like the tips of a five-pointed star, his NOED lit up.

There was no shout to "Call" this time. No warning to prepare. Their Devices would do them no good in this test, it was clear, and anticipation could only ready them for so much.

Indeed, before Rei could really start to gather himself, the countdown appeared before him, mirrored four more times in front of the faces of his groupmates.

5... 4... 3... 2... 1...

0.

A prickling sensation washed in a skyward wave up Rei's bare feet, shins, and hips. Then it was at his finger, traveling along his arms at the same time as it climbed his abdomen and chest. Reaching his neck, he felt every hair on his body stand on end as the tingling spread across his face, over his ears, then atop his head. It lingered there for a bit, uncomfortable, but hardly painful.

Then it began to intensify.

"F0!" Chief Warrant Officer Bretz shouted, and Rei was surprised. *This* was the pressure the average person caved under? Indeed, he looked around, and was interested to see Emble and Gisham—the two cadets closest to him—looking distinctly uncomfortable.

The tingling grew more insistent.

"F1!"

There wasn't pain, yet, per se. Rei *knew* pain, knew it intimately well. There was, however, a heaviness that started to bear down on him the slightest bit, as though gravity itself were steadily increasing.

Which it might just have been, he considered…

"F2!"

Again a jump in discomfort. The same happened again and again, until some 2 or 3 minutes later Bretz passed from F9 to E0. Still not a soul among their five had made a sound, but also still had Rei not yet found himself struggling under more than intense irritation and the ever-climbing pressure of what he was now *sure* was a steadily-escalating gravity quotient.

Then Bretz yelled "E4!"

It started, then. Barely anything at first, but whereas a breath before Rei felt like he'd been in the process of getting buried under a growing mount of living, crawling insects, abruptly several of those insects started to bite. He winced, not having been able to anticipate the minor jolts of pain, but settled after a moment as he grew accustomed to them.

"E5!"

A few more bites, a little extra weight.

E6 was called, then 7, then 8, then 9. The pain was real now, a constant, undulating stabbing that cycled haphazardly around Rei's limbs, body, and head. He tolerated it, setting it aside with well-practiced effort. It was the heaviness, now, that started to concern him. He was already far beyond his own Ranking, and his back was starting to ache something awful. He worked on standing up straight, realizing as he did that his eyes had been closed for some time. Opening them, he let out a shuddering breath as he blinked away the brightness of the subbasement lights.

That was when he noticed Valera Dent.

He hadn't heard the captain arrive, hadn't heard her make her way through their testing rings to join Bretz in the center of the field. She hadn't made herself known to them since the beginning of the assessments, in fact, but the woman stood now with her arms crossed, as appeared to be her fashion.

Stood, and watched Rei unblinkingly.

It took him aback, having not expected the Iron Bishop's attendance, much less her attention. He met her gaze unsteadily, suddenly feeling his body trembling.

"D0!"

The warrant officer's shout was accompanied by a new wave of pain, and Rei could *certainly* feel it now. The constant tabbing at his skin by the "insects" had been replaced by a steady, pulsing burn, like acid splashed against his bare body. His straightening had helped with the weight, but he felt like he could sense his spine compressing.

"D1!"

With a keen of agony, Gisham collapsed on his left, knees slamming to the projected floor under the added pull of the artificial gravity. At once the rings around her blinked out, and she stayed in that kneeling position, trembling under what Rei *hoped* was the ghost of the test's sensation.

Bretz hurried over to her, crouching down beside the girl to put a steadying hand on her shoulder.

"Good effort, cadet," Rei heard the man say. "Take a rest, and gather yourself. That was almost to your Rank. You've got two more tries."

Two more tries.

It registered, then. Not only the fact that Rei had two more attempts—completely forgotten in the single-minded focus to overcome the pain and pressure he was *already* feeling—but also Valera Dent's gaze.

The intent, expectant gaze that had only barely flinched away from him with Gisham's fall.

"S-Sir!" Rei struggled to speak, the movement redoubling the pain around his jaw, his tongue moving awkwardly in his mouth under the restraint of the added gravity.

At his left, Bretz turned to him in surprise. Speaking during the assessment must not have been a common thing.

"I'd l-like to end my... end my a-attempt, sir," Rei ground out.

The warrant officer frowned, hesitating. Then, with a flash of his NOED, the red rings around Rei's feet vanished with a blink.

There was an instant, an odd breath where Rei felt like he was floating. He felt so light he might have been lifting off the field, or been suspended in the depths of an ocean. Steadily his body adapted to standard gravity, though, and he came back to himself, finding his feet and discovering relief as his mind registered the pain having gone.

"I'd like to say that was an excellent first go Ward—seven ranks higher than the average E4—but I have to admit disappointment at the end." Having made sure Gisham was all right, Bretz had stood to approach him. "If you had the strength to *ask* for the attempt to end, I like to think you had another couple levels in you."

Rei had to work hard to keep his lips tight as he offered the man a shaky salute. "Yes, sir. I'll do better by the end of the exam, sir."

Bretz eyed him for a moment, clearly having detected *something* amiss in his answer.

Then, with a grunt, he turned back towards the center of the field, waving Rei down as he walked away. "Take a rest. Try to push yourself a bit more on the next one."

Rei didn't answer, not wanting to lie. Instead, he tried to catch Valera Dent's eye again as he sat down, but the captain had looked away from him once he'd abandoned his first try.

He didn't miss the hint of a smile on her synthetic lips, however.

Fortunately the others weren't long in falling. Sense actually dropped next, at D3, with Warren at D5 and Emble reaching an impressive D7. Bretz congratulated them all, then said there would be a 3-minute reprieve before the start of the next attempt. Rei thought he could hear Gisham mumbling profanity under her breath from his left, but he ignored her, focusing instead on steeling himself for a scathing lecture.

He didn't think their instructor was going to like the stunt he pulled next.

"Second attempt, cadets!" the warrant officer shouted as their break came to an end, motioning for all of them to get to their feet. "Thirty seconds! Up you come!"

Captain Dent still hadn't left, keeping to her spot in the center of the ring as she observed in silence aside from the occasional quiet question or comment to Bretz. As Rei stood up, he was sure he could feel the woman's eyes on him, and he hoped against hope he wasn't about to make a complete idiot of himself. He found his place in the middle of the two rings that had reappeared beneath him, and waited.

At last the countdown appeared.

5... 4... 3... 2... 1...

The moment it hit 0, as the tingling sensation crawled up his legs, Rei took a knee.

"*Ward!*" Bretz bellowed, seeing him end the attempt within moments of it beginning and starting towards him in anger. "What in the *MIND's name* do you think—?!"

"Leave him, Bretz."

The warrant officer stopped short at Valera Dent's steady order.

"Ma'am!" he tried to start arguing, looking around at her still red in the face. "He reached D1 on his first try! If he had it in him he could—!"

"Leave him," the captain repeated, and again her eyes were on Rei. The smile was gone, now, but the expectation had not left her gaze. If anything, it had intensified, almost as though in warning.

I see you, those eyes said. *I see what you are doing. Don't screw it up.*

Silently, Rei promised himself he wouldn't.

Time, it transpired, passes *much* quicker when one isn't being actively tormented by invisible forces, and so the 10 minutes the others took ticked by steadily as Rei observed his groupmates. Again the other four reached the D-Rank together, with Gisham making it to D2 this time before falling. Sense had a similar improvement of achieving D4, while Warren fell at D5 again and Emble only managed D6 on his second attempt. It was this last failing that solidified Rei's resolve, that had him sure he had made the right decision. The test pushed at the body and mind, and while sometimes that led to progress, it could just as well lead to exhaustion. Indeed, Emble looked almost grey as he fell, Bretz hurrying over to the cadet as he shouted that they would get another break. Rei bet himself Emble would fail in the early Ds, maybe even the high Es. The boy had given it his all—reaching a fair bit higher than his rank—but now he was spent.

Rei, on the other hand, was not, and he knew exactly what to expect this time.

"Third attempt," the warrant officer called 3 minutes later. Captain Dent still hadn't moved, and she wasn't even trying to hide the fact that her attention was fixed wholeheartedly on Rei. He didn't know what he had done to earn such study, but he welcomed it. In the CAD-Assignment Exam, he had wanted to fight, had wanted to show that he was more than his body told any bearing witness that it was limited to.

Now the Iron Bishop was watching, and his opportunity had come.

The countdown started, ticked away, and reached zero.

Rei closed his eyes as the prickling sensation crawled up his body. He focused, drowning everything else, trying desperately even to tune out the chief warrant officer's declarations of the climbing ranks. He felt more than heard the group pass steadily through the Fs, then into the Es, experiencing the bite as they moved to E4. Little by little the pain intensified, but he welcomed it, using it as a tool to pull away from the rest of the world and focus only on the next minute, the next moment. Distraction managed to get through only when he heard Elber fall with a cry, and knew Gisham would be next. The girl failed not long after, and by then the sheer effort of standing up had Rei struggling to breath. His eyes still shut tight, he clenched his jaw as he held himself as erect as he could. Though the field beneath him was as solid as concrete, he felt like the projection was going to crack under the downward pressure of his bare feet. And the pain. The *pain.* The bites had become the burn, and the burn had become an inferno. It ripped at him, clawing at his head and face and body and limbs. He felt like his skin was trying to peel itself away, and the escalation of the test presented itself as a growing edge of warning red and black in the corners of his vision.

No, he told himself every time this threat of unconsciousness took him. *Not yet. Not. Yet.*

A particularly excruciating leap in the test's intensity almost had his knees buckling, and from the darkness of his mind—the deep, deep place he had long since learned to bury himself in when the agony of his body was too much—Rei knew that he was having trouble breathing. That was fine. That was fine, he told himself. He would pass out, and the pain would end. There had been times when the black of nothingness had been his *only* reprieve, in the days before his larger surgeries had freed his spine or neck or arms or legs. It was nothing. This he could do. This he could hold.

And then, just as he felt consciousness slipping away, the pain was gone.

Again Rei found himself floating, but the surprise of it brought him far higher this time as his eyes snapped open. He was weightless, still standing on the ground, and yet flying high above every head. For several seconds this time, the sensation lingered.

And then he collapsed.

"I-I wasn't done," he struggled to say, fighting to lift his head as he found himself on all fours. "I wasn't done!"

The *click* of leather boots answered him before anything else, stopping just as Rei managed to look up. Valera Dent was standing before him, staring down at him with an air of such distinct victory, there was no mistaking it this time.

After a moment, she knelt down, lowering herself closer to his shivering height, and reached for his face.

"I wasn't done," Rei repeated with a snarl, shrinking away from her, furious that his opportunity to prove himself had been snatched from him. "I hadn't fallen."

The captain ignored him, and the ache and fatigue of muscles held tense for too long prevented him from moving away in time to keep her from touching him. He felt her fingers slide along the back line of his jaw, under his ear.

Then she brought them back for him to see the blood.

"You did enough, cadet," she said quietly, her NOED flashing in her eyes. From somewhere the buzz of a drone zipping towards them at full speed could be made out, and Rei noticed abruptly that all sound had ceased in the Arena. "Any longer, and I would have had to explain to Lieutenant Colonel Mayd why the *same* first year ended up out cold in his care two days in a row. That—" she glanced over Rei's back "—and the screaming was distracting your classmates."

Rei's breath caught in his throat just as a medical drone dropped in to bob in the air at Dent's left, blue and red lights flashing silently across its forward plating.

He'd been screaming?

Distantly Rei watched the drone trail the captain's reddened fingers with an ion scrub, cleaning and sterilizing her skin in one go as the blood was atomized into dust. He didn't even blink as it turned in the air to do the same to his face, then scanned his head at some input from Dent's neuro-optic. It zipped around the side of his bleeding for a moment, and with a *zap* Rei felt a small needle of discomfort lance through his jaw inside his ear.

He barely registered it.

"No significant concerns noted," the woman told him, dismissing the drone with a final command before her eyes returned to their usual brown. "A ruptured vessel from spiking blood pressure in. You stopped breathing for a bit at the end there. Probably what did it. It's cauterized now, so you should be fine, but have Cadet Arada take you to the hospital if you suffer any headaches or additional bleeding tonight."

Rei nodded numbly, finally managing to ease himself back onto his heels. His arms shook under his weight, and his legs were happy to give out.

"How…?" he started, still processing. He'd been *screaming*? "H-how far did I get?"

The captain smiled at him.

"I'll let Chief Warrant Officer Bretz tell you that. He seemed hard-pressed not to join in the cheering from your groupmates. I would hate to deprive him the satisfaction."

Another surprise.

"They were… cheering?"

Dent chuckled, watching him a moment more.

"Good job, cadet. I'm glad to find you don't disappoint."

And then, with a brush of her uniform as she got to her feet, the Iron Bishop was gone, leaving Rei to watch his sub-instructor marching towards him with a manic sort of pride gleaming in the man's eyes.

C2? C2?! No way…"

They were back in the locker room, the parameter testing having wrapped up some 15 minutes after Rei's completion of the third assessment, with Dent dismissing them after a brief congratulations and encouragement to continue pushing themselves to ever greater heights. Viv was all worried glances until after they'd rinsed off and dried themselves with towels dispensed automatically at the mouth of the men and women's shower chambers. Now that they'd returned to their quiet aisle along the north wall of the locker room, though, she was gaping at Rei with her mouth hanging open, having just been explained what his apparent screaming—confirmed by the odd looks he'd gotten the whole way out of the gym, down the subbasement hall, and even into the showers—had been about.

"Way." It was Sense who assured her from where he was pulling on his uniform. After Rei had recovered enough to stand and walk on his own—or with a little subtle help—the Brawler had collected his things from his own locker to join them in the back aisle. "Our instructor about blew a gasket, in a good way. He kept his cool, but I'm almost sure he would have hugged Rei if there'd been no one looking."

Viv eyed the bald boy suspiciously. She clearly hadn't forgiven him his involvement in the exchange with Leron that morning, even after Rei had assured her quietly the cadet was good in his book. "I would freakin' hope so. I heard Laurent only made it to C1. One of his Brawlers beating out the class C-Ranker… Dude's going to be a celebrity in the officer's mess hall, tonight."

"I'm not much clear on how besting her in *one* test is me 'beating out' Laurent," Rei grumbled, pulling his boots on with some difficulty given his fingers didn't seem to want to work properly. "Let's not forget she turned me into a breathing shish kebab about 24 hours ago…"

He hid a smile from Viv, though. It *had* been amusing to see Bretz—up to that point so rigid and stoic—working hard to keep a tempered expression as he clapped Rei on both shoulders and informed him of how far he'd gone. The looks of awe on the groups' faces hadn't hurt either, with even Warren having taken him in with something of a little more substance than uninterest, for once.

"But seriously, dude… Are you made of iron? That was insane…"

Sense had finished buttoning up his uniform, and was now standing with the cap in hand, watching Rei intently. Viv started to answer, but Rei waved her down.

"It's okay, Viv. Not like I can pretend I have a princess-perfect completion forever." He looked back to Sense, who seemed suddenly nervous.

"If you don't want to explain—"

"It's okay," Rei repeated with a sigh. Finished with his boots, he stood up to pull his jacket from his locker. "I've been… sick, man. For a pretty long time."

Sense's eyebrows would have disappeared under his hairline if he'd had one, but he let Rei continue.

"A disease. Fibrodysplasia oss—" Rei cut himself off with a shake of his head. "It's not important. Long story short, my soft tissue doesn't want to stay soft. I've got—or *had*, hopefully—bone growing in my joints, along with pretty much everywhere else." He slid one arm into the jacket, then the other, wondering if his legs would stop shaking by the time they got back to Kanes. "My… uh… beauty marks—" he held up a hand for Sense to take in the scars along the fingers and wrist as he grabbed his cap with the other "—are the result of surgery. A *lot* of surgery. Between recovering from those and the condition itself, well…"

"Most of that test probably felt like a light tickle," Viv finished for him, herself lagging behind as she only just buttoned up her slacks, having been distracted up until then by Rei's parameter results.

"Damn…" Sense muttered quietly, taking Rei in with a new kind of respect—and possibly just the hint of commiseration. "Not to harp on a touchy subject, but… I'm assuming that's got something to do with your size, too?"

"Yeah," Rei confirmed before Viv could snarl anything. It was all going to get out there one way or the other, and he had a feeling Sense wasn't about to go around disparaging him with what he was finding out. "Damaged growth plates from repeated surgeries. Even the ones that didn't get screwed up on their own over time were deliberately adjusted so I wouldn't grow up lopsided." Pulling the cap over his hair and closing his locker, he gave Sense a crooked smile. "Would have been something to walk around with one leg 4 inches longer than the other, though."

"Ha," the Brawler managed grimly, still looking at Rei with that same odd appreciation. "You've had it rough, man…"

"You have no idea," Rei answered as he threw a thumb over his shoulder at Viv. "Four years with this Amazon following me around like a duckling. It's been horrible."

"Rei, ever wonder what a military issued boot tastes like?"

After Viv had *at last* managed to clothe herself they started for the locker room exit, where they tossed their damp towels in a labeled bin and bid Sense farewell as he told them he was going to wait for Leron and Kay. Leaving the chamber, Rei and Viv chatted animatedly about the test, she sharing her own rather impressive results, he explaining in detail what the Cs of the endurance assessment had felt like. As they stepped back into the hall and the doors swung shut behind them, both ignored the stares they knew were still fixed on their backs. Had they turned around, however, they might have noticed the two pairs of eyes watching them most intensely from among the aisles of lockers, one a black-red sheen glaring from between the chattering bodies of a gathered entourage, the others a fractured, brilliant green lingering on their own at the edges of the room.

CHAPTER 20

"Modern medicine is no miracle. There is yet no money to be made in ridding the world of disease. We may have come a long way from the old ways of corruption and greed in the mega-corporations of the early millennium, but mankind has not yet evolved into a civilization capable of surviving and cyclical charity. I used to think this fair, used to think this a price worth paying for the treatments and tools we do have at our fingertips.

After watching the Stormweaver rise these last years, however, I am forced to consider just how many great talents and brilliant minds our species has sacrificed over the centuries to illness and disease we 'couldn't be bothered' to address…"

Colonel Willem Mayd
Private Journals

I can see some moderate irritation to your anterior tendons, but nothing of concern." Lieutenant Major Ameena Ashton looked pleased as her eyes traveled over the display of her NOED under her short, silvery bangs, shifting the scanning module in her hand over the front of Rei's left ankle just a little as she did. "If there *was* a growth, it's gone now."

Rei groaned in relief, and on the other side of the examination table Lieutenant Colonel Willem Mayd looked quite pleased himself with the news.

"You said you started feeling the discomfort a week ago?" the old man wheezed while Doctor Ashton double-checked her findings over again, moving to the outside of the ankle once more.

"Just about," Rei confirmed. "Not enough to cause me any issues with training, but since it's only gotten a little better I thought I'd stop in to get it looked at."

"Well it looks like the pain is residual from the inflammation," the lieutenant major assured him. With a blink her NOED flashed off, and she offered him a bright smile. "I'm sure there was something there, but your CAD's taking good care of you."

"Understatement of the century, ma'am," Rei laughed as the woman stepped away to place the scanner under a sterilization unit on the counter beside the massive east-facing window-wall to their left. "This marks about thirteen weeks since my last surgery. That's more than a month longer than I can recall ever catching a break."

Ashton looked pained at the idea, pulling off her disposable gloves and tossing them in a bin by the head of the table. "Let's keep that count running, shall we, cadet? I've got no interest in seeing *any* of my charges cut open, least of all one with more scars than I can count already." Picking up a pad from the counter, she turned to Willem Mayd. "I'll see the session record updated to his profile, sir."

"Perfect. Thank you, Ameena."

The doctor saluted her superior, shot Rei another smile, then made for the wide door at the far end of the long room, her nose almost glued to the tablet as she already started reviewing the examination notes.

"I take it you approve of your case worker?" the lieutenant colonel asked after the young woman was gone.

Rei grinned, turning himself off the side of the table to unroll the cuff of his slacks that had been lifted for the scan. "Yes, sir. It's a change from Grandcrest. They were pretty tired of me there, by graduation."

"Try not to think too poorly of them, son," Mayd rasped as Rei tugged his sock out of his pocket and started pulling it over his bare foot. "I think I can say with confidence that they were less tired of you and more exhausted by what they had to put you through. I can only imagine the kind of treatment you required took a toll on those around you as frequently as it did on your own body."

Rei swallowed at that, not liking the unpleasant memories the words brought to mind. Viv had had the worst of it, but Matron Kast and the other Estoran Center staff had hated being a whole planet away, especially following the first couple major surgeries he'd had after leaving home.

"In more pleasant news, however," the lieutenant colonel shifted the conversation abruptly, "I see you've made another jump in your CAD specs since last we spoke."

Rei leapt on the chance to avoid more lingering on the subject of his day's visit. "Yes, sir," he answer enthusiastically, sliding off the table to look up at the man. Despite being some 50 years his senior, Mayd was still several inches taller than him. "E6. I'd like to think it could be more, but Captain Dent and our Type-instructors have kept us limited to tactics and techniques for the last two weeks, even in cross-training. Today is actually the first day we're set to do any real Dueling."

"Yes…" the chief medical officer said slowly, motioning that Rei could go to his boots at the foot of the lone chair on the wall opposite the window, off the back of which his jacket and cap hung waiting as well. In the old man's eyes, his frame was live. "I see… *Particularly* impressive improvement to your Speed and Cognition, cadet! I commend you!"

"Thank you, sir." Rei moved to the chair. Reaching for his boots, he pulled up a Specification Request so he could follow along with Mayd's commentary.

Specifications Request acknowledged.

…

Combat Assistance Device: Shido. User identification… Accepted.
Type: A-TYPE
Rank: E6

…

User Attributes:
- Strength: F8
- Endurance: F6
- Speed: E0
- Cognition: E0

…

CAD Specifications:
- Offense: F9
- Defense: F9
- Growth: S

He looked down as he laced his boots so Mayd couldn't see him fighting off what he suspected was a rather pleased expression. Though Valera Dent hadn't been applying any real combat to their daily afternoon training for the last half-month, Shido had continued to upgrade, demonstrating a bit more of its original rate of growth now that conditioning was against live opponents. Rei had reached a Device-Rank of E6 only the Thursday before, on the very day his Speed and Cognition became his first E-level specs.

He was still a ways behind everyone else in his class, but Rei was *definitely* catching up.

"You're training with the Brawlers currently, is that correct?" Mayd asked, not having turned around as he continued to inspect Shido's stats.

"Yes, sir." His boots tied, Rei stood and took up his jacket, pulling it on. "I've been theorizing it's the reason I'm seeing the steadiest growth in my Speed and Cognition. Shido's form right now will be fairly competitive with the others in terms of actual potential damage output once my Strength catches up, but everyone else has some kind of armor manifestation as well. Tad Emble's Lupinus just evolved Friday, in fact, when he hit D3. They're a *lot* quicker than I am. They've got every other spec on me, too, obviously, but speed and reflexes are where I'm really completely outclassed."

"The best Users are always fast, as I'm sure you know." The lieutenant colonel finally turned a clear eye on him. "Even the Maulers and Phalanxes in the highest echelons of the pro circuits are light on their feet. If you're going to see early growth, Speed and Cognition are ideal places to start."

Rei completely agreed, but he didn't say as much, not wanting Mayd to think he was concurring for the sake of it. The fact was, though, that he couldn't have been more pleased with Shido's improvement, nor the areas in which he had seen the most change. It wasn't *just* his specs, either. His hip hadn't bothered him since Commencement, and the more recent symptoms in his ankle were resolving on their own too. What was more, according to Lieutenant Major Ashton he had grown nearly another quarter-inch since the start of the term, putting him just close enough to comfortably call himself 5'6", even if he still had a few hairs to go. He'd gained a few pounds too, and the reflection he saw in the mirror these days was just starting to present itself as a little too toned for anyone to call him scrawny anymore.

A notification flashed in Rei's eyes, and a quick pull of the message preview had him glancing at the time. With a rush he stood straight and shoved his cap onto his head quickly, saluting Mayd.

"Permission to go, sir?" he asked. "Viviana Arada has informed Captain Dent and Chief Warrant Officer Bretz of the reason for my tardiness, but I don't want to push my luck."

"Ha!" the chief medical officer chuckled weakly. "No, it's best we not keep that woman waiting longer than needed, is it?" He motioned towards the door Ashton had left through. "Keep us appraised of the condition of your ankle, as well as any other concerns. Dismissed, cadet."

"Yes, sir. Thank you."

And then Rei was hurrying out of the room into the clean bright hallway of the hospital—whose every wall was crafted almost entirely of opaque smart-glass—making for the elevator he had ridden up in.

As soon as he exited the building, Rei double-paced for the Arena. While he wasn't able to do more than walk quickly—running in uniform was an offense punishable by a night in the Institute brig—his E0 Speed managed to make even that limited gait carrying him swiftly towards the center of the grounds with nothing more than a disapproving glare from a passing staff corporal. Reaching the Arena, he was up the stairs, around the walkway, and into the underworks in short succession, forcing himself to ignore the Wargames practice one of the third year classes was holding on the main floor. Making the elevators, he summoned a car to bring him down to the SB2, where all of 1-A's training had been taking place every school day afternoon for the last 2 weeks.

10 minutes later he was in his combat suit jogging out into the subbasement proper, hurrying to join the cadets of his class as they stood around the east edge of Field 3. Above their heads, Valera Dent was standing with her sub-instructors in a line at her back, once more lifted a few feet off the ground by the floating projection. She was dressed in her usual regulars, cutting ever the impressive image in black-and-gold before the red-on-white of her subordinates' combat suits.

"You'll start with warm-ups and drilling with your Type-groups." Dent was in the process of addressing the class, her eyes only briefly flicking to Rei as he joined them, and he was pleased to realize he couldn't have been more than a few minutes late. "After that, as discussed last week, we will begin live combat exercises, with FDA set at fifty percent. Today's focus is about application of technique and tactics, not besting your opponents with raw advantage. If you cannot work to apply what you have learned over the last two weeks here in class, then I assure you that whatever victories you have today will be short-lived once the Intra-Schools start next quarter. Commit yourselves to your conditioning. Work to make the habits and practices you have been forming as natural as breathing. Do not scramble. Do not panic. Do not lose your heads. Understood?"

There was an immediate response of "Yes, ma'am!" echoed by twenty-six voices, all well-practiced in decorum by now. In answer, Dent smiled, the black line bisecting her face warping just slightly. "Good. Fight clean. Fight smart." She swept a hand out in broad dismissal. "To your fields."

At once the class separated, and Rei managed to find and catch Viv's eye in the shuffling when she turned around to look for him. She gave his ankle a questioning look, which he answered with a double thumbs up and a mouthed "All clear." She grinned and returned the gesture, then hurried off as one of her groupmates called back for her to hurry up. Rei, in turn, moved south, making for Field 1.

"All right, form up!" Michael Bretz ordered as the four Brawlers and Rei conjoined on him. "Warmups will be half-speed sparring, paired off. Gisham with Emble. Ward with Senson. Warren, Chief Warrant Officer Lake tells me you half-assed Saturday's conditioning with the Lancers, so you're the lucky winner of matching up with me." He eyed them all one after the other. "Captain Dent will announce matches. Six fields. Six bouts at a time, which you may or may not get to observe depending on your practice group. Does anyone need to review Dueling regulations?"

The question was a trap none of them—fortunately—proved dumb enough to fall for. If any one of their group didn't have the basic rulings down for *all* the SCT formats by that point, Rei had no doubt their warmup would have turned into pushups-till-fail and sprints around the Wargames perimeter.

When no one was fool enough to answer him, Bretz smiled wickedly. "Good. Glad to see we're all learning." A flash of his NOED, and the field under him turned solid white, then divided itself into three even distributions outlined in red. "Take a space, and keep to your area. I won't have you lot making me look like an idiot by accidentally running into each other. Go!"

They split on command, Rei nodding to Sense when the taller cadet pointed at the far third with a questioning look. They crossed the circle together, roughly judging where the middle of their portion was before facing off.

"Ready to show off that new E0 Speed?" the bald cadet asked with a grin, bringing his fists up. With a word Scarabus had encased his hands, forearms, and lower legs, its smooth green and black brilliantly outlined in white vysetrium.

"Bring it," Rei snorted, readying himself before calling Shido up. Black plating over white rippled up his fingers and down to the elbow of his left hand, the steel claws of his right manifesting in a blink along with the rest. "If *you* go half-speed and I go no-holds-bars, it might actually be a pretty even fight."

Sense chuckled. "If you say so."

And then he lunged, Rei's NOED flaring red as a green-and-black punch dagger made a line for his right eye.

Among the incredible things about CAD-combat was that the concept of "half-speed" no longer applied in the same way a non-User might have considered it. As they dodged and weaved and struck—Sense being kind enough to slow his pace down to match Rei's lesser specs—someone lacking a Device could have witnessed the sparring without realizing it was a warmup. Even Rei—most recent of all the students in the subbasement to have known baseline human abilities—was still amazed by the swiftness and power of the fighting, even though he for once felt like he was actually contributing just a little to the astounding back and forth. With silent awareness of each other he and Sense took turns kicking or punching or feinting, then blocking or dodging. Some blows landed here or there, but without an active SCT field the neural interruption of their phantom-calls lasted only 10 seconds or so, rather than the length of a match. Still, Rei felt good. With guidance from Bretz he'd done a decent job of adjusting his combat style to the claws, which were a lot harder to ward off or redirect then a simple fist. More than once Sense cursed as a hand or an arm went numb, and every time Rei felt a thrill even in the half-speed.

Of course, for each single blow he landed, his opponent managed about ten, and by the time an alert expanded in their frames letting them know the matchings had posted and warmups were at an end, Rei thought Sense's punch daggers had done a solid job of carving him into a man-shaped hunk of swiss cheese.

"Good fight," Sense told him, breathing lightly and holding out a fist as he recalled Scarabus.

"Good fight," Rei agreed, doing the same to Shido and pumping knuckles. "What field's your group in? I'll come watch if I can."

"Looks like… 5. Huh… They've paired me with Kay. She'll enjoy that, I'm sure."

"Good luck with that." Rei snorted as the two of them made for where Bretz was waving them all over again. Though she'd done a fair job of blending in, it had come to light that Kay Sandree—the girl with blue-and-red hair always hanging out with Sense and Leron—was the third top sixteen ranker in their class, and another attendee of the summer program. She was roommates with the two boys, and Rei liked her just fine, even if he thought her choice of friends was 50/50 at best.

Bretz's lecture was brief and direct, reiterating again that the point of these true combat exercises would be to put into practice the tactics and techniques they'd all been working hard to solidify into muscle memory. Though he didn't say so directly, the chief warrant officer was *acutely* clear that if any of *his* cadets ended up flailing around out there like monkeys wearing boxing gloves, there would be hell to pay in the coming weeks. When he'd said his piece, the five of them saluted the man before breaking off, heading towards their respective fields as others from the different groups made to trade places with them.

Rei had been assigned to Field 4, kitty-corner to 1 and where the Duelists usually trained, and was pleased when he noticed that Viv wasn't moving from the edge of the silver perimeter. Catching sight of him approaching, she looked relieved, then abruptly worried.

"Can't tell if you're happy or horrified to see me?" he asked tentatively.

In answer, Viv made a face. "How about both? Look over my shoulder and take a peek at who's joined us from the Mauler group."

Rei started to groan even before he did as she said. Logan Grant was staring right at them, standing so still he might have been some handsome floor dummy set out to model his grey-and-red suit.

"Fantastic." Rei grumbled, deciding it wasn't worth the effort of trying to stare the asshat down, choosing instead to turn and face the ring. "I swear since the day he caught me checking out Aria Laurent the dude has been glaring daggers at me every chance he gets."

"Oooh so you admit it, then?" Viv latched on, sporting a too-eager grin as she, too, faced the perimeter. "You *were* checking her out?"

"Shut up, you know what I mean." Rei brushed her comment aside, feigning an interest in Field 2 to his right as he felt his cheeks flush a little. "If you want to give someone a hard time for having the hots for her, go pester Grant."

"Nah. I'd have to blame him for it, which I can't. That girl is a *serious* smoke-show. I'd probably make a move myself if I got the impression she'd go for it."

That got a laugh out of Rei, but as he turned back around he found Viv looking over her shoulder. Following her eyes, it wasn't more than a second before he identified her point of interest.

Aria Laurent, like Viv, hadn't moved from her original training ring. Field 5 was the typical home of 1-A's four Phalanxes, and while the rest look to have scattered about the other rings, Laurent was left standing a little apart from other gathering students—including Sense and Kay Sandree—as was her habit. She was as stunning as ever, and stood quietly waiting, bright auburn hair in a bun with her red-gold and green CAD bands gleaming in the overhead lighting.

"I don't know…" Rei said tentatively. "She doesn't seem… aloof, to you? She's always on her own."

Turned away from him as she was, it was hard to make out Viv's expression, but when she answered she sounded… sad?

"No." She shook her head. "If anything she seems kinda lone—"

"Eyes forward, cadets!"

The quick order had Viv, Rei, and the other four students who'd gathered with them—including Grant—snapping to attention as they faced Field 4. Before them Sergeant Major Liam Gross was standing expectantly, his tight tail of pale hair in sharp contrast to his tanned skin and dark eyes. The Duelist Type-instructor, Rei had worked with him twice before during cross training, and his unimpressive showings in those classes was clearly reflected in the subtle frown of the young officer's face when his gaze fell briefly on him.

"At ease," Gross said, and the six of them relaxed at once as he continued. "No preamble, and straight to it. Each of you will have three matches for a total of nine bouts, timed at five minutes with ten minutes of recovery and discussion in-between. Keep in mind you are not just here to practice your own fighting. I want all of you to pay attention to every match-up, and be ready to answer questions as we break down each pairing during recuperation." He checked the time on his NOED. "Let's get to it. Arada and Jax, you're up first. The rest of you have a seat."

So much for going to see Sense fight, Rei thought dejectedly, whispering a quiet "Good luck" to Viv as she stepped onto the field with Adam Jax, a wiry Lancer he didn't know well. Rei was extra disappointed when he realized there would be *two* top-rankers at Field 5 with Laurent and Kay both there, and so it was somewhat dispirited that he sat in one of the six black chairs that had been projected into being at Gross' order, identical to the ones the department and school heads had taken to at the Commencement Ceremony. The others left out of the match claimed their own seats around him, and Rei was wholly unsurprised to find himself sitting between two empty chairs, Grant and another tall boy taking up the far two to his left, a girl with onyx eyes and ocean-green hair a space to his right.

Sighing internally, Rei had to physically stop himself from rolling his eyes.

After his performance in the last assessment of the parameter testing, the Brawlers had largely come around to his presence in their group. Camilla Warren was still stand-offish, and Bretz—undoubtedly subconsciously—went easy on him in the occasional training, but Emily Gisham and Tad Emble had taken to treating him as another member of the group, and Rei had come to count Sense as the only friend he had outside of Viv and Catcher.

Unfortunately, the rest of 1-A still had a tendency to eye him strangely whenever they thought he wasn't looking, particularly after it became common knowledge that he'd become the first of Galen's new class to evolve his CAD in school.

"Cadet Viviana Arada versus Cadet Adam Jax. Combatants… Call."

Distracted by the others' avoidance, Rei had completely missed Gross' instruction for Viv and Jay to take up starting positions, the Arena's voice telling the pair of them to manifest their Devices rousing him abruptly. The field—which would ordinarily have risen up 10 feet while manifesting either a pre-selected or randomized stage— only lifted about a yard, and had taken on the hexagonal patterning and pitching of the Speed & Agility assessment of their parameter testing course. On opposite ends of the ring, 20 yards separating them, the two cadets were facing off in the starting circles, Gemela's two purple-yellow and silver blades already in Viv's hands, while in Jax's a 7-foot spear was in the process of manifesting already held at the ready, its shaft solid green steel, its blade yellow and edged with sky-blue vysetrium.

"Combatants… Fight."

The moment Viv rocketed off her starting point, Rei knew Adam Jax was going to lose.

It wasn't that the guy was unskilled. He'd had the longer weapon in place precisely in preparation for a forward assault, set against an aggressive press that would have immediately lost him any reach advantage he had if Viv had gotten into his range. His positioning forced her around, barring off her momentum as she was made to shift directions over the uneven ground, and Jax even managed the true opening attack of the match, following her half-loop with his eyes and cutting forward at the place she *should* have been in the next step.

Unfortunately for him, the fact of the matter was that Viv was simply too fast.

Seeing the tensing of the incoming strike, she planted and pivoted on the spot, dodging the slash—which caught nothing but empty air—even as she lunged at Jax's body. To his credit the boy corrected quickly, snapping the haft of his spear inward in time to block the slashing downcut of Viv's sword.

Unfortunately, locking up only *one* blade was hardly enough to stop a Duelist.

In a flash Viv's knife vanished into Jax's gut, then was retracted. She'd stabbed again before the boy managed to slam the shaft of his Device into her chest, sending her flying into a rising of white pillars, but the damage was already done. Instead of following up in the opening he'd given himself, Jax's spear was slow in coming up, the grimace on his face apparent as the field registered the injuries to his abdomen and applied the appropriate restrictions.

"Thaaaat's got to hurt…" the blond cadet closest to Rei's left—whose name he wasn't familiar with—muttered with a snort.

Deciding to attempt a conversation, Rei nodded as he continued to watch. "He's done for. She's too fast for him, and that damage is going to bind up his core. He won't be able to move well enough to keep off her next attack."

The boy blinked, then looked at him oddly, as though he hadn't been aware of the fact that Rei could speak. After a moment he turned his attention back on the fight, and said nothing more.

Another forceful avoidance of rolling eyes, and Rei placated his irritation by watching Viv put an end to the bout in style, pinning up Jax's spear with both of Gemela's blades as he attempted a weak thrust at her chest, then delivering a cracking kick to the side of the cadet's head. He fell like a rock, his Device slipping from his grip, and Viv looked about to pounce and finish the job when the Arena spoke again.

"Fatal Damage Accrued: 57%. Winner: Viviana Arada."

"Nice," Rei said under his breath, watching Viv stand straight, breathing lightly as she recalled her Gemela. Jax's reactive shielding appeared to have swallowed most of the ending blow, because he sat looking only a little cross-eyed, and graciously accepted the hand up Viv offered him once he'd regained his bearings.

"Good fight, both of you." Gross—who'd been observing from outside the ring to the right of the chairs—stepped into the Dueling perimeter as the field retracted back into its plain projection plating. "Take a seat."

Viv and Jax did as they were told, sitting to Rei's left and right respectively as the sergeant major continued.

"General thoughts before I ask my questions?"

"Jax was done for the minute Arada stepped onto the field."

Logan Grant's voice was flat, devoid of any sympathy as he spoke, leaning back in his chair with his arms crossed. At Rei's right he felt Adam Jax tense, but didn't look around at him.

He hated to agree with Grant, but the guy had read his mind.

"Elaborate, Grant." Gross said smoothly.

The Mauler shrugged. "Arada is a D7 according to the database. Jax is a D4. It was already a skewed pairing, but Jax's Type is a particularly bad matchup when set against a Duelist. Lancers have to depend on their reach to keep their opponents at bay, using offense as a defense. Arada's Type leans into Speed, allowing her to get inside his guard. The minute she managed that…" He dipped his head at the field, obviously indicating the results of the match spoke for themselves. Then, surprisingly, he looked around at Jax. "You'd probably do a lot better against a Phalanx, or a Mauler like me."

At his right, Rei felt Jax relax a bit, while on his left Viv—like he had—blinked in astonishment.

Not before the heat-death of the universe would either of them have believed they'd hear Logan Grant offer a positive comment to anyone, even as underhanded as it had come…

"Good summary." Gross granted with an approving nod before scanning the group as a whole. "Right now, as you are in the very earliest stages of upgrading and evolution, I would agree that there are ideal and inopportune matchups. A Lancer's reach is at a disadvantage to a Duelist's Speed spec, just like a Mauler's power might be at a disadvantage to a Brawler's reflexes. However, that Brawler's lower Offense will have a hard time against a Phalanx's Defense, who in turn might have that Defense overrun by the Mauler's Strength. For now these are valuable considerations. *However*—" he spoke the word pointedly "—these differences close quickly, as you and your Devices grow stronger. At the System level and above, Type means nothing compared to skill and ability. The Mauler may catch the Brawler, the Brawler may smash through the Phalanx's shield, the Phalanx may withstand the Mauler's assault. Do not lean into or away from the strengths and weakness of your Type as compared to others. Instead, lean into your *own* capabilities, and develop yourself from there. That, of course, includes most and foremost learning from your own failings. Jax—" Jax flinched beside Rei as Gross' eyes fell on him "—give me one thing you would do differently if you could repeat that exact fight."

"My opening attack." Despite Jax's obvious discomfort at being called out, he'd clearly been ready with an answer. "Arada saw it coming. That was when she closed on me, and got inside my range."

Gross looked Viv. "Would you agree?"

"Yes, sir." Viv answered just as quickly, using her hands to demonstrate intersecting paths while she elaborated. "I was actually trying to get further around him. There was a line of raised pillars I wanted to try a leaping attack from, forcing Jax to defend upward, where his spear would have been less stable." She shook the hand pointing away from her, and bent the fingers of the other inward. "When I saw he'd committed to interception, I pivoted. That's when the fight was mine, I think." She—like Grant—looked over Rei's head at Jax. "If I hadn't seen that attack coming, you might have caught me exactly as you intended, or at the very least forced me to back off well out of any optimal range."

"Excellent observations all," Gross said with a bit of a smile as Jax looked to be considering Viv's feedback. "Now, can someone tell me—"

Until the end of the recovery period, the sergeant major grilled them on everything from the field, to where Viv could improve on, to what they each individually would have done under similar combat circumstances. Rei wasn't surprised when Gross pushed him a little less enthusiastically about how he would have dealt with Jax's reach than he did the others, but shrugged it off as they moved on. None of the other Type-instructors had ever been supremely keen on his presence in their cross-training groups, and he had been a good reminder that not *every* staff at Galen's was aware of his Growth spec. Even Bretz seemed pleasantly surprised each time Rei reported an improvement in Shido's performance.

He was in the process of considering that it might have made sense to keep knowledge of his S-Rank as limited as possible when a light cast over the sergeant major's NOED.

"Recovery time is up. Grant. Yang. On deck."

Grant pushed himself up from his chair, mirrored by the girl with black eyes two seats over on Rei's right did the same. They didn't look at each other as they took to the field, only sizing each other up once they faced off in their respective starting points. Once again the projection of the Speed & Agility course rose up around them, here forming the looping staircase of pillars, there dipping down into shallow pitfalls.

"Cadet Logan Grant, versus Cadet Biyu Yang. Combatants… Call."

"By the way… Did you hear he made C0?"

Viv's sidelong whisper had Rei's fingers twitching, and he looked around at her sharply. She didn't glance away from the field, but gave an imperceptible nod of affirmation, and he cursed under his breath. Rei hadn't been tracking anyone's specs aside from his, Viv's, and Catcher's, so it wasn't surprising he'd missed their class' *second* C-Ranked User making his jump out of D9. He stared at Grant, taking in the cold focus that lined the cadet's handsome face while his Device manifested into both hands. Adam Jax groaned in jealousy or disbelief from Rei's right, either of which would have fit the moment.

The Maulers practiced on Field 6, which meant Rei had largely only had occasion to see Grant's CAD from a distance, the two of them having mercifully been spared getting matched into a group together during their Types' cross-training days. Nearly entirely comprised of white steel, the massive axe had a flat, narrow blade that extended halfway down it's 6-foot haft, making it look almost more like a sword than a proper Mauler weapon. Red metal accented the Device's grips and joints, coupled in a rare-double coloring of red vysetrium along the pommel and sharp edge of the steel. His form, too, was armored, with both Grant's arms encased to the shoulders in white-and-red.

Despite having not evolved since arriving at Galens, Logan Grant's CAD looked to be even with Aria Laurent's when it came to its physical coverage.

"Combatants… Fight."

The Arena announced the start of the match, and hardly two heartbeats later Grant and Yang smashed into each other in the middle of the field.

Yang, it turned out, was a Phalanx, her yellow-and-purple shield longer and narrower than most, and whereas Laurent had wielded a spear, the D-Ranker held a double-edged longsword in her right hand, the body of its blade cored with glowing orange. She proved herself the owner of a rather prodigious Strength spec, too, taking her opponent's opening attack head on without flinching.

At least not until he cut straight into her shield.

Logan Grant, it transpired, was a C-Ranked User for very good reason. His two-handed axe cleaved down at Yang's defenses, shearing into the steel of the Device itself. Not pausing to try and wrench his weapon free, Grant twisted and delivered a crushing kick to his opponent's left side. Her defense locked up and her sword on the other side of her body, Yang could do no more than hunch and shift into the blow, which connected with a painful *thud*. She was sent jetting sideways, her shield dislodging with her, but the Phalanx demonstrated surprising agility for her Type when she nimbly turned the momentum into a side-roll and came up ready for Grant's follow-through. He was on her in an instant, leading with a lateral cut that Yang *just* managed to dodge under, and for about a minute the two traded back and forth presses, cutting and stabbing and dodging and blocking as Grant pushed Yang back three steps for every one she got out of him. When the end finally came, it was abrupt, the axe thundering down in an overhead crush, and the Phalanx smashed the blow aside with the combined weight of her shield and sword together. As Grant's white-and-red Device slammed into the field, digging itself 6 inches into the hexagonal pattern, Yang reversed the deflection to bring her weapon cutting up at the Mauler's neck, going for the kill in the opening his failed attack had allowed.

And stepping right into the trap Rei had watched Grant set up for her.

Instead of a clean strike through her opponent's throat, Yang found the momentum of her blow cut short when Grant caught the wrist of her sword arm with a ready hand. Wrenching it out of the way, he didn't give Yang the opportunity to lift her shield in defense of her face before slamming his forehead into her nose. Her reactive shielding accepted most of the blow, but Rei still saw blood as the girl stumbled back, dazed. Jerking his axe free of the ground, Grant's motions were almost lazy as he brought the weapon up, then down on the undefended space between Yang's shoulder and neck, slamming her to the field as most of her body went limp.

"Fatal Damage Accrued: 92%. Winner: Logan Grant."

"Excellent!" Gross called as Grant recalled his CAD while standing over Yang's limp form, the field retracting into itself all around them. "That was well done by the both of you. Give me a moment, and we'll get a medical drone over here for your nose, Yang." The sergeant looked to the four still seated, his NOED blazing as he addressed them. "Did anyone else catch how Grant gained himself the upper hand, in that fight?"

There was silence for several seconds, for once not everyone having noticed the trick. Rei waited, hoping someone else would speak up, but when enough time had passed for the summoned drone to drop down onto the field with its blue-and-red lights flashing, he steeled himself for disapproval and lifted a hand.

"Ward," Gross acknowledged him, perhaps a little more dryly than was necessary.

"That last overhead cut was a ploy," Rei answered flatly, deciding he could meet the officer's lack of enthusiasm just as easily with his own. "Grant brought the weapon down, but released one hand once the momentum was behind the attack already. I'm assuming he knew Yang would try to counter the strike once she deflected it, and if he could negate that counter he would be at advantage. He read her, and used his

Strength spec to exactly that point."

Gross didn't look disappointed at the thorough deduction, per se, but his curt nod was certainly more rigid than any other approval he'd given so far. As he moved on, asking after what they thought could have changed the direction of the fight, Rei watched in astonishment as behind the officer Grant hauled a clean-faced Yang to her feet once the drone had zipped away and the neural interruption faded enough for her to stand.

"He's *still* a dick," Viv whispered sidelong, and Rei glanced to his left to see her watching the Mauler with narrowed eyes even as he silently helped his beaten opponent back to the edge of the field, where she thanked him before moving on her own—a little wobbly—to her chair at the end of the row.

Rei didn't offer a word to the contrary. For one thing he wasn't keen on giving Gross a reason to catch them talking and chew him out for it, but there was also the fact that—if anything—Grant's apparent capability for *some* measure of compassion towards his fellow cadets only brought his treatment of Rei into sharper relief.

After 10 minutes and change had passed in conversation about the fight, Gross' NOED lit up once more, marking the end of the recovery period.

"Third round. Selleck. Ward. You're up."

Rei was relieved, as he stood up with the blond boy whose name he hadn't known, to find himself feeling more excitement than trepidation. Stepping into the Dueling ring, he made for the nearest of the two red circles, "Selleck" already having started for the other. When he was in position he turned to face his opponent, who was taking him in with a bored frown. All around them the field took form again, rising and falling away as the two were lifted a yard off the ground.

"Cadet Mateus Selleck versus Cadet Reidon Ward. Combatants… Call."

"Call." Rei echoed, seeing Selleck's lips move in the same command. The boy turned out to be a Saber-Type, a curved, scimitar-like sword materializing in his hands in a shimmer of red-green steel with blue. His Device crawled up his forearms, too, and Rei could have *sworn* he saw azure, clawed tips at the end of each finger of Selleck's free hand.

Bringing his fists up to his face, Shido's black claws gleaming at the ready, he made a mental note to keep an eye on more than the sword.

"Combatants… Fight."

If Selleck was anywhere around the D4 average for the class, he was almost a full tier higher than Rei, and he proved it out the gate. Sabers were broadly considered the most balanced Type, but the cadet demonstrated impressive Speed by closing the distance between them long before Rei made it to the halfway mark. The scimitar slashed, cutting horizontally at Rei's upper body, and he blocked with the heavy plating along the back of his left arm. Steel met steel, and Selleck's Offense and Strength spec proved themselves far superior when the Saber's blade cut 2 inches into the metal. Pain bloomed from Rei's fingers to elbow, but he ignored the sudden weakness of his fist and the flashing notifications in the corner of his neuro-optic informing him of the damage.

Instead, he swung at Selleck's face, brought within reach by the Saber's opening attack, Shido's claws cleaving at his eyes.

Selleck, predictably, ducked under the blow, and had just enough time to start a gasp of surprise before Rei's right knee took him in his descending face. He wheeled backwards from the hit, pulling his sword free of Rei's left arm as he did, and Rei followed after him with a leaping punch that Selleck barely managed to dodge as he blinked away a watering vision, courtesy what had to have been a painful strike to the nose through his shielding.

Rei ducked and rolled, anticipating the cut at his back as his claws missed, coming up in time to jerk just out of reach of the Saber's chasing slash, then another, then a third. Rei imitated his Commencement dance with Aria Laurent for a few seconds, keeping to the extent of Selleck's range in order to give his NOED and improved Cognition the chance to stay ahead of his opponent's superior Speed. He counted the pattern of hexagons beneath his feet as he retreated, careful to keep some margin of his focus on the rise and fall of the field under him.

Then Selleck lunged at him with every ounce of power the Saber looked to be able to bring to bear, empty hand reaching, clawed fingers extending towards Rei's face.

Not expecting the sudden change in pattern, Rei only managed to get his left arm up in time to keep from being blinded. Selleck was blocked from clawing at Rei's eyes with the blue tips of his gauntlet, but traded that loss for a firm grip of the arm. Rei's mostly limp left hand flopped uselessly as he was suddenly being wrenched sideways with impressive force. He lost his footing, but managed a panicked slash at his opponent that caught the Saber in the chest. Without proper power behind the strike Selleck's shielding absorbed most of the impact, but the claws still cut shallowly along the muscles of the cadet's chest. Landing on his side, Rei felt the hand about his left arm weaken, and he hauled at it, pulling the limb free and starting to roll away, intent on getting clear of his opponent.

Selleck, unfortunately, was too quick by half even injured.

Schlunk!

Rei felt agony erupt through his abdomen, and he took in a hot, hissing breath that only intensified the pain. He flailed, trying desperately to get clear of the Saber, but when his attempts to shove himself further away along the uneven field resulted in only greater torment, he understood.

He had been pinned, the scimitar nailing him to the ground through the torso.

"Fatal Damage Accrued: 74%. Winner: Mateus Selleck."

Mercifully, Rei felt Selleck's sword retract as soon as the Arena announced the victory. Suddenly able to breathe again, he rolled onto his back, coughing and gasping. When the simulated pain had faded enough, he lifted his head to his chest to look up.

Unsurprisingly, Selleck was already walking away, his back to Rei, clearly having no interest in sportsmanship.

Grunting out a dry laugh, Rei pushed himself up to sit, then stand, recalling Shido as he moved unsteadily to rejoin the group himself.

"Break it down for me," Gross was saying as Rei reached his chair again and slumped down into it with a little considerate help from Viv. "What did Ward do wrong?"

"Showed up for class," Grant muttered from the left end of the row.

The sergeant major didn't do more than shoot the Mauler a disapproving glance, taking advantage of Biyu Yang's raised hand to not engage the cadet.

"He allowed Selleck to keep him at distance," the Phalanx stated once Gross had motioned for her to answer. "Ward is a Brawler-Type. Any sort of space his opponents can place and hold between him and them means he became essentially harmless."

"True, though it's important to recall that Ward is an A-Type merely currently presenting as a Brawler. If he achieves greater evolution, he may find his abilities more versatile in the future." The officer looked around again. "What else did he do wrong?"

Choosing to believe the *if* and *may* implications of their superior's previous statement hadn't been deliberate jabs, Rei put his arm up. He could name a dozen things he would do differently having faced a Saber, now, but Gross looked instead to Selleck's lifted hand.

"Grant's joking aside—and I mean no disrespect—" the Cadet stated with the apathetic expression of someone who very *much* meant disrespect "—but stepping onto that field was Ward's first mistake."

"Huh?" Viv snarled, tensing and turning on the boy beside her, but Gross shut her up with a look.

"It's just a fact," Selleck maintained with a shrug, meeting Viv's venomous gaze unblinking. "Ward is an *E*. I'm a D4, *and* his CAD is at a lower evolution. In a competitive setting—or live combat—going up against an opponent that much stronger than you would be idiotic." He paused, hesitating before adding. "Like an E-Ranker publicly challenging a C0."

Viv was on her feet in a heartbeat to tower over the seated Saber, but before Rei could pull her back the sergeant major cut across the tension.

"Arada! Sit!"

Viv didn't look around at Gross, still glaring at Selleck. After a few seconds, though, she eased herself down again, only looking forward again when she'd shoved herself angrily to sit ram-rod-straight in the very back of the chair.

"Selleck, leave your childish sniping out of your explanations next time, or I'll make sure Lieutenant de Soto finds out her Sabers need lessons in manners." This time the sergeant major couldn't ignore the slight, deliberate as it had been made, but he still moved on as soon as Selleck gave him nothing more than a stiff nod. "More importantly, Ward may be at a disadvantage against all of you, but claiming he 'shouldn't have been on the field' is incorrect. Why?"

"Because I had no choice."

Rei, finally getting a little tired of the atmosphere, didn't bother raising his hand again, nor wait for Gross to call on him to continue.

"Selleck used the example of SCTs, which is bull. If your bracket matches you with a higher ranked User, you don't get to put your name back in the hat and pull for a better opponent. As for live combat, I can't imagine you often get the *choice* of when and where you want to engage the enemy, or even what enemy it is you're taking on." He gave a rough laugh. "Then again, maybe Selleck is suggesting he would prefer to forfeit his matches or abandon his duty every time he's faced off with a stronger opponent. That's his prerogative."

"I'm suggesting you don't go *looking* for a fight you can't win, asshole," the Saber snarled in answer, seeming about ready to lunge to his feet. "Only an idiot *asks* to get their face kicked in by—"

"Selleck. Last warning. Keep it civil, or you can go explain to de Soto why I kicked you out of class." Still, Gross' eyes were narrowed on Rei even as he berated the Saber. "The same goes for you, Ward. You might have made Bretz a fan of yours, but don't think you get to pull that kind of shit in my group without consequence."

With some difficulty, Rei sat himself up straighter, placing his eyes somewhere over the sergeant major's left shoulder. "Yes, sir. Sorry, sir."

Gross glared at him a moment more, then grunted in annoyance, moving on to ask another question without addressing Rei's answer, which told him he'd probably been right on the mark.

Not too long after, the fourth matchup was announced, and Adam Jax was pitched up against Grant, who made short work of the fight by overpowering the Lancer within 10 seconds, cleaving straight through Jax's overhead guard to basically split the cadet in half. After that it was Yang against Selleck, and the group had their first lengthy bout of the day, the Phalanx keeping the Saber well at bay, but unable to manage any clean offense without opening herself up to attack. For almost the full 5 minutes the pair went back and forth, until Selleck finally grew impatient. After knocking aside a testing thrust from Yang, he lunged in for a two-handed overhead cut, yelling as he did. Yang, instead of blocking, took the opportunity to power forward, inside her opponent's reach. Selleck slammed into her shield, and with a thrill of déjà vu Rei watched the Phalanx execute the very same dip and press that Laurent had pulled on him. The Saber flipped over Yang, landing hard on his back, and before he could so much as move his opponent had brought her blade arcing around in a downward thrust that speared the boy through the chest, pinning him to the ground.

Rei was pretty sure neither he nor Viv bothered hiding their grins of satisfaction as Selleck walked off the field, red in the face and avoiding both their eyes.

Then, though, it was their turn.

"Arada. Ward."

Their paired names sent a thrill up Rei's spine that he didn't immediately know what to make of. They stood up with nothing more than a quick exchange of looks, and only after splitting without a word to either side of the ring and the red circles waiting for them did Rei realize what he was feeling. When they had faced off, Rei met Viv's eye again, and her unfeigned grin solidified the anticipation. This was the first time the two of them had had the chance to face off inside a sanctioned field.

He might be about to get his teeth kicked in, but Rei was so excited his hands shook as he brought them up in preparation.

"Cadet Viviana Arada versus Cadet Reidon Ward. Combatants… Call."

Gemela and Shido manifested as mirrored blurs of color 20 yards apart from each other. Viv's blades rippled with silver light as she set them at the ready, and Rei had to force himself to steady his breathing.

This was going to be fun.

"Combatants… Fight."

CHAPTER 21

Viv pulled no punches, making the fight about as brief as any they'd seen thus far that day.

Entering it, though, Rei had no expectations otherwise, and so he met her as near the middle of the projected field as he could, managing to block a single testing cut of her sword before taking her dagger to the thigh. He grimaced as the pain had his leg almost giving under him, but didn't lose his focus on the highlighted red of his NOED. Seeing the briefest of chances with both her weapons committed, he punched straight for the body, hoping to catch her in the gut and at least place her under restrictions. Viv, though—too nimble by half—disengaged and bent backwards under the strike before planting her dagger hand behind her to snap her legs up and around in a spinning kick. Rei got a foot to the side of the head, staggering sideways, and this time his injured leg did give, bringing him to the ground. Viv was on her feet again in a heartbeat, lunging at him with both blades leading the way. Rei managed to knock them aside with a heavy swipe of his claws, and was about to bring Shido back to slash at her thighs when Viv used the lateral momentum of the deflection to twist into *another* kick.

This time her shin took him full in the other temple.

Stars erupted in his vision, and Rei felt himself tumbling sideways head over heels to slam in a heap against a raised pillar 15 feet away. He struggled to push himself up onto his hands and knees, practically hearing his neuroline whining in his head as it worked at max to clear his thoughts and vision. Both came back to him just in time to see a shape lancing in from the right, and putting all his Speed and Strength into his legs he threw himself into a forward roll, hearing Viv's sword catch the ground exactly where he'd been a heartbeat before. Spinning on the spot, he reversed course, the steel claws of his right fist leading the way, hoping to catch his friend in a moment of vulnerability.

All he got instead was an elbow to the stomach as Viv ducked under and into his punch, doubling him over straight onto the dagger waiting to cleave through his reactive shielding and slip between his ribs.

"Fatal Damage Accrued: 81%. Winner: Viviana Arada."

"Owwwwe!" Rei hissed after the pain had subsided enough for him to breathe again, pushing himself up onto his knees. "I feel like you cut my lungs out of my chest."

"Quit whining," Viv answered with a chuckle, offering him a hand up, Gemela having already been recalled. Rei accepted the help, watching her carefully avoid his claws as she hauled him to his feet.

"I've been impaled twice in an hour," he muttered with a feigned pout as Gross ordered them back to their seats from the edge of the ring. "I think I'm allowed to whine a *little*, don't you?"

Viv didn't answer, grinning and shoving him lightly towards their chairs. Recalling Shido, Rei let himself to be led off, and partially tuned out the criticism the sergeant major and the others had for him. Nothing they could say was anything he wasn't already aware of, and for once he let himself enjoy the simple fact that the fight had been *fun*.

The recovery period passed, and Jax and Yang were paired for first match of their final round. The Lancer used his superior reach to great advantage, this time, keeping Yang well at bay with relative ease when she proved herself too slow to out-maneuver him. Within 2 minutes Jax had worn the Phalanx down, ending the fight with a keen-eyed stab at an exposed ankle that brought his opponent to the ground with a scream, allowing him to take Yang through the side of the chest as her shield dropped away. Jax looked rather pleased with himself when he stepped off the field, and even accepted Rei's whispered "Nice job" with a grateful nod as he sat down again. This time Rei tried to pay attention when the discussion began, but a thrill of realization struck him as Gross had Yang review where she could have made improvements on her fight.

There were only four of them left. Viv, Selleck, Logan Grant, and himself.

And since he'd already faced both Viv and the Saber…

Rei's escaped groan was fortunately lost to all but Viv, who only glanced at him nervously while the others kept talking around them, likely having deduced the same thing.

It was confirmed not long after, when Gross announced the next pair.

"Arada. Selleck. Second to last match. On the field."

Despite it being one of Viv's fights, Rei found himself having an enormous amount of trouble concentrating. He tried to, *tried* to focus on the pair's fast-paced exchange of blows, the three blades and a clawed hand flashing around and against each other in arching strips of silver and blue light. He just couldn't manage it, though, a weight building in his gut that felt like it was redoubling every second. He was almost disappointed when Viv managed a clean disarming of Selleck's sword when she cleaved through his wrist, then twisted to plant a dagger through his eye. Similarly, he was grateful when it took the Saber a minute or so to recover from the neural scrambling that always followed a Device in the brain, right up until Rei remembered the fights were on a set timer, and nothing could delay the inevitable. He did his best to participate in the discussion, did his best not to let the group—much less the black-haired boy sitting at the end of the row to his left—read his nerves.

He had nothing else to say, however, when time ran out and Gross' eyes lit up.

"Last fight of the day. Grant and Ward. Make it a good one."

Not looking at anyone—not even Viv—Rei got himself to his feet. With forced steadiness he stepped across the silver perimeter of the field, feeling more than seeing his opponent do the same to his left. Rei's heart didn't hammer as he approached the starting circle, nor did his breath come in leaps and jumps. Rather, it was more as though a cold pressure had slowed everything down, as though the subbasement atmosphere had cooled and solidified, making it hard to hear anything but the quiet slap of two people's bare feet across the black steel beneath them.

Reaching the red ring, Rei turned to face Logan Grant with what he hoped was a resolute expression.

And then the cold changed to fire.

The Mauler was watching him with ice in his black-red eyes. That would have been fine—they were hardly friendly, after all—but what set Rei off wasn't the hostility. Until that point, Rei had watched Grant take in his opponents with calm, unwavering calculation. There had been confidence in his bearing as he'd faced off with Yang and Jax, sure, but it had been the steady posture of someone who had absolute faith in their own ability, rather than anything else. Now, though…

Now the look on Grant's face, the sneer so blatant Rei could have counted the Mauler's teeth if he'd tried, spoke only of distaste and disappointment in his opponent.

In an instant the weight was gone from Rei's gut, the cold pressure of the room vanishing as his entire body burned with anger. He could feel his face and ears growing red, but he didn't care. It was rage, not embarrassment, that fueled that flush, and he realized all at once that his temper had been simmering closer to the surface since his earlier head-to-head with Selleck than he'd thought. At his sides his hands balled into tight fists, and his jaw clenched so hard it hurt. None of this was apparently lost on Grant, because the massive boy's lip only curled higher, as though amused by the display.

Rei very nearly called on Shido at that, and the Arena's well-timed voice was all that saved him what he was sure would have been a wealth of ire from Gross, Bretz, and very likely Valera Dent together.

"Cadet Logan Grant versus Cadet Reidon Ward. Combatants... Call."

"Call," Rei and Grant said together, and immediately black-and-white steel faced off with white-and-red. Rei brought his fists up, and across from him taller boy hefted his axe onto one armored shouldered and bent low, obviously preparing for a charge.

"Combatants... Fight."

With the *crack* of breaking flooring the Mauler powered forward like a flaming comet. He barreled across the field in four loping strides, looking like he wanted to use his mass to crush Rei into the invisible wall 5 yards behind him. Rei, for once, hadn't left his starting point, waiting instead as he watched the long shape of Grant's axe blade carefully. The Mauler wasn't stupid enough to put himself in direct contact, where Rei's claws might get a chance to stab into his head or face.

Which meant...

There!

Rei's NOED flared red just as he himself saw the minute shift in Grant's posture. Instead of slamming into Rei full speed, the Mauler twisted at the last moment to bring the axe down in a diagonal sweep from above. Rei's E0 Speed was just enough to dart sideways, the white steel probably cleaving through strands of his white hair as he just dodged the killing arc, and he immediately countered with a punch at the side of Grant's exposed face.

An instant later, Rei was flying through the air, a gauntleted hand having come seemingly out of nowhere to snatch him up by the offending wrist, twisting with the momentum of his own strike to send him sailing with terrifying strength.

It occurred to Rei, as he smashed to the ground some 30 feet from his starting point, that he had just fallen for the exact same trick he'd seen through when Yang had been the victim. Grant's opening blow had been a ploy, a deliberately provided vulnerability even as the Mauler had left himself one hand open to take advantage of the response. From the sidelines it had seemed obvious to Rei, clear as day as he'd watched the Phalanx fall to her own reflexes.

But now here *he* was, tumbling across the uneven ground of the Dueling field, having let himself be caught in the same trap.

Tucking into the toppling roll, Rei managed to get his feet under himself, snapping up even as notifications warned him of strains in his spine and ribs. He ignored them, instead watching Grant already lunging after at him a second time, the cadet's teeth bared, axe forward and at the ready. Thinking quickly, Rei did the only thing he could.

Turning, he bolted for the staggering of rising pillars nearby, ignoring the pain in his back and torso to vault atop the closest of them.

"Running *again*?!" Grant roared from behind him. "Do you even know how to *fight*?!"

Rei ignored him, dexterously taking the rising slope of the pillar-tops that partially circled the field like the looping partition of a wide, spiral staircase. There was a *thump*, and he glanced back to see that Grant had joined him in the climb, the Mauler's Device over one shoulder again in order to make it easier to run.

"What good are you if all you can do is turn your back every time?!" Grant snarled, catching up quickly. "At least have the dignity to die with the rest of—*URK*!"

He didn't managed to finish his statement. Instead of leaping down 10 yards to the field below as he reached the last of the rising pillars, Rei planted a bare foot on the edge of the "step" and—with a strain and a massive shove backwards—reversed directions. He didn't have a chance to spin around, to aim himself properly, but it turned out he'd timed the trap just right when he felt himself slam into Grant's chest.

With a sound like the wind getting knocked out of him the Mauler went toppling off the pillars, flailing as he fell. Rei—unable to stop himself—dropped with him, twisting in the air as they plummeted down. He tried to set himself, tried to position his claws to advantage, but his E0 Speed and Cognition proved no contest against the likes of gravity. The impact actually had Rei bouncing off of Grant's chest, but not before both knees cracked against solid ground of the projection. His reactive shielding and osteoformic integrity boost saved his legs from *actually* breaking, but the notification for bilateral compound fracturing of his femurs flared bright anyway, and agony lanced through his thighs. For a couple of seconds there was nothing more than pained, groaning coughs as the pair of them struggled to gain their bearings, to clear their heads.

Then Grant rolled onto one side, starting to shove himself to his feet with difficulty.

"That's... all you've got?" he wheezed out, glaring at Rei as he leveraged himself up by planting the head of his axe into the ground with a *thud*. "Tricks? Hide-and—*cough*—hide-and-seek?" He straightened, staggering only a little when he wrenched his Device free of the field again. "That's all you've got?"

Rei would have liked to answer him, but the simulated torture of broken bones had his teeth grit tight, so instead he only glowered as Grant took a step towards him, then another. Unable to move as he was, there was nothing left to do but wait for the end, as pathetic as that made him feel.

Grant's neuroline must have cleared his head, then, because the cadet was on Rei in the next blink, the armored fingers of the boy's right gauntlet taking him roughly by the collar of his combat suit, hauling him up. Rei screamed as the movement strained his match injuries, then again when Grant slammed him with one hand against the curved, edged wall of the line hexagonal pillars they had just fallen from.

"You think this is a *fucking game*, Ward?" the Mauler seethed in his face, so close Rei could smell the heat of his breath. "You think this is a playground for tag and ring-around-the-rosie?!"

In answer, Rei raised his right fist with difficulty, intending to punch at Grant's ear. Before he could so much as twitch the claws forward, however, the Mauler rammed the blade of his axe into Rei's elbow, pinning it against the wall to cleave right through the arm. More pain bloomed from the neural interruption, but this time Rei kept his scream to himself, trying instead to bring up his left fist. Barely managing it, he slammed the heavy steel plating down on the armored wrist that had him pinned, trying to break the grip.

Grant didn't so much as twitch in acknowledgement of the pitfall attempt.

"There's a *war* out there, Ward," the Mauler snarled. "And people like *you* get others killed. Did you know that?"

"I know—*urgh*—I know you're a dick," Rei grunted, trying and failing again to break free. "That's about it."

Grant's whole body tensed at the response. His black hair was in his eyes, giving him a crazed look, and Rei was suddenly reminded of pictures he'd seen of the striped white tigers they supposedly still had captive in some zoos in the Sol System.

"*I'm* the dick?" the Mauler hissed. "You're dead weight, and dragging everyone down with you. And *I'm* the dick?"

Rei snapped, the pain fading in favor of returning fury. "I'm not dragging anyone anywhere. You've just got an ego the size of a system, and a jealousy complex to boot, apparently. Get a life, asshole. Your parents must be proud of you. Tough guy, strutting his—"

WHAM!

There was a brief moment of white-hot pain in his throat, then everything went numb. Rei blinked, wondering why he suddenly couldn't feel his body, when he realized Grant had wrenched the axe free from the wall beside them, then punched it horizontally through his neck, interrupting his neural input from the jaw down. Immediately the Arena voice finally chimed in.

"Fatal Damage Accrued: 100%. Winner: Logan Grant."

As the field began to retract around them, Rei found himself involuntarily relaxing. It was over. It was done. It hadn't been pretty, and he'd lost, but he didn't think he'd made a *complete* fool of him—

WHAM!

With an eruption of pain, Rei was suddenly aware that he was flying again. The neural interruption still hadn't resolved, so he couldn't do more than flop and roll like a ragdoll as he landed on plain projection plating. When he stopped, he found himself on his back, staring up at the subbasement ceiling lights, utterly at a loss for what had happened.

Gross' yell brought it all back to him.

"GRANT! STAND DOWN!"

He'd been punched, Rei realized, seeing the motion now as his thoughts cleared. After his killing stroke, Grant had retracted his massive axe, then struck again, even more violently this time. With the pillars at his back dissolving, Rei had been sent arcing through the air, landing a good distance away.

Some feeling returned to his arms and body, and with great difficulty Rei started to sit up, still dazed. He'd only managed to push himself partially onto one elbow when a shadow fell over him, and he squinted at the pair of bare feet that had appeared as though by magic by his side. He peered up, following the lines of the grey-red uniform until he was looking at Logan Grant's face again, and a confusion that had nothing to do with the post-match attack flashed across Rei's mind. It wasn't the Device being lifted overhead with both hands, clearly intent to cut Rei down even as he lay at the Mauler's feet. It wasn't the distant sound of Gross' yells as a whirling in the corner of Rei's vision told him the sergeant major had called on his own CAD.

Rather, what confused Rei the most was the fact that never—not in all his life—had he *ever* witnessed the level of anger etched into Grant's handsome features as he brought his axe down.

With each passing second more sensation had returned to his body, and so it was only *just* that Rei managed to shove himself out of the way, the phantom-call of the vysetrium-lined steel blade ricocheting off the plating with a *screech* of metal exactly where his chest had been a moment later. With limbs that were half-numb he scrambled back, watching Grant lift the Device again and move to follow him, the fury in his gaze not subsiding. One step, then two, and the Mauler had caught up to him, the axe lifting once more. Rei managed to get both arms up, Shido still live around his limbs, ready to take the blow.

It never came.

Instead, there was a tall blur or black-and-gold, and Grant made an "*URK!*" of sound, the axe falling from his grasp as he was abruptly wrenched off his feet by the single slender hand that had taken him by the throat. At first Rei assumed Gross had intervened just in time, but the lack of any CAD colors clued him in before his eyes caught up to his mind and took in the lithe form of a woman with short brown hair spilling out from under her military cap, her back to him as with one arm she held all the collective mass of Logan Grant and his Device 2 feet above the ground like they weighed nothing more than limp cloth.

Captain Valera Dent hadn't even had to call on Kestrel to interpose herself between the two of them. Her own Speed and Strength were enough, and Rei couldn't do more than stare as he tried to process her appearance. It had been so fast. So *fast*. He couldn't begin to count the number of times he had watched and rewatched SCT matches between S-Ranked opponents on the feeds, but this was the first time he'd been witness to that power with his own two eyes. And *without a Device*?

Despite what had just happened—despite Grant kicking and jerking in the Iron Bishop's grip like a fish out of water and the hundred-and-more pairs of eyes Rei knew were trained only on them throughout the room—it clicked, then.

This was what he wanted, he realized.

This was what he aimed to achieve.

"Cadet, correct me if I'm wrong. Your Defense spec is D9, is that right?"

The captain's question was so cold, Grant stopped thrashing in her hand. He looked down on her, and the anger that had etched every line of his face a moment before was suddenly replaced with nothing less that apprehensive fear. He didn't answer immediately, and after a couple seconds of silence Dent jerked him a few inches higher with without so much as a wince of effort.

"Don't make this harder for yourself, Grant. Answer the question. Your Defense spec is D9. Is. That. Right?"

With a visible swallow and a moment's more hesitation, the Mauler nodded.

"Excellent. Then this should only hurt. A lot."

And then, with another blur of blinding power, the captain threw Grant from the field with all the force of a rocket launch.

Like a fired projectile the cadet jetted over the ground, out of the perimeter ring, and beyond the buffer zone that surrounded the Wargames area. The wall of the subbasement was next, and Grant struck it with such a crushing impact that had even Rei wincing as dozens of voices screamed and gasped all around them, watching the Mauler collapse to the floor in a choking, spasming heap.

Dent, though, was hardly done.

"FOR DISOBEYING THE DIRECT ORDER OF A SUPERIOR OFFICER: TWO DAYS IN THE BRIG!" Her voice thundered with what sounded like barely controlled rage, and she started moving steadily towards the boy's twitching form, black boots *clicking* across the steel. "FOR CONTINUING COMBAT AFTER A MATCH VICTOR WAS DECLARED: TWO DAYS IN THE BRIG!" She came to a halt outside the silver lines of the field, some 10 feet from the cadet. "AND FOR *PISSING ME OFF*: TWO DAYS IN THE BRIG!" She looked to her left, in the direction of Field 6, the Mauler's typical training area. "Lieutenant Johnson, you will see your cadet to the Institution hospital, then the Security Center. Grant's training group will be responsible for delivering copies of all of this week's class notes and assignments to him."

"Yes, ma'am!" Lieutenant Kayla Johnson—the Mauler sub-instructor—saluted the captain sharply before hurrying herself to Grant's side, hauling him to his feet with little care for his cries of pain as she did.

"The rest of you!" Valera Dent whirled to face the class, glaring from under the brim of her cap. "Consider this an example of what happens when you elect to *will-*

fully disregard my instructions! You are not animals! You are not children playing at war, allowed to throw a tantrum or let your emotions get the best of you! You are *soldiers* first and foremost, and you are therefore responsible for your own actions before anything else! I don't *care* if your aspirations are wealth and fame in the SCTs! I don't *care* if you never intend to set foot on an actual battlefield! You are not here to prepare for the comforts of the circuits! You are here to prepare for the hardships of the front line! Therefore: *your petty squabbles and infantile feuds HAVE NO PLACE IN MY CLASS*! Is that *clear*?!"

"YES, MA'AM!" every first year in the subbasement—even Rei, from where he was still sitting on the ground—chorused together.

For a few moments longer Valera Dent glared at the collective bodies of 1-A, her brown eyes seeming to burn even if she'd not once called on her CAD. Then, finally, she seemed to relax.

"Cadet Grant's actions have lost this class the remainder of the day's combat trainings. Dismissed. All of you."

There were a few grumbled protests at this from students who hadn't yet had their third match, but the sub-instructors echoed the captain's words sharply, and any complaints came to a quick end. As bodies began to move towards the east exit, Rei finally started to pick himself up, recalling Shido at last as he got to his feet.

Straightening, he found Valera Dent standing not a foot in front of him, staring down at him with the same intensity she'd just lectured the whole of the class with.

"You need to get stronger, Ward," she told him quietly, her face set. "Whatever it takes. I intervened there because you are a student under my purview and protection, and Grant was out of line, but you won't always have someone there to step in for you."

Rei swallowed. "Yes, ma'am." His answer was subdued, and he hated himself for it. He wanted to be able to snap back, but there was nothing to snap back *with*. Valera Dent here. Kana Loren at Grandcrest. Viv for the better part of the last 4 years before that…

If anything, the captain didn't know the *half* of how acutely Rei felt the truth of her statement.

"Tricks have their place," Dent continued, a little more gently this time. "Don't ever lose your cunning. But strategy will only get you so far in this world, or the SCTs Champions would only ever be the cleverest of Users, rather than the strongest. Do you understand?"

"Yes, ma'am," Rei repeated.

"Good. Off with you."

Rei saluted the captain, then stepped around her into the moving mass of the class. Viv had paused to wait for him at a discrete distance, but joined him to pass through the exit together.

"Well that was a mess," she muttered under her breath once they were in the hall. "I knew Grant was an ass, but what the *hell* was that all about?"

It took a moment for Rei to shake his head, the events still tumbling around amongst his thoughts. "I'm not sure. That was… weird, though."

"'Weird'?" Viv repeated in a hiss as they passed with the others into the locker room. "'*Weird*'? The guy tried to cut you down after the match ended, Rei! What in the MIND's name did you say to him to set him off like that?! He looked ready to murder you!"

"I-I don't know," Rei answered truthfully as the pair of them made for the twin showers at the back of the chamber. "He was getting mouthy, so I lashed out. And then he—"

Rei, though, stopped dead so abruptly that some girl following close behind him cursed and had to dodge around him. At his side, Viv halted too, and was about to demand what he was doing when she seemed to take note of the blaze of his NOED.

"Oh boy…" Rei thought he heard her say, but her apprehension was lost on him as he took in the script tracing itself across his frame.

…

Processing combat information.

…

Calculating.

…

Results:

Strength: Lacking

Endurance: Lacking

Speed: Severely Lacking

Cognition: Lacking

Offense: Lacking

Defense: Severely Lacking

Growth: Not Applicable

…

266 I O'CONNOR + CHMILENKO

Checking combat data acquisition.

…

Adequate data acquirement met.

Device initiating adjustments to:

Strength. Endurance. Speed. Cognition. Offense. Defense.

…

Adjustment complete.

Strength has been upgraded from Rank F8 to F9.

Endurance has been upgraded from Rank F6 to F7.

Speed has been upgraded from Rank E0 to E3.

Cognition has been upgraded from Rank E0 to E1.

Offense has been upgraded from Rank F9 to E0.

Defense has been upgraded from Rank F9 to E1.

…

Calculating.

…

CAD "Shido" has been upgraded from Rank E6 to E7.

…

Checking combat data acquisition.

…

Adequate data acquirement met.

Prioritizing reasonable evolution parameters.

…

Selected Prioritization:

Speed. Defense.

…

Recategorizing for future parameters.

…

Processing.

…

Evolving.

…

Evolution complete.

As the protocol came to an end, Rei was left standing with his mouth hanging open, staring at the final line of the script. At his side Viv looked to be vibrating with anticipation, her blue eyes following every passerby, clearly ready to demand if Shido had upgraded again once they were alone in the aisle.

He didn't give her the chance.

"Viv, we've got to go."

Her surprise was only momentary.

Then she glanced around and stepped closer to speak so that only he could hear. "That big?"

"Yeah," Rei affirmed, hardly able to articulate anything else. "That big."

Viv looked at him carefully, taking in what he imagined was the pale shock of his face.

And then she'd taken him by the arm, only having to drag him for a moment back towards their lockers at the north end of the room before he'd turned to join her hurry.

"Fine. But I don't care if all your stats miraculously jump to S. You're still letting me shower before you show me anything."

From the end of the aisle Aria watched Reidon Ward and Viviana Arada turn and rush back towards the exit of the locker room, earning themselves a few dirty looks from the wash of the other students headed in the opposite direction. She'd been following behind the pair unnoticed, trying to eavesdrop on their conversation. This would have been embarrassing enough, but when Ward had stopped dead halfway to the showers she'd nearly run straight into his back, and had to dodge around him and move on as though nothing was amiss. The fact that neither of them seemed to have noticed her sparked Aria's already-smoldering curiosity, and so when she heard two lockers open near the north end of the room, followed by a glimpse of Ward and Arada dashing for the exit together with their regulars folded over their arms, her interest got the better of her. She was alone by then, everyone else already split off into the men and women's chambers to wash off the sweat of the intense training day, so it was with no distraction that Aria pulled up the ISCM database, bringing Ward's information up for what had to have been the dozenth time in 2 weeks.

Seeing the new label of E7 beside his CAD-Rank, she was doubly glad no one was around to witness the stupefaction she knew had to have been printed all over her face.

CHAPTER 22

"Nothing is given, in the world of CAD-fighting. Nothing is handed out. It is earned, rewarded. In some fashion or another, the inches we gain little by little as we climb to the top are always paid for in blood, sweat, and pain."

Dalek "the Gatecrasher" O'Rourke
Post-Match Interview, c. 2435

While moving across campus in your combat suit wasn't strictly permitted unless you were specifically conditioning your Endurance spec, that allowance was enough to get Rei and Viv back to Kanes without more than a few curious glances from some older students. Reaching the dorms, they elected to take the stairs along the west side of the building rather than risk waiting for the elevator, darting up the steps, then down the halls of the third floor until they reached 304. Rushing in slightly out of breath, they slammed the door shut behind them and hurried into the common area.

"My room," Rei said quickly. "You're not going to believe what—"

He stopped, though, entering the living space, because two people were seated across from each other on either couch, looking like they'd just been talking. One, fortunately, was Catcher, who was turning towards the door with his typical beaming expression, obviously pleased to see them.

The other, less-pleasantly, was Chancery Cashe.

"Hey you two!" Catcher greeted Rei and Viv with enthusiasm, his grin fading only a little as his yellow eyes took in their combat suits and the black-and-gold of their jacket, slacks, and caps tucked over and under their arms. "What's with the new look?"

Rei exchanged a glance with Viv. He had completely forgotten, in his excitement, that some of the other four classes would be in leisure hours before their own combat training later in the afternoon.

"Uh…" Rei began, scrambling for an explanation that wouldn't have Cashe snorting at him derisively, but before he could think of anything the silver-haired girl was on her feet. She was—he was surprised to notice—astonishingly red in the face despite her dark skin, and her lips were closed so tight as she looked at him that they might have been glued shut. She stood like that for almost 5 whole seconds, as rigid as a tree, and Rei had just started to wonder if she wanted to say something when she turned away from him and Viv to make—a little too quickly, he thought—for the open door of her room. She stepped inside without a word, shutting it at once, leaving the other three to stare after her.

"What was that about?" Viv finally asked in a pseudo-whisper when they heard the familiar sound of Cashe's study feeds starting up on her window.

Catcher shook his head in answer with a resigned sort of sigh. "Nothing. Don't worry about it. She's just hard-headed." Before either of them could press him, though, he looked around again, smiling once more. "So what's up? You're back earlier than expected. I was just thinking of grabbing a bite before my class' training starts at 1600, if you guys are hungry?"

"No," Rei answered immediately, and it was his turn to know he'd been too fast on the draw.

Catcher raised an eyebrow, his expression growing distinctly more suspicious. "Okay… How about this, then? We *don't* pretend like you're not acting weird, and you guys just tell me what's going on. Hmm?"

Rei hesitated, taking in the blond Saber. Catcher had quickly become the closest friend he had after Viv, but they'd still only known each other for 2 weeks. He trusted him, but there were some things that weren't smart to share with anyone he'd only had half a month to get to know, no matter how much he liked them.

Then again, if Shido's protocol meant what he thought it did, there were also some things that couldn't be hidden one way or the other…

"In here." Rei made his decision and moved for the door of his room, pushing it open. "Come on. Both of you."

Viv—despite her early drive that a shower superseded all other news—stepped in immediately. Catcher only frowned in confusion at the two of them a moment longer before he, too, got up from the couch to join, Rei following in behind him and closed the door at their backs.

In the 2 weeks since term had started, very little had changed in his private quarters. The smart-glass window was opaque and scattered with a handful of notes and references over his desk he hadn't bothered to close out of before leaving for lectures that morning. His bed was unmade and the closet was open, revealing a wanting collection of civilian clothing he'd brought with him from Grandcrest, but aside from that the room was about as sparse as the day he'd moved in.

"Sooo… What's up?" Catcher asked again, watching Rei move to the window, tossing his uniform on the bed as he passed.

Not answering immediately, Rei swiped away the data of the smart-glass, then with a few taps turned it translucent, letting in the light of the late summer afternoon. Putting his back to it, he faced his friends again, meeting Viv's eye first.

"Ready for this?" he asked her.

She nodded just as Catcher started to look—for once—a little irritated at being ignored.

"Ready for what?" he demanded, getting heated now. "Hello? Can someone clue me in on—?"

"Call," Rei said, cutting Catcher off as he focused on Shido's weight around his wrists, bringing his arms up.

The Device whirred into life, as it always did on being summoned. In a blink the now-familiar claws extended from the knuckles along the jointed glove that covered Rei's right hand. At the same time, the white underlay manifested fingers-to-elbow about his left, the heavy steel plating taking shape a blink later. When it was done, Rei took in Shido's form expectantly, seeking what was new, looking for what had changed. He searched, then searched again, and ended up finding…

Nothing.

"Wait… What?" he asked out loud, confused as he turned both wrists over, looking for the promised improvements. Had he not understood? Had the protocol meant something else? No. That couldn't be it. The scripting had clearly stated that Shido had evol—

"Uh… Rei?"

Viv's voice was quiet, and Rei looked up at her more out of reflex than intent. He frowned, at a loss to see both her and Catcher staring wide-eyed at… the floor?

And then it hit him.

Slowly, Rei looked down.

Starting just below his knees, his formerly bare legs were now encased in gracefully plated black-and-white armor. Two pairs of narrow, curved panels of carbonized steel extended to cover the front of each of his shins, bisected by clean lines of glowing, blue vysetrium. The backs, over his calves, were more intricate, made of multiple smaller, thinner sheets layered over one another like long scales, but the armor stopped along the collars of the boots he'd put on to run across campus.

"Take them off," Catcher hissed quickly, like it was a matter of life or death, also looking at his feet. "Take them off, Rei!"

Rei did so immediately, bending to undo his laces in a rush before kicking the boots off one after the other. As soon as he did there was more blurred shifting of metal, and an instant later he felt himself standing half an inch taller on soles of padded steel. The pattern encasing his feet proved the most delicate of the armor, made of several small panes that shifted and moved along more vysetrium jointing as he put his weight on one leg, then on the other, then stood up on pointed—almost-clawed—toes.

"You've got to be kidding me…" Viv breathed, taking him all in, mouth still agape. Then, as though coming to her senses, she snapped out of it and looked him in the face with a scowl. "You evolved *again*? *Seriously*?!"

"You tell me," Rei answered weakly, only barely able to pull his attention from the armor long enough to glance up at her. "Is this real? Or did Grant hit me harder than a thought?"

"Oh it's real," Catcher muttered, he too apparently unable to take his eyes off of the black-and-white steel jointed in blue.

Then he seemed to register what Rei had said.

"Wait… Grant? What's Grant got to do with this? Actually, never mind." He held up a hand to stop Viv when she opened her mouth to answer. "You can tell me later. For now—" he turned back to Rei, staring at him intently "—the more pressing issue. Namely: WHAT THE HELL MAN?!"

The volume and excitement of Catcher's demand finally shook Rei from his reverie with a start.

Still, he hardly had an appropriate reply.

"I don't know. I don't know," was all he could answer. It was *true*, too. He'd deduced that he was obviously going to be ascending through the CAD-Ranks a lot faster than his classmates—probably even well-after he caught up to them—but this was something else. Twice. Twice now Shido had evolved, this second shift in form coming only 2 weeks after the first, and only *three ranks apart*. How was that possible? Most evolutions took months, even years in the top tiers, but more importantly they occurred only every seven to ten levels on average. His had happened in three.

Did this mean there was more to his S-Ranked Growth than the simple matter of improving faster? Did this mean his potential number of evolutions was higher, too? If this gap was anything to judge by, Shido would adapt more than twice as many times as the average CAD, which meant an *enormous* probability of development even *long* before Rei achieved the A- or S-Ranks, if he every managed it.

"Rei! Twice! *Twice in two weeks!*" Catcher had continued his half-excited, half-disbelieving yelling. "That's not unheard of, that's *insanity*! Do the instructors know about this?!"

Rei only shook his head, still contemplating the potential impact and meaning of his new armor.

"We were out of the gym before his protocol triggered," Viv started to explain in his stead, but paused as some thought struck her. "Why was that?" she asked, looking to Rei. "We had more than ten minutes between each match. All of my upgrade protocols trigger whenever I'm out of combat for about thirty seconds."

Rei opened his mouth to answer, anticipating some response to form, but nothing came. He pondered it a moment longer, then shook his head. "No idea." His voice still came unsteadily. "Maybe... Maybe because we were slotted to keep fighting? Maybe Shido was aware of that, and the amount of data it had to process at the end caused the last delay?"

"I'm sorry, 'Shido was aware of that'?" Catcher repeated, looking between the two of them with a blank expression. "Is there a reason I should believe a *Device* suddenly came to life and is taking note of our training schedules?"

"Well... No..." Rei answered, struggling to find a way to explain that didn't have him oversharing just yet. In the end, he decided a kernel of truth was the best solution. "Do you remember telling me you trusted that I had a reason I didn't want to explain why I made it into Galens?"

Catcher nodded, his gaze suddenly very intense.

"Do you still believe that?"

Another nod.

"Good." Rei took a breath, mulling over his words. "I *do* know why I made it into the Institute, Catcher. Viv does too. I'm sorry... I want to explain, but it's..." He paused, struggling.

"It's big," Viv took over, looking at Catcher pointedly. "It's really big. The base truth is that the fewer people know about it, the better for everyone for now."

Catcher's eyes were wide again, and he was studying Viv like he were trying to deduce if she were making some kind of exaggeration. When he apparently found no hint of deceit in her expression, he looked to Rei, doing the same thing.

After several seconds of silence, Catcher took him a heavy breath.

"Is this why Valera Dent sought you out after your Commencement match with Laurent?" he asked carefully.

"Yeah," Rei answered just as cautiously.

"Huh." Catcher looked to contemplate this new tidbit. "Which means the staff know…"

"Some of them," Rei clarified. "I think it's only the higher-ups. I'm almost positive our sub-instructors don't. It's one of the reasons I'm tiptoeing around the bush with this, man. I'm sorry."

Catcher didn't look away from him. "And you wouldn't tell me what was going on even if I asked you straight up?"

Rei shook his head. "No. Not now, at least."

"But eventually?"

Rei considered, then deciding to try for a grin that he was pretty sure came out stiff. "Yeah. Definitely. Though if I had to guess, you'll figure it out before I'm ready to share."

"Along with everyone else and their mothers," Viv muttered. Her eyes were on Rei, and she looked worried. "You need to get stronger. And fast. Before you become more of a target for the class dickwads then you already are."

Rei nodded again. "Dent told me the same thing, after she threw Grant into that wall."

"I'm sorry?" Catcher looked taken aback. "The captain threw *Logan Grant* into a *wall?*"

"At about a hundred miles an hour," Viv confirmed cheerfully. "Then had him tossed in the brig for most of a week."

Catcher blinked at her, speechless. Then, apparently deciding his brain couldn't handle more than one dose of insanity at a time, he looked back to Rei. "Just judging by the hints you're dropping, I think I have a good guess at what's going on with your CAD. If I'm correct, not only do I finally get why you're here at Galens, but I also understand why you'd keep something like that so close to your chest. But you're right. You're *both* right." He glanced between the pair of them. "There is no way in hell you're going to be able to keep your head down with your new kicks, man." He indicated Rei's armored forelegs with a wave. "Come tomorrow, that's gonna be the hottest topic in every ear of every student in the school, and you were only *just* starting to fly under the radar a bit."

"Maybe in 1-C and the other classes," Viv quipped with a snort. "Not in ours. Dent turned Grant into a temporary wall decoration because he went at Rei *after* the match was done. Even ignored Sergeant Major Gross telling him to stand down."

"Damn. *Seriously?*" Catcher looked shocked, his speech derailed. "What the hell was he thinking?"

"I'm not sure he was," Rei was the one to answer, frowning. "The guy looked... demented. I've never seen anyone that mad. I'm just remembering that he said something weird during the fight, too. Something about how I should have the dignity to 'die with the rest of them'?"

"He did?" Viv asked, surprised. "I missed that. Whatever his deal was, he definitely looked pissed. I thought he was going to kill you."

"You and me both," Rei muttered, suddenly glad their lecturers hadn't yet taught the first years how to make a true-call.

"I told you before that dude is bad news," Catcher said darkly, looking between the two of them. "If anything it's even more reason to listen to Dent and Viv, Rei. You *definitely* need to get stronger, or some people might start going out of their way to break you down. Once they realize how fast your CAD is catching up to all of us..."

"Yeah," Rei nodded, having already considered all of what the boy was saying. "Yeah, I know. Which is why I have a favor to ask."

It was Viv and Catcher's turn to blink at each other before looking at him again, apparently not having expected this.

"If you're gonna suggest we sneak into the brig to shank Grant in his sleep, I'll need to change my clothes first," Catcher said with feigned gravity.

Rei stared at him blankly until the boy raised his hands in surrender.

"Okay, okay. No killing off of fellow classmates. Heard." He dropped his arms, managing a smile again. "What do you need, then?"

Rei answered with his own grin.

"Either of you have plans after dinner tonight?"

That's it! Now keep the gap between the two of you tight! Don't let him back away!... Good! Yeah! Just like that! Catcher, speed up a little more. I think he's getting the hang of it."

Rei would have protested, but at Viv's command from the edge of the Dueling field Catcher's longsword began to dance and prod faster, the yellow-and-white blurring of the steel streaked with purple light. Rei—who had indeed *just* been getting a handle on the Saber's speed and openings—suddenly found himself putting all of his focus in nothing more than defending himself, block or slashing away the threatening blade every time it got too near. Before he knew it he was being pushed back, until within 10 seconds Viv was shouting once more.

"Stop! Stop! Rei, you're out of any practical range again."

Rei blinked and looked over the steel shielding of his left arm he'd just been using to defend his face. Sure enough, Catcher was smiling cheerfully at him from some 6 or 7 feet away, Arthus—his Device—held perfectly parallel to the ground at arm's length, the tip hovering inches from Shido's guard.

"Dammit," Rei cursed, dropping his arms to take in the distance he'd been driven back, rending Shido's Brawler-like manifestation useless. "It's his Speed! I can't keep up!"

"Of course you can't keep up." Viv approached from the sideline. She, like them, was in her combat uniform, having switched out with Catcher a quarter-hour before to act as match arbiter and feedback-provider. "Catcher's probably close to C-Ranked Speed—"

"D7," Catcher confirmed for her, tossing Arthus over one shoulder to wait.

"—which puts him a full tier and a half higher than you," Viv finished, motioning to Rei insistently. "We're not here so that you can beat us, right? We're here so that you can *get to the point* of beating us."

"Maybe," Catcher added with a grin, and Viv shot him a glare this time.

They were all three standing near the middle of one of the many Dueling fields available for students in each of Galen's two 24-hour training facilities. East Center—the one closest to Kanes—was a modest structure of steel and polished stone until you *entered* the building. Inside, smart-glass walls made up every surface, kept at a standard-translucence so that newcomers could take in each of the dozen fields that comprised the first floor. There was no staffer, only automated registration systems on pads outside the entrance to each chamber, as well as a trio of dedicated medical drones docked at the end of the hall that divide the fields into two rows of six. The ceiling was only ten feet above their heads—hardly the clearance of a standardized combat-space—but since the facility wasn't designed to hold sanctioned matches it fulfilled its purpose as a training gym perfectly. Even at that moment Rei could hear other pairings and groups in other chambers, hidden from view since the three of them had elected to make their walls an opaque white before getting started.

His consideration of those other noises was interrupted when he flinched as text began to spill down the frame of his NOED.

...

Processing combat information.

...

Calculating.

...

Results:
Strength: Lacking
Endurance: Adequate
Speed: Adequate
Cognition: Adequate
Offense: Adequate
Defense: Adequate
Growth: Not Applicable

...

Checking combat data acquisition.

...

Adequate data acquirement met.
Device initiating adjustments to:
Strength.

...

Adjustment complete.
Strength has been upgraded from Rank F9 to E0.

"Oh, *sweet!*" Rei exclaimed, completely interrupting Viv, who'd apparently continued to berate him for his self-depreciation.

She forgave him, though, as both she and Catcher stiffened in excitement at his words. "What? What is it?"

"E0 Strength!" Rei answered eagerly, lowering his voice a little in case anyone accidentally overheard them.

Catcher groaned, closing his eyes and tilting his head back in jealousy. "Don't get me wrong man, I'm excited for you, but the envy is real. That's the *second* spec you've had boosted tonight!"

"Complain when I catch up to you, Mr. *D7 Speed*," Rei snorted, but he didn't argue further. Indeed, his lagging Endurance had upgraded to F7 about an hour into their session. At the thought, though, his excitement sobered a little. "I really appreciate this, guys, but are you sure you don't mind? I can't be much of a challenge for your spec levels…"

Viv waved his uncertainty off. "Not yet you're not, but it's only a matter of time, right? Besides, this is good for us, too. We should have started taking advantage of our leisure hours weeks ago, especially if we seriously want to catch up with the summer group."

Catcher nodded, looking Viv up and down. "Some of us more than others. You're not that far behind them, entering with a D7…"

"And getting closer to D8 every day." Viv grinned at the pair of them wickedly. "Rei, your specs might be trash, but this is still training. My Endurance jumped to D4 a half hour after yours."

"What?!" Rei and Catcher exclaimed together, and Viv nodded.

"Yup. This might be skewed in your favor for now, but it's not like it's hurting us. And besides—" her smile widened, and she turned on Catcher in a snap to shove him closer to the center of the field "—today gave me a bad taste for Sabers, so I'm glad I get to pick on one for a bit."

"Oh you're *on*," Catcher announced eagerly, catching himself and bringing his sword off his shoulder and at the ready.

Rei let the pair of them go at it for a half hour or so, taking his turn to stand match-side, shouting criticisms where he could. Viv might have been the stronger of the two when it came to rank, but Catcher had learned a thing or two in his 4 years at an ISCM prep. His skill was undeniable, and while Viv could outpace him, he rarely gave her an opportunity to take advantage of her better Speed and Offense. While Arthus' main form was the longsword, the Device also covered Catcher's left arm from elbow to fingers, and he used the purple claws there to much greater efficiency that Selleck had earlier in the day. In the end the two of them were roughly matched at an even level, though Rei *did* think he might have placed his credits on Viv if someone had put a knife to his throat about it.

After Catcher called for a break, Rei stepped in, and Viv gave him the thrashing of his life on repeat. Again he focused on keeping Shido within a usable range, but again he kept getting rebuffed. Gemela had less reach than Arthus did—Viv's sword was about 6 inches shorter than Catcher's longer blade—but her *two* weapons were their own beast to handle, and over and over Rei kept finding himself repelled by the barrage of vysetrium-edged steel.

"Break!" he wheezed after about 15 minutes of near-nonstop fighting, throwing his hands up as he found himself utterly unable to penetrate Viv's slashing defenses no matter how hard he tried. "Break!"

Viv lowered her blades, looking a little disappointed, but when Rei half-dropped, half-collapsed back to the projection plating, she sniggered a little and recalled Gemela.

"I say we call it for the night?" she asked Catcher, who himself was cross-legged nearby. "I think our resident runt is going to pass out if we keep him at this much longer."

Rei didn't have the breath to answer her, so he just held up both middle fingers in response and he tucked his head between his legs, trying to recover.

"Sounds good," Catcher agreed, but he sounded a little disappointed. "Bummed I'm the only one who didn't see any spec improvement, though."

"It'll happen," Viv assured him automatically, wiping sweat from her brow with the back of one hand as she tugged her ponytail free of its hairband with the other. As always, her brown locks fell around her shoulders in perfect form.

"Seriously, *how* does it do that?" Catcher demanded, taking in her curls with genuine amazement.

Viv wiggled her eyebrows mysteriously at him. "If I told you I'd have to kill you." She looked at Rei, then. "You ready to head back?"

It took a moment for him to respond. "Only… Only if you guys promise to come back… tomorrow," he got out through gasps, head still bowed.

Viv and Catcher looked at each other, then shrugged. "We're game. You sure you won't get wiped out for classes, though?"

Rei grinned as his breath finally started to even out. "Even if I do, it'll be worth it in the end."

As he answered, he lifted his face, revealing the flare of the neuro-optic that had just informed him his Endurance had upped again, reaching F8.

Catcher was swearing under his breath the entire way home.

CHAPTER 23

This is the basis of all SCT mechanics at any level." Lieutenant Major John Markus, Head of the Device Evolution department, was pacing back and forth before the layered amphitheater seating of his class while he spoke, as was his usual fashion in the man's infrequent morning lectures. "Through selective targeting and light-speed electromagnetic pulses, the phantom-calls of your CADs are able to interrupt standard activity in both the short and long axons of an opponent's neurological systems. While this is obviously primarily used for the benefit of combat tournaments, it also allows Users to apply non-lethal force beyond such settings when needed. Yes, Kallum." The young, yellow-haired instructor paused to point somewhere over Rei's head. "You have a question?"

"What sort of setting would that be, sir? I thought calling on our Devices outside of sanctioned areas was a criminal offense."

"Extenuating circumstances such as self-defense can be applied," Markus answered. "There have been a number of assaults on popular SCT combatants in the past, none of which have been documented to have gone well for the offending party." A smattering of laughter from the class. "There is also a dedicated unit of Users in the Military Police branch whose sole task is to handle CAD wielders the other disciplinary teams would have no ability to manage. Does that answer your question?" Joshua Kallum—one of 1-A's Sabers—must have nodded, because Markus pressed on. "Good. Then returning to the topic at hand, it is important to discuss the varied lengths of interruption as controlled by Arena fields and—"

As the lieutenant major continued to drone on about the physiological impact of a phantom-call on the human body, Rei tuned the man out, content pretending to be scribbling notes on his pad as he and Viv used it to secretly watch Oraculum taking on Hanson Frost somewhere on Venus. The Intersystem pro match was one of the most highly anticipated of the year—two Rook-Class S-Ranks going head-to-head—and more than once Rei had heard someone suppress a yelp or hiss behind them, not to mention he knew for a *fact* that Sense, Kay, and Leron were sharing a screen two rows below.

"Oh watch this, watch this!" Rei whispered energetically just in time for Oraculum—a Brawler in mostly green-and-black full-body armor—to punch at Frost from nearly 10 yards away. There was a rippling distortion in the air between the two opponents, and Frost didn't move quick enough to dodge the wave of energy. It struck the white-and-silver Lancer full on, slamming him back to bounce off the thick trunk of one of the tall pines that made up their Woodlands field. "*Directional Repulsion.*" Rei could hear the excitement in his own voice. "It's not User-Unique to him, but Oraculum's like one of a hundred registered Users to possess it right now."

"That's a pretty potent Ability to combo with," Viv answered quietly, glancing up like she wanted to make sure Markus hadn't caught wind of their lack of attention. "An S-Ranked Brawler with a ranged attack? That must make him a nightmare to deal with."

"Oh it does," Rei agree, watching Oraculum follow up his Directional Repulsion with a Break Step—a common short-burst Ability that allowed for an extreme boost in speed—to close the gap between him and his fallen opponent in a flash. Hanson Frost went flying as a leg armored in green-and-black took him in the side before he could find his feet again.

Pleased with the direction the fight was going, Rei looked up so Markus wouldn't get suspicious of him staring at his tablet for too long.

It was rare for them to have lectures in the Device Evolution building. Most of their course work was held in the Combat Theory or Tactical Studies departments, but this was the third class by the lieutenant major they'd been made to attend so far that term, and Rei supposed he could see the sense of it. There was value in knowing the *why* and *how* of a thing, especially if said thing had as many questions to be answered about it as a CAD. The talks may even have been interesting—and probably were for a number of people in the class—had Rei not made a study of 95% of the content already.

At the thought, Rei looked over his shoulder, wondering how many eyes would *actually* be fixed on the instructor.

For once, he didn't catch a single glare thrown in his direction.

Shido's second evolution had, it turned out, had the fortune of being made public on the same day that Leda Truant—one of the Phalanxes, and a class gossip that spent most of her time hanging around with Logan Grant's group—made it known to the whole of 1-A that Aria Laurent had ranked up from C0 to C1, re-solidifying her position as the highest level among the first years. As a result—while Rei's new armor had certainly not gone *unnoticed*—many of the curious had been quick to nod along and move on when he played the "an E-Ranker will improve a lot faster" card once again. He got more than a few lingering stares, however, and over the last 2 weeks of class felt like the 1-A cadets had polarized, most finally leaving behind their flame of interest in him at the start of the term, while a few seemed to have suddenly made it their business to watch his every move. To exactly no one's surprise, Grant was among this latter group, his original distaste for Rei having morphed into something altogether more hostile—if also more subdued—ever since their altercation. Stranger, however, was the fact that not only was Leron Joy a part of those watching him like hawks—it was Viv who'd bothered to figure out the boy's full name—but he'd been joined by Kay Sandree. Rei's infrequent interactions with the top-ranked Lancer were still pleasant—he was pretty sure Sense was always putting in a good word for him with the blue-haired girl—but he'd caught Kay studying him on more than one occasion, studying him with something between keen curiosity and suspicion.

No eyes, however, seemed to follow him *half* as much as those of Aria Laurent.

Between the two of them, Rei and Viv had caught the C-Ranker scrutinizing him almost daily, sometimes in passing glances, sometimes frowning at him with such intensity Laurent might have been trying to read his mind. Even Viv wasn't free of her gaze, of late, with Catcher swearing up and down he'd seen the girl watching her on the occasions he and Viv had had to eat without Rei, typically when he took the lunch hour to study or try to find better combat simulations to improve his use of Shido's claws. It had been a bizarre enough feeling knowing several pairs of eyes were always trained on his back whenever he wasn't locked away in the suite, but for the *top* first year to have taken such a poorly-hidden interest in him made Rei feel something between excited and self-conscious.

"Now, there is a very important distinction that is made in neural interruption, particularly when it comes to the simulation of cerebral and spinal injuries. Let's see… Laurent. Can you tell me what that distinction is?"

Speak of the devil, Rei thought as the lieutenant major posed his question.

Aria Laurent had taken a place separate from the others on the far end of a row two aisles up from him and Viv. Ordinarily it might have been odd for Rei to know exactly where another member of the class had placed themselves on any given day, but as the red-headed girl's scrutiny of him had increased, so had his awareness of her. She sat with her back straight and her cap in perfect place, and answered Markus promptly.

"Yes, sir. At its broadest definition, the distinction is typically classified by a separation of the autonomic and somatic nervous systems, allowing neural interruption to solely affect voluntary motor function and somatosensory input."

"Yes. Precisely. Now, if we are to consider—"

Rei wasn't listening again, still studying Aria Laurent as she returned to taking notes. He couldn't claim it completely baffled him. Catcher had stated it best on their first day at school, when he'd said that no one at Galens was going to be any kind of idiot. Rei could understand some notice of him on the C-Ranker's part, particularly following Shido's second evolution.

But Laurent's interest seemed so much so that even now, as he watched her, he caught her green eyes flick towards him, then away again. They hadn't spoken a word to each other—not in the month since the Commencement match—and yet her observation of him only appeared to be growing more and more intense with each passing week. He supposed he should have been grateful, really. Unlike Logan Grant, Laurent's position at the top had made her somewhat unapproachable. She was always on her own. In class, in training, at the dining halls. It wasn't that she gave off any sort of unfriendly vibe, but rather that she just seemed… unattainable. Like sitting down to have a normal conversation with her wasn't something just anyone could do. Even *if* Grant caught up to her rank again, Laurent still had her Third Eye, an Ability that simply outclassed anything any other first year cadet could bring to bear on the field.

In the end, if anyone was going to be watching him as carefully as Aria Laurent, Rei supposed he could count it a good thing she wasn't likely to have ample opportunity to gossip about whatever she deduced.

Thump.

Viv's kick under the desk had him jump, and Rei finally tore his eyes off of Laurent to glare around at his best friend. He was about to demand what she wanted when a booming voice cut him off.

"*Cadet Ward.*"

Rei jerked and snapped about in his seat. John Markus was watching him with narrowed eyes, and by the looks on the faces of every student in the rows before him and Viv—all turned in his direction in their seats—it was apparent the lieutenant major had been attempting to get his attention for several seconds already.

"As on-point as Laurent's answer was," the officer said steadily, his voice threateningly calm, "I hardly considered it fascinating enough to deserve your gaping at her *for a minute after the fact.*"

Rei felt his face go red, and more than a few laughs broke out all around him this time. Even Viv had to fight off a smile, he could tell, seeing her bring one hand to her mouth as she, too, sat rigidly beside him.

"Yes, sir. Sorry, sir," he got out tightly. He wasn't sure what else to say, but apparently his apology didn't satisfy the department head, because the young instructor pursed his lips.

"If you were so intrigued by her response, then perhaps you would like to expand on it? Would you tell me, for example, how exactly the neural differentiation is decided, and why it is so important?"

Rei brightened immediately. "Yes, sir. As far as we are aware, opponents' Devices use a combination of neuron types and information provided by your own CAD to identify how and where to interrupt. I.e.: C- and A-Delta axons for pain and pressure sensation, A-Alpha and Gamma for muscular function, et cetera. As Cadet Laurent said, however, the most important distinction comes in a separation of what neurons work for the autonomic versus somatic nervous system. It would be a disaster if a blow to the head had a User's heart stop, or kept them from breathing, for example." He hesitated, then added: "Or if getting run through the stomach made you lose bowel control in front of your entire incoming class."

The laughs this time were his to claim, and he barely stopped himself from grinning himself as Markus blinked at him slowly, clearly unamused.

"Correct, cadet," the officer said after a moment. "Now imagine how much more impressed I would be with that answer if you *hadn't* spent the entire class switching between ogling Laurent and watching the Venus SCTs with Arada under your desk."

There was an *immediate* scrambling of motion at this, with Viv's quick dropping of Rei's pad not being the only such panicked flinching. All around the class people were hissing along with the sounds of tablets being turned off or stowed away, and it was with an expression of gratified triumph that John Markus returned to his lecture, leaving Rei just one of many embarrassed students.

An hour later the tone of the period ending said that the morning courses were done, and the lieutenant major called out over the bustle of almost thirty cadets gathering their bags and starting to make for the door. "Don't forget that your afternoon training sessions have been canceled, and *all* students are to report to the Arena at 1300 for a special assembly. Also, I expect your papers on the anticipated evolutionary pathways of your Devices by next Wednesday."

There were a scattered chorus of affirmations from the class—Markus was rather lax on demanding appropriate military decorum from his students—before they all filed out of the room, heading for the building lobby. Once outside, Rei and Viv both had to grab hold of their cap brims when a hefty gust of wind cut across the grey of the stormy September day, forcing them to bow their heads against an inconsiderate wash of rain.

"You'd think that after two hundred years of developing CAD technology they'd have figured out a way to turn a Device into an umbrella!" Viv shouted as they joined the others to move as one towards the mess hall.

"I'd take just being allowed to run in this!" Rei answered her, making a face as he felt water trickle down his neck.

"Try it!" she laughed in answer. "I promise I definitely *won't* send you lots of pictures of my hot lunch when the first staffer who catches you makes you bear-crawl a lap around the school in this crap."

Rei chuckled, but said nothing more, letting himself be swept along in the huddled misery of the others. At one point he caught Sense's eye, the bald cadet mouthing a more colorful version of "Screw this!" as he pointed at the sky, which Rei agreed with several fervent nods. Kay Sandree stood beside the Brawler, and Rei saw her looking accidentally, watching what had been a small frown turn into a bright smile as she waved.

It really wasn't just Laurent he had to worry about, he supposed…

They made the mess hall in a few minutes, but that short walk was still enough to see them all soaked to their underclothes. Fortunately, the moment they stepped inside the group was met by several of the service drones who ordinarily cleaned up after the students, and 1-A formed a few fast lines so that the bots could pass over them in quick succession with ion scanners, instantly heating and vaporizing all excess water from their clothes. Viv actually sighed in relief when she was dried off, joining Rei where he'd waited for her before heading for the back of the hall. "As crap as their rules are, can't say the perks aren't worth it, right?"

Rei chuckled, and would have agreed had he not just caught sight of Catcher waving them down from the start of the automated food line.

"Hey," he greeted their roommate as they approached. "You didn't have to wait for us, you know."

"Like I would have," Catcher answered with a mock scoff, grabbing a trio of trays from the dispenser behind him and handing them out. "I just got here. Oraculum took down Hanson Frost in about five minutes, but there were a bunch of great fights on the card after that one. Did you guys get to catch any in class?"

"Most of the Oraculum match, but then Rei got us all caught by 'ogling' Laurent," Viv answered with a snigger, taking the lead ahead of the other two.

Rei rolled his eyes and explained himself in answer to Catcher's confused look. "Turns out the lieutenant major knew a bunch of us were watching the tournament the whole class. He just got annoyed when I got distracted."

"Distracted by… Laurent?" Catcher asked, putting his tray down on the rolling belt of the dispensary and starting to punch his order into a menu that displayed itself across the smart-glass shield covering the food. As soon as he was done a half-dozen automated arms began rapidly pulling his selections from the varied platters of offered food to deposit them one after the other on the tray.

"Yeah—I mean *no*." Rei glared at Viv as he completed his own order right behind Catcher. "Dammit! This is how rumors get started!"

Viv giggled again, already at the end of the line to pick up her laden lunch as it rolled out the other side of the covering. "I wasn't the one caught staring, *Romeo*."

"Whatever," Rei grumbled, watching his turkey breast and Brussels sprouts get piled onto a plate beside each other before getting placed in the middle of his tray. Deciding to change the subject, he turned to Catcher. "Any idea what this 'special assembly' is about, by the way? It doesn't sound like anyone was expecting it when we got our schedules Sunday."

"Not a clue," the blond cadet answered with a shrug, picking up his food to step out of the way and wait with Viv. "There's a rumor that Captain Dent is going to announce a field trip to some old ruin called 'the Colosseum' on Earth, but it sounds like bull to me."

"Has to be," Rei snorted, finally collecting his tray and moving to lead the way towards their favorite table near the edge of the atrium, thankfully still vacant. "The Colosseum got mostly demolished about thirty years ago to make way for Rome's population expansion."

Silence greeted this statement from behind him, and Rei shook his head. He could imagine his companion's stares of empty disinterest.

Viv finally broke the quiet as they reached the table and claimed their usual seats. "If it's nothing special, then… It's got to be an announcement about the Intra-School SCT, right?"

Rei and Catcher both paused, staring at Viv in half-astonishment, half-realization.

"Why are you guys looking at me like you can't believe I said it first?!" she demanded in a huff.

"Cause you're supposed to be the ditz of our happy little company," Catcher was the first to jab back with a grin, taking up his utensils. "If you start being the most on the ball, who's gonna be our stereotypical blonde friend? It sure as hell isn't about to be Rei."

"Meaning it would probably be the only person sitting at this table whose *actually blond*, jerk!" Viv growled, Catcher's enjoyment of her indignation only adding gas to the fire.

"If you're gonna fight, can I at least finish my lunch first?" Rei quipped, tugging off a hunk of turkey with his fork before leaning over the table a little to point it at Viv. "But seriously. That's probably it, isn't it? The tournament's in the second quarter?"

"With Sectionals in the third, and Globals and above happening in the fourth and over the summer, yeah." Viv nodded, her disgruntlement apparently appeased by the shift back to the subject at hand. "That gives us… What? Seven weeks?"

"Six," Catcher barely managed to say through a mouthful of mashed potatoes. "I guess—" he paused, deciding swallowing was better than struggling. "I guess it makes sense. They'll probably want to start us on squad-format training sooner rather than later…"

Beside him, Rei choked, coughing until Viv snagged a glass of water from a passing service drone and handed it over.

"Squad-format?" Rei finally got out after he'd successfully avoided demise-by-sprout. "I didn't know there'd be squad-format events in the Intra-Schools!"

"Cause there won't be," Catcher assured him over his shoulder, taking a water for himself from another bot. "Team Battles and Wargames only start at Sectionals, and each school is only allowed to bring three squads, of which at least half of the members have to be individual qualifiers."

"Wait, really?" Viv asked, clearly only hearing of this for the first time.

Catcher nodded.

"But… That means aside from the sixteen school champions, up to another nine could be participating in squad events." Viv looked astonished by this revelation.

"That's almost a fifth of our entire class…"

"Which gives our lovely instructors ample excuse to start training as soon as possible, not to mention the hard-on Dent has for preparing us for live combat. Users are formed into teams on the front lines, too."

Leaving the two to their discussion, Rei chewed and studied the table as he thought. He'd never really contemplated Team Battles and Wargames much. He loved watching them on the feeds, and knew they were the more popular format outside of high-profile A- and S-Ranked Duels, but combat tournaments in prep school had been all one-on-one bouts, and never more. He wondered what it would be like, fighting a full group.

And *alongside* a full group…

He grinned to himself, shoving more turkey into his mouth, deciding it would probably be nothing short of awesome.

"Wait, they are?"

Rei looked up, having lost track of the conversation.

"Yeah," Catcher was confirming for Viv. "Everyone who goes."

"They're what?" Rei asked. "Everyone who goes where?"

"Catcher's saying everyone who goes to Sectionals is allowed to participate in the Dueling events," Viv said, sounding further surprised. "Even the ones who only go as part of a team."

"Oh. Yeah." Rei nodded to second Catcher before smirking, seeing an opportunity. "Guess you wouldn't know, given you're not a 'fanboy' like us."

Viv rolled her eyes before leaning away from her tray to glare at him pointedly.

"Kidding, kidding," Rei put both hands up—still holding his fork and knife—in feigned surrender. "But yeah. Everyone gets to participate. It's not something you hear about often because anyone who qualifies is technically seeded. I think you have to win two or three matches as a non-qualifier before you're even bracketed in the first rounds you'll see on the feeds."

"But why?" Viv asked, confused. "Why wouldn't they show *all* the matches, then? Sounds like a lot of lost opportunity."

"It's the opposite, actually," Catcher started to explain, breaking off a chunk of bread for himself. "Those Duels happen before any of the other events, so they'd have to be the first fights shown to viewers. Not every school is Galens, much less in this Sector. A lot of those matches are probably…" He paused, obviously looking for a word that wouldn't cast the Users in question in too unfavorable a light.

"Lackluster?" Rei offered.

"Lackluster!" Catcher agreed at once, popping his bread into his mouth victoriously.

"I suppose," Viv muttered, looking a little disappointed. Then she perked up. "Well damn… Even if we don't qualify on our own, maybe we could still be able to go to Sectionals as part of a team."

"You could qualify."

It was, surprisingly, Catcher who stated the fact, beating Rei to the punch.

Viv seemed taken aback. "Huh? You think?"

"Definitely." Catcher nodded with confidence, going for another hunk of bread without looking at her. "We've been doing almost three hours of extra training a day for two weeks now, and you hit D8 last Thursday, right?"

"Yeah…" Viv confirmed a little uncertainly. "But I'm sure there's plenty of people who—"

"Not really." Rei let Catcher chew his food, picking up the explanation. "Have you checked Benaly's ranking lately? Of Lena Jiang's? They're still both D8. A few of the top sixteen have pushed into D9, and Laurent and Grant are both obviously Cs, but you're on pace to pass some of the leaders right now."

"*Seriously?*" Viv hissed, her NOED flaring in her eyes. Rei and Catcher watched her pull up what must have been several profiles for the cadets who'd attended the summer training. After 10 seconds she spoke again. "Oh, whoa… It's not just Benaly and Jiang… *Most* of them are still D8?" she looked surprised, then grinned as she closed her neuro-optic. "See?! I *told* you training with you would pay off!"

Rei smiled without turning to her, his attention back on his lunch. "I'm glad. Then again, your Growth spec *is* slightly above average, so I'm not all that surprised."

"Hey now! I hit D6 the week we started training!" Catcher was probably trying to pout, but his cheek-full of food somewhat ruined the effect. "Even us lowly average-Growthers are getting something out of this, you know?"

"There's a joke in there somewhere, but I don't think I want to go looking too hard for it…" Viv said with a snicker.

As she and Catcher started to bicker amicably again, Rei let them be, his mind elsewhere as he considered their discussion. The Intra-School SCT…

As he was now, there wasn't a User among the first years he thought he had a fair shot of going up against. Even the likes of Tad Emble—who had been a D0 when he'd been accepted to Galens—were still margins more powerful, and ever firmly out of

Rei's reach. His CAD-Rank was bad enough as it was—he was still "the E-Ranker" to some of the less amiable first years—but the real problem lay in the fact that his specs were actually skewed below even his E9, earned up from E7 over the course of 2 weeks hard work both in class and in the nightly after-dinner conditioning with Viv and Catcher. Ordinarily E9 would have put his specification around that rage, but his S-Ranked Growth had skewed all this numbers from the start.

Six weeks… he considered.

Regardless if Viv was right about the announcement, the Intra-School SCT would start in a month and a half. Maybe Rei would get lucky and have an extra day or so if he wasn't in the first round of fights, but that was hardly a game changer…

You need to get stronger.

Valera Dent's words reached him again, and he frowned as he chewed. 6 weeks. He had a 6 weeks to get to a point where he could stand on a field with the other first years without embarrassing himself.

But no… No. That wasn't right. Was that all he wanted? Was that all he was seeking out of his time at Galens? To be just "good enough"? To be just strong enough to stand toe to toe with *some* of the other cadets?

No… No. That wasn't enough.

He'd already told the captain that, in fact. He'd already told her that he wanted what she had had. That he wanted a legend like the one she'd left behind in the circuits when she'd volunteered for the front lines.

And what had she told him? Not to aim to be like her.

"'Aim to be like the ones who beat me'," Rei quoted under his breath, lifting his gaze to look at Viv.

She could qualify. She *could*. He was sure of it. Catcher too, in fact, though that would be more of a gamble.

And Rei had 6 weeks to reach *them*, and higher.

B y the time they finished their meals and left the mess hall, the storm had subsided just enough to make the walk to the Arena bearable. The true rain had turned to an uncomfortable spit, and so Rei, Viv, and Catcher were feeling more damp than wet when the black-and-grey walls of the massive building came into view. Even that didn't bother them, though, because they were too busy looking around as they started along the white marble path.

"Whoa… Isn't that Anatoli Sidorov?" Catcher asked, pointing at a muscular youth with shoulders that would have matched Michael Bretz' for width, the red-on-green band looping his arm marking him as a second year.

"Yeah it is," Rei whispered back, but he was looking past the massive boy to another, shorter figure a ways beyond him. "But look. That's Christopher Lennon."

"No *way*," Catcher breathed, craning to see through the moving crowd.

On his other side Viv finally gave in.

"Who are you guys talking about?" she asked under her breath, looking around in an embarrassed sort of way, like a mother abashed by the behavior of her children. She had reason to, of course, given that they were no longer encircled by the familiar faces of the first years alone.

In a collective bow against the wind, the entire student body of the Galens Institute was in the process of making their steady way towards the Arena. Aside from red-on-green, there were also the blue armbands of third years, along with a few scattered white markings of staffers apparently intending to attend the special assembly as well. Though the older students didn't *look* much different from the first years, Rei couldn't help but feel smaller than ever among them, especially when he caught sight of a few familiar faces.

"Okay, Sidorov I get." Catcher was frowning at Viv in distinct disappointment. "He was the champion of the first year bracket at Sectionals last year, and not everyone watches that. But Lennon is a *legend*! Come on! The guy is one of like *five* to have competed at the Collegiate Intersystems last year as a *second year*!"

"Wait," Viv cut him off, her embarrassment vanishing as she caught sight of the dark-skinned figure in question, a smaller third year with short, grey dreadlocks just making the mouth of the Arena's east entrance. "The Lasher? That's him?"

"*Yes!*" Rei and Catcher both said together, half-exasperated, half-relieved.

"He's incredible," Rei continued. "He was the only second year in the top eight at the Astra Systems, and almost made it to the top fifty at the Championships ahead of a *lot* of third years. He's a favorite to make the top sixteen this year! Oh, and over there there's Wattana Jelani, who—!"

He and Catcher took turns gushing over the famous faces they saw all the way up into the Arena. Unlike most any other day they'd passed through the structure, the roof of the massive building was closed today, the great triangular plates sealing off the cavernous inside from the abuse of the summer storm. Under the bright glow of a hundred solar lights that illuminated the room as brightly as any sun, Rei and the others following the flow of the crowd towards the south end of the stands, which seemed to be the school's standard assembly point. Despite their gathering number tripling the Commencement Ceremony's attendance, among the massive seating designed to accommodate 150,000 people, the collected first, second, and third years still looked like nothing more than a drop of black-and-gold mixed with vibrantly colored hair against the white stone of the seats. The graduating classes had been separated to sit alongside each other in three separate sections, with the third years claiming the central seats, this time. Above this middle gallery the projected image of the red griffin on blue hovered large, while the red-on-green was suspended over the section west of it, and the red-on-grey to the east.

Reaching their area, Rei, Viv, and Catcher took to the stands and found a trio of seats all lined up just a row up from the walkway. They settled in, the physical projection of the supports allowing them to lean back as they continued to talk, their chatter joining the drone of the hundreds of other conversations happening all around them. Every so often someone would peer down into the Arena, where not a soul was present, the lack of officers and NOED indicators a testament to the fact that they had all already been at the Institution for a whole month.

"Oh, that's Lana Archer." Catcher was still fawning over the older students when he could. "She made it to the Systems last year. I've heard she's inconsistent, but a serious danger when she's in the zone. And that's Shoko Komi. She's supposedly too shy to do interviews or anything like that, but you seriously do *not* want to get on the wrong end of her—"

"Dude, do you ever breathe?"

As one the three of them looked around. Sense was grinning down from the seat over Rei's right shoulder. Next to him, Kay gave a brief wave, while on her far side Leron Joy stared resolutely ahead, refusing to look in their direction. Rei returned Kay's hello, but ignored Joy just as stiffly.

"Catcher will tell you breathing is overrated," he addressed Sense instead with a chuckle.

"Highly," Catcher started with what might have been a solemn sort of nod, except he stopped himself to look past their friends. "Rei. Your superfan has her eye on you again."

Rei frowned, leaning sideways a little to follow Catcher's eye around Sense's head. Sure enough, Aria Laurent sat three rows above them, and the moment their eyes met she looked away quickly.

"What is *up* with her?" he asked himself, and before him Sense and Kay both turned to see what he was looking at.

"With whom?" the Lancer asked, her blue-and-red hair tied in a pair of tails under the back of her cap. "Laurent?"

"Yeah," Viv answered, still watching the C-Ranker intently, as though hoping to catch the girl glancing their way again. "She's been watching Rei like a hawk since the start of term."

"Oh?" Kay said, turning to face them with one eyebrow raised. "Guess she's sharper than the rest of us, then."

"What's that supposed to mean?" Viv asked slowly, blue eyes shifting to the Lancer.

Before Kay could answer, though, Sense leaned forward, pointing between their heads towards the Arena floor. "You'll have to interrogate her later, unfortunately. Look."

At the gesture, Rei, Viv, and Catcher all turned about again, just in time for a shout to ring across the conversation and chatter.

"OFFICER ON THE FIELD."

As one, 384 cadets stopped talking and took to their feet, saluting in the direction of the Arena. The silence was so abrupt and absolute that one could actually hear the clip of leather boots over projection plating as six figures made their way across the field. When they reached the center of the Dueling ring, they about-faced, and at once the steel beneath their feet glowed white.

A couple of seconds later, the officers were on level with the bottom row of the stands, the red griffin having once more grown to extend itself against the perfect surface of the suspended hologram.

"At ease, cadets," Valera Dent's amplified voice rang across the quite, one of two among the figures to have stood forward from the other four. "Take your seats."

There was a clattering of noise as the students of every year did as they were instructed.

"You've been gathered here today at the cost of your training afternoon for an important announcement," the captain continued, her brown eyes sweeping slowly over the stands under the brim of her cap. "It has been a month since term started, in which time I have had the great pleasure of seeing most among you make excellent improvements not only in your strength and ability as Users, but in your pride and attentiveness as cadets of the Intersystem Collective Military. Let me first take a moment to congratulate you on that, and say out loud how proud I am of every one of you and your efforts."

She paused as some murmured appreciations broke out in the crowd, letting the interruption settle before continuing.

"I think—therefore—that none of you will be taken aback when I tell you that soon, the focus of your training will shift a little, particularly among the first years. It is time to start preparing you for a true Simulated Combat Tournament."

While none of the other graduating years looked remotely surprised by this, the cadets around Rei and the others were distinctly more enthusiastic of this announcement.

"I told you!" Viv hissed, punching Rei in the arm before reaching across him to do the same to Cather. "I *told* you!"

"Yeah, yeah," Catcher answered her with a smirk, not looking away from Dent as he rubbed his shoulder. "Now hush. I want to hear this."

"In six weeks' time, the first round of the Galens Institute Intra-School SCT will take place." Valera Dent had continued on, ignoring the first years' collective excitement. "It will run the first seven weeks of your second quarter. As you all know, however, *I* am not the officer in charge of the tournament, so I will leave the explanations to someone more qualified." She stepped back with a gesture towards the other figure who had been standing beside her, an older man in the same regulars she sported. "For those of you who do not know him, allow me to present Major Dyrk Reese, who will be handling all brackets and arbitration for this event."

"Thank you, captain," the major said politely, and as he took center attention Rei recognized the man with a frown. Head shaved and with deep set eyes, Dyrk Reese was the very officer who'd looked to disapprove of his participation in the demonstration match at the Commencement.

Suddenly, Rei got a bad feeling.

"As your Chief Combat Officer has just stated, my name is Major Dyrk Reese, and I am the coordinator and principle arbiter of the Galens' simulated combat tournaments, including the Intra-Schools. Most of you are already familiar with this event, but I will nonetheless explain it for the benefit of our first years." Reese turned to face the east section, and Rei saw his dark gaze scanning the young cadets intensely. "The Intra-School SCT is a double-elimination tournament *all* students are required to participate in, which will end when sixteen qualifiers have been selected from each year to represent this academy in Sector 9's sectional tournament. In the second week of October, you will receive a notification of the time and date of your first match, all of which will happen here, on the floor of the Arena proper." Reese lifted both hands slightly to indicate the massive Wargame space that extended north of the raised platform he and the other officers stood upon. "After that, your pairings will be assigned again several days in advance, and are dependent on the outcome of each of your bouts. Every cadet will at the very *least* have two fights, which will only occur if you lose both of your initial matches. Should you go undefeated, four matches—" he held up a hand, and Rei had his NOED zoom in on the man to make out four fingers held up above a CAD made of grey and green steel with pale yellow vysetrium "—will be all you need to participate. Should you lose, however, you may have up to seven matches over the seven weeks if you still intend to qualify."

The major paused at this point, glancing over his shoulder to one of the four lesser officers waiting in an attentive line behind him and Valera Dent. At once the woman's NOED flared, and below the suspended platform the Team Battle circle lit up in green, and a moment later the entirety of the rest of the Wartime field beyond it blazed blue.

"As our older students are already aware," Reese continued on as—once again— only the first years gasped in awe at the sight of the entire Arena floor set alight, "the Intra-Schools are not judged *only* on bracket results. After the top sixteen quali- fiers from each year are decided, myself and Captain Dent will make a selection of three cadets from every class. Each of these individuals will be tasked with forming a six-person squad, at least three of whom—including the squad-leader—*must be individual Sectional qualifiers.*"

He stopped again, and this time Rei could tell it was with deliberate intent. All around him the first years were suddenly truly abuzz, this announcement apparently very much news to a vast majority of them.

"Wait… Does that mean we can still go to Sectionals even if we don't make top sixteen?" Behind Rei, Sense sounded floored.

"Yeah." Rei half-turned to answer over his shoulder, not taking his eyes off Dyrk Reese. "You also get to compete in the Dueling brackets if you get selected by a squad-leader."

"*What?*"

It was, surprisingly, Leron Joy who spoke up then, his demand coming in a hiss of disbelief. Rei actually turned in the other direction to meet the boy's gaze, managing to keep his frown at a minimum.

"Look it up. There have even been some cases of non-qualifiers winning the SCTs, even if it's rare."

"It's truuuue," Catcher chimed in right on time in a sing-song voice. "Look up Emilia Soból. She ended up winning the Centauri System Collegiate SCTs in 2378 after not qualifying for her local Sectionals except for as a squad-member."

"They're not lying." Kay came to their assistance, her eyes alight as she did as Catcher suggested. "There are others, too. Even on Astra. A couple years ago someone made it to the Intersystems after not qualifying."

"How did we not know about this?!" Joy demanded heatedly.

"Because if you lose in your school's tournament, you're not usually likely to do well enough at Sectionals to make mention of it," Rei answered plainly, turning to face the Arena again as Dyrk Reese started up once more.

"Yes, that *does* always get a few people excited," the aging man said without humor. "Starting at Sectionals, Team Battle and Wargame formats will begin to take precedent over individual Dueling matches. With this in mind, I encourage you to not only consider the implications of training your own capabilities, but also the reflection of your conditioning efforts in the eyes of your fellow cadets. While you yourself may not qualify, if you can prove able and team-oriented, you might have a place on a qualifier's squad." He looked over his shoulder at Dent, who picked up for him at once.

"On the front lines, squads may be assigned based on who is available, but given the nature of CAD-warfare the ISCM will always attempt to deploy its Users with a group-combat in mind. This means that individuals who have already been shown to work well alongside each other will often be prioritized. Many combat teams enter the war effort together, and are *kept* together." She brought a hand to the gold buttons of her chest. "When I joined, I was placed in a five-man team that consisted entirely of classmates and former professionals I'd fought with in the circuits even years prior." She dropped her hand, looking steadily across the rows of the first years. "The bonds you make here at Galens may well extend beyond the walls of this Institute. Take care to remember that. Your friends now could be your comrades-in-arms in the future, whether on the battlefield beyond Sirius, or in the SCTs."

As soon as she was done, Reese started up again. "As I hope *all* of you are aware, baring extraordinary circumstances, first year cadets are also bracketed separately from the rest of the tournament, and are essentially treated as a separate event. You will therefore be facing off against what similarly ranked students other schools can offer, so I would remind you that you all bear the symbol of the Galens Institute on your arms. For those of you who are our future squad-leaders, that responsibility weighs particularly heavily, and consider it carefully when making your team selections come the time. You *will* be allowed free selection—so long as those you approach agree to participate—but bear in mind that the results of Team Battle and Wargame matches reflect more severely on this school than the results of your individual combats."

"So don't just pick your friends," Viv translated under her breath, and Rei nodded beside her.

"Second years!" Dryk Reese turned to face the students seated beneath the red-on-green projection of the school emblem. "One could argue that you face an even greater challenge. As opposed to last year, those of you who qualify for Sectionals now will be participating in the tournament proper. You will not-infrequently be faced with opponents with a year's worth of training and growth on you, and you are expected to face them with the same dignity, strength, and confidence you would any other enemy. The Intra-School tournament will select sixteen from your number, as well as any additional elected teammates, but prepare yourselves. Recall there are members of the class above you who reached as far as the Intersystems as second years, and I have great faith that there are many among you with the same aptitude and ability."

He turned to the center group, now. "And finally, for those of you to whom this is your last opportunity to participate in the collegiate tournaments: I remind you only that your turn has arrived to be the head of the spear. You are the flag, the waving banner of the Galens Institute, and it is on you that the eyes of the ISC will be most closely as you climb this seasons circuit levels. You have prepared for this. Some of you more than others, but all of you with intensity and dignity worthy of this school. I anticipate great things from you, and look forward to seeing the heights the best among you will attain this season."

The bulk of his speech apparently at an end, he resumed a wider scan of the stands. "Should you have any questions, Captain Dent and your Type-instructors will field them in your next training session. For now, strive—each and every one of you—to better yourselves. For your own benefit, for your chance at joining a squad, for the griffin on your arms, and for the ISC as a whole. May the strongest rise victorious."

Rei might have imagined it, but as the major spoke these final words, he could have sworn the man's dark eyes looked in his direction, and not in any sort of benevolent way. Before he could ask if Viv had noticed the same thing, however, one of the attending officers behind Reese and Dent bellowed their orders.

"CADETS, YOU ARE AT LIBERTY FOR THE REMAINDER OF THE AFTERNOON!" The projected disc that had held the six of them aloft was already descending slowly. "DISMISSED!"

At once there was a great swell of voices and noise as nearly 400 students started to climb to their feet within their three divided sections. Rei, Viv, and Catcher were among them, along with Sense, Kay, and Leron Joy at their backs.

"We're out a day of training for *that*?" Leron demanded bitterly as they moved parallel to one another towards the stairs. "Couldn't they have just sent us a notice with our week's schedule?"

"They wanted to impress upon us the importance of the event," Rei responded evenly, waiting for the cadets in front of him to push into the orderly line. "This is our first shot at fighting under the Institute's flag in front of the masses. Not to mention sponsoring families and brands."

Reaching the steps first, Leron descended past Rei, snorting as he did. "You've got your head more firmly stuck in the clouds than I thought if you think you're ever going to get a sponsorship, Ward."

"It's happened before," Kay tried to placate gently. "I hear the Lasher had families fighting over him even before he qualified for the Intersystems."

Leron waved her comment away dismissively. "Sure. But when they do the same for some nothing E-Ranker, I'll eat my right boot."

"Leron!" Kay hissed indignantly, but the pair of them were too far away a moment later for Rei to hear anything else, trailed by an embarrassed-looking Sense who grimaced apologetically back at them before letting himself be swallowed by the tide of bodies.

"Rei, forget what I said about getting stronger to keep people off your back." Viv's voice was astonishingly level when she spoke up from behind them as they, too, finally reached the steps. "Do it so you can feed that douche his own footwear."

Rei laughed out loud, and was about to answer when a hand—its fingers as strong as steel wires—took him by the arm and pulled him straight across the stairs and into the empty row of the opposite section.

"Owe!" he shouted, completely taken aback. "What the hell are you—!"

And then he stopped, not even hearing Viv and Catcher's shouts of surprise from behind him, nor the complaints from the cadets higher up on the steps to "Get moving!" and "Get out of the way!" as his friends half-blocked the stairs to chase after him.

He was too busy staring into a pair of green eyes, their brilliant patterns reflected a hundred different ways, like the intricate cuts of clean, clear gems.

"You and I should talk," Aria Laurent, the most promising cadet Galens had seen in a generation, told him quietly.

CHAPTER 24

"Luck comes to those who wait.

… Or those willing to get up and get shit done."

-ancient Earth proverb

t had taken her most of the morning, lunch, and the entirety of the special assembly to build up the nerve, but Aria had found it in the end. As soon as Dyrk Reese had dismissed them to leisure hours, she'd been the first on her feet, striding down her row and causing several of her classmates to shrink back into their seats in surprise. The most eager to leave had crowded the steps, but as always the students gave her room the moment they realized who she was, and it took all of 5 seconds to descend and step out of the line again.

Then, when Reidon Ward and his usual band had joined the throng, she'd plucked him from among them with no more effort than might have taken the plucking of a flower.

"You and I should talk," she said, cutting off the short cadet's yell of alarm. As she expected, Ward's grey eyes went wide as he registered who she was.

Then, less expectantly, his face stilled, and he wrenched at his arm in her grasp. "Yeah, we should, but how about we do so when you're not in the process of *actively shattering my elbow?*"

Taken aback by the boy's intensity, it was a moment before Aria could think to release him. By the time she had, Viviana Arada had navigated the current of the students descending the steps to join them, Layton Catchwick right on her heels.

"Hey! What the hell are you—Oh!" Arada stopped short when she caught sight of Aria. Then she looked at Ward, then back to Aria. "Ooooh."

Then, with the faintest glimpse of what could only have been a wicked smile, the Duelist spun around again, pushing Catchwick back towards the stairs. "Come on, we're going."

"Wait, what?" the tall Saber demanded, surprised as he himself stared at Aria in something between awe and alarm. "Hold on! What's—?"

"Viv, you can stay," Ward told Arada, but the brown-haired girl only smiled at him over her shoulder with a little *too* much enthusiasm.

"Oh no. No no. You two have fun. Catcher and I will be at the East Center when you're… uh… done here."

"We will be?" Catchwick—"Catcher" apparently—asked, bewildered.

"Might as well take advantage of the free afternoon!" Arada said brightly, but Aria suspected the girl would have used any excuse available to her to make her and Catchwick scarce. Indeed, despite a chasing protest from Ward and more confused questions from the blond Saber, a few seconds later the two of them had been swept into the departing first years again, leaving Aria standing awkwardly with the white-haired Atypical.

Awkwardly?

But yes, it was. The *moment* Arada and Catchwick were gone, Aria suddenly became aware of the staring eyes of her classmates as they filed by. A few—like the dark gaze of Logan Grant and a couple others—took the two of them in rather distastefully, but most of the rest only gaped in interest or astonishment. Abruptly Aria felt the weight of the last month, 4 weeks spent without anyone but her uncle, Maddie, and the occasional calls to her siblings to pass the time.

For a moment, she forgot how to speak.

Reidon Ward, on the other hand, obviously suffered no such affliction.

"Well? What did you want to talk about?"

Aria started, her attention drawn back to him. Despite being some 5 inches shorter than her—had he grown since they'd last faced off?—the boy met her gaze almost fiercely, without a blink of hesitation or apprehension. She was surprised, but also… oddly pleased? It was an odd sensation to experience, but when most of the rest of the class either refused to look her in the eye or only wanted to stare her down in challenge, this sort of directness was refreshing.

"Oh… Uh…" Aria struggled to find her words, her flare of built up confidence shaken by the spectators still spilling by. "You… uh…"

She trailed off, and could feel her face going red as her gaze flit from Ward to the other first years, then, back again.

Unexpectedly, the boy looked over his shoulder, taking in the others without any sort of hint that their staring bothered him.

"Oh." He paused, considering for a moment, then looked to the Arena floor. "No officers. Good."

Then, without another word, he turned and started to jump up the white marble ledges that formed the Arena's cushioned seats.

Aria watched him go, completely nonplussed, until Ward was some ten rows up from her. Stopping there, he glanced back at her with a bemused expression. "Come on!"

A second's more hesitation, and Aria made up her mind.

Between her C3 Strength and D8 Speed, it took all of four jumps to reach Ward, clearing two or three aisles of seating at a time. When she caught up to him—well-clear now of the rest of their classmates—he looked her up and down with measured appreciation.

"To have your specs. Seriously..." He studied her a moment more, then turned with a sigh to plop down onto one of the nearest cushions. "So? What did you want to talk about?"

Though she could still feel the last eyes of the dispersing crowd below them, separating herself from the others had brought back Aria's nerve.

"In class. This morning... You've been watching me, too."

Immediately Reidon Ward's cheeks flushed pink, and all of a sudden he seemed to be having trouble meeting her eye.

"What? No—Well, yeah, but—*Hold on.*" He caught his scrambling answer, lifting both hands with palms out in front of his face as though to ward off any additional embarrassment. "Okay. Yeah. I might have been eyeing you a little too long this morning, but it was nothing like *that!*"

Aria frowned, confused. "Nothing like what?"

"Like... well... like *that,*" Ward tried again, floundering.

"What are you—?" Aria started to ask a second time.

And then it clicked, and she felt her own ears go red-hot all at once.

"I didn't mean it like *that!*" she exclaimed, panicking a little. "I just meant I've been watching you and it sounds like—" She froze, the heat redoubling.

"You're not helping!" Behind his own embarrassment, Ward had cracked a smile. "At all! At *all!*"

"Shut up!" Aria squeaked, turning her back on him and marching off to drop down onto a cushion some five or six separated from his own.

Then Ward started laughing.

She couldn't say why, but the sound actually made Aria feel better. She thought she *should* have felt annoyed, maybe even angry, but for some reason she didn't get the impression the boy's amusement was at her expense.

"I didn't mean it like that…" she muttered once he'd settled down again, not looking his way.

"I know. I get it." Ward was still chuckling, but seemed to have gotten himself under control. "I'm sorry. I guess I know now why Viv like's making fun of me so much."

Aria didn't answer, turning her face away from him to hide the color she knew was still lingering on her cheeks.

"I'm *sorry*," Ward said again. "I *do* get it. I guess I have been keeping an eye on you, this last month, in a way."

"In a way?" Aria asked.

"Well… Only because you've been watching me so closely it's started to give me anxiety."

Aira's mortification in that moment was so extreme, if she could have dug a tunnel into the marble to disappear into, she would have. She actually considered it for a second, wondering what kind of damage she could do to the stone with Hippolyta.

It took her a full 10 seconds before she was able to speak again.

"I thought I was being subtle," she mumbled quietly.

"HA!" Ward's exclamation was so loud it made her jump, and the following gale of renewed laughter finally itched at her enough to get her to whirl around.

"It's not *that* funny!" she shouted, frustration at last draining off some of her embarrassment.

"It's pretty funny," Ward managed to get through a broad grin, wiping his eyes like a tear of amusement was threatening to escape. "Between the two of us, Viv and I considered starting a game of over-under to see how many times we'd catch you looking in a given day. Even Catcher's taken note, and all four of us are only in the same place at meals and the dorm."

"Oh nooo…" Aria moaned, resting her elbows on her knees to bury her face in her palms as the heat returned.

"Oh yeah," Ward assured her unnecessarily, and she could still hear the smile on his voice. "Can't say I blame you, though. I'm a pretty interesting guy."

Aria cracked one eye through her fingers to glare at him. He was indeed smiling, but the way he'd phrased those last words…

Whether or not he had *meant* to give her an opportunity to change the subject, Aria took it with enthusiasm.

"'Interesting' is an understatement, Ward," she muttered, dropping her hands to look him dead-on, now, uncaring of her flush. "It doesn't take much to get the distinct impression you're anything but an idiot, so I'm going to assume you know the *actual* reason I want to talk."

Down the row from her, Ward's expression hardened a bit.

"That's a big assumption," he said, a little coolly, now, but there wasn't so much as a hint of confusion teased in his features. "Why don't you enlighten me anyway?"

Aria glared at him. She wasn't a fan of games. Not when it came to matters as tremendous as this.

Still, if she had to play along to get a straight answer, she was willing to humor him.

"Remind me. What was your CAD-Rank when we fought at the Commencement?"

Ward frowned a little, and looked to chew on his repy for a moment.

"E3," he finally admitted, though he didn't sound like he wanted to.

"E3," Aria agreed with a brief nod. "And what, could you tell me, is your CAD-Rank now?"

"E9." The answer was more prompt this time.

"Yeah. E9..." Aria pushed herself up to cross her arms and lean back. Behind her, the support projection of the seat manifested to accept her weight. "In a month—a *month*—you've gone from a low-E-Ranker to nearing the minimally accepted level of a traditional Galens cadet. Six ranks. Before that, in ten weeks you went from an F8 on assignment to that E3 I saw at the ceremony."

Ward's brow creased. "You looked up my baseline?"

"You're damn right I did. You *had me* in that fight, Ward." Aria hated to admit it, but it was true. "If it wasn't for Third Eye, you had me. Even if you ended up losing, that's the closest I've come to getting my ass handed to me, before or since." She peered at him more intently. "I checked your profile the minute I had the chance, and you'd jumped to E4. Then the following day you show up to parameter testing with an *evolved* CAD. *Hell* of a coincidence. You're damn right I checked your baseline."

She didn't feel it was any kind of important to mention she'd pulled his assignment specs *before* she'd seen the physical upgrades to his Device.

Ward watched her levelly, clearly thinking quickly. In the end, he put on an unconcerned air and shrugged. "You just admitted you know I was F-Rank at assignment. With the right training and enough hours put in, it shouldn't be surprising I've caught up a little to everyone else in the—"

"Ward. Don't bullshit me."

Aria said it calmly, but the boy went so still she might have threatened him with a called Device.

"Most of the others don't care," she continued. "You were a curio for a week, but the minute you gave them a semi-plausible reason not to think of you anymore, they took it. All that's left from ninety percent of our classmates seems to either be indifference, apathy, or just disappointment at your presence. But not *everyone*." She felt her frown deepen. "Some people are paying attention. You've climbed *eleven* CAD Ranks in less than four months, most of them recently. That would be impressive enough, except you *didn't* get 'the right training', did you?"

The change was subtle, but distinct. Whereas one moment Ward was watching her with careful attention, the next his gaze was sharper, more dangerous.

Choose your next words wisely, that look said.

Aria softened her tone. "I'm sorry. I don't mean to be insensitive. It's just… I know what your surname means, Ward. If you tell me I'm wrong, I'll believe you, but if I'm right then there's no way you had the network or the funds to find trainers for an *A-Type* CAD. My brother is an Atypical, too, and my parents had to spend a fortune on finding him a couple of decent instructors." She did her best to get across her genuine empathy. "I'm not trying to call you out. I'm just asking you not to lie to me."

There was a long, heavy silence. All of a sudden Aria realized that they were alone in the Arena, the rest of the Institute's student body having finally cleared out. Her voice had carried, echoing back at her slightly in the vast emptiness of the covered stadium, and the quiet that followed extended so long she started to get nervous again.

Then, finally, Ward exhaled in a resigned sort of way.

"I didn't lie to you," he grumbled, sitting back in his own seat and crossing his arms to mirror her. "And I haven't lied to anyone. Well… Maybe some half-truths here and there. I just gave them a plausible reason, and let them run with it."

"You're good at the bait-and-switch," Aria acknowledged with a nod. "I've experienced it for myself."

Ward managed half a smirk at that. "Maybe. Still… Can't say I'm all that surprised some people are watching me as closely as you claim. It's not like I can hide my CAD-Rank."

"Or your evolutions," Aria added with a snort. "*Twice.* Twice in the first two months of term. I'm half-expecting to see another change any afternoon, now."

Silence answered her.

"Wait. Seriously?!" Aria demanded, leaning towards him across the cushion next to her. "I was just kidding!"

Ward shrugged again. "My first change was six ranks after assignment. My second was three after that, at E7. I'm due to hit D0 any day, now. Won't be surprised if it's sooner than later."

Aria gaped at him. She supposed she shouldn't have been that taken aback—she'd already been aware of everything he'd just said, after all—but still... To hear the confirmation of it from Ward's own mouth...

"It's the top rankers, isn't it?"

His question cut across her bewilderment.

"What?"

Ward wasn't looking at her again, frowning at the ground between his knees. "The ones who are keeping an eye on me. It's the top rankers?"

"Oh," Aria caught up. "The ones I'm aware of, yeah, though you shouldn't limit watching out just for them. There's a lot in the higher levels that are eyeing the first year bracket at Sectionals. I'll bet most of them are keeping tabs on you."

The boy nodded slowly, still staring at the marble. "I guess if they do the math, I *would* be some kind of threat. Guess that explains Kay's sudden interest in me... Dammit." He grimaced. "This is *exactly* what she warned me about."

It was Aria's turn to frown again. "Who did? Kay Sandree?"

Ward opened his mouth to answer, then shut it again. "No. It's not important. Just someone who's keeping track of me as closely as the rest of you lot, I think."

"Are they the one helping you grow so fast?"

Ward blinked at that, then looked around at her. "Helping me?" Something seemed to click for him. "Is *that* what people think is going on? That I'm getting outside help?"

It was an unsettling response, and Aria watched the boy much more carefully as she answered. "I couldn't tell you what anyone else is thinking. It's not like I rub shoulders with a lot of our classmates. But if you'd asked me ten seconds ago what I thought was going on with your CAD, I would have said you have an impressive Growth spec, and someone powerful willing to help you take advantage of it."

Ward's face darkened as he registered his slip up. "And now?" he asked her.

"What if I asked you what you thought is going on now?"

"I'd say your Growth spec is probably more than impressive, and you just have the temperament to squeeze every ounce of value out of it."

They stared at each other for a long moment, Ward's grey eyes meeting her green like slate scraping against emerald. She could tell he was sizing her up, trying to read her expression, but Aria made sure not to let so much as a hint of her internal amazement shine through, much less her suspicious confusion.

He was the first to speak again.

"Let's say you're right. Theoretically. What of it?"

Aria opened her mouth to answer, but no words came out. She tried a second time, and again only silence offered itself to her.

This was the hard part. This was the point in the conversation she had been dreading.

"Laurent."

Ward said her name like a warning, his eyes narrowing a little, and she knew then he wasn't about to let the subject go. Why would he? *She* had been the one to finally break her distant study of him after a month. His being called out by John Markus that morning had done the trick, had given her the courage, but it was *she* who had broached the topic.

What of it? Ward had asked.

And yet the words just wouldn't come.

After another 5 seconds of tense silence, Ward grunted, then pushed himself to his feet.

"If all you wanted was a confirmation of your suspicions, I could have saved you the time. I'm not gonna pretend those watching my rank closely enough won't know something's going on, but I'm also not about to put a target on my back by explaining to you why the admissions board let me into Galens. Not even Catcher knows that."

"But Arada does?"

The question eked out unbidden, and Aria wished she could have snatched it back, feeling the blood creep once more into her cheeks.

This time, though, she didn't hide her face.

Ward frowned down at her. "Viv and I have known each other since we were fourteen. We got our CADs together. So yeah. She knows."

Aria nodded, still struggling to form the question she wanted to pose. It was important. *So* important. Ward was obviously on edge about being marked by the other top rankers for the speed at which he was catching up to the class, but he didn't seem to have registered yet that there was more than one way in which he could be targeted.

First. She had to be the first, or at least find a way to put herself at the front of the line.

"Listen, if you got what you wanted out of me, I'm gonna go. Viv and Catcher are waiting for me to—"

"Wait!"

As the boy turned away from her—offering nothing more than a lifted hand in farewell and taking a step towards the stairs—need outweighed pride. The earnestness in her exclamation must have come through, because Ward looked over his shoulder at her, and Aria found herself getting to her feet to face him.

"Look…" she started, hands in fists by her sides as she fought to get the words out. "I… I don't have a lot of friends…"

Ward watched her blankly for a moment, clearly expecting more. When nothing else came, he cracked an uncomfortable grin. "Yeah… I kinda noticed that. You're a little…" He hesitated.

"Unapproachable?" Aria finished for him, feeling a lump build in her throat. "Yeah. I know. I don't *mean* to be. Everyone in our class just… doesn't seem keen to try and talk to me."

The grin fell into a frown, and Ward turned to look at her head on. Before he could say anything, though, Aria continued.

"I know I should try more but… I have a hard time feeling like I need to get closer people who shrink away from me whenever I get too close. Don't get me wrong," she brought up a fist to look at it, "I'm proud of my rank. I'm proud of my specs. But how would you feel if all anyone ever seemed to want to do was either avoid you or crush you on the field?"

"Kinda shitty," Ward answered promptly. "I get that… Actually, I kinda got that impression the first time I saw you, when Captain Dent put you on display in front of everyone at the Commencement Ceremony."

It was like a cool breeze had suddenly churned itself into being within the bright confines of the Arena, sweeping over the stands to set Aria's skin atingle. She stared at the short boy, momentarily at a loss for words, recalling the exact moment he was describing. She remembered how she'd felt, standing in front of everyone like some prize fighter put to auction, remembered the jealousy she'd harbored for the students she could see exchanging whispers and quiet laughter as Valera Dent had spoken at her side. It had been her responsibility—her *duty*, rather—to hold herself tall and proud before her class and show them what could be, what should be. Still, it had made her feel like a mannequin, dressed in the black-and-gold of the ISCM, envious of the living souls ogling her from their seats.

And here was someone who had seen right through all that…

"I…" she started, finding it hard to speak again. "I… Yeah…" It was all she could manage, but Ward seemed to be picking up on her struggles now.

"Honestly… It was one of the reasons I was so eager to fight you," he said with a sigh, reaching up to pull his cap off and run a hand through his white hair as he looked away from her, like the admission was a little embarrassing. "I remember thinking it must have felt kinda cheap to be put on a pedestal like that. I wanted to see what you could do." He snorted at the ground. "Earned me a spear in the gut for my trouble."

"It was fun."

Again the words slipped out, but this time Aria wouldn't have taken them back even if she could. As Ward looked up at her in surprise, she pressed on.

"It was fun," she repeated. "That was the first time—the *only* time, actually—I've had fun in a real match. I know it sounds stupid, but that was… It was important to me. It's the reason I started watching you in the first place." *This* confession she thought might chagrin her later, in the solitude of her room, but in the moment she only kept on, latching to the momentum behind her words. "All summer all I'd done was train and sleep and train and sleep. I was looking forward to the camp. I was *so* looking forward to it. But when I got there…"

"The other top rankers weren't keen on making nice," Ward said with a nod. "I've been getting that impression, yeah."

"Exactly. And then term started, and Commencement happened… I admit I wasn't thrilled when the captain matched us up at first, but by the end of our fight…" Aria trailed off for a second before finding her courage again. "It's not even that I almost lost to you. I mean that's a part of it, but… The moment you threw that damn hat." A smile tugged at one corner of her lip. "I don't know… I guess I kinda realized you weren't on that field with me because you wanted to beat me—well, not *only* because you wanted to beat me." She corrected herself as Ward opened his mouth to interject. "I felt like you wanted more than that. Or something different. Does that make sense?"

"Not even a little bit," Ward said with a light laugh.

Aria exhaled in frustration. "Ugh… Well it's not like I've figured it out for myself completely, so I guess that's hardly surprising. But listen…" She took a steadying breath, and finally offered the most important of the questions she had come to ask. "Could we fight again, sometime? It doesn't have to be anytime soon, but—"

"Hell yeah!"

His eager answer cut off what was likely to have been a list of rambling excuses in case he didn't want to, and Aria gaped at him. She'd expected to have to convince him, had expected the difference in their ability to have translated into anything but enthusiasm. She was a C-Ranked User, and he hadn't even made D yet. For her to be challenging him, even informally… If anything, anyone who caught wind of it would have just called her a bully.

And yet there Reidon Ward stood across from here, grinning like a madman with an equally manic glint in his eyes, having just fervently agreed to face her on the field again.

"… Really?" she asked, and she hoped to the heavens the question didn't come out as disbelieving as it sounded to her own ears.

"*Absolutely*!" Ward practically yelled back, his voice almost shivering with excitement. "Is *that* what you wanted to ask me?! You should have just come out with it! I'll take you on anytime you want! Right now, even!" He looked down at the field, his face alight with anticipation. "Maybe we can even use the main floor to—!" He stopped himself, some of his excitement draining away. "Oh. Damn."

"What?" Aria squeaked, afraid he had changed his mind. "What's wrong?"

"I can't right now," Ward grumbled, eyes lifting to the Arena's far exit. "I just told Viv and Catcher I'd meet them at the East Center to train."

"Oh," Aria made sure to sound disappointed, but in truth she was just relieved he wasn't bailing on his assurance. "No problem. We can always have a match another day." She hesitated, but couldn't to stop herself from asking. "Do you… Do you and Arada train a lot?"

"Every day." Ward nodded absently, his mind still obviously on his dissatisfaction with the fact that the two of them couldn't have it out there and then. "Whenever we can."

"Oh…" Aria couldn't decide if she was more impressed or alarmed. "Well… I guess that's one way to spend time together…"

Ward appeared about to agree with her again, but stopped, then slowly looked at her, his expression bewildered.

"What's that supposed to mean?"

"Oh…" *Curse* her pale complexion and easy embarrassment. "I mean… It's got to be hard to find time, right? For a couple to get to see each here at school must be… be…"

She trailed off, because even as the words had left her lips the look on Ward's face flashed a myriad of emotions. Confusion turned to realization, realization to horror.

Then horror to hilarity.

"HA!" he howled, covering his mouth with the back of one hand to try to stem the laughter that followed this. His amusement was as confusing at is was awkward for Aria, and she had to shout to get him to stop.

"What?! What's so funny?!"

It took a moment for Ward's apparent delight to subside enough for him to look at her straight, and when his hand fell from his face he was smiling so wide he looked like his cheeks were hurting.

"Do me a favor: don't *ever* let Viv hear you thought we were dating, okay?"

Aria blinked, surprised. "You're… not?"

"*No,*" Ward almost started laughing again, but managed to control himself. "*Definitely* not. She's like an overprotective sister, and I am *so* not her typical type, in more ways than one. Oh." He seemed to shiver. "I got a cold chill just thinking about it. No way." He cocked his head at Aria. "What gave off that impression, though? I don't think we've done anything that would make people thing we're going out?"

"Uh…" Aria squinted at him, not sure if he was serious. "Are you joking?"

His utterly blank face spelled out very much that he was *not* joking.

"Okay… You always sit in class together. You always eat together. You walk everywhere together. You just told me you two train together every night. You *change together* in the locker room—that's not suspicious *at all.* I heard you somehow ended up as *roommates.* You two are never far from—"

"Okay, *okay!*" Ward interrupted her in alarm, throwing his hands up and waving them frantically to get her to stop. "Man… When you phrase it like that you make me feel like we *are* dating…"

"Uh… Yeah. That's kind of my point."

Ward nodded, then snorted. "All right. I admit to fueling the confusion, then. But no. Definitely not dating. We've just known each other forever, and she would get seriously more grossed out that I am if you suggested otherwise to her. Also," he cocked an eyebrow at Aria and crossed his arms again, "you've been conveniently leaving out the fact that I said I train with Viv *and* Catcher every day. We also eat together most of the time. So unless you think all of this—" he gestured to his short frame with one scarred hand "—is sexy enough to be seducing two *very* good-looking examples of opposite sexes *at the same time*, you really should reconsider your theory."

Aria gave herself a moment to clear *those* images out of her head before trying to navigate the conversation to more manageable waters.

"All of you train together? When?"

"During evening leisure hours."

Aria frowned. "What about studying?"

Ward shrugged. "We get it done. Mostly on Sundays."

"That's it?" Aria demanded in disbelief. When the boy nodded slowly—like he didn't understand why she sounded so confused by the concept—she considered finding something to throw at him. "No way. There's no way."

"I make a pretty mean tutor," Ward answered her incredulity with a chuckle.

Aria could only shake her head, half in disgust, half in disbelief. "Seriously, what *are* you?"

"Viv would tell you I'm an overdeveloped six-year-old. Catcher would be nicer. He'd probably just call me 'still growing', or something."

Aria couldn't help it, and she sniggered. "They sound fun."

"They *are* fun," Ward assured her with a smile. Then he paused, taking her in more intently all of a sudden, as though struck by a thought.

"What?" she asked him, abruptly nervous again.

He hesitated a moment more, but when he spoke Aria felt a small flame of excitement leap into being in her chest.

"Well... About East Center... Want to join?"

CHAPTER 25

"... if you make it, remember that good friends can be hard to find in the world you're about to share."

Major Albert Connelly

Okay. So I'm going to summarize, and you're just gonna stand there and tell me if I have this all straight or not. Got it?"

"Got it."

"Great. So Aria-friggin-*Laurent* drags you off after the special assembly, and ends up admitting that she has, indeed, been basically stalking you?"

"That's a pretty extreme exaggera—"

"Yes or no answers only, Rei."

"... Yes. But that's still an exaggeration!"

"Fine. Regardless: she *then* asks you—*you*, an as-of-yet *E*-Ranked CAD-User—if you could have a match."

"Well I'm basically a D0 at this—"

"Dude. For being so smart, you're *really* bad at following directions."

"Sorry. Okay. Yes. She did."

"Mhm... Then—because all that's not weird enough already—she assumes you're dating Viv—who *will* kill us both if she finds out I heard that, by the way—admits to not having made a lot of friends at school, and confesses that you almost beat her at the Commencement Ceremony."

"Yes. But you're getting things way out of order."

"Doesn't matter. What does matter, on the other hand, is the fact that—after all that—we somehow ended up... here."

"... Yes. Yes we did."

Catcher nodded slowly, like an old man finished with lecturing a reckless child, not looking at Rei. Instead, the pair of them stood in their combat suits just beyond the perimeter of their usual Dueling field in the East Center facility, watching with dismay as Viv and Aria Laurent went at each other with astounding ferocity, Viv's Duelist Speed and Cognition having proven themselves the only specs that had a chance of standing up to the Phalanx's numbers for more than 15 seconds or so. It was like witnessing two tigers tearing at each other, except said tigers were armed with vibrantly glowing steel weapons and armor. As Rei's neuroline had improved, so had his ability to follow the blur of such fighting, and so it was in silence that he and Catcher watched the two girls strike and slash at each other, Laurent's shield and spear meeting Viv's two blades every time they sought an opening.

It was genuinely breathtaking.

Gemela's sword lanced in, but was slammed aside by Hippolyta's shield. Laurent's spear thrust forward, nearly taking Viv through the chest, but she dodged under it to take an opening, slashing at an exposed thigh. The Phalanx reacted by kneeing upward, accepting the cut of the slighter blade along the steel plating of the red-and-gold greaves that covered her lower legs, turning the clever block into a kick that would have taken Viv in the chin had she not spun out of the way. She was forced to duck again immediately following this, because Laurent's spear whirled in an arc over her head to cut horizontally once, twice, three times, and Viv eventually had to leap backwards to be clear of the weapon.

All of that, of course, took about 3 seconds.

The two went on like that for almost a minute more, back and forth again and again over the center of the neutral white field they tended to prefer for sparring practice. They all knew Laurent was handicapping herself, not calling on Third Eye in the moments things got dicey, but Rei didn't think anyone much cared. He and Catcher stood mesmerized to the side, watching with rapt attention.

The two girls, meanwhile, were both grinning ear to ear even as they tried their absolute best to kill one another.

As was not uncommon in CAD-fighting, the end of the match came abruptly. Viv's Endurance was higher than Rei's by far, but it was still her weakest spec, making her ill-suited for drawn-out combat against an opponent she couldn't put down within any reasonable time. Rei noticed her getting slower some two and half minutes into the fight, and it was shortly after that Catcher started muttering under his breath, apparently seeing the same thing. Viv's dodges became less deft, her strikes less accurate. Before long Laurent was steadily beating her back, towards the edge of the field. Rei and Catcher watched the press happen, waiting for the moment.

When Viv's back bumped up against the invisible wall at the extent of the ring, the fight ended in a flash.

Laurent lunged forward, slamming her shield straight into Viv to flatten her against the wall. Before her momentarily pinned opponent could respond, the Phalanx shortened her grip on her spear and stabbed it into Viv's hip, earning herself a scream of agony. The pain was so much that Viv looked to lose concentration for an instant, her weapons going limp in her hands, and Laurent pulled off in a blink, drawing her left arm back, then driving the bottom of her shield into Viv's throat with a *wham*!

"Fatal Damage Accrued. Winner: Aria Laurent."

"*Damn*," Rei heard Catcher mutter under his breath after the field had announced the end of the match.

"Yeah," he agreed, starting towards the pair as Laurent recalled Hippolyta in time to catch Viv when she started to fall, having undoubtedly lost all motor control from the neck down.

It didn't take long for the neural interruption to fade as the field de-pixilated around them, and by the time Rei and Catcher reached the two girls Viv was standing mostly on her own again, all smiles as she talked with surprising energy.

"That was *amazing*," she gushed, swinging her left hand in an imitation of half of Laurent's killing combination. "You have better wide control of your Device's parts than I do even as a Duelist."

"Don't forget that I've had two full months of additional one-on-one training," the red-headed Phalanx said, sounding rather pleased to be able to talk so casually in the aftermath of the fight. "You've got a lot of skill. I hope you plan to take the Intra-Schools seriously. You could totally make it."

"That's what we told her," Rei said, coming to a halt by the pair of them as Viv's brown eyes lit up with excitement. "Judging by that expression, though, I get the feeling she might take your word a little more to heart than ours."

"Judging by that match, she—" Viv pointed at Laurent enthusiastically "—could take you both on blindfolded. All three of us if she decided to use Third Eye. You'll pardon me if I measure her opinion with just a liiiiitle more weight."

"Sure, sure," Rei said with a roll of his eyes, but he laughed regardless. "You know, that's actually the first time I've ever seen you lose a fight, now that I think about..."

"What are you talking about? Jenny Costa whipped me up and down the gym constantly my first year in combat team."

"A *CAD*-fight, dummy. Also Costa was a fourth year and five inches taller than your skinny fifteen-year-old ass."

"Well *ex-cuuuuse* me for not reading your mind. How about you call up those pretty little kitten claws of yours and help me restart my winning streak, then?"

There was a giggle, and Rei and Viv looked away from their banter to see Aria Laurent watching them brightly.

"You two have *definitely* known each other a while. You're like an old married couple."

"Ew," the pair of them said together, then snorted at the same time.

"You guys are gonna make me feel like a fourth wheel, at this rate," Catcher muttered, looking Viv up and down as he spoke. "You up for another match? I have a feeling my Speed is like two fights from ranking up, so you'd make a good partner."

"Give me a minute. My fingers are still a little numb." Viv looked between Rei and Laurent. "You guys okay to pair?"

"Definitely," Rei answered, not displeased to see the Phalanx perk up at the suggestion. They'd sparred a bit to warm up, but hadn't had their promised match yet. "Can you split the field?"

Viv's NOED flared—she was the one who'd booked the space for them—and a moment later the Dueling circle had divided itself into two equal portions. Rei supposed they could have moved to another room, but it was more fun to stay together, even if it meant letting Viv and Catcher watch him get absolutely pancaked what was likely to be several times in a row.

Fun...

The thought caught him, and he looked at Laurent, who was answering some question Catcher had asked her about her Device. It was strange, given they'd all only spent the last hour together, but the girl seemed somehow... happier. She was smiling through a sheen of sweat built up from the match, her red hair in a bun behind her head in her typical fashion, and abruptly Rei recalled something Viv had told him once, or had tried to. It hadn't registered, then, but it came to mind now, her answer when he'd asked her if she thought the girl was aloof. Lonely, Viv had told him.

Rather than aloof, she had thought Laurent was lonely.

He must have been sporting a rather pleased expression, because Laurent cocked her head at him once Viv had told Catcher she was good to go.

"What's that look for?" she asked him curiously.

"Nothing," Rei answered quickly, raising an eyebrow at her. "You sure about this rematch? By your own admission I almost beat you last time we met on the field."

The girl's amused snort was half-endearing, half-terrifying.

Sure enough, he didn't last more than 5 seconds in their first encounter.

With nothing but the flat semi-circle of space around them, Rei had no tricks to pull, no schemes to weave. All he could do was meet Laurent head-on in the middle of their half of the field, and he was rather pleased with himself when he managed to dodge the opening thrust of her spear.

Pleased, that is, until Hippolyta's waiting shield caught him a titanic blow in the chest, sending him careening 10 yards back to slam with a *crunch* into the perimeter wall. He hit the barrier so hard he saw stars, and barely made out the red warning lines that marked him having suffered a crushed sternum, broken spine, and collapsed posterior skull.

"Fatal Damage Accrued. Winner: Aria Laurent."

"Ah! I'm sorry!" The C-Ranker came rushing over, her Speed bringing her to his side in a heartbeat. Her Device already recalled, she started to reach for him. "I'm sorry! I'm so sorry! I should have held back! It was just a reflex to—!"

She stopped short before she could touch him, Rei's raised hand cutting her off as the pain of the simulated injuries subsided.

The moment his neuroline had cleared his mind enough to think straight, he grinned up at her.

"Again," he said, making sure she heard every ounce of his enthusiasm.

She blinked at him, surprised.

Then she smiled back just as eagerly.

"Okay."

They went again, then again, then again. Each time Rei found himself absolutely outmatched in every possible way, but each time he also lasted just a little longer, survived for just a few more seconds. By his sixth defeat—courtesy of a spear through the heart—he had forced Laurent to chase him down for a full 20 seconds, even managing a few clever deflections and testing jabs that had had her bringing her shield to bear in protection of her face or vitals.

After his chest had stopped hurting so bad he couldn't breathe, he lifted his head to find the Phalanx looking down on him, something like awe sketched across her face.

"What's that look for?" he echoed her early question with a pained chuckle, starting to push himself to his feet.

Laurent shook her head a little. "It's just... You're kind of incredible, aren't you?"

Straightening up, Rei glanced at her sidelong. "Hardly," he snorted, rubbing at the place Hippolyta had skewered him, willing away the fading simulation of discomfort. "All I can do against you is provide a moving target."

"That's not what I meant." She was frowning at him, and her eyes—perhaps unbidden—had drifted to the scars made easily visible in the sleeveless fit of the combat suit. "I might be able to win again and again, but... I don't know. You just make me feel like I can't *beat* you, if that makes sense. It was the same thing at the Commencement. Even after Hippolyta took you through the stomach..."

Rei winced, recalling the unpleasant memory. "No idea what you're talking about. Pretty sure that fight ended with me as a scrawny decoration on the end of your spear."

"I'm *serious*. You don't really give up easily, do you?"

At that, Rei managed a grim laugh. "No. I don't. To my endless regret." Then looked her in the eye. "Again."

By the time they called it an end to the evening, Rei had lost no less than twenty times to Laurent's superior ability. He'd never gotten to mark even a scratch on the girl—much less force her to call on Third Eye again—but his last couple of matches he had averaged nearly 40 seconds each time. He could read her better and better, and adapted a little more each time to her combat style.

"Phew!" Catcher groaned, letting himself fall back to lay on the cool surface of the black projection plating once Viv had recalled the field. He was sweating profusely, but looked all too pleased with the night's results as he stuck a thumbs up straight into the air above him. "Rank up in Speed! Yeah!"

"Congrats," Laurent said as she cocked an eyebrow down at him in surprise. "I didn't realize you could make that kind of progress with sparring. No wonder you guys are all catching up to the curve."

"Some of us more than others," Viv told her, and through his distraction Rei saw her nodding towards him. "Like the half-pint over there. Watch this."

Laurent turned to Rei, but he was too preoccupied to pay any of them any mind. In the frame of his neuro-optic, text was spilling across his vision.

...

Processing combat information.

...

Calculating.

…

Results:
Strength: Severely Lacking
Endurance: Severely Lacking
Speed: Severely Lacking
Cognition: Severely Lacking
Offense: Severely Lacking
Defense: Severely Lacking
Growth: Not Applicable

…

Checking combat data acquisition.

…

Adequate data acquirement met.
Device initiating adjustments to:
Strength. Endurance. Offense.

…

Adjustment complete.
Strength has been upgraded from Rank E2 to E3.
Endurance has been upgraded from Rank F9 to E0.
Offense has been upgraded from Rank E2 to E3.

…

Calculating.

…

CAD "Shido" has been upgraded from Rank E9 to D0.

Grinning hard, Rei dismissed the notification with a blink. His attention returning to his present soundings, he looked around to find all three of the others watching him, Viv and Catcher with eyes narrowed in suspicion, Laurent innocently and obviously a little confused.

"What?" he asked, trying to play it off.

"Don't *what* us," Catcher scoffed, sitting up again and pointing at him like some lawyer accusing a suspect on trial. "You managed it, didn't you?"

"No idea what you're talking about," Rei said with a shrug of feigned virtue. "Nothing to see here."

"Bull," Catcher said, pulling up his own neuro-optic. A few seconds later and he gave a dry laugh. "Yup. Called it."

"Called what?" Laurent asked, looking between all three of them at a distinct loss. "What did he manage?"

"Check his ISCM profile," Viv told her, sounding like she was holding back her own smile as she, too, read over the script that was scrolling by her eyes.

Laurent frowned, then did as she suggested, the light flashing across her vision making their fractured green sparkle and dance.

Then her mouth fell open.

"D0?!" she demanded, dismissing the text and whirling on Rei. "D0?! Are you kidding me?!"

"The database doesn't lie," Catcher answered her darkly. Then, though, he managed an honest smile and looked up at Rei. "Congrats, man. That's amazing."

"Thanks," Rei answered appreciatively. "A little bummed Shido didn't achieve an evolution, but I guess I can't complain."

"C-can't complain?!" Laurent stuttered, still gaping at him. "That would have been your third evolution in a month!"

"Yup," Viv told her, shaking her head and turning to make for the door as she spoke over her shoulder. "Don't worry. Keep hanging out with us and you get used to it."

"To an extent," Catcher grumbled good-naturally, pushing himself up to his feet. Once standing, he clapped Rei on the back and gave him a wink. "Just remember your first training partners when they make you a King, got it? I don't need my own asteroid or anything, but I won't say no to a nice estate on Earth or something like that."

"You bet, man," Rei answered with a laugh, and Catcher let his hand drop to follow Viv towards the exit and the promise of a hot shower. Rei, in turn, looked around at Laurent, intending to ask her if she wanted to walk back with them.

He stopped, though, when he saw the look on her face.

It wasn't… elation, per se. That would have been exaggerating. It was more of a sort hopeful excitement, her bottom lip between her teeth, her eyes bright as they watched Viv and Catcher chatting by the door.

"What's up?" he asked her, and the girl jumped at the sound of his voice.

"Oh," she squeaked, and she flushed red. She seriously got embarrassed way too easily. "Uh…" She looked to be struggling to find the words, and Rei waited patiently.

If he'd learned anything that day, it was that Aria Laurent—C-Ranked User and top combatant among the first years by a mile—was about as much a tongue-twisted teenager as any of the rest of them.

"Do... Do you guys mind?"

The question came haltingly, and Rei didn't follow.

"Mind what?"

Laurent squirmed before him, not meeting his eye, and her shy discomfort struck an unfamiliar chord with him. Something pinched in his chest, and it took him a moment to realize that he thought the girl was cute.

Way cute.

"If I... If I came back with you? The next time you guys train together? Do you mind?"

Her question, voiced in a tone that was somehow excited, embarrassed, and scared all at once, brought Viv's words to bear again.

Lonely, she had said.

Lonely.

Rei could only smile.

CHAPTER 26

The next day proved a little more awkward than anticipated, starting with breakfast. Rei, Viv, and Catcher sat at their usual table, but despite each agreeing they had caught sight of vibrant red hair under the flat-top cap, Laurent never made an appearance, much less moved to join them. First lecture was being held in the Tactical Studies building, which was a hike from the mess hall, so Rei and Viv split off early, promising to see Catcher at lunch.

Getting to class, they found themselves among the first to arrive, and so took their usual spot towards the front, close to the bottom of the theater. The rest of 1-A arrived steadily, and they traded hellos with Sense and Kay when they appeared—alongside a silent and stiff-faced Leron Joy—then glares with Logan Grant and his posse when the group of four or five—including Mateus Selleck and Leda Truant—strode in like they owned the place. It was almost time for the tone that marked the start of the period when Laurent finally appeared, cutting it close, and she beamed when she caught sight of the pair of them, lifting a hand to wave good morning as they did the same.

Then, before either of them could say a word to suggest otherwise, she hurried up the steps along the side of the theater to take her typical seat at the edge of the class, separate from everyone else.

"Wha—?" Rei started to ask, but a nudge from Viv shut him up.

Still, she was obviously trying not to laugh in exasperation as she shook her head at him. "Leave it alone. She probably doesn't want to bother us."

"'Bother us'?" Rei repeated, completely dumbfounded by this. "Why in the MIND would she think she'd be bothering us?"

"Cause—you adorable dolt—she's a shy girl who just made her first friends at school and doesn't want to overstep and freak them out," Viv told him calmly. "Since you seem impervious to the concept of a lack of self-confidence, just trust me: leave it alone."

"Oh," Rei answered dumbly, considering this point.

Just then Captain Sarah Takeshi, Head of the Tactical Studies Department, entered the room, and every member of 1-A was on their feet and saluting. The woman returned the gesture, then had them all sit again before turning to the large smart-glass wall that made up the lecture hall's display.

While Takeshi was preoccupied, Rei glanced over his shoulder. Almost predictably he locked eyes with Laurent, who must have been watching them, but this time instead of looking away the two of them exchanged smiles, and he turned back to the front rather high-spirited as their instructor pulled up the first slides of a presentation called "Basics of Wargame Stratagems".

He supposed he had no right to be *too* disappointed…

After that first lecture came to an end, they had another in a classroom on the fifth floor of the same building, then a joint double-period lesson on military law with 1-B, held in the Combat Theory Department. Each time was the same, with either Rei and Viv taking to their seats before Laurent, or vice versa, always separated by several rows and chairs. The girl didn't even try to walk with them between classes, and when Rei made the suggestion of calling out for her since she was alone, Viv took him by the sleeve and told him to be patient.

Not about to pretend he had *any* experience in deciphering the silent understandings of girls, Rei offered no other objection.

It was lunch, at long last, when Viv made her move. Rei saw it coming, because as they met Catcher inside the mess hall's entrance he could see her gaze following Laurent even as they traded stories about the morning's lectures. They got in line a ways behind the C-Ranker, with Catcher chatting away happily between them, all the while cheerfully oblivious to the goings on. Rei humored him, but he, too, kept an eye on Laurent, watching the girl pick up her tray of food from the end of the belt and head off towards the south wall of the arboretum without a glance back.

Catcher only stopped talking when Viv interrupted him after they'd all collected their own respective lunches.

"Come on. Follow me."

"And the look on his face when—Hold on, where are you going?" the Saber's story about Jack Benaly answering a question wrong in class was cut short as he looked around in surprise, already having taken two steps in the direction of their usual spot. "Our table's over here."

"Not today it's not," Rei said brightly, stepping in behind Viv to let her lead the way.

They navigated the hall in a file, avoiding bumping into other students of every year and ignoring the curious—and occasionally nasty—looks thrown their way. It had become such a habit for them to claim the same place among the palm trees every day that Rei realized he'd never actually bothered to explore the extent of the mess hall, and discovered that this had been to his loss. Whereas on the east side of the large building the curated plant-life had always been tropical and bright in nature, as they passed into the southern quarter of the expansive biosphere the environment shifted quickly. Even the temperature dropped, as though the dome was subdivided into climates, and it fit the cooler, darker evergreens they suddenly found themselves standing under, their great, pointed tops looking like they could have scraped the glass of the atrium high above.

Pine trees, Rei recognized them, noting too the mossy undergrowth and themed blue-green coloring of this section of the building.

The space, unfortunately, was only slightly less jam-packed with students—mostly second years—and so it was that the three of them ended up having to search for a little after Viv had explained to Catcher what they were about. It was fortunate she had, too, because it was he—tallest of them as he was—who spotted their goal first.

"Hey, over there," he told them, using his elbow to gesture towards the wall of the dome. Rei—who couldn't see anything through the crowd—trusted in Catcher's vantage and began to press in the indicated direction as best he could. A few seconds later the trio were free of the bulk of the milling, chattering cadets, finding themselves looking at a quiet corner with a single table half-hidden behind the low branches of one of the smaller evergreens.

And there, smiling to herself as she contemplated some private thought, Aria Laurent sat alone with her chin in hand, elbow on the plasteel surface by her tray of food, cap on the bench by her hip. She was looking out over the Institute grounds, and the sun through the clear triangular panes of the arboretum was alight in her eyes and hair like fire and green glass.

"Stop staring, moron," Viv snickered under her breath as she pushed by him, and Rei realized with a jolt he'd stopped short at the sight of the girl.

"Shut up," he muttered back, embarrassed at having been caught, but following all the same.

Reaching the table first, Viv paused behind Laurent's shoulder, waiting a moment to see if the girl would notice. When she didn't, Viv followed her gaze out over the campus and the southern skyline of Castalon rising high above them in the distance.

"You know, if you've been hogging a view like this to yourself this whole time, I'm gonna be kinda upset."

Before her Laurent jumped, whirling around. Her eyes went wide as she took the three of them in.

"Oh," she breathed, clearly surprised, watching in astonishment as Viv put one leg then the other over the bench by her side to take a seat "Hi... Sorry. I didn't know if you guys would want to..."

She trailed off, looking unsure of herself.

"Please. I've spent the last month having to deal with these two on my own." Viv selected a French fry from her plate to wave it at Rei and Catcher before popping it into her mouth, continuing as she chewed. "If you think for a *moment* I'm about to let my first opportunity to share a little girl time get away from me, you're insane." She feigned a glower at the boys. "Even *if* thing one and thing two here decided to follow."

"Oh please, you would get bored within a day without us," Catcher played along, sitting opposite Viv as Rei did the same across from Laurent. "You should think of us as free entertainment."

"Just cause I don't pay for it in credits doesn't mean I don't pay for it *at all*," Viv jabbed back, reaching across to steal one of Catcher's fries, this time. "Though I admit to the probable boredom part."

"Hey!" Catcher protested, making a snatch for Viv's hand and losing to her Speed. She winked at him, taking a bite even as he cursed her and promptly thieved one of hers in retaliation.

Leaving the two of them to their antics, Rei took in Laurent as she watched the exchange with hesitant delight, like she'd not expected to be having lunch among them.

Which she obviously hadn't, he reminded himself.

"You could have sat with us, you know," he said after a moment, putting his own elbow on the table and leaning a cheek into his fist. "This morning. In class. You're gonna make us feel like you're too cool to hang out with us."

"What?" Laurent demanded, whirling on him in absolute mortification. "No! That's not what I was trying to do! I just thought—!"

She stopped herself as Rei started to laugh across from her.

"I'm just teasing," he told her with a grin, finally moving to pick up his fork and knife as the squabble between Viv and Catcher beside them turned into an all-out war for ultimate french fry dominance. "Viv figured you out, even if I was a complete dunce about it."

Laurent's expression grew relieved.

Then she scowled at him. "That was mean! You about gave me a heart attack!"

"I can see the headline now." Rei started to dig into his steak. "'First year Prodigy Dies of Embarrassment at Galens Lunch Table'. At least you'd go out in style…"

"Shut up," Laurent mumbled, but he glanced up to see her forcing away a smile.

Tugging free a hunk of meat, Rei chewed on it in silence, looking out over the southern grounds while Catcher cried mercy behind him as Viv must have gotten ahold of his fingers. When he swallowed, he looked around at Laurent again.

"Did you not have a lot of friends at your last school either?" he asked.

He knew it was an awkward question—what idiot wouldn't? Still, despite whatever she might say to the contrary, it made little sense for Aria Laurent—Galens' top recruit—to be so secluded like this. Even Logan Grant, who—in Rei's opinion—possessed the personality of an ill-tempered toddler, had formed something of a group, and had started to do so from the very first day of classes. Rei expected Laurent to blush and freeze up, or to maybe see a bit more of the fiery presence she'd cut when he'd first stood across the Dueling field from her, or when she'd pulled him out of the assembly crowd the day before.

In the end, he got a bit of both.

"No. Not really." Laurent's cheeks were indeed a little red as she answered quietly, but when she looked away from him towards the grounds again Rei got the impression she was less embarrassed than…

Was that anger?

"I mean… I guess I did," the girl kept on after a moment, frowning at the grass and trees and buildings outside. "Not really sure you could call them 'friends', though."

"Why not?"

Laurent made a face. "I feel like friends are people *you* get to pick, right? People *you* decide you want to spend time with? I… uh…" She looked a little uncomfortable, but continued. "I didn't really have a choice in who I got to associate with."

"Ah," Rei nodded in understanding, cutting another chunk out of his steak. "One of *those* families."

Laurent blinked in surprise, looking around at him. "How did you know?"

"Because he's been dealing with mine for years."

Viv was leaning victoriously over *two* plates of fries when she reentered the conversation, Catcher grumbling curses and nursing a few twisted digits across from her.

"Your family…?" Laurent echoed tentatively.

Viv nodded. "Yup. We went to the same preparatory academy. Hitched onto each other in our first year at Grandcrest, when we figured out we were the only two in the grade who were serious about becoming Users." Without looking she smacked Catcher's good hand away from her tray as he made a sly attempt at retrieving his plate. "My parents weren't super pleased when they found out who I was hanging out with at school."

"Still aren't," Rei said with a snort, giving her the stink-eye over a forkful of meat and broccoli. "Four years, and I've never met them."

"Well that's crap of them," Catcher decided to chime in, shaking the sting off before freezing and looking slowly at Viv. "I-I mean I'm sure they're great people in their own way, of course…"

"It's fine," Viv shrugged the slight aside, finally reaching for her own fork. "They *are* great. They're just… a little too stuck up for their own good."

"But you guys were allowed to keep spending time together…?" Laurent asked tentatively. "I mean, obviously you were, since you're here, now…"

"Nope," Rei and Viv both said in unison, and with matching amusement.

Laurent looked promptly confused.

"My parents tried to put their foot down when they first heard I was 'hanging out with a Ward'." She made air-quotes to either side of her head as she said it, nearly spearing herself in the ear with her fork. "Told me it was fine to take an interest in CAD-combat, but that I should pick my friends more carefully."

Laurent stared. "And what did you do, then?"

"She told them to shove it, and hung up on them." Rei grinned as he recalled the moment. "I was there when she ended that call. One of the only good memories we have together."

"You're hilarious, jerk." Viv made a face and gave him the finger before scooping up some mashed potatoes. "But yeah. What he said, essentially. If anything the last 4 years are their fault. Weird as he is I might have ditched him on my own eventually, but the moment they told me I wasn't allowed to hang out with him…" She shrugged. "Pretty much sealed the deal."

"They were all kinds of pissed for a while," Rei continued the story for Viv as she started to eat. "Took them the rest of the year to get over it, and that's only because I ended up with the best grades in the class. They must have thought I had *some* value to her, at that point."

"That *is* awful, though," Laurent said quietly, but she was staring at Viv, watching her shovel down potatoes in a very un-ladylike fashion. "I guess you're kind of amazing, too, huh?"

Viv paused, cocking an eyebrow at the C-Ranker above overstuffed cheeks. She swallowed, and continued to look perplexed as she answered. "I don't know about that. If anything I was just an overly rebellious brat who *happened* to make out with a smart-ass genius as a best friend in the end. Imagine what would have gone down if Rei had been someone else. Like Catcher."

She grinned as, across from her, Catcher spit and coughed into the water he had just accepted from a passing bot.

"*Ahck*—That was—*cough*—That was rude." He scowled over the table while dapping at the wet spot of his uniform with a napkin. "I'll have you know *my* parents think I'm something of a catch, thank you very much."

"Well someone's got to…" Viv said under her breath.

"Woman, I will cut you."

As the two started going at it again good-naturedly, Rei returned his attention to Laurent.

"I get the feeling it would take me being crowned an Intersystem pro-circuit Champion to get Viv's parents to want to bother with meeting me, but they've long-since given up on stopping us from hanging out, even before we both made it into Galens." He studied the Phalanx's face carefully. "Sounds like you've had a tougher time, though…"

Laurent didn't say anything for a moment, still watching Viv with a bit of a sad frown.

Finally, she nodded.

"My family—no, my *mother*, if I'm being honest—can be… a bit overbearing." She exhaled in resignation, turning to face him. "She has… expectations. I suppose both my parents do, but my father prefers a more… uh… *extreme* hands-off approach." Laurent did a good job of keeping her expression set, but the disappointment didn't escape her voice. "My mother raised me and my siblings pretty much on her own, and I think she got used to a little too much control." The girl seemed to sag slightly, and appeared to have difficulty meeting his eye again. "I hope I don't sound ungrateful. I know she loves us in her own way, but…" She trailed off, leaving Rei to wait.

"I actually didn't want to come to Galens, if you can believe it," she started again when she was ready. "I wanted to go to an inner-system schools, maybe one of the academies on Mars, or even Earth. But *Mother* had to have her way again." She spoke bitterly, then her eyes fell to the table, and her voice grew more subdued once more. "Still... I can't complain. At least here I'm not surrounded by instructors and headmasters ready to bend over backwards to make sure they meet all of her ridiculous demands."

Rei whistled. "That bad?"

Laurent nodded, and said nothing more, still staring at her plate.

Rei, though, chuckled. "Don't worry. You've got the wrong lunch buddy if you're looking to be judged for a little parental baggage. At least your mom and dad didn't leave you at the hospital the day after you were born."

The *girl* looked up sharply, eyes wide. "You're kidding..."

Rei snorted. "I wish. I was born with a nasty case of boneitis. The happy couple decided they couldn't handle it."

"Bone...itis?" Laurent repeated uncertainly, clearly having trouble balancing his humor with the gravity of his statement.

"His body's soft tissues like to calcify and turn into splinters that have to be removed," Viv spoke up, glaring at Rei as she pointed her fork at him. "If you're going to explain things, do it properly."

"Okay, *Mom*," he grumbled in answer, but across from him Laurent looked to be making a realization.

"Is *that* what your scars are from?" she demanded. "I've been wondering what—!" She caught herself, looking suddenly distressed. "I-I'm sorry... I didn't mean—"

"Don't sweat it," Rei interrupted with half a smile, not even pausing in his cutting into his lunch again. "My point, though, is that you don't need to feel bad about venting. *Especially* about your parents. You're in the right place for that, Laurent."

He stuffed the steak into his mouth and looked away from her, studying the flyers and transport vehicles that cut across the sky high above them in a perfect grid of air lanes. For a while the only conversation was Viv and Catcher's typical back and forth, and eventually Rei took to watching the pair go at it with amusement as Laurent sat quietly opposite him, hardly touching her food.

Then, out of nowhere, she spoke again.

"Aria."

Around the table, the other three all paused. As one they turned to her, taking her in intently.

"What was that?" Rei asked, though he was quite sure he'd heard her clearly.

When the girl looked up, one might have mistaken the redness in her eyes were it not for the brilliant smile she met them with, bright as the sun high above.

"Aria," she repeated, her voice just a little hoarse. "My friends call me Aria."

CHAPTER 27

"Despite the formation of the ISC in 2182 following the New London Treaties, it was nearly 100 years before the Intersystem Collective Military was established, and for good cause. With the signing of the Treaties, war had become largely non-existent across the civilized planets of mankind, what revolutions, conflicts, and uprisings did occur typically easily handled by local peace-keeping forces or un-manned global defense systems. Only after humanity's first attempted expansion into the Sirius System, and subsequent encounter with the archons, was the need for a force capable of large-scale combat reestablished, if rapidly so.

Now, 200 years later, the ISCM is the single largest branch among the governing systems of the Collective, its exclusive funding by the SCTs making it nearly au-tonomous from the tedium of Intersystem administrations, lobbyists, and private interests intent on pressing their own agendas..."

A History of the Collective
Gilbert France, M.S., Ph.D.
Distributed by Central Command, Earth

I don't know where you're getting your information from, but I find it simultaneously infuriating and amusing that you think I would divulge a student's particulars without their permission."

"Oh save me the speech. She's my daughter. I have the right to know."

"She may be your daughter, Salista, but as of the moment she accepted enrollment into this Institute, she also became *my* cadet. My highest obligation is to protect her and her education, even if that is from the meddling of well-intentioned parents."

"Don't give me that bullshit, Rama." Salista Laurent's voice was seething. "If you were interested in protecting her education then you would take a greater inter-est in who it is she is spending her time with. Viviana Arada is one thing. The girl seems to have promise and comes from a good family. Layton Catchwick I'll allow as well, but I will *absolutely not* allow Aria to be wasting her year with a ward of the government, much less a D1 who—"

"D2."

On the other side of the call, Salista paused.

"What was that?"

"D2," Rama Guest repeated firmly, staring at his reflection in the black sky beyond his office window as his NOED spelled out "Voice Call Ongoing" across his vision. "Your informants are behind the ball, whoever they are. As of yesterday evening Reidon Ward reached a D2 CAD-Rank, *and* achieved his *third* evolution since arriving at Galens at the beginning of August, which is already more than I should tell you."

"What do I care if he's a D2? That just makes Aria a full *tier* above him as of last week, which means he hardly measures up to her. That boy has no business fraternizing with my daughter, particularly if they are training together on a nightly—!"

"Who my charges choose to 'fraternize with', as you say, is their business, and theirs alone," Rama rumbled, feeling the twinge of impatience beginning to grow. "I accepted this call because you are dear to me, Salista, as your own person *and* as the wife of my greatest friend. I did *not* take it to be lectured on how to conduct the affairs at my school, nor to be instructed on how to impede in the growing bonds of the cadets under my care. If this is the way our conversations are going to go from now on, then I will instruct my chief assistant to refuse all communications from you henceforth, and you will be forced to rely on your spies for all updates on the progress and wellbeing of your daughter. Is that understood?"

There was silence on the other end of the line for a long few seconds.

"I just want what's best for her, Rama…" Salista's voice was cool, hard even, but not absent a certain taste of what might have been sadness.

Rama Guest felt the fire leave him all at once, and his shoulders sagged as he sighed.

"I know. I know, Salista. But this is not the way. They are not my children, so I am hardly fit to lecture you, but I can say with certainty that you are toeing the same path you took with Kalus and Amina, and risk similar results."

Another silence, this one so thick Rama could almost taste the tension.

Then, with a tone, the connection cut off, leaving him to stare off into the darkness as his frame scripted a "Call Ended", then blinked out. He took a deep breath, allowing for a moment to center himself, studying the stillness of the stars against the trailing lights of the moving traffic beneath them.

"She hang up on you?"

Rama looked around. Maddison Kent stood a little to the side, a stylus still held over the wide pad nestled into the crook of her elbow, ready to take notes as he directed.

"She did," he muttered, gesturing at the tablet to indicate it wouldn't be needed. "Though whether out of anger or because I struck at a guilty nerve, I couldn't say."

"That woman is a force of nature," Maddison grumbled, stowing the stylus behind one ear and relaxing. Rama gave her a warning look, which she met without so much as flinching. "Oh please. Like you disagree."

"Perhaps I do, but I hoped a year of working together has not given you the impression I am frequently one to speak ill of those not present to defend themselves." Rama turned away from the window at last, making for the broad chair behind his desk. It was getting late, and he still had to run through the day's requisition forms from Bashir Sattar.

"That's fine. I've heard ill enough from Aria." Maddison followed him as he settled in, coming to stand across the desk. "In fact, these last two weeks have been the first time since summer training started that she and I haven't spoken daily."

Rama raised an eyebrow at her. "And that's... a good thing?"

"Of *course it is*!" The younger woman looked like she wanted to roll her eyes, but seemed to think better of it. "Consider it: that girl has been starved of true companionship most of her life. If she's not coming to me, then she's finding it somewhere else, isn't she?"

"Hmm... Perhaps." Rama contemplated this news a moment, then eyed Maddison carefully. "I'm *still* not sure how I feel about you being so friendly with one of our students, by the way."

"Then you should have hired a member of the military to be your assistant, rather than a civilian," the woman told him sweetly, grinning in a knowing sort of way. "Then you could have ordered me to stop spending time with the poor girl."

"None of the other applicants could manage half the work you do in *twice* the time, and you know it," Rama grumbled, knowing better than to engage in *that* losing battle. "But still, it may not be seen as appropriate by some."

"Oh? But they would be fine with two months of daily morning training with the Institute's commanding officer, as well as not-infrequent audiences just to say hello?"

Rama coughed to clear his throat, knowing he was cornered. "Yes… Well… If Aria isn't reaching out to you as often, I suppose it is likely only a good thing…"

"It is," Maddison assured him, seriously this time. "She's making friends, Rama. Real friends. Isn't that the whole reason you pushed to have her brought here?"

"It is *one* reason I pushed to have her brought here," Rama was careful to clarify. "One of *many* reasons." Then he sighed. "But yes. In the grand scheme of things, I suppose you're right… If Aria can find a place at Galens, then perhaps she won't go the same way as her siblings."

"And perhaps your best friend won't be left heartbroken," Maddison added, blunt as ever.

Rama glared at her, and this time his assistant had the sense to look a tad sheepish under his gaze.

"Sorry," she said with a bit of a grimace. "Just slipped out."

"Yes… As it seems to more and more frequently of late. I can see your beau's fiery personality has been rubbing off on you."

Maddison grinned at that, but only lifted her pad in question. "Will that be all, colonel? It's getting late, even for you."

Rama grunted in agreement. "Yes. Thank you for your work today. You may go."

The woman nodded in acknowledgement, turning to leave. She'd made it as far as the door, pulling it open, when Rama found himself calling after her again.

"Maddison…"

His chief assistant looked over her shoulder at him questioningly.

"She… Aria knows what she's doing, doesn't she?" he asked, chewing nervously on the inside of his cheek. "I know I defended her choices on that call but… Ward is a wild card. She knows what she's doing, right?"

Maddison offered him a smile he wasn't sure he liked. "Of course she doesn't. But why is that a bad thing?"

And then she was gone, leaving Rama Guest to regret ever having been fool enough to ask.

CHAPTER 28

"It is not his victories that make a man. It is his defeats."

Golden Child
Pierson Maron

The day the troubles began started off on such a positive note, Rei would never have guessed he was going to find himself waking up in the hospital later that evening.

He'd always been the earliest riser of the five cadets in 304. Viv, Catcher, and Benaly tended to sleep in, while Cashe kept to her room in the morning, and so it wasn't unusual for him to get the common area to himself for a good hour before anyone else made their appearance. Getting up when his NOED alarm went off at 0600, he started by making himself coffee in the kitchen, then settled onto a couch in the living room before pulling up his school texts and lecture notes on the smart-glass wall to review.

It was a chore, for once, to study. For one thing he'd stayed up late the evening before finishing a paper for Captain Takeshi on "Team Coordinations in Multi-Squad Matches", and for another he had to consciously stop himself from calling on Shido, wanting to examine his newest evolution for what had to have been the hundredth time since the changes had taken place two nights before, on his reaching of a D2 CAD-Rank. The adaptations hadn't been as extreme as either of his previous two shifts, but the fact that he'd achieved a third evolution *at all* was enough to distract him from his review of molecular compression equations. More than once he found himself staring at the complex formulas blown up in white lettering on the semi-transparent wall before him, and each time he had to refocus, to work to keep his mind on task. It was hardly easy. Apart from his own elation, Viv, Catcher, and Aria had all been ecstatic at his progression, while in combat training yesterday afternoon every eye had been on him again for the first time since earlier in the term. Rei frowned, remembering the whispers that had started up once more. He understood, of course. When he'd been an E-Ranker it had been easier to pass off his progression as "catching up". Now that he'd been in the Ds for half a month, however, his jump up of two levels in that period had likely only gone largely unobserved because no one but a handful of the top students were bothering to keep an eye on him.

Now that Shido had evolved this third time, though... well... People had started to take notice again.

Rei blinked and cursed himself, realizing he'd once more been doing nothing but staring blankly at the function for carbonized steel decompression with Device calling. He tried to set his mind to task again, and for 2 whole minutes managed to review the numbers in detail, partially committing them to memory.

It was so dull that he was more than pleased to hear the *click* of a door opening behind him.

Rei turned on the couch, hoping to find Catcher making an early morning of the day, or even Jack Benaly, with whom he could have at least made some scattered conversation. He was disappointed—and a little alarmed—therefore, when he found himself looking at Chancery Cashe, the girl's silver hair in a messy tail behind her head, purple-green eyes sleepy over a loose shirt and pajama shorts.

Her expression cleared, though, the instant she realized who she was sharing the common area with.

For a time the two of them did nothing but look at each other, Rei frowning around at her, Cashe looking stricken at finding herself alone with him, even in the shared space. Eventually—unwilling to start the day off on the wrong foot—Rei mumbled a minimally-polite "Morning" as he returned his attention to the smart-glass display.

His jaw almost hit the floor when the Lancer answered with a quiet "Good morning..."

Unable to stop himself, he twisted to look over his shoulder again, eyeing Cashe in confusion. Not since their first day on campus had the girl spoken so much as a word to him, and he'd only ever seen her exchange more than a passing greeting with Catcher, who seemed not to give her any other option. As such, Rei didn't quite know what to say as he took in his generally silent suitemate, who was suddenly looking everywhere but at him.

"Um... Is that coffee?" she asked after a moment, clearly hesitant, eyes finally settling on the mug resting atop the table by his knees.

Rei was so dumbfounded it took him a second to answer.

"Oh… Yeah. There should be some left in the pot, if you want it…?"

She nodded, still refusing to look at him again, and moved awkwardly to the kitchen, where the sliding and clinking sound of a cupboard being opened and a mug getting retrieved told Rei he'd been taken up on his offer. His distraction now utter, he could only listen to the coffee being poured, and a few seconds later Cashe reappeared, making back for her room in a hurry. Reaching the door, however, she paused in the opening, and appeared to be steeling herself for something.

Then, all at once, she whirled.

"Ward, listen…" the girl started, her expression pained, but she seemed unable to continue. Still completely at a loss, Rei only watched her, allowing her to gather herself, somewhat reminded of Aria as he did.

"Listen…" Cashe tried again, but once more appeared incapable of getting out whatever words she was going for.

In the end her eyes started darting around, settling on the mathematics displayed on the room wall.

"Are you… um… Are you done with the paper for Takeshi?" she finally managed, and Rei would have bet both arms and the CAD attached to them this was *not* what the Lancer had been intending to say.

Still, he wasn't about to give her a hard time for even this meager olive branch.

"I am, yeah," he answered, turning around a little further to face her more fully. "Finished it last night. Why?"

Cashe looked to be struggling with herself. "Would you…? I heard you're good with… with the coursework… Would you be able to look at mine? I'm not really happy with some of my deductions…"

She trailed off, fidgeting with the handle of her mug in distinct discomfort.

Rei, though, offered her a smile. "Sure. Can you bring me your pad? I was about to fall asleep to this crap anyway." He indicated the compression formula with a grimace.

Cashe looked briefly surprised, then brightened. "Oh… Yeah. Okay!"

She vanished into her room, reappearing a moment later with her tablet in one hand, coffee still held in the other. Moving around the couches to sit opposite him, she put her mug down to wake the device up and swipe across its contents for a while before handing it over.

"I'm having trouble with ideal coordination on the 'Asteroid Mines' Wargames field," she told him, more confidently now as she pointed to a place on the wall of text she was presenting. "If your whole team gets dispersed across a series of blind tunnels like this, I can't figure out how to quantify whether or not you're better off engaging individually, or trying to regroup…?"

"Oh, yeah that's definitely a tricky one, because it actually comes to event probability. If you try to attack on your own, the best you can hope for is a one-on-one fight, right? If you think of it that way, you have to consider the likelihood of encountering worse conditions, like two-on-one, three-on-one, et cetera. By attempting to engage on your own, the probability of your elimination increases since the best you can hope for is equal odds. *But*, if you try to regroup first—"

For a good quarter hour Rei reviewed Cashe's paper with her, and by the time anyone else stirred the silver-haired Lancer was almost animated in their discussion. Unfortunately, Viv was the next to open her door drowsily, though she woke up fast upon taking in the pair of them seated near enough to hand the tablet back and forth across the table.

"What the…?" Viv muttered, dumbstruck, and her astonishment was apparently enough to remind Cashe of the situation. The girl blanched, pulling the pad away from where she had just been about to pass it back to Rei, and stood up at once.

"Th-Thanks for the coffee," she stuttered, once again having lost the ability to look him in the eye. "A-And the advice. This was… really helpful."

Then, so swiftly Rei was sure she had engaged her Speed spec, the Lancer was gone, the door to her room closing with a quick *clack*.

You told Cashe, didn't you?"

Walking at Rei's right, Catcher glanced at him sidelong.

"Told her what?"

"About me."

"Ah," Catcher looked away again with a shrug to peer up into the clear sky of the early day, hitching his school bag higher onto his shoulder. "No idea what you're talking about."

"Bull," Rei snorted. "I spent part of the morning with her going over our Tactical Studies paper. I think she tried to apologize before that, but asking for my help was the best she managed to get out."

"Well that was certainly nice of her," Catcher said with feigned approval. "I guess she must be warming up to you."

"Like she would do that without someone pushing her." Viv looked around Rei to peer at the blond Saber suspiciously. "I don't know if you've taken too many blows to the head since the start of term, but I seem to recall Cashe looking about ready to throw Rei's ass out of school herself, if they'd have let her."

There was a quiet gasp from Viv's left.

"That happened?" Aria asked, eyes wide under the brim of her cap and she, too, bent to look between Rei and Catcher as they walked. "I haven't heard any of this!"

"Because you're lucky enough to have no drama in your suite," Viv replied, turning to her with a jealous expression. "Want to switch? Cashe leaves her room so little I'm basically living with two boys and Catcher."

"Hey!" Catcher exclaimed in indignation, finally look down at them again and earning a laugh from everyone.

Everyone except Aria, who was gazing at Viv with dead seriousness.

"Are you actually offering?" she asked as the mess hall came into sight at last. "Cause I can make that happen, and I think I've *yet* to exchange more than ten words with any of my roommates at his point."

"Oh," Viv looked taken aback. "Uh… No. Sorry. I was just joking, and I don't think—"

She stopped at the grin that split Aria's features.

"That's not fair!" Viv exclaimed with a laugh. "You're too good at saying stuff like that with a straight face!"

"Don't hate the player," Aria answered with a giggle, moving slightly aside to let a couple of third years pass along the path in the opposite direction. "No one said you could be the only tease of the group."

"Yeah, but it's no fun when *I'm* the one getting teased…" Viv grumbled, pouting. Then she perked up. "Weren't we interrogating Catcher? How did this get turned around on me?"

"Oh, there's some friends from class!" Catcher exclaimed suddenly, waving in towards a group of first years who were distinctly *not* looking at him before taking a step in their direction. "Guess I'll catch you guys later! See you at lunch!"

"Yeah, no." Rei said, snagging him by the gold stitching of his collar before he could get away. "Nice try, but you still haven't answered my question."

Catcher seemed to deflate a bit, then sighed as he stepped back to walk alongside them again. "Okay, yes. I told her a *little bit* about you—but nothing too important, don't worry!" he added in a hurry when Viv glared at him sharply. "I wanted to clue her in before she put her foot even deeper in her mouth. Cashe is… kinda behind the ball on a few things."

"Like what?" Viv pressed him in a slow, menacing voice.

"Like the fact that accusing Rei of having his family get him into school was kind of the epitome of a faux pas," Catcher answered quickly, lifting both hands in a sign of peace. "That's basically it, though, okay?"

"She did *what*?" Aria hissed from Viv's left.

"Oh this is a fun story," Viv replied with a grin, and proceeded to launch into a retelling of their first afternoon in 304 that was—in Rei's opinion—rather hyperbolized. Regardless, by the time they reached the hall, Aria had been caught up, and she looked somewhere between livid and mortified as Viv finished describing that initial exchange with Chancery Cashe.

"You're kidding me," she seethed as the doors to the arboretum slid open for them. "How could she say something like that? Did she not know?"

"No, she didn't," Catcher explained calmly. "And believe me when I say she regrets it. Cashe has a chip on her shoulder when it comes to Users—not even just getting into Galens."

"Why?" Aria pressed him, falling in behind Rei and Viv along the breakfast line.

"Her business," Catcher said firmly, and quailed only a little under the look Aria gave him, then. "It *is*. If you want to know, ask her yourself. How would you guys feel if I went around spilling the beans about Rei's fibro? Or the fact we basically had to *chase you down* before you would be seen in public with us?"

Aria, predictably, flushed crimson at that.

Then she relaxed. "Fine. I guess I can't argue with that."

Viv, on the other hand, was less placated.

"Nuh-uh," she said, looking at Catcher sharply. "I don't buy that *any* Galens cadet could be so far removed from reality. Spill."

In response, he only stared her down.

Breakfast that morning was spent in an unusual fervor of Viv grilling Catcher for more information, and him refusing to bend as stoutly as a steel rod. By the time they had to split for lectures, the two of them looked about ready to *actually* kill one another, and it was with some relief that Rei and Aria said goodbye to the Saber before chasing after Viv, who was already stomping off in the direction of the Tactical Studies building.

"Come on, *relax*," Rei told her with a smile once they'd caught up. "It's not that big a deal. If Cashe was willing to open up a little like she did this morning, you'll get your chance to interrogate her as thoroughly as you want at some point, I'm sure."

Viv grunted noncommittally, not so much as glancing at him over her clenched jaw.

Aria edged in between them, giving Rei an "I've got this"-look before slipping an arm into the crook of Viv's stiff elbow.

That got her to turn around, finally.

"He's right, you know," Aria said with a smile, matching steps so the two of them could walk side by side as they approached the Department. "It's not worth getting upset over."

"Yeeeah, fine," Viv grumbled. After a moment she glanced down at their joined arms, then grinned back up at Aria. "But if I get to walk to class like this as a reward, I might just have to get pissy every morning. Gotta make all those suitors jealous."

Aria laughed, disengaging herself and shoving Viv away playfully. Following behind the two girls as they started talking about the day's courses and their planned training that afternoon, Rei couldn't help but smile.

For someone who claimed not to have made many real friends in her life, Aria Laurent had found her place in their little group with surprising ease. Whether it was a proper social upbringing or just her bubbly nature, it hadn't taken more than a few days for her to come out of her shell enough to join in with the trio's banter, to everyone's shared delight. Far aside from being the first year's prodigal top ranker, she proved herself equally smart and quick-witted, and could keep up with their jabbing dynamics even when Viv and Catcher managed to get on each other's nerves, like that very morning. Rei had had no regrets in his choice of new friends so far in the term, but he didn't think there would have been any argument if he'd said the last 2 weeks had been more fun than any of the previous since arriving at Galens.

Fun…

Rei caught himself smiling a little, watching Aria from behind while she and Viv continued to chat. It felt good, somehow, seeing the girl happy. Before she'd bucked up the courage to approach him, he'd never considered the fact she may have been anything less, but witnessing her now had opened his eyes to what her school life must have been like before he'd invited her to join them. It was an astounding change, and if he'd thought Aria alluring then, his interest in the girl had only redoubled with seeing her bloom, especially around Viv. It was like watching two grade-schoolers meet and make friends for the first time, the enthusiasm and energy infectious. He might even have been a little jealous, actually, were it not for the fact that—in reality—*he* was the one who probably spent the most time with Aria Laurent.

As excitable as she was—as happy and full of life as she seemed when they were all together—not even this talkative, laughing version of the girl compared to the one he faced off with on the Dueling field almost every night. When Hippolyta was live over her limbs, Aria always changed in an near-indescribable way. She was terrifying, yes, *always* terrifying, but she was also mesmerizing, and the sole reason Rei thought his growth hadn't slowed down much since hitting the D-Ranks budded from her endless intensity. As odd as it was to say, Aria *thrived* on the battlefield, her technique and ability all grace and all power *all* the time. The two of them had become habitual sparring partners—though they all four cycled a bit throughout every training session—and for the first week of her having joined them Rei had argued that Aria should have spent more time matching off with Viv or Catcher, who could have at least provided *some* kind of challenge.

Aria, though, refused to hear any of it, insisting that he was simply more fun to fight.

Rei chuckled to himself, considering this. On the one hand, he imagined there was some amusement to be had in his amounting to what was essentially a living punching bag for the girl—though she'd obviously blushed and squeaked to the contrary the one time he'd joking accused her of sporting a rather wide sadistic streak. On the other, however, he supposed he could credit himself with posing a different kind of challenge, and one Aria might not have had the opportunity to face off with often even during the summer training months.

While he couldn't meet her strength for strength, Rei could match her now for more than a minute at a time, *every* time. Despite their difference in specs, despite their difference in experience and rank, he'd slowly over the course of 2 weeks gotten to the point where he could stare down the length of Hippolyta's spear and say with confidence that he wasn't about to be taken down without a fight. He never actually *won*, of course—*never*—but he took in, processed, and adapted to Aria's style a little more with every encounter. It had been the same for Viv and Catcher before the Phalanx had joined them, but between their constant cycling and the fact that they were a bit closer to his own ability, Rei hadn't been nearly as purposeful with his observation, nor his responding to the pairs' styles. Against Aria, though, he had had no choice but to deliberately tailor his combat if he ever wanted to last more than a few seconds, and as a result improvement was more measurable, his growth more apparent against the height of their clearer mismatch. In the end, it was against her that the realization had come:

Of a fashion, Rei could *study* his way to advantage in a fight.

Then again, he supposed there was no real surprise there. He'd adjusted to more than a few opponents in his time on the training fields under Valera Dent and Michael Bentz's watchful eyes, and he couldn't imagine competitive SCT combatants didn't agonize over any footage of upcoming adversaries they could get their hands on. Still, it was a concept Rei hadn't thought to consciously apply until matching so consistently with Aria, and he suspected it was these subsequent adaptations that provided challenge enough for her to come back again and again, even against a low D-Ranker like him.

He tested her, he had realized, helping her identify her own weaknesses by finding them for himself.

They reached the Tactical Studies Department, climbed the several floors to their classroom, and took their usual seating three-abreast along the center of the lower rows, Rei in the middle of the two girls. Viv made some last-minute adjustments to the paper they had due that day with his and Aria's input, and once Takeshi arrived the course passed quickly, as did the rest of the morning's lectures. Lunch proved a bit more of an awkward affair, with Viv and Catcher refusing to look at one another and staring daggers when they did happen to catch each other's eye, and it was with a further wash of relief that they split once more to head for the Arena and their afternoon training. Taking the elevators down to SB2 together, neither Rei, Viv, nor Aria noticed the eyes that followed them into the locker room, or out again and down the hall to the combat area.

It was only as they stepped into the cavernous expanse of the underground field space that the three of them got their first surprise of the day, and anything but a pleasant one—at least by Rei's estimation. It had become standard protocol for Valera Dent to wait for the class to gather around the elevated platform for Field 3, sometimes reviewing the day's program with her sub-instructors, sometimes standing silently while the cadets arrived in a steady trickle. For this reason, the initial oddity they noticed was that 1-A appeared to be congregating around Field 2, to their left.

The second was that it was not the chief combat instructor who overlooked them from the raised projection, but rather an aged man in standard regulars, his temples clean-shaven under the ridge of his cap, eyes deep-set and dark.

It took Rei a moment to recognize him.

"Is that… Reese?"

Viv and Aria nodded together to his left, and the three of them exchanged a confused look before joining the steady flow of their classmates towards 2. They found a space in the groupings wide enough to accommodate, and all around them there was excited murmuring from the other cadets. Rei caught Sense's eye, giving him a questioning look, but the Brawler only shrugged as though to say he had no idea what was going on either.

"What do you think this is about?" Viv asked in a hushed voice, taking in the major as he stood with the sub-instructors in a formed line at his back.

"No idea," Aria whispered back, she, too, observing the higher officer with a mix of interest and confusion. "The Intra-Schools aren't for another month, but maybe there's a second announcement?"

"Maybe…" Rei said uncertainly, studying the major for himself. He actually had his own suspicions, and a twinge of excitement thrummed at his insides as he considered it. Hadn't Reese and Dent told them squad leaders for team events would be selected from the Sectional qualifiers? If that was the case, it might make sense if those involved with that decision saw the cadets work, and not *just* in the tournament…

Before he could voice his hunch to either of the girls, though, Dyrk Reese's dark gaze found him in the gathered students, and the anticipation in Rei's gut turned abruptly to stone.

Twice now he'd gotten the impression that the major wasn't his biggest fan. The first had been at the Commencement, when the man had obviously tried to intercede when Dent had granted him the demonstration match against Aria. The second had been 2 weeks ago, when he'd thought Reese's disapproving gaze had picked him out of the crowd at the special assembly.

Now, though…

Now, Rei's misgivings were instantly etched in steel.

He had seen the look Dyrk Reese was giving him before. He had seen it a thousand times. Leron Joy. Logan Grant. Mateus Selleck. It was the same look the students who'd never accepted his presence among them had been shooting his way since the start of school, the same distaste and disgruntlement of an ego forced to bend, rather than allowing itself to. It wasn't the first time Rei had been greeted with a similar treatment from a staff, even—Liam Gross and several of the other sub-instructors had never really warmed up to his lagging behind the rest of the class—but at least *those* officers always made even *some* minimal effort to hide their disappointment.

Reese's disapproval, on the other hand, was so blatant that Viv spoke up from

Rei's side.

"What's *his* deal?" she half-whispered, half-snapped

Rei was about to answer that he didn't know, when a voice rose up from behind them.

"Apparently the man's got half-decent standards."

Together Rei, Viv, and Aria all turned on the spot, finding themselves facing off with a tight-lipped Logan Grant. His usual entourage looked to be scattered among the other students behind him, but Rei didn't miss Selleck's cold stare from a nearby group of Sabers, nor Leda Truant's from where she stood with the class's other two Phalanxes.

"What do *you* want?" Viv spat, and Grant actually blinked at her, like he hadn't expected the venom.

After a moment, though, he looked instead to Aria. "I thought you'd eventually get over your phase, Laurent, but it doesn't look like it. What the hell are you doing?"

"What are you talking about?" Aria's face was already growing pink, but she didn't look away from the tall Mauler.

"I mean that if you were looking for a decent sparring partner, you could have just asked," Grant snapped back, taking them all off guard. "You're going to ruin yourself training with this asshole." He gestured at Rei dismissively.

Rei, for his part, could only take the black-haired boy in in confusion. Was Grant... angry?

"Are you that willfully ignorant?" Viv snarled, taking a step towards the Mauler. "Since you seem to have your head buried under a *rock*, maybe someone should clue you in on the fact that Rei's already practically—"

"Caught up to some of the others?" Grant finished for her in a low growl, narrowing his black-red eyes at Viv. "Don't treat me like an idiot, Arada. Obviously I'm aware. I also don't give a shit. All I've ever seen Ward do on the field is run away and try to pull the wool over his opponents' eyes. Super impressive. Real quality fighter." The bitter sarcasm of his last words came through hard.

"I'm sorry, where the hell did *you* get a leg to stand on when it comes to criticism?" It was Rei's turn to join in. "I seem to recall you getting a week in the brig for trying to cut my head off *after our match ended*."

"Yeah, well maybe next time you'll think twice about mouthing off about my parents, dickwad." Grant didn't even glance at Rei as he spoke, his eyes still on Viv, and it was she he addressed again next. "It's not just Laurent. What *you're* doing with him has me at a loss, too, Arada."

"Excuse me?!" Viv seethed, but before she could get another word in Rei held her up with a hand on her arm.

Not that his own anger had subsided in the least.

"Dude, you've got serious issues," he growled at Grant. "I don't know what stick was shoved up your ass as a kid, but you should see about getting that removed."

The Mauler at last turned his attention on him, and he sneered. "Maybe I'll take advice from you when you can hold up your promises, Ward. What was it you said you would do to me, last time we talked like this? 'Grind my face into the field', I think it was? How'd that work out for you in our last match?"

Rei, for once, had no response to give, and he felt his cheeks follow the direction of Aria's as the heat built up.

Grant, seeing his victory, smirked, then looked between the two girls again. He seemed almost disappointed. "Whatever. I guess it's not my place to butt in. Just remember I warned you from the start when he—" he gave Rei an eyeful over a clenched jaw "—drags you both down with him."

And then, before any of them could protest this statement, he stepped by, shouldering Rei out of the way to move closer to the front of the group.

"I swear on *Gemela* that I'm going to make that shit-stain *bleed* one day," Viv fumed, watching Grant's broad back walked away from them.

"*Viv*," Aria hissed in warning, only for Viv to whirl on her.

"Oh come on! Like he deserves any better! You can't seriously be so cool-headed that—"

"*Viv!*" It was Rei's turn to whisper urgently, hoping to get her to shut up. It worked this time, fortunately, because when she looked around at him Viv, too, caught the glower they had earned themselves from Dyrk Reese, the major's attention leveled on them with distinct displeasure.

The three of them stood quietly for a long moment—the closest other students pulling away as though they might get contaminated with the officer's disapproval—until Reese finally turned his attention elsewhere.

"Funny how he didn't give *Grant* any kind of stink eye," Aria grumbled in annoyance behind Rei's shoulder, and he had to suppress a snort.

Not wanting to push their luck, they shared a silent agreement not to speak again until the training started. Fortunately it wasn't more than another minute or so before the stragglers arrived from the locker room, and as soon as all twenty-six of them were gathered Reese began to address them in a clear, steady voice.

"Good afternoon, cadets. Once again, I am Major Dyrk Reese, coordinator and head arbiter of all Galens SCTs, including the Intra-Schools. For those of you wondering at Captain Dent's absence, I'm afraid you will have to suffer me as a replacement today, as well as frequently over the next fourteen weeks."

There was a muttering of curious whispers at that, but the major didn't let it slow him down.

"This afternoon I am present only as an observer. You will attend to your regular groups without interruption, and I hope you'll manage to ignore my attendance and examination of your forms and abilities. It is not absent purpose, obviously." His eyes moved steadily across the group, lingering a little too long in Rei, Viv, and Aria's direction. "As Captain Dent is new to the Institute this year, along with my SCT responsibilities I am seeing to the oversight of your initial Team Battle and Wargame training regimen." He had to raise his voice as 1-A *immediately* broke out into excited whisper. "This means that—starting next week—*I* will be your instructor every Tuesday, Thursday, and Saturday afternoon, allowing the captain to spend additional time with the second and third year students who are expected to compete at the highest level in this years' collegiate Dueling circuits. This *also means*—" he pressed on as the hubbub of anticipation pitched "—that I will be taking advantage of this opportunity to make a personal assessment of your capabilities, which I hope you are all smart enough to understand may have its own impact in the coming weeks."

With those words, Rei knew that he had been right.

Reese was already on the hunt for squad-leaders.

Unable to help himself, Rei glanced at Aria, on Viv's other side. The way she was frowning up at the major before them, he suspected she'd deduced the same thing.

"Coinciding with your review of squad formats under Captain Takeshi, we will begin Team Battle training Thursday." With a wave of his hand, Reese released the Type-instructors to their duties, and they started moving at once. "I hope you will all think to review your Tactical Studies materials before then."

As soon as he was done, the lesser officers began their usual shouting.

"Maulers on 6!" Lieutenant Johnson called out, already hopping off the platform.

"Duelist to 4!" Gross announced.

"Sabers—!"

Telling Viv and Aria he would catch them after class, Rei started jogging towards 1, Sense—who had lingered to wait for him—stepping in at his side.

"Squad formats," the bald Brawler said under his breath as they approached the field Michel Bentz was already waiting by. "Awesome. I've been looking forward to this."

"Don't get too excited," Rei told him as they joined Tad Emble, Emily Gisham, and Camilla Warren in a semicircle around the chief warrant officer. "I don't imagine they'll be tossing us into a Wargame on day one."

"You would be correct."

Bretz was watching the pair of them, and appeared to take advantage of their conversation to kick-off the morning's lecture.

"As Ward just said, while I know that the major's announcement may get everyone a little hot and ready for some action, temper your expectations. Trial by fire has its place, but Team Battle and Wargame formats require precision and planning more than they do power and luck. As such, do not expect us to toss you in green and tell you all to have fun and get along. That's just a good way to get you all developing some bad habits. And I do *not* intend to have any of my students developing bad habits." The Brawler instructor glared at his five charges one after the other. "To do that, of course, means I need to hammer in some *good* habits. Your Tactical Studies courses have been reviewing squad formats for some time. Who can list the critical concepts of ideal group-based combat for me?"

Rei's hand—as was a standard in the group—was up first.

"Let's hear it, Ward."

"Communication, positioning, and advantage," he listed at once, and Bretz nodded predictably. At Rei's elbow, Warren told him "Nice" under her breath, and he almost looked around at her. It was a day for pleasant surprises, apparently. The dark-skinned girl had never paid him a compliment before, even as meager as this one.

"Communication, positioning, and advantage," Bretz was repeating. "Exactly. Simple on paper, less so in practice. Communication is handled by your Devices, and something I can only instill in you so much. Tags. Labels. The common diction of the ISCM. After that, though, you'll have to find the right squadmates, and figure out things on your own from there. Advantage is all about taking the opportunities presented to you in combat. Situational changes. Surviving team numbers. Terrain. Everything. Again, something you will learn and develop on your own and as a squad with practice." Bentz grinned. "Positioning, however... That's a different story."

With a flash the chief warrant officer's NOED flared, and a moment later the field beneath their feet was shifting and shimmering. As the white palettes of hexagonal pillars began to show themselves, Rei at first thought Bretz was pulling up the Speed & Agility course from the parameter testing again, and frowned. They'd been cycling into a variety of more complicated fields for weeks now, and he wasn't keen on duking it out again somewhere so—

He stopped, though, when he realized that the projection manifesting before him was only vaguely similar to the exam zone, and even then just in the basic building blocks of it. Indeed, as he watched, the outside thirds of the field rose as solid wedges, forming a sort of path that cut through the middle of them in a perfect line, like a sheer valley cleaved through white stone. There was nothing special about the hologram otherwise, and Rei glanced about to see that all around them the Lancers, Sabers, and Duelists areas had taken on the same strange manifestation.

"Position in team-based formats can further be broken down into two parts," Bretz was continuing his lecture, which was steadily turning into an explanation of what Rei was starting to think was going to be a very interesting training afternoon. "Information, and mobility. As Brawlers—and friends—" he added this last part with a fond smirk at Rei "—you on average possess the highest Speed and Cognition spec of every Type other than Duelists. This makes you among the most ideal of candidates for flanking, and even scouting if necessary."

Rei could feel the excitement bubbling up again.

This was *definitely* going to be an interesting afternoon.

"Senson," Bretz addressed Sense as he moved to step outside of the zone perimeter. "Take a starting position, if you would. The rest of you, off the field with me."

As he spoke, the typical red starting circle appeared about 5 yards up the path from where they stood. Sense obeyed at once, moving into the marker, then looked around at the chief warrant officer curiously.

"What am I supposed to do, sir?"

"First, call your Device," Bretz said, smiling at some private amusement. "Then… Don't mess up."

As he said it, his NOED flickered, and under Sense's feet the field began to move.

"Whoa," the Brawler said in surprise as he started sliding away from the starting ring, which stayed projected where it had been despite the shifting of the floor. He was barely 2 yards from the perimeter and the rest of the group when he seemed to catch on, because with a shout he summoned up his CAD, hurrying to return to the red circle. Reaching it, he started walking with the passing of the floor to stay within the marker, like he was ambling along on the world's largest, whitest treadmill.

"All of you, on me."

Rei looked away from Sense to see that Bretz was moving south, along the solid wall. After a moment he turned, and momentarily vanished up a set of steps Rei hadn't noticed rising into the side of the uniform pillars. At a jog he and the other Brawlers followed their instructor, taking the stairs in a quick line to find themselves atop the flat semicircle to the left of where Sense was still pacing quickly in place some 10 feet below them.

"Senson. The course will speed up now. Be ready."

The Brawler's confusion at Bretz's warning was apparent, but he only raised one green-and-black gauntlet in acknowledgement, the ivory vysetrium along the point of his punch daggers bright even against the field. As soon as he did so, the path under his feet began to move a little faster, and pretty soon he was jogging instead of walking, eyes forward on the empty "course", as the instructor had called it.

And then, from the end of the lane, a horizontal barrier about 3 feet tall appeared, sliding towards Sense at the same rate as the hexagonal paneling beneath him.

"Dexterity and speed are assets every User should cultivate, but as Brawlers in particular you need to use them to your advantage." Bretz had continued his lecture as they watched Sense vault over the low barrier with ease to stay within the red ring under him. "All of you have already experienced the value of mobility in one-on-one combat, but in squad format that mobility becomes doubly important, particularly to positioning." At the end of the path, a flat barricade diagonally bisected the way, coming at Sense a little faster this time. "This course was initially designed as an alternative to your agility parameter test, but couldn't be standardized without making it too easy for students to memorize the run." As it reached him, Sense was forced to jump and push off the left wall to clear the obstacle. Landing, he almost stumbled, the path having sped up a little once again. "As it gets faster and faster, it will become more and more challenging. Your responsibility is to last as long as you can without failing. Dueling fields are often static, but in Wargames in particular the environment of the event—be it elimination or objective-based—will not be so plain. Multi-level. Shifting terrain. Ample placement for ambushing and being ambushed. You will need to be able to take it all in and adapt to it as opportunity presents itself."

As he said this, the end of the path arrived in a sudden staggering of lifting and dropping pillars, reaching Sense at the speed of a light run, now. The cadet managed the variation with ease, demonstrating a good eye for his foot placement and a solid Cognition spec, and eventually the obstacle flattened out again, to be replaced by a series of wide beams that bisected the path a different angles, forcing Sense to dip and dodge and jump. Managing this, he was running in full, now, and the next barrier came in the shape of two flat, triangular white sheets that rotated like fan blades across the path. Sense timed the approach right and dove through the opening, rolling and coming up on his feet in time to vault and duck into a trio of over-under repetitions through a series of low and high barriers. Clearing this, a solid wall 15 feet high came barreling at him, and the Brawler leapt to catch the lip of it with both hands, clearly looking to haul himself overtop it.

Unfortunately, that was his first—and final—mistake.

Sense's Device lacked the individual jointing along his fingers that Rei's and some of the other Brawlers enjoyed. As a result, his left hand failed to get a good grip on the top of the wall, slipping off even as the cadet tried to pull himself up. The ended with a yelp of surprise and a heavy *thud* of muscle and steel hitting the still-moving ground, and Sense yelled again as he was hurtled backwards towards the open rear end of the path, shoved along by the solid obstacle like a hand sweeping a table clean. When he was a single yard away from the silver line that marked the edge of the field the entire projection flashed red, and everything came to a sudden stop.

Everything except Sense, of course, whose inertia had him hurtling over the perimeter at breakneck speed.

There was a distortion of light, like a clear film of plastic being impacted, and a semi-solid projection caught the boy as he looked about to be catapulted across the buffer zone into Field 2's space. It accepted his weight with an eerie lack of sound, slowing then stopping him, then apparently turned solid as Sense slid out of the dent he'd made in the strange wall in a tumble of CAD-clad limbs. Coming to a stop on his back, it seemed to take him a moment to catch up to what had happened, but when he did he picked his head up to look at his groupmates, all of whom were staring down at him with a mix of interest and alarm.

"WOOH!" he whooped. "LET'S DO THAT AGAIN!"

Rei wasn't the only one to laugh, and even Bretz cracked a smile.

"You'll get your turn again, don't you worry," the instructor called down, but he was already looking around at the others. "Remember that mobility is essential, particularly for you lot. If you can make yourself fast, you can make yourself invaluable. Master your Speed. Master your Cognition. If you can do that, you will *never* be useless."

It struck Rei, then, the understanding of what exactly it was that Bretz was doing. He was already thinking ahead. He was already planning for them, planning a future in which they were essential to a squad.

He was believing in them.

The fire in Rei's chest—that need to become stronger, to become better—burned just a little brighter as he watched Michael Bretz cast his confident gaze over all of his students.

"Now," the man continued after a moment, "after that lovely little demonstration... Who wants to go next?"

Unsurprisingly, every hand shot up into the air at once.

"Let's see... Gisham. Take the lead. Then it will be Emble, Ward, and Warren."

Emily Gisham barely subdued an excited exclamation before she jumped off the 10-foot drop of the wall to land lightly on her feet. Sense—who'd recalled his Device and gotten to his feet—gave her a thumbs up before himself crouching and leaping *up* the sheer cut of the field, making it over the top to join the others. Rei, abruptly, realized that the stairs had likely been for his benefit alone, and didn't know whether to feel embarrassed or grateful for the fact.

Soon, he told himself. *A little more patience.*

It was likely only a matter of time, after all, before he would be able to show off similar acrobatics.

"Call, Gisham," Bretz told the cadet below them, and as soon as her Device was live the field began to move. The chief warrant officer made no comment as Sense cheered the cadet's easy managing of the first obstacle—a suspended rectangle that forced Gisham to duck under it—and not long after the rest of the Field 1 group was shouting right along as she leapt and vaulted and dove her way faster and faster along the course. She made it a good while longer than Sense had, but eventually got tripped up when a series of moving pillars dropped out from under her, causing her to lose her balance and fall. She, too, yelled in alarm as the path hurtled her backwards, but with a similar distortion of light the barrier at the end caught her safely, and she tumbled out of the rigid dent her body had made laughing.

Emble was next, and unfortunately his run didn't go nearly as well. He didn't make it more than 30 or 40 seconds before his Speed failed him as he attempted to leap over a sudden swell in the path. One foot caught the lip of the hill, so instead of clearing the obstacle he ended up tumbling down the other side of it. He managed to get to his feet quickly, starting to run again, but before he could gain any momentum his slip-up had pulled him back within the invisible one-yard marker inside the perimeter, and with a flash of red Emble struck the barrier listlessly. The others, including Bretz, tried to cheer him up as the cadet rejoined them on the wall, and Rei offered him a grin as they crossed paths that Emble didn't return.

While getting back up would undoubtedly prove more of an issue, Rei was confident in his specs enough to drop straight down to the path below. Tucking into a roll, he came up easily enough, stepping into the starting ring.

"Call, Ward."

"Call," Rei echoed, and with a thrill he watched Shido take form around his arms and legs.

While his third evolution hadn't been as substantial a change as his first two, it was nonetheless enthralling to take in the upgrades. At his right the Device now extended down from the half-gauntlet it had once been to cover the entirety of his right forearm and elbow, the intricate black steel there not as thick as the defensive plating of his left, but still a cry better than the emptiness of scarred skin. His other elbow, too, had been covered, as had both of his knees, forming true half-greaves around his legs that matched Aria's own set, now.

It was a good thing, too, because as the path began to move under his feet, Rei got the impression the upgrades to his lower extremities where about to become particularly useful.

The first obstacle, luckily, was a simple one. From the end of the path a single broad pillar appeared in the middle of the way, forcing him to make a quick decision to move right or left. Choosing the latter, he flattened himself and half-skipped through the high gap of space between the wall and the barrier, letting it pass him by without issue. He heard Sense whoop from above him, and would have grinned had the hologram beneath his feet not started speeding up at that moment, demanding that he concentrate.

Next came an up-down repetition that had him jumping, then ducking over and under several flat half-walls, followed by the short rise of an awkward staircase that cut across the path at an angle. Clearing both, he hit the ground at a jog, now, and momentarily had to dive through a broad ring that only offered its center as a reasonable place to pass. Rolling to his feet once again, he found himself facing a hill like the one Emble had stumbled over, and so instead of trying to leap over the incline Rei simply took it at a run, dropping down the other side with a little more momentum than he would have liked. It was fine, though, because the path was now moving at a true clip, and as he dodged a wall that bisected the way Rei found himself soon almost sprinting.

Before he could get going all-out, though, the path fell out from under him.

"WHOA!" he yelled as he stumbled, then fell, and shouted again when all of a sudden he was being flung back *up,* into the air, even as the track continued to race by beneath him. He realized, flailing in nothingness, that he'd been duped by a series of rising and falling pillars just like the ones that had beaten Gisham, seeing them piston up and down below him for a moment before his momentum brought him slamming back down to the ground just past the obstacle. The landing hurt, but wasn't unbearable, and Rei shoved himself to his feet as quickly as he could.

Just in time to take a broad, flat wall straight to the face.

As the barrier impacted him, he heard the rest of his group "Ooooh…" from above, but his reactive shielding had long since risen enough to take this sort of hit without too much trouble. Any concern about the wall fell away as Rei found himself being bulldozed backwards at a breakneck pace, and he yelled again as he registered just how fast the path must have been moving beneath him.

A flash of red, then an odd, wrapping pressure that was first soft, then hard, and Rei rolled out of the catching perimeter wall a little stunned. Once his neuroline had helped catch his thoughts up to what had happened, he started to smile, completely getting the thrill Sense and Gisham had enjoyed.

His amusement, however, was cut short when he realized that a figure was frowning down at him, standing with his arms behind his back in full regalia just outside the limit of the Dueling field.

"Your course time was barely forty-seven seconds, cadet," Major Dyrk Reese said dryly. "I can't imagine why you would appear to have any cause of amusement when two of your group mates ran for nearly twice that long."

Scrambling up, Rei rose in a stiff salute before the higher officer.

"Yes, sir. Sorry, sir. It was my first attempt."

Reese's dark eyes flashed, and Rei knew at once that he had said something wrong.

"Do you always give excuses when criticized, cadet, or do you ever consider opening your ears and actually *listening* on occasion?"

It was Rei's turn to frown, but he said nothing in reply. The accusation was hardly fair. He hadn't been attempting to make any excuse, just stating a fact. And besides, if what Reese said was right, hadn't he just run for longer than Emble had? So why was *he* the one getting reamed out?

"No answer? Good. Maybe that means you'll think twice before being impressed with yourself next time. Get back to your group."

Rei had to work *very hard* now, not to snap something back, but managed to control himself.

"Yes, sir," he answered simply, dropping his salute to turn and move swiftly back to the stairs, where he took them two at a time in quick succession. Reaching the top, he recalled Shido quietly, his mellowed mood not helped by the grim looks on the faces of his groupmates.

"What did the major want?" Sense asked him as he reached the Brawlers.

"Apparently he wasn't a fan of the fact that I looked like I was having fun," Rei answered, unfortunately unable to keep some bitterness out of his voice. "Guy seems like kind of a d—" He caught himself, looking sheepishly around at Michael Bretz, who was eyeing him in warning. "Uh… Sorry, sir."

If Bretz had known where he was going, however, the man chose to feign deafness, because he looked instead to Camilla Warren. "Warren, you're up. After that it'll be Senson again for a new round."

"Yes, sir!" Warren answered cheerfully, and as she passed Rei she treated him to a dazzling smile and quiet "Nice job. Keep it up."

It surprised him yet again, though not unpleasantly. Of the Brawlers, the dark-skinned girl had been the last holdout to treat him like one of their own, so it was a nice change to see. A little abrupt, maybe, but if she was coming around to his presence among them, then his concerns about the attention Shido's progression was gaining him might be less warranted then he'd thought.

Then again…

Feeling eyes on him as Warren dropped down to the field—glancing briefly as she did to where Major Dyrk Reese still stood in rigid observance at the starting end of the path—Rei looked around to find Emble watching him. It startled him a little, because beneath his rows of brown hair the boy's expression was tight, unsettling. They locked gazes for only a moment, then Emble offered what had to have been the most stiff attempt at a nod Rei had ever seen before looking away again.

It struck Rei, then. Harder than he had thought. 47 seconds… If Reese had been right, and his own guestimation of Emble's run was correct—which he suspected it likely was—then Rei had just, for the first time since the start of term, bested another User specifically…

It was a pathetic comparison, in the grand scheme of things. The course was as far from combat as one could get. It wasn't even one of the parameter tests Rei had failed so abysmally on the first day of classes.

And yet… It was still his first real, tangible victory. His first real proof of his own improvement.

A little at a loss as the realization took him, Rei looked away from Emble's turned back to take in Shido's band around his right wrist. The black-and-white steel of its slim rings hadn't changed—nor would they ever, he knew—and the glimmering blue of the vysetrium, bright with the Stryon particles that gave the loops and diamonds their light, seemed to wink up at him knowingly. For a moment that constant, un-erring heat that had driven him so hard so fast dimmed just a little, allowing him to experience in truth the wonder of his own accomplishment.

It was happening… He was actually, truly climbing…

And then the exclamations started up around him, and Rei shook himself free of his awe to hurry to the edge of the wall, joining the others in cheering Warren on as she ran.

CHAPTER 29

In an odd display of awkward balance and counterbalance, Emble's displeasure at Rei's performance over the course of the rest of the training session seemed only to swell even as Camilla Warren grew more and more excited for him. Not really sure what to make of either of these two shifts in treatment, Rei took Warren's compliments and cheer in stride, and chose not to make comment on Emble's sullenness. The boy's black mood didn't go unnoticed by the others, either—especially after their second and third runs had Rei basically tying with him despite all efforts otherwise—and while Sense had the wherewithal not to push Emble on the topic, Gisham was less tactful, asking him if everything was okay several times throughout the period. Michael Bretz, too, seemed to take note of the shift in tone, but like Sense he appeared to read the situation a little better, Rei catching the instructor's sharp gaze shifting from him to Emble on occasion over the course of the class.

Altogether they each got a good half-dozen attempts at the run before Dyrk Reese announced with a booming voice from the center of the combat space that the training session was over. The major had lingered near Field 1 for nearly a third of the class—then passed by several more times even after finally taking rounds about the other groups—but Rei had been careful to give the man no more cause to snap at him, and Reese had never bothered making too much of a comment on anyone else's performance. Indeed, when they finally called it a day, Rei and the Brawlers—apart from Emble, at least—had long since been having an excellent time once again, and it was in high spirits that Bretz dismissed them back to the locker rooms with words of praise for their day's work.

Sense clapped Rei on the shoulder as they started along the wall of the sub-basement, choosing to go around the outside of the Wargames zone rather than cut through the fields where the Lancers and Duelists were wrapping up their last runs. "I don't think I've had that much fun since school started!" the tall boy said excitably. "Nice job on those attempts, by the way. Another few tries and I feel like you were gonna get close to passing *me*."

Rei laughed. "Fat chance. Pretty sure you and Gisham both had the rest of us by a good twenty seconds or so."

Sense smirked amicably. "Maybe. Still... You're a far cry from parameter testing, isn't it?"

Rei opened his mouth to answer, about to admit that he certainly wasn't *displeased* with his progress over the last 6 weeks, but a girl's voice cut in from behind them before he could say a word.

"Seriously, Ward. It's pretty damn impressive! I feel like you'll be better than all of us in another month!"

Rei and Sense looked around together to find Camilla Warren tailing them closely. Gisham was nowhere to be seen—having stayed behind to ask something of Bretz—but Emble was following rigidly along a ways back, and didn't meet either of their gazes when they glanced at him.

"I don't know about that..." Rei replied tentatively. "Getting through the Es was definitely a lot easier then climbing the Ds has to be."

Another half-truth, but a necessary one. He wasn't strong, yet. Not even close. Even if he had to start lying outright, he was going to buy himself every day he could, for as long as he could.

"Sure, sure," Warren nodded along with a bright smile. "Whatever the case, Senson's right. It's seriously impressive how far you've come. I kinda feel bad for giving you the cold shoulder at the beginning of the year, now..."

At Rei's side, Sense frowned, eyeing the girl curiously.

Rei, though, had decided it was clearly a day for extended hands.

"No problem." He did his best to return her smile. "You were hardly the worst of it. And it's not like it wasn't weird of me to be here. Even now I'm still behind the curve, what with all of you gaining two or three ranks since the start of term."

"Yeah, well..." Warren grimaced a little. "It's not like you deserved any of it. I really could have been nicer."

"It's seriously no problem," Rei insisted, looking forward again and catching a glimpse of red hair near the opening to the hall. "Things have worked out pretty well anyway."

No one said anything else, after that, because at that moment the rest of them, too, noticed Aria Laurent leaning against the wall beside the exit. With a muttered excuse Warren vanished rather quickly, as did Emble. Gisham hadn't yet caught up to them, so by the time they reached her only Sense was still at Rei's side, and even *he* seemed a little hesitant.

"Hey!" Rei said, catching Aria's attention as she scanned the departing students.

"Oh. Hey. How'd training go?" Rei might have imagined it, but he thought the girl looked relieved when she caught sight of him, stepping away from the trickle of cadets to meet him quickly. He was sure of the fact when Aria started looking Sense up and down nervously as she approached.

It was amusing to witness, like watching a lioness pawing at a housecat in trepidation.

"Fun times, but I think I might have rubbed one of my groupmates the wrong way." He glanced around to find Sense standing tensely at his side, having some obvious difficulty being so close to *the* Aria Laurent as his gaze darted about. Smirking, Rei decided it was safe to make introductions. "Aria, this is Bahnt Senson. He's a Brawler in my group." He turned a sharp eye on Aria in mock warning. "Behave. He's a nice guy."

Expectantly, Aria's cheeks flared *immediately* red as she sputtered. "W-What? What's that supposed to mean?!"

Rei, unable to help himself, grinned and looked to Sense, now. "You can stop shaking in your boots. She's seriously too easy to tease."

Aria tried to splutter out another protest, but failed to do so, and the sight of her in that state seemed to do the trick. Sense relaxed a little, looking like he was taking the girl in in a whole new light.

In the end, he even managed a crooked grin.

"I-If he's ever too mean to you, just let me know. I… uh… I've got some pretty good stories of Rei's training fails I could share with you."

It was Rei's turn to stiffen, and all at once he realized his potential mistake. "Whoa! Wait! Hold on!"

Too late, though. Aria stood with her mouth open a moment, looking between the two of them.

Then her green eyes settled on Rei with a gleam he *distinctly* did not like.

"Oh *really*?" Aria followed up with interest, sheer anticipation bloomed into a wide smile. "One of these days we're going to have to have a chat, then. I can use as much ammunition as possible, with this guy."

"For what?!" Rei demanded, distinctly regretting having acquainted the pair. "Blackmail?! You've *definitely* been spending way too much time with Viv if that's the first place your head goes!"

"Who's been spending too much time with me?"

Rei started, whirling to find Viv coming up behind him, pulling up one shoulder strap of her combat suit to wipe sweat off her cheek as she approached.

"Rei's just been kind enough to introduce me to Cadet Senson," Aria answered, motioning to Sense as the boy stood sheepishly by, and Rei thought he could *hear* the evil in her voice. "Apparently there's anecdotes to be shared about his struggling in class."

"Oh, *this* I gotta hear," Viv joined in eagerly, stepping up beside the Brawler and slipping an arm flirtatiously into his. "Spill, big guy."

Sense had literally opened his mouth to answer—his face going so red at Viv's touch that even his shaved head flushed—when Rei interceded.

"NOPE!" he exclaimed, taking Viv by the other arm and lugging her off the Brawler, moving towards the exit. "*HARD* NOPE!"

"Awwww!" Viv protested, but even without looking around he could hear her grin. "You're no fun!"

"It's okay, Viv," Aria said, sounding like she'd stepped in behind the pair of them. "Now we know who to go to when we need dirt."

"You two are the worst," Rei muttered, glancing around. Sense was standing where they had left him. "You coming?"

The cadet—who'd been watching the three of them go with an awestruck sort of expression—seemed to rise out of whatever reverie he'd fallen into. "Uh... Nah. I'm going to wait for Leron and Kay."

Rei waved an acknowledgment as he hauled Viv away, Aria right behind them, both giggling, and as he led them around the corner of the exit he could have *sworn* he'd heard Sense mutter "Lucky bastard..." under his breath.

It wasn't until after they'd showered and regrouped at their lockers that the girls finally managed the stop laughing, but even then Rei could still hear the pair whispering behind his back as they all got changed. He would have rolled his eyes, but again he was visited by that odd sense of content, listening to the two of them chattering quietly. As fun as training had been, it had proven a wholly unproductive day when it came to Shido's improvement, and his disappointment at the lack of spec progress was outweighed a little by the sounds of the girls having fun, even if it was at his expense. Aria's grin—as wicked as it had been—was stuck in his head a bit, and Rei smiled to himself as he pulled on his boots, eyeing the lines of his pant legs hovering a little too high above the laces. At last checkup, Willem Mayd had measured him at gaining nearly another half-inch and a few more pounds.

He was going to have to get his uniform adjusted again, pretty soon...

"Dinner, then East Center?" Viv asked suddenly, and Rei took her addressing of him as an indication that he could look around without fear of being murdered in his sleep later. Sure enough, plucking his jacket from the steel locker and turning to face the girls, he found them in the process of tucking their shirts in, Viv with her feet still bare, Aria with her hair wrapped up in a towel to help it dry.

"Eh. Not hungry just yet." He pulled on the jacket one sleeve at a time. "I actually kinda want to head back to the dorm and get some reviewing in for Markus' class. I got interrupted this morning."

Viv looked immediately downcast at this suggestion, but Aria perked up.

"Are you doing the compression equations? Can I join?"

Rei, not expecting such interest, was about to answer with an eager affirmative when he hesitated. He blinked at Aria, considering the fact that it was extremely unlikely Viv or Catcher would want to join them.

Which meant they'd be alone together in 304...

A slight pressure took ahold of Rei's chest unexpectedly, then, surprising him. It occurred to him that, unlike the other two, he had never been on his own with Aria, and for some reason had trouble imagining it.

"Uh... Sure! I got a start on them, but definitely haven't put in the time I should yet." He paused, considering. "Maybe we can meet in the lobby? Claim one of the couches or tables?"

Aria shrugged, finishing with her shirt to turn and reach for her own jacket. "I don't mind studying in your suite. I'm actually curious to see if all of them are set up the same."

Rei swallowed nervously, and didn't *remotely* miss Viv cocking an eyebrow at him as her eyes slid from him to her and back again.

He actually saw the moment the lightbulb went off in her head, and would have cursed her to a hundred terrible deaths then, if he hadn't thought it would look too suspicious.

"One of our suitemates uses our wall display a lot," Viv said smoothly, managing to keep her voice completely even despite grinning at Rei while Aria had her back to them. "Might be best if you guys study in Rei's room, just in case."

Aria visibly froze at that, her jacket halfway pulled onto one arm. When she started moving again, Rei got the impression she was very deliberately not turning around to face them. "O-oh. Well that's fine, I guess. Are you going to come, Viv?"

"Nah," Viv answered, still smiling at Rei as he glared at her with what he hoped was all the fire of every star in the universe. "I actually just remembered that Catcher and I promised to meet some people before 1-C's session."

Aria half-looked around at that, and Rei could have thrown himself at the girl and hugged her when she asked her next question.

"Really? Aren't you two fighting right now?"

Viv's gleeful expression stiffened as she saw the noose she'd accidentally set for herself. "Uh… Yeah." She reached down for her boots, obviously trying to give herself a moment to think. "Like you guys said, though, I shouldn't have gotten that worked up over Cashe. I'll apologize, and we'll get over it. I've been looking forward to meeting some of his friends from his class, anyway."

"Yeah, sounds like fun." It was Rei's turn to go on the offense. "Tell me… *When* exactly, did you guys make these plans? It's the first I've heard of it. Aria too, apparently."

Viv glowered at him as best she could without showing her face to Aria. Before she could come up with an answer, though a voice called out from the end of the aisle.

"Ward! Bretz has asked all of the Brawlers to meet for a minute."

Rei, Viv, and Aria together looked about to find Warren had poked her head around the far edge of the line of lockers. She was already dressed, her hair tucked neatly under her cap, and was smiling again.

"Bretz did?" Rei asked, surprised. It was the first time the instructor had ever requested an after-class meeting of any kind. "What for?"

Warren shrugged. "No idea. Apparently he told Gisham to have everyone gather up downstairs. Sounds like there's something he wants to review about the Intra-Schools."

"Huh." Rei frowned, but he pulled his own cap out from his locker to pull it over his white hair. "Okay. Just give me a second."

"Sure," Warren answered, beaming. "I'll wait for you."

She disappeared around the end of the aisle again. Rei was really having trouble acclimating to this new-and-improved personality. He wasn't about to complain, but it was still strange to consider when he compared the Warren now to the stand-offish classmate she'd been only a few days before.

"Sorry, sounds like I've got to run," he told Viv and Aria, looking to the latter. "I can't imagine this will take too long. You okay to meet in the lobby at Kanes?"

"Definitely," Aria answered only a little too quickly, and Rei suspected she, like him, was happy to dodge the trap Viv had set up for them. "I'll spin by my room to change, but then I'll be good to go."

"Awesome." Then Rei smirked, his eyes falling to Viv. "Have fun with Catcher and his 'friends'. I'll be sure to ask you guys all about it at dinner."

He thought he might have seen Viv start to give him the middle finger from where she was still bent lacing her boots up, but before she managed it he closed his locker with a *bang* and started up the aisle, smiling to himself. Reaching the end of the row, he found Warren waiting for him as promised, looking in the other direction towards the exit, knee bouncing nervously on the wall she'd leaned up against.

"Everything okay?" Rei asked, eyeing her fidgeting.

The Brawler started, jerking around to face him, eyes a little wide. It took her a moment, but the smile returned once more.

"Yeah! Sorry. Was just stressing over what it was that Bretz wants to talk to us about."

"You mean about the SCT?"

Warren nodded. "Yeah. Yeah… Hopefully it's good news. Brawlers tend to be at a disadvantage early in their development, so I'm a little worried we might be a bit handicapped for this first Intra-School…" She trailed of, apparently losing herself in thought as she looked at him.

Then, all at once, she was back and bright, pushing off the wall again to start making for the locker room entrance, waving for him to follow. "Not like we can do anything about it right now, though, so no use stressing. Come on. Emble's waiting in the hall."

"Oh. Great." Rei tried to sound enthusiastic, but suspected he didn't manage it. As they strolled by the other rows, he peered through the pockets of changing students. "Should we tell Sense where we're headed?"

"Gisham said she was going to find him," Warren responded quickly, moving with a little more purpose for the door. "We're gonna meet them downstairs."

Rei nodded absently, distracted at the thought. He'd never been to any of the other sub-levels other than SB2, and was definitely curious to find out what secrets lay further beneath the Arena. Was it possible there were other layers of Wargame fields? If so, just how *big* was the actual building?

Reaching the exit, the doors slid open for them with a hiss, and they stepped out in the hall. As forewarned, Emble was waiting for them, his arms crossed and his mood not improved in the slightest judging by the somber look on his face as he caught sight of them. Falling in on Warren's other side, the boy didn't say a word as the girl prattled on enough for all three of them put together.

"So today's training was fun, wasn't it? I had a hard time getting the hang of the course at first—especially when it kept changing like that—but it was *definitely* good practice. It made me really think on what Bretz was saying about taking advantage of our strong points as Brawlers—our Speed and Cognition and whatnot. I mean I always knew we were the fastest aside from the Duelists, typically, but I never really considered how we could use that."

"Yeah, it's definitely important to be aware of, especially in squad-formats," Rei agreed somewhat weakly.

Warren, though, clearly needed no more encouragement to keep talking as they reached the elevators.

"*Exactly*. And if squads are so important for Sectionals, maybe there's a way we can seriously use that. Like, what team *wouldn't* want someone who could get a good sense of a field, especially a Wargame zone. And then you could kite opponents to lead them into ambushes and the like. There's so much I haven't really thought about when it comes to—"

She didn't stop talking even after they stepped inside and Emble had punched the symbol for "SB7" that appeared in the smart-glass wall of the car, the lowest level displayed. They dropped quickly, Warren chattering all the way, requiring only the occasional "Uh-huh," or "Yeah, definitely," from Rei to keep her momentum going. It was honestly impressive, in a way, and he couldn't help but wonder how many other students—even just in 1-A, he really had yet to get to know.

His impression changed rather abruptly not a second after the elevator settled and the doors opened on a wide, open lobby that could have been identical to SB2's above.

WHAM!

The blow came as a foot slamming into Rei's lower back. It took him so suddenly that he didn't even have time to yell as the Strength behind the kick sent him flying out of the elevator to tumble and slip across the polished floor of the subbasement, his cap flying away. Confusion lasted only a moment—his neuroline and decent Cognition keeping his head clear—and it was long before he came to a sliding halt that he'd registered what had happened.

"Emble, what the hell?!" he snarled, shoving himself up, intending to glare back into the car at the brooding Brawler who'd been standing behind him while they'd descended.

As he stood, though, Rei registered at once that Tad Emble was the least of his worries.

Warren had finally stopped talking. She'd stopped smiling, too, and the expression she graced him with as the two of them stepped onto the landing was anything but friendly. Her mouth was tight, orange eyes narrowed, taking him in with nothing short of angry disdain. It was a look Rei had seen before.

And it was mirrored on the features of the other four people standing in a box around him, surrounding him in the wide space of the lobby.

It was as he recognized the faces of this group that true understanding of the situation he had found himself in dawned on Rei. Two of them he only knew as Gathers and Perez, from 1-A's Lancer and Mauler groups respectively. The third was Leda Truant, the Phalanx and class gossip.

And the fourth, who moved in a blur even as Rei took in the six to land a heavy punch to his torso, was Mateus Selleck.

"Oomph!" Rei gasped as the Saber's strike hooked him in the gut. His reactive shielding absorbed most of the impact, but not all of it, and he staggered backwards several steps, just able to keep himself from doubling over. He only barely caught sight of Selleck's bared teeth when a second punch took him in the face, landing across his left cheek, and this time he stumbled and fell again, slamming his temple against the wall of the lobby opposite the elevator he'd been kicked out of.

Even as he curled over himself, though, clutching at his head as his neuroline worked once more to try and clear his thoughts, Rei could only laugh.

A pair of large hands took him by the collar of his uniform, and he was hauled roughly to his feet and shoved up against the wall.

"Mind explaining what's so funny, Ward?" Selleck asked through gritted teeth.

Rei grunted in discomfort, unable to keep from clutching at the blond Saber's wrists as he blinked through faint stars to meet the cadet's eyes.

"A little surprised, that's all. I honestly expected Grant to show his ugly mug when he finally decided to stoop this low."

Selleck sneered. "Logan's got better things to do than deal with a shit-stain like you. That's kind of the point, actually, since you're apparently too thick to realize it: we *all* have better things to do than deal with a shit-stain like you."

As he spoke the others gathered up around and behind him. Rei looked past the Saber, meeting first Emble's dark gaze, then Warren's.

"Pathetic," he spat. "From my own group, too. Then again, I guess I'm the idiot for not seeing it. I should have figured the bubbliness was an act."

"Shove it," Warren snarled back, every ounce of friendliness and cheer gone, to be replaced by irritated contempt. "If you're looking for an apology, go find it somewhere else. Do you have any idea how much of a pain in the ass it's been, having you in our group?"

"Let me guess," Rei grunted, still gripping at Selleck's wrists, "I'm dragging you all down. I'm dead weight."

"You're damn right," Warren answered, color darkening her cheeks. "Why are you still here, Ward? Why can't you see you don't belong at a school like—?"

"Bullshit," Ward snarled across her. Then, turning his glare on Selleck, he let go of the boy's wrists with his right hand, forming a fist under the Saber's forearm. Not a one of his assailants had summoned their CADs, and for good reason. Devices weren't tracked on the regular, but the ISCM could and did keep tabs on every manifestation in order to prevent abuse of power by Users. If any of the six drew out their phantom-calls, there would be a record of their pinged location, which wouldn't have suited the nature of this particular kind of ambush.

Rei, on the other hand, was under no such restrictions.

"Call."

Shido took form in a blink, covering his arms and forelegs. The Device felt uncomfortably tight over his uniform, and hadn't manifested at all over his boots, but the important part was that the razor claws extend even as they formed, the phantom-call punching up through Selleck's bone and flesh. The boy screamed in pain, but managed to keep his head about him, twisting and rolling Rei over his shoulders to slam him with a crunching *thud* into the ground.

"Hold him down!" the Saber bellowed even as he wrenched his arm free of the Device. Immediately the others piled onto Rei, who kicked and cut and slashed at any and every limb that reached for him. He managed a good few hits before their numbers completely overwhelmed him, and it wasn't more than 15 seconds before Gathers and Perez were kneeling on his arms, pinning them spread-eagle, while Truant, Emble, and Warren did much the same to his legs.

"Bullshit!" Rei yelled it, this time, lifting his head awkwardly to glare at Brawlers. "You had your chance to tell me to go screw myself, to chase me out of this school. You had *six weeks* of chances. But you didn't do *shit*. Not until you realized that you're not as high above me on this mountain as you thought!"

WHAM!

The kick took Rei in the side, his shield barely keeping the power of it from bruising his ribs. He coughed and wheezed, blinking as he grimaced and found Selleck standing between Gathers and Warren at his left.

"Shut up!" the Saber spat at him, shaking his arm at his side as the last of the neural interruption faded quickly outside of a sanctioned field. "You want to pretend it's some big achievement to crawl your way out of the Es? What a joke! If anything the fact that you spent all that time around Users who could break your damn neck with barely more than a thought should have woken you up to the reality that *you don't belong here!*"

Rei sneered, wrenching at his arms and legs to no avail. "Do you—*cough*—Do you have any of your own thoughts on the matter, or are you just going to repeat Grant this entire time?"

Another kick, and this time Rei felt his shield giving a little, not pleased with the repeated abuse.

"Guess that… answers that question," he croaked. "Do you even… see the irony in saying any—*cough*—any of you could break my neck, but need six people to pin me down?"

Before Selleck could answer, though, Rei had managed to lift his head again to address Emble, who was leaning on his right leg. "And *you*. You're the—*cough*—the proof, you know? If it was the rest of these… losers, I might even believe it. But you." He did his best grin at the Brawler. "You're just scared. All of you are just scared. Pathetic. What a pathetic bunch of—"

This time Selleck came around to drop his heel right onto his face.

Rei's head cracked against the floor, this time, and for several seconds his vision went dark. He could taste blood in his mouth, and the Saber's screams that *he* was the pathetic one were utterly lost to the pain and nausea of what felt like a concussion. Another impact, and this time he felt his shield give even more, his nose making an unpleasant *crunching* sound as boot met cartilage and bone. The shock of pain had him thrashing, and at a word from someone Rei's limbs were freed, but he was too shocked to put them to any use. All of a sudden the kicks doubled, then tripled, until Rei realized all six of his classmates were stomping and striking at him, and all he managed to do before his shielding gave way completely was roll over and curl into a ball, protecting his head and face with Shido's steel plating. He dove, then, into himself, into the distant place where he always went when the pain became too much. From deep within his own head he watched as though from above as he was battered and bruised, watching the six cadets kick and beat at him without mercy. It was a good thing none of them could call on their own Devices to amplify the torture, but he doubted it wasn't for lack of desire on any of their parts. He guessed, too that there were no eyes to see them, in the lobby of the bottom floor. No cameras. No witnesses.

No one would know.

He considered—with the startling clarity only one who had already known every kind of pain the world could grant—trying to call up his NOED and make an attempt at recording the assault, but decided it wasn't worth the risk to his face now that his shield was gone. He considered calling for help, too, but he knew no one would be able to reach him in time. He wanted to lash out, want to cut at his assailants again, but without Shido's reactive defenses he knew his body wasn't up for the task anymore. Selleck and the others were conscious enough not to go so far as break any bones, but just the same he was a huddled, bloody mess by the time someone started shouting that that was enough, *enough*! Most of the kicks subsided quickly, though a couple more landed shortly thereafter for good measure, but only after a few seconds of silence did Rei allow himself to return to his waking consciousness, to slide back into the present.

The present, and the pain.

He moaned as he felt every inch of himself trembling, felt the throbbing, pulsing ache of battered muscle and bloodied skin through the torn fabric of his uniform. Barely able to move he did his best to shift one arm, to clear his vision enough to see by. Dimly all he made out where the blurred shapes of booted feet stepping by him, the faint echoes of voices telling the others it was time to go. His neuroline could only do so much, and only as he registered the sounds of the elevator doors sliding open and several people filing in did any single voice reach him.

"This time, learn your damn lesson," Selleck growled.

And then Rei was left alone, shivering and groaning, on the lobby floor.

Almost at once the edges of his vision began to darken, and alarm at the prospect of passing out in such a secluded place offered Rei a surge of adrenaline that had his eyes opening wide. He could still feel unconsciousness coming fast, his body unable to tolerate the shock of bruised flesh and organs, and so he did the only thing he could.

Pulling up his NOED, he flicked to his contacts, struggling to focus on who he could call.

In the end, he selected the first name, at the top of the list, ordered alphabetically.

"Calling" an automated voice spoke into his ear just as the same message flared across his frame. The line rang once, then twice. At the third, Rei started to fear there would be no answer, but just as he began to lose the ability to keep his eyes open there was a *click* of acceptance, and the words changed to "Voice Call Ongoing" under his drifted lids.

"Hey!" The enthusiasm in the girl's voice was so jarring it might have made him smile under any other circumstances. "This is a surprise. Are you done already? I'm just heading back to the dorm to get changed and meet you in the—"

"S-Subbasement 7," Rei gasped, cutting her off, and as he spoke he tasted again the blood between his teeth. "E-Elevators. Sub... Subbasement... 7."

He didn't hear the answering demands, the confusion and fear that replaced the eagerness. He didn't hear the repeated questions, didn't hear the requests for an explanation, nor the eventual promise that she would be right there, that she was on her way, that he needed to hang on. Rei was already starting to drift, tugged down into the darkness, beneath any place where the girl's voice could reach him.

Before the blackness took him in full, though, he blinked as his frame flashed one last time for him.

...

Processing combat information.

...

Calculating.

...

Results:

Strength: Severely Lacking

Endurance: Lacking

Speed: Lacking

Cognition: Lacking

Offense: Lacking

Defense: Severely Lacking

Growth: Not Applicable

...

Checking combat data acquisition.

...

Adequate data acquirement met.

Device initiating adjustments to:

Strength. Defense.

...

Adjustment complete.

Strength has been upgraded from Rank E6 to E7.

Defense has been upgraded from Rank E3 to E4.

"Huh," Rei muttered to himself. "Not a complete waste of a day after all."

And then even the lights of the lobby above him went black.

CHAPTER 30

Rei came to in the dark, and the first thing he registered was that he was in only slightly less discomfort rising out of unconsciousness as he had been falling into it.

He blinked several times as he slowly woke, taking in a dim, vaguely familiar tiled ceiling, illuminated only by the faint presence of a blue-orange light coming from his left. He made to turn his head to see where he was, but hissed and groaned as even this simple motion caused his neck to pulse and ache in discomfort. In the end he used only his eyes to look, and found himself gazing out a translucent window-wall that offered a handsome view of the Institute grounds at night, complete with the soaring glow of the Castalon's towering skyscrapers—bright despite the late hour—rising like a crown across the horizon.

"Rei?" a tired voice asked quietly.

Rei had smartened up, and didn't glance around too sharply, now. He shifted his head as far as he could to his right, in time to see a dark figure lifting from one of several chairs along the far wall of the large suite he'd woken up in. They left behind a second form, curled up and apparently asleep in another of the seats, and as the person approached the light of the distant city reflected off the gold buttons of a wrinkled uniform, then caught in blond hair and yellow eyes.

"Catcher," Rei groaned, doing his best to offer his friend a grin. Even his *face* hurt, dammit. "Funny running into you here. Did I miss dinner?"

Catcher's answering smile was so tight, it might have been chiseled on. "Afraid so. Too bad, too. It was steak day again." Before the joke could continue, though, he reached the edge of the bed, taking Rei in critically. There was something new in the usually cheerful Saber's face. Something dark and hot, and it took Rei a moment to place it.

Fury.

It was guarded, but present, a seething anger hidden behind a mask of calm.

"Do you remember what happened?" Catcher asked him quietly.

"Oh yeah," Rei answered with a grimace. "Head as hard as mine, would be difficult to forget."

Catcher nodded slowly. "Grant?"

"More like his fan club. Asshole didn't even have the balls to show up himself." Rei flinched as the angle of his neck started to ache. Rolling his head forward again, he stared at the ceiling once more. "Hospital, I'm guessing?"

Catcher nodded again. "You've been out for about ten hours, though I think most of that is the lieutenant major's work."

"Ashton?"

"Yeah. Apparently she took over your case the moment Aria carried you through the front doors."

"Oh god," Rei groaned, closing his eyes. If he could have covered his face without feeling like his arms would fall off, he would have. "At least tell me it was over her shoulder or something…"

"Nah," Catcher's usual smile sounded like it had returned a little. "Princess style. Full on. Heard it from the multiple students taking pictures."

"Dick," Rei snorted. Then he opened his eyes again. "Where is she? Is that her by the wall?"

"No, that's Viv. We came running as soon as we got the call. Basically fought off Willem Mayd with a stick when he told us we could go home, and he ended up getting us some extra chairs to try and sleep when it got late."

Rei took in the slumbering figure hidden in the dark at the back of the room. Indeed, peering closer, he could make out the shape of perfect curls, and the glow of the vysetrium in the CAD bands about the girl's wrists was distinctly silver.

"Aria's close by, though. Don't worry."

They way Catcher said it, like he was trying to hide a laugh even as he whispered, had Rei frowning at him. Catcher pointed to something on the wall behind Rei's head.

"Want me to try sitting you up? This looks like the bed's positioning controls."

Rei started to nod, but when his neck protested this, too, he merely grunted an affirmative.

Catcher pressed a finger to some panel hidden from view, and with the subtle whirling of machinery the top half of Rei's hospital mattress began to lift. It wasn't the most comfortable transition—even this slow shift made his back and hips ache—but he was grateful for it nonetheless when Catcher brought him up to about 45 degrees of incline, giving him a better view of the room.

The room, and the girl in a plain shirt seated by his knees to his left, bent over the edge of his bed to rest her head on crossed arms atop his blankets, clearly fast asleep as her red hair cut a pattern over the green glow of her CAD bands.

"Like I said, she's close by," Catcher repeated with a quiet grin.

Rei didn't answer him, looking down at Aria with a conflicting mix of emotions that had no business pressing at him in the situation at hand.

"Has she been here the whole time?" he finally asked, letting himself believe the hoarseness of his tone was related to the beating rather than anything else.

At his side, he caught Catcher's face falling slowly back into the lines of anger.

"The whole time," he confirmed. There was a heavy moment of silence before he seemed able to continue. "When Viv and I got here they'd already whisked you away. But Rei… Aria was a bloody mess. I mean literally. The doctors took her jacket away as a bio-hazard precaution. What the hell did they do to you?"

"Kicked the shit out of me and then some," Rei grunted. "Six of them. Camilla Warren and Tad Emble among them."

That seemed to take Catcher aback, and his eyes blazed as he stared at Rei dead-on, then. "Warren and Emble? From your *Type-group*?"

"Yup," Rei said matter-of-factly, still not having looked away from where Aria slept by his legs. "Them, and four of Grant's regular entourage." He grit his teeth. "I should have seen it coming. Warren was suddenly acting like my best friend, and Emble was pissed about training."

"What happened in training?" Catcher asked with surprising intensity. In the grand scheme of all Rei had just told him, Emble's behavior seemed hardly the most pertinent topic.

"I beat him," he answered simply. "Once, at least. After that we probably tied run-times for most of the other attempts, too."

"Times? What did you guys do in training today?"

Rei frowned, finally glancing around at the Saber. "You guys didn't do the agility course?"

"Agility course? Dude, do you think I went to combat training today? I've been here with Viv since Aria called and told us she found you beaten to a pulp."

For a long few seconds Rei stared at Layton "Catcher" Catchwick, then. It dawned on him, in that moment. It dawned on him that—while he didn't know if anyone would ever be able to the match the stone pillars of the relationship he and Viv had built over the years—he really, *truly* had more than one friend in the world, now.

Catcher was chasing his own dreams, just like Rei. Just like every cadet at the Galens Institute. And yet, despite that, he had come running at the drop of a hat, and didn't seem to have thought twice about missing a valuable day of conditioning, even in a world where that conditioning could prove the edge he needed between a life spent in ease and luxury, and one battling the archons beyond the boundaries of Sirius.

Rei made his decision, then.

"Catcher, pull up your NOED for me."

Catcher gave him a puzzled look. "My NOED? Why?"

"Just do it, man."

Catcher continued to watch him in confusion for a moment, but—with a bit of a resigned shrug—eventually brought out his frame as Rei did the same.

It proved trickier than Rei had anticipated to grant the Saber viewing permissions. His battered right arm barely wanted to lift on its own so he could focus on Shido and bring up the CAD's spec options, and Catcher had tried to protest when Rei had started struggling with doing so. Ignoring him, Rei made the changes quickly, then returned his attention to the blond boy at the side of his bed.

"Before I send you this, swear to me you won't yell and wake up the girls."

Catcher, apparently, had gleaned what was going on, because he'd lapsed into silence again as Rei had gone about granting the permissions. He looked a little amused, though, at the request.

"You want me to promise I won't yell? That's it? You're not gonna make me promise not to tell anyone?"

Rei managed a tired grin. "I'm not worried about that anymore, man."

It was Catcher's turn to stare, then, and Rei suspected the Saber might have been having the same sort of epiphany he'd just come to. After a few still seconds, Catcher brought up a pinched thumb and forefinger to draw them across his lips in a zipping fashion, then raised one hand like he were pledging wordless fealty.

"Good enough for me," Rei chuckled.

Then he sent the scripted permissions over, and Catcher immediate looked down at Shido intently, his NOED blaring in a wave of up-scrolling text.

Reaching the bottom of the lists, he froze.

It was like seeing Viv take the numbers in for the first time all over again. Rei watched Catcher's eyes trace the fateful line once, then twice, then three times. Eventually his gaze stopped moving all together, finally processing what he was seeing, and after a good 15 or 20 seconds Catcher's neuro-optic blinked out. Even then, however, he didn't so much as twitch, staring at nothing, his jaw hanging open in disbelief. When he at last started to turn to Rei again, he mouthed at the air, like he was trying to find the words.

Eventually, as their eyes locked, Catcher settled for making a pained face, shutting his lips tight and letting out a strained, keening sound not unlike the screeching of a teakettle.

It was honestly a more contained response than Rei had anticipated for the boisterous cadet, and he couldn't help but smirking as Catcher finally found his words.

Or some of them, at least.

"I... You... Your CAD... I..."

He seemed unable to string together a coherent sentence, but Rei sat patiently, knowing too well the incredible nature of what he'd just revealed. There were several more attempts at speech made, but finally Catcher took a breath, steadying himself, and got out a single, straight statement.

"Tell me you're not pulling my leg."

"I'm not pulling your leg," Rei responded dutifully, which didn't seem to please the Saber in the least.

"Seriously, Rei. Tell me you're not messing around. You didn't spoof that, did you? Because Viv's told me you've talked about messing with your NOED, and—"

"It's not faked, man. It's one hundred percent legit. Honestly I kinda thought you'd have already had your suspicions. You said a month ago you had an idea of what was going on."

"And I was right on the money! But *this*..." Catcher shook his head slowly. "I thought there was something going on with your Growth man. I nailed that. For the admissions board to let you in, I figured you had to have the potential to really blow the roof off this place in the long-run, or they wouldn't have taken a risk on you. But I thought you might be in the high Bs. *Maybe* an A by some miracle of the MIND." He was still shaking his head as he repeated himself. "But *this*..."

"Yeah," Rei said under his breath, nodding. "It's something else..."

Catcher seemed to have nothing to say to that, and the two of them stood—or reclined, in Rei's case—in silence for a good long while again.

Eventually, though, the Saber looked to come to some private conclusion, visibly mulling over his thoughts before sharing them.

"Well I guess that gives cause to why people are scared..."

Rei frowned around at him. "Scared?"

Catcher gave him a sidelong look as though not believing he didn't know what he was talking about. "Oh yeah. Like Emble. I've got no idea what you mean about the agility course, but if it's anything like what our parameter testing is like... Wouldn't this be the first time you'd caught up to the class? Or someone *in* the class, at least?"

Rei grunted an affirmation. "Yeah, I actually thought the same thing. Selleck and the others made a big deal about making sure I knew how much 'I didn't belong', but I've heard that noise before. I told them it was just cause they didn't like that I was catching up."

"Exactly," Catcher said. "They don't like it because they're scared."

Rei looked at him blankly, and the Saber sighed, giving in. "Dude... You've climbed from the low Es into the low Ds in less than two months. A whole *tier*. There's also a rumor going around that before *that* started you rose up four or five ranks on your own out of the Fs. Add in Shido's evolutions... How do you expect people to react? Do you think everyone is going to applaud you?"

"Well... Not everyone, no, but—"

"Hardly anyone, man. I'm gonna be honest with you: I'm incredibly grateful you and Viv ended up in 304 with me. I haven't had friends like you guys in, well... ever, probably. But despite that, even *I'm* pretty jealous. Even I'm a little scared. Not of *you*, per se—I don't really see you going all 'evil ruler of the galaxy' on everyone—but more of what you mean for the rest of us." Catcher grimaced the smallest bit, suddenly looking far away, obviously taken by his own thoughts as he spoke. "For lack of a better way of putting it: you're about to make us look bad, Rei. *All* of us, and *really* bad. *I'm not saying you should change anything,*" he made sure to add quickly as Rei opened his mouth to interrupt. "I'm honestly not even saying it's a bad thing. All I'm saying is that... that Rank..." He exhaled as he started to struggle again, blowing his cheeks out in disbelief. "Wow... Voicing it out loud really sounds absurd... All I'm saying is that *S*-Rank comes with a lot more weight to it than you might think, and not all of it on you."

Rei sat, looking at Catcher somewhat at a loss for words. On the one hand he wanted to protest, to deny that Shido was anyone's responsibility but his own, but on the other his friend's argument had struck deep. Considering it all, Rei looked from Catcher first to Viv, curled up by the wall, then to Aria, her head still on her arms over the edge of the bed, her back rising and falling steadily as she, too, slept on.

More weight than I might think... he repeated to himself silently.

He'd contemplated it before, of course. But not to this extent. He'd pondered on the reaction people would have if—*when*, rather—they figured it out, even if "it" was less the specific facts and more just the base version of the truth: Rei was on a path to outstrip them all and then some. He'd known there would be dissent, of course, known there would be bad apples, but now he wondered if it wasn't more likely to be the other way around. Had his time spent with his friends corrupted his understanding of the Users he was surrounded by? Of the cadets that made up his class and the Institute as a whole? Was Shido's growth, even as it brought him soaring with each passing week to new heights, also going to see him dragged down by reaching, jealous hands no matter how high he climbed? He hated that visual, hated the idea that—as much as he tried to keep to his own business—there would always be others who would want to intercede.

But, at the same time, he realized that it could only be true.

Tad Emble's face, twisted from his usually benign pleasantness first to the black frown as he'd been outstripped on the course, then furthermore as he'd held down Rei's leg while Mateus Selleck had kicked his face in, told him it could only be true.

Rei let his head fall back to the bed with a dull *thump*, cursing as he did. "Shit…"

Catcher smirked by his side. "Get it now?"

"Yeah… I guess I do… I mean I *knew* their bitching about me not belonging was old news, but when you put it all together like that…"

"It's the excuse you're gonna get until you prove you can beat every one of their asses into the ground, man. It's the easy excuse to give, instead of admitting that they're scared. And they are *definitely* scared, man. If Grant's gotten around to sending his minions after you, even *he* has to be beginning to feel the fear."

Rei managed a chuckle. "He did admit that I was catching up, before training started and—"

"It was Grant?"

The question, asked as keenly as a knife, sliced through their conversation with all the cool precision of cold steel. Catcher whirled, and beyond him Rei saw Viv getting to her feet, obviously having woken just in time to overhear precisely what they both would likely have rather explained more carefully.

As she approached the bed, she spoke again.

"Rei. It was Grant?"

Rei gaped at her, thinking fast, trying to come up with an answer that wouldn't be adding gasoline to the fire. Catcher's fury had been intense, a smoldering, burning anger, but it had been controlled, roiling beneath a calm, composed exterior.

In comparison, Viv's face was an inferno.

Her eyes seemed to blaze as she stared him down, waiting for an answer. Her jaw was clenched, hands in fists by her sides once she came to stand at Catcher's side, and it was like Rei could *feel* the heat of her rage emanating in waves, as though Gemela was manifesting its User emotions into true energy.

"He wasn't there," Rei finally decided on. "Just some of his tag-alongs and a couple Brawlers from my group."

"But he was involved? He was the one who told them to do this?"

"Th-they didn't say," he answered carefully.

Viv's lip curled. "Of *course* he was," she spat venomously, and her eyes had glazed over, no longer seeing Rei as she worked herself up. "Of *course* he was. I'm gonna kill him."

"Viv—" Rei started to try to calm her down, but she cut him off before he could say anything else.

"No. Don't you dare. Don't you *dare*, Rei." Viv's glare could have scorched the earth. "It's one thing to pick fights and badmouth you. You can handle yourself, even when you lose. It's another to send lackeys to beat you half to death without so much as having the guts to show his own face!"

"Viv. I'm okay." Rei lifted both arms as best he could, trying to hide the strain this took as he attempted to prove that he was alive and whole. "I'll be back on my feet before—"

"SHUT UP!"

Viv's scream was so abrupt, Rei and Catcher both jumped while Aria came to with a start at his legs.

"What? What happened?" she demanded, her head jerked up, red hair falling across her freckled face while she blinked away sleep. Catching sight of Rei—awake and well—she froze, taking him in with wide eyes that glimmered green in the faint light.

Viv, though, didn't let her get another word in.

"Enough, Rei," she seethed. "Enough. Even you can only take so much, and you'll be *so* surprised to hear it turns out I'm not good at watching any of my friends get turned into the class punching bag. I'll handle this."

With that, she whirled on her heel and started for the door.

"Viv, wait!" Rei croaked, reaching after her in vain from the bed.

Fortunately Catcher was largely more able-bodied, in the moment.

"Viv, hold on," he said, grabbing her by the arm and stopping her short. "What are you going to do?"

"Did I stutter?!" Viv snapped, wrenching herself free of the Saber's grasp. "No one should be able to get away with this kind of shit!"

"But how?!" Catcher demanded, starting to get equally riled. "What are you planning to do?! Walk up to him and punch him in the face?!"

"And more, if I can manage it!"

"He's a C-Rank, Viv! You'll get beat to a pulp!"

"I'm a Duelist! I'll run circles around his cowardly ass and cut him down—!"

"*What in the MIND's name is going on in here?!*"

In a blaze of white the room's ceiling lights came on, and Rei, Aria, Viv, and Catcher together all winced and squinted under the sudden illumination. In the doorway a tired looking woman in a rumpled doctor's coat was standing, taking them all in furiously from under her disheveled silver bangs.

"You are disturbing the *entire floor*!" Lieutenant Major Ameena Ashton snarled, thundering towards Viv and Catcher with a purpose. "And in a room with a sleeping patient, no less! What are you—?!"

She paused, catching sight of Rei sitting up and alert, blinking at him in surprise.

Then she rushed to his side in a flash.

"Ward!" she breathed. "You're awake! Excellent. How are you feeling? Do you know where you are?"

"I-I'm okay," he said at once, wincing as the doctor started poking and prodding at his scarred arms. "I've been up for a little bit."

"You have?!" Ashton demanded, and she half-whirled, obviously intending to rip into Viv and Catcher some more.

Both of them, however, were gone.

"Those two!" Ashton growled, snapping around to glare at Aria, who was still sitting—quite plainly at a complete loss for words in the confusion she'd woken up in—by Rei's other side. "Cadet Laurent! Care to explain why I wasn't summoned the *moment* he came to?!"

Aria's mouth opened and closed, obviously having no answer to give.

"It's not her fault, ma'am!" Rei interrupted at once. "She was sleeping until just a few seconds ago!"

Ashton continued to frown at Aria for a moment, then grunted to face him again. "I suppose that Arada and Catchwick woke her up as well, did they? The next time

I see them…" She trailed off, starting to study Rei's face. Reaching into the chest pocket of her wrinkled coat, she plucked up what might have been a stylus, except a twitch of her fingers had a small light glowing at its tip. "Eyes forward, Ward," she ordered, and Rei looked dead-ahead, letting her test his ocular responses with several flicks of the instrument across his pupils. "Hmm… Good. Reactions are fine. That's good." Tucking the device away again, she reached for his neck with both hands, feeling along his spine and the sides of his throat. "Any loss of sensation anywhere? Any tingling, or pain down the arms?"

"Too much sensation, and lots of pain, but not what I think you're looking for, ma'am," Rei attempted some light humor, trying for a grin. It wasn't the best he could do, but he was distracted. If Viv had run off to hunt down Logan Grant…

He knew all too well that Catcher didn't have a prayer of catching her.

"Good," the doctor said again, releasing his neck. With a flick of her hand and a flash of her NOED a stool Rei hadn't noticed in the dark zipped across the floor from the far corner of the room. Seating herself upon it as it reached her, Ashton looked to Aria again. "Laurent, I'm going to ask you to step outside. Ward and I need to speak in private."

"Yes, ma'am," Aria was on her feet at once, her usual alertness having returned pretty quickly, but Rei stopped her before she took so much as a step towards the door.

"Aria, hold on." He looked to Ashton. "Ma'am, if you're planning to ask me what happened, I'm going to tell you straight up that I can't answer that."

Ashton's face darkened. "Can't, cadet? Or won't?"

Rei chose not to reply to this. If he could avoid lying, he would. "I won't insult you by telling you I fell, or something, but I also won't tell you who did this."

"And why not?"

"Are there cameras in the lobby Aria found me?"

Ameena's frown deepened, but she shook her head. "No. Major Barnes has already told me as much. It's the reason he asked me to ask you to—"

"Then there's no evidence. Nothing but my word." Rei shook his head. "I'm sorry, ma'am. They set up their ambush in a place with no eyes. They didn't call on their CADs, so they can't be tracked. They hit me hard and fast, and while most everyone was still changing in the locker rooms, so I doubt they even came or went outside of an inconspicuous window other cameras might have picked up. There's no evidence."

"You don't know that unless you tell us what happened, cadet. I'm giving you an order, now. Explain."

"Then I'll claim I don't recall, ma'am."

"Which will lead to my recording you as having suffered significant head trauma, and ordering you to bedrest until you *do* remember." The woman's face was stony. "Are you willing to sacrifice days of training so close to the Intra-Schools, cadet?"

Rei swallowed at that. He hated this. *Hated* it. Ameena Ashton had been his case worker since he'd arrived at school. They'd met three times already to review the progression—or regression, rather—of his fibro, and he very much enjoyed having her on his side.

But… If he didn't do this…

"Yes, ma'am," he said after a moment.

"Rei!" Aria hissed from his other side. "What are you talking about? If you know what happened, just tell her!"

Rei looked around. Aria's expression was mournful, like she didn't like witnessing the exchange before her any more than he liked participating in it.

"I can't," Rei said miserably. "Think about it. There's no evidence. Catcher said I've been out for half a day. If there was proof, Major Barnes and Campus Security would have already found it, the students involved would have been rounded up, and you guys would have been updated."

Aria looked pained. "There has to be something… We can't just let them get away with this…"

"They won't," Rei answered through clenched teeth. "I'll pay them back, but I'll do it the right way. On the field. I just need to get stronger. For that though, I need *time.*"

Aria's eyes widened at the words, but Rei had turned his attention to Ashton again. "I'm sorry, ma'am, but I'm already at the very bottom of the barrel when it comes to the first years. In more ways than one. If I accuse my classmates without evidence other than my say-so, it will just give the ones who did this more ammunition, not to mention hand plenty of others an ample reason to dislike me. I can't let myself be slowed down by something like that."

Ameena scowled. "You should have more faith in your classmates, Ward."

Rei almost scoffed, but managed to turn it into a cough at the last second. "*Ahem…* I just got beatdown by a half-dozen members of those very classmates you're talking about, ma'am. And I can tell you they're just the bravest of the assholes who would be happy to take a piece out of me."

Ameena blinked at that, and looked abruptly troubled.

"Ward…" she eventually started again, sounding hesitant. "If things are that bad, that's all the more reason to tell me what—"

"He's fine."

Aria's statement was sharp and clear, and both Rei and the lieutenant major looked around at her in surprise. Immediately her cheeks flushed, but she held her ground firmly, her gaze clearer now than it had been all night.

"He's fine," she repeated. "He just needs time, like he said. He just needs to get stronger. I'll help him."

They continued to stare at her, and her words seemed to register as her faced reddened even further.

"I-I mean *we'll* help him," she corrected, voice pitching into a squeak of embarrassment. "Viv. Catcher. Myself. He just needs to get stronger, ma'am."

Ashton glanced at Rei, giving him a questioning look he thought he could read. *Does she know?* the doctor was asking him.

He offered only the briefest shake of his head in answer.

Ashton grunted, addressing Aria again. "Intentions being all well and good, cadet, what happens in the meantime? What happens if this group decides to come after him again? I don't expect even Ward is likely to get strong enough to fight off six first years at once anytime soon." She gave Rei a poignant glance sidelong, letting him know she had picked up *some* clues, at least, from their conversation. "Are you intending to shadow him for the next twelve months until he is?"

Rei registered the oddity of the question, only barely noticing Aria stiffening from his left. 12 months until he was? Did that mean Ashton—and probably Willem Mayd, therefore—thought him likely able to take on multiple opponents his age within a year's time? It was a shocking prospect to consider, and he wondered if the doctor knew she, too, had let slip more than intended.

"If I must," Aria finally answered evenly. "But I don't think that will be necessary. Rei only needs to get to the point where he can prove himself on an even playing field with the class. People won't be so quick to discount him, then."

"And how do you propose he does that?" Ashton asked, raising an eyebrow.

"The Intra-School SCT."

Rei didn't realize he'd been the one to answer until Aria and the lieutenant major both turned to look at him. Ashton frowned, forehead creasing, but Aria beamed like he had read her mind.

Which, given her words had put the pieces together, he basically had.

"The Intra-Schools?" Ashton repeated. "You plan on getting yourself on level ground with your class in a month?"

"Yes ma'am," Rei answered. "I can do it. I know I can."

Another half-truth. By the time the second quarter started, most of his classmates would likely be D8 or D9, with not a few among them ranking in the C's. Already Kastro Vademe, the Lancer from 1-B, had joined Aria and Grant in that prestigious ranking, but in 4 weeks he certainly wasn't going to be the only one to manage it. Rei would have to climb six—no—*eight* levels to put himself on similar footing, given his other specs were skewed downward by his S-Ranked Growth. Eight levels in 4 weeks, through the D-Ranks no less, when he'd only managed nine in 6 weeks mostly through the Es. He *could* do it, he knew.

It would just be a month of hell the likes of which he suspected would push him, mind and body, to his limits.

Ameena Ashton was still watching him, very clearly anything but pleased.

Eventually, however, she only sighed with a shake of her head. "Well, I can't exactly *make* you tell me anything, though I suspect Major Barnes will do his best when he arrives to talk to you. Oh, speaking of." With a blink her NOED blazed, then went out again. "He asked me to let him know when you woke up. As you've deduced, he and Campus Security have nothing else to go on but your testimony, which, if you're not willing to give..." She frowned again.

"I'm sorry..." Rei said again, and he truly felt it.

Ashton contemplated him for a moment, taking him in with something between sadness and resignation.

Then, without warning, she reached up and flicked him in the forehead.

"Owe!" Rei yelped, wincing twice as he instinctively tried to lift a hand to where her finger had struck. "*Owe!* What was that for?!"

"For making me worry," Ashton grumbled, but she looked to be smiling a little as she scooted away from his bed. "You're supposed to be my miracle case, Ward. I can't well ride your future to fame and glory in the medical field if you get your face kicked in before you even finish your first quarter of school, can I?"

Rei, with nothing to say to this, only mumbled his understanding, and from his left Aria spoke up eagerly.

"Does that mean you won't keep him on bedrest, ma'am?"

Rei perked up at once to hear the answer.

"So long as he's brave enough to tell Major Hadish the same thing he just told me, it's not like I actually could. Hippocratic Oath, and all that." She narrowed her eyes at him. "Pretend you don't remember, though, and I will see you strapped to this bed myself until your graduation. *As a third year*. Is that clear, cadet?"

"Yes, ma'am," Rei said quickly.

Glaring at him a moment longer, Ashton finally shook her head and got to her feet. "I need to get a medical drone. We'll do scans again, and if everything is still clear I'll discharge you after the major has his go."

"Discharge?" Aria asked only a second before Rei did, clearly as surprised as him. "In his condition? Is that a good idea?"

The lieutenant major cocked her head at the girl. "Do you have a medical license and board certification of User-specialized care, cadet?"

Aria reddened yet again, averting her gaze to look at the bed as she mumbled her answer. "No, ma'am…"

Ashton, though, only smiled in truth, finally. "Oh don't pout, I'm only teasing." She looked to Rei. "Most of your damage is superficial. Severe dermal and muscular contusions. You have some mild bruising of the liver, and likely some strained ligaments in your back and ribs, but your CAD will help deal with all of that fairly fast. The best thing for you to do is help it by getting up and moving when you can, for as long as you can. That being said—" she continued quickly as Rei opened his mouth to voice his excitement at this news "—I *am* ordering you to sit out of training for the next forty-eight hours. I will pass this on to the chief combat instructor who I *assure you* cares more about your health than your CAD-Rank."

An image of Logan Grant being thrown into a wall at a speed that might have been measured in Machs flashed across Rei's thought, but he decided that wasn't the best time to be arguing opinions. Instead, he just nodded. "Understood. Thank you, ma'am."

An unhappy grunt was all Ashton offered him in reply, turning to head for the door. "I'll be back soon with the medical drone. Laurent, if he tries to do anything stupid—like get out of bed before I scan him—I am *ordering you* to pin him down by the neck until I get back."

"Yes, ma'am!" Aria answered with a little too much enthusiasm for Rei's comfort, even throwing the woman a salute as she left.

The moment she was gone, Rei pulled up his NOED and drew up Viv's contact, calling her with a quick eye command. The line rang.

And rang.

And rang…

"Come *on*, Viv," Rei hissed as the call went to voice mail, closing it and making to try again.

"Rei," Aria caught his attention before he could. Her own eyes were alight, and with a wave of one hand she shared a screen with him.

Catcher, looking winded and sweaty, was on the other side of the video call, breathing hard somewhere under one of the outside lights that illuminated the campus paths at night.

"Catcher!" Rei exclaimed. "Where's Viv?"

"Long gone, man," the Saber got out through gasped inhalations. "She lost me near the Arena. Obviously she's headed to Kanes, but I think even her Endurance out-does mine, at this point. I won't get there before she wakes up half the dorm to figure out where Grant is, if she doesn't know his room number already."

"Shit," Rei muttered. "That's not good. We've got to find her."

"*We* don't have to do anything," Aria corrected, staring at him evenly through her frame. "Catcher, the lieutenant major wants to make sure Rei's clear, and he needs to speak to Hadish Barnes, but after that he's being discharged. Once I get him back to his room I'll come join you. If shit hasn't hit the fan by then, I'll drag Viv off the hunt myself until she's cooled down."

"He's being discharged?" Catcher asked, surprised. "Already?"

"Apparently," Aria said with a shrug. "Might be a while, though. Are you okay to go keep after her on your own for now?"

Catcher paused, looking suddenly conflicted. "I mean… yeah, but…"

"What?" Rei asked him, concerned at the hesitation. "What's wrong?"

Catcher shook his head. "Nothing. I'm just… Thinking about it, I'm not sure I *want* to keep after her. You have to admit the girl's got a point, man. Grant can't be allowed to get away with this…"

"Catcher!" Aria hissed in disbelief. "If she calls Gemela on a fellow cadet without good reason, she'll be lucky to get half a month in the brig!"

"I know!" Catcher looked pained, and the video spun dizzyingly around him as he turned his head in what must have been the direction of Kanes. Sure enough, the silhouette of the Arena loomed behind him, now. "And I know that's not what I said in the hospital, but *honestly*… If anyone that's not *you* is gonna pick a fight with the guy, Aria, it might as well be Viv, right? And he *can't* get away with this!"

"He *won't*," Rei promised, feeling his ears grow hot. He didn't like being fought over like this. It made him feel like a child. "But Viv can't be the one to pay him back, man. It's got to be *me*."

Catcher grimaced at that, but after a moment appeared to see Rei's point, because he nodded slowly. "Yeah... Okay. I get that, I guess." He groaned, and seemed to steel himself to start running again. "Urgh... All right. I'll try to find her, but no promises. Just meet be back at the dorms as soon as you can?"

"Okay," Rei and Aria answered together, and Catcher ended the call with a muttered curse as he began moving again.

"He won't be able to stop her," Rei said the moment both their eyes were clear.

Aria made a face. "No, he won't," she agreed. "But maybe he can get in her way long enough for me to get there. I meant it when I said I'd drag her off myself if I have to."

"I know you did." Rei laughed grimly. "Maybe you should go now? He could use your help."

Aria looked at him like he'd started speaking in some alien language. "And leave you to hobble your way back in the dark? You wouldn't get back till morning, if you made it at all."

"I can *walk*," Rei insisted. Then he paused. "... I think."

It was Aria's turn to laugh. "We'll find out when Ashton and Barnes are done with you, won't we?"

Rei chuckled at that, letting his head fall back to the pillow. After a moment Aria sat back down, crossing her arms and looking around the room. Rei watched her, but the few times she glanced in his direction she looked away again quickly, turned once more into the shy, awkward girl he'd started to come to know.

"I'm glad you're okay."

Aria spoke so softly, Rei almost missed the words. She was turned away from him, watching the room door, but he could tell she wasn't focused on it. Her hands were gripping the sleeves of her plain button-down shirt, and Rei was reminded of the fact that her jacket had been taken away from her because of the blood.

Something pressed at his chest again.

"Thanks," he said quietly. "For coming to find me, I mean."

Still not looking at him, Aria gave a small shrug with one shoulder. "Did you think I wouldn't? You scared the hell out of me, when you called."

"... Yeah... I suppose I must have." Rei, for some reason, couldn't take his eyes off her red hair. "I'm sorry. I didn't mean to. You were just the first—"

He stopped himself. He had been about to say, "the first person in my contacts", but something told him that wasn't what Aria would want to hear in that moment. It wasn't necessary, either, nor did it devalue in any way the fact that she had not only come running when he'd needed her, she'd also carried him across the campus at what he could only imagine was breakneck speeds to get him to the hospital.

"Thanks," was all he managed to say again.

This time Aria nodded, though he thought he saw her swallow first. After a few more seconds of silence, she finally looked around at him.

"I'm serious, by the way."

Rei blinked. "About Viv? Yeah, I know. She could—"

"No. About the SCTs."

"Oh. Right..." Rei's mouth went dry, and for once he was the one who turned away, staring down at his lap. "I know you are, but you don't need to take on that responsibility. You already work three hours basically every night with me. More would just—"

"Help me as much as it helps you, Rei," Aria interrupted him. "I don't train with you guys because I need playtime. I mean—" she reached up to brush a hair out of her face "—it *is* fun. And that's important to me. You know that. But you also challenge me, Rei. Not in the traditional sense. You're basically a wet noodle when it comes to durability—"

"Gee, thanks," Rei muttered.

"—but there's more to a User's potential than the numbers on their CADs." Aria finished with a smile. "You... I don't really know how to explain it... I think you force me to take note of my own weakness. The way you adapt. The way you learn. The way you *fight*. If I don't change in response, I feel like one day I suddenly won't be able to keep up with you."

"Because Shido changes so fast?"

"Because *you* change so fast." Aria was watching him intently now, he could tell. Even still averting his gaze he could feel her eyes on him. "D-Rank or not, if I didn't bother correcting the things you take advantage of... It would be like Commencement all over again, only this time you'd be ready with a way to get around Third Eye."

Rei smirked, now absently studying the scars along his right arm. "Impossible. Not like I am now. I've got a ways to go."

Aria laughed quietly behind him. "Meaning you've already figured out how to get past it. Fine. I concede that maybe you still have some growth before you really have a shot at taking me down head on, but that doesn't change what I'm saying."

She started to reach out, pausing, then rested a hand on his thigh over the blankets, just above his knee, and Rei finally looked up at her again. "You *push me*, Rei. In a way no one else does—or at least has ever tried to. Sure, maybe Hippolyta would grow a little faster if I found a training partner closer to my CAD-Rank. But despite that… I *learn*, with you. I learn a *lot*. I feel like a better fighter, after these two weeks, and it's not like Hippolyta's *not* progressing. I'm probably not more than a week away from C2."

"It's still not your responsibility," Rei said slowly, trying hard to ignore the tingling pressure of her fingers on his leg, even through the fabric.

Aria huffed, and her hand retracted as she pouted. "Fine. Then how about you think of it this way? Do you know any other students who train an additional three hours a day?"

"I'm sure some of the Sectional hopefuls are doing a lot of extra—"

"Yes. They are. But not three hours' worth, *every day*. And if you seriously want to make a showing at the Intra-Schools, I know you've already done the math. You're going to have to train even more, even harder. Right?"

Rei hesitated, then nodded.

"Therefore," Aria stared, as though entering the closing arguments of a court case, "can you tell me of a single partner I could find *in the entire school* who would push me as hard as you're about to push yourself?"

This time, Rei had no argument to give. He just watched her for a time, taking her in, gratitude and amazement mixing together in a strange cohesion in his chest.

He didn't hate the feeling in the least.

After a while, Aria started to go red again.

"What?" she asked quietly. "Why are you looking at me like that?"

Rei didn't answer for a moment, pondering.

Then he opened his mouth.

"I still think you just get off on treating me like you're personal punching bag."

When Ameena Ashton returned with the medical drone, tailed by the lumbering form of Hadish Barnes, the two of them were dumbfounded to find Aria Laurent, C-Ranked prodigy of the Galens Institute first years, in the process of soundly beating an already-injured Reidon Ward with his own pillow.

CHAPTER 31

As Rei had anticipated, Major Barnes had proved a *much* tougher character to crack than the good doctor. He played his role as the chief of campus security well, and while in the end even he admitted he couldn't *force* Rei to reveal his attackers, it had come after a solid half hour of assurances, orders, and a scattering thinly veiled threats of extended time in the brig if Rei kept "withholding evidence". Giving up at last, however, Barnes had left dissatisfied, muttering something about "your funeral, kid", though Rei was pretty sure the major had seen reason in his argument that accusing anyone would only lead to more trouble in the long run.

"I can't decide if you're stupidly brave, or bravely stupid," Aria muttered after Barnes and Ashton had left them alone again, the lieutenant major having told them they were dismissed shortly after scheduling Rei for a follow-up the next day. He was seated at the edge of the bed—having achieved such a position on his own, by some miracle—and as Aria looked the other way had managed with great difficulty to tug on the pants of the new uniform Barnes had had one of his men retrieve from the stock depot while they'd talked. His boots had taken longer, and giving up on lacing them Rei had finally relented to assistance when it came to pulling on the fresh shirt and jacket. His old one had been unsalvageable, which was scary, but there was a slim silver lining in the fact that the uniform had obviously been selected according to his newest measurements, and fit him like a glove.

He wouldn't have to bother Quartermaster Sattar for another month or two after all.

"Probably the worst half of both options," Rei grunted in answer, working through the discomfort of holding his arm up so Aria could help get the second stiff sleeve of the white shirt over Shido's bands.

"Stupidly stupid?" She smirked, managing the rest before straightening his collar for him. Rei thought her fingers might have lingered over the open buttons, but in the end seemed to decide he'd have to manage that task on his own, for which he was grateful.

Between Viv running off to hunt the mastermind of his thrashing and Aria helping him to get dressed, he wondered if he wasn't experiencing a little *too* much of the doting parenting he'd lacked in childhood.

"There are those who wouldn't argue that," he got out, letting her reach for his new jacket while he struggled with the buttons. He managed three, his fingers trembling as his arms hurt just from being bent at the elbow, and decided that was good enough. It was the middle of the night. If anyone was going to yell at him about a half-open shirt as he limped back to his dorm from the hospital—undoubtedly with *more* of Aria's help—they could go and shove it.

"Yeah, I'm getting that impression," Aria muttered, holding up the jacket for him. He got an arm in easily enough, but the second was the struggle again, and Rei was pretty sure all his grunting and groaning by the time they managed it had probably woken up any patients left on the floor Viv and Catcher's earlier screaming match hadn't.

"Rei... Are you *sure* about this?"

In the process of struggling with even more buttons—though merciful the sizable gold decorations were less numerous and easier to manage—Rei glanced up. Aria had taken a step back from the bed and was frowning down at him from under the brim of her re-donned cap. Her own jacket had been yielded to her cleaned—or a perfect replacement had been found—and she looked completely the part of a Galens cadet once more while she took him in carefully.

"Which part?" Rei asked, more to give himself time to think than anything else as he returned his attention to the buttons.

"Not telling them."

"You were pretty steadfastly on my side about it while I was arguing with the lieutenant major."

"Yeah, cause you seemed resolute on the idea, and I know better than anyone— okay, maybe not better than *Viv*—that you're not one to stay down even when it's good for you. So I'm asking you straight up: are you sure about this?"

Slowly, Rei nodded. He understood her concern, but he could see the pattern of events play out in his mind's eye. "I don't want you to think I'm not pissed. I *am*. Or I will be, once I have the energy to feel anything other than sore and tired. But there's jack to be gained for reporting Selleck and the others."

"Mateus Selleck?" Aria asked sharply, and Rei recalled that she'd been asleep when he'd filled Catcher in. "The Saber?"

"Yeah. We kinda… didn't hit it off, last time we were in a cross-training group together. Looks like I left a bad taste in his mouth."

"Who were the others?"

"Does it matter?"

"It does to me."

Rei frowned, managing finally to close up his jacket. With a breath of relief he let his arms relax, reaching for his cap, the only part of his original uniform left to him once again, retrieved by Barnes' team from SB7's elevator lobby. Unfortunately, he found himself unable to lift it higher than his nose, and after a few seconds of awkward struggling felt it tugged gently from his hands.

"Who were the others?" Aria asked again, sliding it carefully over his white hair.

With a sigh Rei filled her in on the details of the ambush, from Warren and Emble's betrayal to the beating itself. While she didn't rage and scream like Viv, Aria demonstrated herself at least less able to keep her emotions in check than Catcher.

"I hope they find Grant dead in a ditch tomorrow," she hissed, face contorted in such fury her eyes seemed to glow the same shade as the green vysetrium of Hippolyta's bands. "It would serve him right."

"Not for me, it wouldn't," Rei growled back. He had found, as he'd finally voiced in detail all the events of the afternoon, some of the anger he thought wouldn't hit him until he'd spent a good night in his own bed. "I'm not just keeping this from the staffers because I don't want my school life to get more complicated, Aria. I'm gonna pay those assholes back and then some. Grant needs to be alive for me to do that to my heart's content."

Aria snorted. Apparently unable to help herself, she reached up to straighten his jacket for him. It was oddly in her nature, Rei was discovering. So quick to blush and stutter, right up until the moment it was time to take action. Indeed, once she was satisfied with the state of his uniform as a whole, she offered him a hand to stand.

"I'm hoping you still mean on the field. I would want to be there, and I'd want every member in our class to watch it happen."

Rei accepted her assistance gratefully, wincing as he let himself get pulled to his feet. His legs shook, but held. "You're seriously bloodthirsty. Has anyone told you that?"

"You really know how to flatter a girl, Rei."

Rei couldn't help it. He sniggered, and was pretty sure he would have gotten himself whacked with the pillow again had it been within easy reach.

While standing had been simple enough, walking proved an entirely different matter. Rei made it to the wall on his own, guiding himself along it to the door at a snail's pace, but Aria seemed to give up on patience when it took them a minute to make it 10 feet down the hall. Initially he grunted in discomfort when she looped her arm under his, helping to hold him up, but when he found they could move along at more than a crawl with assistance he made no other complaint, and settled into hoping they would make it outside before Aria noticed the color of his ears as she held him close to her.

The night sky was a brilliant cacophony of lights and darkness, the city rising up in a staggering of well-lit towers like a mountain range of steel and glass to ring them on all sides. Directly above, the crossing patterns of the air-lanes mixed with the still stars that hadn't been swallowed by Castalon's light. It made for an amazing view as they turned left out of the hospital to follow a northeast path that would take them first to the Arena, then on to Kanes.

Or *would* have been an amazing view, rather, had Rei had any focus to give to it.

Everything hurt. Everything. He trusted Ashton when she said that getting up and moving was what he needed to assist Shido in repairing his battered body, but the longer he walked, the more he ached. Within a minute his side was throbbing to an excruciating point, and he had to admit that—for all the agony his fibro had caused him—the discomfort of a bruised internal organ was new to him. His legs pained him with every step, and he was breathing hard before they were so much as out of sight of the hospital.

"Swear to me you won't tell the others about this," he groaned as he continued to entrust his weight onto Aria's arm. In answer the girl only looked around at him, hesitated, then made a quick motion with her eyes he recognized even before her NOED flashed briefly.

"Did you just take a picture?! What the hell?!"

Aria laughed. "If you've got breath to yell, you've got breath to walk. Come on, gimpy."

Rei grumbled, but allowed himself to be led on, mercifully distracting from the betrayal of his body for a moment, which he suspected had been Aria's intention.

In a silence broken only by his occasional groans and curses the pair of them cut across the darkness of the campus together. It was past midnight, which meant the evening patrols were out and about, but fortunately they were lucky enough to make it to the Arena without running into anyone. It wasn't like Rei expected them to get into any trouble, but he didn't fancy the idea of having to call up an already-exhausted Ameena Ashton to have her explain why two cadets—one of them arguably only partially-dressed—were walking arm-in-arm across the campus in the middle of the night.

It was with no small measure of relief, therefore, when Kanes finally came into view along the path. The squat dorm was mostly dark except for a scattering of lit windows that marked late studiers and the like, and as they approached Aria said that she would let Catcher know that they'd made it back. Sending off a message through her neuro-optic, Rei saw the reply arrive quickly, but was taken aback when Aria stopped short some yards away from the dorm doors.

"What is it?" he asked with difficulty. "Did he find her?"

"No, but…" Awkwardly, Aria turned them around, looking back in the direction they had come. Rei was about to demand what was going on when he saw a figure hurrying towards them at a jog, coming along a south branch in the path they'd crossed. It took him a moment, but as the person passed under one of the solar lights suspended over the pale stone of the walkway, he recognized a sweating Catcher.

"I take it you didn't happen to run into her on the way here?" the Saber gasped, breathing even more heavily than Rei as he met up with them.

Aria frowned. "No, but where were you looking? Wouldn't she be in the dorm?"

Catcher shook his head, leaning over to hold himself up against his knees in an attempt to catch his breath. "Yasiin Najjar from 1-D told me he saw her leaving with Logan Grant and a few others shortly after I got back. I went to the suite first, then checked every hall of every floor before I asked Najjar. He's a Duelist too, so he recognized her. We must have crossed paths."

"She left *with* Grant?" Rei demanded, not comprehending. "And 'others'? Was it Selleck and the rest?"

Catcher's face was glistening, and it was obvious he'd been looking non-stop since he and Viv both bolted from the hospital. "I assumed. I didn't waste time asking, after hearing that." He groaned, and eased himself down into a squat to lift his head and look up at them in distress. "What the hell is she doing? Was she planning to take them all on at once?! I ran to the East *and* West Center to see if they'd booked fields to make it all at least semi-official…"

"And Najjar didn't say if she looked like she was being forced to go with them?" Aria asked, sounding worried.

Catcher shook his head again. "No, but I feel like he would have noticed that, right?"

They were quiet for a moment, each contemplating their own fears. Rei could feel concern and anger bubbling together to make an ugly mess of his thoughts. If Grant helped Selleck and the others, then Viv was likely to end up in even worse shape than *he'd* been left in.

No. That couldn't happen. He wouldn't let that happen.

Ignoring the pain it caused him, he tried to ease his arm out of Aria's. She started to fight him stepping away, holding on more tightly and giving him a sharp look, but Rei met her fiery gaze evenly.

"We need to find them," he said as firmly as he could manage, standing tall and pushing down the throb this caused his liver in particular. "I'm not much use, but I can push through for now."

Still Aria hesitated, clearly not keen on the idea of leaving him on his own in his given state. Eventually, though, she relented, and let his arm go.

"Thanks," Rei told her quietly, then looked between his two friends both. "If they weren't at one of the training facilities, they'll have gone somewhere with no cameras, like the elevator lobby. Any ideas?"

"Arena locker room," Catcher offered at once.

"Too many eyes in and out of the place. At this time of night there would be no mistaking them coming and going."

"Bathroom somewhere," Aria said next, but shook her head. "No. Same issue…"

"It's got to be on the grounds then, right?" Catcher posited with a contemplative look. "There's cameras in every building, but there's got to be blind spots on the campus greens…"

It was a good suggestion, but had Rei's stomach tied in knots. If they were going to have to search the entirety of the premises for every quiet nook a small group of students could have gone to brawl, they wouldn't be at it until morning and then some.

It was Aria who alleviated a little of his worry.

"They won't have gone far. Grant wouldn't want to risk getting caught by the evening patrols. They'll be nearby."

"Which means they're probably already done…" Catcher muttered gloomily.

"You don't know that," Rei told him quickly, unwilling to consider the prospect as he shoved an image of a beaten and battered Viv laying in some random hedge row somewhere from his mind. "Viv's quick, and she's smart. I'll bet she's got a plan up her sleeve, if she left with them all so willingly."

Catcher nodded slowly, elbows on his knees as he looked at the ground.

"Regardless, we should get moving." Aria's eye was bright, and Rei thought he could make out the pattern of a map on her frame. "There's not much available space between Kanes and the east wall. Rei, you check that, and call if you need help. Catcher, you go north, and I'll go west. South is mostly campus, so it's the last place we should check."

"Agreed," Rei answered, turning at once to start heading for the grass area to the right of the dorms. Behind him he heard Aria take off in the other direction, but before either had gotten far Catcher yelled after them.

"Wait!"

Together Rei and Aria whirled around again. Catcher was standing once more, and looked to be reading a thin line of text off his NOED with wide eyes. Before either of them could ask what the holdup was, he blinked the frame away.

"That was Cashe," he said a little breathlessly. "She says Viv's already back in 304. And she's not in good shape."

The first thought to pass across Rei's mind as the three of them burst through the door of the suite and rushed into the common room was that he regretted casting aside his pride to let himself be half-carried, half-dragged by Aria and Catcher. As they came together to a screeching halt on the hardwood floor, they took in the oddity of the scene before them with utter astonishment.

Chancery Cashe sat on the couch closest to them, looking around in alarm at the sound of the entrance *banging* open followed by the pounding of running feet. She was dressed only in a plain white shirt and black boxer-shorts, and the disheveled state of her silver hair told Rei she'd most certainly been asleep at some point in the night already. On the smart-glass wall, a scattering of articles on "Connor Galt"—a User who'd been tried several years prior for war crimes and desertion—were projected, and Rei could only imagine Cashe must have been having trouble sleeping and gotten up to study. He only had eyes for the Lancer for a moment, however, his attention sliding quickly instead to the girl next to her, who'd only partially glanced around at their arrival.

"Not in good shape", it turned out, was a matter of perspective. Viv's perfect curls looked untouched, the skin of her face and cheeks unblemished. There wasn't a speck of dust on her uniform, much less any rips or tears, and where Rei had expected blood and bruising he found nothing more than some faint cuts on the knuckles of her right hand that looked to have already been cleaned.

Viv was—on the other hand—trembling.

"Viv!" Aria hissed, leaving Rei's weight to Catcher in favor of moving around the couch to quickly take a seat on Viv's other side. "What's wrong? Are you okay?"

Silently, tentatively, Viv nodded once.

"I-I kinda found her like this," Cashe tried to explain, looking between all of them nervously. "I woke up when something broke in the kitchen. When I came out to see what had happened—" She paused suddenly, staring at Rei for a second as her face drained of all color. "Ward! What happened?!"

Rei was confused for only a moment.

"Aria didn't tell you your face looks like the ugliest side of an old eggplant?" Catcher tried to joke, his smile too strained to manage the humor.

"Oh. That. Don't worry about it." Rei waved Cashe's alarm aside nonchalantly, disengaging from his friend to limp towards the kitchen. Sure enough, a puddle of water in the middle of the white tiling was littered with the shattered remnants of what must have been a glass. Taking it in only briefly, he turned back to the couches, putting one hand on the wall and the other on his side as his liver protested again. "Viv. What happened? Someone in the lobby said they saw you leaving with Grant and his friends. Did they do something?"

A pause, then a quiet shake of Viv's head.

"You can tell us the truth…" Aria said softly, a shift in her shoulder telling Rei she'd put her hand on Viv's. "You had us really worried. Catcher's been looking everywhere for you…"

That seemed to bear some fruit, because Viv lifted her head slowly and looked around at Catcher.

"… Sorry," she mumbled. "I'm really sorry… I'm okay, though. Just… Just a little shaken…"

"By what?" Catcher asked, getting heated. "Viv, if Grant did something, I'll—!"

"He didn't do anything," Viv cut across him, almost desperately. "Anything, I swear." She looked back down at her hands. "… He didn't do it at all, actually…"

There was a confused exchange of looks between Rei, Aria, and Catcher.

"Viv…" Aria spoke gently. "What do you mean? What do you mean he didn't do it."

Viv took a shaking breath, still not looking at any of them. "We messed up… *I* messed up, actually. He didn't do it."

It was at that moment, at last, that Rei understood.

"It wasn't him," he translated, and Aria, Catcher, and a very confused-looking Cashe all turned to him. "The ambush. It wasn't Grant."

A pause, then another nod of Viv's head.

The others, then, appeared to catch on as well—with the exception of poor Cashe, that was. They gaped at Viv, Aria from beside her and Catcher from behind.

Fortunately, in the presence of her friends, Viv seemed to be calming down enough to find her voice little by little.

"I-I found him," she explained. "I didn't have to pound on more than two doors before someone told me what room he was in, on the fourth floor. When I reached it, he must have been the first one to wake up, because he answered." She swallowed. "I punched him. The instant I saw enough of his damn face to know it was him." She lifted her right hand for emphasis, showing off the injured knuckles.

"She was bleeding when I came out of the room," Cashe told them all, still confused but obviously keen on helping now that even this meager explanation was in process. "I thought she'd cut herself on the glass, so I helped her clean up. There's more, though." She looked at Viv pointedly. "Show them."

Immediately, however, Viv shook her head.

"Arada, *show them*," Cashe insisted.

"Show us what?" Aria asked when Viv didn't answer this second request at all.

Rei, though, had already noticed. As she'd lifted her hand, her sleeve and CAD band had slipped down. They covered most of the skin of her wrist, but not all of it.

Ignoring the protesting scream of his body, he pushed off the wall, crossed the floor in three quick steps, took Viv's hand firmly in his.

"Wait! Don't—!" Viv tried to stop him, but even her Speed wasn't enough to prevent him from wrenching her sleeve down for all of them to see.

Aria hissed, and Catcher swore in fury.

Under her uniform, Viv's wrist was blue. It wasn't broken, but it didn't have to be.

All Rei needed to see was the distinct imprint of fingers over pale skin, where a big hand had wrapped itself around Viv's slender forearm and squeezed.

"I'll kill him," Rei seethed, letting Viv tug the limb free to cover up the bruise again. His own agony was utterly forgotten, eaten away by the heat of his anger. "Where is he, Viv? What room?"

"I'm not telling you," she said quietly.

"Why not?!" Rei thundered, feeling himself start to shake. "Why the hell not?!"

Viv didn't answer.

"Viv…" Aria started slowly, though Rei could hear rage barely hidden in her own voice. "He can't get away with this. Why don't you—?"

"BECAUSE *I* ATTACKED *HIM*!"

Viv's yell had them all jumping, and Cashe positively jerked away, even further when Viv shoved herself to her feet and whirled to look them all in the eye at last.

"*I* attacked *him*, all right?!" she shouted again. Her face was pale, and while her trembling had stopped she looked to be holding it back only by keeping her hands clenched tightly at her sides. "It wasn't his fault, it was *mine*! I punched him, and then I punched him, and then I punched him again! I would have kept going except he caught my arm and stopped me! That's how I got *this*!" She reached around to pull the sleeve up herself, this time.

"I don't care if you came after him with Gemela true-called and an army at your back," Catcher snarled. "He hurt you. He can't keep getting away with this!"

"He's not 'getting away' with *anything*!" Viv answered just as heatedly, letting the sleeve fall again. "That's my whole *point*!" She looked to Rei, almost pleadingly. "He didn't do it Rei. He didn't. I'm sure of it."

This, Rei hadn't expected.

"How?"

"He proved it. After I told him why I was there. Wasn't hard to get it out of me. I was practically screaming it as I punched him. He dragged me off to gather up the others." Abruptly, Viv's fire suddenly winked out, and her face went white again. "Grant went straight to Selleck first, like he knew he'd be involved. Got him to explain exactly what happened. Asshole was smirking the whole time, like he was proud of it. After that, it wasn't hard to find the others." She counted them off on one hand all while looking Rei in the eye, unwavering in her conviction. "Truant. Perez. Gathers. Emble. Warren. Was that everyone?"

Rei nodded slowly. Indeed, along with Selleck, that was the six of them, and he hadn't spoken all their names to anyone other than Aria yet that night.

Viv seemed darkly satisfied. "Yeah… He assembled them like they had business to attend to. I even got worried he was playing me at one point, and they were all gonna gang up on *me*. But…" She shivered. "Grant seemed… *angry*. Like nothing I've ever seen. It was like the time he went after you in training, Rei, when you set him off. He kept it pretty composed, right up until he led us all out to a field north of the dorm."

She paused, here, and Rei could see in his mind's eye the eight figures all together in the dark of the grassy grounds, out of the sight of any cameras, just as they'd suspected.

"And then what?" Aria pressed gently. "What happened, Viv?"

Viv shook her head slowly, but it was more in awe as her blue eyes appeared to be looking at something far off rather than any of them.

"I've never seen anything like it. Not without a called Device. I thought *I* was good on the combat team, but Grant…" She seemed in awe of whatever she was recalling. "There's a reason he competed at the Intersystem level. He put half of them down before anyone knew what had happened, including me. The others didn't stand a chance even all together, and they ended up on the ground too." She shook her head again, and didn't finish the sentence.

"Logan Grant took down his own group?"

It was Chancery Cashe who asked, sounding dumbfounded. Rei could appreciate the emotion, given that he was at a bit of a loss himself. That Grant hadn't been behind the attack on him that afternoon was plausible, if a little hard to swallow. Rei supposed he could believe he and Shido had bred enough bad blood for someone like Mateus Selleck—or even Camilla Warren—to take their own initiative against him and his growth.

But to hear that Grant—the same Grant he'd been warring with since the start of the term—had then turned around and punished those very people…

That was an altogether different matter.

And yet… Here was Viv, his best friend in the world and beyond, practically swearing to that very fact.

What the hell is going on? Rei could only ask himself.

"We… spoke, after that." Viv had found her voice again. "After he was done. Then he told me to go back to the dorm." She frowned, eyes still far away. "It was so *fast*. I didn't expect it, and by the time I'd figured out what was going on it was already done. I came back here, then, just like he said." She frowned, as though not sure how she'd ended up following Grant's orders. "I tried to get a glass of water to help calm down, but…" She waved absently at the kitchen, and the rest of the story fell into place.

"I cleaned her up," Cashe wrapped in her stead. "That's when I saw the bruise. Ward," she looked to Rei, "what is going *on*? And also…" her purple-green eyes flicked to Aria briefly, "can someone explain to me why Aria *Laurent* is sitting on our couch?"

"I helped Rei back from the hospital," Aria answered her promptly, as though there were nothing more typical in the world. "We're training partners, so it's pretty normal."

"You're-Wait... Training...?." Cashe tripped over her own words, gaping between Rei and Aria. "Hold on... *What?*"

"You heard her," Rei said with a shrug, not interested in arguing the facts again in front of everyone, especially after Aria had so vehemently fought him on the subject once that night already. "As for the rest... In case my face wasn't clue enough, I got jumped today. By some of Logan Grant's regular entourage, plus a few... uh... unexpected additions."

"Oh," Cashe said simply. She looked to be processing his words, and a few seconds later her eyes went wide in understanding. "*Oooh!* I'd *heard* you and Grant had gone at it a couple time..."

"Glad to hear my misfortunes are making the rounds," Rei muttered under his breath, though a subtle smile from Aria told him he'd been overheard.

"So now what?" Catcher asked of the group. "We just swallow that Grant had nothing to do with this? Even if that's true, he's still been sticking it to Rei all year so far!"

"And he can keep sticking it to me, if all he's interested in doing is mouthing off and humiliating me on the field," Rei said, putting a hip on the back of the couch with a groan to take his weight off his aching legs. "I can handle that bullshit."

"And if that's not all?" Catcher demanded, clearly still hot-headed. "Even if he didn't tell them to do it, his minions wouldn't have had the guts to ambush you like that if he wasn't always tearing you down, man. If we don't do something about it—"

"We don't need to," Viv said firmly. "Grant took care of it."

"How could he take care of it when he's the *source of the problem?!*" Catcher was clearly having trouble controlling his fury. "That doesn't make sense!"

"It will in the morning," Viv promised him, but her eyes fell on Rei. "He wants to talk to you."

Rei felt a knot form in his gut. "Me? Why?"

"I don't know. But he said you wouldn't have to worry about this sort of shit again. At least not from anyone he's close to."

Rei, for once, wasn't remotely sure what to make of that. Logan Grant was by the minute turning out to be a more confusing character than he'd anticipated, and he wasn't sure how to handle it. While he wouldn't be complaining about hearing that Selleck and the others had gotten as good as they'd given, it was truly bizarre for that repayment to have been doled out at the hands of the cadet who'd been going for Rei's throat all term, sometimes literally.

"*Ugh!*" Catcher groaned in annoyance, shoving his hands into the pockets of his slacks and seeming less than satisfied with the evening's developments. "I can't handle this. I'm going to bed." He didn't turn away just yet, however, looking Viv up and down carefully. "You sure you're okay…?"

Viv gave him the first—if strained—smile Rei had seen from her all evening.

"Yeah," she promised. "Just a little shaken up. Grant was…" She didn't finish her sentence, but Rei caught the subtle changes in her expression. He stared at her, bewildered.

"Must have been scary, yeah," Catcher finished for her quietly.

Rei didn't bother correcting him, watching Viv carefully, abruptly wondering what else she and the Mauler might have talked about after he'd put down Selleck and the others.

He decided this was neither the time nor place to ask.

"Well, since we're all in one piece, I'm calling it," Catcher reiterated after a moment of quiet. "Goodnight, all."

"Night," came the mumbled responses from everyone as he made for his room and disappeared inside. The door was about to shut behind him when Catcher's head reappeared around the edge, looking a little embarrassed.

"Uh… Rei… I'm *really* hoping you don't need help getting undressed or anything like—"

"Good*night*, Catcher!" Rei cut across him loudly.

Catcher grinned, vanishing again as the door shut with a *click* behind him, with Viv and Aria managing matching snickers.

"It was a fair question," Viv said after she'd regained control of her face. "Not like you'll get either of us to help you shower in the morning or anything like that."

Rei didn't know if he had ever rolled his eyes so hard, given the act *actually* hurt—though that might just have been residual soreness in his face. Looking around at the three girls remaining in the room, however, he almost choked to find that Aria's face had gone bright red at Viv's suggestion, and she was staring at him with nothing short of trepidation.

"Get your mind out of the gutter! Both of you!" he half-yelled, half-squawked. "I can handle putting on pajamas, *thank you very much!*"

"Forget pajamas, how the hell did you get across campus?" Cashe breathed, taking him in again more critically this time. "You seriously look like you let an S-Rank Brawler use you as a training dummy." She turned to Aria. "Like actually. Did you carry him?"

"Not from the hospital," Aria answered with a quick shake of her head, obviously eager to change the subject. "When I found him, though, he was unconscious, so I kinda—"

"Okay, that's enough!" Rei cut in, nothing short of desperately by now. "Between the lot of you I might just leave school *voluntarily* and save myself the injury to my reputation."

More grinning—from *each* of them this time—and Rei sighed with a shake of his head.

"You're all gonna be the death of me," he grumbled.

"So long as you don't get yourself killed by our classmates first, apparently." It was nice to see some of Viv's usual pep had returned.

"Too true," he admitted, wincing as he recalled the sight of Selleck's boot coming down on his face. Deciding he'd had enough reminders for one day, he looked over the three of them. "I think Catcher had the right idea. I'm gonna call it a night, especially if I want a prayer of making it to class in the morning."

"Oh, is it that late?" Chancery Cashe asked absently, checking the time. Seeing the lateness of the hour, she started, then leapt up off the couch like it had bitten her. "I'll be heading to bed as well!" she said in a rush, and for the first time all night, Rei was reminded a little of the rigid facade she'd shown off when they'd first met, the afternoon of the Commencement ceremony.

It made him feel like laughing, for some reason, and he stopped himself only to spare his cheeks the discomfort.

Cashe was around the couch and passing Rei in a heartbeat, headed straight for her room. She reached it, and had settled a hand on the handle when Viv called out to her.

"Cashe."

The Lancer paused, looking around tentatively. Viv was watching her, and looked to be struggling with something.

"Thanks," she finally mumbled. "For sitting with me. For worrying."

A look of surprise passed over Cashe's features, and it was a moment before she seemed able to answer.

When she spoke, however, she did so with a faint smile.

"Anytime. I'm pretty sure I owe you guys at least that much, after the idiot *I've* been."

And then, with a wave to Rei and Aria as well, she opened the door and stepped inside, leaving everyone feeling like maybe the day hadn't been such a complete mess after all.

CHAPTER 32

Shido proved itself even more indispensable than Rei had previously imagined when he woke up the next morning feeling—while far from whole and healthy—significantly better than he had the evening before. He made it out of bed and between the bathroom and the kitchen without too much trouble other than some further protests from his liver, but he decided not to push his luck when Viv and Catcher checked on him as they were about to head to breakfast. Telling the former he'd see her in class and the latter they'd meet up at lunch, he let them go in favor of giving himself some much needed extra time to shower and get dressed.

As he moved around Rei steadily loosened up even more, and so it turned out not to be too much of a task to pull on his pants, shirt, and jacket. His boots proved themselves only slightly less tricky than the night before, unfortunately, with his fingers fighting the dexterous movements of tying them up, but he managed it in the end. Donning his cap, however, demonstrated itself to be completely out of the question, because every time he tried his shoulders absolutely refused to cooperate, locking out and burning in protest with each attempt. Eventually he gave up, tucking the cap under one arm and taking up his pad in his other hand before heading for the Tactical Studies building, hoping anyone who questioned him on his inappropriate dress would take his explanation in stride given his face was still black-and-blue.

He was, in the end, grateful he'd skipped breakfast, because the walk to the day's first class took three times as long as it should have. His legs—while able to tolerate his weight now—still ached after a minute or so, and he had to take frequent breaks to catch his breath and give himself a rest to recuperate. Once he'd reached the Tactical Studies Department, he allowed himself to circle the long way around the first floor to the elevators at the back of the building, which carried him to the third in a gracious sparing of the torment him imagined the stairs would have been.

Reaching the classroom at last, Rei found that he'd arrived a little earlier than most of the other students, but by some fortune of the day had still been beaten by Viv and Aria. They were talking across his empty seat in their usual place, and only noticed him once he'd started the arduous climb up the six whole steps that led up to their aisle.

"Oh, Rei, I'm so sorry." Aria jumped to her feet and hurried over to help him. "We should have sat on the first row."

"Nah, it's good for him," Viv said nonchalantly, though she eyed him sidelong when he reached the chairs and he eased himself down—with a hand from Aria—between the pair of them. "What's with the cap?"

"Couldn't get it on," Rei admitted dejectedly, breathing a little easier once he was seated and giving Aria an appreciative smile as she took to his other side. "Apparently even a CAD and the best medicine in the system can only do so much."

Viv grunted in understanding. Then, before he could say a word in protest, she plucked his hat from under his arm and pulled it over his head, straightening it with a twist.

"Thanks," Rei snorted.

Viv shrugged like it was no big deal, reaching down to her bag for her pad. "Don't thank me. I'm not the one that brought you breakfast."

Rei blinked, then turned. Aria was indeed in the process of retrieving a parcel wrapped in paper towels from her own bag, pulling it open a little nervously.

"You didn't have dinner yesterday," she mumbled, "so when Viv and Catcher said you were skipping breakfast too…" She didn't finish, presenting him with several pieces of buttered toast and roasted ham, which Rei could only stare at for a few seconds.

Partially because it was only in that moment that he realized he was indeed, absolutely starving, and partially because that pressing on his chest returned as Aria averted her eyes from his, holding out the food to him silently.

"*This* is the part where you say 'thanks', idiot."

Viv's stage whisper made Rei jump, and he reached up to accept the parcel at once.

"Th-thanks!" he stuttered, though not unenthusiastically. "You're a lifesaver. Literally."

Aria nodded shyly, but continued to refuse to look at him. He wanted to say more, but Viv's hiss in his ear again cut him short.

"Eat. Before Takeshi gets here and yells at you. You two can flop around each other like fish out of water later."

Next to each other Rei and Aria both sat up straight as boards, mortified, snapping around at once to face the front of the class and *mutually* avoiding each other's eyes, now. Rei's cheeks were on fire, he knew, and he could only imagine what Aria's looked like. He didn't know whether he wanted to punch Viv or hug her, but decided he could debate the topic with himself after he'd settled the rumbling of his stomach that had started up the moment he had seen the toast.

He'd wolfed down the majority of it, fortunately, by the time Logan Grant arrived, tailed by the usual suspects.

The Mauler's entrance was announced by a sort of stilling of the class all about them. The sudden drop in the chatter and noise claimed Rei's attention from his breakfast, and he looked up and around curiously. The first thing he noticed were several people staring at him, which he supposed was fair given the rearranged state of his face, but others appeared, instead, to be gaping between him and the room door.

That was when he saw Grant.

Handsome as he was with his strong jaw and dark hair, the bright bruise that covered the Mauler's left eye and cheek somehow only seemed to make the massive cadet *more* striking. He stood rigidly, glaring at Rei from the base of the stairs, but then turned to start climbing upwards, snarling under his breath at the group behind him to "Come on." Dutifully, six other students followed him, not a one meeting Rei's gaze, nor any other cadet's in the class.

"Whoa…" Aria muttered, which pretty well summarized Rei's own feelings at the sight.

To a one Warren, Emble, Gathers, Perez, and Truant looked not much better off than he himself did. Only a couple of them appeared to be limping, but *all* of them sported some combination of a black eye, a bruised nose, or a nastily cut lip. Trailing at their end, Mateus Selleck appeared to have gotten the absolute worst of it, most of his face battered like he'd had his head slammed into a wall several times, and when he didn't look in their direction Rei considered it was possible the Saber was having trouble seeing much of anything through blackened, swollen lids. Mouth agape, he and Aria watched the group climb in silence along with the rest of the class, and only when the seven of them had settled down in a back corner at the very top of the lecture hall did anyone have the sense to look forward again.

"You weren't kidding," Rei hissed quietly to Viv, who—of every person in the class—hadn't once looked in Grant's direction. Indeed, she appeared to be deliberately focusing on the opposite wall of the room, like the white plasteel paneling had suddenly become the most fascinating thing in the world. She jumped a little when he addressed her, and again Rei had to wonder what it was she and the Mauler had talked about the night before.

"What?" Viv asked, apparently having been doing her best to ignore the whole proceeding. "Oh… Yeah. No, I wasn't."

"He did all that with his bare fists?!" Aria demanded, leaning to speak around Rei in an alarmed whisper. "Through their reactive shielding?!"

Viv nodded, and the fact that she didn't want to talk about it was apparent even as she spoke. "Yeah… His Strength spec must be through the roof. Catcher had it right. It was scary…"

"I'll bet…" Aria mumbled, stealing a glance back towards Grant and his group, but looking straight again with a snap. "Damn. He's staring at us. Why do I feel like a snack for some monster?"

Viv managed to crack a smile at that, a little of her usual life returning. "Don't tell us that! If you're a snack, what the hell would that make us? And besides, he's probably not staring at 'us'."

"He's staring at *me*," Rei grumbled, resuming the wolfing down of his toast in order to give his hands something to do other than twitch nervously on the desk in front of him.

He had just finished his breakfast—shoving the napkins into his pocket—when Sarah Takeshi entered the classroom. He was a little slower than Viv and Aria in standing, and his pitiful salute could only reach his chin, but the captain had either already been briefed on the situation, or took pity on him after glancing over his bruised face. She gave them leave to sit, then her gaze lifted to the rest of the 1-A slowly, lingering in the top corner where Grant and the others were sitting.

She made a face like a disapproving mother, glaring up at the row in question long enough for every student to know she was *not* pleased about something, then turned and swiped at the smart-glass wall to bring up the starting slides of a lecture on "Multi-Level Field Management."

Class passed at a crawl, with Rei having difficulty keeping enough of a focus on the lesson to do more than take passable notes. He didn't volunteer for any questions—thinking it best not to draw any more attention to himself than necessary, for the time being—and didn't meet Takeshi's gaze despite him feeling like the captain had spent much of the hour and a half with one eye on him. When the tone for the end of the period chimed, he gathered up his pad quickly to limp with all speed from the class alongside Viv and Aria, not wanting to be called back and berated with any questions or lectures that day.

They'd made it to the hall, and Rei had just started to breathe easy when a hand caught him by the arm.

Groaning internally Rei turned, expecting to find Takeshi looming over him, ready to lay into him. He was surprised, therefore—and a little relieved—to discover Sense taking him in sharply, having pushed through Viv and Aria alongside Kay Sandree, who stood at his elbow taking in Rei just as critically.

"Spill," the Brawler said simply, not letting go of Rei's arm, as though to imply he wasn't going anywhere until the pair of them had heard the story. At Sense's back, Rei caught a glimpse of grey-orange hair, and realized even Leron Joy was lingering near enough to hear the exchange.

"Nothing much to say, man," Rei answered with the best shrug he could manage, wincing as his shoulders complained in response. "Got into a bit of a disagreement after training yesterday."

"That's some disagreement," Kay said with a frown as the other students moved around the group, stealing glances at Rei as they passed. "Your face looks like one of those ancient Picasso paintings."

"You guys are seriously creative with these descriptions," Rei muttered, trying for a smirk that he didn't think came off as anything more than a pained expression. "It's not as bad as it looks. I'll be fine in a day or two."

"Was it Grant and his posse?" Sense growled. "Are you the reason they showed up looking like that this morning? And when the hell did Warren and Emble start hanging with those guys?"

Rei couldn't keep his face from darkening, and he hoped his irritation at the mention of the two Brawlers stayed hidden in his bruising. "You'll have to ask them."

"Grant had nothing to do with it," Viv said from beside Sense, speaking quietly again. This back and forth change in demeanor was seriously starting to worry Rei.

"How do you know that?" the bald Brawler asked, turning on her and finally letting Rei go. "That jerk's been laying into Rei all term, from what I've seen and heard."

Viv opened her mouth, looking like she were trying to come up with a good answer, when a different, deeper voice spoke up in her stead.

"Because I already made that clear."

As one all six of them—Leron Joy included—whirled to find Logan Grant lumbering towards them like a thundercloud. Behind him Selleck and the others lingered meekly, kicked dogs told to stay, and the Mauler's approach was so unexpected that no one moved as he shouldered his way between Sense and Kay.

Then, grabbing Rei by the collar of his uniform, he twisted and shoved him up against the nearest hallway wall.

"Grant!" Aria snarled in warning as Viv, Sense, Kay, and several other students passing nearby shouted in alarm.

"Oh shove off, Laurent," Grant snapped back, not looking at her. "I'm not interested in breaking your boyfriend when he's already been kicked to shit, don't worry."

Rei thought he saw Aria's teeth bare at the retort, and he held up a hand—as best he could, at least—to stop her escalating. She came up short, but Rei only had eyes for the massive boy in front of him, the pair of them glaring at each other with angry fervor.

No... Maybe—for once—"angry" wasn't quite the right word...

There was something different about Grant's expression, this morning, something... off. He looked like he was *trying* to come off as furious, but it was tinged with something odd, something Rei would never have thought possible given his understanding of the Mauler's character.

Shame.

"You're a waste of damn space, Ward," Grant hissed in his face, his left eye bloodshot from where Viv must have indeed repeatedly punched him the day before. "You're a *anchor*, and you have no business being here. I despise you. I despise everything about you, from the way you fight to the way you talk to the way you've got your friends wrapped around you finger with charm and smiles. It's pathetic, and if I ever get the chance to wipe you off the face of this fucking world I'll take it in a heartbeat, and make it a better place for it."

He continued to stare at Rei, black-red irises burning.

Then, with a jerk, Grant let go of his collar.

"But... When I put you down, it'll be on the field. In front of everyone. *Again.* It won't be some back-alley beatdown or some half-assed ambush." Grant looked like he wanted to spit, like the words tasted bad in his mouth. "My 'friends'—and I use that term loosely, right now—won't be bothering you again. If they do, Arada can let me know, and I'll take care of it."

"Like I need your help, asshole," Rei grunted, fighting his discomfort and reaching up to straighten his uniform, which had twisted around his neck under the taller boy's abuse.

Grant's lip curled in irritation. "I'd say the state of your face right now says you could use all the help you can—"

"In your own words, Grant: shove it." Rei cut the Mauler off sharply, his patience for wordplay at an all-time-low that morning. "Play the hero all you want. Doesn't change the fact that *your* attitude is what breeds people like Selleck and those other cowards, and if you're unwilling to realize that, then you're not doing anything more than patting yourself on the back for addressing the symptoms instead of the problem."

It happened for only the briefest of moments. Grant's face contorted, twisting into a picture of such an astounding emotion, Rei's jaw almost dropped.

Was that... regret?

Looks like he'd hit the nail on the head...

In an instant, though, Grant's facade of rage was back, and he shoved one long finger into Rei's chest, pressing him into the wall again.

"I'll handle Selleck and the other idiots. You just do your best not sink your little group. I don't care if you're getting stronger, Ward. I don't care if you're catching up. You run when you should fight. You hide when you should face. You've tricked and connived into every small victory you can claim so far this year. Your way of doing things is a disease, and you're going to kill the potential of your friends if you keep it up."

"Oh shut the hell up, Grant."

It was, to everyone's surprise, Aria who chimed in at that moment. Rei and the Mauler both turned to look at her, but there was no hint of the shy, uncertain girl she tended to live off of the battlefield. Instead, Aria stood now with all the erect surety of the ace of Galens first years, green eyes narrowed at Grant with such intensity they might have cut through flesh.

"You're quick to dismiss Rei's ability just because you don't like the way he does things," she snarled. "You're so damn sure of yourself that you lack even an ounce of self-awareness. Maybe consider the fact that you're *not* the smartest person in the room. Maybe consider the fact that Viv and I—who I think you know are both going to be top contenders at the Intra-Schools—are intelligent enough to know what's good for us, and what's bad. Wake the hell up, and stop insulting everyone around you with your misplaced masculinity issues."

She spoke with such burning sharpness that neither Rei nor Grant appeared to have anything to say in answer, both of them staring at her in surprise. After a second Aria's face flushed with embarrassment as she returned to herself, and she took advantage of their astonishment to grab Rei by the arm and pluck him from between Grant and the wall.

"Keep assuming your enemies are nothing more than what you see at first glance, and one day you're gonna be left bleeding by someone unexpected," she muttered as a final statement, pulling Rei past the Mauler firmly. He let himself be led away without a word, watching Grant's eyes trail them as the Mauler tried to hide the astonishment that lined his half-opened mouth. After a second Sense, Kay, and Leron all moved to follow.

Rei didn't miss, however, Viv's hesitation, her blue eyes finally lifting to look at the back of Grant's head.

Nor—when she finally hurried to follow them—the fact that boy's own gaze broke from him when she passed, watching Viv herself go with what could only have been called disappointment.

CHAPTER 33

Squad-formats have long been a favorite of tournament enthusiasts, arguably even before the SCTs became a sanctioned event by both the ISC and the ISCM. Given the nature of the archons and their existence only at the extent of our expansion into the reaches of space, the military deemed it safe to share footage of combat exercises and team training with the masses as a form of morale boosting, a way to raise the spirits of the billions across the six—now seven—systems. The commanding officers of the armed forces underestimated the effect these feeds would have however, particularly when it came to instances of squad-based mock battles.

Within a few years, the Simulated Combat Tournaments were born, with Team Battle and Wargames formats drawing views and crowds second only to the very highest echelons of individual Duels.

Essentials of Simulated Combat in Military Training
Lieutenant Colonel Hana von Geil, Ph.D.
Distributed by Central Command, Earth

Dammit!" Lena Jiang's angry voice cut through the chaos of the com noise. "Dorne got by us! Ward! Lancer headed your way! Just hold them off long enough for reinforcements to get back to you!"

"Got it," Rei answered dryly, trying not to sound too annoyed as he shifted his attention from NOED-linked communications to the trees around him. Under his feet the shin-high grass weaved and danced in the simulated wind, and the forest that surrounded the clearing he stood in bent and swayed in the same rhythm. Birds traced graceful arcs across the sky overhead, where only the occasional cloud patterned the clear, endless blue. It should have been mesmerizing.

Regrettably, though, the distant sounds of battle—steel clashing against steel and people shouting as they fought—somewhat ruined the scene's peaceful effect.

Around Rei's arms and legs, Shido's phantom-call gleamed in the daylight. He could actually feel the heat of the sun on the back of his neck, but after weeks spent in squad-training with the other classes the realism of the projection no longer astounded him. He truly placed himself mentally in the field, ignoring the fact that it was all a hologram, eyes sweeping the tree-line around him as he took two steps back, closer to the plain black pole that was Red Team's objective "flag". It was still strange to witness the CAD pulsing crimson rather than blue about his limbs, the vysetrium having adapted to the side-designation, but Rei set this small distraction aside, looking for a glint of light in the woods, listening for the approaching crack of disturbed underbrush.

Sam Dorne of D-1, however, proved himself a slippery bastard for a Lancer.

The flash of metal catching sunlight alerted Rei to the User before anything else, and he whirled to his left. Dorne had managed to sneak around to the north side of the clearing without him noticing. He was barreling from under the cover of the trees to make a direct line to the flag, his Device glowing blue over orange-and-black steel, spear tucked at the ready under one arm. With a *crunch* of the loose earth shifting under his soles Rei was between the boy and the objective, Shido up and set. Dorne didn't so much as pause, but why would he? Rei had only reached a CAD-Rank of D5 two days prior, while he knew for a fact the Lancer had hit D9 around the same time Viv had done the same. Their gap in power was substantial—even more than Dorne knew, given Rei's skewed specs—and it was with a confident shout that the boy brought his weapon around in a diagonal strike aimed at Rei's thigh.

Unfortunately for the Blue Team member, Rei had long since made a point of studying the art of spear-wielding, and even with his better specs Sam Dorne couldn't have held a candle to Aria if she'd fought him barehanded.

Speed was where Rei could meet the Lancer most closely, and he applied this fact by twisting and bringing one leg up, into the inside arc of the spear's strike. The haft caught on the steel plating of his shin, impacting harmlessly, and Rei continued the turn even as he planted the defensive leg again. His other foot came around in a whirling heel kick, and Dorne was forced to duck to ensure his head would stay fixed on his shoulders. The Lancer cursed, leaping back, but the moment he could Rei followed, practically hearing Viv's constant criticism to keep his opponents within assailable range of Shido's claws. He punched out, going for Dorne's exposed chest, but with a twisting snap of the spear the Lancer smashed the strike aside. Again Rei turned the momentum into a spinning kick, and this time he caught Dorne in the side.

The Blue Team member hardly budged, having planted and braced, but by closing the distance between them Rei had eliminated the boy's most significant advantage.

People were shouting across the coms again, but Rei didn't have time to be distracted. He kept his focus on Dorne, intent on staying between him and the flag as they traded blows back and forth. With his reach stolen, the Lancer's ability was severely reduced, and Rei could see the awareness of that fact bright in the boy's face as they fought. Good. That was good. If he was distracted by his own failing, then maybe—just maybe—Rei had a chance to turn their power mismatch on its head.

He stayed tight to Dorne as they circled the clearing, not letting him get out of range for even a moment. He was struggling to land any kind of significant blow, but all he would need was one opportunity, one shot. His opponent's strikes were short, concise in his limited range, and while they looked well-practiced they subsequently lacked the speed that would have had the Lancer outclassing him. Dorne wasn't adept at close-quarters like this—what User of his Type was, at their level?—and if Rei could just force him to grant him an opening…

And then, from the east, there was a blurred flash of familiar purple-and-yellow, and all at once Rei's right leg failed him as a burning pain cut across the back of his thigh.

"*Urk!*" he managed to quell the scream, but he could do nothing to stop himself from collapsing as his knee gave out. Dorne, to his credit, didn't hesitate to take advantage of the surprise assistance, his spear coming around in a blur before Rei had even hit the ground. The glowing-blue of the blade took Rei a little above the heart, and a searing burning enveloped his chest. As a last resort he tried to yell, tried to get the word to the rest of his team.

"Objective compromised!" he wheezed into his coms. "Objective compromised! There's two! There's two!"

But then he saw the damage notifications flashing across his frame, and knew it was too late.

Right hamstring severance registered.
Applying appropriate physiological restrictions.

Ascending aorta severance registered.
Fatal Damage Accrued. Communications interrupted.
Removing "Reidon Ward" from combat.

As Dorne wrenched his weapon free of Rei's chest, the pain vanished all at once, as did most of the sensation throughout his body. A moment later he found himself sinking, sinking down through the grassy ground, his vision of the projection distorting as he slipped beneath the hologram into the 10-foot space under the elevated field where "killed" combatants waited out the end of a Team Battle. He regained feeling in his limbs as he continued to descend, and by the time he was deposited gently onto the plain black of the projection plating Rei could shove himself up with a bare grunt of effort.

He found his feet just in time to hear the Arena announce the end of the match.

"Contact with Red Team's objective maintained for 15 seconds. Winner: Blue Team."

Looking up, Rei couldn't help but chuckle as above him the field started to dissolve. At the same time, the scattered members of the opposing squads began descending across the broad expanse of the 70-yard Team Battle zone, including the two directly above him. Sam Dorne recalled his Device as he descended, the CAD vanishing to leave the boy in only his grey-and-red combat suit.

Beyond him, though, the real culprit of the fight was also floating down gracefully, one gauntleted hand still raised to her side where she'd touched the black pole and maintained the 15-second contact needed to win, the modified red glow of her weapons turning back to sliver before Rei's eyes while she grinned down at him.

"Two on one's not very fair!" Rei called up, feigning irritation.

From the air, Viv laughed, letting her hand drop. "I just gave you a love tap. Dorne would have had you soon enough, I'm sure."

In addition to sword and knife, Gemela gleamed around her forearms as the light of the true day caught on the gauntlets, brand-new additions when the Device had become one of the first—outside of Shido—to evolve among the first years, upgrading when Viv had hit D9.

"I hate to say it, but I'm not so certain," the Lancer himself said with a frown, finally reaching the plating lightly as the last of the Woodlands field faded above them to reveal the open canopy of the Arena proper. Looking around, he nodded to Rei in a rare show of respect "I've got to admit you're a lot tougher than I'd heard, Ward. We rushed because we thought you'd be a pushover when we realized you were on defense. Good fight, though."

"Good fight," Rei returned the nod before recalling Shido. After the CAD had dematerialized into its bands, he continued. "Probably just luck, though. I managed to stay inside your optimal range. *Someone*—" he offered Viv a mocking glare as she came to land and started approaching as she recalled Gemela in turn "—has been drilling it into my head non-stop for six weeks now."

"Well don't complain about it too much. It worked on me." Dorne frowned, brushing a hand across a sweat-dampened head of red-brown hair as he looked Rei up and down. "That being said, isn't it weird to have you defend? Especially on your own as a Brawler? Why weren't you on recon or the like?"

Good question, Rei thought angrily, but decided on a more diplomatic answer instead as he offered what he hoped was a passable shrug. "I'm technically an A-Type, so maybe my squad-leader was under the impression I'd have something hidden up my sleeve?"

"Clever of her," Viv answered sarcastically as she came to stand beside the pair. Then her blue eyes narrowed a little. "Then again, maybe you should ask her yourself, Dorne. Looks like she's on her way over here."

With a sinking feeling Rei looked around the Lancer to indeed find a tall, black-haired girl approaching at a clip that said she was not planning to have a friendly, post-match chat.

"Great," he muttered. "This'll be fun. You two want to do me a favor and get back to the Blue Team? I need to deal with this."

With a look that said "Good luck" Dorne turned and hurried towards the far side of the field perimeter, where the Red Team was gathering. Viv, for her part, hesitated a moment, then seemed to decide this was indeed a battle he'd have to handle with on his own.

"Have fun," she said with a snort before starting to jog after the Lancer.

Rei only grunted a sardonic thanks, and had only just enough time to plant his feet before Lena Jiang was on him.

It was a good thing, too, because he was shoved—*hard*—the moment she reached him.

"What the *hell* was that?!" the Saber half-screamed, half-hissed, following him when he staggered a step back. Before he could answer she'd shoved him again, and this time he almost tripped onto his ass as she kept after him. "All you needed to do was keep them off the damn pole long enough for us to get there! Are you *completely* useless, Ward, or did you just want to throw the game to *piss me off?*!"

"Lena, calm down!" Gillian North—a muscular Mauler with green hair who Rei was pretty sure was part of the B-1 class block with Jiang—exclaimed, reaching them in time to pull the Saber away from pushing him a third time. "Calm down! I'm the one who let Arada get by me before we could regroup!"

Jiang, conveniently, seemed not to hear the girl. "You're basically a Brawler!" she growled at Rei. "If you'd gotten inside Dorne's range, you should have been able to take him down, and then you could have distracted Arada long enough for us to get there!"

Rei, though, wasn't about to let himself get steamrolled. "I *am* basically a Brawler, which skews me heavily towards Speed and Offense specs!" he snapped back. "I'm a *stupidly* poor choice for a defensive position, which *I told you at the start of the match*!" He pointed a finger at Jiang. "*You're* the one who made the call to keep me back. *You're* the one who refused to listen to me when I said I wouldn't be able to hold a position long, especially if I got outnumbered!"

"I kept you back because you would have been *useless* in actual combat, but apparently you were *useless* everywhere else, too!" Jiang's free arm was tense at her side, like she wanted nothing more than to shove North off and lunge for Rei's throat. "We lost because you couldn't hold the objective!"

"We lost because your positioning decisions resulted in not one, but *two* enemy team members getting by you!" Rei snarled back. "Don't put this on me because you can't deal with the fact that *you* messed up, Jiang! Maybe learn from it, and next time we can—!"

"What is going on here?"

The slow, deathly calm voice had Rei starting, just as it did Lena Jiang and Gillian North. Behind the two girls Emily Gisham, Mirnov Yurievich—a Duelist from D-1—and Conrad Fae—a Phalanx in the same C-1 block as Catcher—had just reached them, but instead of the fight they were looking apprehensively over Rei's shoulders. Whirling, Rei was unsurprised—and hardly pleased—to find himself on the receiving end of the sour glare of a familiar pair of cold, deep-set eyes.

Major Dyrk Reese, who had been arbitrating the match—as he always did on their squad-format training days—had appeared behind him like a ghost in the night. In his officer's regulars he stood with his hands clasped at his back, and his expression was one of such disapproval that even Rei felt like shrinking down into himself a little.

"Cadet Jiang—" to Rei's surprise, he wasn't the first to be addressed, the major's gaze lifting to the girl "—you may be among the top rankers of your class, but that is no excuse to lay hands on a fellow student. If I catch you doing so again, I will have you cleaning every one of the first year bathrooms for a week. Understood?"

"Yes, sir," came Lena Jiang's resentful reply, and it was apparent Reese didn't miss the tone as the major arched an eyebrow at her.

"Congratulations, you've just lost your team valuable feedback on their match." From over Rei's shoulder, Emily Gisham started to protest, but Reese cut her off. "No. If a cadet under my purview can't be bothered to treat their fellow students and instructors with respect, they hardly deserve my criticism, especially if they've been assigned as squad-leader for the match. Convene amongst yourselves and discuss what you could have done better. Maybe next time—" the major continued to glare at Jiang "—you'll have the sense to address your officers more appropriately. Dismissed, all of you."

In disgruntled silence all six members of the team saluted. Rei, in retrospect, probably could have done a better job of hiding his satisfaction at seeing the Saber reamed out, because as he was turning away with the others to make for the tunnels that would lead up to the stands, Reese addressed him directly.

"Not you, Ward. Stay."

Rei felt a chill, but he faced the major again dutifully, standing at attention before him. Reese waited for the others to move out of earshot, watching them go before speaking.

"Let me clarify something for you, cadet," the aging man said slowly, his gaze so unwavering as it fell on Rei again that it might have been chiseled out of angry stone. "As arbiter and instructor of this course, it is my responsibility to ensure your safety and monitor the behavior of my students. For this reason, and this reason alone, Cadet Jiang's actions were addressed. However… Do not for a moment misunderstand the fact that I agree with her *wholeheartedly*."

Rei had seen it coming, but he still had to bite his tongue to keep from retorting. It had been 2 full weeks since Reese had taken over half their training days, and—just as the higher officer had done on the first day he'd shown up to class, when they'd run the agility course in preparation for maneuvering large fields—he had always gone out of his way to keep an unfairly sharp eye on Rei's performance.

"You seem to fail to grasp the fact that until the day arrives where you have caught up to your classmates completely, you are a burden to them. You slow them down. Jiang's frustration is utterly understandable. You *did* lose your team that match. Your CAD is currently manifesting as a Brawler-Type Device. You managed to get inside of Dorne's defendable range. Had you been even on a level with the *average* member of your class, you should have had no trouble at least injuring your opponent enough to render him impotent to the outcome of the match. Then you would have been able to engage Arada, and perhaps kept her at bay long enough for your teammates to retreat to your location and provide reinforcements." Reese made a face that seemed to be masking disgust with disappointment. "I admit that Valera Dent's interest in you has not been without merit. You have certainly come a long way since the start of term. However, had it been my decision, you would never have set foot on these grounds. The admissions board has seen fit to prioritize your potential—a *single* cadet's potential—over the rest of all of your classmates'. Even should you eventually outstrip every one of them, you will have cost many of the other first years valuable time and energy."

"So you *do* think I could outstrip them, sir?"

The snide question didn't so much slip out as Rei more let it loose. It wasn't smart of him, he knew—and the flash in Reese's eyes told him he was wading into dangerous waters—but he was getting rather sick of hearing how much he "didn't belong" at Galens. He was fairly sure he scored the best grades of the first years in classwork, and he had continued to beat out Tad Emble—who, along with Warren, refused to look him in the eye anymore—with more and more consistency in combat training. Michael Bretz had let slip that he had high expectations for Rei's upcoming parameter testing, and he'd even started landing the occasional hit on Sense and Emily Gisham, the latter of which was quickly rising in prominence as one of the best Brawlers among the first years.

More than anything, though—more than all of that—he, Aria, Viv, and Catcher had all been getting up early, going to bed late, and giving up their Sunday leisure days in favor of even more additional conditioning, nearly doubling in the last 2 weeks the hours they'd been putting into their extra training.

He was sick—so, *so* sick—of being told he "didn't belong".

"Of everything I just said, *that's* all you registered?" Reese asked dangerously.

Rei didn't even bother trying to stop himself.

"It seemed all that was important, sir."

The major stared at him for a long, *long* time. A full 10, maybe even 15 seconds passed as the man took Rei in with dead eyes, like a vulture looking at carrion.

When he spoke, anger had finally snuck its way the slightest bit into his words.

"Two days in the brig for sheer cheek, Ward," Reese breathed. "Ever disrespect me like that again, and I will make it a week without training privileges. Is that understood?"

"Yes, sir," Rei said, keeping his face blank and lifting his eyes to look beyond Reese. He hid a smirk, deciding he'd done enough standing up for himself, for the moment.

"You will report to the Security Center after class." Reese, for his part could have murdered with the quiet venom dripping from his voice. "Someone will be assigned to deliver your coursework to you. Dismissed, cadet."

Without hesitating Rei snapped up the expected salute, then spun on his heel and made a line across the field for the tunnel entrance. Beyond the perimeter of the Team Battle area most of the twelve first years who were slotted to fight next gawked at him as he passed, obviously not having missed the tone of the exchange even if they hadn't been able to make out the individual words.

Only Aria, standing slightly to the side of the rest of one group, shot a curious look at him, and Rei could only roll his eyes at her to indicate his irritation before he was across the silver border, beyond the new Red and Blue Teams, passing out of the larger Wargames field to cross the 5-yard buffer zone and slip into the underworks.

All of their Squad-training had so far been held on the main floor of the Arena, which had yet to stop making Rei feel giddy every time he stepped out onto the field. As an additional bonus, however, the first years had also steadily become intimately familiar with the tunnels and halls beneath the expansive stadium seating of the massive structure, and so it was without much thought to where his feet were carrying him that Rei took the ramp down through the automated double doors into the back passages. A sharp left to pass the seemingly endless smart-glass paneling that depicted Galen's most celebrated Users and SCT combatants, then another left to start up the steep set of stairs leading into the stands. A few seconds later and Rei was in the open air again, stepping out of the stairwell into a space between the white marble seating sections, and he barely blinked at the daylight once more as the fervor of the noise around him drowned out the distant sound of Dyrk Reese telling the squads to take their position.

Despite the major's handling of the training, squad-format days had quickly become something the entirety of the first year class had taken to looking forward to. For one thing, it made for an excellent change from the more direct conditioning and repetition of the one-on-one Dueling that Valera Dent still drilled into them

Mondays, Wednesdays, and Fridays. For another, they incorporated true fields into the practice, and Rei could now say he'd fought in more than a dozen different settings, though today's Woodlands area had been a new first for him.

Perhaps most interestingly of all, however, was the fact that squad-format days were held collectively with all class-blocks present, making them the busiest—and liveliest—trainings they'd had all year.

A notification pinged his NOED, and Rei opened it with a quick command.

Above you to your left.

Rei closed his frame and looked around. Two sections over and some rows above him, Viv was waving in his direction, looking to have already found Catcher in the scattered crowd. Their 128—or 116, rather, given Aria and another eleven students were currently prepping to fight down in the Arena below—looked like nothing more than a spattering of grey-and-red combat suits against the ivory of the seats, but since matches were happening one at a time in the south Team Battle field, most everyone was gathered in the lower aisles of the areas closest to that zone. As a result, the ensuing conversation and discussion regarding the day's battles so far reverberated and echoed in the vastness of the Arena, even with the ceiling plates raised to frame the open sky in the now-familiar black crown high overhead.

Ignoring multiple sets of curious glances as people caught sight of him, Rei began moving toward Viv and Catcher's section. Since the day they'd started these joint trainings he'd been one of several students from 1-A that tended to get gaped after by the other blocks who had had—until that point—limited contact with their class. Aria always got an eyeful wherever she went—half because her looks had guys and girls alike fawning over her, and half because she was Aria *friggin'* Laurent—as did Logan Grant for similar reasons. Rei, on the other hand, knew it was neither stunning handsomeness nor any overwhelming power that made him the center of attention when he passed, so he didn't deign to meet any of the new gazes that still followed his every move 2 weeks into the squad-format training. It had taken 1-A months to get used to his scars and diminutive stature, and he didn't think anyone— himself included—would ever really become accustomed to Shido's meteoric growth.

Rei supposed he could give the rest of the first years a little time before their staring started to piss him off.

"Yo," Catcher greeted him cheerfully from where he was leaning back in his seat, lifting a hand in a friendly salute as Rei finished climbing the stairs to reach them. "What was Reese chewing you out for this time?"

"If I had to summarize: being a plague on all life as we know it." Rei dropped down onto the cushion to the Saber's right with a disgruntled sigh. "Any idea if they expel students for the murder of teachers, here?"

"More like *attempted* murder," Viv said from Catcher's other side, and Rei looked around the back of the boy's head to see her watching the Arena. "Don't know if you've checked, but the ISCM database has Reese ranked as an A4."

"Seriously?" Rei grumbled, pulling up his NOED, intending to tap into the major's public file to check Viv's assertion—for no good reason other than his unwillingness to give Dyrk Reese more credit as a User and instructor than he absolutely *had* to.

Before he could, however, the neuro-optic started scripting off on its own, interrupting him.

...

Processing combat information.

...

Calculating.

...

Results:
Strength: Lacking
Endurance: Adequate
Speed: Adequate
Cognition: Adequate
Offense: Adequate
Defense: Adequate
Growth: Not Applicable

...

Checking combat data acquisition.

...

Adequate data acquirement met.
Device initiating adjustments to:
Strength.

...

Adjustment complete.

Strength has been upgraded from Rank E8 to E9.

"Nice," Rei muttered to himself as the upgrade script winked out, Major Reese's CAD-Rank forgotten. He wasn't unenthusiastic about the Strength boost—it certainly would have come in handy trying to break through Sam Dorne's guard—but what was more exciting, ironically, where all the "Adequates" of his other specs. Despite the fact that the Lancer had been a full 5 levels higher than him—not to mention with un-skewed stats—Rei had held his own well enough for Shido to judge most of his measures as balanced to the point of not requiring modification. Maybe it was due to the brevity of the fight—Rei couldn't help but wonder who, in the end, would have won their clash had Viv not arrived to interrupt them—but it still had him feeling good about himself.

Finally, at long last, his stats were starting to look like he was actually catching up.

"Another spec upgrade?" Catcher asked.

Rei nodded without looking around, pulling up a Specification Request. "Yeah. Strength, this time."

"'This time'," the Saber repeated mournfully, shaking his head. "Could you try not to rub it in, at least?"

"Sorry," Rei said with a grin, looking over his numbers quickly. It was the second adjustment Shido had made since the evening before—Endurance having ranked up shortly after Aria had drilled his face into the field for the fifth time that morning—and he wanted to see how things were shaping up.

Specifications Request acknowledged.

…

Combat Assistance Device: Shido. User identification… Accepted.

Type: A-TYPE

Rank: D5

…

User Attributes:

- Strength: E9

- Endurance: E6

- Speed: D1

- Cognition: E9

…

CAD Specifications:

- Offense: E8

- Defense: E7

- Growth: S

Rei, despite himself, frowned just a little.

"What's with the long face?" Viv asked, apparently taking note.

"I'm behind," Rei grunted honestly. Casting about to make sure there was no one seated close enough to be eavesdropping, he dropped his voice. "There's only two weeks left before the Intra-Schools start. I wanted to be at D6 by now, and C0 by the time the second quarter hit."

"*Dude*," Catcher breathed in exasperation as below them the field on which Aria and the rest of the Blue and Red Teams stood started to glow. "What did I *just* say? If talking about hitting C0 before I do—much less *Viv*—isn't the definition of 'rubbing it in', I don't know what is."

"Sorry, sorry," Rei muttered with an apologetic grimace. "If it makes you feel better, though, there's not a lot to it. If you discount Growth, all my specs have me sitting at an average closer to E8. Speed is my *only* D-Ranked stat, actually."

Viv snorted, turning her attention to the field again as the Arena announced the match would be an Elimination-type bout. "Somehow I get the feeling you'll be just fine, Rei."

"What makes you say that? E8 is a full tier behind any of the competitive first years, and that's just right now. If you're not C-Ranked by the time the Intra-Schools kick off, I'll shave my head."

"You should do that anyway. Your hair's getting out of control again." Viv eyed him sidelong across Catcher, Rei's straight white locks having indeed grown out quite a bit since the start of the term. "But as for the SCTs... Sam Dorne is one of those 'competitive' first years, Rei, and you held up pretty decently against *him*."

"Only because he can't use a spear half as well as Aria," he replied as the Arena told the combats to call their Devices.

"Which essentially means that so long as you know your opponent, I'll get to keep saying it: you'll be fine."

Rei, unfortunately, had no answer to give out loud to that. Viv's words touched on the very mentality he'd been building up since Aria had started training with them. If he was honest with himself, he had *never* been the 'stronger' fighter. Not once in his less-than-illustrious career on the combat team at Grandcrest, nor since he'd been assigned Shido. He'd *always* had to out-think what opponents he'd managed to beat, which he supposed was exactly what Viv was attempting to argue.

This wasn't combat team, though. This was CAD-fighting, and he would need more than just his wits to go toe-to-toe with most of the Galens first years. Valera Dent had said as much already, the day Logan Grant had tossed him around the field like a rag doll.

Strategy will only get you so far in this world...

As much as he took Viv's confidence in him as a sign that he was headed in the right direction, he still needed to get stronger, and—in that respect—Rei knew he was behind. What's more, his inability to keep his tongue to himself had now earned him two days in the brig, setting him back even further...

Rei frowned, realizing he hadn't told the others about his upcoming punishment. Before he could open his mouth, however, the Arena's final announcement distracted him.

"Combatants... Fight."

"Ha! There she goes!"

Catcher's laughing exclamation echoed Rei's studying of the 70-yard Team Battle space as the match began. The combat area looked to be an interesting variation of the Mountainside zone, with two flat-topped cliffs rising 30 feet in the air above the spectators, bisected by a 10-yard canyon at the bottom of which ran a shallow river that appeared to carry a fast current. As with every match that involved visual obstacles or multiple levels, the field was semi-translucent, allowing the onlookers to see each combatant from both teams even when the Users themselves didn't know their relative positions. For the moment, the fighters had been cleverly divided equally between the two cliffs and the river in three separate two-on-two matchups.

If he had to guess, though, Rei would have bet the Red Team was about to be put at a significant disadvantage.

Outpacing her partner easily—a Mauler Rei didn't know, who sported a massive hammer of white-and-purple steel—Aria was powering up the flow at the bottom of the canyon like the fighting water was nonexistent. Hippolyta's red-and-gold greaves gleamed around her legs, and her shield was held at the ready even as she charged towards the two Red Team Users running to meet her from the other end of the field. Her spear was retracted, ready to strike at a moment's notice, but Rei knew better than to think Aria Laurent would be arrogant enough to throw herself at a pair of opponents without good reason. As she closed the gap quickly, the Mauler some 5 or 6 yards behind her, he could guess what was about to happen, and almost laughed.

Sure enough, just before the Red Team's fighters—a Saber and Brawler named Clement Easton and Archie Brawn respectively, Rei thought he recalled—hurled themselves into Hippolyta's reach, Aria's rush turned into a deep coiling of both legs.

Then, with a powerful thrust upward, she launched herself into the air.

In a graceful, twisting flip Aria arched over Easton and Brawn, keeping her shield between herself and them the entire way over. She landed in the river again with a *splash* on the other side of the pair, and as could be expected the two cadets whirled to face her, ready for Hippolyta when the spear lanced forward in a blur of blue-adjusted vysetrium almost before Aria had touched down. Easton's sword knocked the longer weapon upwards and out of the way, and Brawn lunged directly at Aria's shield, obviously intent to try and overpower her defenses.

Unfortunately for them both, in their moment of distraction the two failed to keep an eye on the *other* Blue Team member barreling up on their back.

Easton went down in a single blow the instant the Mauler reached him, the massive hammer taking him in the side of the head so hard it sent his limp body crashing into the canyon wall. While the Saber's FDA was announced to the spectators, the Users on the field were mostly too preoccupied to take account of their notifications, and so Brawn didn't so much as glance around as his partner was killed off. The Brawler was already committed, intently focused on his own rush, and with thick, piston-like punch daggers of black-and-blue steel he struck at Aria in a series of gatling blows that came so fast she actually took a step back, then two as her shield accepted the majority of the punishment. Pressing his advantage, Brawn lunged, putting a full shoulder into the red-and-gold steel, obviously expecting Aria to stagger.

He found himself mistaken, however, when she didn't so much as budge.

Rei almost thought he saw a smile on her face as Aria closed the trap she'd set for the Brawler, the snare of confidence she'd offered by feigning the knockbacks. As Brawn bounced off her shield like he might have a solid stone wall, Hippolyta's spear lanced out in a blurred trio of thrusts, taking him in the thigh and abdomen before he managed to smash away the blow that would have skewered him through the throat. Undeterred, Aria turned the deflection in a spinning over-cut, the spear coming arcing around her head once before slashing horizontally at the Brawler's left side in another blur of blue. Despite his injuries, Brawn managed to turn and bring both arms up, ready to block the heavy blow, but at the last second Aria retracted the spear.

Instead, with a blast of strength she powered forward, shield leading the way.

The steel took Brawn just below the shoulder, and he went flying head-over-heels. The Brawler landed in a heavy spray of water, floundering for a second as he sunk under the weight of the current. He managed to find his bearings impressively quickly, getting his feet under himself to start to stand again.

Amusingly, *that* was the point the boy seemed to register he had landed in the shadow of a tall form wielding a massive hammer, and many of the spectators laughed as the Brawler's yell of surprise reached them even in the stand when the Mauler brought his white-and-purple Device down on his opponent's head with all of the force of a falling boulder.

"Poor guy," Catcher snorted. "Both of them, really. Aria was pulling their strings from the start."

"Maybe, but what's she doing now?" Viv asked, bringing up her NOED to zoom in on Aria and the Mauler as they convened and started pointing up the sides of the cliff.

Doing the same, Rei found himself missing the live commentary of a professional SCT match. Spectators didn't have access to the combatants' coms, but the announcers did, and would often clue viewers in as to what was going on. Dyrk Reese was arbitrating as usual, floating above and slightly behind the field on the same white projection disk Michael Bretz used to observe training sessions, but Rei had a hard time imagining the unpleasant old man going out of his way to explain what was happening even if it was requested of him.

Still, in this case, Rei thought he could guess what Aria and her teammate were about.

"They're trying to figure out how to get out of the canyon," he explained, focusing in on the pair just in time to see the Mauler—his wavy black hair streaked with blue—shake his head in disappointment as Aria continued to indicate the cliffside with her spear. "Looks like her teammate doesn't think he can make it, though."

"That's unfortunate," Catcher muttered, his own eye blazing, now. "Oh, that's Casey Foreman. He's in 1-C with me. Nice guy."

"Nice guy who's about to get abandoned in the river," Viv said with a smirk. "If Aria can make it up, Blue Team will be fine. The others are holding their own for now. She'll be all they need."

It was true enough. Lifting his attention to the flat half-circle plateaus that topped the cliffs, Rei saw that all the other combatants were still kicking, having matched off into four pairs of one-on-one fights. If Aria could get out of the canyon herself, Blue Team would certainly have the advantage.

On the other hand…

"She's gonna figure out how to get them both up," Rei said.

To his left, Viv blinked and looked around at him. "Seriously? Why?"

"Because she might not know the situation right now," Catcher was the one to explain, once more showing off an understanding of CAD-fighting that often matched Rei's own. "I doubt anyone is yelling into their coms at the moment given they're all engaged, so for all she knows her whole team is down and she'd be jumping into a four-on-one fight. Aria's badass, but those are odds even she wouldn't have a prayer of handling."

"But how?" Viv asked, frowning once more down at the Arena. "If the Mauler can't make the jump…"

Rei, though, was watching Aria heft Hippolyta's spear as she pointed with her shield, now, at a place about midway up the north cliff.

When it clicked, he laughed.

"She's gonna ditch."

On his left, it was Catcher's turn to look surprised. "You think? Why would she—Ooooh…" He seemed to catch on, peering down at the pair as the Mauler—Foreman—nodded enthusiastically. "That could work…"

"What? What could work?" Viv appeared distinctly confused. "What's a 'ditch'?"

Rei shot her a feigned glare. "Viv, if you're gonna make us explain every fight we watch, I'm *actually* gonna strap you to the couch with your eyes taped open the next time there's a System SCT on the feeds."

Viv made a face. "If someone is gonna strap me to a couch, Rei, I'd prefer it be *anyone* but you. But seriously—" she looked between him and Catcher as Rei rolled his eyes "—what's a 'ditch'?"

Catcher, in answer, nodded towards the field. "Pretty sure you're about to find out."

Sure enough, Aria and Foreman seemed to have agreed on a plan. Rei watched with anticipation as Aria crouched again, looking like she was eyeing the uneven cliffside carefully.

Then she jumped.

With a spray of water she shot straight up into the air, barely a foot from the wall, clearing more than half the distance to the top canyon with relative ease. Viv started to groan when she didn't make it all the way up, but stopped abruptly as—in the moment gravity began to pull her back down again—Aria thrust Hippolyta out in midair with a ripping twist of her body. The spear pierced the stone of cliff with a *crack* of breaking earth, the carbonized steel coupling with her Strength spec to drive the weapon what must have been nearly 2 feet into the projected rock. Instead of falling, Aria ended up hanging from one hand, then two, from Hippolyta's haft.

Then, with a grimace and a strain, she pulled up with such force that she launched herself the last 10 feet to clear the top of the canyon completely, landing in a roll on the north side of the clifftop.

"Oh!" Viv exclaimed in astonishment, jumping up from her seat as all around them several other people did the same. "OH!"

But the spectacle wasn't done. From the river, it was Foreman's turn to crouch, then spring upward. While his Strength likely matched or outstripped Aria's, his Speed clearly did not, nor was he helped by the weight of the hammer. Indeed, there was no way he would have been able to make the top of the wall on his own, but his free hand *did* just reach Hippolyta's haft, still sticking perpendicular out of the stone. It was less graceful than Aria's clearance, but with a few swings of his legs Foreman managed to pull himself up to straddle the spear, then stand on its narrow length by stabilizing himself with one hand on the wall.

Then, at last, he leaped again, and this time the last 10 feet to the top were manageable even for a Mauler.

"What?!" Viv demanded, and her shout of confused amazement wasn't the only one to be heard echoing about the Arena. "WHAT?!"

"Now watch Aria," Rei told her, turning his own attention away from Foreman as the Mauler picked himself up to charge immediately at the closest of the Red Team combatants. It took a second, but as expected…

Hippolyta vanished off Aria's body, the shield and greaves whirling out of existence back into the form of her CAD bands.

"Wait, *what*?!" Viv hissed, stepping so close to the edge of the seats before them that Catcher actually reached out to grab her by the wrist, stopping her from falling on her face in her amazement. Viv's astonishment was so extreme that she didn't even noticed. "She recalled her Device? Why?"

Neither Rei nor Catcher answered, waiting for the reasoning to present itself. In nothing but her combat suit and bands, now, Aria turned to the canyon, took two steps back and—with a spray of projected dust—took a running leap over the fissure. Rei could see her face as she flew, arms wind-milling while she arced over the 10-yard expanse, and he thought he caught her lips moving even in midair.

Sure enough, there was another whirling and twisting of steel, and by the time she landed and rolled onto the south clifftop to join the other half of the fight, Hippolyta was live in her hands again, greaves, shield, and spear in all.

"Oh," Viv said weakly, much of the tension leaving her as she watched Aria lance into the fighting as Foreman did the same on the other side of the canyon from her. "Oh… I get it." She stepped back, not looking away from the field, or at least the zoomed-in projection of it on her NOED. Catcher let go of her as she sat down slowly. "So that's a ditch."

"That's a ditch," Rei and Catcher confirmed together, but Rei let the Saber continue the explanation.

"It's not common, but it can be useful in the right circumstances. Some top-level Users use it in combo with certain Abilities, like Magnetic Hunt or the like. 'Ditch' part of your Device for some reason or another, then recall and call it again. See—" he pointed towards the canyon "—the spear's gone from the wall, obviously."

Indeed, where Aria's weapon had been protruding from the rock only moments before, nothing but a cracked hole in the stone remained.

"It pretty risky," Catcher continued, "especially against opponents who can react in a blink to your recall if they catch you doing it. It takes a second to get the Device back, and even longer if its far away, then you have to call it again. Against a User with A- or S-Ranked Speed and Cognition, that's like voluntarily dropping your weapons, stripping, and waltzing around naked for them with a target painted across your ass."

"But if you do it right, it can come in handy," Rei added as Viv nodded along on Catcher's other side. "There was no way Foreman was getting out of that river on his own, but they managed it together. And in the case of Magnetic Hunt: imagine if you were under the impression your opponent had thrown their weapon to have it chase after you, only for them to cut you off as you're running and cleave you in two."

"You guys are making me feel like I should study chess just to get through my Duels," Viv muttered darkly.

Catcher chuckled. "Wouldn't hurt. In your case I'd start with checkers, though. Or maybe tic-tac-toe?"

"Son of a—!"

As Viv and Catcher started to go at each other in their usual fashion, Rei watched the Team Battle wrap up in the Arena. Aria's appearance on the south cliff had proved a rapid end to the two Red fighters there, and Foreman's support on the north side was in the process of doing the same. Indeed, even as Aria turned, looking like she was ready to jump the canyon again, the last of the Red User's fell to a spear between the eyes, and the Arena voice chimed in mechanically.

"All Red Team combatants eliminated. Winner: Blue Team."

Whereas there hadn't been much celebration following most of the other matches that day, this flawless victory—with all six of the Blue Team members left standing—earned a resounding cheer from the gathered first years. From the shouts and comments thrown out by the cadets, Aria in particular appeared to have garnered a significant amount of praise, and who could blame her? Rei was sure someone like Reese would have found some comment to make to the contrary, but in Rei's opinion the execution of the match as a whole had been brilliant, and he looked forward to telling Aria as much.

The crowd quieted as the field dissolved, carrying the remains combatants down to the Arena floor slowly. Aria and the others took their leave of the Team Battle area, allowing for yet another group to gain starting positions while the major himself descended to offer criticism. After a little while Rei realized that he was still focused in on Aria—and had been for a good while now—and with a cough to cover his jolt of realization he blinked his NOED away and looked around, hoping the other two hadn't noticed. Almost predictable Catcher was doing nothing more than muttering to himself, apparently taking in the newest first years to step onto the field and trying to discern what tactical approach their team makeup would allow for.

And Viv, of course, was grinning around the Saber at Rei, very obviously not having missed him staring.

Rei shot her a glare, and she raised both hands as if to say "I saw nothing" before settling back in preparation of watching the new fight. Satisfied with not being teased, Rei shook his head, and decided he, too, should probably get his thoughts out of the clouds and focus.

It was 2 or 3 minutes later that Aria appeared out of the same tunnel entrance Rei had taken into the stands, expectedly trailing a little behind the other cadets who'd made up her combat group. She found them easily enough when Rei, Viv, and

Catcher all waved together to draw her attention, and it wasn't long before she was climbing the stairs to join them.

"That was awesome!" Viv said excitedly as Aria started up the row in their direction.

"Agreed," Catcher added enthusiastically. "Nice ditch. Totally badass."

"Thanks," Aria said brightly, tucking a strand of red hair that had escaped her bun behind one ear as she sat down on Rei's right. "It was a bit of a gamble. I wasn't sure I'd manage to wedge Hippolyta like that, but our teammates weren't responding to coms and Foreman was pretty sure there was no way he'd be able to get up the cliff on his own. Apparently his Strength is actually pretty low for a Mauler…"

"Well you definitely figured it out," Rei told her with a grin. "Not to repeat dumb and dumber over here—" he tossed a thumb at Catcher and Viv as they both sputtered out a protest "—but that was seriously amazing. Perfect victory, too. I don't think we've seen one of those yet."

Oddly, Aria made a face at this. "You could have fooled me, given Reese's feedback. You would have thought my team had won by the skin of our teeth the way he told us off. I'm *really* not a fan of that guy."

"Neither is Rei," Catcher chimed in with a snort. "He got a *personal* chewing out, after his match."

"Yeah, I saw that…" Aria frowned at Rei. "What was he on about? It looked like Jiang was trying to pick a fight."

"She was," Rei muttered. "She wasn't happy with the fact that I couldn't take down Dorne before Viv managed to hamstring me."

"No way," Aria said in disbelief. "Isn't Dorne 4 or 5 ranks above you? And what the hell were you doing as defense anyway?"

"Exactly," Rei answered simply. "Don't try explaining that to *her*, though."

"She was kind of a pain all summer, come to think of it. Not really good at taking criticism."

"She's been like that as long as I've known her, period," Catcher added as the field below shifted into the stark white form of a flat Neutral Zone while the two teams faced off across the empty expanse of the rising projection. "If you guys were hoping to make nice with her, I'd recommend against it. She's never been one for friends."

"Huh," Rei frowned and turned to the Saber. "I totally forgot you guys are from the same system. Didn't you say you'd fought her before? On combat team in prep school?"

Catcher looked a little embarrassed. "Yeah. And lost. Repeatedly."

"So we can agree she's a pain in the ass, got it." Aria was looking at Rei impatiently. "If anything I'm even more at a loss as to why *you* ended up getting an earful, given that?"

Rei gave a noncommittal shrug, waiting for the Arena to finish announcing the start of the Team Battle—another elimination bout—before answering. "The major just wanted to tell me how much he's looking forward to seeing me grow."

There was an empty pause as Aria stared at him blankly.

"I don't believe you," she said at last.

Rei snorted. "You shouldn't. But what he actually said doesn't matter. The guy's a prick, and I ended up letting him know."

This statement was followed by a very different kind of silence, and Rei saw both Catcher and Viv turning slowly in their seats to look at him.

"And…?" Viv asked pointedly. "How did that go?"

Rei hesitated, suddenly not wanting to say.

Under the blistering gazes of the other three, however, he finally caved.

"… Two days in the brig. Starting after class."

"What?!"

Viv and Catcher yelled the question together, and he cowered away from them both as they leaned closer to him in unison.

"Two days?! But it's the beginning of the week! He's taking away two full days of combat training!"

"Rei, are you serious?! What the hell did you say to him?!"

Rei explained as best he could, and by the time he was done repeating the post-match conversation, the two of them were grimacing.

"Dude…" Catcher muttered. "Were you *trying* to pick a fight?"

"Don't know. Maybe." Rei shrugged and crossed his arms to lean back into his seat. "I'm just getting sick of it. It's one thing for Grant and the others to give me a hard time—and we haven't even heard jack from *them* in two weeks. Reese is supposed to be our *instructor*. If he didn't want me at the school, he should have tried harder to keep me out in the first place, rather than this backhanded bullshit."

He was getting angry again, and found himself glaring at Dyrk Reese as the major oversaw the combat now ongoing below them. The man stood erect and stiff, dark eyes flitting from one fighter to the other, and Rei felt something that might have been a pang of jealousy cut across his chest.

He would bet anything the teams battling it out now—win or lose—would get more value out of their post-match conversation with the arbiter than Rei had out of half a month of training.

A light pressure came to rest atop his right arm, pulling Rei out of his dark musings to look around. Aria was watching him with a sad, crooked smile.

"He's not worth getting worked up about," she said gently. "Not to rub salt in the wound, but you can't afford to be losing days of training like this right now."

Rei stiffened, and was on the very edge of snapping back something about whether she'd heard what he'd just said, but Aria kept on before he could get a word out.

"I *get it*. I do. It's frustrating, and I'm—*we're*—" she gestured to Catcher and Viv on his other side with a dip of her head, not having taken her hand off his arm "—frustrated for you. But rising to Reese's bait is only going to end up with you making his point for him, isn't it?"

Rei's mouth dropped open, the words like a knife in his gut.

And then, as though the hole there had punctured his anger, he deflated.

"Fine," he admitted darkly, taking a depressed breath. "Sure. I can't pretend I wasn't already worried about falling behind as is. Losing two training days is gonna be a bitch. Any more would probably sink any chance I have of lasting more than two matches at the Intra-Schools."

"Did he take your privileges?" Aria asked, finally drawing her hand away now that he'd calmed down.

The place where her fingers had touched his bare, scarred skin seemed to tingle even in their absence.

Rei blinked, recalling something Reese had said on that very subject.

"… No," he answered after a moment. "But he said he'd do it next time. What does that mean? What privileges? I've never been brigged before."

"Have any of us?" Catcher asked with a snort before answering more seriously. "Galens is pretty serious about keeping their students in top shape, so even if you're being disciplined you're allowed *some* training hours. I think two?"

"Three," Viv corrected him. "It was basically the first thing I looked up when I got accepted."

As one, the rest of them all blinked at her.

"What?" she huffed as below them someone screamed when a sword cut through one of their legs. "Let's be real. Do any of you think I'm going to graduate this place with a perfect record?"

A picture of Logan Grant's black eye from 2 weeks past flashed across Rei's mind, and he almost laughed.

"Point made," Catcher admitted. "Okay. Three hours of training a day. Plus feed access for coursework, I think."

"That's not so bad…" Rei muttered, more to himself than anything. It didn't compare to the total additional conditioning and sparring they all did on top of their regular school training, but at least it wasn't nothing.

"You think that, but unless you can get a partner for your assigned hours, you're gonna be swinging at simulations for the next two days, brother." Viv made a sour face. "And to get a partner…" She let his explanation trail, clearly not eager to continue. After several seconds in which Rei, Aria, and Catcher together all glared her down, however she finally gave in. "You need permission from the disciplining officer."

Rei groaned, his eyes drifting once more to the tall, stick-straight form of Major Reese hovering high above the chaos of the match.

"Can we talk about that murder plan, again?" he grumbled, and Catcher and Viv both smirked grimly from his left.

None of them, however, noticed Aria watching Rei, brow pinched together in consideration.

CHAPTER 34

Two days for disrespecting an officer. Let's see…" Sergeant Amelia Becker snorted at the small pad in her hand. "Major Reese? And in combat training, too? What made you think it was a good idea to piss off the guy who's going to be overseeing your Intra-Schools, cadet?"

"Slip of the tongue, ma'am," was all Rei could say to that, standing at attention with his eyes on the grey, polished concrete wall of the hall behind the woman, his bag over one shoulder.

It was his first time in the Security Center, having never had reason—or the desire, rather, given the hospital visit from Hadish Barnes—to frequent it before. As opposed to most of the other structures on Galens' grounds, the place was more stone than steel or glass, apparently designed to fit the aesthetic of the Institute's grand encircling walls. It was one of the larger buildings on campus, broad and four stories tall, and from the outside had the appearance of a modern fortress, complete with heavy steel doors that reminded Rei of the school gates. Inside had been less imposing, at least in the lobby area, where a gleaming granite floor had reflected several soft solar lights set in the high, arched ceiling, complimented by a few thick windows in the east and west walls.

After he'd presented himself for discipline to the staffing officer at the front desk, however, Rei had been directed to follow Sergeant Becker into the building's back halls, which proved to be *much* more in line with the prison-like environment he'd envisioned as he'd made the dreary walk across campus after training had wrapped for the day.

The brig, it transpired, took up the second floor of the Security Center, and consisted of some forty modest cells split along two halls. The walls and floor on this higher level were concrete that had been sanded and polished to a sheen, the only variation in their medium being the heavy, 3-foot thick panels of glass that made up the doors of the lockups themselves. Rei was now standing in front of one such room—unit 026, according to a plate set in the ceiling above them—at attention before Sergeant Becker while the woman read off his docket.

"Well, at least you've got balls," she said, eyeing his uniform as she tucked her pad into the pocket of her own black-and-gold slacks. "Your release is set for 1800 on Thursday, meaning you'll miss two days of classes. Was someone assigned to send you your coursework?"

"No, ma'am, but I expect my friends will be happy to do so. Am I allowed to contact them?"

The sergeant nodded. "You weren't stripped of privileges, so you'll have partial NOED access. It will be monitored, but that includes communications. Keep it to school discussion, and we won't have any issues." She reached out to tap the door with a knuckle. "The inside layer is smart-glass. It's meant for use in school work only, but we're lenient about SCT feeds and the like so long as you don't give us trouble. There's a half-dozen of you in here right now, though, so your training hours will be limited to early morning and late evenings, since you're a first year. I can waive them for you, of course." She eyed him critically, then, obviously intent on gauging his reaction to this suggestion.

"No thank you, ma'am," Rei said at once, still looking above the woman's shoulder. "I appreciate any and all field time I can get. Could you tell me the exact hours I'll be allowed?"

He might have imagined it, but he thought the sergeant looked rather pleased with his response. "0600 to 0730, and 2030 to 2200. Someone will come fetch you a quarter-hour before your times, and escort you upstairs. Did you bring your combat suit?"

"Yes, ma'am," Rei patted his bag with one hand, having been smart enough to pack it after training.

Becker nodded. "Then make sure you're changed *before* you're called on. If any of us see more of you than we want to when we come to fetch your ass, losing privileges will be the least of your problems. Any other questions?"

"No, ma'am."

"Good." With a flash of her NOED there was a hiss of releasing pressure, and the heavy glass of the door to Rei's right began to retract silently downward, into the floor. "Then in you go. Meals are delivered at 0800, 1300, and 1900." She pointed to the back wall, where a steel toilet, a sink, and simple ion shower took up each corner. "The shower can be used for cleaning and drying clothes and bedding. If you require assistance, there is a function in the menu of your wall for that. I don't recommend crying wolf, though."

"Yes, ma'am." Rei turned as the door lowered until the top of it was even with the hallway floor, creating a flat, 3-foot wide threshold into the cell. He marveled at the thickness of the glass as he passed, but supposed it made sense. The best of Galens's third years graduated in the high A-rankings or above. In case imprisonment was ever seriously needed, it wasn't like ordinary walls would do much to restrain someone with a Strength spec approaching—or encroaching—S-level.

Once he was inside, the sergeant must have input another NOED command, because the glass began to rise again behind him. Rei didn't turn around until the sound of a vacuum seal being applied to the door announced that it had finished closing, and when he did he found himself staring at a projection of a wall the exact same color and texture as the cement around him.

"*Too* depressing," he muttered to himself, reaching up to tap at the smart-glass. At once a familiar menu popped up—with the addition of the "Assistance" command Becker had mentioned, and after a few seconds Rei had pulled up a few recordings of old S-Ranked SCTs and swiped them here and there over the surface of the wall if only to give it a bit more life.

Then, feeling a little better, he looked around to face the cell again.

Aside from the shower, sink, and toilet, only two objects took up most of the minimal space. On the right side of the room a narrow bed that appeared hardly long enough to accommodate Rei—much less a monster like Logan Grant or the like—had clean sheets, a blanket, and a pillow neatly folded atop it. Opposite this, a small, desk—barely more than a 2-by-3 table—took up the left wall, with a chair tucked underneath it. It might have seemed a quaint, even comfortable little space, were it not for the fact that *everything*—down to the stitching in the mattress—was the same slate grey monotone as the cement all around him.

"*Seriously* too depressing," Rei said, a bit more loudly this time, and he didn't like in the *least* the way his voice felt flat in the small chamber, like the walls were designed to absorb all sound.

All of 15 seconds into his stay, and even with NOED and feed access Rei could already understand why this was called punishment.

At the thought, he tossed his bag on the desk and pulled up his frame while he moved to the bed, intending to make it. As he pulled apart the bedding and flattened out the sheets, he sent out a quick group message, keeping to the point.

Communication allowed as long as it's related to school. Would one of you guys be able to send me any assignments we get between now and Thursday night? Class notes would be cool, too…

Unsurprisingly, he wasn't long in waiting for a reply, having barely folded down the corners of the fabric before Viv answered briefly, absent her usual animations and pics, clearly getting the hint.

I'll cover you.

Rei had to admit it to himself: he was the slightest bit disappointed it had been her who'd gotten back to him first. Feeling that pressure in his chest again, there was no use in pretending he hadn't been hoping someone else might have taken up the opportunity before her.

Another pinged message, and Rei felt his heart jump a little before realizing it was from Catcher.

How's the slammer? Remember: find the biggest, baddest mother in there, and take them out first. Only way to survive.

Despite a wince of trepidation at the thought of a staff monitor frowning at this message in some office downstairs, Rei had to laugh.

Will do. Keep it to school stuff only, though. I don't want to be stuck in here longer than I have to.

Given the radio silence that followed this, Rei thought Catcher had understood this time—or more likely been *made* to understand by Viv. He felt a little lonely, all of a sudden, registering the quiet of the room and the absolute solitude of it. Taking solace in activity, he finished making the bed, peeled himself out of his jacket and hat to toss them on the back of the chair, then flopped down on the freshly-tucked blanket with a bored huff. Finding himself staring at the ceiling—and its single light that he hoped wouldn't be kept on all night—he stared at the pattern in the cement for a time, contemplating the events of the afternoon.

And his own stupidity.

He wanted to kick himself for having almost bitten Aria's head off for calling him on it. He was out of time. In less than 2 weeks the Intra-Schools would start, and he was behind in his growth. And yet, despite that, he'd managed to get himself locked up for 2 days, and in exchange for a single moment's satisfaction.

"Moron," Rei muttered to the emptiness.

Friday and Saturday, all of Sunday, then the following week, one afternoon training of which he was pretty sure would be set aside from parameter testing. With any luck he wouldn't be matched with an opponent early, but given Reese was in charge of the whole event Rei couldn't escape the feeling that not only would he *definitely* be fighting, but he'd be presented with a hurdle he wouldn't like.

He was out of time…

What could he do? Was there something he hadn't thought of? Something he hadn't considered. Shido's improvement had been as steady as ever over the last couple of weeks, but there had to be *some* way to take advantage of his *S-Ranked* Growth that he hadn't thought of, right? Rei wracked his brain, trying to think of anything, deciding that if he was going to be stuck alone in a grey hole for 2 days he might as well try to do something productive with his downtime.

Unfortunately, no stroke of genius claimed him.

Including class time he was training 7, sometimes 8 hours a day, he and the others pushing their bodies, minds, and schedules already, even with the assisted recovery offered by their CADs. What's more, he'd somehow gotten himself paired off with Aria Laurent, Galens' most impressive student in decades, according to Valera Dent herself. Measuring his improvement in the last month compared to the 2 weeks prior to that—in which he'd only trained with Viv and Catcher—Rei could say for certain that pitting himself against the strongest his class had to offer him had certainly offered a significant advantage to his progress.

Something tickled at his brain, then, and he considered that thought. Could he find a way to make his sparring with Aria *more* challenging? Maybe he could ask Michael Bretz to teach him how to make a partial-call, and try to take her on without his greaves, or defenses?

No. That was stupid. He'd never landed a blow in any match against Aria, much less put up enough of a fight to think he could take on *more*.

Still… There was something there… Wasn't there?

After another minute of struggling with his own thoughts, Rei gave up with an aggravated "Ugh!", shoving himself off the bed again to pull out the chair and take a seat at the desk as he tugged his pad free from his bag. Setting an alarm for himself for 2000, he considered taking advantage of the time before training to finally make adjustments to his NOED—he hadn't yet had any real cause to play around with the software—but decided the campus *Security Center* wasn't the place to be making possibly-illicit changes to his school-designated neuro-optics. In the end, he settled instead for starting on what classwork he already had. It felt weird being *glad* John Markus had assigned them a paper on "Varied Evolutions Within Types", but Rei was happy to have anything to think about as he pulled the research prompt up.

As the SCT feeds continued to flit and flicker in the corner of his vision to his left, Rei started working, only barely able to suppress wondering if he'd screwed himself more badly than he was willing to admit.

The fact that the brig's food was as good as the mess hall's was the first—but hardly the last—pleasant surprise Rei received that initial night in lockup. At nearly exactly 1900, about an hour after he'd reported for discipline, a tray of beef stew, bread, and varied roasted vegetables slid into the room so abruptly he'd almost fallen out of his seat when he'd jumped. As he'd stared at the dinner he only just caught a narrow slot in the bottom of the glass wall vanishing from sight again, and he realized that some kind of solid projection must have shielded the opening at all other times.

He worked as he ate, content in losing himself in research on how Sabers could either sport a narrow, single-handed blade—like Catcher or Mateus Selleck wielded—or a larger two-handed weapon closer to a Mauler's Device—like the one Major Albert Connelly had shown off at the start of the CAD-Assignment Exam. It was lucky, in the end, that he'd had the earlier wherewithal to set an alarm to remind him to get changed, because he was in the middle of a fascinating account by a former Intersystem Champion who'd been able to use Arsenal Shift to change back and forth between these two forms freely—and to great success—when the notification that it was 2000 blazed across his frame. Deciding he could call it a night on his schoolwork, Rei put his pad away before pulling his combat suit out of his bag, grimacing as he realized he hadn't had a chance to wash it after Squad-training. Running the fabric through a quick cycle in the ion shower, he changed quickly, folding his uniform onto the table before starting to warm up in what little spare space the cell had to offer.

He had 3 hours a day. Even if it was only going to be against simulations, he wasn't about to waste even a second of the time he had to not fall even further behind.

2015 arrived, and almost on a timer the feeds Rei still had running on the entry wall flickered and vanished as the glass become translucent again. The officer who greeted Rei with a nod from the other side of the barrier wasn't Becker, but instead a stout, young man who addressed him the moment the cell began to open.

"Cadet Ward, I'm Warrant Officer Jetson. It's your allotted training time. Follow me."

Rei wasn't given the opportunity to salute or agree as the man turned and started moving north up the hall before the wall had even completed its opening. Hopping over the last foot of descending glass to hurry after the warrant officer, Rei fell in behind him wordlessly, allowing himself to be led to a stairwell at the back of the building. They took one flight, then another, almost reaching the landing and the door that must have led to the fourth floor before his escort spoke again.

"You have until 2200, at which point either myself or another observational staff will escort you back to your cell." Jetson made the landing. "Any interaction with other cadets other than your training partner is strictly prohibited. Is that understood?"

"Uh… Yes, sir," Rei answered uncertainly, a little confused as he, too, cleared the top of the stairs. "Am I being assigned a partner, then? I was under the impression I would only be able to use simulations…"

The warrant officer paused, looking around at him even as he reached one hand for the door hand. "Assigned? No. We don't assign partners. Yours arrived a little while ago." He looked Rei up and down, then, appearing to break form a little as he frowned. "I have to say, though… The lot of us were surprised when she showed up…"

"What do you—?" Rei started to ask, but then the door was being opened, and the room beyond it blazed bright enough for him to take it all in at a glance.

Four standard-sized Dueling fields comprised the entirety of the massive, open chamber, each claiming one corner of the floor with a bare buffer area between them. The ceiling was low—even lower than those of the East and West Centers—and crossed with dozens of lights to illuminate every corner of the space, as though the observing officers standing on each wall Rei could make out wanted to offer no shadows their charges might try to hide in. Three of the fields were already in use, manifesting in the standard neutral-white of a flat training ring. A pair of second years—a Saber and Lancer, identifiable by the red-on-green of their combat suits under their Devices—had each claimed one area, and were moving in arching blurs against multiple simulated enemies who looked a good deal more competent than the martial-arts projections Rei had been forced to battle with in his last months at Grandcrest. On the third field, two third years in impressive full-body CADs were sparring so ferociously it took Rei a moment to make out the heavy axe and sword-and-shield of a Mauler and Phalanx.

And on the edge of the fourth field—the one closest to the door Jetson led Rei through now—Aria stood waiting, her red hair already in her fighting bun, Hippolyta's bands gleaming green from where she had her hands on her hips as she watched them enter.

"Hey," she said cheerfully, like nothing at all was strange about her appearance. "Glad to see you haven't been shanked yet."

Rei, for his part, could only mouth at the air as he gaped at her, not comprehending. How in the MIND's name had she managed to pull *this* off? To convince Reese to give her permission…

"I remind you that Cadet Ward is being disciplined for violation of student code, Cadet Laurent," Warrant Officer Jetson spoke up firmly. "You are here to train, not banter. Keep your jokes for his release, if you would."

"Ah," Aria's face went a little red, and she saluted the man briefly. "Yes, sir. Sorry, sir."

Jetson nodded before looking to Rei. "As I said, you have until 2200. All of us observing are B- or A-Rank Users, and you have permission to request feedback and instruction if you desire it. Someone will tell you when your time is at an end."

Then, before Rei could thank the young man, he was walking away, moving to take an empty place along the closest wall so that four correctional officers in total now stood to watch the training silently.

Deciding he was being left to his own devices, Rei hurried over to Aria.

"What you are *doing* here?" he asked in as quick a whisper as he could, not wanting to be berated for delaying. "How did you get Reese to give you permission?"

Aria's flush of embarrassment hadn't quite left her cheeks, but she managed a mischievous smile all the same. "Not telling. Girl's got to have her secrets."

"You sold your soul, didn't you? There's no other explanation."

Aria sniggered. "Sure. Let's go with that. Now come on. You're gonna get me yelled at again."

Indeed, despite the brevity of their exchange, Rei could tell every eye of the observing officers—including Jetson's—was trained on them in disapproval.

"Do you have field control?"

Aria nodded, and with a flash of her NOED the plating under their feet glowed white, then lifted a yard off the ground.

"Standard FDA?" she asked as a small menu of options scrolled over her frame.

"Yeah. I get the feeling our spectators won't be pleased if we try anything fancy."

Aria nodded, making a few quick selections. "I'm very likely a little out of favors after this, so that's probably a good call."

Behind her Rei saw a red starting circle begin to glow against the white of the solid hologram under their feet, but he was too busy frowning at her to notice, voicing his question just as the NOED vanished from her eyes.

"Aria… Seriously… What did you do?"

Aria's smile fell a little as she met his gaze, and she looked to be considering saying something.

Unfortunately, however, that was when they clearly reached the limits of the correctional officers' patience.

"You two!" Jetson barked. "If you're going to do nothing more than stand around talking all night, I'll have you both removed and Ward's training privileges revoked for the rest of his brigging!"

Rei and Aria both jumped, stepping away from each other at once.

"Don't worry about it," she answered him in a hiss. "It's not a big deal."

Then she turned and jogged to her starting position, forcing Rei to do the same, leaving him less than satisfied as he followed her retreating back over his shoulder.

Rei was pretty sure, after the first couple of bouts, that he'd done a decent job of alleviating some of Jetson's and the other officer's confusion as to why he—of all the first years—had earned himself the coveted position of Aria Laurent's training partner. It wasn't like he miraculously managed to land his first blow on her that evening, or anything of the sort. As his specs improved he felt like he was getting closer to forcing her to use Third Eye again, but he was still a ways from that yet. Rather, it was more the struggle *Aria* had in taking him down that Rei thought might earn him at least some measure of approval from the observers.

Phalanxes—even prodigies—were not built for speed. Their Cognition was excellent, coupling marvelously with the innate Defense value of their Devices, but if Aria could be called lacking in an area it was her ability to end a fight with a faster opponent. Rei, of course, was *not* faster, but he was fast enough, and it was—after all—how quick he was in *other* ways that had proven the challenge for her, that had made her fight to keep him as her partner that day in the hospital.

She'll change her pattern now.

The thought flashed across his mind even as Hippolyta's spear came a hair's breadth from gutting him. Rei leapt back, keeping an eye on Aria's right leg. On cue his NOED flashed red around the limb as the kick came at his face, but it wasn't this blow that worried him as he bent away from it. The last two times she'd used this combination of moves, Aria had followed up by turning the momentum into a twisting lunge straight for his abdomen. He'd deflected both attempts, having seen this exact pattern before in their recent sessions, but this time he suspected a variation.

Sure enough, instead of a lancing strike, Aria powered forward with her shield shouldered, looking to slam him further back.

Rei sidestepped, dodging the devastating power of the charge by inches. He punched at Aria's exposed shoulder, but unsurprisingly the shield was already being repositioned even as he drew his arm back, and Shido's claws bounced harmlessly off the red-and-gold steel. In close proximity Aria had lost her reach advantage, and so she ducked and swept at his legs with her spear, trying to knock him off balance. Rei sprung back to flip onto his left hand, simultaneously clearing the weapon and putting some distance between them again as he finished the somersault to land on his feet. He would have preferred to stay close, obviously, but if he'd jumped straight over the sweep Aria would have caught him with the shield in midair, just as she had numerous times before.

The spear wasn't far behind him, and Rei was forced to dodge and weave as he kept his arms up to defend his face, his D1 Speed finally enough to avoid some of Aria's attacks. Quickly, though, she drove him back, and before he knew it Rei was being herded around the outside edge of the field, unable to stand his ground for more than a second under the barrage of blows. Still, he waited, expecting her to go for a wide sweep at his left side in an attempt to slam him into the perimeter wall, which would undoubtedly win her the fight shortly after.

He was surprised, therefore, when the finishing blow came from head-on.

The cut swept up from below, the spear blade arching from Aria's shins to try and catch him low, where his guard was lacking. Rei barely managed to dodge out of the way, waiting for the twist that would bring the spear around from the side. Instead, however, as the weapon curved up and missed, Aria shifted and spun into the blow, and Rei thought he caught an odd movement of her hand along the shaft of the spear.

That was only an instant before the bottom of the haft, the blunt end of the solid steel rod, caught him squarely under the chin as it ripped up in the exact same arc the blade had taken.

Rei was glad for his steadily improved reactive shielding, because otherwise he was pretty sure he would have bitten half his tongue off. As it was the weight of the hit lifted him clear off his feet, almost straight up in the air as his head snapped back, and he didn't have a moment to register the red script that announced whatever injuries he'd sustained when a crushing force took him in the abdomen. He realized—through a rapid muddling of his thoughts as his neuroline adjusted his cognitive function in response to what had to be a simulated concussion—that Aria had followed up this successful attack by backhanding him with her shield even as he'd been in midair.

The result, of course, was Rei flying backwards, ricocheting off the curve of the invisible wall inside which they'd been dancing around, then landing to tumble once, twice, three times over the projected white of the floor.

Through the haze of the concussion Rei scrambled to get to his feet, but even as he managed it a blur of green light told him it would be too late. He was actually able to dodge the first follow-up blow and deflect the second, but his limitations failed him when he was too slow to see the shield swing around at him low. The edge of the heavy steel caught along the outside of the knee, and this time he *did* make out the injury notification as the leg erupted in pain.

Right femoral fracturing registered.
Right knee soft-tissue damage registered.
Applying appropriate physiological restrictions.

Rei felt his leg go mostly limp, but it was irrelevant given the fact that he was already falling. Indeed, he hit the ground hard, but the impact wasn't fractionally as painful as Aria's shield fell after him, slamming into his chest even as he bounced off the field floor.

Mercifully, the match ended there.

"Fatal Damage Accrued. Winner: Aria Laurent."

"Ugh!" Rei coughed, rolling around on the ground for a few seconds and clutching at his heart until the simulated pain subsided. "You—*urk*—you always go for the chest. My poor ribs are—*cough*—actually going to break, one day."

"I doubt it," Aria said with a snort, offering him the end of Hippolyta's spear. "Every week you get a little faster. I'm not going to be able to catch you at *all*, pretty soon."

"Just keep surprising me, and you won't have any trouble." Rei found his breath again, and eyed the blade of her Device warily before grabbing hold of the haft and allowing himself to be hauled up. Once he was standing, he rubbed at his chin pointedly. "That up-cut with the butt of your spear was excellent. Totally blindsided me."

"Variety is key against you, I'm learning." Aria grinned. "But thanks. Lieutenant Imala has been pushing her spear-using Phalanx to take advantage of the fact that we have reach to play with."

"Ah, so *that's* what happened…" Rei said with a nod, recalling the odd shift he'd seen in her Device before it had clocked him in the jaw. "You slid your grip up as it spun, so the range changed on me. Damn… Your sub-instructor is good."

"Really good. She sometimes takes three of us on at a time. We've never won, and she doesn't even bother with a full-call."

They chatted like that for a little while, giving themselves a brief reprieve to recover. Their bouts were getting longer and longer, with Rei typically not letting Aria take him down in less than a minute and a half anymore, and despite their earlier disapproval the observing officers seemed willing to turn a blind eye on reasonable conversation so long as it was between matches.

If anything, what was stranger was how every time they separated to start a new fight, Rei felt that same disappointing twinge he'd experienced when Viv had been the one to answer his request for coursework…

Despite his urgency, despite his feeling that every minute of training he could get in was going to count if he wanted to overcome whatever Dyrk Reese threw at him in the first round of the Intra-Schools, Rei could not find it in himself to care about these breaks they took. It had occurred to him, after their second or third bout, that this was the first time he'd actually gotten the chance to be alone with Aria. Maybe not in the true sense of the word—four observing staff and the other students hardly allowed for any real privacy—but it was the first time he'd stood on a field with just her, the first time they could count themselves to be doing something simply "together".

The concept pressed at his chest a little every time he considered it.

Eventually, of course, they always had to return to training, and in that the two of them were even more fervent than their chatting. Again and again Aria came after him, Hippolyta flashing and screaming, and again and again Rei dipped and dodged and smashed aside the advances with Shido's claws and steel plating. He always lost in the end, but never without giving a good showing of himself. Occasionally he even left Aria winded, and after some score of lost battles they both had opportunity to celebrate.

"Oh!" Aria exclaimed quietly as her NOED lit up where she sat across from him, both having taken to the floor to recover from their most recent exchange. "Endurance ranked up!"

"Cognition for me!" Rei told her just as enthusiastically, watching the script scroll across his vision telling him he'd hit D0.

As though forgetting her own excitement, Aria actually squealed at this news. "Rei! That's great! Your improvement rate is incredible! I'd trade you half my stats for whatever your Growth spec must be."

Rei laughed nervously, watching her scroll through what had to have been a Specification Request as she reviewed her new numbers.

He wasn't sure why he hadn't told Aria the secret behind Shido's upgrades. It wasn't that he didn't trust her. He did. Implicitly so, even—to a point that it alarmed him sometimes given they'd only *really* known each other a month. It wasn't that he didn't *want* to tell her, either. Again, he did.

But...

For some reason, the idea of giving Aria access to Shido's spec felt different than when he'd granted Catcher permissions, or even Viv. It simply didn't seem like something he should "just do", something he could just spill out when the opportunity presented itself. He was aware—intimately so, in fact—that there was no logic to this feeling, and had more than once tried to convince himself that sooner was probably better if he didn't want her getting to the point of asking him awkward questions down the line.

But, every time, he realized that if Aria was going to ask him those questions, she would have done so already.

This very fact, actually, was one of so many reasons why revealing Shido's specs to her felt... complicated. Even Catcher had pressed a little, had admitted curiosity in Shido's extraordinary rate of growth. As for Viv, had she not known from the start

Rei thought he could say with confidence that his best friend would have been the pushiest of them all, demanding to know the secret even if she had to threaten him at the end of Gemela's blades. That was simply her personality.

But with Aria... With Aria, it wasn't that she appeared not to care...

It was just that Rei felt like it had always been him, and him alone, she'd been curious about from the start.

Yes, it *had* been Shido's rapid improvement that had driven her to reach out to him, to join their merry little band, but it hadn't been the Device that had caught her eye. She'd said it herself, when they'd first talked, when she'd admitted the fact that she had had *fun* in their fight at Commencement. It was after their match that she'd started keeping tabs on his CAD-Rank, after their match that she'd found herself watching him carefully. They'd been sparring partners for a month now, and she'd had ample opportunity to grow bored of him, to trade him for a stronger pairing. Logan Grant himself had offered, right in front of Rei.

But she never had.

There was a small, pessimistic side of Rei that told him she could just be waiting. Aria was smart—*every* cadet at Galens was smart—and it was possible that she'd just deduced that a little patience would pay off in dividends if Rei and Shido continued to grow at the rate they were. It was possible she was just getting in on the ground floor, possible she'd conned him and Viv and Catcher from the start.

Pessimism, however, never held up long to the facts.

It was late evening. Only a few minutes until their hour and a half was up, in fact, Rei realized as he briefly pulled up his frame to check the time. Viv and Catcher would undoubtedly have claimed a field at East Center, as they had every afternoon for 6 weeks straight now, and Aria could have gone with them without issue, without going out of her way. They were both strong opponents, in their own right, and while they might not have been able to read and challenge her in the same way Rei did, they could certainly have provided enough of a trial to make up for the mere 2 nights without his presence.

And yet, despite that, here Aria was, having very obviously leapt through at least one substantial hoop only to break up her evening, limit her training time, and go through whatever other hassles she'd undoubtedly had to manage in order to be allowed the designation of "training partner" to a brigged cadet...

"What? Am I sweating that much?"

Rei blinked at Aria's question, then realized with a wash of embarrassment that he had been staring at her for some time now as he'd thought. She'd set Hippolyta's spear down to wipe at her forehead, grimacing when the back of her hand came back shiny and wet.

"N-no," Rei said with a quick shake of his head. "It's not that…" He considered his words, finding himself unable to look away from her as he did. Her hair was falling out of her bun, strands sticking to her cheeks and ears and face. Her Endurance was more than impressive—especially with this new upgrade—so she was breathing lightly, but all the same she was hunched over from the exhaustion that followed 90 minutes straight of intense combat. Her red-and-grey suit was damp, and riding up her legs and chest, and Rei thought her left arm might have been trembling a little from bearing her shield for so long. In short, she was a mess.

She was also beautiful.

"I'm just feeling lucky," Rei decided was the safest way to express himself, offering her as bright a smile as he could.

When she returned it, the pressing in his chest came back.

"You should! You're training into Speed and Cognition, right? If you keep developing that way, you're gonna be a terror of the field, Duels and squad-formats both!"

Rei chuckled and shook his head. "Not what I meant, dummy."

Aria looked confused. "Oh? Is getting brigged that much fun?"

"Getting brigged is no fun at all," Rei snorted. "My cell is a single shade of grey, I can't talk to anyone about anything but school, and in the *one* hour I spent locked up before training I got so bored I started actually enjoying working on Markus' paper on evolutionary deviation."

Aria gave a dramatic shiver. "Remind me never to get myself tossed in here, then. It sounds awful."

"It is," Rei chuckled. "But that's not why I'm feeling lucky." He eyed her a moment longer. "Can I ask you how you got Reese's permission, now?"

Once again, Aria's face fell a little. Rei had expected her to look hesitant, maybe even a little annoyed that he was pressing the issue.

Instead, though… Aria looked scared.

Rei was dumbfounded, and started backpedaling immediately. "It's okay if you don't want to! I've just felt like Reese hasn't been *your* biggest fan either. Which is probably my fault, too. So I was surprised, is all. But you don't—"

"I didn't get his permission."

Aria's quiet answer cut off his rambling, leaving Rei with his mouth open as he blinked at her. She wasn't looking at him, eyes on the white field between them, and had pulled Hippolyta's spear across her lap to thumb at the Device's haft nervously.

"You... didn't?" Rei finally asked, his confusion overpowering his concern. "But... Then how are you here?"

Aria held her answer for a moment, biting her bottom lip as though debating saying anything at all.

After a little bit, though, she finally lifted her gaze to him.

"If I told you a secret, could you keep it?"

Rei frowned. This was hardly a question he'd anticipated.

Still, the answer was simple enough.

"Yes."

There were no ifs, ands, or buts about it. He trusted Aria. He trusted her as much as he trusted anyone, Viv and Catcher included. His hesitation to reveal to her his own secret had nothing to do with faith, after all. If this was a chance to make sure she could trust *him* just as much, Rei would take it without pause.

What was more... He was certainly curious as to what sort of revelation could drive Aria to swear him to secrecy.

She nodded and managed a little bit of a smile, like she hadn't really expected any other answer. "Not even a pause. Could have guessed..." She took a breath, and seemed to be steeling herself. "I told you I never actually wanted to come to Galens, right? I'm glad I did!" she added quickly. "Really glad. Honest. But... It wasn't *my* dream, per se."

"Your mom's?" Rei asked, suspecting where the conversation was headed. Aria had never been keen about talking about her family. Though they'd questioned her a little bit—and by "they" Rei meant "Catcher"—she'd never really opened up more than she had that day in the mess hall, the afternoon after their first training session together.

Still, her reluctance to talk about the Laurents—particularly her parents—spoke plenty as to her feelings.

"My father's actually," Aria answered. "At least I think so. Not that he'd ever say as much, but between the two of them he's only the navigator. Mother is the engine, the one who gets things done."

"And they wanted you to come to Galens?"

She nodded. "We kind of have a history with the school. My father—Carmen—is a graduate of the Institute. His mother was before him, and my brother and sister are, too. It's… I guess you could call it 'tradition'? And one I honestly wanted noth-ing to do with."

"Can't blame you… I'd want to get away as well, I imagine…"

"Exactly. I had my eye on some schools in the inner systems. Even one of the top academies on Earth. It's not like I couldn't have made it in, either, but Mother wouldn't hear of it."

"Because of 'tradition'?" Rei asked, finding himself getting irritated.

"Well… Yes… But for other reasons, too…" Aria took a breath, and seemed to steel herself. "The most important of those being that Rama Guest is my uncle."

Rei, following this, could only gape.

It clicked, then, of course. He recalled, suddenly, that he had once been surprised that someone of Aria's caliber was at Galens. Even as one of the top schools of the Astra planets, the Institute didn't carry the weight of the academies in the Sol Sys-tem, like the Military College on Venus, or Annapolis on Earth. It made sense, too, how Aria had bypassed Reese's permission, because if he was honest with himself Rei knew full-well that the major wouldn't have let anyone—even the favorite of the first years—pry such a consent from his cold, dead hands.

And it *certainly* made sense why Aria would want to keep that kind of knowledge under lock and key.

"Whoa…" Rei finally managed to get out, and he couldn't help but look around them to make sure no one was nearby to overhear. They were the final two in the training chamber—the older cadets having been escorted away steadily over the last hour—and only Warrant Officer Jetson was left to supervise them from his wall some 20 yards away.

Looking back at Aria, Rei still dropped his voice. "Are you serious? The com-manding officer is your *uncle*?!"

"Yeah," Aria nodded, looking a little forlorn. "Don't get me wrong. He doesn't play favorite, or anything… Not really, at least. It's just… helpful to have him around, I guess you could say."

"Like when you need to go over your dickwad instructor's head about some-thing?" Rei suggested.

Aria managed a little bit of a grin at that. "Exactly. And when you need to figure out when your brigged partner's allotted training times are. Uncle Ra—the colonel—" she corrected herself quickly "—was my father's roommate when they were at school. All three years. After that they both served on the front lines. Not frequently together, but always in touch." She shrugged. "I didn't even realize he wasn't my *actual* uncle until Kalus told me when I was, like, eight or nine."

"Your bother?" Rei asked, more to give himself time to process than anything. She nodded.

Rei sat quiet a moment, thinking.

"I'm assuming you haven't told anyone else?" he asked eventually.

"Not a soul. Maddie knows, obviously, and I'm sure some of the higher officers have to be aware, but like I said: he doesn't really play favorites."

"Who's Maddie?"

"His chief assistant. Maddison Kent. She's really nice. My favorite person on campus." She managed a real smile at Rei, this time. "Don't worry. You're a close second."

Rei felt his ears grow hot, and was happy that his growing hair now covered them.

"Still… That's a big deal, Aria. If people found out—if the other cadets found out—a few people might call foul. Even for little stuff like this." He tapped the field between them pointedly. "Don't get me wrong, I'm really happy you're here—*really* happy—but you've got to be careful…"

Immediately Aria's face darkened.

"You don't think I *am* careful?" she demanded. "I just said you're the only person I've told. I *know* what people might think. It's one of the reasons I'm so *pissed* at my mother in the first place!"

"I'm not trying to call you out, I'm just—"

"No. Stop. I know." Aria looked suddenly regretful. "I'm sorry. I didn't mean to snap." She sighed. "I am careful. I really am. It was easy, over the summer. We each had our own suite to stay in so no one missed me when I would go visit. I never had reason to ask for anything, either, so there was nothing for me to worry about. Now, though…"

"You had the colonel give you permission to train with me," Rei finished for her, feeling suddenly guilty.

Aria shrugged. "That and a couple other favors here and there. Nothing major. Nothing related to school or training or anything. Just… satisfying curiosities, I guess?" She was eyeing him as she spoke, and Rei took the hint.

Him, he understood. She'd asked her uncle about him.

With a chill Rei couldn't help but wonder if the reason Aria had never asked him outright about Shido was because no one posed a question to which they already had the answer to…

"Ward. Laurent. It's 2200."

Together Rei and Aria looked around. Jetson was pushing himself off the wall to approach them, his face set into the impassive expression of a good soldier.

They were out of time.

"Recall," Rei muttered, and Shido vanished into its bands in a whirl of metal and blue vysetrium as Hippolyta's did the same around Aria's wrist. He got up first, offering her his hand to help her up, which she accepted gratefully.

Once she was on her feet, though, he didn't let go.

"Listen," he said quickly, meeting the brilliant green of her eyes again. *God* she was pretty, and looking at her made it hard for him to concentrate as he tried to be as concise as possible "Thank you… For telling me. For trusting me."

Aria's cheeks had gone a little pink, glancing down at their hands briefly, but she smiled. "You're my second favorite person on campus," she joked under her breath. "Why wouldn't I?"

To Rei, though, it was all anything but a joke.

"Aria…" Rei hesitated, practically feeling the warrant officer approaching behind him. "Do you know?"

He took her in as he asked the question, studying her expression, her eyes, her mouth, her cheeks. He took her in, seeking any indication of the truth, even if he was answered with falsity.

"Know what?"

The perplexion, printed against her slight smile, couldn't have fit more appropriately on the innocent faces of the paintings of angels Rei had seen in texts of long-dead old religions.

Still, he had to be sure.

"About Shido? Do you know?"

At this clarification, her eyes widened. It was minute, infinitesimal even, but Rei caught it.

When she answered, it was with an intensity he'd only seen her show off in combat.

"No. But I've got my suspicions…"

He nodded slowly. She had shared something so important with him, had divulged something that could make her school life hell, maybe even end her time at Galens altogether. He didn't believe she was lying to him now.

Which meant it was time he gave her the same gift.

"I'll show you," he said, dropping her hand and lowering his voice to a whisper as Jetson closed in on them. "Not tonight. Not while I'm brigged. Thursday, after I'm released."

Aria stared at him, clearly not having expected such a promise. Jetson, though, reached them before she could say anything more.

"Cadet Laurent, Ward's next training will be at 0600 tomorrow morning. If you intend to be there, I suggest you get back to your dorm before anyone questions why you're out so late."

Aria started, jerked out of her astonishment at the warrant officer's cool statement.

"Y-yes, sir!" she stammered, snapping him a salute. After a moment's hesitation she took two steps backwards, looking at Rei again in lingering surprise.

She had just turned around, making for a wider set of doors in the south wall of the chamber when Rei called after her.

"Aria!"

Aria looked back at him over her shoulder.

"Thanks. For coming… For everything."

It took a moment, but the smile he got back was worth Jetson glowering at him all the way back to his cell ten times over and then some.

CHAPTER 35

Aria indeed showed up the following morning despite the early hour, as she did the next evening. Their sparring was more subdued, their breaks shorter and their chatter somewhat less involved, the pair of them very clearly adjusting to each other a little after Aria's spilling of her secret and Rei's promising he would reveal his own. To his surprise, this atypical quiet between the two of them didn't bother him. There was a new weight to their relationship, Rei had realized, one he'd come to notice as he'd lain in his narrow bed after showering that first evening. As he'd stared at the darkness of the cell's ceiling—whose single light had, mercifully, been extinguished not long after he'd returned for the training chamber—he came to the understanding he *had* trusted Aria, before, and that she had very likely trusted him in kind.

But now that trust was manifesting itself, and as it became iron, so too did his confidence in it.

In spite of the extreme hours of their allotted time on the practice fields, Rei looked forward to Jetson's—or one of the other correctional officers'—arrivals more than anything during the 2 days he was confined to his cell. The solitude was bad enough—by dinner on Wednesday Rei was pretty sure he would have been glad for even a glimpse of *Logan Grant's* face—but the monotony was the truly frustrating part. After months spent in the company of friends submerging himself in the world of CAD-fighting and the intricate complexities of Devices and all their nuances, the muffled, eerie silence of his lockup was oppressing in a way Rei had had no way of preparing himself for. Even the volume of the feeds he kept running at all times other than when he slept could only be turned up so far, resulting in a dim, swallowing sort of soundlessness that made him feel small and claustrophobic. His assignments, in the end, were largely his only saving grace in these long periods between training and meals, giving him something to focus and think about.

Unfortunately for Rei, his knack for classwork backfired terribly, for once, when he not only finished his paper for Markus before his second night in the brig, but also completed everything Viv sent to him from the lectures he was missing.

With nothing left to distract himself with—and fighting again the urge to take a peek at the coding of his NOED—Rei turned to the feeds, deciding if he was going to have them on as background noise, he would just as well do to make something of them. On a whim he pulled up all the records on Dalek O'Rourke he could find, thinking he might glean something from the man who had been Galens' Intersystem champion. Regrettably, "the Gatebreaker" turned out to fight more like a Mauler than a Brawler, laying into his opponents with an obscene Strength and Endurance rather than leaning into the Speed and Offense specs most of his Type relied on. In the end, it had still been an educational study, and while he doubted he'd have opportunity to make much use of it, Rei couldn't help but marvel at the complex possibilities CADs had provided for their Users, even in the limited confines of an SCT Arena.

His second and final night in the lockup came and went, and Rei slept fitfully, his rest interrupted by dreams of a red-headed girl with her back to him, refusing to look his way even as he called out to her. Rei woke up to his NOED alarm at 0530 feeling distinctly unrefreshed, and had to fight off his fears as he showered clean of a cold sweat and changed into his combat suit in anticipation of being fetched for training. At 0545 his wall turned clear, and Rei found himself rather pleased when Sergeant Becker nodded at him from the other side of the glass as she gave the command that his cell be opened.

"Training time, Ward," she announced unnecessarily. "Your partner's already waiting, so hop to it."

Rei wasn't surprised at the buzz of excitement he experienced at the words, though he decided not to examine too closely if it was the opportunity to fight or the mention of Aria more acutely that had his heart pumping.

Down the hall, up the stairs, and into the fourth floor training area Becker led him with hardly a word. Stepping out into the light of the massive room, he was pleased to find it was only the two of them in the space, in addition to the familiar figure waiting for him with her hands on her hips, as seemed to be her habit.

"Morning," Rei said with a wave after the sergeant had given him the usual "you have an hour and a half" spiel before making for the closest wall to observe. "Ready to kick my ass up and down the field again?"

"More than ready," Aria answered, returning the gesture as she moved to where the starting position on her side of the field would show up. "It might be my last chance to embarrass you in front of an audience that isn't our class. Gotta take advantage of it."

"Pretty sure second and third years get preferred training hours, so could be a minute before you have any more witnesses…"

Aria shrugged. "That's fine. Need to warm up anyway."

Rei chuckled, stepping himself towards where he knew the red ring on his side of the area would project itself.

This was how their last two sessions had been as well. A quick hello, then straight to business. It had been nice, in its own way. It had kept the correction officers off their backs, and Rei had been less stressed about taking advantage of what time he had to prevent himself from slipping further behind. Shido had hit D6 only last night, in fact, which had made him feel a little less like he was still trailing the pack that was the first year class.

Today, though, was different, and Rei felt his cheer slip away a little as across from him Aria pulled up her NOED and started up the field.

Today was the day it was his turn to bear all, and—even through his conviction—the trepidation that had had Rei tossing in his sleep all night only clawed at him deeper now that he stood across from the source of his fear.

Aria, too, must have been feeling some measure of apprehension, because—despite the warmth of their initial greeting—they fought in near silence for a majority of the allotted time, only occasionally voicing feedback or congratulating one another on a particularly skillful exchange. The hour and a half slipped by—with Rei feeling like he would never be able to step foot on a field without hearing words "Winner: Aria Laurent" again—and steadily the other three fields filled up with older students. An additional officer escorted each individual—as well as the one second year who had a partner, today—and by the time Rei and Aria lined up for what was likely to be their final bout the audience they had been joking about was well and truly present.

"Oh, hold on!" Rei called out as his NOED flared into life unbidden before Aria could start the match.

…

Processing combat information.

…

Calculating.

…

Results:

Strength: Severely Lacking

Endurance: Lacking

Speed: Lacking

Cognition: Lacking

Offense: Lacking

Defense: Lacking

Growth: Not Applicable

…

Checking combat data acquisition.

…

Adequate data acquirement met.

Device initiating adjustments to:

Strength.

…

Adjustment complete.

Strength has been upgraded from Rank E9 to D0.

Rei almost whooped out loud, but thought better of it, glancing past the script to Becker and the other officers, who included Jetson, now. Aria, meanwhile, had paused with her NOED alight, and despite their subdued mood she looked like she was having a hard time containing her curiosity.

"What was it this time?" she asked after a second, giving in.

"Strength again!" Rei answered with a grin. "You can tell Viv I can officially bench more than the average three year-old!"

For a moment—just a moment—Aria beamed, appearing to forget for a second the weight of the day Rei knew she shared with him. It returned all too quickly, though, her face settling again into more of a forced smile, and she triggered the match before blinking away her NOED.

"Sparring bout," the field announced mechanically. "Cadet Aria Laurent versus Cadet Reidon Ward. Combatants at the ready…"

"Congrats," Aria told him, settling down into position. "Now let's see you do something with it."

Rei blinked at the challenge, considering it.

By the time the call to the start of the match came, he'd made his decision.

"Combatants... Fight."

The moment the red ring disappeared, Rei blasted towards Aria, launching into an aggressive offensive. He *was* typically the one to open combat between the two of them—Phalanxes were hardly built for initiating engagement, after all—but instead of relying on his Speed this time, Rei channeled his study of Dalek O'Rourke and barreled in straight and true. As he'd anticipated—or hoped, at least—he caught Aria as she prepared to defend his usually more-calculated assault. Her spear was up, set to strike the moment he gave her the opening, and her shield was hiked but loose, ready to adjust for whatever lateral shift he made in the initial salvo.

Instead, Rei crossed Shido's steel-plated sleeves and slammed straight into her defenses at full speed.

For what had to have been the first time ever, Aria let out an "*oomph*!" as the impact took her hard enough to steal her breath away. As he felt her left arm give under his weight, Rei knew he'd succeeded in taking her by surprise. He heard the shifting of steel against steel from below, and her entire body gave way as he drove her a step back, then another. This was a victory all on its own, and Rei felt an excited fire building in his gut as she ceded a third pace to his rush.

No... Not his gut, actually...

His... side?

Realization took Rei in a cold wash even as he looked down. From around the edge of her shield, Aria's *empty* right hand was gripping him by the ribs, fingers digging into his reactive field and body with terrifying strength. Rei's NOED flashed red, and he had only an instant to grant himself the briefest of thoughts.

Ah, shit.

With the wrenching pull and what felt like the force of a catapult, Aria flung him one-handed to the side, tossing him 20 feet across the floor as if he weighed nothing more than the cloth of his combat suit. He managed to adjust on the fly, tucking as he landed and rolling to come up on his knees, but a throbbing agony in his left side had him wincing and struggling to push himself up.

He didn't need the notification to tell him he'd suffered several cracked ribs.

"With her bare hand?" he muttered to no one in particular, glaring at Aria. "Are you kidding?"

Sure enough, she hadn't chased after him, having to pause and stoop to retrieve the spear she must have dropped not a moment after he'd initially impacted her. Armed once again, she met his eyes, then lowered herself into her favorite defensive stance, weapon lifted over the top lip of her shield, which she brought up to the bridge of her nose. Even without seeing her mouth Rei could tell she was smiling.

He snorted, supposing he could grant her a little amusement.

Then, steeling himself for the world of pain he knew was about to descend on him, he tried again.

Rei feigned going straight for the shield this time, though he had no intention of trying the same trick twice. If he had, there was no doubt he would have bounced off it like a wall, the same way Cadet Brawn had during the Team Battle training where Rei had earned himself this stint in the brig. Instead, as he came into range, he waited for the spear strike, reading Aria's posture. It came head-on in a blaze of red across his NOED, lancing straight forward like the waiting sting of a scorpion. Rei dropped under it, falling into a slide that had the steel of his greaves whining across the solid projection of the white field. He'd been aiming for Aria's legs, hoping to kick them out from under her, but the restrictions placed on him by his wounded side slowed his movements too much, thieving whatever chance of success he'd had.

Seeing him fall, Aria planted her shield. The uneven kiting of its base made an imperfect seal with the ground, but it was enough to cause Rei a jarring impact when he slammed into it with both steel-clad feet. Undeterred, he let his knees accept the collision, shoving himself up with both hands. His D0 Strength allowed the inhuman feat of launching himself upward from what was almost a seated position, using his planted feet as a pivot point. Again Aria's incredible Cognition saved her as she adjusted instantly to bring the shield up once more, blocking the clawed punch that had been aimed at her face. Rei found himself slamming into the steel a second time, on this occasion with the better half of his body, and he immediately felt the familiar drop and push of Aria's favorite throw. The smooth metal became a platter for his torso, and Rei knew he would be slung overhead in a heartbeat. Usually he would have let himself be tossed, would have done his best to correct his landing or roll to his feet in time to meet the follow-up assault.

This time, though, he decided to try holding on.

Only his left hand got around the edge of the shield before Aria shoved upwards on powerful legs. The result was an awkward snapping of his body off, but instead of flying away, Rei's grip held. There was another "*oomph*!" as Aria's arm was wrenched by the unexpected weight added to the throw, and while Rei slammed down uncomfortably onto his broken ribs, she was pulled to one knee right after him, her surprised expression distinct as their eyes met.

Without an instant to lose, Rei slashed at Aria's exposed face. She jerked back, only avoiding Shido's razored claws by what had to have been a thread, then cut at Rei's left arm with her spear, the limb still extended as it clutched the steel of the shield. Unable to let go in time, Hippolyta's blade dug deep into the defensive plating, cleaving halfway through flesh and bone, and through an explosion of pain Rei felt his fingers fail and give, releasing the Device. Aria shoved herself up and back, trying to put some space between them again, but Rei did his best to chase after her, scrambling to his feet to follow before she could regain her optimal range.

For nearly a minute more they exchanged near-constant blows. Between his ribs and ruined left arm Rei's offense was severely limited, but he stayed at it all the same. It was interesting, watching Aria's adjustment to this abrupt change in pacing, this aggressive assault. Despite his injuries he kept her on the defensive, never once managing to crack her walls again, but still pressing her in a way he'd never managed before. Rei decided, even as she fought, that he might take a page out of her book a little more often, from then on.

It would appear that variety *was* key, after all…

At least for a time.

WHAM!

Had Aria given him moment to, Rei might have screamed, then. He'd been too slow with his footwork, to focused on coming at her again and again and again. While it had certainly paid off in its own way, his weak Endurance had shown itself more quickly than usual, reaching the breaking point when mounting fatigue caused Rei to overstep as he swung a haymaker around at Aria's head. She ducked the wild blow, but at the same time punched down with her shield, slamming the heavy steel edge into the top of Rei's foot. Red notifications informed him of several shattered bones, and immediately his leg gave out under the shock of pain that lanced up his body all the way to his head. Staying crouched, Aria executed a low backspin that brought her a clean pace away, and finishing the turn she brought Hippolyta's spear around in a blur of green. The blade caught Rei in the side of the gut, carving clean through almost to the spine, and only Shido kept him from vomiting at the explosion of agony and nausea the injury triggered.

Fortunately, an opened abdomen coupled with shattered ribs, a broken foot, and a half-severed arm seemed to be enough for the system to call the match.

"Fatal Damage Accrued. Winner: Aria Laurent."

As the simulated wounds began to deaden, Rei gave himself leave to collapse all the way to the ground, sinking into the numbness and extremity confusion of the neural interruption. He rolled onto his back, breathing like the bellows, and was taken by surprise when a heavy *thud* told him Aria had done much the same nearby. Rolling his head as he continued to gasp in lungfuls of air, he found her seated only a few feet to his left, eyes closed as she leaned back on her hands, chest heaving from exertion.

"No... way," Rei struggled to get out between breaths. "Did I... finally... tire you out?"

At first all Aria seemed to be able to do was let out an eruptive laugh and a smile, still fighting to recover herself. With her Endurance, however, it wasn't more than 10 or 15 seconds before her heaving settled, and she started breathing a little more regularly.

"Yeah," she managed. "You could say that." She cracked an eye at him. "What the hell, Rei? What was that?"

Rei gave himself a few seconds, his own Endurance comically lagging in comparison.

"Change of... pace," he wheezed out eventually. "Did it... work?"

Aria nodded aggressively. "Definitely." She was breathing normally in record time. "I don't know if it compares to your regular style, but you took me by surprise."

"That was... the goal." Rei nodded in agreement, rolling his head forward and closing his eyes as the lights above began to spin. "You told me to... do something with my Strength."

"Well it worked. I think I could deal with it easily enough if I'd known it was coming, but if you can change up your pacing like that within a fight... Scary."

"I'll keep that in mind." Finally he felt like he was catching his breath. "Still didn't put a scratch on you, though."

There was a pause.

"You did, actually."

Rei's eyes flew open at once, and he looked around at Aria with a snap.

"What?!"

"Yeah." She was rubbing at her right cheek. "After you pulled me down by my shield when I tried to throw you. You slashed at my face, and Shido caught me here." She drew a line across the edge of her top lip. "It was shallow, but my mouth was killing me for most of that match."

Rei stared at her, hardly believing his ears.

Then, unable to contain himself, he *did* whoop, this time, punching at the air repeatedly with both hands in excitement.

"Cadet Ward!" Jetson yelled from the south wall. "Contain yourself!"

"Yes, sir!" Rei called back without looking at the officer, grinning like an fool at the ceiling. "Sorry, sir!"

"Idiot," Aria told him under her breath, but he could tell she, too, was smiling. "You're gonna get yourself brigged until next week if you do that again. And it's not like it's *that* big a deal."

"Lies," Rei snorted, looking around at her again. "We've been partners for a month. I've lost probably a half a *thousand* matches to you, at this point. And this is the *first* time I've landed a hit."

"A scratch," Aria corrected him, raising an eyebrow in warning. "I don't want to be hearing around the mess hall tomorrow that you took my head off or something."

"Still counts!" Rei said excitedly, not in the mood to be deterred.

Aria laughed at that and shrugged before going quiet again. After a few seconds of shared silence, Rei realized they'd just slipped back into their usual habits, if only for a minute. The weight had faded, even briefly, allowing them both to forget the shift that was happening between the two of them.

The scary, incredible shift.

Checking his NOED, Rei saw that it was only 2 minutes until 0730, the end of his allotted training period. With no time left for another bout, he decided it was the moment to set things in motion.

"I get released at 1800 today," he said quietly, looking to the ceiling again. "Same time you'll be getting out of squad-training. I'll meet you guys at the Arena, after."

"You want Viv and Catcher, there, too?"

As expected, Aria hadn't missed a beat as to what he was talking about.

Rei nodded. "Yeah. I think they'd want to be there, and—not to be dramatic— you're gonna need them to verify that I'm not pulling your leg."

"You could just tell me *now*, you know."

"I really couldn't." Rei shook his head before looking around at her again. "No time, and this isn't the place for it. Trust me on that, okay? You'll see."

Aria grumbled something unintelligible in response, then sighed. "Okay. Fine. I think I'm just impatient. It's been almost two and a half months since Commencement, you know? Give a girl a break."

Rei grinned. "It's worth it, I promise. You won't regret hanging out, after today."

I hope, he corrected himself privately, seeing again Aria's back as it had been turned away from him in his dreams. If he was honest with himself, he wasn't sure what to expect of the moment he finally shared Shido's secret with her. Viv had been explosive, while Catcher—oddly enough—had been fairly level-headed about it.

But Aria was different. Aria was a User of a caliber above. He *thought* he knew her, *thought* he could trust their relationship not to change after today, but he couldn't be sure of it.

"I've never regretted hanging out. Not once."

Rei blinked, pulled from his fears to find Aria looking at him intensely.

"Is that what you're afraid of?" she asked quietly, frowning a little. "That I'll be disappointed? That I'll leave? Whatever your secrets are, Rei, I'd like to think you could have a little more faith in me…"

Rei looked at her for a moment longer, taking Aria in carefully.

"I'm not afraid you'll be disappointed," he answered finally. "I… Honestly, I don't know what I'm afraid of. But I *like* spending time with you. Viv and Catcher do too. I guess… I don't know…" He grunted in frustration as words seemed to fail him. "I'm afraid to give you a reason to think of me as anything else than I am on my own. As me."

To his surprise, Aria cocked her head at him as she started to smile again. "You mean how someone might feel if they admitted to being let into a prestigious school not on their own accolades, but on their family's whims?"

Rei stared at her, registering her words. They hit him like a hammer, and he almost had to laugh at himself for not seeing it.

Here he was, afraid Aria would see him as someone different after today, when she most certainly could only have been suffering the same fears…

Rei chuckled. "Yeah… I guess so."

"Ward! Laurent! Time's up!"

Rei pulled himself into a sitting position as Aria looked around next to him. Becker was standing at the edge of the field at ease, watching them both expectantly.

"Guess that's it for prison-yard training," Rei grunted, getting to his feet as he recalled Shido. The moment the Device had withdrawn from his limbs he offered Aria a hand, and she took it as soon as Hippolyta, too, had returned to its red-gold-and-green bands. She got up with his help, rising to stand a good 4 inches taller than him.

And it was *her*, this time, who held firm to his fingers.

"I'm not going anywhere," she whispered, meeting his gaze intently as Rei felt his face warm. "I promise."

Then, finally, she let go, stepping by him to make for the main doors of the chamber.

"See you after squad-training."

Time—as it is wont to do—passed at a crawl for the rest of that day. What minimal breakfast Rei managed to get down offered hardly any distraction, arriving shortly after he'd had returned to his cell and showered, and he spent most of the morning fighting and failing to study more of O'Rourke's matches, unable to concentrate long enough to glean anything of use from the recordings. A-1's morning lectures, mercifully, provided some small diversion in the form of several assignments Viv pinged him with a little before noon, but even this work collectively took less than an hour after the two or three weak bites of lunch his stomach could tolerate. In the end, Rei was left to stare blankly at his feeds again. Between the grey monotony of his quiet cell and his mounting anticipation—and trepidation—that last half day passed with almost-sickening sluggishness, most of the time spent with him struggling *not* to dwell on his fear despite Aria's assurances.

For this reason, Rei was already dressed in uniform, his pad and combat suit tucked into the bag he had over one shoulder, when 1800 rolled around and the glass wall of his cell turned clear.

It was Jetson who was waiting for him, this time, and the young officer eyed Rei with what might have been amusement through the glass as he commanded the door to open. With the sound of a releasing vacuum it descended, the warrant officer addressing him at the same time.

"Cadet Ward, you've completed your assigned isolation time. I'm here to escort you out. You are to return to your normal academic schedule as soon as possible, and any class absences, tardiness, or missed assignments recorded from this point as being due to disciplinary measures will be marked on your record." Strangely, Jetson offered him a smile. "Basically: you're free, and everyone knows it, so starting now don't try to get out of anything by claiming you were brigged."

"Oh. Uh… Yes, sir," Rei answered, a little thrown by this shift in tone given the sergeant's typical formality.

Jetson didn't miss his confusion. "You're not a disciplinary charge anymore, cadet. Being a hardass is exhausting, so if you've served your time, I'm not gonna waste the energy." He jerked his head to indicate the hall to his right. "Come on. I'll show you to the Center lobby."

He actually waited, this time, for Rei to clear his cell door before they made for the stairs along the south side of the building. Rei didn't speak as he was led out, trailing behind the officer down to the first floor, then out of the Security Center's plain, polished cement backworks once more into the handsome front lobby. A Sergeant he didn't recognized was staffing the front desk, and she looked up questioningly as Jetson led Rei across the marble flooring towards the front doors.

"Cadet Ward: time served," he called over his shoulder to the woman, who nodded without a word and marked something on a wide pad floating against a lift-desk at her elbow. After that they reached the entrance, the heavy steel opening quietly at their approach, and Jetson motioned for Rei to pass through. "Try to stay out of trouble, cadet. Believe it or not, we don't *like* having repeat offenders."

It was Rei's turn to manage a grin, and he threw the man a quick salute. "Yes, sir. Will do my best, sir."

And then, turning, he stepped out into the warmth of the late afternoon, onto the stone path that led to the broad campus road just outside the building, hearing the doors slide shut at his back.

As strange as it was, the *sun* was the first thing Rei took notice of, feeling it play on his cheeks. He shifted his face to smile up into it, noting that he was likely catching the last rays of the day before the shadows of Castalon's towering skyscrapers reached the Institute from the west. It was odd to feel so pleased about something so small, but—though Rei had only been confined 2 days—there hadn't been a window or breeze to be found in those 48 hours. He felt some small measure of weight lift off his shoulders, and breathed a little easier as he turned east and started for the dark building whose flat plating shined and reflected in a hundred different ways in the very center of campus.

The Security Center had been built with easy access to the Institute as a whole in mind, so it didn't take him more than a few minutes to reach the Arena at a quick pace. By the time he made the gaping maw of the west entrance, it wasn't even 1815 yet, and so he was hardly surprised after climbing up the stairs out onto the viewing way to find the south end of the main floor still busy with some scores of first years who'd lingered after training had wrapped. At a glance Rei could tell Reese had already taken his leave, fortunately, and so it was more-casually than he might have otherwise that he made for the bend and the seating sections they always claimed on squad days.

"Oh! Check it out! The former convict!"

Approaching the end, Rei paused just as the walkway began to loop, looking down at the Arena floor. Sense, Kay, and Leron Joy were still in their combat suits, seated and stretching on the projection plating of the Team Battle field, though the bald Brawler was climbing to his feet.

"Hey," Rei greeted them, leaning over the rail to take in the trio. "I just got let out. Did I miss anything interesting?"

"Nah." Sense shook his head, approaching the 10-foot wall and shielding his face as the sun glared off the Arena's steel crown high above them. "Haven't you realized yet *you're* the sole source of quality entertainment in this place?"

"Hardy-har-har," Rei answered sarcastically, lifting his eyes to look over the other cadets scattered about the stadium. "Have you seen Aria and the others? I'm supposed to meet them here."

"Laurent was in the final match," Kay answered him with a smile and a wave. "Her and Catchwick. They're probably still in the locker room."

"Which means Viv, too," Rei finished, returning the hello. "Thanks. I'll just let them know I'm here, then."

He was in the middle of pulling up his NOED, planning to send them all a group message, when Leron Joy spoke up.

"You training with them for the Intra-Schools, Ward?"

The question was posed mildly, almost civilly, but looking past his frame Rei could see the tightness of the Saber's expression, the rigidity of the barely controlled irritation there.

"Who I train with isn't anyone's business but mine, man," he decided to answer just as evenly, typing out a quick "*I'm in the stands.*" with his left hand before sending the message off.

"It is when you're involving Laurent and Arada, *man*," Joy responded pointedly, dropping the façade to scowl in truth, now. "Don't know if you've been paying attention, but they're favorites to qualify."

"I've been paying attention," Ray said steadily, blinking his NOED away to meet the Saber's gaze. "And? So what?"

"So maybe you should consider the impact you could have on Galens' standing if some of our best first years don't have enough of a chance to get properly ready before Sectionals."

Rei would have rolled his eyes if he'd thought that would help the situation. Despite how nice it felt to be out of his bleak cell, he supposed it would have been a pipe dream to hope anything might have changed during his 2 days of confinement. "Sure thing. You go ahead and tell Aria Laurent who she should be spending her time with. I bet that'll go over reeeeally well, don't you?"

Joy's cheeks tightened as his jaw clenched in irritation. "You selfish son of a—"

"*Anyway*," Sense called loudly, cutting his friend off from where he was still looking up at Rei from the floor below. "Good to have you back, man. Bretz was almost in tears yesterday when he realized his favorite student wouldn't be showing up."

Rei snorted, taking the opportunity to ignore Joy as Kay worked to calm the Saber down. "That's an image I'll hold onto for a while. Was Reese the same?"

The Brawler chuckled dryly. "I'll spare your ego and choose not to answer."

"Thanks," Rei said with a laugh. "I don't know how much sparing you're doing, though, considering the major's the one who tossed me in the brig in the first place."

Sense frowned a little. "Yeah. Heard about that. What the hell happened?"

"Let's just say your third wheel isn't the only one to have a bone to pick with me, these days." Rei inclined his head in Joy's direction, which did nothing to help Kay's attempts to calm the cadet down. "As it happens, it transpires that Reese isn't a fan of mine."

Sense sighed, then made a face. "I'm sorry, man. With any luck the Intra-Schools will get people to shut the hell up, finally."

Rei looked at him curiously. "You think so?"

"Yeah," Sense nodded with a crooked grin. "I've got a good feeling about them, when it comes to you."

"Ah, well so long as you've got 'a good feeling', I guess I'm in good shape!" Rei laughed.

Before Sense could respond, though, Leron Joy had apparently had enough of Kay's shushing.

"If you get anywhere, it's gonna be on the backs of everyone who's helped you so far, Ward!" he half-shouted, half-snarled.

Fortunately for everyone involved, that was the exact moment Rei caught a flash of red hair appearing from one of the underwork entrances.

"If you say so, Joy. I guess the SCTs will have to decide that, won't they?" He nodded across the way. "There's my group. Maybe I'll catch you guys at the mess later."

It was almost fortunate that he didn't have the focus—or the energy—to rise to the Saber's idiotic indignation. As soon as he'd seen Aria, Rei's mind had whirred back to his reasoning for being there, and so he waved farewell to Sense and Kay and made his way around the south bend of the walkway. The stands, fortunately, had mostly emptied out as he'd been chatting, with the lingerers likely making down to the locker room to shower and change before heading to dinner. For this reason, Rei didn't have to point too high up into the stadium to indicate a solid block of empty seating once Aria, Viv, and Catcher had caught sight of him, all of them nodding their understanding together and starting to climb to meet him higher up.

Rei didn't jump up the white marble, this time, not wanting to catch more attention from the remaining first years than he already had with his mere presence. Instead, he took the stairs quickly, passing one section, then another, then a third. Halfway to the top he found a promising row, turning into it and marveling privately at the thought that such an ascent would have—not so long ago—left his legs aching and lungs burning.

Despite whatever anyone might say, despite Logan Grant's hostility, Dyrk Reese's distaste, and Leron Joy's irritation, Rei couldn't help but take pride in the fact that Shido had already very much transformed him into an altogether different person.

"You're alive!" Catcher exclaimed with feigned relief the moment they joined up, throwing his arms around Rei like a heart-stricken wife welcoming home a soldier. "Oh thank the *MIND*!"

"Get off me, jerk," Rei snorted, pushing the blond Saber off with a smile. "It's nice to see your face too."

Catcher grinned at him, yellow eyes bright, but a moment later he was shoved aside as Viv pushed by him to come to stand in front of Rei with a scowl marring her pretty features.

"I hope you realized you left me and Aria high and dry, getting locked up," she said crossing her arms. "We've been having to deal with this idiot—" she elbowed Catcher again for emphasis "—for two days without you."

"Wow, life must have been *so* hard for you," Rei teased. "Next time Reese throws me in a cell, I'll make sure to offer to trade places with you."

"You better," Viv said, a little too serious. Then, after a moment, her face softened.

"It wasn't too much of a pain?"

Rei shook his head. "Nah. The cell was kind of miserable, but other than that it was fine. Besides—" he glared around his best friend to the girl waiting behind her "—I had a frequent visitor."

Even after he addressed her, it took a moment before Aria met his eyes. For once, she wasn't flushed, looking—if anything—a little pale as she stood holding one elbow nervously. She was chewing on her bottom lip—which Rei was sure he would certainly have found adorable had her obvious apprehension not sent his own worries and fears back into overdrive. Viv, it appeared, noticed his shift at once, because after a second of studying his face with a furrowed brow she stepped closer and bent down to speak quietly into his ear.

"Are you sure about this? There's no rush, you know..."

Rei wasn't in the least bit surprised that she seemed to be aware of why it was he'd gathered them all together. He supposed there was always the chance Aria had explained what had been discussed in the Security Center training chamber, but Rei thought it more like she'd only said they would be meeting in the Arena, leaving out the rest of it so as to avoid proving questions. Viv, if anything, probably only had the clues set before her now, in that moment.

They were clearly more than enough.

"Yeah," Rei answered her quietly, ignoring Catcher's odd looks over her shoulder. "Yeah. It's time for her to know too."

Viv pulled back, appraising him a moment more.

Then—either because she saw his conviction or knew better than to argue when Rei's mind was made up—she nodded.

"Come on, you," she said to Catcher, reaching back to grab the Saber by the sleeve, hauling him past Rei quickly. Rei didn't turn to see where they went, but judging by Catcher's confused protests, Viv had only dragged him to the end of the row.

Leaving him alone, once again, with Aria.

Facing her now, Rei's mouth was dry. All the weight, all the doubt and concerns, bore down on him at once. Again he saw her back, saw her turned away from him, as she had been in his fitful dreams. Again he tasted that fear. In her face now, too, he could tell that she wasn't without her own worries, her own uncertainties, and all of a sudden he started to question if he was, in fact, ready for this.

His answer came from Aria herself.

She hadn't looked away from him, even as Viv had done her last diligence. She hadn't looked away, even as he stood sweating silently before her. Her green eyes watched him steadily despite her nervousness. She was taking him in, her forehead wrinkling a little in what might have been concern. He wondered what she saw, there, wondered which of his dreads she could make out.

Whatever they were, they seemed enough to spurn her into action, because suddenly she took two steps forward, halting now no more than a foot from him.

"Rei... It's okay. I'm not going anywhere."

The words, a repeat of the very promise she had made to him that morning, turned out to be exactly what Rei needed. The assurance settled into him, and like a key clicking into place he felt the latches of his hesitation open and fall away in slow succession. Taking a breath, then another, he lifted Shido's right band to his face, pulling his NOED as he did.

Rei didn't tell her not to shout. He didn't swear her to silence, didn't instruct her not to speak to anyone of the information he was about to share, or warn her of the potential repercussions if she did. He didn't say anything, in fact.

He just input commands to grant Aria viewing permission, then swiped them over to her in silence.

The script popped up in Aria's frame instantly, and she squinted a little as she took it in. Realizing what was expected of her, she accepted the allowances, then looked down at Shido's black-and-white steel, the glowing blue of its vysetrium bright in the fading light of the day. Rei watched, feeling like he couldn't have moved even if he'd wanted to, as the Specification Request scrolled up over Aria's green irises, her pupils flicking back and forth in quick succession as she read each line carefully.

Then, at last, she reached the bottom of the list.

As with Viv, as with Catcher, Aria froze. She didn't reread the line, didn't trace it again and again, as though unsure if she had taken it in correctly. Instead, she just stared, transfixed on what had to have been a single character, the one letter that popped out to anyone who had access to Rei's numbers.

S.

He said nothing. At his back he didn't even notice that Viv and Catcher, too, had gone quiet. Rei only lowered Shido, watching Aria stare in shock at his Growth Rank. Not counting Valera Dent, she was the third, now, that he had shared it with, but there was nothing less concerning or alarming about seeing someone register the truth of the situation, understanding the reality of Shido's true strength:

Potential that might very well be without limit.

Finally, at long last, Aria closed her frame with a slow blink, though she kept staring at the same spot she had before, like the text had been burned into her version. After another few seconds she turned, still gazing off at nothing, and eased herself unsteadily to the nearest cushioned seat. Once settled, she was quiet for a time yet.

Then she opened her mouth.

"Ooookay, then… *Wow…*"

That was all she said for nearly half a minute, her mouth and cheeks twitching as she obvious struggled to come to grips with Shido's specs. Eventually her face shifted up towards Rei—though she kept staring at the same spot, as if her mind couldn't quite let go of what it had seen—and asked the eternal first question.

"That's real, right?"

"It's real," Rei answered with simply.

Aria nodded slowly, pausing once more before speaking again. "And… it's been like that since your assignment?"

"Since day one."

Another nod, this time coupled with a second "*Wow…*"

The silence this time only held for 10 seconds or so. Then—with a sharp inhalation—Aria seemed to come to herself a little.

"Well I get why you would be worried about showing me," she got out with a strained smile, looking at Rei directly, this time. "That… That's a lot to trust someone with…"

"I told you already. That's not why I'm worried about…"

Aria managed a tight grin. "Well you *should* be. This is a big deal, Rei. A *really big deal.* Telling more people than already know is… well…"

"Necessary," Rei finished while she struggled to find the words. Before she could obviously insist that that was very much *not* the kind of statement she'd been trying to make, he pressed on. "For my own sake, Aria, it's necessary. We're too close. I don't mean that in a bad way, mind you. I just mean that there's no separating us anymore. You, me, Viv, Catcher. To pretend like everything is fine and normal, all while Shido grows like it has been… I would feel like the relationship I've developed with you guys—with *you*—" he couldn't help but make her distinct, even in some small way, "—would all be structured on a lie. For my own sake, it's necessary."

Aria had watched him carefully as he'd spoken, and when he was done it only took her a second or two before she nodded slowly. "I get that, I suppose… It's not like I didn't know *something* was going on, but this…" She shook her head in disbelief.

"*S*-Ranked Growth, Rei? I was betting you were A. I've heard it happens on occasion. But *S*?"

"It's a first," Rei admitted, feeling a little of her amazement himself. Despite the five months they'd had together, now, Shido still didn't seem quiet real to him if he thought too much about it. "At least according to Valera Dent."

"The chances of that…" Aria murmured, her gaze drifting while she considered. "I was one of the top assignees in the ISC, this year, Rei. After I developed Third Eye, I honestly probably became one of the top hundred in the galaxy, maybe fifty. The likelihood of that was astronomically enough, even with my family history. But *you…*" She blinked, then looked at him sharply. "Have you thought about what this means? Like *really* thought about it? Do you understand what Shido is going to become?"

At this last question, Rei felt his heart sink a little. This. *This* was what he had been afraid of. Aria had asked him what Shido was going to become. Shido. His CAD.

Aria, though, read him like a book.

His face must have fallen, because she narrowed her eyes at him, scrutinizing Rei so intensely she might have been trying to make out his thoughts. Something seemed to click with her after a moment, because her expression softened, and she even smiled again—with a bit less difficulty, this time.

"Let me rephrase: do you understand what *you* are going to *make* Shido become?"

Rei felt his jaw drop halfway open, catching himself in his surprise. Again, however, Aria didn't miss it, and she laughed.

"Ah. I get it. *That's* what you meant when you said you were worried about me seeing you as someone else." She contemplated him a little more, her face drifting back towards serious. A moment later she stood up, coming to stand in front of him again, even closer this time, like she wanted to make sure he could hear her every word. "Rei… As much as I would get flack for saying it from every instructor I've ever had: Shido is *not* a part of you. It's a tool. A learning one, sure, but at their core our Devices aren't anything more than weapons and armor we get to disguise as fashion accessories." She lifted Hippolyta in example, the CAD's green glowing over its red-and-gold. "You're being unfair—to both of us—if you think I'm ever going to think of you as anything but yourself. When I told you—" She paused, her gaze lifting briefly to where Viv and Catcher had to be waiting a ways behind Rei, and when she spoke again her voice was lower. "When I told you about the colonel, I was worried what you'd think of me. I was worried if it would change your opinion of me. It's why I've been… been quiet, since Tuesday night…"

Her face flushed a little, but Rei pretended he didn't notice as he nodded.

"I know. I'm really happy that you trusted me with that, but…" He smirked. "If it's unfair that I'm worried about *this*, then it's unfair that you were stressing about—"

"No." Aria cut him off. "Not it's not. I'm not going to go so far to claim that I *wanted* this situation with my uncle—with my family—but it's still something I had a say in. Something I've taken advantage of, if only in small ways. If someone was going to judge anyone, *you* should be judging *me*, not the other way around." She smiled again, and it was definitely starting to come easier, now, the warmth of it spreading through Rei's chest and into his limbs. "But—since you decided to show me that—" she glanced down at Shido "—I guess I was worried about nothing."

"You were," Rei assured her. "Your family pressured you, Aria. And it's not like you've needed help getting to where you are. You didn't want to come here. You would have been happier in the Sol System, right?"

Aria's smile turned crooked, and she shook her head. "No… No, I don't think so. I'm *glad* I came here, in the end. You and Viv and Catcher…" She hesitated, and something like sadness flashed briefly across her face. "I haven't had friends like you guys in a long time, Rei… Maybe ever. And now this." She looked down at Shido again. "I'm excited about this. I admit that, but not because you're something more, or less, or different. It's not *you* that's changed. CAD-assignment isn't arbitrary, or randomized. Our exam wasn't just to separate us into 'yes' and 'no' categories. We were assigned based on aptitude, based on potential. Shido shouldn't make you *you* in anyone's eyes." She was meeting his gaze steadily now, and Rei managed to keep himself only a little distracted by how close they were. "If anything, the fact that it has specs like that says more about the kind or person *you* are—and might become—than it says about your Device alone."

Though she'd spoken quietly, once she was done Rei felt like his ears were ringing. Far below, Sense, Kay, and Joy were the only three left in the Arena with them, still warming down after their matches, but the distant echo of the trio's conversation and occasional laughter was lost to him.

He had eyes only for Aria.

Like a vast weight had been lifted off his shoulders, Rei felt like he could have leapt off the marble seating and taken flight, then. He felt… hot. Energized. As though he'd been released from chains he'd only been partially aware of. His fears melted away, letting her words sink in as he took her in, and when he could let out a shaking exhalation Rei became aware of a distinct, almost-painful clawing in his chest.

Unbidden, he found himself lifting one hand to grip at the fabric of his jacket, over his heart.

"You're gonna be trouble for me," he muttered under his breath.

"What was that?" Aria asked with a faint smile.

"Nothing," Rei answered quickly. "Just… I'm happy. I think I was more worried than I realized, about all this…"

"About revealing to me that you're probably a unique case among every User to have ever lived, and that your CAD likely has the potential to become an engine of destruction of un*godly* proportions?" Aria cocked her head at him in feigned confusion. "Can't imagine what there was to be worried about…"

"Hey! I thought *I* was the one with potential!" Rei retorted with a mocking frown, crossing his arms and going for a pout. "Wasn't that the whole point of your speech?"

Aria laughed. "Sure was. But I didn't think calling *you* an 'engine of destruction' of *any* proportion would have come out right…"

Rei almost choked, and it was his turn to feel the heat of his face. "Yeah… Okay. Maybe not."

Aria continued to grin at him. After a few seconds, though, her expression shifted, her gaze sharpening.

"You didn't answer my question," she said. "You have thought about it, haven't you? Where you could take Shido?"

"Yeah…" Rei nodded unsteadily. "A lot. Like… a *lot*, a lot. I try not to, anymore, actually. It becomes hard to process."

"Of course it does," Aria said gently, and for a moment Rei thought she might reach out and touch him. Her hand twitched, but if she'd been considering anything she seemed to think better of it, because she only repeated herself. "Of course it does. All the Users I've ever heard of who've been assigned B-Ranked specs end up impressive, in one way or another. I can only imagine the As are the same. So you…" Her expression shifted into something between pained and excited. "You're kind of in your own class, aren't you?"

Rei snorted, gracing her with an uncertain smirk. "Are you trying to make me feel better? Cause if you are you should go back to telling me again how you'll never see me as anything thing less than *me*."

"Sorry!" Aria said quickly, realization dawning on her face. "Sorry! I just… I got caught up in it, I think…"

"It's okay," he assured her with a light laugh. "Trust me. I know the feeling. But yeah… I've thought about it. For days on end, especially after Shido started to grow. You might not believe it, but I started in the low Fs. Like… *really* low Fs."

"I definitely believe it." Aria nodded. "For a D6 most of your stats seem to average closer to E9, if you exclude your Growth Rank… If you *started* at F8, that means everything else must have been abysmal to being with. What did you start with? F3s? F4s?"

Rei made a face. "Try F0s. Almost unanimously across the board. But it's okay," he kept on quickly as Aria looked shocked. "It's okay. Shido grew fast, even just against simulations. By the time I got my letter from Galens, everything was a lot higher."

Despite his assurances, Aria's surprise only faded a little. "F0s… Seriously?"

"Seriously." Rei answering, waving her incredulity aside. "But it's *okay*. It didn't take too long for me to get some sense of what was happening. Maybe not as in-depth as I do now, but I had a basic grasp. If anything, to say I've only *thought* about it would be an understatement…" He sighed, recalling the constant state of astonishment he'd been in, in those early weeks. "Honestly, I don't want to brood over it anymore. If I did, I would start obsessing, and I can see that being a spiral I could take downwards really easily, really fast. So trust me. Trust that I've considered, okay?" He grinned a little. "Or at the very least trust that Valera Dent and the rest of the higher officers who know my specs are watching me close enough to make sure I don't go all 'evil ruler of the galaxy' all of a sudden, or anything."

Aria blinked. "Evil ruler of the… What now?"

Rei grimaced. "Nothing. Forget it. Something Catcher once said."

After a second of quiet, Aria giggled. "I'll have to tell him you're quoting him. He'll be way too pleased."

"Don't. You. Dare. Don't get him started."

"Or what? You'll go 'evil ruler of the galaxy' on me?"

"If you force my hand, you never know…"

Another pause, then the two of them burst out laughing together. Rei felt the last of his trepidation melt away. This was how it was supposed to be. This was all he could have hoped for. No more secrets. No more invisible chains.

No lingering on Shido's heavy truth.

As though it had been waiting patiently in the wings for him to take notice, Rei's stomach decided that was the moment to let him know with a rumble that his appetite had returned.

"Oh man…" he muttered, recalling how he'd only picked at his breakfast and lunch for nerves, that day. "Pseudo-tyrant or not, I'm still starving." He glanced to Aria. "Want to head to dinner?"

"Definitely," she answered brightly. As Rei turned to make the aisle, though, she stopped him with a word. "Wait."

He looked around at her again curiously. She was smiling at him, and there was something even warmer about her, now, something that seemed to have her glowing.

"Thanks," Aria said softly. "For telling me. I feel… It makes me happy, knowing a little more about you…"

Rei had to stop himself from snorting again. "If you think this 'a little', you're gonna be really disappointed when you find out that's all the fun and secrets I have to doll out."

"I don't believe you."

"Huh?" Rei frowned. She'd spoken so quietly, he hadn't quiet caught what she'd said.

"Nothing," Aria told him quickly, stepping forward and prodding his shoulder to get him going. "Now move it. You're not the only one who's hungry."

Rei didn't need telling twice, and together they made for the end of the row. Viv and Catcher had taken up the last seats by the stairs, and didn't bother hiding the fact that they'd clearly been waiting for them anxiously.

"So…" Catcher started up as soon as Rei and Aria reached them, looking between the pair. "Should we make up a cool ritual, or something? Like a 'welcome to the super-secret Rei-Is-a-Freaking-Monster club' party, maybe?"

"Oh, I want a party!" Aria exclaimed enthusiastically, sounding like she was only half-joking.

"Don't encourage him," Viv said with a sigh before looking at Rei, who was watching her blankly. "I had to tell him, sorry. He was starting to make up all kinds of stupid reasons why you two were chatting alone."

"Like wha—?" Aria started to ask, stepping around him to stand at his side.

"Nope. Not going there." Rei managed to cut Catcher off before he could answer, the wicked look that overtook the Saber's face making him think he could guess all too well what sort of debauchery might have been theorized. "*That's* how rumors get started. I've also barely eaten today, so I'm starving. You guys good to head to the mess?"

"Sure," Viv answered readily enough, pushing herself to her feet.

Catcher, on the other hand, looked distinctly disappointed. "What? That's it? No fanfare? No celebration?" He frowned at Rei. "This is a big deal, man!"

"So you guys keep telling me," Rei muttered, forcibly stopping himself from rubbing at his temples with thumb and forefinger. "Which—if you think about it—is all the more reason to *not* make a scene, wouldn't you say?"

Catcher looked unconvinced.

"Come on, pouty face," Viv told him placatingly. "You can have my dessert. How's that?"

"Deal," Catcher answered at once, bouncing up from his seat. He paused, though, just as he started to hitch his bag over his shoulder. "Oh… Wait. On second thought, scratch that. I'm gonna be skipping the sweets for a few days."

Rei gave him a funny look as he moved around the blond boy, deciding his stomach wouldn't survive waiting for anyone else to get moving.

"Why? You worried about your love handles, all of a sudden? Pretty sure there's no one in the *galaxy* in better shape than most Users…"

Catcher shook his head. "Nah. Just wanna stay clean for Monday. Figure a few days of salads and protein won't kill me."

Rei frowned, looking around to Viv and Aria. "What's happening Monday?"

"Oh, right, you wouldn't know," Aria said, looking apologetic. "Sorry. I should have told you."

"Told me what?"

It was Viv who answered, grinning at him evilly.

"Parameter testing. First thing Monday afternoon. Not even giving us part of the week to prep ourselves."

Rei's curse echoed so loudly, several cadets walking along the outside of the walls glanced up at the Arena's open crown in confusion.

ria didn't realize she'd paused, when the others started making down the steps. Her eyes were on the back of Rei's head, watching him descend as he grumbled in annoyance at the news. Only when Viv stopped and looked around at her, clearly a little worried, did Aria realize she hadn't moved from the end of the row.

"You okay?" Viv asked quietly, so that the boys down the stairs from her couldn't hear.

"What?" Aria flinched. "Oh… Yeah. Sorry."

She started after Viv at once, who lagged behind to let her catch up.

"You sure? I mean… When Rei showed *me*, I'm pretty sure I was semi-catatonic for a couple of days…"

Aria laughed discreetly at that. "No. No, I'm fine. Like I told him, I already knew *something* was up. Everyone does. How could they not? I just didn't expect… that."

"That," Viv repeated with a snort. "Yeah… You can't really, right? No one would expect *that*."

"No one," Aria agreed enthusiastically.

Ahead of them, Catcher and Rei had started up a conversation regarding something about the projection plating of the Arena floor, so Aria and Viv were content in trailing behind a little, choosing instead to chat about their training that day. It had been an intense one, with Reese laying into most everyone in the class over the course of the 3 hours of matches, and the two of them had even come head-to-head at one point. Despite all this, Aria found herself distracted as they spoke, having repeatedly to pull herself back to the topic at hand while Viv largely carried the conversation. More than once she caught herself looking at Rei again.

A tiny pulse of something warm, light and deep, pressed at her chest.

Absently, Aria lifted on hand, lightly touching the black fabric of her jacket just over her heart with the tips of her fingers.

You're gonna be trouble for me, too, she thought, echoing the realization for only her to hear.

CHAPTER 36

"Growth is the measurement by which we quantify your ability to survive."

General Shira Abel
Central Command, Earth
Annapolis Commencement Speech, 2465

Watching Sense tackle his final attempt at the Speed & Agility test was like taking in a completely different human than the one who'd run this exact course 10 weeks prior. Though Rei new the bald cadet had only climbed three ranks to D8 over the length of the first quarter, his CAD had evolved recently to encase his full legs, and he'd obviously developed a much better sense of his abilities since the start of term. Whereas Sense's speed and nimbleness had already seemed impressive before, he moved now with a grace that appeared even to impress Michael Bretz—hovering high above them as he administered the testing—because the sub-instructor nodded along steadily for almost all of the allotted 15 seconds.

Sense danced more than ran across the staggered form of the exam field, deftly handling the rise and fall of the hexagonal patterns that made up the projection like his feet had memorized the troublesome terrain. He jumped and flipped and spun with all four limbs, the black, rapidly moving discs vanishing one after the other after the other in quick succession to his swipes and kicks and strikes. There was never a pause in Sense's movement, never a hesitation or a hitch. Like water around rocks he flowed, claiming every target within reach of any limb as he did.

"Time!" Bretz bellowed from overhead. "Total: 37 discs! Up thirteen from your initial test, Senson! Excellent work!"

"Thank you, sir!" Sense called back with a casual salute to the man, already starting to jog off the field. Despite his increased speed and maneuverability, it looked to have been in Endurance where the Brawler had made the most improvement, because he didn't even appear winded. On the contrary, he'd barely broken a sweat as he stepped out of the parameter ring and off the raised field to trade grins and thumbs up with

Rei and Emily Gisham before taking to his assigned circle outside the ring.

"Emble!" Bretz was yelling. "On deck! And I want to see a better effort this time."

The only indication Tad Emble made that he had heard the chief warrant officer was a darkening of his face as he stood up. Rei, for his part, just couldn't bring himself to feel bad for the boy, and he watched the brown-haired Brawler step up onto the field with interest, barely noticing Bretz reset it. Emble's last count had only been 26. If he didn't make too much of an improvement this time around…

"Cadet. Call."

Emble called his Device, and a second later the red 5 appeared in front of his face. When the count hit 0, he was off in a blur.

Had Sense not just performed his feat, Rei was sure Emble's attempt would have been more impressive. In comparison, though, the slighter boy's movement and dance were stiffer, almost clunky. He swiped more than struck, jumped more than leapt, hurtled more than ran. The attempt, rather than focused and clean, appeared to be fueled more by desperation than focus, his pattern and movements unsteady and lacking.

It showed, in the end.

"Time!" Bretz's announcement matched the vanishing of the discs, the black circles blinking out of being just as Emble had been pouncing towards another group. "Total discs—" the Warrant officer didn't hide his frown "—25. Step off the field, Emble. We'll speak after all tests are complete."

The Brawler looked stricken. As he turned to do as instructed, recalling his CAD in the same motion, he seemed unable to keep his eyes from meeting Rei's. The two of them might not have been on the friendliest terms for obvious reasons, but Rei still tried not to be blatant with his elation on his face. 25! That meant Emble's top count was 26! If the adjustments Rei had planned for after his first two tries paid off…

"Ward! You're up!"

Rei might have seemed a little *too* enthusiastic as he leapt to his feet, because he could have sworn he heard Sense snigger. Ignoring his friend, he hurried onto the field and to the starting circle.

"Cadet. Call," came the order, and with a word Shido was around Rei's arms and legs, black steel gleaming over white as the Device's blue vysetrium glowed.

The countdown started, but Rei mostly ignored it, carefully studying the mapped directive his NOED had plotted out for him, highlighted in red. He could do it. He knew he could.

At 2, he settled down, planting the clawed toes of Shido's steel boots firmly.

At 0, he rocketed out of the starting circle like an arrow flying from its bow.

Four discs flashed out of being before he'd even reached the rising sweep of the pillars that partially circled the field to his right. He managed the climb at a sprint, downing another three as he did, then took a flying leap without pausing to launch himself in a massive arc through the air. It wasn't the highest jump he could have made, but was instead calculated meticulously to cross his path through as many of the shifting targets as possible as he rose and fell. With intricate precision born from a new D2 Cognition Rank—and two previous failed attempts—Rei twisted in midair and swiped out in perfect synchronization with every extremity. His only clue that he'd struck true came from the echoed *bzzts* of discs pixilating out, then twice more as he slashed with his claws and left leg before hitting the ground in a roll that brought him up barely a foot from the field perimeter. Not stopping, Rei launched himself forward, cutting left and right, then planted and pivoted to barrel straight at the staircase's final pillar once more. Reaching it—and taking another disc as he did—Rei leapt again, praying to the MIND his plan would work better this time. Ignoring the target zipping by to his left ear that had broken his focus on his last two attempts, Rei thought of nothing but his footing, willing his neuroline to concern itself only with the landing. He hit the pillar halfway up its height, some 6 feet from the uneven ground.

And this time, he didn't slip or slide as he shoved off again, keeping his momentum upward, arching out and away in a graceful backwards flip as his hands and feet struck out again.

"Time!" Bretz voices called 2 seconds later, just as Rei made his landing. "Total discs: 26! *Brilliant* improvement, Ward!"

Rei couldn't stop himself from grinning like a maniac while he got to his feet, hearing Sense and Gisham both whooping his triumph from the sidelines. He might still have been far behind either of them—Gisham had come in second with a still-impressive 35 discs—but he had nearly *tripled* his count of 9 from the first parameter test, *and* tied for last place. What's more, Warren had only scored 32 points.

Given that she looked about as sullen as Emble, sitting at the far end of their line of five circles outside the perimeter, Rei was pretty sure she, too, had realized it was only a matter of time before he caught up to her as well.

"Bravo, cadet."

Rei looked around, feeling the field start to sink beneath him. Michael Bretz was stepping off his floating disc nearby, and looked to be having trouble concealing a rather pleased expression.

"Pretty sure Captain Dent saw that as well," the chief warrant officer said, jerking his head over his shoulder in indication. "Caught her looking after I made the call. Excellent work. I'm glad to see my hopes for you haven't been wasted so far."

Rei's cheeks ached from smiling so hard. "Thank you, sir." He saluted, being careful of Shido's claws as they came close to his hairline. "Hasn't been an easy go of it."

"I know." Bretz looked a little more serious, and he studied Rei carefully for a moment. Them he leaned in, dropping his voice. "I'm aware of all the extra training hours you and your three suitemates are putting in. Keep at it. It won't just be the tail of the class you'll catch up to, at this rate."

Before Rei could say anything in reply—like correct the man on the fact that Aria didn't share a suite with him, Viv, and Catcher—Bretz had pulled back and spun about to address the rest of the Brawler group.

"Break, then prepare for Offense & Endurance!"

"Yes, sir!" the collective response came—even from Warren and Emble—and as one the Brawlers started to stand from their designated spots as the circles vanished beneath them.

Rei moved quickly off the projection plating so Bretz could begin setting up the second test, recalling Shido as he did. Sense and Gisham convened on him at once, grinning almost as broadly as he still had to be.

"That was *awesome!*" the bronze-skinned girl exclaimed enthusiastically. "We might have gotten more discs, but that was so *clean,* Ward! Did you miss a single target?!"

"There was one by that last pillar I think I could have gotten if I'd been given another try," Rei answered eagerly enough. "It messed me up on my first two runs, though, so I didn't go for it this time."

"Seriously badass, man," Sense agreed, snatching a trio of waters from a passing service drone and handing them out. "At this rate, if you haven't caught up to me by end of the calendar year, I'll be disappointed."

"Get ready to be let down, then," Rei lied with as straight a smile as he could manage, cracking the top of the drink to gulp it down.

The truth of it was that he had somewhat higher expectations of himself, if all went according to plan. He'd hit D7 over the weekend, with nice spikes in his Speed and Cognition bringing him to D3 and D2 respectively. He was hoping for another rank by the end of the week—or at least before his first Intra-School match—and he was due for a fourth evolution soon if Shido kept up its current pattern.

If he was being honest, Sense's level was one he hoped to surpass within 6 weeks or so, much less the entirety of the coming quarter.

The three of them spent the break chatting about the Speed & Agility course, as well as what their approaches were going to be for the Offense & Endurance test. Given his already-impressive score in the Defense assessment that would come last, this next exam was the one Rei had been most looking forward to. He'd maxed out at E5 last time, his Speed and Endurance failing him as he'd taken on the first opponent of that level. Now, however, Endurance alone was more than a full tier higher than it had been, and that was the spec that had seen the *least* improvement over the course of the last 9 weeks.

Strength. Offense. Speed… Every other relevant stat had made even greater leaps.

C0, Rei told himself as he swigged from the water again, setting his goal while Sense and Gisham talked about what changes they would see in the projected opponents at the higher Ds. Reaching C0 was a realistic goal if his adversaries were only defending, he thought, and would make him feel a little better about the upcoming SCTs if he could beat it…

C0, he told himself again, visualizing the black digits on grey, simulated clothing.

All too soon, their short break was over, and Bretz was calling them to attention again.

"Eyes forward!"

The moment they'd all snapped to face him—Rei, Sense, and Gisham standing a little separate from Warren and Emble—the sub-instructor started his review.

"You know the deal, but quick refresher: opponents start at F0 and go up in increments of five, two fights at each rank. They will alternate back and forth across the field, and won't attack. Only dodge and defend. Your job is to FDA as many as you can, with how fast you can manage it as a secondary factor. Attempt ends when any of them last more than thirty seconds. Any questions?" He didn't give anyone the chance to lift a hand. "Good! Order will be the simple reverse of the last test. "Ward, Emble, Senson, Warren, Gisham. Ward, you're on deck."

Glad that Shido was now at a point to allow him a full recovery after only their brief reprieve, Rei capped his water, tossed it to Sense when the Brawler held an offering hand out for it, and stepped onto the flat white field. Moving quickly he took up a position in the center of the wide circle, turning to face the black outline to the north of him, where he knew his first opponent would appear.

"Cadet. Call."

"Call," Rei echoed, and he felt himself lift fractionally on steel heels as Shido took form around his limbs again. Almost at once the counter started, and this time he watched it carefully, only looking through the transparent red numbers once the shape of the female projection appeared, her monotone grey broken up by the clear "F0" that labeled her chest in black.

The numbers hit 0, and Rei was pretty sure she was "dead" before the countdown had even faded away completely.

He didn't hesitate. Not in lancing at her. Not in plowing Shido's claws through her bare defenses to cleave her face into equal partitions. Not in whirling as the second opponent—the man, this time—manifested to the south. Rei thought it couldn't have been more than 10 or 11 seconds by the time the F5 woman appeared, and another 15 or so before the first E0 showed up. Within a minute he had cut them and the following E5s to ribbons, blasting past his previous record.

At last, the first D0 made her appearance.

This was new territory, and Rei felt the faintest hint of anxiety as he rocketed towards the projection, watching her bring her hands up, ready to defend. His concerns faded when she blocked his opening, clawed punch, only to be too slow to stop his left hand from grabbing her by the arm just below the shoulder. With a quick twisted and a violent heave Rei used the limb like a handle, putting all of his Strength to pulling the woman down and slam her as hard as he could to the ground. She bounced and convulsed, but when no FDA was announced Rei brought a foot down on her neck.

"Fatal Damage Accrued," he heard this time, and with a thrill knew he had—at the very least—surpassed himself.

Then Rei realized he'd wasted a second grinning at nothing, and he launched towards the D0 man.

It took a few moments more to down this opponent. Rei tried to replicate his last kill, but the man's thicker arm proved less conducive for grabbing hold of, and he couldn't get a good grip before the D0 smacked his hand away. The projection blocked another blow, then another before Rei changed tactics on the fly. Jabbing in a blurred thrust at the man's face with the claws, he read the sidestep intended to be a dodge. Rei's left leg swept around with a sharp twist of his body, flipping up the heel of the D0's weightbearing limb to bring him crashing to the floor. From there, a few seconds of ground-and-pound had the Arena speaking up again.

"Fatal Damage Accrued."

Rei didn't let himself get distracted this time. Leaping off the defeated man as the hologram depixilated, he barreled at the D5 who'd just materialized. He opened with a standard punch, testing his opponent, only to have the strike batted away like it had been nothing more than annoying. Gritting his teeth, Rei hunched and set himself.

Then he launched into a furious flurry of strikes that might well have made the Gatekeeper himself proud.

Quick and nimble as the D5 was, she wasn't fast enough to move completely out of the way, and couldn't back-peddle without breaking her defenses. 10 seconds passed, then 15. Finally, a dozen small wounds from near misses against the claws took their toll, and the woman failed to bring an arm down in time to block a low haymaker to the side of her chest. Steel cleaved open her shielding to cut into ribs and muscle like paper, biting through projected lung and heart. The D5 went rigid from simulated shock, and could do nothing to stop the steel-clad knuckles of Rei's left hand that collided with her face with all the force of a sledgehammer.

"Fatal Damage Accrued."

Rei wrenched Shido free and whirled, definitely a little winded now. Just the same, he bolted across the field, making his choice as the D5 man bent behind his hands, ready for the incoming volley.

Instead of throwing any kind of strike, though, Rei full-on tackled the projection around the waist.

They went to the ground together, tumbling over each other in a jumble of confused limbs, but Rei didn't let go. The D5 thrashed in his bear hug, and he realized he probably would have been dead had his opponent been armed—or even just been willing to attack him. Ignoring this twinge of guilt, Rei threw his body sideways and tossed the man over until he was on top of him.

When the D5 was struggling between him and the ground, Rei jerked Shido loose from where it was pinned under his opponent to deal three quick punches to the man's undefended side.

"Fatal Damage Accrued."

Rei staggered to his feet, *definitely* feeling the fatigue now. He turned as quickly as he could and ran at the C0 woman who stood waiting for him. With his arms starting to fade, he could tell the drawing back for his opening blow was sluggish.

It was rendered all the more useless when the C0 stepped *into* his range, rather than dancing away.

Rei was so surprised that he hesitated in his punch, nearly slamming into the woman before finally bringing the strike down. As close as she was now, though, he didn't have half the force he wanted behind his fist, and the C0 had little trouble deflecting the claws past her, leaving Rei to stumble sideways a step. He caught himself, then came in again, going low this time. The woman stepped back, and his first slash caught air, as did the spinning kick he turned the missed strike into. Within seconds Rei found himself chasing his opponent backward, the grey feet prancing below her like she was some professional acrobat. He didn't have a prayer of catching her, her Speed and Cognition simply out-performing him on every level. He ended up cursing his reach, cursing the lack of range Shido's form limited him with. If she'd wanted to—or been programed to, rather—the C0 could have run circles around him from 20 feet away, and he would have never gotten close enough no matter how hard he pushed himself.

He certainly still had a long way to go...

"Time!" Bretz's shout came in the same instant the woman blinked out of existence, marking the 30 second mark to the fight and the end of the attempt. "First C0 reached! Total time: 4:42.87! *Excellent* first run, Ward! I want to see that same effort on the next two!"

Breathing like the bellows, Rei didn't have the ability to do more than raise his hand in thanks as he took a moment to bend over his knees, gulping in air. Only when he heard the pat of bare feet on the field did he force himself to straighten, finding Emble making for the center of the ring with a determined look on his face. Deciding trying to catch the boy's eye was in no one's best interest, Rei took the shortest route out of the ring, then walked around the outside buffer zone as Bretz told Emble to call.

The other Types were about their own business, as ever, but it was fun to take a few seconds to see how the groups were faring. Most of the other fields were into the Offense & Endurance test, like the Brawlers, and Rei had a chance to glimpse Viv going at what he thought was the second C0 before he reached his ring and took a seat again. Looking to Emble, he found the cadet cleanly dispatching the first F5, moving on to make short work of the second, then the E0s and on.

Rei might have imagined it, but he rather thought the Brawler ended up having a harder time of the D5s than he had. Perhaps it was only that Emble was trying to be more careful—likely trying to make up for his blunder during his third attempt at the Speed & Agility course—but his strikes, as clean and calculated as they were, seemed forced, even a little rigid. He managed the tier in the end—taking out the D5 man via a heavy knee to the forehead after doubling him up with a punch to the gut—but as soon as he engaged the C0 woman Rei knew with a thrill that they were going to be a match in this test as well, if only for the first attempt. Sure enough, Emble's rigidity cost him, and despite being able to keep up with his opponent better than Rei had been, he still didn't manage to land any sort of finishing blow before his 30 seconds were up.

"Time! First C0 reached! Total time: 4:41.43! Not bad, Emble. Senson! Up you get!"

Perhaps in part due to Bretz's rather lacking praise, Emble looked a bit disheartened as he walked off the field, deliberately avoiding all eyes again. Rei couldn't blame him, of course. The Brawler had *technically* bested him with his faster time, but it was by less than 2 seconds, whereas Rei's first-quarter parameter testing had had him losing by a minute.

It would be interesting, too, to see how the rest of the attempts went...

Sense tore through the ranks in two-thirds the time either Rei or Emble did, then took down the two C0s in about 20 seconds each. Even *his* improved Endurance had him gasping for air when the first C5 showed up, though, and barely 10 seconds into his allotted 30 Sense's swings were wild and unfocused, costing him the tier. He wrapped at just over 4 minutes, though, and collapsed to his spot with a groan after giving Rei a weak grin of thanks for a congratulatory thumbs up.

Gisham, in the end, was the one who surprised them all.

"Time! First B0 reached! Total time: 5:04.98! *Great* job, cadet!"

She had *barely* managed it—just as she barely managed to make it back to her seat without crumpling from exhaustion—but it was still a well-deserved record. It had taken nearly a full minute for Gisham to take down the C5s—applying what had to have been an exceptional Speed spec to excellent use—and the B0 had outpaced her like she'd been nothing more than an annoying fly. As she half-sat, half-fell to her ring, Rei tried to catch her eye while he stood for his second attempt, but she was heaving in breaths from her back too desperately to take note of anything else.

The F0s fell for him without issue, as did the F5s, then the Es and D0s. He took a little more time with the D5s, this time, trying to pace himself, and he faced the man head-on rather than tackling him to the ground. It took some time, but Rei managed to down him with three claws to the heart in the end, and when he turned around to face the C0 woman he was a bit less exhausted then he'd been upon reaching her during his first attempt. He hated to think it, but maybe Emble had the right of it…

Still… Even with his reduced fatigue, the C0's Speed proved too much to overcome, and his run ended with Bretz's call once again.

"Time! First C0 reached! Total time: 4:56.05!"

The chief warrant officer pointedly made no address of the slower time, though he did raise a questioning eyebrow when Rei had caught his breath enough to lift his head from between his legs. Rei only shrugged, hoping his silent attempt to say "was worth a shot" got through, and Bretz offered no additional comment before he called for Emble.

Emble, this time, took things even slower. After tearing through to the D5s, he took nearly 30 seconds on each of them, dropping the pair so late in Rei's mental count he started to wonder both times if the boy was going to fail to even make the C0s this attempt. Emble managed it, though, and demonstrated his strategy when he launched himself at the C0 woman with everything he had, barreling into her so fast that even her superior Speed and Cognition failed to get her out of the way in time. A feigned jab at her face had the projection flinching back, and Emble took advantage to drive his other fist into an exposed thigh. Immediately the woman's agility reduced, leaving her limping as the simulation must have registered damage to the tissue and bone below her hip. She was left with little more than her blocking and deflection speed, which might have been enough had Emble not redoubled his assault, then, tearing at his opponent with a gatling flurry of blows that started to blur as they came. At the very tail end of his allotted time one punch finally got through, taking the woman squarely in the temple, and the call of "Fatal Damage Accrued" was echoed by a quiet hiss of "Yes!" from Camilla Warren.

She shut up quick, though, when Rei saw Sense give her a glare from where he sat to the girl's left.

On the field, Emble was out of gas. He managed a good sprint towards the second C0, but his fatigue—which had obviously built up fast with his newfound aggression—proved the end of him. The C0 man gave him no opportunity to limit his mobility, and as soon as the projection was out of reach Rei knew the fight was done.

Sure enough, Bretz's call came not long after.

"Time! Second C0 reached! Total time: 5:10.46! Good improvement, Emble! Let's see if we can't do the same a little faster, next time."

"Yes, sir!" the Brawler actually managed to wheeze out, looking all too pleased with himself. As he started moving off the field, he actually looked directly at Rei this time, smirking.

Rei stared him down until the Brawler had glanced away again, feeling an anger he'd only just begun getting over gutter, then blaze to life in his chest.

Two can play at that game, shithead, he thought quietly, making up his mind.

Sense managed to reach the second C5 this time, and after him Gisham shaved a few seconds off her run in reaching the B0s. It felt like too soon before Rei was walking across the field to take his starting position, calling Shido up at Bretz's command. The countdown started, and at 3 the first F0 materialized.

At 0… Rei jogged towards her.

There was a choking sound that probably came from the sub-instructor, as well as a laugh that might have been Gisham's, but Rei ignored them. It wasn't the first time he'd taken advantage of the parameter testing's design, and he very much doubted it would be the last. As expected, the F0 didn't move from her starting place in the black circle that marked where she'd materialized, watching him approach with eerie, unblinking grey eyes. When he reached her, Rei didn't pause to drive Shido straight into her chest, his Speed not even allowing her to dodge or drop her hands in time to block.

The moment FDA was announced, Rei turned and trotted over to the F0 man, taking him out in much the same way.

By the time he'd downed the E5s in a similar fashion—and with only minutely mounting difficulty—more than 4 minutes had passed. Rei could practically *feel* the chief warrant officer's eyes on him, and suspected that if this gamble didn't pay off in some way that he would get an earful come the end of the attempt. There was no changing things now, of course, but he *did* pick up his pace a little as the first D0 showed herself. He was still careful to conserve his energy dealing with her, on the other hand, overpowering her with the same grab-and-pull he'd used to deal with the D5 woman in his previous attempt. She went to the ground hard, dying to a steel boot crushing through her chest, and the D0 man fell much the same, with Rei careful to go for his *wrist* rather than his arm, this time. The D5s required a bit more intent, of course, but three chances were more than enough opportunity for Rei to learn from his successes and mistakes.

As well as those of others.

The moment FDA was announced for the second D5, Rei whirled and put every ounce of Speed and Endurance he'd been saving up into launching himself at the female C0. His approach must have been minutely different, this time, because she didn't dodge into his range, and instead hopped back a step away from him, batting away his testing slash at her face.

Rei, though, had done everything he could to stay as fresh as possible for this fight, and so it was with a different level of fire that he chased her down.

He didn't go for the launching, sweeping kill this time. Emulating Emble's tactic, he led the C0 back, waiting for the right moment, studying the pattern of her movement, of her retreat. When the opportunity came, Rei put just a bit more power into his forward lunge, gaining himself no more than 1 or 2 unexpected inches on the D0.

It was enough for Shido's middle claw—the longest of the three—to catch her trailing leg just above the knee as she stepped back once again.

The effect was immediate, even more-so than when Emble had managed the same trick. Rei must have severed the heavy quadriceps muscles of the woman's thighs, because the instant she tried to put weight on the limb it collapsed under her, bringing her to the ground. Rei was on her in a blink, and despite superior Defense and Strength specs the C0 only last a few seconds against razored steel, awkwardly immobilized as she was.

"Fatal Damage Accrued."

Rei whirled and sprinted full tilt across the field at the second C0. This was his chance, his one opportunity. That fight had taken its toll on him—chasing the projection around like that after what had to have been nearly 6 minutes of fighting—but it didn't matter. All he needed was a little more. Just a little longer.

In the back of his head he counted, closing in on the C0.

1 second. 2 seconds. 3.

He slashed, and his opponent sidestepped even as he batted aside the blow. Rei punched, and the projection dodged backward.

6 seconds. 7.

A kick, and another dodge. Rei could feel the threat of fatigue building in his arms as he slashed again.

12 seconds. 13. 14.

At last the pattern shifted, the C0 starting the backpedal with every striker.

18. 19. 20.

Rei chased, forcing himself to be patient, looking for the opportunity.

22. 23.

There.

The right time. The right moment. A back step that left the projection's right thigh exposed, if only for a half a breath. Shido slashed, and the man's thicker leg proved a disadvantage as the precise cut of the claw split even more muscle and tendon. Like an echo of the first C0 the man brought his ruined leg down as he finished his back-step, the limb immediately crumbling underneath him.

26. 27.

Rei lunged, leaping at the C0 even as he fell, desperately leading with Shido at grey eyes, taking the opening offered.

28. 29…

"Fatal Damage Accrued."

The projection flickered and faded on the end of the black claws. Rei was gasping again, heaving in air as he shoved himself to his feet. He pushed down the excitement, swallowed the elation. He wasn't done yet. Not yet. Some distance from him the grey woman had risen on the north starting point, the black "C5" contrasted against her chest. Gathering himself, Rei forced his legs to move, forced himself to take a step, then another, until he was running at the woman.

30 seconds later—and not even a hint of a landed blow to his name—Rei heard the merciful call of the attempt's end.

"Time!" Bretz yelled, and before him the woman blinked into nothingness. "First C5 reached! Total time: 6:47.82! Way to finish hard, Ward!"

Rei just barely managed to throw the man an almost-proper salute, grinning at the disgruntled smirk playing across the sub-instructor's face. He might not have been impressed by the *method* of the attempt, but he didn't seem too keen on arguing with the results.

Nor, clearly, was Bretz intent on cutting him any slack.

"You can gasp your lungs out off the field, cadet. Emble! You're up!"

Rei was still smiling when he passed the brown-haired Brawler, who'd finally come out of his shell of self-pity enough to glare in annoyed frustration as they crossed paths. Rei couldn't stop himself from mouthing a sarcastic "Good luck"—earning himself an even deeper glower—before stepping outside the perimeter and taking a seat in his ring. He didn't look around at Sense and Gisham this time—though he thought he could tell they were trying to catch his eye to shoot him silent congratulations. He was too focused on watching what was about to happen, too interested in seeing if Emble could rise to the challenge.

Almost unfortunately, just as the boy started to tear into the F5s, a familiar notice began to script itself across Rei's NOED.

...

Processing combat information.

...

Calculating.

...

Results:

Strength: Adequate

Endurance: Lacking

Speed: Adequate

Cognition: Adequate

Offense: Adequate

Defense: Adequate

Growth: Not Applicable

...

Checking combat data acquisition.

...

Adequate data acquirement met.

Device initiating adjustments to:

Endurance.

...

Adjustment complete.

Endurance has been upgraded from Rank E7 to E8.

With all the *more* reason to be grinning, now, Rei dismissed the upgrade notification in time to see Emble launch himself at the second D0 with a fervor. He wasn't proud of it, but Rei couldn't help but think the Brawler looked desperate again, his combat less clean than it had been in his second attempt.

Sure enough—in what appeared to be a fatal flaw—Emble once again showed a penchant for getting flustered all too easily.

"Time! First C0 reached! Total time: 5:05.75! I wanted to see more out of you, cadet!"

Emble, for his part, stood heaving with his Device-clad hands in fists at his sides, staring at the place the woman he'd been fighting had abruptly disappeared. He seemed not to hear Bretz's comment, nor the follow-up order to vacate the field, not even flinching until Sense passed him as he made for the center starting point. Only then did Emble whirl, his eyes finding Rei's, and the two of them stared each other down while the chief warrant officer started barking at the Brawler with increasing annoyance.

For a few seconds Rei wondered if Emble was going to lunge at him, and he pushed himself to his feet in preparation. Since being assigned Shido, he'd grown just over a quarter-inch a month—at least according to his regular checkups with Ameena Ashton—but his new five-foot-six-and-a-half frame, solid as it might be, still only came up to the livid cadet's mouth.

Just the same, he would have happily provided the fight Emble was looking for, if he'd been given the opportunity.

Then, though, the Brawler paled and looked away, hurrying off the field with his head lowered like a cowering animal.

"Keep your head, Ward."

The voice, steady and calm, was like cold water in Rei's ear, and he went rigid for a moment. When his body allowed him to move again, he looked around slowly, unsurprised to find the tall, short-haired woman standing just behind his shoulder, her brown eyes on him with something like an amused smile playing at synthetic lips beneath the black line of her prosthetic that made up half her face.

It had been some weeks since he'd spoken to Valera Dent directly. It wasn't so much that the captain had seemed to be going out of her way to avoid him, but rather that—since her pressing him to get stronger after the incident with Logan Grant— the Iron Bishop had treated him with the same hands-off approach she'd graced the rest of 1-A with, preferring to leave the direct teaching to her sub-instructors except in rare occasions. It had been nice, in a way. Between Shido's growth and evolution, his training with Aria, and his encounter with Mateus Selleck and the others, Rei thought he had enough jealous and curious eyes watching his every move.

He was always pleased to be addressed by the woman, but he didn't look forward to the mutterings and rumors that would start if Dent's personal interest in him was made any more obvious.

"You reached the C5s? Did I hear that right?" Dent's eye was alive with text as she stepped to stand beside his circle.

Rei swallowed, then nodded. Despite the fact that they'd talked several times, it still felt bizarre to be approached by "the Bishop" so directly.

"Yes, ma'am. The first one. Just now."

"Impressive. Up from… E5? *Very* impressive."

Rei wasn't sure what to say to this other than "Thank you, ma'am."

"Seems you took my advice to heart. I'm glad. How has training with Cadet Laurent been going?"

"Uh… Good, ma'am…" Rei hesitated, briefly wondering if he risked toeing a line before voicing his own question. "Are *all* the instructors aware of our pairing?"

Dent chuckled, and Rei thought he heard Sense slamming one body or another to the ground from where his test had started on the field. "We are aware of *every* pairing and grouping of *every* student, Ward. Not just yours. No need to feel so special. Squad-formats at Sectionals are taken very seriously. We like to know who plays well with who."

That made sense, Rei admitted privately, looking around to watch Sense's run. The Brawler was already into the Es, and didn't look to be slowing down.

Though Major Reese was the one in charge of the Intra-Schools, it *was* the captain who oversaw all levels of Galen's involvement in the SCT levels above that. It had been implied, when the upcoming tournament had been first announced, that the three squad-leaders would have their pick of teammates, but Rei supposed it was only logical Dent, Reese, and whatever assistants they had would want a say in the groups who would be representing the Institute beyond the walls of the school…

"Are you ready for next week?"

The question was easy and pleasant, as though Valera Dent was striking up a casual conversation with a friend. Her tone, however, did nothing to stop Rei from suspecting there was more interest in his answer than she was letting on.

"Yes, ma'am," he said firmly, watching Sense take down the first C0 with a punch-dagger to the throat. "I'm a little behind where I wanted to be, at this point, but I'll be in fighting shape by Monday."

Dent nodded slowly beside him, her own eyes on Sense's test. "Excellent. Initial pairings were made up Saturday. They'll be sent out soon. Do you have an inkling of how you'll deal with your first match?"

It was asked in that same light tone, but Rei froze, and he had to stop himself from looking up and around at the captain. Her choice of words had been… odd. An 'inkling'? As though to suggest he should already have an idea of how to handle the upcoming pairing? Rei would have bet his damn *CAD* there was more to this question than there appeared, more to be read between the lines.

He got a bad feeling he was—in the fairest way Valera Dent could manage—being warned about something.

"I… do," he got out eventually, lowering his voice a little. Sense was squaring off with the first C5, now. "My CAD-Rank might have caught up to the tail of the class, but my individual specs are still a ways behind. I'm operating under the impression my first match will be stronger than I am. Possibly *much* stronger than I am."

"Probably a good assumption," Dent said, and Rei saw her smile a little in the corner of his eye. "I caught a bit of your Speed & Agility test earlier. I'd say you've figured out where your strengths lie, as a User. Now it's just about taking advantage of them.

"Yes, ma'am. My Speed and Cognition have always been my stat leaders. If I can tap those properly, I can put myself on a more-even playing field."

"I like the way you think, Ward." Then Dent, too, lowered her voice. "Just don't forget what the name of you CAD means. Your tree's growing, but you have yet to form your first branch."

Rei frowned, and couldn't help but glance around at the Bishop, this time. She made no indication that she noticed, however, instead stepping away from him as Bretz called "Time!" and announced that Sense had reached the second C5. She intercepted the Brawler as he staggered off the field, and looked to be congratulating him and giving him a little feedback following his performance.

This left Rei with ample time and excuse—as Warren reached the starting point—to consider the brief exchange he'd just had.

He knew it. He *knew* it. If he wasn't overthinking things, Dyrk Reese was going to throw him a curveball as his first matching. Rei might have been improving fast, might have well surpassed Emble—and probably many others on the tail end of the first years—in *every* parameter test, now, but he still had a long ways to go before he thought he would feel confident enough to pair up against the likes of some of the others in their class. He found himself considering, trying to guess who he would set against, trying to figure out who would be sent to deliver Reese's message. There was Grant, obviously, but the two of them hadn't had much interaction since the morning after Rei had woken up in the hospital, and regardless he doubted the major would have been willing to be so apparently heavy-handed. Similarly, he discounted Aria, as well as Viv and Catcher for the same reasons. There were plenty of others as well, and Rei looked over his shoulder to where Mateus Selleck was sitting with his back to the Brawlers' Field 2, wondering if enough rumors about the bruises they'd all shown up to class with that day would be enough to spark suspicion if the two of *them* were paired up.

Then, though, Rei realized that the gap between someone like him and Selleck was no longer so wide that the Saber would prove a definitively overwhelming opponent…

With that thought, the realization clicked, and Rei groaned.

As much as he looked forward to sparring with Aria every evening, he was pretty sure he was going to have to ask Catcher to spare some time for him, this week…

Warren, in the end, only reached the first C5, just like Rei, but did so more than two and half minutes faster than he had. Still, she didn't look too pleased with herself, and was gritting her teeth as she ceded the floor to Gisham, who proceeded to cut another few seconds off her run in reaching the first B0. Dent had lingered to give fair feedback to both of them, and stayed to join Bretz on the field after the chief warrant officer had called them to break. Rei was watching the back of her head, wondering what a "normal" level of help was for higher officers to provide their students, when someone punched him in the arm.

"Owe," he grunted, looking around at Sense and Gisham's grinning faces. "That hurt. Reactive shielding doesn't do shit for that kind of thing, and you know it."

Sense snorted. "Says the guy who's probably about to hit the S-ranks on this next test. Pretty sure your pain tolerance is gonna be a thing of legend, after today."

"You say that like it isn't already," Gisham said with a jealous expression, looking Rei up and down. She was still sweating from her attempt, water bottle back in hand. "What did you hit last time? C2, right? Unbelievable…"

"I'll trade it for my childhood back?" Rei joked, lifting and showing off one scared arm to make his point. "Forget *my* testing, though. B0! That's amazing!"

Sense jumped immediately in on fawning over the girl, and Gisham was blushing and glowing within seconds, seemingly happy to be the one basking in the attention for once. That suited Rei just fine. While he *was* looking forward to seeing how far he could push himself on the Fortitude test, he was also nervous. Not of the pain, of course. He could deal with the pain—though Warren's green face from where she sat silently with Emble didn't help. More so, Rei was concerned much for the same reasons he'd felt a little relief once Valera Dent had walked away from him.

He really, *really*, didn't need any more rumors flying around.

Still… That didn't mean he was willing to cut himself short on seeing how far he'd come.

"Okay! Everyone pick a space! Let's go!"

Bretz's shouted order marked the end of the break, which came almost 2 full minutes after the Sabers, Lancers, *and* Duelists had started their own Fortitude assessment all around the Brawlers. Rei would have felt bad—given that the delay in wrapping the Offense & Endurance test was very much *his* fault, and his alone—but he was too caught up in the clenching of his stomach as the group as a whole started onto the field.

He might be able to handle the pain, but that didn't mean he had to look forward to it.

Emble and Warren crossed the field together quickly, clearly trying to put some space between them and the other three. As a result, Rei, Sense, and Gisham were left with the trio of closest standing markers, the double layer of red rings against the white of the field. Despite the shade of lighting being the *exact* same as the starting circle for every SCT matchup, Rei couldn't help but think the glow felt ominous as he approached his spot after offering the other two a tense "Good luck" when they split to either side of him.

He'd just settled into a set stance, shaking his arms and neck loose to prepare himself, when he found Bretz approaching him.

"Ward," the man said so that only Rei could hear him once he was close enough. "The captain wants me to pull you at C5, if you make it that far."

"What?!" Rei hissed angrily, gaping at his sub-instructor. "No! How is that fair?!"

"Priority has to be given to your class as a whole over you," Bretz said automatically, like he was repeating an answer he'd been fed, and he looked none-too-pleased with the situation himself. "Dent says you didn't realize you were screaming by the end, last time?"

"Oh…" Rei's indignation dried up all at once, but came back as resolution a moment later. "Is that the only reason? If I can keep my mouth shut, will you let me keep going?"

"*Can* you keep your mouth shut?" Bretz asked intently.

Rei hesitated. Keeping his focus would mean not pulling away from the torture of the test, not curling into himself. He would feel *everything* this time.

Then again, it wasn't like he hadn't experienced it all before.

"Yes," he said finally, hoping to convey his conviction as he met the chief warrant officer's gaze. "Yes. I can. I swear."

Bretz frowned, studying him closely. Then his NOED flashed to life, and he looked over his shoulder to where the captain stood scanning the other Brawlers from the center of the field. At once Dent's own eyes blazed, and she paused as she read the message. Turning her head to take in Rei waiting by the sub-instructor, she seemed to be contemplating him, looking him up and down like she was trying to read what his body was capable of.

Then she held up one hand, forming an "O" shape with her fingers, and nodded.

"Okay," Bretz said, turning his attention on Rei again as the his frame faded from his retinas. "B0. That's the best you're going to get, cadet, so I suggest you take it."

"Yes, sir," Rei said at once with a quick salute. The B-Ranks had been his goal anyway, so he wasn't about to push his luck if Dent would at least grant him that.

"Okay!" Bretz roared as soon as they were done talking, pulling away from Rei to look around at the group as a whole. "I doubt you've forgotten this particular drill, but quick recap of the Fortitude test: pain and sensory stimulation will start at an F0 Offense level, and increase a rank at a time from there. Muscular load will do the same. Attempt ends when you fall, or—" he smirked at Rei for a moment "—you take a knee. Questions?" Again he didn't wait for any hands, his NOED popping up in his eyes again. "Excellent. In that case… Here we go!"

The countdown appeared, flicking down in front or Rei's eyes. When it hit 0, the chief warrant officer shouted once more.

"F0!"

Contrary to what Dent and Bretz might have been expecting, Rei didn't immediately end the test as the prickling started teasing the ends of his fingers. He let it go for some time, in fact, passing through the Fs until he finally felt the pressure of gravity start to weigh on him in the low Es. Another couple of minutes he let the sensations press on and over him, waiting until the pain began just after D0, this time.

Only when the irritating, snipping bite of the simulation started did Rei drop, earning himself nothing more than an exasperated look from Bretz and a crooked smile from Dent. The feelings faded almost at once, and Rei breathed easier.

Good warmup, he thought, seating himself more comfortably to wait for the others to finish.

He was, therefore, a little amused when Sense dropped to one knee not a rank after him, following closely by Gisham.

Rei gave them each a questioning look, but the pair only answered with matching shrugs that said something like "Hey… If it works for you…", and he had to stop himself from laughing out loud. Bretz looked a little peeved, but seemed to know better than to say anything by now, but Captain Dent was looking between the three of them curiously, her brown eyes lingering a while on Sense and Gisham each.

Whatever she was thinking, Rei wasn't sure he wanted to know, in that moment.

Warren and Emble, predictably, appeared to want nothing to do with the shared strategy of the rest of the group, holding out for as long as they could. Warren fell first, giving a decent show of herself by reaching D8—three ranks higher than her initial results a quarter prior, if Rei remembered properly—while Emble stayed standing nearly a full minute more to reach a very respectable C1—*four* ranks higher than his already-impressive D7 record. As with the first test, however, the boy looked drained after he collapsed to the floor, and Rei knew that was the extent of his body, for the day.

He almost wished Emble would take a knee for the next two attempts, if only to spare the rest of them the discomfort of watching the Brawler force himself through the agony.

"Second attempt!" Bretz yelled after their short break, shooting Rei, Sense, and Gisham *all* an exasperated look this time, like he thought he knew what was coming. "Thirty seconds! On your feet."

Rei obeyed at once, as did the two on either side of him.

And all three of them took a knee together again the moment the countdown reached "0".

Bretz's glare was more threat than anger, speaking to the fact that they would be running laps around the campus for *days* if they didn't prove their point in the third attempt.

Rei only smiled when he was graced with his warning look, and could have *sworn* he'd seen the chief warrant officer roll his eyes while Captain Dent appeared to be trying to hide a smile by very deliberately *not* looking in the direction of the three cadets already planted on their asses as the F-levels went by.

It was Warren's turn to pull an impressive feat, this time, falling only after reaching C0, tacking another two to her record. Emble, on the other hand, dropped only seconds after her, not even reaching C1 again.

The break came and went, and when Bretz called for the final try, Rei fought down his nerves as he stood with purpose, this time.

The countdown came, ticking by, and he forced himself to breathe.

"F0!" Bretz's call came, and the tingling started to take over.

Even before he was in the Es Rei closed his eyes, shutting out every distraction he could, fighting to block out the moans and cries of the other groups closest to them, all of them a ways further into the third attempt. He welcomed the prickling, crawling sensation as it climbed his arms steadily, then his legs, then his body. He welcomed it as it reached his neck, sliding up his face and scalp under his hair. As the weight of gravity became magnified, he welcomed that too, mindful to keep himself upright with his head held high.

When the pain started, on the other hand, he did everything he could to simply block it out.

It was strange to him, not being able—or willing, rather—to crawl away from his own conscience as the discomfort grew more intense. By the time Bretz called D6, Rei's teeth were clenched and he was only breathing through his nose, eyes screwed tight. The biting became the burn, then the burn became the searing, bone-deep ache, like hot knives digging into his body. Rei found a strange kind of solace in focusing on *not* curling into himself, the odd battle with instincts born of nearly two decades of endless pain keeping him both grounded and distracted.

D7, came the call. Then D8. D9. C0. When C1 was announced, Rei heard a cry from his left, and knew Sense had gone down. At C2, it was Gisham, the only indication of her fall being the heavy *thud* of her knees on the field. Rei didn't open his eyes, didn't look to see if Warren or Emble had managed to keep up, by some miracle.

He was too busy hating himself for his own conviction.

He understood, now, why Dent had pulled him at this point last time. Long before then he'd wanted to scream, wanted to cry out, and at the start of the quarter the pain could only have been worse for him. Now, facing it, the intensity of the experience was so much that he felt his stomach roiling, agony mixing with nausea all while the endless, Atlantean weight of gravity did everything it could to pull him down.

"C3!" came the call, and Rei almost—*almost*—collapsed, a desperate part of himself whispering that beating his record was enough, *enough.*

"C5!" a little while later, and Rei's nausea was complimented with a knifing pain through his abdomen that reminded him of the time Aria had impaled him on her spear in front of the entire first year class.

"C7!"

Even with his eyes closed, Rei could tell his vision was going dark.

"C8!"

Never again, he told himself, redoubling his effort not to pull away from his physical body, from the torment of the test. *Never again.*

"C9!"

He was *definitely* blacking out, now, and it was nothing less than pure willpower that had Rei keeping his knees locked as the gravity pressed down on him so hard his jaw started to pull open under the pressure.

And then, at last…

"B0!"

The only plus of the additional gravity, it turned out, was that when Rei fell, he dropped so hard his reactive shielding actually triggered to protect his knees as he struck the field. Lucky for him Bretz was quick on the trigger, because the added weight and agony vanished before his upper body and face slammed down right after his legs. Rei caught himself barely, just managing to keep from smashing his nose against the ground, then let himself drop the rest of the way down a little easier.

He could *feel* the eyes on him, and he realized he had yet to open his own as his body shivered and trembled. He tried, made the best attempt of it he could, but found himself unable to do more than blink unsteadily as his limbs spasmed and twitched.

"Easy, Ward. Easy."

Bretz's voice, followed a moment later by Valera Dent, echoing distantly to him.

"Medical drone. Now. I want to make sure he didn't tear himself apart."

5 seconds later Rei heard the whir of the bot approaching, and soon the flashing red and blue lights cut through his closed lids.

It was the push he needed to come back to himself a little.

"I'm okay," he managed to grumble, groaning as he worked to get his arms to bend. Barely managing it, he had a lot of trouble pushing himself up, getting back onto his hands and knees only with the assistance of what felt like a lot more than just two people.

"You're *actually* insane."

The familiar voice finally had him opening his eyes, and he blinked blearily towards where a blue-eyed face swam across his unclear vision at his left.

"Oh. Hey." He tried to smile at Viv, but only managed a grimace. "Did you guys finish? How'd you do?"

"She did fine," another voice, this time from the right, spoke up gently, sounding anxious. "We all did. How about you worry about yourself, you incomprehensible *moron*."

Abruptly Rei's mind cleared a good bit, and he turned to find himself almost nose-to-nose with Aria, who was looking at him with such concern she didn't seem to notice how close their two faces were. It took several seconds of him staring, in fact, of him registering that she had her hands under and over his right arm and shoulder—Viv holding onto his left—before Aria's cheeks flushed, and she jerked away a little in realization.

Catching himself, Rei blinked again, then looked around.

He was surrounded, it transpired, by a veritable throng of people. Before him Bretz and Dent were both pulling back from where they'd clearly pushed him upright by the chest, and standing behind them Sense and Gisham were taking him in with expressions somewhere between impressed and horrified. Even Warren and Emble lingered not a few feet further back, though Rei couldn't tell if their frowns were disappointment at the fact that he'd reached the Bs, or that the test hadn't outright sent him into cardiac arrest in the process.

It was what he heard *behind* him, though, that had Rei looking over his shoulder in alarm.

At his back, the majority of the Lancers, Sabers, and Duelists had apparently gathered to witness the final leg of his Fortitude assessment, keeping just beyond the edge of Field 1. The Phalanxes and Maulers, too, were grouped up past them, with a few who couldn't see over the heads of their classmates jumping up and down and asking loudly what had happened. Rei wondered why their sub-instructors hadn't called the various groups back, but with a throb of surprise he realized he could see most of the trainers standing at the front of the gathered crowd, watching him with mixed expressions of astonishment and disbelief. Even Liam Gross—the Duelist instructor who had never been any great fan of his—was taking him in with wide eyes, and Rei almost groaned aloud.

"So much for minimizing the whispers," he mumbled instead, slowly feeling

Shido assist his body in a rapid recovery from the ordeal of the Fortitude test.

"What was that, cadet?" Michael Bretz asked, still squatting in front of him opposite the captain.

"Nothing, sir," Rei assured him quickly, rolling his shoulders and trying to push himself up to a high kneel, at least. Managing this, Viv and Aria followed him up, and he glanced at the pair of them hopefully. "Would you guys mind helping me—*Whoa!*"

He didn't have to finish before the two girls had him on his feet, lifting him from the ground with no more effort than if he'd been made of straw.

CADs seriously were an amazing technology.

"How are you feeling, Ward?" Valera Dent asked after she and Bretz had stood themselves, bending to peer first into one eye, then the other, obviously checking his pupils. "The drone scan has you clear of any soft-tissue or skeletal injury, but you pushed yourself pretty hard."

"Don't know any other way of doing things, ma'am," Rei joked while the medical bot indeed continued to buzz overhead. His attempt at humor seemed to fall on deaf ears, because the captain just stared at him pointedly until he caved.

"Fine. I'm fine. Don't think I would have gotten any further even if—" he caught himself as Dent raised a brow in warning, realizing it probably wasn't a good idea to let everyone else know he'd had a safety limitation placed on him. "Uh… Even if my body had held out. I was close to passing out at the end, there."

"We thought you *had*," Viv snorted from his left, slowly letting him go to try and stand on his own. "If you'd hit the ground any harder you would have dented the field."

"How long were you guys watching?" Rei muttered, not sure he wanted to know the answer.

"Since the Ds," Aria spoke from his right. She seemed much more hesitant to let him go, for which Rei was grateful. The moment Viv had released him, his legs had started shaking under his weight.

"Great. *That's* not at all embarrassing, or anything…"

"Are you kidding, man?" It was Sense who spoke up enthusiastically. "You hit the Bs. The *Bs*! What the hell do you have to be embarrassed about?"

At this exclamation Rei heard several whispers of awe start up from those gathered at his back, those who apparently hadn't caught the results of the test itself.

"How about the fact that your bald ass is one of thirty people currently *still* staring at me," Rei said with a better grin this time. Then he looked to Bretz and Dent again. "Am I the last tester? Could I request a dismissal? I could… uh… sit down, for a while."

Bretz snorted. "I'll bet." He glanced at the captain. "Permission to dismiss my group, ma'am?"

"Granted." Dent finally lifted her gaze from Rei to look over his head to where the rest of the class and their instructors were gathered. "The rest of you, too! Excellent effort today, everyone! Dismissed!"

The moment she gave the leave the muttering and conversations rippling from the crowd of students redoubled, but Rei still made out the coordinating dispersal of bare feet over the steel plating. Bending his knees a little, he found that his own legs had gathered a bit more strength, and he looked at Aria again with a smile.

"I'm good, you can let me go."

She did so so quickly his bare arm might have suddenly been burning white-hot.

"Ward."

Rei looked around to find Dent watching him again. Bretz had finally turned away to address the Brawlers—congratulating them himself on the day's successes—allowing for a moment where only Rei, Aria, and Viv could hear the Iron Bishop.

"You did good," the woman said quietly. "Keep it up. Got it?"

Rei smiled, thinking he could probably translate the encouragement for himself. *You're on the right path. Keep going.*

"Yes, ma'am."

Despite all of Shido's assistance—and occasionally that of the walls of the hall and locker room—it took Rei at least 20 minutes to wash up and get changed, kept company by Aria and Viv all the while, other than in the showers. By the time he got his uniform back on, his legs were at last starting to feel normal again, and so it was finally at a good pace that the three of them were joined by Sense and Kay as they made for the elevators that would carry them out of the Arena subbasements levels. Even Leron Joy—attached to the other two as always—fell in with them, but for once seemed to have nothing ill to say at Rei's expense. It was possible Aria's presence was too intimidating for him to mouth off around, but—judging by the glances he kept shooting in his direction—Rei rather suspected the boy might at last just be giving him at least a *little* bit of credit as a Galens cadet, after the Fortitude test they'd all witnessed.

"B5 in under five minutes?!" Kay was half-squeaking, half-shrieking at Aria as they walked, mouth hanging open. "Come *on*! I thought for sure I'd at least be able to beat you in Offense & Endurance!"

"Sorry," Aria answered a little shyly, though she didn't look displeased with herself. "My Endurance spec is in the high Cs, so I don't ever really tire out if I pace myself. Add that to Hippolyta's reach…"

"*Don't* talk to me about reach!" Kay huffed, shaking her head in disappointment. "I've *got* reach! I'm a friggin' Lancer! I've got *all* the reach!"

"And she's *the* Aria Laurent, Kay!" Sense cut in good-naturally as they finally reached the lobby. "Come on. Give yourself a break. I bet she even beat Rei's stupid score." He looked to Aria. "How'd you do in Fortitude?"

Aria paused before answering.

"… C7," she said sheepishly.

Sense's grin froze on his face, and he was silent for a second.

Then, turning on Kay again, he frowned at her. "I was wrong. Do better."

"You son of a—!"

Rei chuckled to himself, summoning a car for them all to take via a pad in the left wall. Viv was laughing as Leron Joy tried to intercede between Sense and Kay's banter, giving Aria a chance to escape the conversation and join him by the time the elevator doors opened for them.

"Are you actually all right?" she asked him quietly as they led the way inside together. "Viv's not wrong. I seriously think you're insane."

"Someone's jealoooous," Rei whispered playfully as the others piled in behind them, Sense breaking off from his harassing friend to punch in their top-floor destination.

As they started to climb, Aria scowled at him. "As if. I'm just not as much of a masochist as you."

"*No one's* as much of a masochist as Rei, Aria," Viv snorted, overhearing. "Dumbass did combat team for 2 years while his body literally tried to kill him with bone knives from the inside out."

"Bone knives?" Leron Joy only muttered his confusion, but in the confines of the elevator everyone overheard him.

Viv, though, ignored the Saber so firmly he might not even have been there.

"Don't try competing with him. Seriously. You'll end up with a headache at best, and probably missing limbs at worst."

"Damn, Viv," Rei made a face as they reached the Arena underworks, the door opening for them silently again. "The hell do you think I spend my time doing?"

"Your utmost to kill yourself," Viv snorted back as they started filing out of the elevator.

"No one's competing with anyone," Aria assured her before Rei could offer any retort. "Well... At least not with who has the harder head."

"Ah..." Rei nodded sanctimoniously. "*This* is what Catcher must feel like, when we gang up on him."

The two girls turned on him as one, speaking in unison. "We are *not* ganging up on you."

They froze, glancing sidelong at each other as Sense and Kay both covered laughs from where they walked in front of them.

Rei put up his hands in surrender. "Sure you're not. My mistake. Just saying I'm the only one limping here, so maybe I deserve some slack?"

"You're limping because you thought it would be a good idea to beat your chest at B0-Ranked Offense damage and muscle load," Viv told him with narrowed eyes, following with Aria as the others took the first ramp up towards the stands. "You get no sympathy from us."

"None," Aria agreed shortly.

Rei gave her his best hurt look. "Et tu, Brute?"

"What?"

"It's a quote. The fall of Ceasar on Earth, in Ancient... Never mind. I'm just saying you guys are doing a lot of ganging up for not ganging up on me."

The argument, fortunately, came to an end with that, because the six of them cleared the tunnels onto the open walkway, then, stepping into the shadows of the western stands of the Arena. The late-afternoon sun had already dipped below the edge of the open roof high above them, and it was the first truly crisp day of fall, leaving all glad for their uniforms in the shade. Before them, the entirety of the main floor was in use as the second years partook in a Wargames exercise, four teams of six combatants distinguishable via the modified vysetrium glow of their Device collectively lighting up as red, blue, green, or yellow respectively. The field was a Desert variation, a massive, sprawling rise and fall of sandy dunes and powerful winds that buffeted those fool enough not to fight and run in the lower valleys, but then Rei supposed nothing less than a tornado would faze the cadets battling it out on the projected space.

They all, to a one, bore Devices that were more than half-complete, the colored plating of their armors covering every inch of most every limb, with many of them sporting helms or visors, or else abdominal or chest shielding. Even used to watching A- and S-Ranked Wargame matches, Rei thought it was an impressive sight, hardly convinced otherwise when a Mauler timed the colossal swing of his hammer perfectly to send two opponents flying overtop the crest of the nearest hill in unison.

"Lucky," Kay muttered enviously, and Rei realized he was hardly the only one who'd come to a stop to watch the fighting. Indeed, all six of them had paused, with Viv and Joy's expressions matching the Lancer's for jealousy.

He supposed he couldn't blame them. They'd been doing squad-training for two weeks, now, and not once had there been any mention by Dyrk Reese about expanding out of the Team Battle formats. For once Rei had had no complaints with this decision, mostly because he thought the first years all—including himself—had a lot of work to do before they were ready for the breadth and chaos of a Wargame, but also because he didn't see his still-lagging Endurance spec doing him any favors on a field that size.

"We'll get there," he told the group bracingly, making the first move to the left, heading for the western Arena entrance. "It's only been half a month since we started squad-training."

"But it looks so *fun*." Viv was the one to whine in response even as she and the others started to follow Rei.

"Become a squad-leader, then," Aria said over her shoulder, hurrying her pace a little to catch up and walk beside him. "I bet you'll get all the Wargames practice you want, then."

"Really?" Rei had to admit that had peeked his interest. "Why's that?"

"There's a *lot* of focus on squad-formats at Sectionals," Aria started to explain, repeating Dent's own words from weeks ago, but paused after that. Rei thought he could guess where her hesitation was coming from, and his suspicions were confirmed as she continued. "I, uh… I heard from some third years that first years who make a team spend the entire winter break basically doing back-to-back squad-training. To make up for lack of experience."

Rei hid a smirk, surmising that said "third years" probably happened to sport the rank of Colonel.

"Oooh that makes sense," Kay said as they reached the Arena entrance and started down, Rei swallowing his pride and taking hold of the railing that bisected the stairs as his legs protested the descent. "But that means we just have to make a squad, then, right? Not necessarily squad-leader?"

"Oh… Yeah, I guess." Aria flushed red again, and Rei knew she was realizing she'd been speaking as a probable shoo-in for getting her own team.

"Sweet!" Viv exclaimed as they reached the base of the steps, skipping up to walk on Rei's other side and leaning around him to look at Aria. "So that means I just have to punch enough faces in during the Intra-Schools to make *you* want to take me on, right?"

Aria looked delighted. "Would you want to be on my team? Oh that would be so much—!"

Rei coughed pointedly as they started north along the west wall of the Arena, bringing her up short again.

"Oh… I mean… There's no guarantee I'm going to get a squad, of course." She managed to compose her face, but couldn't hide her excitement as she kept on. "But if I do, I would *totally* want you!"

"Nice!" Viv punched the air in success.

"You should pick your teammates based on merit." Leron Joy had finally decided it was time to sour the mood, and Rei looked back at him to find the Saber scowling between Viv and Aria. "Not on the fact that you're friends."

"Viv is probably gonna hit C0 before her first match," Rei told him coolly, turning forward again. "That would put her neck-and-neck with Zain Kadness and Laquita Martin among the Duelists, both of whom were part of the summer training group. Still think Aria shouldn't take her?"

"I *think* Laurent should pick *after* the SCTs," Joy replied just as evenly from behind. "And maybe it's not Arada I'm worried about her weighing herself down with, *Ward.*"

Rei had opened his mouth to answer, but Aria stole the opportunity by halting and whirling. As one the rest of the group came to a stop together, and Joy—though he stood a good 3 or 4 inches taller—suddenly found himself leaning away from her in alarm as she took a step towards him.

"How about doing me a favor and not worrying about me weighing myself down with *anyone?*" Aria told the boy with venomous cheer. "I appreciate your concern, Joy, but you've apparently mistaken me for someone who needs help making her own decisions." She met his gaze evenly. "Do I *look* like someone who needs help making her own decision, Joy? Do I?"

The Saber's mouth opened and closed several times, struggling to find words to answer with for a while before Sense tried to come to his rescue.

"He didn't mean anything by it, Laurent," the Brawler said with a placating—if strained—smile, stepping close to the pair. "Leron just doesn't always know when to shut his trap, that's all."

Joy glared at his friend, though clearly more to have an excuse not to look at *Aria* than out of any real annoyance.

That was the moment, however, that a notification pinged Rei's NOED. He glanced at the subject line out of habit, not thinking anything of it, and did a double take as Viv stiffened beside him, her own eyes on her lit frame.

As his mouth went dry, Rei managed to get the news out. "Ease up, you guys. We just got our pairings for next week."

Instantly the tension of the party shifted, and as one Aria, Sense, and Joy all pulled up their NOEDs. Kay was a step ahead of everyone, already scrolling through a heavy list of text as it scripted across her vision, and as Rei selected the notice he was greeted by a similar wall of names, dates, and ranks.

"They've packed everyone into *two* days?" Joy was the first to speak, obviously looking over the fact that the entire first round of first year pairings was to take place over the coming Monday and Tuesday. "What the hell's up with that? That's thirty-two matches per afternoon!"

"Lose fast then, and save us all some time," Viv told him coolly. "Wednesday and Thursday are probably second year pairings, with Friday and Saturday left for the third years. That lets them get all the matches done in seven weeks."

"Which leaves three for squad-leader selection and team building before the quarter is over," Rei added with a nod, scrolling down. His last name would be at the very bottom of the list, which meant he should be around…

He groaned as he found his matchup, seeing that he'd been right on the money with his earlier guess.

He was *definitely* going to have to ask Catcher for some help, between now and… Monday? Damn. Only 1 week left to train.

Out of curiosity, he started to look at the other pairings, scrolling back up to find Viv's first.

"Why do they have to make it double-elimination?" Joy was still grumbling, pupils moving across the lines as he looked for his own name. "Seems pointless to me. Just cut it to singles and save everyone the time."

"Double-elimination means reduced chance of unfavorable early knockouts,"

Sense explained. Then he made a face. "Damn… I'm up against Kastro Vademe. He's three ranks higher than me…"

"Bad luck," Joy said, clearly not really listening. "But who cares about early knockouts? If you're strong enough to make it, you make it. Simple as that."

"Nothing's that simple."

It was Aria who answered, and Rei looked past Viv's match-up against some D8 he didn't know to see her face had gone stony as she stared at one line in the roster.

With a frown, he decided to skip Catcher's name for the moment, and scrolled to look for "Laurent".

Viv beat him to it by seconds.

"Well shit…" she muttered, glowering herself as the others looked around at her in confusion.

"What?" Kay asked. "What is it?"

Viv didn't answer. Nor did Aria. In the end, it was left to Rei, who himself had to read the bracket three times to make sure he wasn't misaligning things.

"Grant," he told the other three shortly, nervous excitement clawing at his insides. "First round has Aria matched up against Logan Grant."

CHAPTER 37

"It's honestly small wonder that the SCTs so rapidly captured the interest of the masses. Pinnacle examples of CAD-combat can sate even conflicting urges the human mind is capable of possessing. Users are dancers in their own way, a good match like watching the choreographed ballets of the planetary companies. They are social events, a hub for interaction and engagement both locally and across the systems, with public feeds gathering masses and private showings being the center focus of parties and outings and soirees.

And, of course—at the heart of it all—there ever remains the fact that the tournaments scratch that itch so many of us suffer, that ecstatic enthusiasm for violence and energy that has had man's blood boiling since the concept of competition was first conjured up in the primitive minds of our most ancient ancestors…"

A Consideration of SCTs and Their Intersystem Influence
Lieutenant Colonel Hana von Geil, Ph.D.
Distributed by Central Command, Earth

CLANG!

For the umpteenth time Aria felt her left arm jar painfully as she accepted the cut of Logan Grant's axe, ducking low and angling her shield above her so that the white-and-red weapon screamed and skittered off the red-gold steel over her head. She swept Hippolyta's spear low, aiming for his ankles, but Grant leapt up and away, avoiding the follow-up smash she'd been hoping to catch him with in midair.

Apparently Rei wasn't the only one clever enough to study up on her moves.

Landing some 5 feet back, it wasn't more than a blink before Grant plowed forward again, wet sand spraying up from under his bare feet with every broad step. Once again Aria accepted the initial attack, dissipating some of the heavy blade's impact by letting herself be driven back a foot, further into the ankle-deep surf already lapping at her shins.

They were dueling on a Sunset Beach variation, half the field consisting of the uneven incline of the sandy shore, the other half the washing in and out of a shallow tide. Ordinarily most Users would probably have done everything they could to stay *out* of the water, wanting to keep their feet and legs free of the clinging sand and surf to use their Speed to every advantage on the firmer beach. Aria's first act when the Arena had called the start of the match, though, had been to make for the waves. For one thing she was a Phalanx, and the impairment of her own mobility by the tide would only be minor compared to the impact on most opponents forced to wade in after her.

For another, the "Sunset" part of the field title meant the projected horizon was at her back, shining—if even only dimly—in Logan Grant's eyes.

Seeing a chance, Aria thrust straight for the Mauler's gut, but the massive boy twisted with shocking dexterity, avoiding getting impaled by inches as he swung at her right side. Turning with her whole body Aria caught the axe on her shield and deflected it upward, retracting her spear in the same movement. Tucking the haft under her arm, she snapped it sideways, using her ribs as a lever point. The resulting slash could hardly have been considered a true hit—the majority of the weak cut absorbed by Grant's reactive shielding—but her C4 Strength still sent the Mauler staggering to the side with a grunt of pain that told her she'd done *some* damage, at least.

More importantly, it gave her the chance to adjust her stance again, settling back into her favorite defensive posture as her opponent came again.

The axe fell and was deflected. The spear thrust and was dodged of smashed aside. In a furious blur the pair gave and took, cutting and slashing and stabbing at each other in a dance through the shallow current that had rainbows misting all around them against the dusk light. It was—for all intents and purposes—a solid match-up, and Aria admitted she would have bet any number of credits in the world Grant was going to end up qualifying as a Galens representative for Sectionals.

More than a month of training with Rei, though, had given Aria a new perspective on the rhythm of battle.

Grant was fast, and *terrifyingly* strong, but in the end he was also consistent. There had been a good breadth of variety in his attack patterns at first, using the full extent of his Device—not just the head of his axe—as a mix of assault points. If anything, Aria suspected he was likely among the more versatile of the first years. A dozen times over she had had to deflect or dodge or block a punch or a kick or a knee that came at her in a blur of white steel and red vysetrium. The closest Grant had come to landing a good hit had been with the butt of his weapon, in fact, having surprised Aria and barely giving her enough time to duck and avoid getting smashed in the temple with it. For the first good minute or two of the fight Grant was a guessing game, and it was only her stellar Cognition and endless hours of training that kept Aria in one piece.

Then, though, the patterns had started to emerge.

Fast as he was, strong as he was, Grant didn't hold a candle to Rei when it came to inscrutability. Just as Aria had had her own habits discovered and torn apart, so too had she picked up a bit of a talent for doing the same herself, cultivating it over time in their afternoon classes, or whenever she went up against Viv or Catcher in their extra conditioning hours. It might have been a useless measure against *Rei*— who she suspected still didn't comprehend the entirety of his value as a training partner—but against anyone with a lesser talent for battle Aria was steadily finding she could apply it with ever-increasing efficiency.

And Logan Grant—though most, Rei included, would deny it—absolutely had a lesser talent for battle.

Right feint into a wheel kick.

The understanding presented itself less as a thought and more as the blink of a moving image, and Aria lifted her shield accordingly toward the axe swinging in from her right. At the last moment Grant pulled the weapon down and away, twisting into a massive kick that would have sent her staggering had she not appropriately braced already, leaving the Mauler the one stumbling back post-impact. He managed to deflect her follow-up thrust, then brought his axe overhead.

Full downcut. No feint.

Aria timed her arcing wrench of Hippolyta's shield upward, smashing the cleaving strike aside even as she slashed with her spear. Again Grant's attack was foiled, but again he displayed astonishing dexterity by accepting the deflection and turning it into a diving roll that brought him up to his feet—wet and spitting out sea water—half a dozen feet away.

Of course, he made no hesitation of lunging once more.

Again and again Grant came, and again and again Aria rebuffed him. With every passing second she felt like she understood more, could read a little further ahead. The broad boy seemed out of tricks, and he knew it, too, his normally prim black hair plastered over eyes so filled with blistering frustration, Aria was surprised Hippolyta didn't melt off her body. Again he came, and again she sent him staggering back.

Still, she wasn't really getting anywhere herself, walling up to camp like she was…

Her Cognition provided her with the opportunity within seconds of setting itself to the task.

Rei's gonna like this, Aria thought, allowing herself a grin.

Inadvertently, the smile turned out to be the perfect bait for the already-irritated Mauler.

She thought she heard Grant snarl and curse as he lanced forward again, bringing his axe around in a cleaving blow at her left side. Aria saw the trick even before her NOED lit the lower half of the weapon up in red too. She saw the shift in the strike, the redirection of the momentum only capable by a User with tremendous Strength and Speed. Instead of the blade cutting at her side, Aria found the butt sweeping up towards her face.

Too bad it was the second time he'd gone for this exact trick in the 4 minutes they'd been fighting.

Aria dropped like a stone, extending one leg for stability and trusting the other to accept her and Hippolyta's weight. The axe's haft *whooshed* overhead uselessly, and before Grant could bring any kind of defense to bear Aria powered upward again, at an angle this time. The Mauler was too close to be in any kind of feasible range for her spear, and Aria didn't have time to draw back her shield. Instead, she simply drove her head into Grant's stomach, slamming into him with such force she felt his feet exit the water as the boy gave a loud "*OOMPH!*" of sound. He catapulted backwards, barely managing to hang onto his axe, landing and tumbling into the surf again some ways away. Aria chased after him, powering against the waves, already knowing she wouldn't reach him in time to get a killing blow in. Sure enough, Grant hardly thrashed before he was on his feet.

Aria, though, bent once again, then slammed the edge of her shield into the ocean.

A massive spray of salt water erupted outward away from her, half-wave, half-mist. Grant actually yelled as the assault caught him full in the face, the hand he instinctively brought up to protect his eyes utterly worthless.

For Aria, though, it offered just the time she needed to close the rest of the distance, and she gave a war-cry as she plunged her spear at the griffin stitched across Grant's chest.

She had actually just felt the impact the blade cutting through the shielding, just felt the resistance of flesh and bone as the tip started to drive into skin, when

Grant's hand snapped down, grabbing it about the haft just below the weapon's head and stopping it dead.

He had *caught* the spear.

What the—?! Aria started to think in alarm, but a moment later she was forced to wrench back as the axe came driving around crosswise, very nearly taking her head off. What was going on? How was that possible? Grant had a fist around Hippolyta's haft! How could a Mauler manage to swing his Device if he—

And then Aria registered the sizzle of evaporating water, and an instant later she saw the flames.

Crimson ion fire was flickering off of Grant's vysetrium lines, setting the water droplets that had built up over the white steel to boiling. His entire Device was glowing a brilliant red, cutting through the dim colors of the sunset to their left. He held firm to her spear, refusing to let it go even when Aria wrenched at it, and his eyes were alight with angry focus as he lifted his axe again in one hand.

Overclock, Aria realized.

The understanding clicked, and she made the decision to let go of the spear in favor of throwing herself backwards as Grant cut at her wielding arm, this time.

She could imagine the sounds the crowds must have been making, then, as she found her footing in the water. Armed with nothing but her shield, now, she stood facing a monster of steel and muscle and fire. That Grant had developed his first Ability was news to her—as it was undoubtedly to the spectators—and despite the field cutting them off from the stands Aria knew people would be shouting themselves deaf in that moment.

Especially after Grant pulled Hippolyta free of his chest with a tug to cast the weapon into the water, then launched himself after Aria with the bellow of an angry titan.

With nothing left for it, she decided it was time to use her own trump card.

Third Eye!

She trigged the mental command just as Grant reached her, literally feeling the dormant parts of her neuroline tingling into life in her head and down her spine. All of a sudden Aria's left arm felt... not her own. Like a prosthetic that granted her sensation, but no muscular control.

That was all well and good, though, when Third Eye brought her shield up in a snap to defend from the incoming axe at a near-perfect angle.

Forcing herself to trust in the Ability, Aria instead focused on retaliating in any way she could. Grant's assault was fearsome, but if she could cause him further injury she could probably cut into what time he managed to maintain his Overclock. With this in mind she flung a punch the moment Third Eye blocked another blow, turning it into a heavy forward kick when Grant's free hand swept her arm aside.

For about a minute more they ripped into each other like that, Aria swinging and striking with armored fists and legs whenever she got the chance, Grant cutting down at her with such savage repetitions, the edges of her shield were soon gashed and dented a dozen times over by the falling axe blade. Aria kept herself in one piece, but only barely. What was more, she didn't manage to land so much as a single blow the entire time Grant's Device burned red, the ocean boiling into steam around his ankles and hissing off his armor.

That was fine, though. All of that was fine. All she needed to do was survive, was outlast him. If she could do that… If she could be ready…

And then, with a sputtering gasp from the Mauler, the end of the fight arrived.

Just as he pulled his axe back for another hacking chop at her head, Grant's flames flickered, his vysetrium dimming momentarily. His handsome face twisted into a grimace, like he was willing the Overclock to continue with pure resolve, and for a moment the Ability held, the fires rippling back into life. The Device came around as intended, and Aria's Third Eye bent her arm to meet it. The burning red of the blade encountered a battered steel shield for what might have been the hundredth time. They impacted with another ringing *CLANG* of metal striking metal.

This time, though, the axe rebounded back, ripping itself from Grant's hand, and went flying to join Hippolyta's spear somewhere among the waves.

There is no time for mercy in CAD-combat, no time for hesitation. Even as Grant's whole body spasmed before her, the ion flames winking out in truth now as he reached the limits of his Ability, Aria didn't so much as blink. She lunged, driving a free fist into the Mauler's gut to double him over with another "*OOMPH!*" of stolen air. Her shield came around, then, smashing into the side of his head and sending him flying so violently his entire body whipped about to trail water through the air in all directions before he crashed facedown well onto the beach again. Not waiting to hear if that had been enough to win her the match, Aria plunged after the Mauler, powering through the waves. She saw him still moving, saw him struggling to push himself up onto all fours.

With a yell Aria took a flying leap, closing the last 10 feet of distance in a catapulting arc, and drove the bottom of her shield into the back of Logan Grant's skull, smashing his head back into the sandy ground.

"Fatal Damage Accrued. Winner: Aria Laurent."

And there we have it!" the augmented voice of Captain Sarah Takeshi, acting commentator of the day's matches, reached the entirety of the stands from where she shared the observation platform with Major Dyrk Reese on the far side of the field. "Aria Laurent brings it home in the end with a *brilliant* combination of quick thinking and Ability triggers! Congratulations to Cadet Laurent!"

If Rei had thought the gathered assembly of staff and students had been loud when Grant had revealed his Overclock, it was nothing to the absolute *eruption* of noise that followed this announcement. Despite there being only some 400 people seated in the lowest rows of the south end of the stands, the cheering and applause exploded from the gathering to echo and reverberate through the stadium, the great roof above closed against the chill of the fall afternoon. As the Dueling field below them dissipated, Aria and Grant both drifting down the 10 feet to the projection plating, many cadets—particularly among the first years—were standing up quickly to clap and yell.

Rei, for his part, stayed seated, suspecting Aria would have preferred a more subtle congratulations if possible. Viv did the same to his left, but on her other side Catcher was showing no such restraint.

"WOOH!" The Saber punched the air and looked to be doing his best to stop himself from jumping up and down with enthusiasm. "THAT'S WHAT I'M TALKING ABOUT! WAY TO PUT HIM IN HIS PLACE, ARIA!"

"Dude, take a breather," Rei laughed, waving him back down as several other first years turned in their direction from the aisle below, some amused, others less-so.

"Sorry," Catcher apologized, though he was still grinning from ear to ear as he sat again, not looking away from where Aria was offering Logan Grant a hand up after the boy appeared to have regained control of his limbs. "I just *really* needed to see that. Didn't you?"

"Maybe," Rei answered noncommittally. He himself wasn't actually looking at the Arena, but was instead taking Viv in sidelong. She was sitting quietly, surprisingly subdued. He hadn't really noticed it at the time, but Rei realized her cheering, too, had seemed a little low-spirited compared to the day's previous bouts, and the look on her face now as she watch Aria and Grant limp off the field in opposite directions was odd.

She looked almost… concerned.

"You okay?" he asked, unable to help himself while Catcher continued to whoop and holler.

Viv started, jerking out of whatever reverie she'd been in to immediately plaster an alarmingly convincing smile across her face.

"What? Yeah! That was awesome, wasn't it?!"

She began shouting along with Catcher, not missing a beat, leaving Rei to take her in with his own frown. He didn't like this, *hadn't* liked this for a month, now, ever since Viv had come back from witnessing Logan Grant put the beatdown on his entourage. He hadn't pushed her for more information—and hardly thought this was the time—but still… He was starting to have solid suspicions as to what the pair of them discussed, that night.

He just hoped Viv would eventually realize it was okay to talk about…

"Next match: Conrad Fae versus Casey Foreman. Combatants, approach the field."

Sarah Takeshi's amplified announcement brought Rei back to the present, and he turned his attention to the Arena again in time to see the next two first years step into view from where they'd likely been hugging the wall of the floor. He just caught a glimpse of Aria's red hair vanishing under the east walkway, and as she left the noise of the spectators finally started to ebb, allowing the atmosphere to return to one of tense anticipation.

The elevated projection Takeshi and Reese stood upon at the far end of the Dueling field was much like the one Michael Bretz and the other instructors sometimes used to oversee their training from above, if a little wider. Below the two officers, Fae and Foreman were standing rigidly just outside the east and west ends of the silver perimeter, waiting to be called on.

Reese didn't keep them long.

"Combatants, take position."

As one the two first years stepped over the perimeters, taking to their starting circles in near-choreographed unison. Though Rei was loath to credit the man any positive attributes, Reese definitely knew how to run a tight ship when it came to the first day of the Intra-School tournament.

"This is as an official Duel." The major repeated his arbiter's speech for what had to have been the fiftieth time that day already. "It will therefore be subject to regulation ruling. Once the field is formed you will be ordered to call, then engage. Premature Device manifestation will result in a penalty. Premature approach, attack, or the like will result in a match loss. Understood?"

Together Fae and Foreman nodded. Rei saw Reese's eyes flicker briefly, and at once the field began to come alive.

In a steady, graceful rise the area built itself up beneath the two boy's feet, pixilating into being. As they had been all afternoon, Rei, Viv, and Catcher immediately started guessing what the zone would be, trying to piece it together as parts fell into rapid place.

"Is that white?" Viv asked, pulling up her NOED to zoom in on the growing projection. "Is it a Neutral Zone variation?"

"Nah, too uneven," Catcher said with a shake of his head. "Looks like… snow, maybe?"

Rei was the first to put it together.

"Tundra," he told them, grinning as he felt a sort of devilish pity for the two boys.

Sure enough, about 10 seconds later the field solidified, and the matched combatants now faced each other across a frozen incline of slick, snow-blown ice. From the stands the projection seemed to extend beyond the far perimeter of the area, stretching into a frigid, empty whirling of grey and white that nonetheless allowed for a decent view of Reese and Takeshi, their platform distorted by what could only have been a blizzard, shrieking and biting. Indeed, the raging sounds of a harsh wind had filled the Arena, lashing in what had to have been cruel blasts over Fae and Foreman.

Rei was anything but envious of them.

"Field: Arctic Tundra."

It was the Arena's voice, now, that took over the announcements, speaking up in the smooth, mechanical intonations that were uniform across every planet of every system.

"Cadet Conrad Fae versus Cadet Casey Foreman. Combatants… Call."

The two first years' commands were lost to the shriek of the storm winds, but—like it did for more solid obstructions—the field projection adapted for the viewer, allowing Rei to clearly see the glimmering blur as CADs were summoned. Casey

Foreman, he recalled then, was the Mauler Aria had once helped out of a ravine during squad-training. His hammer and armor gleamed white and purple, with the grey glow of his vysetrium only barely distinguishable against the background of whirling snow. Across from him, Conrad Fae was a Phalanx Rei had actually teamed up with before himself, a spear-wielder like Aria. His orange-and-silver weapon, however, was a bit longer and far more slender than Hippolyta, the black vysetrium tip more like a sharpened stake than a blade.

Almost the moment the match started, though, Fae proved his battle-instincts went beyond the delicate appearance of his Device.

"Combatants... Fight."

It was over so fast Rei was sure he could have blinked and missed it. Poor Casey Foreman orchestrated his own defeat, in the end, charging forward across the ice with a howl that could *just* be made out over the blizzard. Not only did Fae let him come—as Phalanxes often tended to when faced with a more aggressive opponent—he actually started retreating immediately, backing up in quick steps that had most of the rest of the stadium laughing.

Except—Rei noticed—the third years' section.

That was when he decided to pay close attention, and he was glad for it not a few seconds later.

"Fatal Damage Accrued. Winner: Conrad Fae."

"*WHAAAAT?!*" Viv's confusion was echoed hundreds of times all around them, and for once even Catcher seemed at a loss on her left. Below them the field was already dissipating, with Fae retracting his spear from where it seemed to have materialized to stick out the back of Foreman's skull, having taken him through the eye before most of the viewers could deduce what had happened.

"Oh, and there's the fastest end to a match we're likely to see for some time!" Takeshi's voice called out, the sounds of the storm fading away with the dematerializing of the field. "Quick thinking and appropriate use of the environment will do that, on occasion! Congrats to Cadet Fae!"

"But what happened?!" Viv demanded, looking between Rei and Catcher almost desperately, the latter of whom could only shake his head.

"Looks like Foreman impaled himself?" he tried uncertainly.

Rei was about to come to his rescue when a familiar voice answered from the right.

"That's exactly what happened. Fae's pulled that move before, though never quite this efficiently. You'd think that spear of his was too thin to be much use against a Mauler like Foreman, but he sure knows how to use it."

All three of them turned, and Rei did his best to keep his face steady as Aria settled down in the empty seat he'd been saving for her at his elbow. She was still in her combat suit, and he had to chuckle at the sweat on her brow.

"Did you run up here?"

"Damn right. Didn't want to miss the match. Barely caught it as is."

Rei laughed louder this time, allowing Viv to look around him hopelessly.

"But how? How do you run yourself onto your opponent's weapon like that?"

Rei didn't miss the fact that she didn't congratulate Aria on her fight.

If Aria herself noticed this, though, she chose to make no comment of it. "Lieutenant Imala calls it a 'pike dig'. Apparently it was used against cavalry in ancient warfare. Butt the end of your spear into the ground, and let your opponent's own momentum impale themselves."

"Fae was really clever about it," Rei agreed with a nod, continuing for her as she started to pull out the tight bun of red hair behind her head. "The ice wasn't ideal as a support for his weapon, so he withdrew, sliding the end of it back until it caught, probably on a crack or lip or something. Then he aimed for Foreman's face."

"Straight on, it would have been hard to gauge the distance from the tip of the spear," Viv wrapped for herself, understanding dawning. "That's why Fae aimed at the head, instead of the body. It was so slender, depth perception would have basically been nullified until it was already in Foreman's eye."

"Exactly," Aria finished with her hairband between her teeth, running her fingers through her locks to tug them free of knots. "Add that to the wind and snow blowing in their faces, and Foreman's only chance would have been if he'd taken things a little slower from the start."

"Which Maulers are sooo good at doing," Catcher said sarcastically, leaning back to grin at Aria from behind Viv and Rei. "You got a taste of that too, didn't you?"

At his left, Rei felt Viv tense, but pretended to make no note of it.

"You bet I did," Aria grunted, popping her hairband over one wrist before shaking her left hand with a grimace as below them Sarah Takeshi called on "Kasper Valente" and "Janice Owens" to approach the field. "Dude did *not* want to lay off me even for a second! How is having that much Endurance for a Mauler fair?! And then the Overclock?! He about gave me a damn heart attack!"

"Yeah but you kicked his ass in the end!" Catcher looked like he was having a hard time staying in his seat again. "That was a match and a *half*, girlfriend! When he tossed your spear... man!"

The pair of them chatted across Rei and Viv for a while more, until the field under Valente and Owens began to shimmer and rise. As a variation of Cargo Bay formed—manifesting into the spacious storage area of some massive intra-system transport ship or another—they settled down to watch.

Only then did Rei lean over to whisper sidelong to Aria.

"Good fight. I figured you had it in the bag, but still... Nice job."

She looked rather pleased at the compliment. "I channeled you for half that match, you know," she muttered back as the combatants were told to call. "By the end I was reading him like a damn book. At least until he pulled that Ability out of his ass."

Rei snorted. "That's got less to do with me and more to do with the fact that you've put more hours into training than anyone else."

"With you, dummy. Putting more hours of training in with *you*."

Rei shrugged, unwilling to concede the point. Both grinning, they lapsed into silence for a bit, watching Owens—a Duelist—launch herself across the largely-empty bay space with both blades at the ready the moment the Arena called for the start of the match.

Valente met her nearly in the middle of the field, his Saber's Speed not quite matching his opponents, but impressive, nonetheless. His Device was of the two-handed variation, and while it packed less of a punch than a Mauler's axe or hammer, it could be wielded much more freely, even single-handed for brief periods if needed. In the end the pair appeared to make a good match, because a minute into the fight neither had demonstrated any sort of significant edge on the other.

"Is Viv okay?"

Aria whispered the question in a short lull in the match, as Owens pulled away from Valente to circle him a bit, looking for a better opening than she'd found close up.

It took a moment for Rei to answer. He was hardly surprised Aria had noticed—Viv was usually her most vocal cheerleader, so long as Catcher wasn't caffeinated—but he just wasn't sure how to best put his suspicions into words.

Or, indeed, if he should at all.

"Yeah, she's fine," he finally decided, responding just as quietly as Viv and Catcher yelled beside him when Owens ripped inward to engage the Saber again. "I think she just… I think she might see Grant in a different light from the rest of us. After whatever happened that night…"

"Ah," Aria caught on quickly, and bent just a little to study Viv's face from around his own. "*That* night, yeah… I've asked her about it, but she's been pretty tight lipped on telling me what happened."

"You did?" This *did* surprise Rei, and he snapped around to look at her directly. "What did she say?"

"Hey. Eyes forward. You're gonna give us away."

As she said it, Aria pushed his face back around with a smirk.

Rei's cheek burned where her fingers had touched him, and he *willed* himself not to go red.

"Like I said," Aria continued, "she hasn't told me much of anything. Nothing more than she explained when we got back to your suite that night."

Rei grunted, happy to get his thoughts on track again. He recalled the shaken state they'd found Viv in. Most of that could probably have been assigned to the shock of watching Grant flatten the better part of his entourage bare-handed, but he'd never believed that explained everything…

Still… In the end, it was her business, and if Aria couldn't get her to open up during what little girl-time the two of them got, it was clear Viv wasn't looking to talk about things until she was good and ready.

As though to complement this temporary resolution of his curiosity, Rei's NOED chose that moment to alert him to a notification. Seeing it, he felt his stomach do a sort of weak backflop before curling in on itself uncomfortably.

It was time.

"Looks like I'm up," he said out loud just as Valente managed to deny Owens of her off-hand knife with a lock and twist that cut clean through her left wrist.

Around him, the other three all tensed, but it was Catcher who spoke up first.

"Keep a cool head, man. Remember what we went over. If you outmaneuver her, you've got a good shot at coming out on top."

"Yeah. You got it." Rei didn't actually believe his friend—he'd spent too many hours over the last several nights going over all the possible outcomes in his head—but that didn't mean he was any less resolved to make a good show of himself.

And whatever he managed to do, Catcher would have been integral in it, this time.

"Kick ass," Viv told him plainly, looking around only long enough to punch him—

lightly, for once—in the arm. "Don't bother coming back if you lose. I'll disown you."

"I'd rather you didn't? It would make things awkward in the suite, you know?"

Viv gave him a wicked grin. "Then don't lose."

"Right. Duh."

Grinning despite his nerves, Rei bent to retrieve his bag from where it had been stowed between his feet before standing up. As he turned to make down the row to the right—towards the east side of the underworks the notice had told him to report to—he caught Aria's eye. She smiled, a brilliant, natural smile that was only tinged the slightest bit with concern.

"Good luck," she said.

Rei cocked his head at her, pretending to be hurt. "That's it? No speech? No epic send-off?"

She laughed. "I can give you one if you want, but don't pretend you're not twice as aware of anything I could say than any of us are, Rei."

He smirked, granting her that. "Fine. In that case… Thanks. And save my seat for me."

"You got it."

Allowing himself to trade smiles with her only a moment more, Rei finally managed to turn away and head for the stairs at the end of the row. Without a glance back he descended to the walkway below as the fight between Valente and Owens raged on, then turned right to make for the closest entrance to the underworks. Reaching it, Rei finally paused, unable to keep himself from looking up and southward, back towards the others.

He didn't miss Viv and Catcher turning away quickly, having clearly been watching him go with hopeful trepidation.

In the end, only Aria met his eye, and after a second she lifted a hand to wave, then made a gentle, encouraging shooing motion.

You got this, Rei translated for himself.

With a nod and his own brief wave back, he allowed himself to be swallowed by the passages under the stands.

CHAPTER 38

By the time Sarah Takeshi finally called his name 45 minutes later, Rei had gotten control of his nerves. After changing into his combat suit in one of the subbasement locker rooms, he'd returned to stand silently at-ease along the wall of the Arena floor, waiting in the steadily moving "on deck" line with a cycling of five others under the watchful eye of Claire de Soto, the Saber sub-instructor. He hadn't looked left or right the entire time, had barely registered the faces of the comers and goers, of the winners and losers of their matches. In his own head Rei stayed, preparing, readying himself as best he could.

So, by the time his name was up, he felt he had steeled his resolves to every extent his current abilities would allow for.

As he approached the field he saw in the corner of his eye another form in grey-and-red striding towards the opposite side from the west wall. He forced himself not to look, forced himself to keep his eyes forward, on the platform where Sarah Takeshi and Dyrk Reese hovered several feet above the ground while they waited. Rei didn't lift his gaze to the major's either, not wanting to know what sort of expression—or lack thereof—graced the aging bastard's features as his plans took form. Instead Rei watched the silver line of the perimeter approach, reaching it and rounding the area until he was roughly near the east point of the circle.

Only then did he lift his eyes to his opponent, waiting for him 30 yards away.

Lena Jiang was glaring at him with as much distaste as he'd seen from most anyone in all his time at Galens. At C1, the black-haired girl had officially come to be the class' top Saber a week or so before, matched for CAD-Rank with no more than two or three others, and trailing only Logan Grant's C2 and Aria's C3. She was *technically* only three ranks higher than Rei, now—who'd hadn't quite managed to crack D9 despite a full schedule of near-*endless* training the week before—but with his true specs lingering closer to a D1 or D2 average, the girl was practically a full tier higher than him when it came to capability.

Silently, Rei apologized to Valera Dent. If he was going to get through this match without being used like a living practice dummy, he would still have to rely on will and wiles for the time being.

"Combatants, take position."

Reese's command was as clear and unfazed as any Rei had heard so far that day, and he again had to grant the man a begrudging level of respect. While no doubt the major had been anticipating this particular fight all afternoon, by the tone of his voice he might have been on the same mechanical repeat as the Arena.

Stepping over the perimeter, Rei crossed quickly to the red starting ring that had only just manifested atop the black steel of the floor. Reaching it at the same time as Jiang across from him, he met the Saber's gaze unblinkingly, unwilling to give the girl so much as an ounce of satisfaction by looking away.

"This is as an official Duel." Reese performed the arbiter's speech once more, and Rei wondered if it was customary to give it before every match in the Intra-Schools. "It will therefore be subject to regulation ruling. Once the field is formed, you will be ordered to call, then engage. Premature Device manifestation will result in a penalty. Premature approach, attack, or the like will result in a match loss. Is that understood?"

Rei nodded, and Jiang did the same. There was a moment, half a breath, in which the Arena went silent, even the stands going quite as the promise of another fight settled.

And then the world began to shimmer and shift around Rei.

Since starting squad-training, the first years had been privy to a much greater variety of fields than the Neutral Zone variations they'd always used in Dueling practice. Still, despite this, zone manifestation was yet a fascinating experience to experience, particularly from *inside* the projection.

The first thing that shimmered into being was a billowing black sky of smoke and orange and red fire. Not a hint of the heavens was visible, and Rei wouldn't have been able to guess if it was day or night no matter how long he'd attempted to catch a glimpse of sun or stars through the roiling smog. Next came the floor, rising dark from the plating as it lifted Rei and Jiang more than the standard 10 feet, telling him immediately they'd be fighting on some kind of incline. Sure enough, a rough, crumbling rock formation pixilated into being beneath them, and he found himself standing at a steep angle of some 30 degrees.

That would have been bad enough, had it not been for the running lava that boiled and bubbled in a dozen streams of varying curvatures and breadths down the slope of the field.

Unable to help himself, Rei—and Jiang across from him, he was glad to catch—turned north, where the spot around which Reese and Takeshi had hovered was now completely overtaken by the very-convincing rendition of an active volcano in process of steadily erupting high, high above them.

Rei couldn't help himself.

"Holy shit."

"Field: Volcanic Slopes."

Rea had seen the variation of the zone before, of course, witnessed it some scores of times over in the SCT feeds. That, though, was an altogether different experience to *standing* in the shadow of the spitting, trembling mountain, all while feeling the burn of the molted rock and the blow of hot wind through his hair.

"Cadet Lena Jiang versus Cadet Reidon Ward. Combatants... Call."

At last Rei recalled where he was, and turned to face forward again. "Call," he echoed, and in a whirl of metal and light Shido was around his arms and legs. Black steel over white reflected a bloody red sheen in the dim illumination of the field, the claws protruding from Rei's right knuckles flickering like solid flames with every subtle motion. Around and through the armor the vysetrium strips felt even brighter than usual, rippling their icy blue light outward as the Stryon particles within whirled into life upon the Device' summoning.

And across from him, blazing in the smoke, Jiang's CAD was outlined in similar brightness, a stunning white that made her rather easy to distinguish from the trailing whisps of all around them.

The black-haired girl stood—20 yards away now—in greaves of a brilliant, rainbow-blue offset by dark purple, the interlocking armor reaching all the way up to her hips. Her right arm, too, was encased almost completely by her CAD, trading off for nothing more than a glove of steel plating over her left hand, though each finger was tipped with a glowing white claw. Her sword too, was edged with white, a single-handed variant like Catcher's, and it left a trailing wash of bright light across Rei's eyes as the Saber twirled it at her side a few times to limber up her wrist.

He'd have to watch out not to be blinded, if he wanted the fight to last more than a few seconds.

Then, at last, the final command came.

"Combatants… Fight."

There was the *CRACK*! of shattering stone, and Jiang erupted forward in a blaze.

Rei, fortunately, had already made the decision to hold his side of the field by the time she moved, which turned out to be the right call. Despite his top spec being his D4 Speed, he didn't think he would have made it more than 5 or 6 yards towards the middle of the zone before the Saber caught him, and likely flatfooted. Set as he was, his Cognition was high enough to see her coming, and so Rei managed to settle and spot the opening blow before Jiang was on top of him.

CLANG!

His new D0 Defense, it transpired, was on par enough to handle a direct blow from Jiang's sword. The Device hit the heavy plating of his left arm, biting in only barely before rebounding. Jiang cursed, smoothly jumping back several feet to accept the momentum of the ricochet, then lanced forward again, sword straight before her. It was a direct thrust Catcher had used more than once, and Rei bashed the assault aside with practiced familiarity, letting it slide by him. Unfortunately, he didn't have time to launch a counterstrike before the Saber's opposite leg came up to kick at his face. He blocked the blow only barely, finally staggering sideways out of his starting place.

"I get it! It's run away or turtle up now, huh, Ward?!"

Rei was so caught off guard by Jiang's question he very nearly let himself get impaled as another thrust came. Barely dodging it, he had to fend off a series of quicker, shallower strikes in rapid succession, the girl prying for an opening through his swift adjustments.

"See?! You've gone from a mouse who couldn't stand and fight to a wall that doesn't know how to! Is this why you can never hold your weight in squad-training?! Because you're too scared to throw a punch?!"

This time Rei registered Jiang's seething words more clearly, and he felt a pang of irritation. While it wasn't strictly against the rules to taunt an opponent in sanctioned matches, it *was* considered pretty shit form for a member of the ISCM, not to mention incredibly disrespectful. The spectators wouldn't hear anything, of course—not unless something was yelled loud enough to reach the stands over the rumbling of the volcano—but the Saber's words *would* be clear to Reese and Sarah Takeshi.

Then again, Rei doubted the major cared, and the captain's job at the moment was only to provide good entertainment for the crowd.

A cut from the right ripped around, and Rei barely managed to catch and redirect it with his claws. This turned into another kick he turtled against, which unfortunately left him open for a slash from Jiang's claws at his face. He wrenched back, avoiding getting blinded, though the distortion of his reactive shielding as the vysetrium tips just caught the field told him just how close it had been.

"Oh, look at that! You're still slippery as ever! Good for you, asshole!"

Rei grit his teeth, ducking a cross-blow from the left before spinning sideways to avoid the following axe-kick from above. Jiang was *relentless*. Worse, she was sure-footed despite it. Even on an incline of 30 degrees her attacks came quick and clean with hardly a pause, while Rei was having a hard-enough time holding onto his bearings while keeping himself from getting chopped to pieces. He could feel his neuroline tingling as his Cognition took on this problem, but he was challenged by another furious volley of blows before he came up with any ideas.

"Seriously?! Is that it?! All that growth you've been rubbing in our faces, and all you can do is huddle up and take a beating?!"

Oh, and on top of everything else, Rei also had to fight to keep his cool, which helped nothing.

Crunch!

As he stepped back yet again, ceding once more to Jiang's intensity, Rei felt the stone beneath his feet crumble and give, and he fell into an awkward half-split when his back foot slid down the hill over the resulting rubble and debris. He only flailed for a moment to keep his balance, but it was all a quick fighter like the Saber needed, and she stepped in quick to cleave down at his right shoulder. Unable to get the defense plating of his left arm around, Rei did the only thing he could, blocking with his right. He cursed internally as the blow landed, fearing what would happen once he lost the function of his offensive hand. There was a *CLANG*, and he braced for the pain of the phantom-call cutting through the thinner steel into flesh.

Instead, Jiang cursed as her strike rebounded yet again.

That, at last, was when his still-struggling Cognition finally clicked.

As Rei found his footing once more, so too did he see the advantage he might be able to take hold of. Jiang was built for Speed, and clearly had a respectable Endurance to boot. Her strikes were quick and endless, absent any indication of slowing down after what was probably a minute of ceaseless hacking at Rei. To have such advantages, there had to be a balance, right?

If even his lighter carbon-steel plating could handle a blow from the girl, then didn't that mean her Offense—and Strength, too, therefore—were probably severely lacking?

Oh this is gonna suck, Rei moaned silently to himself, setting his feet.

Then it was finally *his* turn to lunge.

The surprise on Jiang's face as he turned the fight on her was apparent, and immediately made the incoming pain on the horizon worth it. She slashed at him, from below this time, and Rei brought up a steel-clad shin to deflect the strike as he threw his first punch, claws going straight for her face. The Saber dodged back, cutting downward as she did, but in her retreat her range fell well-short of a killing blow.

And Rei let the slash fall even as he followed after her.

The tip of the vysetrium-edged blade bit into the top of the left side of his chest, cleaving shallowly through the knotted muscle he'd been steadily building up over the last 5 months. Rei ignored the blaze of pain, taking advantage of not having to defend to close the distance between them in a blink. Her sword was in a bad position after the blow, and Jiang tried desperately to dodge as Rei punched again. The move saved her life, but only kept the hammering claws of his fist from taking her through the chest.

Instead, Shido slammed into Jiang's shoulder, cutting deep through muscle and bone as it impacted with a *thud*!

D2 Strength was nothing to scoff at, even if it was well-shy of the average Galens cadet's specs, and the Saber was launched sideways several yards, tumbling to the ground and rolling down the hill in a shower of crumbling black stone. Rei started after her, but found the footing too precarious to handle the decline in a rush. Making a split-second decision, instead of chasing he rushed west along the incline, towards the middle of the field, leaping several of the flaming streams of magma until he was roughly in the center of the zone. Touching down in a wide delta between the two thickest lava flows, he finally turned to see what had become of Jiang.

Had he been any slower about it, that would have been the end of the fight for Rei.

Rainbow-blue steel flashed behind its white edge, and Rei brought his arm up just in time to deflect the cut that would have taken him in the side of the neck. The Saber wasn't finished, though, keeping with her momentum to slam a shoulder into his chest, sending him staggering backwards. He caught himself only inches from stepping into the slow current of molten stone, and managed to rebuff her next attack more solidly, accepting the blow on both arms before wrenching forward to force her back.

Idiot, he cursed himself as Jiang staggered two steps before stopping herself from tumbling back down the slope again.

He hadn't been thinking, had he? He had been *trying* to set himself up in an advantageous position, a place where his willingness to wall up worked in his favor. Among the lava streams, another slip-up on Jiang's part might very well mean FDA by environmental factors, or at least severe limitations due to burns or lost limbs. He hadn't been thinking, though, when he'd turned his back on her.

It had been her shoulder he'd hit, not her legs.

C5, Rei decided the girl's Speed had to be. Maybe C6. Indeed, despite the fact that her left arm hung limply by her side, now, Jiang had closed the distance between them in barely 2 seconds, and that had been uphill, not to mention starting from where he'd sent her to the ground. 6 feet away she stood, glowering behind loose strands of disheveled hair, her sword held before her at the ready. Though her teeth were bared, she was watching him more carefully now, dark eyes trailing his body to taking in his steel-clad shins, knees, arms, and elbows. Her gaze drifted over him, lingering eventually on the left side of his chest, and the expression that crossed her face was distinctly irritated.

Rei thought it was a good opportunity to grant himself a little payback.

"What? This?" He pointed at his breast, where her sword had cut into the skin and muscle beneath his intact combat suit. "Oh, sorry. Did you expect something impressive? Your hits have been so weak I figured I could brush one off without much issue." He nodded towards the Saber's useless left arm. "Think I ended up with the better end of that deal, too."

It was only a half-truth. It had been a gamble to begin with—and one he intended to take again, if the opportunity presented itself—but the cut *had* set him with limitations, if minor ones. His shoulder was stiff, and moving it was painful.

But it had been a long, long time since anything like that had been much of an issue for Rei.

Jiang's eyes blazed, fury steeling her face into something demonic.

Then she lunged.

Rei had found his footing now, though, had learned her tricks. He held his ground again as their fight devolved into a lashing mirage of white into shielding blue, streaks of light arching and jolting in endless cuts through the air. The Saber didn't give him a moment this time, not even a chance to look for an opening. She had been played a fool—and knew it, too—and now she attacked his quick defenses with a savage anger that Rei for once thought wasn't entirely directed at him. He let the assault come, let himself take the beating. Shido's plating began to grow steadily more chipped and dented, and he took one, then two, then three more shallow wounds across his shoulder, thigh, and face as the battle stretched on.

With every passing moment, though, Rei learned a little more about Lena Jiang, noted bit by bit the pattern of her movements, the rhythm of her blows he and Catcher and reviewed and practiced in intimate detail.

WHAM!

When he finally got a chance to retaliate, it was unfortunately only with his left fist, but the blow still landed. His NOED and Cognition both registered the repeated form, the down-slash, then up again, then looping over and around to come from the right. Reading it, Rei swiped out with his claws to catch the sword, powering forward at the same time with his free hand. Steel-plated knuckles caught Jiang in the gut, and she went lurching backwards down the hill, feet slipping over loose stone while she obviously fought hard not to double over. He followed after quickly, but once more the crumbling footing made closing the distance too precarious before she was up and at the ready again.

Still, two of the fight's three real blows had been his, now...

Jiang was even more careful in her approach after this second rebuttal. She didn't lunge at him, but instead came steadily, cautiously. She tested him first, snapping and feigning the blade up at his face, then his groin, then the shoulder she'd already dealt a minor would to. Rei didn't take the bait, didn't let himself get reeled in, nor fall for any of the deceptive blows meant to trap him into committing to a block. *He* had the advantage—had had it from the moment he'd robbed the girl of her left arm—and he wasn't about to give it up in a sprint for the finish. Jiang was hot-tempered. He'd seen that more than once, now. If he could be patient...

Sure enough, the Saber's lip started to curl up again not 30 seconds into her testing games, and soon after she was barraging him with cuts and sweeps and slashes again, falling into now-familiar patterns.

WHAM!

Another left-handed blow, but this time straight to the solar plexus, stealing the wind from Jiang's lungs as she was sent flying backwards to tumble and fall down the incline once more. Again Rei didn't chase her, content to wait, content to let his stronger opponent cut herself to death against his wall. The Saber rolled onto her stomach as pebbles and broken rock spilled around her, and she was slower in gaining her feet, now, likely suffering the limitations of bruised ribs that made it hard to breathe.

When she managed it, though, something had again changed in her face as she looked up the mountain at him from below. The fury had lessened, oddly enough, fading to be replaced by something calmer, something more reserved. Jiang looked resigned, but not as though she were giving up on the fight.

Rather, she looked like someone ready to do something she would rather have avoided.

All of a sudden Rei was on edge. An image of Logan Grant's Overclock flashed across his mind, and he immediately hunkered and stepped back again, closer to the flow, closer to where Jiang's mistakes could cost her dearly. She didn't climb up after him, a frown pulling at her mouth. He watched her, scrutinizing her more carefully than he had all match.

Then, with a strain of concentration mapping itself across her face, Jiang hauled back, fighting obvious pain as she opened up her chest, drawing her sword behind her in a powerful sweep.

And then she threw the weapon in a whirling arc, sending it spinning high, high over Rei's head.

Instantly he knew what was going to happen. Before he heard the words, before he caught Jiang's voice yelling over the rumble of the volcano, Rei knew what was about to happen.

"MAGNETIC HUNT!"

In a scrambling blur Rei whirled, looking for the blade. Narrow as it was, it might be hard to make out, hard to distinguish against the fires and flames. Desperately he cast about, seeking the white blaze that would mark the Device's hurtle towards him. Finally he found it, catching the streak of light directly in front of him, some ways away.

Catching it, and only just in time to see the sword splash harmlessly down into the lava in a faint spray of molten red and orange.

WHAM!

As the force of a sprinting body took him in the back, Rei cursed his own stupidity for the second time. Jiang's shoulder slammed into him, smashing against his spine with all the hurtled weight of the girl and the rest of her Device, and only then did

Rei's Cognition register the signs. Once already the Saber had surprised him with her Speed, hadn't she? And why had she yelled the Ability trigger when her chest was injured? A simple voice command would have been enough.

As he was launched forward, turning as he flew and limbs flailing in a desperate attempt to find solid ground again, Rei understood. The glimpse he caught of Jiang's face—that same resigned, regretful look—echoed his certainty.

You're not the only one with tricks up their sleeve, that look said.

And then, with a searing, blinding flash of agony that was fortunately kept mercifully short by the fast-acting Arena, Rei tumbled into the boiling lava with a heavy *splash*.

"Fatal Damage Accrued. Winner: Lena Jiang."

From her secluded vantage along the walkway that crowned the highest point of the stands, Valera Dent watched Reidon Ward thrash only for a moment before the Arena eliminated his sensory input and began to dematerialize the field. As the boy started to sink towards the ground—Lena Jiang dropping with him—Valera couldn't decide if she was disappointed or thrilled with the match's results. On the one hand an early defeat like this put Ward in the loser's bracket from the go, meaning he would have to take part in—not to mention *win*—six more pairings in a row if he wanted to qualify as one of the sixteen first years guaranteed to make it to Sectionals.

On the other, Ward's CAD was growing splendidly, and despite the discrepancy in their levels the boy had had his *much* stronger opponent on the ropes more than once during the match.

Was it the end of the world if the boy didn't qualify? Doubtful. Not anytime soon, at least. If anything it wasn't unlikely he'd be asked to join one of the Sectional squads regardless, and Valera was pretty sure she could guess who of the likely leaders would be first to approach him.

But she knew, too, that Ward *could* make it on his own, that he had the ability, and certainly the will.

Valera—after all—had been tracking the boy's additional training hours more closely than anyone, using the Institute's log and recording systems. That was saying something given just how many silent eyes the cadet was steadily accruing, within Galens and without. Valera had known him capable—had deduced that the day his file had fallen across her desk—but even she had expected to have to steer him along now and then, to guide him here and there. Instead, not only had Ward taken it on himself to push his body, mind, and CAD together to limits that outpaced all but one single other member of his class excluding his training partners, but he had managed to recruit *Aria Laurent* as one of those partners. If anything, Valera had been starting to wonder if she would be nothing more than a passenger along for the ride since she'd gotten Ward into the ISCM system.

Now, though, watching the boy pick himself up from the ground and stagger as his opponent swept unceremoniously from the ring, she decided the time had come to meddle a little.

"Kel," Valera spoke to the air, "where's Lennon?"

It was only a moment before her NOED lit up on its own.

In a brief blur a myriad of hundreds of familiar faces from a dozen angles whirled dizzyingly through a small window in the corner of her vision. The features and expressions of the Institute's gathered cadets were a varied mix ranging from bored to elated as they waited for the next fight to start, and after a second the flashing images cut from every recording device in the Arena stopped. One young man's soft face remained, black-skinned and strikingly blue-eyed under a wash of designed, iron-grey hair braided into dreads that reached his shoulders, and Valera wasn't surprised in the least to find him watching the upcoming fighters intently.

Despite the fact that the day's combatants were first years, he never did miss an opportunity to try and learn…

A pause, then two perpendicular red lines traced across her retinas, interlocking over a point in the third years' section. Zooming in on the spot with a quick command, Valera found him highlighted near the end of an upper row.

Perfect.

Blinking away the zoom—but keeping the trace on—Valera made no attempt to hide her speed as she moved. High up as she was, no one was likely to notice her with all eyes on the floor below, and so it was in hardly a breath that she was at the top of the stairs in question, then another before she was halfway down. Only then did she slow her pace to that of the average human—as was expected of all Users in polite company—the heels of her leather boots clicking over the stone as she descended the rest of the way.

Finally reaching the highest row of the third years, she dismissed the trace, noting her interest's position herself.

"Cadet Lennon."

At the sound of her voice several of the closest students started and whirled, not having heard her coming. Ignoring them, Valera watched the grey-haired young man turn with a confused expression, one that shifted into surprise the moment he saw her.

Leaping to his feet, he saluted sharply. "Ma'am?" came the curious question as below the newest pairing were told to take their starting positions.

"Come with me," Valera told him simply.

Then she started down the rest of the stairs, not looking back to see if the third year was following her.

At the bottom of the steps she went left along the walkway, making for the nearest entrance to the underworks. Reaching it, she slipped in for a bit of privacy, then finally turned around. As expected, the young man had been on her heels without pause, and had already come to a halt just inside the frame of the tunnel.

Christopher Lennon, unlike many Users, did not possess any overly imposing presence. He was shorter than most of his classmates—even the girls—standing under 5' 10" with narrow shoulders that had him looking rather diminutive in his Galens uniform, complete with the red-on-blue griffin about his left arm. Aside from the grey dreads that clashed handsomely with his dark skin, his features were rather plain as well, his blue eyes watery and his cheeks stubbornly holding onto a little fat despite his CAD's genetic correction and the Institute's intense training regimen.

All in all, his countenance did an excellent job of disguising the monster within.

"Lennon, I'm going to get right to the point." Valera had little patience for pleasantries now that she'd made her decision. "You asked me at the start of the term if I would be willing to train you personally. Do you recall?"

The question could have been rhetorical, of course. Despite the hassle her fame could cause her, Valera was not *un*aware of her value as a Knight-Class S-Rank.

Sure enough, the abrupt resuming of the topic took even the stoic Lennon aback.

"Uh… Yes, ma'am," he said, clearly doing his best to hide the hint of hope in his voice. "You told me I would be better served to focus on my instruction in class, as I remember…"

"I lied," Valera said flatly. "The truth is that I was too busy to take on a student for individual practice. I'm *still* too busy, to be honest. However…" She paused, looking him up and down. "Are you still interested?"

"Yes, ma'am!" the cadet answered at once, snapping up straight as his hopes were realized. "Very much so!"

"Good. I'm willing to take you on, but you will need to free up your schedule two nights out of the week for the next two months. Mondays I will work with you independently here in the Arena, in SB3."

Lennon looked delighted, but also a little confused.

"And the other night, ma'am?"

Valera smiled.

"The other night will be spent with you paying the favor forward."

CHAPTER 39

"I find the stories irritating, in their own right. They so often paint the image of some lone hero, some singular legend left to his solitary climb, bearing on his own the building hardships of a violent life.

It's all ludicrous. It's not even that I never would have made it alone.

I never would have even taken the first step up…"

The Stormweaver

c. 2495

Unbelievable behavior!" Major Reese snarled in Rei's face. "If you think base insults are appropriate to bear in an official match, cadet, then I'm of a mind to throw you back in the brig until your next pairing!"

To her credit, Sarah Takeshi attempted to come to the rescue at once. "All due respect, major, but Cadet Jiang is the one who instigated the taunting. If anyone is going to be lectured, it should be—"

"Cadet Jiang at least has a win to her name *to show for it*, captain," Reese snapped without looking around at the woman. "Given the means of her victory, I'm inclined to believe her words were calculated to get Ward here to drop his guard."

Rei's ears burned with angry impatience. He had better things to do—*such* better things to do—than to sit here and get reamed out like this. Beside, logic like that could be applied to *any* instigating commentary in a match, if the major was going to go that far.

At his elbow, Takeshi seemed to be thinking the same thing, because her face darkened, though she opted to say nothing more.

"In this instance, I will consider your defeat punishment enough for the disrespect you've leveled at my feet, and that of this Arena and school." Reese's lip curled at the words, like they left him with a bad taste. "If you deign to lower yourself to such a level again, I will have to have a discussion with Captain Dent as to what lessons *she has been teaching her trainees."*

That spiked at Rei's fury, and not for the first time he almost snapped back. Threatening *him* was one thing, but implying that *Dent*—the chief combat instructor of the Galens Institute—was doing anything less than a superior job in her assignment was asinine and disrespectful.

Still, getting him to rise to the bait was *exactly* what Reese was trying to do, Rei knew, and he wasn't about to give the man the satisfaction this time.

Besides, the unblinking tab in the corner of his vision—indicating the script he had minimized quickly when the major had come storming up on him while he'd been recovering in the east tunnels post-match—really meant that he had *better things to do.*

"Yes, sir," he said simply, still standing rigidly at attention with his eyes fixed on the wall of the underworks behind the major. "Sorry again, sir."

Reese's irritation visibly peaked at this lack of response, and he looked about to say something more before deciding better of it. Instead, he just whirled and marched back up the ramp towards the Arena and the SCTs he'd paused for the sole purpose of ripping Rei a new one.

"You're dismissed, cadet," Takeshi said, waiting—very obviously deliberately— until the major had vanished back onto the floor above them.

Rei gave her a stiff salute, and had snapped around—eager to get to more pressing matters—when she brought him up short by speaking again.

"Also… Good fight, Ward. Even as a loss. It was a very good fight."

A little of the anger drained from Rei. Turning around again, he offered the woman a more genuine salute, as well as what vestiges of as grateful a smile as he could muster up. "Thank you, ma'am."

With a nod the captain turned and followed Reese's path up the ramp, disappearing into the impatient hubbub of the cadets looking forward to the closing matches of the afternoon.

Rei waited—wanting to make absolutely sure she was gone—before finally giving in and pulling open the script again.

…

Processing combat information.

…

Calculating.

…

Results:

Strength: Lacking

Endurance: Lacking

Speed: Severely Lacking

Cognition: Severely Lacking

Offense: Lacking

Defense: Lacking

Growth: Not Applicable

…

Checking combat data acquisition.

…

Adequate data acquirement met.

Device initiating adjustments to:

Strength. Endurance. Speed. Cognition. Offense. Defense.

…

Adjustment complete.

Strength has been upgraded from Rank D2 to D3.

Endurance has been upgraded from Rank E9 to D0.

Speed has been upgraded from Rank D4 to D6.

Cognition has been upgraded from Rank D3 to D5.

Offense has been upgraded from Rank D1 to D2.

Defense has been upgraded from Rank D0 to D1.

…

Calculating.

…

CAD "Shido" has been upgraded from Rank D8 to D9.

…

Checking combat data acquisition.

…

Adequate data acquirement met.

Prioritizing reasonable evolution parameters.

…

Selected Prioritization:

Speed. Defense.

…

Recategorizing for future parameters.

…

Processing.

…

Evolving.

…

Evolution complete.

Closing the script, Rei realized that his hands were shaking. He knew why, of course. For one thing it had been a while since Shido had made a really solid jump like that. It was strange that the Device didn't manage these sorts of improvement against Aria—aside from in their first match—but he supposed it had to pay off to face a variety of strong opponents with scattered skillsets and specializations.

More importantly than the specs, though…

Rei paused for a second, debating what to do. The underworks housed any number of side chambers he could have snuck into. Team locker rooms for visiting combatants. Break areas. Classrooms. All Rei needed to do was follow the hall down a ways, and he knew there was an auditorium under the south stands where Michael Bretz had once had him and the Brawlers watch over an hour of repeated Team Battle positioning. He could bolt down the tunnel, slip inside, and a moment later…

But no. No. That felt wrong, somehow. Maybe it was the fact that Aria, Viv, and Catcher had all been there for Rei's last evolution, with the latter two witnessing the one before that. Or maybe it was that they'd all also shared their own moments of change as their CADs had one by one gone through their first changes—or second, in Aria's case—in the last month.

Either way, doing it without them just didn't sit right with Rei.

And so it was for that reason that—15 minutes of forced patience later, after he'd showered and changed back into his standard uniform—Rei stepped out into the stands again and started making up towards the seats where he knew his friends would be waiting for him.

Aria was the first to notice him climbing up the steps in their direction, still in her combat uniform as she waved him down. Viv and Catcher found him only a moment later, and grinning up at them made avoiding the eyes of the other first years easier while he ascended to their row. Reaching it, it only took him a few seconds before he was sitting between Aria and Viv again, forcing himself to keep a level expression as he looked to the Arena, where what had to be one of the last matches of the afternoon was just getting started. "What did I miss, anything good?"

Silence greeted him, and after a moment Rei looked around at his friends. To a one all three were staring at him, bearing not even a hint that any of them were buying his nonchalant attitude.

"How you doing?" Aria was the first to ask him, and he turned to find her studying his face with a little concern. "That was a really good fight, you know…"

Oh. Right. It struck Rei as amusing that he hadn't even given the fight a single thought since Reese's lecture. He supposed, though, that from their perspective Aria, Viv, and Catcher would all be thinking he was trying to play off the disappointment of his defeat.

He did, after all, have reason to be disappointed…

"Uh… I'm okay. A little bummed, I guess."

Catcher—ever the optimist—reached around Viv to slap him on the chest genially. "Dude! You stood nose-to-nose with the top Saber in our class, and *almost* had her! I mean seriously! You *almost* had her!"

"More than once," Viv agreed rather fervently. "That was a great fight, Rei. Anyone weaker than Jiang and you would have had that match in the bag."

Rei snorted. "Hardly. She ended up beating me at my own game, didn't she? Pulled the wool *right* over my eyes at the end, there."

"Maybe, but Viv's not wrong. Most anyone else would have gone down before they had the chance to trick you." Aria spoke firmly, like she *really* wanted him to listen. "The majority of the summer training group is going to pass through to the first round of the winners bracket. Your matchup for next week isn't likely to be as tough a pairing. You've got this."

Rei was starting to feel bad. They were so concerned about his potential dispirited-ness, and all he could do was sit there waiting anxiously for the first day of the Intra-Schools to wrap so he could drag them all somewhere and share his exciting news.

"I know," he tried to assure Aria with as winning a smile as he could manage. "Don't worry about me. Reese was never going to pitch me into a match I really had a chance of coming out on top of, was he? Next week will go better. And that's more time for me—for all of us—to train."

"*Exactly.*" Catcher was nodding along vehemently to his left as below them a Lancer Rei didn't know fell to Biyu Yang's sword and shield. "Keeping your chin up and your head high is what you need."

Viv nodded as well, but was still watching Rei in concern, and as he looked from her to Aria he realized she, too, appeared largely unconvinced of his "okay-ness".

The guilt was finally too much for him.

"Look," he lowered his voice to avoid being overheard, pulling up his NOED as he did. "Sorry. I'm a little distracted. I'll probably beat myself up a bit about Jiang later, but for now, well…" He swept through his script history, snagging a screenshot of the Shido's most recent notification and sending it to the other three in a group message. "Like I said. I'm a little distracted."

Taking in the range of reactions from his friends was as amusing as it was affirming of his own excitement. Viv smirked as she read over the evolution notice, apparently hardly surprised. Catcher groaned with envy and leaned back to cross his arms over his chest as he rolled his eyes at the ceiling.

And Aria—newest to the phenomenon that was Shido, and therefore still impressionable—squeaked with such exhilaration that most of the heads in the row before them turned around in confused alarm.

"Sorry, *sorry*," Aria whispered, first to the students in front of them, then to Rei and the others. "I just… I've only seen one of your evolutions!"

She *barely* managed to keep her voice under control this time, and Rei couldn't help but laugh quietly. "Don't get too excited. Just like when it added the elbow and knee guards, there's never been anything special about Shido's physical changes."

"Not yet," Catcher grumbled. Then, with a sigh, he uncrossed his arms and sat up straight again to look at Rei. "So? What is it this time? Did your greaves fill out? I feel like Shido is definitely leaning towards a Speed specialty."

Rei shrugged. "Don't know yet."

There was a blank staring from the others, all three of them looking at him like they didn't understand.

"What you mean, 'don't know yet'?" Viv repeated in a low hiss, glancing around to make sure no one was trying to eavesdrop. "Could you not tell? Maybe it's something to do with Shido being an A-Type?"

Rei shook his head. "No. I mean that I haven't checked yet. It didn't feel right, running off to see what had happened without you guys."

Viv gaped at him with her mouth open for a solid 5 seconds. Catcher did the same, and glancing over his shoulder Rei saw Aria was no different.

"Rei… Are you *insane*?!" Viv finally got out, somehow managing to both yell and whisper at the same time. "This is an *evolution* we're talking about! Why would you wait?!"

Rei squirmed uncomfortably. "Well… I mean… I've been at all *your* evolutions, so I guess I just thought it would feel weird if you guys weren't there…"

Viv's eyes went so wide they looked like they were about to pop out of her head, and Catcher decided to try and intervene with a strained grin.

"Dude, it's not like it's the birth of your first child. You don't have to wait for us for anything like that."

From Aria, too, there came something like an exasperated giggle. "Rei, you've only been with us of ours because the majority of our training happens as a group, in extra hours. I'm sorry, but if Hippolyta evolved during Duel- or squad-practice, I'd probably fake sick just to get to the locker room as fast as possible and see what happened."

Rei sunk down into the projected back of his Arena seat, feeling somewhat embarrassed. "Well fine. Next time I'll know better. Maybe I just *wanted* you all to be there, I guess."

Though it hadn't been his intention, Rei couldn't deny some amusement when these words wiped the grin from Catcher's face and had Viv looking a little less frustratingly-astonished. Aria, too, sobered a little as she traded a pained look with the other two before speaking again.

"Sorry. We didn't mean to tease." She tried for a smile. "If it means anything, it definitely makes me happy." She was quickly regaining a bit of her original excitement. "Ooh, I can't wait to see!"

Catcher sighed again. "Yeah, it makes me happy, too, I guess. Way to guilt that out of us."

Rei snorted as Viv mumbled something quietly from where she sat between the two of them, making Catcher frown at her.

"What?"

Viv didn't repeat herself, so Rei was left to translate the words he was sure had been spoken.

"She said she's glad I waited, too. She just didn't want to say it out loud."

Viv gave him the evil eye, and Rei, Aria, and Catcher all enjoyed a rare laugh at her expense before more glares from the row in front had them shutting up to wait in eager silence for the afternoon's matches to end.

Four fights later and the last pairing of the first day of the Intra-Schools ended in an exciting upset when Aadhik Khatri, a Mauler in the same class block as Catcher—and one of the top sixteen from the summer training group—got taken down with surprising ease by a Brawler from D-1 called Misha Fethers. After the field they'd been having it out on—an interesting, multi-level variation of Abandoned Depot—had dissipated, Sarah Takeshi announced a wrap to the day in a clear, cheerful voice that only barely managed to mask her fatigue.

Commentating on thirty-two fights in a row could only have been exhausting, after all.

"And with that, we conclude our first day of the Galen's Intra-School SCT! Attendance at 1300 will be mandatory for the remainder of the week as the rest of you have your own shot at showing off! Look forward to commentary by Lieutenant Kayla Johnson tomorrow, and you are all dismissed!"

With the final word, the suspended disc the captain and Reese were still standing upon started to descend to the floor, and a thrum of conversation picked up at once among the Institute cadets, the mass of the first years discussing the excitement of the matches they'd watched, or debating if it was too early for dinner, or if their regular groups wanted to go grab a training field in the East or West Centers. For their part Rei, Aria, Viv, and Catcher were relatively quiet, exchanging nothing more than a whispered affirmation that they would accompany Aria downstairs to SB2, where her uniform was still in her locker.

The lines down the steps grew quickly, but emptied just as rapidly as the walkways designed to accommodate 150,000 people funneled barely 400 out through the Arena's two entrances. As soon as they could Rei and the others stepped out of line into the underworks—empty aside from a couple other first years that still needed to get changed—and it wasn't long before they were down the elevator, around the hall of the subbasement, and shoving open the locker room doors.

The moment they were inside—and with no one having followed them down— Aria turned on Rei in a whirl.

"Okay! I can't take it! Show us! Show us now!"

Rei laughed. "Go get changed! It can wait till—"

"*Nope!*" Aria cut him off, putting her hands on her hips and fixing him with a glare that said she would bear no additional argument. "Show. Us. Now. Rei."

Rei only cast around to Viv and Catcher for a moment before he realized they were both staring him down with the same insistence as Aria.

Then again, it wasn't like anyone really needed to tell him twice.

"Hold onto your socks," he muttered, more to himself than any of his friend as he focused on Shido's weight and spoke the word.

"Call."

The last time his CAD had evolved, it had taken him a moment to realize the change, to identify the growth of his armor up his arms and over his knees and elbows. The time before that, he'd only noticed the metal encasing his legs after Viv had pointed it out to him.

This time, on the other hand, Rei started to see the change even in the blink it took Shido to whirl into being over his limbs.

"Oh holy fu—," Catcher began in a hiss, staring wide-eyed right along with the others once the call was done, but Rei didn't hear him finish. He was too busy gaping at both his hands as he raised them up to look at.

Both his *clawed* hands, now.

In what was distinctly the greatest evolution the CAD had yet demonstrated, the Device designs around his arms looked to have combined, then mirrored. The heavy defensive plating originally along his left forearm and elbow had slimmed and softened to smooth, cleaner layers, and now covered his right as well. Similarly, the curved, black lengths of sharpened steel that had before only protruded from one set of knuckles now extended from both. Along the limbs the white of the underlayer was a little less visible beneath fluid, polished metal, but the blue vysetrium now ran between the plating even more intricately, like a dozen lines of glowing thread that moved smoothly with his careful flexion and extension of elbows, wrists, and fingers.

"Whoa…" was all Rei managed to get out, and the other's echoed his amazement only with their silence.

The armor about his legs too, had changed, though not as significantly. There had been no growth, with Shido still only extending up to cover Rei's knees, but the metal had taken on the more polished look of the steel about his arms. He kicked off his boots to let the CAD encase his feet, too, then tried standing on his tiptoes, then jumped up and down a couple times, and he hoped he wasn't imagining it when the Device felt more responsive, more intrinsically entwined with his own motions.

In one go, Shido's Defense, Offense, and possibly Speed had made collective, massive bounds…

A strong hand took him about the arm, then, and Rei was pulled from his astonishment as he was suddenly being dragged backwards, towards the locker room entrance again.

"Hey! Hold on!" he started to protest, but Aria didn't so much as look around at him as the doors slid open once more for them. "What are you doing?"

"Oh like you aren't curious," she said over her shoulder, and Rei caught a glimpse of a wide, excited grin as with her free hand she started twisting her red hair into a single tail again. She'd turned them right, pulling him north along the tunnel so quickly Viv and Catcher were having to jog to keep up with them.

"Aria, you won't be able to fight down here," Viv told her with a frown. "Rei calling Shido on his own might not draw any attention, but if *both* of you summon your CADs, there could be trouble."

"Not on a sanctioned fiiiield," Aria answered in singsong as Rei caught onto why he was being led towards the main combat floor of the subbasement.

"But none of us have access to the projection flooring!" Viv continued to argue, starting to sound a little concerned.

Aria didn't answer. Instead, they reached the great gap in the left wall that led unceremoniously onto the main gym floor, and she pulled Rei without pause to the closest of the zones—Field 4, where Viv and the other Duelists always trained. Only once they'd crossed the edge of the silver perimeter did Aria finally let go of him, but not until after she'd steered him to right around where the east starting ring would be.

Then she started tying her hair up in truth again, her NOED blazing as she did.

"Whoa!" Catcher exclaimed in surprise as the field beneath their feet suddenly began to glow white.

"Sorry," Aria said, still grinning and blinking away her frame to look at Viv. "The summer training group was given access permissions to every field on campus, other than the main floor of the Arena."

It took a moment for Viv to answer, frowning down at the projected area incredulously. "Wait... Then why haven't we been training here instead of in the Centers? We could have had our own zones instead of splitting one!"

"Oh..." Aria's excitement shifted into something almost alarmed. "Uh... We aren't really supposed to use them often. Or at all, honestly... Not without prior permission..."

She glanced at Rei with a pleading expression, and he suddenly understood. He doubted very much the entirety of the summer group had access like this.

He doubted anyone other than Aria specifically, in fact, had access like this.

Doing his best not to smirk, he nodded and attempted to cover her ass. "Makes sense. Dent's said from the beginning those who earn them will be handed advantages, but I bet the higher-ups don't exactly want unsupervised combat running amok in the school every day."

"Why not?" Catcher laughed. "I hear the Battle Royale Wargame format is gaining popularity in the System and Intersystem tournaments. Setting everyone loose could be the best training!"

Viv looked less convinced, and had continued to frown at Aria a little suspiciously, so Rei decided it was a good opportunity to redirect the conversation to more appropriate—and interesting—waters. Lifting his hands to his face, he eyed Aria through the crossing lines of his now-mirrored claws.

"Don't know about a Battle Royale, but I'd definitely be down for a little one-on-one to see what this baby can do."

The smile came back, tinged with the focused, savage excitement that always—*always*—made Rei's spine tingle whenever the two of them faced off.

"Oh, bring it," growled Aria Laurent, just before the Arena's voice started up.

"Sparring bout. Cadet Aria Laurent versus Cadet Reidon Ward. Combatants…
Call."

CHAPTER 40

The next day, Viv dominated her match against Gillian North so thoroughly, the fight ended about as quickly as Conrad Fae's against Casey Foreman. The Mauler came head-on across the Grasslands field, and Viv's Speed had placed her behind the broader girl as North had swung and wasted her opening strike, burying the head of her axe into the soft ground of the windy plains. Bilaterally severing her opponent's hamstrings with a flash of Gemela's sword, Viv barely missed a killing blow with her dagger at the back of North's head when the Mauler tucked as she dropped, trying to roll out of the way.

Unfortunately for her, useless legs made her an easy kill for a Duelist who could run circles around her prey even when they *weren't* crippled.

Catcher's fight, not long after that, concluded in victory as well, if by a much narrower margin. He ended up pitched against a Phalanx Rei had never met—a boy from 1-D named Jae-Song Gwan—and initially had a hell of a time breaking through Gwan's defenses. A sword-wielder variation of the Type, the Phalanx was clearly familiar with standard Saber combat, and used that to his advantage as he let Catcher come again and again to break against his shield, retaliating only when a true opening presented itself. Further complicating things, the Deserted Settlement field only accentuated Gwan's defensive tactics by providing him plenty of obstacles to put between himself and Catcher, most of which included the crumbling, worn walls of the abandoned huts and shelters that took up most of the zone's dry, barren landscape.

In the end, though, Catcher had smartened up, and actually pressed Gwan into a corner of one such building before collapsing part of the ceiling on the boy with several careful strikes to the rotting crossbeams that held up the fragile roof of the place.

After that, a few more interesting bouts took place, keeping everyone in the stands on the edge of their seats all afternoon. Sense's match against Kastro Vademe of 1-B didn't go well, but that was hardly unexpected. Not only had the Lancer been among the summer training cadets, he was also quietly regarded as the third most powerful User of the first years, trailing only behind Aria and Grant, and the latter not by much. After that fight, though, Kay Sandree's match had been the complete opposite, her superior Offense breaking through everything Clement Easton—a Saber also from 1-B—could throw up against her.

In what felt like rapid succession Rei saw those he considered friends and enemies alike rise and fall, as well as everyone in between. Emily Gisham rose victorious, and Leda Truant fell. Leron Joy claimed a close victory, followed by a brutal loss served to Sam Dorne. Mateus Selleck continued on to the winners bracket, but both Camilla Warren and Giano Perez—one of the lackeys who had weeks ago held Rei down as his face had been kicked in—lost one after the other. Tad Emble had barely eked out a victory for himself the day before, but the fact that there were at least a *couple* people in the losers bracket with him who Rei desperately wanted a solid excuse to punch in the face had him so excited he even forgot about Shido's evolution for a bit.

Once the day's brackets wrapped, though, it was straight to the East Center with Aria, Viv, and Catcher, followed by an evening of solid training interrupted only with an hour for dinner after the mess hall had emptied from the late-afternoon rush.

Rei suspected he'd adjust to it within a day or two, but for the moment Shido's adaptations still felt like a solid leap forward in his total power. Whatever the upgraded design of the steel was, it hadn't lost any of its defensive value despite a thinning of the metal, and the jointed action of his greaves as he moved was more fluid, more natural. His claws punched and cleaved with no more efficacy than before, but he could now slash and strike with *both* hands rather than having to focus on independently attacking and defending with the right and left respectively. In their bout the night before Rei had still been a long way from taking Aria to the ground, but the doubling of his offensive options had earned him not only his second hit ever on her, but also his third.

Of course, some bare scrapes to her thigh and side hadn't amounted to much when she'd decapitated him with a blurring cross-sweep of her spear.

Still, it certainly amounted to *something*, which showed particularly well when they'd traded partners a little later that night. For the first time ever Rei had found himself fighting Catcher to a stalemate when the pair of them battled it out for *seven* minutes before they both agreed to the draw, neither able to break through the other's defenses. Viv had still nailed him to the ground a little while later, but it took her a full *five* minutes, and she hadn't walked away from the battle unscathed. What was more, by the time their second afternoon of training after Shido's evolution had wrapped, Rei's Endurance had notched up once again, as had his Defense. The CAD's new versatility allowed him even more variation in his tactics, and he could only believe the change of pace had to feed well into the Device's Growth. Rei suspected he might hit C0 before his next match, even with their standard training classes canceled for the week in favor of mandatory attendance to the opening matches of the Intra-School. Combining his steady spec improvements with Shido's evolution, by Wednesday he was already starting to feel a building anticipation for his next fight.

It worked out well in the end for him, because they were on their way from lunch after morning lectures, heading to the Arena, when the first years received their second-round assignments.

"Oh this is gonna be so *sweet*!" Catcher was in the middle of saying. "Not like they're gonna be S-Ranked matches, but some of the second years are high in the Bs, which will definitely make for some cool—Oh! Hello!"

Rei had been mulling over his own thoughts, only half-listening as Viv and Catcher discussed the afternoon's upcoming tournament, when the notification that must have stolen the Saber's attention flashed across his own vision. As one he, Aria—who had been walking along beside him listening—and the other two all stopped short, as did the majority of other first years trailing along the path with them from the mess hall towards the center of the campus.

Viv was the first one to find her name, and she groaned. "Well that's gonna be awkward. I'm up against Benaly…"

"*Jack* Benaly?" Rei asked, scrolling all the way down. "Oof… Good luck."

"Thanks for the vote of confidence," Viv muttered, closing her frame and looking around. "What about you guys?"

"Someone named Candice Brett?" Catcher asked hopefully of the group.

"She's a Duelist in 1-D, I think," Aria answered him, her eyes tracing what must have been her line. "Not a pushover, but definitely someone you can handle. I'm up against Adam Jax."

Viv grimaced. "That's two in a row from our own block for you. Damn. Reese isn't pulling any punches." She looked to Rei. "What about you? If you say Log—if you say Grant I swear on the MIND I'll—"

Rei only gave her the briefest of raised eyebrows before he shook his head, deciding it was best to pretend he hadn't heard the slip-up. "Nah. Not Grant. Turns out the major's not that ballsy." Then he grinned. "Next best thing, though."

"Who?" all three of them asked with a range of anticipation and exasperation at his stalling.

"Warren," Rei told them, working hard to hold at bay the excited energy that had coursed through him at the name.

There was a trading of glances by the others, and Viv smirked viciously.

"Camilla Warren?" she growled with distinct pleasure.

"Yup," Rei answered just as excitedly.

"Wait. The bitch who tricked you into getting jumped by Selleck and the others?"

To a one Rei, Viv, and Catcher all looked around in surprise at Aria's angry snarl.

"What?" she asked irritably. "I'm not allowed to get pissed?"

"No, you are…" Rei told her slowly, grinning a bit. "I just don't think I've ever heard you curse…"

Aria's cheeks went a little pink. "Yeah, well… My sister would say a proper lady knows less how not to say something, and more *when* exactly to say it. So that's her, right? The Brawler in your group who got you ganged up on?"

"Yeah. It's her." Rei blinked his frame away. "Probably the best Reese could line up: someone who has a bone to pick with me."

"Aside from Grant and Aadhik Khatri, all of the summer group made it through the first round," Aria agreed, indicating the path again with a questioning dip of her head as she spoke. "I suppose it *would* have looked a bit too suspicious if he'd pitched you up against either of them, though. Two top rankers in a row…"

"But how could he have known about Warren's issue with Rei?" Catcher asked as the four of them started moving towards the Arena again. "He didn't even tell Hadish Barnes, and *we* sure as hell didn't say anything." He looked between Aria and Viv. "Did we…?"

"Not me." Aria shook her head.

"Definitely not," Viv answered much the same.

"No need to go on a witch hunt, guys," Rei said with a snort as a pair of second years who looked late for their matches brushed by them as quickly as they could get away with without jogging. "At this point Warren and Emble's issue with me is an open secret in our group, and probably most of the class. Not to mention who knows who Selleck or any of *them* told? Reese isn't dumb. None of the staff are dumb. It might even have just taken the six of those guys showing up to class all bruised like that to clue most everyone in."

Viv grunted in agreement, but frowned at the shape of the Arena as it showed itself once they'd taken a bend around through the campus path. "Probably. Still…

If that's the case, you'd think someone would catch on to what he's doing, right? Even if he's being careful, the dickhead is definitely stacking your fights against you."

"Who says no one's caught on?" Aria asked quietly, and Rei was pretty sure only he had made out the question.

Shortly after that the pooling of students and staff near the mouth of the Arena made it a little too loud to talk easily, so with nothing more than furtive glances around by Rei and Catcher they waited for the crawl of the controlled lines to reach the building. No famous faces they hadn't already identified among the older years leapt out from the crowd by the time they mounted the entrance steps, though, and so it was a little dejected that the boys took the lead south, along the walkway. A couple minutes later they were climbing the steps to the row they'd been lucky enough to claim for the last two days, and took a seat in the hubbub and noise of the gathering students and staff.

As with Monday and Tuesday, the Intra-Schools kicked off exactly at 1300, with laggers unfortunate enough to suffer the stares of the already-attending as they hurried into the Arena in singles and pairs. The clock struck the starting hour, and two shapes appeared from the tunnels under the stadium to cross the field from opposite sides. Meeting in the middle of the Dueling field that would host the day's matches, the officers turned to face the stands, and Rei heard a shout of laughter from who might have been Sense below them. Then he, too, recognized Michael Bretz standing beside Dyrk Reese, looking distinctly unusual in the traditional black-and-gold of the ISCM, rather than the typical red-on-white of his combat suit.

"Guess we know who the day's commentator is now," Rei chuckled to the others, pointing the Brawler's sub-instructor out to them.

That was the moment that Reese's eyes blazed, the NOED distinguishable even so far below them, and a then the two men were rising rapidly on the projected disc they would share the rest of the afternoon. Bretz's frame followed suit, and he looked to take a deep breath before opening his mouth to speak in a rather impressive announcer's voice, amplified by the Arena's systems.

"Cadets! Welcome to the third day of the opening week of the 81st Galens Institute Intra-School SCT! As—we hope—all of you are aware, today marks the starting bracket of the second year matches! First years—" he turned to the east section of the three areas the students had taken up "—this will be an excellent opportunity to observe the level and ability you are expected to have achieved in the next twelve months! Third years—" he looked now to the middle section "—enjoy how far you've may have come, but take account also of the talents you might find yourself facing in the future! It is not unheard of for those younger than you to rise far into the Global, System, and even Intersystem tournaments! And as for you second years—" his eyes fell on the west section "—fight hard, and fight well. Take this chance to study your classmates, to observe those who will be both your team-mates and your rivals in the coming weeks, months, and years. You will never have a greater opportunity than this!"

There was a pause as Bretz's opening speech—hardly as involved as Takeshi or de Soto's in the previous days, but no less poignant—rang in echoes through the Arena. After a few seconds the chief warrant officer put on a smile that looked only a little forced, and dove right into the day's event.

"And now that that's out of the way… Let's all give a big cheer for our first combatants of the day!"

Immediately there was a resounding roar, and Bretz's actual calling of the pairs' names was lost to the shouts and applause as two students in red-and-green—a girl with pinkish-blue hair and a boy with dark skin and with a shaved head, like Sense's—stepped into view and onto the projection plating. They both approached the Dueling field with calm confidence, heads held high, and only once they were standing on opposite sides of the silver perimeter did the noise from the crowd die down. Major Reese waited deliberately, it seemed, until it was so quiet someone's cough from the second years' section reverberated through the vastness of the still Arena.

"Combatants, take position."

The red rings appeared, and the second years were standing in them a heartbeat later. As soon as they were in place, Reese continued only briefly.

"This is an official Duel. Do you condone and agree to the rules of this fight?"

There was a grouping of low muttering from the first years all around them, and Rei saw Viv and Catcher exchange a look of surprise to his left, but he himself said nothing. Indeed, he was relieved to hear the traditional question being asked, rather than the longer arbiter's speech the major had been insisting on for the last two days.

Apparently the second years were deemed experienced enough not to be made to suffer anything more than the standard protocols of CAD-fighting.

The two cadets nodded together, and at once Reese's NOED flared once more. There was a building rush of sound, and beneath the feet of the fighters the projection plating swelled upward in a torrent of liquid, washing blue.

As one Rei, Aria, Viv, and Catcher all called out the name of the recognizable field together.

"Flood Zone!"

A classic of the SCTs, the variations of the Flood Zone field were favorites of many viewers because of their simple obstacles. Like the Neutral Zone they didn't often offer much in the way of barriers or levels of complexity, but they were also just a notch more involved than the plain white of that most basic of combat areas. As the two second years were lifted up from the plating, so too did the water rise about their feet, then their ankles, then their shins. By the time the field was in place, the combatants stood in a knee-deep rush of what might have been mistaken for a shallow river were it not for the scenery projected behind them. A grey, boiling storm brewed and flashed lighting across the distant horizon, and the lashing pound of a torrential rain must have had the two fighters feeling soaked to the bone within seconds. They stood in what had likely once been a grain field—judging by the shape of an old-world style farmhouse in the distance—and even before the match began Rei could tell the two were fighting the force of the flood about their legs.

"Field: Flood Zone."

Fortunately for them, the Arena didn't keep them standing in the abuse of the elements for long.

"Cadet Omara Ejua versus Harper Heton. Combatants… Call."

The combatants—Ejua and Heton, Rei now knew—did as instructed, and from his left Viv shouted in excitement.

"Oh! This will be interesting!"

"You've got that right," Aria muttered from Rei's right, and he caught the flash of her NOED zooming in on the field even as he pulled up his own to do the same.

Ejua and Heton, it transpired, were both Duelists. The former's Device was a sleek, silver-blue overlaid with red vysetrium, and his two blades were identical, a pair of matching, curved sabers about 20 inches long by Rei's guess. A visor covered the top half of his face, the opaque glass alight with red lines the same color as his vysetrium, and the CAD enveloped every inch of both arms and legs, leaving only his torso and abdomen unprotected, along with his neck, chin, and mouth. Heton, on the other hand, stood in white-and-green with glowing orange lines, her Device having encased her body, neck, and head to just below her eyes, as well as from her knees and elbows down. Only her upper arms and thighs were bare, along with the crown of her pink-blue hair, and in her right hand she held a long, double-edged straight sword, complimented by a shorter parrying dagger in her left.

Though the two might only be second years, Rei got the impression they were still about to see a really, *really* good fight.

"Omara Ejua is a B4, and Heton is a B5." Catcher, meanwhile, looked to have pulled the cadets' profiles for them. "If I had to guess, I'd say that's pretty above average for the class at this point. These two might be in the top tier of the second years."

Viv made a squealing sound, and Rei had to stop himself from laughing out loud. His best friend had always been enthusiastic about becoming a CAD-fighter herself, but it could be hard to get her excited for any fight she wasn't taking part in.

Then again, the moment the Arena announced a start to the match, Ejua and Heton proved that Viv's glee was anything but misplaced.

"Combatants… Fight."

WOOSH!

Water sprayed in mirrored fins from either side of the field, tracing the flashes of red and orange that were Ejua and Heton. Duelists were generally the fastest of the User Types, of course, but if it could be assumed that the B-Ranked fighters had Strength of any respectable degree, it would have made the obstacle of the rushing water nothing more than a nuisance for the time being. Sure enough they met in the middle with a keen scream of steel cracking against steel, the whine of their blades ringing off each other so loud it could be made out even over the storm. From the crowd another eruption of enthusiasm echoed, and all around them Rei saw people leaning forward, undoubtedly zooming in on the fight themselves. He kept his own focus steady on the pair, watching and studying them as best he could. The spray of the water and the blur of their Devices made visibility minimal, but his decent Cognition spec allowed him to just make out most of the details.

It was an acrobatic dance of death.

Neither Ejua nor Heton ever stopped moving. Not as they struck, not as they blocked, not as they parried and deflected and dodged. Red and orange streaks of light reflected in the water and the spray as their legs stepped and flipped and kicked through the flood, and pretty soon Rei was seeing afterglow until the colors formed a sort of temporary cage about the two Duelists with every engagement. It was—without a doubt—a cut above the rest of the combat they had seen so far. Even Aria's match against Grant—as enthralling as it had been—suddenly paled in comparison to this incredible performance, this impromptu choreography of sword and light. Rei could only take it all in with bated breath, not realizing the stands had gone silent, not realizing nothing could be heard now but the ringing of weapons, the roar of the storm, and Michael Bretz's colorful commentary from his and Reese's place above the fight. For a minute or so that was all to be seen, all to be taken in.

And then the water started to rise.

No. It had always been rising, Rei knew. That was a common theme of the Flood Zone field. By the time he tore away from the fight long enough to take notice, the rush of the current had gained 4 or 5 inches up the length of both combatants' thighs, and looked only to be climbing quicker.

"It's rising fast…" Aria commented from his left.

Rei, along with Viv and Catcher, all nodded, but the fact only had them watching more intently. With Endurance likely in the B-Ranks, it would be a long while before Ejua or Heton started to tire, even at the pace they were going.

The field had other plans for them.

By the time the water reached their waists, mobility between the two fighters had become limited, and even as Duelists they were soon almost entirely immobilized for fear of losing their footing in the current. It hardly stopped the pacing of the fight, however, as their blades only started to blur faster and faster in an endless cacophony as the evenly matched pair both tried and failed to sneak in a blow, to apply even some minimal restriction that might just gain them the advantage. Neither managed it, however, and the water kept rising, kept climbing.

It had reached their midriffs before Heton made the first major move to turn the tides in her favor.

WHA-BOOM!

There was a blast of noise, and all the water for about 5 feet in every direction around the girl exploded up and outward in a massive, rippling wave. Ejua appeared to have been caught unawares, because through the spray Rei saw the shape of the dark-skinned boy catapulted backwards, looking to be absent his weapons.

"Oh, and there's Cadet Heton's Repulsion Ability!" Bretz shouted out over the storm as the stands exploded into cheers. "Electromagnetic energy from CAD-usage stored up in the Device, and then released in all directions! Looks like Ejua might be in trouble!"

"Looks like?" Viv snorted. "Dude lost his blades. He's done for."

"Nah," Catcher disagreed with a shake of his head. "He'll pull a ditch. Recall and call them back. Heton won't be able to get to him in time in the water to take advantage of the delay."

Rei had to agree. He didn't know if the girl's plan had been too well thought out. Repulsion was a limited Ability that had to be charged up to be potent. On any other field it would have combined well with her Speed, but restricted as that was...

And then, incomprehensibly, Rei saw Ejua stand up from where he'd been swept by the rush of water to the south edge of the field, still in his called Device, and still sans-weapons.

"What the...?" he and Aria both hissed together, leaning forward in tandem, so bewildered neither even noticed when they brushed shoulders to peer as close as possible at the goings-on below them.

"What is he doing?!" Catcher demanded, watching Ejua lift both hands up, almost like a Brawler, as Heton charged at him through the flood.

Then, from behind the girl, Rei saw two twin shapes lifting out of the water, and he shouted in understanding just in time for Ejua's matching swords to fling themselves at his opponent's back with nothing more than a pull of his fingers.

"Invisible Hand!"

Heton, too, seemed to have recognized the danger of the telling motion, because she threw herself sideways only a blink before she might have been impaled through the spine from behind. Rei saw one of the sabers catch her a glancing blow to the shoulder, but it must have been a shallow one because she shoved up out of the water again with both blades held ready, pink-blue hair soaking and plastered to her face and forehead and the white-green Device that covered her neck, cheeks, and shoulders. It was a good thing she did, because immediately she had to defend from an assault by Ejua's weapons, spinning and whirling in the still-climbing current as the sabers cut and slashed from every direction and angle even though their User stood a good 15 feet away.

"And Ejua pulls out his own stops!" Michael roared to match the crowd's enthusiasm. "Invisible hand! A rare Ability similar to Magnetic Hunt, but requiring the User's deliberate focus and attention! It puts a heavy burden on the wielder, but the control you get in exchange looks worth it to me!"

"Whoa!" Viv shouted, sliding to the very edge of her seat. "I've never seen anyone below the A-Ranks with Invisible Hand!"

"Me neither!" Catcher squealed in positive delight, fists balled over his knees while Heton fought for her life below them. "That is so *cool!*"

"And might be the end of the match," Rei muttered with a slight frown. "If Ejua can keep this up long enough for the water to slow—"

"Oh!" Aria's exclamation cut him off, however, and for good reason as it was echoed hundreds of times through the stadium, even from the third years.

As one of Ejua's sabers had descended, Heton had done something both foolish and incredible. The minute the enemy blade had sliced down towards her she'd dropped the parrying dagger in her left hand and—with a well-timed snap and twisting dodge—*caught* her opponent's saber by the handle. Ejua wasn't quick enough to stop the second of his blades, and without having to defend from two sides all of a sudden Heton whirled and slammed both her longsword and the boy's own stolen weapon into the Ability-controlled Device. There was a *pinging* sound, and the heavier weight of the two blades together sent the saber flying across the field so far it actually hit the opposite wall of the perimeter with a *bzzt* of pixilated energy.

And then, without pausing even a moment, Heton pulled her feet up from the ground, dropping into the rush that was now nearing her chest, and let herself be swept up by the current.

Swept up, and hurtled by the grace of nature right towards the very place her opponent stood near the curved edge of the south wall.

To his credit, Ejua had begun the process of salvaging the circumstances the moment his second saber had been sent sailing. His Device withdrew in a whirl of metal and red light as he recalled it, then started to take form again when he promptly summoned it once more. The ditch, however, came too late, because even though the CAD reappeared with both weapons back in his hands, it wasn't in time to stop Heton from triggering what turned out to be a very well-thought-out plan. Rei saw it at last, then, understood the circumstances the girl had set up for herself only as she erupted from the water again, barely feet from Ejua and his recovered sabers. The Repulsion she'd used had seemed a waste, earlier, had seemed a squandering of valuable energy.

Now, though, Rei saw it had been the key to getting Omara Ejua exactly where Heton had needed him.

WHA-BOOM!

The second Repulsion caught the boy as point-blank as the first, but this time there was no empty space behind him to accommodate Ejua's flying body. Instead he was slammed into the invisible wall of the field at devastating speed, the built-up energy of the released Ability flattening him for the briefest of moments against the gentle curve of the barrier as the water of the flood exploded outward once more. For a blink Rei saw Heton lunging freely forward, having immobilized her opponent *and* cleared her way to victory of all obstacles for only the briefest of moments.

It was all that was needed, in the end, for her longsword—the only blade left to her, now—to take Ejua cleanly through the heart, impaling him to the wall of the field as the weapon flashed and warped the barrier slightly when it erupted through his back.

"Fatal Damage Accrued. Winner: Harper Heton."

The fading sounds of the storm and flood were nothing compared to the eruption of cheers from the stands. Even many of the third years were on their feet, and nearly *every* first- and second year had leapt up the moment the victory was announced. Despite Heton's win, Rei knew the applause was for *both* Users, then, and he found himself looking forward to more of Omara Ejua's matches just as much as his victorious opponent's.

Michael Bretz seemed to be of a like mind.

"Congratulations to Cadet Heton, and a *brilliant* fight by both combatants! Let's all give another cheer as they take their leave of the field!"

The roar came again, even louder this time, as Heton put an arm around Ejua's waist to help him stagger out of the perimeter. Having already recalled their CADs, they both lifted hands in thanks before disappearing beneath the edge of the walkway, earning another spike in noise.

"That was bad-*ass*!" Viv's shout was barely audible despite the cheering finally starting to die. "Forget Break Step! I want Repulsion!"

"It would be even better for you in a more open field!" Rei agreed loudly, trying to make out Bretz's next announcement. "But yeah! You wouldn't think it would necessarily be ideal for a Speed-focused Type like Duelist, but it's what you do with it!"

"Valera Dent has it too," Catcher added eagerly as everyone finally gained their seats again. "And she's pretty much as fast as they come! Check out her retirement match against Alex Rightor sometime! It was really useful to her."

"I saw that fight live!" Rei exclaimed excitedly as Viv looked to be taking a note of the recommendation in her NOED. "Man, that was a great—!"

"Next match—" Bretz's voice cut across the lingering conversations "—Caleb Asino versus Kirill Viktorovich. Combatants, approach the field."

The second pairing of the day ended up taking place on a variation of Woodlands, and was both shorter and more brutal than the first when Viktorovich, a Phalanx in near-full Device armor, outmaneuvered Asino's limited Brawler's reach with the length of his spear. After that, the third, fourth, fifth, and several more matches passed without too much additional fanfare, none of the pairing being able to hold a candle to that first encounter between Ejua and Heton. They were all enthralling, in their own way, the speed and power of the weakest of the second years seeming still to outmatch the likes of Aria and Grant, but a combination of duller field selections and a lack of grace and fitness as compared to the opening Duelists made most of the fights lack in comparison.

And then, as the twelfth winner strode out of the ring while his defeated opponent limped away in shame, Bretz announced the contenders of the day's thirteenth pairing.

"Next match: Anatoli Sidorov versus Jasmine Song. Combatants, approach the field."

Immediately the Arena seemed to gain a new energy to it, an aura of excitement which—while never having fully departed—had lacked some presence following Harper Heton's win. The change was so palpable that on either side of him Rei saw Aria and Viv both frown and look around, clearly unsure of what to make of the shift in the stadium's aura.

"I'm guessing one of these guys is good?" Viv asked of Rei and Catcher after a moment.

"Very good." Catcher was the first to answer with a nod. "Sidorov. We already pointed him out, remember? At the announcement of the Intra-Schools."

"Dude. That was *six weeks ago*. The only reason I can remember what I had for *lunch* this morning is my Cognition spec!"

"He won the first years bracket at Sectionals last year," Rei repeated for her, watching the tall, somewhat-lanky form of Anatoli Sidorov make his calm way from the southeast wall towards the Dueling field, long bronze locks tied in a ponytail at the base of his neck. Across from him a shorter, stockier girl with short-cropped reddish hair—not unlike how Emily Gisham kept hers—was moving to stand on the opposite side. "Pretty handily, too, if I've heard correctly."

"Ah, I *thought* I knew his name from somewhere," Aria said with a nod before glancing at Rei in surprise. "You didn't watch the tournament? I would have expected you too, given Galens' presence in this Sector…"

"It was on the feeds at the same time as a couple of Earth's Sectionals were underway." Catcher said, watching Sidorov and Jasmine Song being told to take their positions in the ring. "I'm guessing he had to prioritize."

Rei, grateful he hadn't needed to explain himself, only nodded.

"Lucky," Aria grunted, sounding a little irritated as she leaned back and crossed her arms over her chest. "My mother gave me no choice. And I wasn't even *home*."

Rei grimaced. "Well she never gave you an option as to where you were going after preparatory school, so I can't say I'm surprised she wanted you as familiar with Galens as possible."

"Maybe," Aria grumbled over Reese's asking the combatants if they condoned to the rules of the Duel.

"If it makes you feel better, Sidorov is expected to be a shoo-in for the Systems this season," Catcher offered in a clear attempt to cheer her up. "Maybe even the Intersystems, like Lennon did last year. If you got to see *his* fight, then you didn't miss much by skipping the Sol Sectionals."

The Saber's assurances seemed to help a bit, because Aria looked a little less disappointed. Shortly after, though, her irritation with her family was likely forgotten, because the Arena began to glow.

Anatoli Sidorov, it transpired, was expected to climb high in the collegiate SCTs that year for very, *very* good reason. A Lancer-Type, his silver-grey CAD encased every inch of his body except the outer parts of his chest, with the tower-like helm that shielded his head bisected by a horizontal line of the same yellow vysetrium that edged the narrow blade of his simple spear. What the Device's weapon lacked in ornamentation, however, its owner more than made up for in fluid skill and ability, taking on his opponent with a careful, crafted approach to the Duel the likes of which Rei had yet seen. The fight did last nearly 2 minutes, but it was obvious from the go who would come out the victor. Sidorov didn't toy with Song, didn't play or mock her in that time. Rather, it was more like he would bare nothing but perfection in his engagements, like he could suffer all patience as he waited for the exact right moment to strike, the exact right moment to pounce. Song, a Brawler, was no common fighter herself, but the disadvantages of her CAD—a brilliant yellow Device interspersed over a black under-layer with green vysetrium—played right into the Lancer's strengths. Sidorov kept her nearly constantly at bay with superior reach, alternating between calmly fending off a barrage of pressing blows and pushing Song back himself with his own volley of flawless patterns and combinations. Even though not a single hit landed over the course of their exchanges, the Duel had the entire Arena holding its breath in the silence of the Neutral Zone the combatants had risen upon.

And then Song attempted to trigger what must have been Overclock, and the moment Sidorov had been so meticulously waiting for came in a blink.

The Brawler had kept him on his toes for nearly 20 seconds in a row, proving an incredible Endurance spec with a seemingly-endless gatling of punches and kicks against which the Lancer calmly stood his ground. The combination of strikes ended with a front-kick from Song that Sidorov caught—almost-casually—on the haft of his spear, but the block had clearly been read by the Brawler. Without hesitation she used her opponent's steadfast stance to plant and shove off of, soaring back more than 10 yards. Song landed lightly after an arching backflip, and there was a rippling of brightening green light.

Before Michael Bretz could so much as announce the trigger of the girl's Overclock, however, the Arena's voice rang clear over the silence of the stands.

"Fatal Damage Accrued. Victor: Anatoli Sidorov."

It had happened so fast, it took a full few seconds for anyone—including the chief warrant officer—to make sense of it. One moment Song had clearly been preparing to bring the full brunt of her Overclocked Device down on Sidorov's immovable facade of calm calculation.

The next, she was falling, twitching and limp, over the Lancer's shoulder, his spear having taking her through the sternum with such force, the yellow blade and half the shaft had punched out her back.

"OH!" Bretz finally boomed just as the crowd, too, erupted in ecstatic cheering. "And *there's* the impeccable timing Cadet Sidorov is known for! A little distance seems to have been all he was waiting for! Break Step is a dangerous Ability if you know how to use it, and this Lancer sure does!"

The applause redoubled, and Sidorov could be made out recalling his CAD so that it vanished from Song's chest as his silver-grey armor, too, whirled away into his CAD bands. He helped the shorter girl stand until she seemed to be regaining control of her feet again, then took his leave from her and the field with the same quite confidence with which he had fought, not even looking up into the stands.

"I can't tell if I think he's hot and arrogant or hot and shy," Viv said, watching Sidorov's bronze hair slip below the lip of the lower walkway. "

"He kinda reminds me of the Bishop," Catcher muttered. "The way he fights."

"That's fine." Viv shrugged. "Dent's hot, too."

"I *don't* recommend hitting on our instructors," Aria said with a giggle that had Rei rolling his eyes.

Viv, though, only grinned and said nothing more.

The rest of the day's fights passed in relative—if energetic—monotony, with none of the matches carrying half the excitement of either Ejua versus Heton or Sidorov's cool trouncing of Song. Nearly 2 hours later the cadets were once more released from their attendance, and Rei, Aria, Viv, and Catcher took advantage of their afternoon and evening in the same way they always enjoyed what late leisure time the Institute allowed them: training. Claiming their favorite field in East Center, they sparred and conditioned non-stop until the four of them decided collectively no one could put off dinner any longer. After a relatively brief meal—over which they mostly discussed the variety of Abilities they'd been privy to during the second years' fights that day—they returned to the Center and practiced again until they knew they were pushing having to run to get back to Kanes in time for curfew.

The next afternoon—Thursday's—proved a little more widely entertaining than the first of the second year's days. A good few more of the class' top-level Users took to the stage over the 3 or 4-hour tournament, and while there lacked any match quite as astounding as Sidorov's, Liam Gross had ample opportunity to comment on some half-dozen pairings that matched or surpassed the excitement of Ejua versus Heton. Nearly every fight involved one or more Abilities being triggered, and Rei and the others were treated not only to further impressive uses of common skills like Overclock and Break Step, but a few rarer ones as well. Magnetic Hunt was employed by two different Users on the second day—a Mauler name Benson Hert and a Phalanx name Fara Saberu—and a Saber named Johnson Robel applied Distortion to his sword, causing the length of the blade to vanish unless it was in motion, when it would appear only as a dense blurring in the air. All in all it was not an afternoon without lessons, and after another evening of practice and training Rei, Aria, Viv, and Catcher went to bed with the combined giddiness of the day's fights and the anticipation of the morrow's.

Friday, after all, was the start of the third year bracket…

As good a student as he liked to think himself, the next morning Rei could not have focused on John Markus' discussion on "Device evolution as related to improving specifications" even if the lieutenant major had been stripped naked, danced the macarena, and told them all their CADs were actually self-aware. Similarly, a lecture by Quentin Alphonse—a staff captain in Galens' Combat Theory Department—passed with such dull enthusiasm from 1-A that the man had eventually given up and granted them all permission to review the third year roster in preparation of the day's event. As a result, by the time lunch was done and the entirety of the Institute's student body was once more gathering inside the Arena, there was much speculation being thrown around about who would be seen on the field that day, and what possible pairings would make for the most brilliant fight.

"We should have started a betting pool," Catcher could be heard muttering to himself while Viv was still scrolling through the class roster.

"I think you said Archer made it to Systems last year, right?" She had taken on a more enthusiastic interest in the fights since the second years had started—particularly when it came to Duelists—and had been not-infrequently grilling the rest of them for any bit of information they had for 2 days now. "If they pit her against Hamilton, who do you think would come out on top?"

"Kevin Hamilton?" Rei asked. "He's another Duelist, right? A2? That puts him a rank above Archer, but I'm pretty sure he didn't make it higher than Globals last year so…" he considered a moment "…Archer."

"How do you *remember* that stuff?" Aria asked him, almost indignantly, as she looked him up and down from her usual seat at his right, like she wasn't sure if he were impressing her or freaking her out.

Rei would have settled for both, and he grinned at the thought.

"Don't look at me like that. I'm not some weirdo. If you're as into the SCTs as I've been my whole life, stats like that just stick with you naturally. Watch this." He turned to Catcher. "Catcher, what CAD-Type is Anthony Weston, and what's his rank?"

"No idea. I'm not a weirdo."

Aria and Viv both snorted at the answer, and Rei glared at his friend, who was looking at him with a perfectly innocent smile behind his live NOED. A second later, Rei got a private message.

Lancer. A1.

"Traitor," Rei grumbled, blinking out of the message as Catcher stifled a chuckle on Viv's other side.

At that moment, though, the clock struck 1300, and on cue the observers stepped out from under the walkway.

Dyrk Reese looked the same as he always had, walking briskly with his shaved temples gleaming beneath the lip of his military cap. On the other side of the field, however, a woman was matching his pace, and the already-vibrant thrum of the stands redoubled with excitement as the student body recognized Valera Dent herself even from behind. Upon reaching a common point, the two officers about-faced to stand at ease looking slightly away from each other, and Rei wondered if he was the only one to feel a sort of tension in the flawlessly composed expressions masking the pair's features.

"Those two do *not* like each other much, do they?" Aria muttered from his right.

Guess that answers that, Rei thought, trying not to smirk.

Soon Reese and Dent were in the air. They had only just reached the apex of their climb, the projected disc stabilizing under their booted feet, when the captain stepped forward and delivered the most to-the-point opening speech of any commentator thus far.

"Today, as you all know, marks the opening day of the third year bracket of the 81st Galens Institute Intra-Schools. Those of you seeking to climb as high as you can in this world would do well not to look away from the field for so much as a moment, this afternoon. This is the day you will understand how the difference in the time and effort you put in *now* will affect you in ripples and waves for years in the future."

For a while silence greeted her, the audience transfixed by the cool, steady words. After a time, her composure finally broke a little, and the Iron Bishop managed to crack the smallest of smiles, one corner of her synthetic lips curling upwards ever so slightly.

"Then again, there's always value in simply allowing yourself to be entertained. Therefore, and without further ado, please welcome to the stage your first combatants: Mira Esku and Sabina Thren!"

As the audience responded to the warmer shift in the woman's tone, the Arena erupted in cheers, spiking and fluctuating when two girls, both pale-skinned with blonde hair, stepped into view. Rei, for his part, sat quietly, watching Valera Dent with a frown.

To their credit, Aria, Viv, and Catcher all did the same.

"Cuts right to it, doesn't she?" Viv was the first to speak, not looking away from the captain as the two girls—Esku and Thren—came to stand opposite each other along the east and west edges of the Dueling field.

"Yeah, she does," Rei grunted, zooming in on Dent's face, where the thin smile was still suspended. "Call me a pessimist, but I'd be willing to swear that opening speech was the only bit of honesty we're gonna hear from her today."

"And I'd bet you're right," Aria muttered, finally uncrossing her arms to sit forward in her seat a little. "She's been pretty clear she's not the biggest fan of the SCTs."

"I think it's less that she's not a fan, and more that she thinks there's better things to be done with our time," Catcher said, looking around Viv and Rei's backs to the girl.

"Is she wrong?" Aria answered. "Twenty percent of the ISCMs Users are in the circuits, rather than the front lines."

"The *top* twenty percent," Viv added, and she lifted a hand to draw a line horizontally across her face with one finger. "And we all know Dent's probably got more reasons than most to wish there was more firepower aimed at the archons…"

Rei stayed out of the conversation, reminded a little too vividly of a certain interview he'd been forced to sit through, nearly 6 months ago now. Not for the first time he suddenly found himself wondering how many eyes and ears there were in his immediate vicinity, and how many of those were trained on him in a single given moment.

Fortunately for Rei, all involved in the conversation were given an excellent reason to forget about it the moment Dyrk Reese finished the customary questioning of the combatants' understanding of the rules, and the field began to rise.

It took them longer than usual to guess the stage, this time. There were no markers, no rising obstacles, but neither did the lifting ground beneath Esku and Thren's feet give any indication that it was a plain Neutral Zone that was coming into being. Instead, the projected sky above the combatants turned a clear, aquamarine-blue without so much as the hint of a cloud, and only when the two cadets had reached the 10-foot ascent did the floor of the field seem to shimmer into view.

No… No. It didn't *seem* to shimmer.

It *actually* shimmered, reflecting Esku and Thren in a rippling distortion, like an imperfect, twisting mirror.

"Field: Salt Flats."

The Arena's announcement brought a muttering of excited conversation and a few *whoops* of anticipation, which Rei found amusing. The ISCM was—like any entertainment behemoth before it—constantly reviewing and refreshing the parameters of its business. The Salt Flats were one of the most recent additions to the SCTs field-types, having been added to the rotation along with the much acclaimed Zero-Grav and Free Fall zones only a month or two prior. In Rei's opinion it was by far the most mundane of those three inclusions, but the masses would always find something enjoyable in anything shining and new.

At least for a time.

"Cadet Mira Esku versus Cadet Sabina Thren. Combatants... Call."

The two girls—standing 20 yards apart from each other as their reflections danced beneath their feet—did as commanded, and *this* time when the crowd cheered, Rei was right along with them.

Among the third years, there was as wide a discrepancy in rank as there was in both classes below them. The difference, however, was that the amount of training and discipline it took to catch up from D6 to C3—the current gap in power among the first years, as far as Rei knew—was a world of difference compared to what was needed to rise from *B*6 to *A*3. This, of course, was what Valera Dent had been alluding to in her opening speech. The discrepancy in the third year class, the silent awareness that those not in the highest tiers among themselves had fallen behind, and had likely fallen behind a long time ago. There would be duds, in the coming 2 days, Rei was sure. Matches in which the lower ranks were pitched against each other or—even worse—where one of the overwhelming strong would be paired with someone with far lesser ability. There wasn't a single student among the third years who wasn't *terrifying* of course, but it had to be acknowledged that those who'd fought and struggled and shed blood for every moment of every day of their time thus far at Galens had risen higher and farther than their less-willing classmates.

And what had excited the crowd was that Mira Esku and Sabina Thren were very obviously in that higher category both.

Though Rei had seen full-bodied CADs before, it had exclusively been through feeds, and certainly never in a setting of such trembling energy. Esku, it transpired, was a Mauler whose heavy Device was grey-white with murky blue vysetrium teasing its joints and lines. Her armor was layered and built up, much like the thick plating of the knights of ancient Europe on Earth that Rei had read about. The massive hammer she lugged over one shoulder with both hands had an uneven, jagged head, and could have been a solid hunk of some deep-sea glacier strapped into place atop a long haft by threading steel ribbons. Her form-fitting helmet had a decorative tail of projected blue light, and a single flat, circular viewing scope was embedded in the center of its faceplate, just between where her eyes would be. Its lens, glaring in the sun, was trained on the other cadet standing 20 yards across from Esku over the shimmering salt flats.

Much like everyone else's eyes in the stands.

While the Mauler's armor and weapon were indeed impressive, it was Thren's CAD that was swallowing all the attention, taking the form of a Lancer-Type in a whirling blink. A rare solid-green with vibrant yellow vysetrium detailing, the Device was leaned away from Esku's heavy plating in favor of slighter, slimmer steel that appeared almost skin-tight around Thren's legs, body, arms, and neck. Her head, too, was enveloped, with her face shielded by a pane of opaque yellow that curved overtop to cover her hair. In her right hand Thren held her weapon casually, a massive, tapered lance of green steel and bright vysetrium that looked far too heavy for any single person to be carrying so easily, counterbalanced by a shorter, heavy base that had to have been as thick as Rei's calf.

The girl's armor and armaments, however, was not what had everyone's attention.

Over Thren's shoulders, a solid half-loop of thick green steel lined with yellow floated like some broad, suspended collar. It drifted, seemingly lazily, shifting gently this way and that with every subtle movement of its User's body, appearing benign to any uneducated eye.

Well… Technically it *was* benign, but that hardly made it unworthy of attention.

"Is that an *external?*"

For once it was Viv who posed the question first, hissing out loud as the very query was repeated in a hundred different ways from as many mouths among the first- and second years. Her disbelief was well masked, but not completely hidden. Rei, too, couldn't help but gape in amazement and delight down at Thren, focusing his NOED in on her Device to observe it in careful detail.

"Has to be, right?" Catcher answered Viv after a second. "But for an A-Rank to have one? That's impressive!"

Very impressive, Rei agreed, taking in the odd, looped component floating above and behind the Lancer's shoulders.

External modules—or simply "externals", as they were much more commonly known—were hardly common as it was. Aside from usually being exclusive evolutions achieved by S-Ranked Users, they weren't even developed by *every* such CAD-fighter. Even as high as the Intersystems not all combatants were lucky enough to wield an external, much less more than one. It was unfortunate, too, because the modules provided an incredible advantage to any User who possessed them:

Flight.

Well, not *true* flight, exactly. Even Valera Dent—whose Kestrel held the living record of *eight* externals, as far as Rei knew—couldn't achieve that. What they *did* allow for, however, was near-flawless mobility, applying anti-grav tech to the User's Device that allowed them to skate over even—and sometimes uneven—ground like a dancer sliding over smooth ice. The more powerful—or numerous—the modules were, the greater the effect achieved, or at least the lesser the impact such mobility had on the User's neuroline. Rei was astounded to find Thren in possession of even a single external, and wondered if it hadn't been a recent gracing of a new evolution by her Device.

As far as he'd been aware, there was supposed to have been only *one* third year at Galens with such an advantage.

Rei's musing, though, were interrupted by the Arena's cool, calm voice.

"Combatants… Fight."

CRACK!

The speed at which Esku and Thren launched themselves towards each other in that moment was so astounding, it took a moment for Rei to convince himself one or both of them hadn't just broke the sound barrier. Two lines of disturbed earth and settling dust suddenly appeared in the originally perfect surface of the flats where the girls had rocketed towards each other from either side, and even in the brilliance of the sun the flaring, flashing colors of their Devices shown blue and yellow through the air.

"*Both* combatants open with a Break Step, looking to catch the other by surprise!" Captain Dent's voice cut over the *clanging* of metal and the roar of the crowd. "They've met dead-center, and are now putting their all in a close-quarters match!"

Rei heard Viv shout in astonishment at the announcement of the early triggered abilities, but he ignored her. Even Esku, a *Mauler*, cut and cleaved so fast that he doubted an opening Break Step would have put much strain on her body. More interesting to him, rather, was the fact that the fight had indeed immediately devolved into one of incredibly close proximity. Despite the pair possessing what was arguably the greatest standard range among CAD-Type, they had stepped well into each other's reach, exchanging a furious flurry of sweeps and blows that left him dizzy as he tried to follow them. He wondered, abruptly, how he had for so long been able to appreciate CAD-fights at this level and beyond before he'd developed a decent Cognition, and could only imagine it had been a simple, potent fascination with the sheer power and speed A- and S-Ranked Users could bring to bear.

Now that he could actually *follow* the fight, though… Rei found himself stricken with an awe the likes of which he had never before experienced.

Despite the irregularity of the combat, despite the proximity of Esku and Thren, despite neither of them being able to bring either of their weapons to bear to any appropriate extent, their exchange was fluid, flawless, and seemingly without end. In consecutive volleying back and forth the two third years twisted and swung and slammed the broad-sides and butts of their Device hafts at each other, almost appearing to take it in careful turns to duck and dodge and dance out of the way. The whole time, however, neither girl stepped beyond the disadvantaged range they shared, like they both held more faith in preventing the other from bringing the full might of their weapons to bear than they did in having the chance to applying their own true strength. To the casual observer it might have seemed like fear, like cowardice.

To Rei, however, it spoke only to the absolute acknowledgement by each combatant of the other's ability.

Wham-WHAM!

Thren was the first to land a real blow, the paired kicks happening so fast Rei almost missed the combo despite having been watching with riveted, rapt attention. As Esku had adjusted her footwork, taking a small approaching step over the dust-choked flat, Thren had hooked her heel with the crook of an ankle, jerking the leg forward. In a blink the Lancer's foot was back up, slamming into the Mauler's chest even as she just started falling from the surprise off-balancing. Esku rocketed backwards, limbs and still-held hammer trailing after her body like the tails of a kite. She hit the ground only a few yards from the field perimeter, tucking and rolling and coming up on her feet in time to deflect the driving point of Thren's weapon, thrust forward in a graceful assault as the Lancer had zipped across the flat ground with nothing more than a shove of one foot and a pulse of yellow light from her external. Despite the failed attack the crowd roared in approval as the first use of the module occurred, the mere effect of it enough to send screams of excitement rippling through the crowd.

Rei forced himself not to get caught up in the energy, forced himself not to get lost in the avid exhilaration of witnessing such a battle with his own two eyes for the first time.

Thren recovered from the deflection in a blink, keeping behind the momentum of the skating lunge to drive a narrow shoulder into Esku's armored side. This turned out to be a mistake, because while the Mauler slid several feet across the salts, she herself hardly shivered from the impact. Instead, she took the opportunity to release the haft of her hammer with one hand, slamming the back of a clenched fist at Thren's face. The Lancer blocked only barely in time with a raised arm, but the minimal Defense her slim Device must have offered was highlighted when Esku's blow landed hard enough to drive through, catching Thren in the head anyway and sending her staggering sideways. Rei thought he saw something like shards of yellow glass raining to the floor of the field, and sure enough when the Lancer looked up the right side of her visor was mostly shattered.

Well… At least it wasn't her face.

Unperturbed by the damage to her Device, Thren thrust herself sideways. Any other User would merely have made an awkward hop with such a motion, but the third year instead slipped over the ground in a graceful arc around Esku, salt dust rising in wisps after her trailing foot. The Mauler—not to be outdone—looked to time the angle of the circle, then blurred forward to try and catch Thren by surprise.

It didn't work, but it did provide Dent another chance to shout about the second Break Step usage.

Over several minutes the fight continued to evolve, growing more and more vicious at every opportunity. Thren managed to drive the point of her lance into Esku's side, earning herself the advantage for a time before the Mauler caught her left arm in a downward chop of her blue hammer. A minute later the Lancer had demonstrated that she also possessed the Repulsion Ability, but Esku looked to have read some sign in the shifting of her opponent's body, because she leapt clear of the blast radius only an instant before the energy was released. It was the Mauler's turn after that to unleash Mirage—an Ability that briefly projected an autonomous-but-harmless second copy of herself—but Thren used the advantage of her reach to keep the two mirrored images of her enemy at bay long enough for the hologram to flicker and fade. Not long after that the two girls looked to be reduced to nothing but their own physical ability, the fight ramping up in both speed and savagery as the pair grew desperate to end the match before either of them reached the limit of their Endurance.

In the end, it was Thren's body that failed first.

Not for a moment had the Duel slowed down. Not for a moment had the two girls disengaged, or had one retreated in an attempt to catch a breather and recover. On the contrary, the paired third years had gone after each other like beasts lost to bloodlust, hacking, slashing, and stabbing all while throwing dust and sand into the air in great clouds as they steadily ruined the perfection of the salt flats between them. For this reason, it surprised no one when the end came abruptly, when the loss was delivered only after body, mind, and Device alike had been pushed to their limits, and very likely beyond.

PING!

The sound of loose steel ringing clean echoed the flashing, whirling form of Thren's green-and-yellow lance flying point-over-end through the air, knocked out of its User's grip by a massive up-cut from her opponent's hammer the Lancer had tried desperately to deflect. She managed to save herself the impact of the blow, but her Strength failed her in that moment, her weapon sailing well-clear of her reach. Immediately she launched herself backwards, skating in reverse without taking her gaze off of Esku, obviously making a play to retrieve the lance.

Unfortunately for her, she chose to withdraw in a straight line.

Rei could forgive her the mistake. According to his clock they had been fighting for nearly 6 minutes now, and the girl had to have been exhausted. Still, not only did he wince as he watched the retreat, but on either side of him he saw Aria, Viv, and Catcher alike all share in his moment of realization.

When Esku lunged forward in her third Break Step of the match, it came to no one's surprise.

The Mauler's ability caught her up to Thren so fast, she would have actually *passed* her opponent had it not been for the hammer swinging horizontally at her side. The massive, uneven head of blue vysetrium caught the Lancer full in the chest, and between the momentum of the Break Step and the blow itself, Rei could only whistle in astonishment when Thren was sent catapulting back so fast it wasn't even a heartbeat before she slammed into the perimeter barrier with a shuddering impact that sent a wide ripple of static along the projection in all directions. She slid down the invisible wall from there, the shattered parts of her external tumbling about her shoulders to fall to the ground. At once she was struggling, and the girl found her feet for a moment. Just a moment.

In CAD-fighting, there is no mercy.

WHAM!

Esku's hammer, thrown with the confident precision of someone who had practiced the exact motion ten thousand times before, took the beaten Lancer squarely in the head, crushing it against the wall. As a phantom-call Thren was obviously spared the ugly, eruptive decapitation this would have earned her otherwise, but just the same there was a collected "OOH!" of sympathetic pain from the crowd on impact.

Then, as User and hammer alike tumbled to the ground, the Arena spoke.

"Fatal Damage Accrued. Victor: Mira Esku."

The absolute explosion of cheering that followed this announcement was so loud, Aria started and covered her ears in surprise at Rei's right, only lowering her hands again after the initial wave of screams and applause had died down. Over the noise only Dent's voice could be heard, amplified as it was.

"An excellent fight to both cadets! A flawless demonstration of positioning, Abilities, and prowess! Congratulations, Cadet Esku, on your first victory of the season!"

The cheering rose again, and from the left Viv had to holler to be heard.

"That was brutal!" She, like Rei, was watching Mira Esku wave to the crowd, face glistening with sweat over a broad smile now that her grey-white Device had been recalled. At her back Sabina Thren looked to be having trouble getting to her feet, and in a blink of impressive Speed an officer of the Institute was by her side, steadying her.

"As it should be!" Catcher howled ecstatically before whistling his approval along with the crowd.

"They were basically an even match!" Aria seemed to think Viv's statement deserved more of an answer. "Once you get to that level…"

"Unstoppable force. Immovable object." Rei nodded. Thren looked to be recovering from the cerebral scrambling her FDA had caused, because she was trying to make another attempt to stand—with help this time. "A-Rank. S-Rank… Down where we are you'll get plenty of matches that end fast. It's normal. In the grand scheme of things we're brand-spanking new at all this. After a few years, though…" He waved a hand to where the Lancer was being led, leaning heavily on the assisting officer, from the southeast side of the field, all while Mira Esku continued to wave as she walked off in the opposite direction.

"Maybe." Viv was able to speak in a normal voice as the applause finally subdued. "But still… That was brutal."

Whether fortunately or not, this fact didn't change for the rest of the afternoon.

After Esku versus Thren, a consecutive series of equally devastating matches took place in rapid succession, each seeming more awesome than the last. Tim Greyson— a Duelist whose twin scimitars had blades made of pure red vysetrium—narrowly beat out David Jenson after almost falling prey to the Brawler's nasty combination of Overclock and repetitive Strike Pulses—an Ability that extended the reach of a User's attack by combining it with a short burst of electromagnetic energy. After that, Verah O'Donnel took the win over Jasper Serent after nearly 10 whole minutes of the two Sabers managing a treacherous, mountainside variation of the Northern Tundra field. Next came the upset of Karen Behst—an A3 Phalanx—giving up a win to B9 Mauler Elizabeth Aaron when a distinctly cocky attitude cost her first her right leg, then the match in quick order.

After that the pairings became a little more varied, the fights a bit more scattered now that Major Reese's selection had caught the attention of the crowd. An A4 Duelist made short work of his B8 opponent, ending the match with such quick ferocity there were nearly as many boos from the crowd as cheers. Two fights later, an A3 Lancer took his time dismantling the B7 Brawler he'd been pitched against, earning much appreciation from the stands, but glares of disapproval from both Reese and Captain Dent after the match was done. From there the up and down of the pairings became almost consistent, with breathtaking battles interspersed with brutal defeats that left Rei feeling sorry for the weaker party.

Still… No one missed the hammering in of Valera Dent's earlier point.

"Remember when I told you you'd make a good training partner if only because of the number of hours you were going to force me to practice?" Aria asked Rei under her breath at one point, as another mid-A-Rank Brawler punched the lights out of the B7 Lancer she'd been set against.

Rei nodded without looking away as FDA was announced.

"Do you feel a bit better about that now?"

He smirked, but didn't answer.

The afternoon pressed on with its undulating excitement, though the energy of the crowd as a whole never fell below a certain level. Even when the matches set two

B-Ranks against each other the fights were as intense as the top-level second year's had been, leaving no one wanting for so much as a moment for entertainment. By the time the thirty-second—and final—pairing concluded with a 9-minute match between two A-Ranked Phalanxes, even Rei found that he had shouted himself hoarse despite every attempt made to keep focused on the fights rather than the outcomes.

Sore throats, of course, didn't stop any of them from conversing enthusiastically as they finally made their exit from the Arena some 10 minutes later, following a brief call for a last applause for the afternoon's fighters from Dent. As always, the four of them made a line immediately for East Center, the path to the facility a bit more well-trafficked than they were used to at this hour.

"That was *amazing*!" Viv did her best to exclaim once they were free of the bulk of the crowd, trailing the path east only with the other students who looked to be of a same mind as them. "I get it. I've got to say it. I get it. I finally understand why you two fanboy so hard about the SCTs."

Rei chuckled, glancing back at her from under the brim of his cap and pulling the collar for his uniform jacket up around his neck to fight off a chilly autumn breeze. "*This* is what convinced you?" he asked, amused. "Don't get me wrong, it's definitely badass and all, but I've been forcing you to watch S-Ranked matches with me since we were *fourteen*, Viv!"

"It's different in person," Aria chimed in. "At least in my opinion."

"*Exactly*," Viv agreed, puffing into her cupped hands to keep them warm as they walked. Despite a healthy late-afternoon sun still lingering over the skyscrapers of Castalon at their backs, her breath misted through her fingers. "This is my first-time seeing matches like this up close!"

"It is?" Catcher sounded astounded. "Seriously? Then what was it that got you so interested in becoming a User in the first place?"

"I was good at fighting," Viv told him with a perfectly straight face. Only after Catcher had blinked at her in confusion did she break into a smile. "It was the excitement, man. The energy. I mean, I *was* good at fighting—"

"She was," Rei agreed as they took a turn in the path, passing beneath a copse of overhanging willows.

"—but my family are all bureaucrats and politicians. *Not* something I would be good at."

"She wouldn't." This time Rei grinned as he chimed in.

Viv glared at him a moment, but it was Catcher who spoke again first.

"Okay... Sure. I guess I see that. But still... You've *never* seen an SCT in person?!"

Viv shook her head, and for some reason Rei found Catcher staring at *him* in amazement.

"Can you believe that? If I'd had nothing but the feeds to watch, I don't know if I'd be here, today."

Rei smirked, looking forward again. "You're asking the wrong person to back you up there, man. The feeds are all I ever had, and I used to have to sneak into the Matron's office to steal her pad to watch before the Estoran Center let me go to Grandcrest."

There was a *smack* from behind him that could only have been Catcher face-palming.

"Sorry, man," the Saber grumbled apologetically. "That's me being an ass."

Rei laughed. "How? By *forgetting* that I come from a different place than most of the other cadets here? If anything I wish more people would do the same."

There was a rare pause in the conversation as Catcher—mollified but obviously still embarrassed—held his tongue, and it was Aria who spoke up from Rei's side as the East Center came into view a ways ahead of them.

"I think it was freedom, for me."

Rei looked at her sidelong. "The reason you got interested in becoming a User?"

Aria nodded, her pale, freckled cheeks flushed in the bright cold.

"Not your family?" Viv's expression was inquisitive.

Aria gave a dry laugh. "If you asked them they'd definitely say otherwise, but if anything my mother's pressure was more of a constant reason I sometimes considered *not* pursuing a career in the ISCM."

"You would have ditched the military just to spite her?" Catcher had clearly recovered from his faux pas already. "That's a serious grudge, Aria..."

Aria shrugged. "It's a seriously *earned* grudge. At least I didn't flee to the front lines to get away from her, like Amina did. Not yet, anyway."

Rei looked at her side long. "Just make it big in the SCTs. She won't be able to pull on your leash then, will she?"

Aria gave him a look that was both appreciative and exasperated. "Tell that to my brother."

It was Rei's turn to shut up, knowing he'd put his foot in his mouth as they reached the training facility, the doors of the building hissing open for them readily. He knew the story, of course, knew the tale of Kalus Laurent at this point. Though not as much of a prodigy as Aria, her older brother had still achieved Pawn-Class certification almost straight out of school, 2 years prior, becoming a rare S-Ranked A-Type at the *very* impressive age of 22. He wasn't yet a regular of the Intersystem circuits, but there was no doubt he would be soon enough.

And yet, despite that mounting success—or *because* of it, perhaps—Kalus had cut off all ties with his family for no other reason than to escape the whispered words of Salista Laurent.

And that was *still* a better option than the eldest child, Amina, had ended up taking in order to slip loose of the family's clutches.

Feeling a bit of an idiot, Rei let the others talk amongst themselves as they changed in the Center's single large locker room, then headed for their favorite training room hall. The facility was busier than usual—with nearly every practice field claimed by cadets inspired by the opening weeks of the Intra-Schools—but Viv had started making a habit of booking their time each morning in the ballpark of when they expected to need access to it. The variation in the days' match-lengths had made this tricky, but whether because it couldn't be bothered or because they were already frequent customers, the system had never given them grief for the occasions they were late to their reservations.

For the usual 2 hours-plus the four of them sparred, Rei taking on Aria for most of the time, Viv against Catcher. They swapped up on occasion for a change of pace, but on the whole kept to their routines, stopping only to give each other feedback or inquire from someone about a particular problem their respective Type might cause in a fight. Aria was skilled enough with her spear to fill in for a Lancer's consideration, and Catcher could help out when it came to studying up on taking on a sword-wielding Phalanx, but Rei had to admit they lacked a Mauler's eye in their conversation, something that had been brought up not-infrequently before.

Given the nature of Shido's growth, however, none of them had every managed to come up with the name of anyone they felt comfortable adding to their little group.

After their first training round was up, they changed, showered, and broke for dinner, wolfing down a quick meal of chicken parmigiana and pasta in the mess-hall as they discussed their pairings that coming Monday and Tuesday. Aria and Catcher felt confident enough with their brackets—having been matched with opponents they had no reason to think they couldn't manage—so most of supper was spent focused on Viv and Rei's potential trouble.

"I mean it's not *impossible*," Viv said for the seventh time that evening, handing her empty tray to a passing service bot and sounding more and more like she was trying to convince herself of the fact rather than anyone else. "Right? I've practically caught up to him in Rank. So what if he was in the summer training course?"

"It's *not* impossible," Aria agreed with a serious nod, offering her own tray, too. "You'll just need to be careful, and be aware that you won't be able to rely on the advantage of your Speed quite as much. Jack Benaly might be built like a wall, but he's still a Brawler. He'll be able to go toe-to-toe with your agility, and probably has better Endurance to boot."

"Thanks," Viv grumbled dejectedly. "Don't know if that was supposed to make me feel better, though…"

Aria laughed, pushing her chair back to stand as she looked questioningly between them all and motioned towards the door. As Rei and Catcher nodded and got to their feet to join her, she kept on. "Don't pout. You know that's not what I meant. You've got plenty of other advantages to play into, and you're a *better fighter*, Viv, simply put. Jack Benaly won't know what hit him."

Viv shrugged, clearly still unconvinced as she, too, stood.

"Maybe Rei should spend some extra time with her this weekend?" Catcher suggested to the group as they started for the mess hall exit. "Just to get her more used to fighting a—"

"No!"

The echoed answer came from Viv and Aria both, the two girls glaring back at Catcher while Rei led the way through the pine woods-section of the arboretum once more into the tropical area where most of the other first years typically ate.

"It was just a thought," Catcher corrected himself quickly, tossing both hands in the air so that Arthus' bands slipped down his wrists into his sleeves. "No need to take my head off, I promise."

"Rei already has one loss," Viv growled, apparently not remotely placated by the Saber's show of submission. "If he gets another, he's out of the running completely. He needs as much time pitted against the biggest challenge we can get him. Presently, that's Aria."

"That's me," Aria herself agreed. The statement wasn't haughty or self-important. It was merely fact, a truth they were all intimately aware of.

Rei gave a light laugh as he dodged Sam Dorne walking by with a teetering tray of food, accompanying a girl he didn't know. "Lay off Catcher, guys. He's got a point." He looked around at Viv behind him. "It won't kill me to take an hour or two to work with you over the weekend. *If anything*—" he had to put an emphasis on the words as both Viv and Aria seemed ready to interrupt him "—your Speed matches Aria's, and your fighting style is closest to a Brawler's. It might do me some good in preparation for Warren."

Viv continued to look unconvinced, but Aria seemed suddenly less sure of herself.

The discussion lasted them the brisk walk back to East Center, hands in their pockets and chins tucked against an evening wind that was particularly cold in the artificially early sunset provided by Castalon's encircling presence around the school. It took Rei and Catcher both to convince Viv to accept Rei's help, only managing it with a further heavy emphasis on the fact that changing partners up was not without its advantages to all parties involved. By the time they reached the training facility and changed once more back into the they grey-and-red combat suits, Viv had finally caved.

"Fine, fine!" she threw her hands up in surrender as they exited into the Center's main hall and made for their training room. "I give up! I will graciously accept your assistance and wisdom, oh wise and powerful Reidon."

Rei grimaced in amusement, not looking back around at her. "I don't know… That didn't sound very 'gracious' at all to me. What do you think, Catcher?"

"Not gracious in the least!" the Saber echoed dutifully.

"You two are going to rightfully earn yourself each half of Gemela in the back, one night," Aria said with a laugh even as Viv started something much to the same purpose. "I wouldn't blame her either, if you keep up this—"

She cut herself short, though, as they came up to the room. With the fading of the day, many of the enthusiastic cadets who had previously occupied the rest of the East Center's field had called it an evening, likely with much self-congratulations and bolstered confidence in their futures as Users. There were still a few fields occupied, of course, but all of these rooms were—like Rei and the other's kept theirs when training—set to opaque walls that barely allowed for any more than a blurred silhouette and *maybe* the faint streak of some particularly bright vysetrium. The other unused chambers were dark, their solar lights having dimmed to off not long after whatever occupants had previously been putting them to use had vacated. It was, for this reason, especially odd that the room the four of them tended to prefer was not only well-lit, but had also had its smart-glass walls set to clear.

It made the two figures conversing on the other side of the wall, near the edge of the field perimeter closest to the ajar door, immediately identifiable despite being turned slightly away from them.

"Holy hell…" Catcher whispered in disbelief.

He was the only one among them who managed to get so much as a word out.

Slowly, tentatively, Rei approached the entrance to the room, pushing the cracked door further open as he took an uneasy step inside, his eyes never leaving the two people. He must have made some noise he didn't notice, because the pair cut off whatever quiet discussion they had been having to look around at him and the others.

Valera Dent, as was her habit greeted the four of them with the faintest hint of a smile.

"Good evening, cadets. I was getting worried you would pick *this* night in particular to skip your usual hours."

She was dressed in her regulars, complete with cap and the red-on-white armband below her left shoulder. She stood with her arms crossed—cutting a casual air that made it clear this was an informal visit—and around her wrists the white vysetrium in Kestrel's bands shone bright against its blue-and-red steel.

For once, however, it was not the Iron Bishop that drew the attention in the room.

"Holy shit…" Catcher could be heard muttering again as he too, undoubtedly, took in the second, slighter figure standing by the captain's side.

The young man was an inch or two shorter than the woman, this accentuated by the fact that he was not wearing a military cap. He wasn't wearing *any* article of ISCM regulars, in fact, standing at ease by Dent instead in the red-on-blue combat uniform of a third year cadet. He had dark, almost-black skin, complemented by designed blue eyes and deep-grey hair threaded into dreads now tied behind his head in a short tail. His face was soft—strangely so for a User who underwent intense physical training—and his shoulders were narrow, making him seem almost diminutive in stature alongside the presence of the Iron Bishop.

And yet, despite this, it remained a fact Rei—and no doubt Aria, Viv, and Catcher right along with him—had recognized the young man before he'd so much as turned to face them.

"Christopher Lennon…" Aria was the one to speak this time, so quietly she sounded like the name might have been a slip of the tongue.

At her words, Lennon looked directly at her. "You know me? Good. That will keep introductions simpler." He studied her a moment more before speaking again. "Aria Laurent. Phalanx. C3." His blue eyes flicked to Viv. "Viviana Arada. Duelist. C0." He turned to Catcher. "Layton Catchwick. Saber. D9." Then, finally, his cool gaze—steady as that of a predator that did not belong in his slighter frame and build—fell on Rei. "And Reidon Ward. A-Type. Also D9."

After this listing, there was a quiet pause that might have been misconstrued as awkwardness by an uninformed observer.

Anyone who could have glimpsed the thoughts of Rei or any of his friends, however, would have known the lot of them to be merely dumbstruck by the fact that Christopher Lennon—"the Lasher" himself—knew their faces from the door they still all stood dumbly in front of.

Eventually Valera Dent seemed to take pity on them, though when she spoke it was with a much more pronounced smile. "Close your mouths, you lot. You'll drool on the projection plating. We have barely two hours until your curfew sounds, and I'd like to take advantage of every minute possible."

"T-Take advantage, ma'am?" Rei stammered, only able to look away from Lennon for more than a glance as he struggled to process what she had said. His mind was a muddle. Despite his Cognition, he couldn't decide if he should be trying harder not to stare, if he should be saluting the captain, or if he should be pulling his pad out to ask the third year for his autograph.

"Yes, Ward. I'm hijacking your extra training hours tonight. I've decided you four—" she waved a hand to indicate him and the others without uncrossing her arms "—are in need of a challenge. Something to *really* get your engines going."

"A-A challenge, ma'am?" It was Aria's turn to stammer, though Rei was convinced she had to be doing a better job of not gaping as she asked.

"Me." Christopher Lennon said simply, looking slowly between them all again.

There was a moment of truly stunned silence this time.

"What…?" Viv's squeak of incomprehension—and maybe a little apprehension—broke the quiet.

Captain Dent smirked. "You heard him, Arada. Cadet Lennon here has graciously agreed to do me a favor. You four have been training against each other for some time now. I decided you needed a change-up."

"Against *him*?" Catcher demanded in a hiss. "All due respect ma'am… Are you trying to kill us?"

For the first time, Lennon showed a hint of amusement, one corner of his lip lifting into a crooked smile. "Hardly any danger of that in sparring matches, isn't there, Catchwick? Or do they no longer teach the basics of phantom-calls in first year anymore?"

"Don't tease them," Dent told him, but she looked to be hiding her own amusement as she looked to Catcher. "Kill you, Catchwick? No. Not at all." Her face grew suddenly serious. "*Push* you? Yes. *Hone* you, yes? *Temper* you all into something more than you are now? Yes."

"In two hours?" Rei asked her, not understanding.

"For starters," the captain answered back cryptically. "You might be surprised what two hours can teach you, under the right circumstances."

"That's assuming you *have* those two hours, ma'am," Lennon said without looking away from where he'd taken to studying Rei. "At this rate we'll be lucky to finish warmups before you have to send them to the showers."

"True enough," Dent agreed with a nod, meeting Rei, Aria, Viv, and Catcher's eyes one after the other. "It's hardly my intention to force this on any of you. I can guess that by your responses, you all have some idea of what is about to happen. If any of you would rather spend your evening otherwise, I'll arrange for combat simulations on another field." She paused, letting the offer sink in. "Anyone want to get off this train?"

"No, ma'am!"

The response was immediate and collective, Rei and the others all straightening to attention at once at the woman's question. They might have shared in mutual disbelief—they were standing in the same room as the *Lasher*, after all—but Rei knew that not one among them was fool enough to pass up such an opportunity, unexpected as it might be.

Dent looked to repress another smile.

"Good. I thought not."

A brief flash of her NOED, and behind her the field came to life, blooming solid white for a moment before five red starting circles appeared in the projection, four staggered at even points 5 yards from the inside of each cardinal direction along the perimeter, with the final dead center in the middle of the combat zone.

"I think you can figure out your positions, right?" the captain asked when the field was through manifesting.

"Are… Are we taking him on all at once?" Viv's question came tentative. She might ordinarily have been the fiery one among their group, but at the moment she seemed to have all the fight of a kitten.

Even Viv, apparently, needed no clueing in as to what they were about to face.

"If you had half your class with you, it still wouldn't be enough, Arada," Lennon told her plainly, turning away from them and taking a step up onto the field. Just like Aria's early statement, there was nothing conceited about the proclamation, no bravado.

It was—as they all knew—merely a fact.

Lennon was in the center of the space before any of the four of them had reached their own starting rings, arms loose by his sides and watching them spread out around him after dropping their bags by the door to climb onto the field. When Aria—who'd made for the furthest ring across the perimeter—finally reached her place, he turned in a slow circle to address them all.

"First, you'll show me what you can do. One at a time. I've seen you fight, but that's hardly any way to take your measure. Besides—" his eyes fell briefly on Rei "—there's always the chance one or two of you might have learned a new trick since the start of the week."

He smirked, apparently unsurprised as all three of the others glanced at Rei in mutual surprise.

Then his gaze flicked to Catcher. "You. Catchwick. Come at me with everything you've got."

"Uh, m-me...?" Catcher asked, pointing dumbly at himself as his face paled.

In answer, however, Lennon looked to Dent, standing silently at the edge of the field. After a moment's hesitation, the captain nodded.

Instantly, Lennon vanished.

WHAM!

Catcher went flying, impacted by the third year's punch with all of the force of an orbital train. He slammed into the invisible wall nearly 10 yards at his back so hard the projection actually warped outward a bit, then rebounded, tossing him into the boundary like the field were spitting him onto the floor in disappointment.

"Is there another Catchwick in this room, first year?" Lennon asked evenly of the gasping, wheezing boy, red light fading from his eyes.

Rei's hands had gone numb. He should have been concerned, should have been worried as Catcher struggled to breath, rolling slowly over onto his hands and knees. The Saber coughed, then gagged, one hand coming up to clutch at the fabric of his combat suit just below his chest. Rei should have been worried.

But all he could do was stare.

It had been so *fast*. Lennon had triggered a Break Step, sure, but Rei hadn't so much as seen him move. What was more, the third year hadn't called on his Device, at least not fully. There had been no physical summoning, phantom or otherwise, the red glow which had already winked out in the older boy's eyes the only hint that he'd used anything more than his natural ability to move.

He had tapped into that much Speed with nothing but the barest brushing of his CAD's potential.

"If this is how serious you're going to take me, then maybe I *should* have introduced myself," Lennon decided aloud, looking around at Rei and the others as Catcher continued the fruitless fight to find his feet. "My name is Christopher Lennon, though you might know me as 'the Lasher'. I'm an A-Type, like Cadet Ward here. My CAD-Rank—" he smiled a little as he spoke, the predator roaring forth in his gaze again as he looked at Rei "—is A8."

W hat followed were the 2 most grueling hours of Rei's—and he suspected any of his friends'—life. Forget the pain of post-op recovery. Forget the fatigue of Michael Bretz' training, or the intensity of the Intra-School fights. Despite everything they brought to bear, not only did all four of them together fail to put so much as a single scratch on Lennon, but they did so in cohesion with the fact that the third year never once called on his CAD again for the duration of the training session, not even partially.

For the first half hour or so Lennon took them on individually in bouts of several minutes, shouting and goading them into challenging him with everything they had. Despite having no assistance from his Device, there was no doubt he *allowed* Rei and the others to dance around the field with him for a bit each time, always ending the practice bouts brutally, oftentimes resulting in the registration of concussions, broken bones, or ruptured organs despite the fact Lennon was using nothing more than his bare fists to fight. All the while, too, the young man kept a steady, inscrutable expression, the only shifting in his face coming as a slightly raised eyebrow when Rei called on Shido for the first time, the Device whirling into its newly mirrored form around his arms. Of course, this didn't make any difference in the outcome of their bout, nor their next three.

What was more, that first 30 minutes turned out to be the *easy* part of the night.

Christopher Lennon was a legend—on Astra-3 and far beyond—for good reason. Qualifying for the Collegiate Intersystems as a second year wasn't unheard of, but of the *hundred*-plus cadets from across the ISC to come together for that highest-level of tournaments, *maybe* a half-dozen weren't in their third year of whatever academy they were receiving their schooling in. Lennon had ranked in the top eight of the Astra Systems the season before—the only second year to do so—and had almost made it into the top fifty overall Users in the civilized *galaxy,* not even speaking of the expectation people had for his showing in the coming tournaments.

Handling a foursome of D- and C-Rankers—with or without his CAD manifested—posed no more of a challenge to Lennon than Rei might have had ignoring a swarm of gnats in the summer sun.

They fought with hardly any breaks, hardly any pause. As one they attacked the dark-skinned third year again and again, and as one they were rebuffed in rapid succession every time. After his initial inspection of their abilities, Lennon took on a roll not unlike the grey projections of the Offense & Endurance parameter tests, always defending and never attacking.

And still he found a way to ensure all of them—even Aria—spent more time on the ground then on their own two feet.

"Ooph!" Viv grunted, falling flat on her face as Lennon sidestepped the point of Gemela's lunging sword at the last possible instant, hooking her ankle with a trailing leg to trip her up. In the same motion he redirected Catcher's down-cut with an open palm, deliberately guiding Arthus' purple blade to the side so that Aria was forced to bring Hippolyta's shield up to defend herself from the adjusted attack. Rei, too, was in the midst of the melee, ducking low to slash at Lennon's exposed knee.

His blow jarred to a stop when the third year's bare foot found the crook of his wrist, then Rei was yelling as he was pulled down by the stamping leg, finding himself pinned by the forearm to the floor for a moment.

He didn't stay there long, of course. Lennon didn't stay there long, after all. The third year was like water given will. It wasn't just *speed* that he moved with, wasn't just *guile.* There was a grace in his body and limbs that spoke half of sheer, natural skill, and half of unwavering, unending conviction and training. Rei had to consider more than once, as they all fought, that *this* was what it was like to face someone in the highest tiers of the SCTs, collegiate or otherwise. Though Lennon wasn't an S-Rank yet, he was damn close, and might very well be by the time the season's Intersystems came along, much less by the end of the school year. Despite any lesser demeanor the young man's appearance might cut, Rei knew he was standing in the ring of one of the future greats of the Simulated Combat Tournaments, both collegiate and beyond.

It was the only thing that kept him going, that kept him in the fighting even long, *long* after his Endurance and body were spent.

"That's enough."

Valera's call to end came in the middle of a complex engagement involving all four of them closing in on Lennon from every direction, looking to make a mark on the third year more by sheer luck than any significant measure of skill, given that even Aria looked to be ready to keel over from exhaustion. The moment the captain spoke the words, however, he was gone from their midst, triggering another Break Step to blur between Catcher and Viv and come to stand just inside the invisible wall beyond which Dent had been watching them all evening. With a collective yelping and pained grunts, Rei, Aria, Viv, and Catcher together all collided with one another, everyone but Aria ending up on their asses to rub at bumped heads or offended anatomy where friendly weapons had inadvertently cut.

"Cadet Lennon," Dent said as the field faded under them, sharp eyes trailing across the group while they helped each other to their feet. "Your impressions, if you would."

Lennon didn't hesitate, coming to stand at ease as he spoke, eyes on Aria first.

"Laurent, you depend too much on your defensive posturing. You have a favorite stance, which will be your end as soon as you come across an opponent who knows how to get around it. Vary your combat more. The advantage of surprise can be hard to come by in a Duel, but a Phalanx going on the offense—especially a spear-wielder like you—can certainly achieve that. Catchwick—" Lennon's gaze fell on Catcher "—your technique is excellent, but it's also textbook. Take a lesson out of Ward's style and learn to be a little more unpredictable. Arada—" Viv's turn "—you're chaotic. I like that. But you also leave yourself open a lot. That's all well and good when you're the fastest on the field and can correct for it, but the moment you're not you'll lose, and you'll lose quick."

Finally, Lennon looked to Rei, and when he spoke it was slowly, like he was considering every word.

"Ward... You're simultaneously the one with the least to work on, and the most improvement to make. Despite what I just said to Catchwick, *you* could learn from him as well. You've got the Brawler technique down, I can tell, but when you have the opportunity to apply it you tend to think yourself too far outside the box. Occam's razor: when you hear hoofbeats, think horse, not zebras. Sometimes the basics are exactly what you need."

He paused, then, considering Rei for a moment before continuing.

"Also... Is what you've shown me really the extent of what your Device can do?"

Rei, still breathing hard as he and the others struggled to stand up straight under the weight of extreme fatigue, tried and failed to answer. He knew what the third year was getting at, though, and in the end just nodded, his sweat-soaked hair sticking to his ears and forehead.

Lennon frowned, eyes dropping to Shido's black-white and blue, tracing the steel patterns with something like disappointed consideration. Rei was sure he knew what the A-Ranker was thinking, now, watching Lennon study the Devices claws for a few seconds.

Shido *wasn't* a Brawler-Type, after all.

"Well, I suppose you're still a little low in the ranks," he said at last. "The Cs are more promising. I guess I'll just have to be patient." Then, abruptly, he smiled, the first *true* smile the young man had graced them with the entire evening. "Also, you need to improve your Endurance. It's blatant from a mile away that your opponents only have to run you ragged if they want an easy time putting you in a hole."

The breaking of the Lasher's stoic exterior at long last felt—in a very strange way—like a rather healthy reward after the brutality of their session. Rei returned the smile, as did Aria, Viv, and Catcher at his side.

"Yes, sir," he was able to get out this time, unsurprised to hear his voice come as a croak from a parched throat.

The others managed to echo Rei's words, and Lennon looked around at Dent with raised eyebrows.

"Hear that, captain? At some point I earned enough respect to be called 'sir'. I feel so special."

Dent snorted. "I'll allow it, given the circumstances." Then she grew serious, not looking away from the Lasher. "So? Do we have a deal?"

The question puzzled Rei, and he knew he wasn't the only one as Aria and Viv exchanged a confused look at his side.

Lennon, though, didn't answer at once. Instead, his gaze fell on Rei, and despite his face having fallen back into its standard expression of military-apathetic, he couldn't hide the glint of interest in those brilliant blue eyes.

"Yes, ma'am, we do. I even get the feeling this won't be a complete waste of my time, by the time we're done."

CHAPTER 41

Seven weeks!" Catcher half-squealed, half-groaned for what could only have been the ten thousandth time in 12 hours. "Seven *weeks*!"

"You're making it hard to tell if you're miserable or excited," Aria said with a quiet laugh, cutting into her pancakes with an enthusiasm only barely hidden behind what Viv teased was her "ladylike comportment".

"I can't be both?!" Catcher demanded, leaning over the table in his eagerness. "We're going to train with Christopher—!"

"*Catcher*!" Viv hissed in warning, elbowing him in the side from where she sat on his right, across from Rei.

Catcher lowered his voice, but the pitch of his words made the attempt at subtlety all but useless. "We're going to train with Christopher Lennon for seven weeks! Seven *weeks*, guys!"

"Six, if you discount last night," Rei said with a grin. "And it's only two hours one evening a week, man. No need to get so worked up about it."

Catcher glared at him from over his waffles and bacon. "Rei, I will bet my breakfast that you were up all night screaming with excitement into your pillow, so don't give me that bullshit."

Viv guffawed and Aria nearly choked on her pancake at this, then all over again after they both caught sight of the flush Rei could feel creeping up his neck.

"Give me your breakfast, then," he said, trying to save face.

Catcher raised an eyebrow. "Yeah?"

Rei grinned. "You said *all* night. I managed to get some sleep at around 0400, I think."

They all shared a good laugh at that.

"It *is* a little surreal, though, isn't it?" Aria carried on the conversation a bit later, after they'd handed their trays to the service bots and started making for their morning classes. "I mean… It's the *Lasher*. What the hell does he have to gain from working with us? *Why* is he working with us?"

"Dent," Rei and Viv said together. He was pleased he wasn't the only one who'd come to the conclusion, and he waved for Viv to go ahead as they approached the doors of the mess hall.

"They said it last night," she explained, taking the lead both in the conversation and out into the cold of a grey, chilly morning, complete with a biting wind that shook the trees around them and stung at the cheeks and ears. "They've made some kind of deal. I'm thinking *she's* training *him*, or at least found someone to do it for her."

Aria's eyes went wide, and she looked to consider the point as she tucked her chin into her jacket and pulled the regulars a little tighter around herself to help ward off the cold.

"I guess that makes sense…" she agreed at last. "If you think about it there's not too many staffers who could give Lennon much of a challenge, are there? I'm pretty sure Lieutenant Imala is an A7…"

"Bretz is an A8," Rei backed her up with a nod, hitching his bag over his shoulder as they turned southeast, towards the Device Evolution Department building where one of John Markus' rare lectures was going to be taking up their whole morning. "Not to mention Lennon is an A-Type. Pretty sure we're the only three in the school. I'll bet anything he trains with the Duelists, just like I train with the Brawlers."

"Which would make Dent an ideal instructor…" Aria said with a nod. "She and the colonel are the only S-Ranks in the school. I'm not even sure there's an A9 among the staffers." She looked up at Viv. "Yeah… I'm sold. She's definitely training him, or finding someone from outside campus to do it. Probably in exchange for him working with *us*. Which means my questions doesn't change that much, though…"

"Why is the captain bothering with us?" Catcher offered helpfully.

"Exactly."

"Seek advantages, and you'll earn them," Rei told them as a group of third years passed going in the other direction, looking to be headed for the Arena.

Aria and Catcher both glanced around at him, only confused for a moment.

Then understanding dawned on them.

"Yeah." Rei nodded along as they clearly followed his meaning. "It's not exactly what she said, but it amounts to the same thing. I don't know if we need to dwell too much on the mystery of it. There hasn't be a *day* since the middle of the first quarter that we haven't spent grinding at our Ranks." He grinned. "I think we've *earned* some training time with Christopher Lennon, don't you?"

Judging by the matching smiles on his friends' faces, then, he was pretty sure the silence that answered him was one of unanimous agreement.

For once, Markus' lecture was anything but dull. Smartening up to the fact that they still had the second day of the third year's opening bracket coming up that afternoon, the lieutenant major had polished the topic of his class, making sure it was something they could all be enthusiastic about. In the end the morning passed pleasantly enough, the double period with 1-C—which meant even Catcher got to sit with them that day—spent following the Device evolution of several of Galens' most esteemed graduates—including Dalek O'Rourke—over the first 5 or so years of their careers via combat recordings. It was *fascinating* seeing where some of the ISCM's historical greats had started, then where they'd ended up by the time they reached the middle and upper classes of the S-Rank. Everyone—even Viv—had heard of most if not all of the Users Markus covered that morning, but Rei would have given up Shido if *any* of them had been privy to these earliest recordings of the fighters. O'Rourke, it turned out, had started out like him, with Cerebryx nothing more than a single-handed punching weapon that had eventually become the great, bullish Device which had earned him his "Gatecrasher" combat-name. Serena von Bor, "the Ivory Shield", had begun with a small buckler and shortsword, and it was thrilling to watch her CAD evolve into the mountain of regal white-and-yellow armor, complete with a tower shield and curved saber. James Wicky's first manifestations had been almost identical to Viv's, his Duelist's blades transforming over time into the twin rapiers that had seen him nearly crowned champion of the Intersystems a half-dozen years in a row.

By the time class ended, both the 1-A and 1-C class blocks were abuzz with refreshed excitement at the future of their careers, their energy only accentuated by the fact that no one could wait for the noon leisure to wrap.

At last, after an hour lunch that felt at least thrice as long, they were headed to the Arena for the sixth and final day of the Intra-Schools' opening week. Rei, Aria, Viv, and Catcher followed the throngs out of the mess towards the center of the school in a rare silence, all of them sharing in the same anticipation they had built up talking over the meal. It had been exciting before, this particular afternoon. Before, there had been much to look forward too already, much to await. Dyrk Reese—as ever—had been masterful in the design of the brackets, leaving one final treat for the last day of the first pairings. Before, there had been much to look forward to.

After the previous evening, however, Rei and the others were suddenly waiting with absolute impatience for the first of what was undoubtedly going to be a short series of highlights in the tournament.

Reaching the Arena, they let themselves be swept up in the entering ground, climbing the stairs and trailing the walkway before climbing to claim their usual seats in the first years' section. Rei might have been imagining it, but he thought the noise of the gathering students was different, today. It wasn't *subdued*, per se—that was the wrong word for it. It *was* quieter, *was* a little easier on the ears in the echoing expanse of the great open chamber, but it was also more intense.

It was like *everyone*, rather than just most, were conversing now, but only doing so in lowered, exhilarated voices.

"Sounds like we're not the only ones looking forward to this," Cather muttered on cue.

Together Rei and the girls nodded in agreement, but said nothing more.

1300 approached, and for once there were no stragglers, no latecomers to the day's events. Not a soul moved along the walkways or stairwells even 5 minutes before the hour, and the Arena had actually gone quiet well before the clock marked the start of the day. Indeed, it was in almost utter silence that the afternoon's observing officers started across the pitch from opposite sides, though more than one voice *did* pick up in pleased surprise as Dyrk Reese's companion was recognized.

"Oh!" Aria exclaimed with hushed interest, and for good reason.

After all, her uncle—the commanding officer of the Galens Institute, and the only S-Ranked User in the school other than Valera Dent—had apparently taken the time out of his busy schedule to commentate for them that day.

"Good afternoon!" Colonel Rama Guest's booming voice echoed across the renewed buzz of the students and seated staff once he and the major were floating above the field on their projected viewing disc.

"Good afternoon!" the crowd answered with impressive cohesion, though a few awkward "sir!"s followed this from here and there.

The colonel offered them a tempered, amused smile. "No need for that, fortunately. For the next three or four hours I heartily give you all the great privilege of treating me as nothing more than your tournament commentator. I'm not well-practiced as an announcer—which I hope you'll forgive and understand—but Major Reese told me a few weeks ago that my presence might well add a little panache to this final day of the opening week. Oh—" he paused and looked around at Dyrk Reese with dramatic apology "—was I not supposed to tell them that?"

There was a rolling wave of laughter from the crowd, Rei and Catcher included as Aria and Viv hid smiles. From behind the colonel, Dyrk Reese hadn't moved, though one might have thought one of the man's eyebrows had twitched in irritation at the jest.

How he'd got that stick shoved so far up his ass, Rei could only imagine.

"Now, then," Guest returned his attention on his audiences, and his light-hearted air sobered a bit, "you're hardly here for my stand-up routine, I think. Five days. Five days you have watched and witnessed and learned as cadet after cadet has climbed and fallen on this Arena, has won and lost and fought for the chance to move forward, ever forward. Five days some of you have taken in where you've ascended from, while others have only come to understand how far they have still to go. I have yet to see a match end without earning commendations for both fighters in some form or another. I've yet to hear of a student who has not given it their all on this field, even when the bouts were brief. This week has been spent in intensity: in intense enjoyment, in intense study, in intense strain. You who have already faced your opponents have earned a respite, and earned a reward. It is no secret, I think, that there is one match left that each and every one of you awaits with anticipation. I understand, and I assure you it will arrive. However... I would remind you all that the cadets who will face each other for you in the meantime are no opening act. They are no warm-up, no appetizer. Every student who takes the stage today is here for one purpose, and one purpose only: to climb higher, to reach for the stars, and seek to start their journey towards their place in history, their place on the walls of this Arena's underworks. You are allowed to be excited. You are allowed to anticipate. But do not forget that every moment—not just the one you await—is an opportunity to learn, to grow. This is true today, as it is true for every second of you life as a User, as a soldier of the ISCM."

Guest paused, allowing his magnified words to resonate over the crowd, now silent again.

Then, when he seemed sure he had gotten his point across, he smiled once more.

"And so, without further fanfare... Cadet Caleb Ensure! Cadet Wattana Jelani! Please approach the field!"

Not long after, the final day of the opening week of the Intra-Schools started with a roar.

The first match of the afternoon was an absolute massacre, at least in Rei's opinion. It might have seemed a balanced fight if one judged only by the full 3 minutes it took Wattana Jelani—a Saber—to plant her two-handed greatsword into Caleb Ensure's gut, but the reality of the exchange was that Jelani had only been taking her time with the heavyset Brawler. Despite the weight of her orange-and-white weapon, the girl had wielded it with deadly skill, deflecting and redirecting every punch Ensure threw at her with ease, right up until the perfect moment arrived. Then, as though it was nothing more than an afterthought, Jelani stepped into her opponent's swing and ran him through with deft grace, putting an abrupt end to the fight.

The next match too, was a bit one-sided, as was the third. After that, though, there was a solid string of consecutive pairings that had the crowd on their feet more than once as the combatants blurred and blazed across different fields, their arsenal of Devices flaring lights of every color through forests and cliffs and buildings, then over snow-blown ice and ocean tides. The Flood Zone field made an appearance again, this time as a tidal rush of water passing under a stone bridge that looked to be moments from being swept away. The two cadets who had their stand there—a Mauler and Duelist named Schmidt and Heatley respectively—had to battle an ugly mess of wind, rain, and slick footing as their CADs lit the grey storm in arcs and flashes.

That was one of the fights that had gotten a standing ovation, when Heatley had used a rare Ability called "Puppeteer" to remove himself from his armor, leaving an autonomous shell that ended up getting ahold of Schmidt's legs and immobilizing him just long enough to lose the Mauler the match.

In the end, the colonel's fear of misplaced attention turned out to be baseless. The third years—even the weaker end of the class—all made a good showing, not a single User allowing their fight to be ignored in favor of a future treat. One by one the bouts came and went, and one by one the applause rose for the winners, in tandem with sympathy for the losers. Over the course of three hours or so Rei sat in rigid attention as he had the opportunity to see names he knew fight, and even more to learn some fresh ones. Lana Archer—to Viv's great delight—proved an absolute menace with a pair of blades she applied Magnetic Hunt beautifully, trapping her opponent by willing her Device to close in on him from both directions. The underdog Noah Wagner surprised everyone when he viciously battled his way into overcoming a Phalanx that was four ranks higher than him. Saber Samar Bandi ended his bout in less than 10 seconds, triggering a Break Step right out the gate that—judging by the shouts of enjoyment from the third year section at this—was a recent evolution, and certainly a surprise to his opponent.

One by one the bouts came and went.

The thirty-first fight of the afternoon was a particularly enjoyable one. Two Phalanxes named Liu Jie and Paul Williams—both A4s—faced off on a variation of the Neutral Zone, the entire zone one flat plane other than a single thick pillar of white in the very center of the circle. More than once Rei had glanced over to see if Aria was watching as intently as he hoped, because the battle was a perfect chance to check out exactly what higher-levels of her Type could do when going on the offensive. It took nearly 10 minutes of back and forth, but even as defensive specialists neither of the two Users ever allowed themselves to completely wall up, ever allowed themselves to be driven too far back towards the walls. Jie employed Mirage several times over the course of the match, which Williams handled with well-timed triggers of his Third Eye—the only other cadet Rei had seen all week with Aria's Ability. In the end, *both* Phalanxes called on Overclock as they entered the 9th minute, and the stands were on their feet well-before the match ended, the crowds howling with glee and awe as the pair cut and slashed and slammed into each other with terrifying, breathtaking power.

Eventually, though, it was Williams who was left standing, thrusting his spear in the air over Jie's fallen form before promptly keeling over from exhaustion just as the Arena called out his victory.

"And a *wonderful* showing from our second-to-last combatants!" Rama Guest rumbled as the two third years reached the projection plating together, both staying prone for a few seconds while they caught their breath. Despite his earlier implication of his lack of ability, the colonel had proven as capable an announcer as any of the other commentators all week. "It goes to show that Phalanxes aren't all shield, and it's important to remember that you sometimes have to get aggressive if you don't want to get knocked on your tail!"

There was a light rolling of laughter from the crowd—something Guest had achieved several times over the course of the afternoon.

"Isn't the colonel a Lancer?" Viv asked over the noise. "What's with his thing for Phalanxes? That's like the fifth time he's talked them up today."

Rei only grinned and shrugged, looking sidelong and being utterly unsurprised to find Aria hiding her face with the brim of her cap as the cheek he could see flared red with quiet embarrassment.

"Now then!" Guest resumed after the laughter had subsided a little. "You have all been patient! You have all been enthusiastic! I could not have asked for anything more from the proud students of this school!" Though he spoke in the jovial exultations of an announcer, perhaps out of habit the man had come to stand at ease with his chin up, and he very much cut the image of Galens' Command Officer despite his smile. "As promised—if by absence alone—there *is* one last fight for you all to enjoy today. One last match for you—every one of you, now, without exception—to learn from." Guest raised one hand. "From the right, allow me to introduce Cadet Annika Ivanov!"

Immediately a tall, slender girl appeared from under the edge of the walkway, striding forward with stern confidence as her black hair, streaked with artful white lines, swayed in a braided plait behind her neck. There was a healthy toll of clapping and whistling, mostly from what was likely Ivanov's class block among the third years, picked up by others in the crowd.

All eyes, though, were only on her until the colonel lifted his other hand.

"And from the left, Cadet Christopher 'Lasher' Lennon!"

The eruption of heightened applause that followed Lennon's name didn't wait for the boy to step out into the open. People in every class, first, second, and third alike, were on their feet as he made his appearance, walking towards the west edge of the field. It took Rama Guest lifting both hands in the air with a commanding glare into the stands before the students—and some staff, Rei noted with amusement—settled again. Who could blame them, though? Lennon was the only cadet at Galens who bore an official field name, approved and sanctified by the ISCM. Most of the *officers* didn't sport such an honor, and yet the unimposing boy with black skin and grey hair who now stood calmly just outside the perimeter of the Dueling ring had earned it.

And earned it as a second year User.

Once the crowd was calmed, Guest stepped back, allowing Reese to take command of the formalities for the thirty-second time that day.

"Combatants, take position."

Together Lennon and Ivanov crossed the silver line and made their way to their respective starting circles. The moment they stood within the red markers, the major continued briefly.

"This is as an official Duel. Do you condone and agree to the rules of this fight?"

Two nods. So opposed to the intensity of the enthusiasm not a handful of seconds ago, the tension of the silence now felt like it could be tasted on the air.

Reese's eye flared, and the field began to change.

It was *immediately* apparent—at least to anyone who had been keeping up with the professional circuits of late—what the zone was going to be. Instead of an upwards swelling of color and material like there usually was, the projection plating seemed to vanish as its black faded into absolute darkness, like a bottomless pit. Lennon and Ivanov, meanwhile, started to rise, each lifted above that void atop a hunk of warped scrap metal. As they climbed, more such junk materialized in the emptiness around them, and by the time they came to a hovering stop 10 feet above the field enough of the scene had come together to form a full picture as what looked like a broken, crumbling ship floated slowly across the backdrop of the projection.

A space wreckage.

"Field: Zero-Grav."

The Arena's cool voice cleaved through the palpable, vibrating quiet of the stands, managing to draw out two or three excited shouts here and there, but only those few.

Everyone else was busy watching Lennon and Ivanov drift off their respective hunks of debris, the physics of the zone taking over even before they got their devices out.

"Cadet Annika Ivanov versus Cadet Christopher 'Lasher' Lennon. Combatants… Call."

That, Rei knew, was the moment the spectators got their first taste of the experience they had been anticipating all day.

Ivanov, it transpired, was a Lancer, but clearly not just *any* Lancer. Almost every third year had had a completed Device—the full armor that covered every inch of their skin in addition to their weapons—but Ivanov's proved… something else. As the CAD whirled into being from the bands around her wrists, the girl appeared to grow.

No… She actually *did* grow, Rei realized.

Such a change wasn't abnormal, to a certain degree. Shido added a solid half-inch of height to his still-short frame, after all. Ivanov's Device, on the other hand, swelled in a way that *no one* would have classified as "normal".

The CAD was formed of silver-and-white steel accented with purple vysetrium. It manifested in layers of plating, the pieces looping and locking into themselves until the girl's slender frame had broadened to more than half her original width again. She grew taller too—though it was a little bit harder to tell free-floating like she was—the Device's feet elongating slightly as clawed, weight-bearing toes made their appearance. The helm came into being last, a slim framing of metal that first tapered, then widened again at the top, the forward edge of which was lined in a glow of purple. In her right hand a halberd with a blade that might have been the size of Rei's whole body came up to be taken in a double grip, held before the girl defensively.

All in all, the Device was an impressive piece of tech, clearly sporting evolutions for Speed and Defense that probably outstripped most other Lancers of Ivanov's age.

It was almost a pity, therefore, that the opponent she faced that day was aptly called "the Lasher".

Lennon's Device had not expanded his form, as far as Rei could tell. The black steel, interlaced over a grey underlay, had not made him taller or broader or more menacing. If anything, in fact, the boy's armor very much matched his usual physical appearance: unimpressive, unintimidating. Even the glowing red of the vysetrium wouldn't have helped, though the trio of illuminated lines that cut vertically down the clean metal of his oblong helmet *did* have a certain flair to it.

There were, however, two things that *did* make Christopher Lennon stand out from the crowd.

The first came in the form of a mirrored trio of black-and-red modules that hovered just behind him, one longer, broader shape like a shield floating above his upper back, the other two angular, outwardly pointing triangles a little closer to his shoulders. The externals didn't move, didn't so much as twitch from their position, so still was Lennon keeping even as he floated.

The other difference of note, of course, were the weapons.

"Holy hell..." Viv could be heard whispering at Rei's left.

Christopher Lennon was a true A-Type, the wielder of a Device that did not physically fit any classification among the other standard Types. Instead of a blade or spear or hammer, a thin hilt was held in each of his fists from which a long, drifting tail of black steel and red light floated in the zero-gravity environment. About 12 feet in length each, the weapons would best have been described as massive, flat swords that had been broken into even, angled segments, until Lennon was left with two chain-like apparatuses with razored edges and broad, tapered points. With the barest flick up of his wrists the third year drew the floating steel linkings closer, the weapons drifting upward like the universe's most dangerous rope cast to water.

Abruptly, in the space of the blink that was all it took for a Device to be called on, "the Lasher" had come to be among them in truth.

"Combatants… Fight."

CLANG!

It was Ivanov who made the opening move. The moment the match start was announced, she twisted her halberd and punched it into the torn platform of metal she'd been slowly drifting away from. Sinking the purple blade in deep enough to get traction, she pulled herself down until her broad clawed toes made the surface.

Then, almost as soon as she'd landed, she was gone again.

"WHOA!" Catcher yelled, taken aback, and Aria and Viv both gasped.

Rei made no sound, however. He was too focused on trying to see everything, to take in every moment, every second of what he could tell was about to be a titanic matching.

Clearly the mass of the wreckage Ivanov had launched from had been enough to bear her weight, because it only drifted slightly away as the girl catapulted across open space in a silver-white blur, as bright and powerful as some great steel arrow fired from history's most terrifying ballista. The purple halberd led the assault, bearing down on Lennon with all speed.

So when he twisted aside in midair—echoing a short pulse of his externals—to let Ivanov flash by him into nothingness, it was with such snapping reflex that Rei thought he'd blinked and missed it.

Ivanov must have anticipated this, however, because when she slammed into the invisible wall of the field perimeter it was with both feet, and she was lancing at the Lasher again so soon after she might as well have just rebounded right off the projection. Again Lennon skated aside, then a third time when the girl ricocheted off a passing hunk of hull, then a forth when she launched from the wall again.

The fifth pass couldn't have happened 6 seconds into the match.

Rei had never witnessed anything like it. *Never.* He'd seen a few matches on the Zero-Grav field before, but most had been inside ships' hulls that had been simulated to have lost their artificial gravity, allowing for more intimate combat. Here, though, the open vacuum of space called for something altogether different, and Ivanov was using the lack of friction and the power of her Device's adapted legs to great advantage.

Meanwhile Lennon had done nothing more than engage his modules to move him this way and that just enough to miss death by inches every time.

It was on the sixth pass that the game changed. Ivanov cut at Lennon horizontally this time, and at last the chain-swords came to life. With a ripping jerk of one arm the drifting steel blades sped upward in a blur, moving with such force they deflected the slash. Ivanov wasn't done, though, because her halberd almost immediately sank into a passing mass of steel and loose wires. The debris accepted her weight, allowing her to spin around the haft of her weapon like a gymnast and bring both legs wheeling about at Lennon's face. The Lasher blocked with crossed arms, and though he himself didn't look to so much as wince under the blow, the impetus of it sent him tumbling head-over-heels through space with dizzying speed. Ivanov found her footing—standing almost upside down to Rei and the other spectators' perspective—then launched off again, clearly hoping to take advantage of what had to have been a loss of her opponent's bearings.

Unfortunately for her, she'd underestimated who it was she was facing.

An instant before the Lancer's halberd might have cut into Lennon's body, his form seemed to expand outward with explosive growth. One moment he'd been a tumbling figure heading for the wall, and the next he was a flashing, rippling sphere of black and red.

Red?

Rei understood just as Ivanov's weapon *pinged* away, and it was only with a violent bend and twist of her own body that the girl managed to avoid getting cut to ribbons. She hit the wall before Lennon, but leapt clear of the blurred shape that was the young man before he collided with the limit of the projection himself.

Collided, but only after snapping his chain-swords out and away to keep them from collapsing in on him.

It was awesome, seeing it now, realizing the optical illusion. Lennon *had* likely lost his bearings—at least for a moment—tumbling as he'd been. It hadn't mattered, however, because he had started swinging, whirling his fluid weapons about himself with such blinding speed that the trailing metal and vysetrium had briefly looked like a rough shell about his body, practically impenetrable even as he'd flew.

He wasn't an S-Rank yet, and *still* the move was unlike anything Rei had ever witnessed.

"Incredible," Aria whisper breathlessly from his right, giving voice to his silent amazement. "His Device *has* to have crap Defense with armor like that, and yet he can still mount a *total* guard despite lacking footing. Incredible…"

Rei was about to agree, eager to share his own wonder, when Ivanov started her assault again.

In a dizzying series of jetting leaps the Lancer shoved off the wall, then off the body of an empty escape pod, then off another hunk of hull. This trio of directional shifts took barely a second, but just the same the red lines of Lennon's helmet never lost her as she moved. Her attack came in a flash and was promptly deflected, but this hardly mattered when she bounced away again in another blinding line.

In 5 seconds she had attacked four times, then twice that in 10. Ivanov was nothing more than a streak of silvery steel, ricocheting again and again and again off the wreckage and wall her opponent still had his back to. It was like watching trailing lightning that flashed purple here and there, matched with black and red when one of the chain-swords snapped into position to slash away a cutting strike.

"Does she have a plan?" It was Viv's turn to voice her thoughts, peering with her NOED live in her eyes into the exchange. "I get that he's dangerous, but this doesn't seem to be working…"

"It's probably all she can do," Catcher answered before Rei could, leaning forward on her other side. "The size of her weapon… She can't be used to having someone with a reach advantage on her, even among other Lancers. Plus, Lennon's chain-swords are *just* as versatile in proximity as they are at range. He's quick, but the nature of those weapons means a delay between strike and impact." He slashed a hand in front of him in emphasis. "They trail. So Ivanov has adapted."

"She's got Speed herself, so if she can attack and get out of the way in time to avoid getting caught…" Viv nodded catching on as Ivanov continued to blur about the wedge of the field she'd effectively trapped Lennon in. "I get it. Makes sense. But still…"

"It doesn't seem to be working," Rei repeated, finishing for her in agreement.

It was true. As impressive a feat as the Lancer's blistering assault was, it was obvious she was having a hard time getting through Lennon's active defense. She cut and she stabbed and she thrust at him with every pass, but not one blow broke his guard, not one attack wasn't rebuked in a snap of black and red.

On the other hand, Lennon seemed to have spent the entirety of the match on his back foot. Not once had he done anything more than take Ivanov's aggression, accepting it as those red lines followed her movements like a trio of angry eyes. Was it possible the girl's tactics had boxed him in a corner?

No. No, definitely not. Rei had only caught one or two of the Lasher's fights in the previous collegiate season, but even those fleeting experiences were enough to tell him there was more going on. Christopher Lennon was waiting, he knew. He was waiting, but not in the way most Users waited, seeking the moment of mistake, the chance their opponents would give them to break the stalemate. Lennon was more than that. His legend alone dictated this.

Slowly, Rei smiled.

"What?" Aria asked him, having apparently caught the expression in the corner of her vision. "What? Did you figure something out?"

Rei nodded. "Yeah. And you're gonna like it."

"What? Why?"

"'Cause it's a lesson we already know."

And then, like the words were the key to the flood, the Lasher turned the tides of the battle with a single snap of one wrist.

It was the fact that Ivanov was leaping *away* from him when the chain-swords started to move that had Rei knowing he was right. She'd just bounced off the wall in the direction of another chunk of debris, glancing off this to the heavy shape of what might have been a torn ship wing, then off a painted plate of solid steel. From there she lanced right at Lennon once more…

And found herself streaking towards the broad point of the chain-swords as *it* rushed at *her*.

There were screams from the crowd as Ivanov fell for the trap. She managed to recover, but barely, slashing the segmented Device aside but ruining her attack in the same go. She landed in half a crouch by Lennon, unable to strike before shoving off again to keep from getting slashed at. She bounced off the wing again, then another pod, then at the young man once more…

And found herself on the business end of the *other* set of chains, this time.

"*Damn!*" Catcher shouted, jumping to his feet with dozens of others as Ivanov once again only just managed to defend herself from the attack, slamming shoulder-first into the wall before scrambling to jump away and be clear of Lennon's attack range. "How is he doing that? How is he *doing* that?!"

Rei smiled, waiting as he watched the Lancer try again, then again, then again, finding herself cut off every time.

Finally, Aria answered, coming to the understanding just as he had.

"He's reading her," she groaned, like she wasn't surprised despite the awesome-ness of the situation. "That's what he's been doing the whole time. He's been figuring out her patterns."

Exactly, Rei thought.

Again and again and again Ivanov tried once more to regain her advantage, but even as he pressed off the wall to float gently towards the center of the stage, Lennon never let her find her edge. It was like he could see the future, reading her direction from the moment she leapt away from him, positioning one chain-sword or the other exactly where the Lancer was going to be a heartbeat later. Most of the time it was the sharpened tip she had to fend herself against, but more than once Ivanov was batted out of the air as the Lasher's Device caught her crosswise. Each time this happened, the impressive Defensive spec Rei had suspected the girl of possessing showed itself off, because her reactive shielding flashed when the chain swept around the blocking handle of her halberd to cut at her anyway.

Still, even that had to give eventually, and it was when Lennon's counterattack finally broke through the shielding that the match was forced to change again.

CLANG! WHAM!

He caught her early, this time, slashing with both chain-swords. The heavy steel segments arched like metal whips, slamming into Ivanov as she leapt from one piece of wreckage to another. She hadn't expected the blow, didn't have time to bring the halberd up to defend herself. The Lasher's Device took her full in the chest, and Rei saw silvery metal shards scattering into space as the Lancer was sent flying, her body driven hard into the massive form of a free-floating container that had just drifted into the field from beyond the wall.

Shouts of disappointment and thrill alike resounded from the third years' section, while the firsts and seconds only yelled in excitement, Viv and Catcher among them. They had good reason to, because not only was Ivanov extracting herself from the healthy dent she'd put in the metal siding of the container, but Lennon was finally on the move.

For the first time all match, he truly went on the attack.

With a slash of one chain-sword he drove the tip into the broken mess of passing fuselage, hauling hard at it to send his body careening across the debris-scattered space. Just as he reached the extent of the weapon's length he slashed to embed the other chain into another hunk of junk, combining his momentum and heavy pull on this second anchor point to wrench free the first. In two more such movements he had closed the 15 yards or so on Ivanov.

And all in about 3 seconds.

Reaching the Lancer just as she finally got her feet under her—the chest of her armor a mostly-broken mess—Lennon didn't offer her any additional reprieve. His free weapon cut in a horizontal streak, and it was only Ivanov's atypical clawed toes that saved her likely getting slashed in two, allowing her to grip, tuck, and roll down into space off the container. The slashing chain-sword cleaved into the wall she'd just vacated with a screech of tearing metal, and Rei had just enough time to be amused at the fact that the Arena was projecting sound in what should have been vacuum when Lennon pulled hard on his anchored point. The weapon came loose, but brought him rushing back towards the broken ship wall that had housed it, allowing him to land in a crouch.

Then he shoved off again, and the crowd finally got the chance to witness a clean exchange between two Users possessing S-Ranked Speed, or something very near it.

Despite the disadvantage of having only one weapon, Ivanov initially did an excellent job of defending herself as Lennon gained on her through the void. The halberd slashed left and right and up and down with blinding precision, adjusting minutely to every shift in the zero-gravity each strike made to her suspended position. Lennon's chain-swords didn't stop, however, and he used his externals to stabilize himself as he streaked after the girl, allowing for a constant barrage of attacks.

They slammed into the east wall of the field one after the other, Ivanov shoving herself out of the way to keep from getting shoulder-checked into the projection. She tried to escape by pushing off as hard as she could, but Lennon twisted and slashed, the chain-sword of his left hand wrapping about her ankle before she could pass out of range. He hauled at her, bringing her wrenching back, and Ivanov made the mistake of prioritizing the freeing of her leg by slamming the butt of her halberd at the entrapping Device, setting the chains loose.

It didn't much help when Lennon's right fist—wrapped about the handle of his other weapon—slammed into the already-damaged armor of her chest to send her careening again with another scattering of shattered metal.

"OOOOH...!" came the collected moan of hundreds of voices as Ivanov's head struck a passing hunk of the wreckage with a painful *clang*. The blow, combined with the weight of the Lasher's punch, had the Lancer taking her turn to spin wildly through space, limbs flailing as she tried to find anything that would allow her to stabilize. Lennon was on her, though, streaking after the young woman with a powerful leap off the invisible wall. He caught up in a heartbeat, both chain-swords slashing inward from either direction. They caught Ivanov mid-flip...

And passed through her harmlessly, the form of her spinning body glitching, then pixilating out of being.

Then—mirroring the enthusiastic roar of a surprised crowd—the *real* Ivanov launched into view, streaking at the Lasher's exposed back from the other side of the very hunk of debris that had appeared to send her flailing not seconds before.

"Oh! Now *there's* a clever combination of Abilities!" Colonel Guest's announcement—which Rei had largely been tuning out in favor of taking in the fight for himself—finally reached him. "Mirage we've seen several times in the last several days, but Ivanov's 'Cloak' is the first on the field, I believe! Allowing her to go nearly-invisible so long as she remains still, it's an Ability usually better suited for ambushing in Team-Battle and Wargames, but here she is wielding it masterfully in a one-on-one Duel!"

It was a fair assessment, to be sure, but Rei thought the celebratory tone might have been premature. The Lancer had been quicker than any of them had noticed—even Christopher Lennon, it would have seemed. In a blink after the impact to her head she had triggered both Mirage *and* Cloak, and so fluidly that no one had been any the wiser. She must have flipped around the edge of the wreckage, then waited, invisible, for Lennon to pass her as he chased after the false projection. Against anyone else, it would have earned her the match.

Unfortunately for Ivanov, though, she wasn't facing anyone else.

She reached Lennon, who'd been doing his best to spin about using his externals. Even to Rei it seemed that the boy was too slow, but something bit at him, an awareness that he knew he shared with anyone else who had studied up on the Lasher. Lennon still had a lot of tricks up his sleeve, especially now that his opponent had triggered not one, but *two* abilities. In a flash, Rei suddenly suspected that they were about to witness something incredible.

An instant later, his hope was met and then some.

Ivanov's halberd fell, slashing down at Lennon's exposed body before he could fully turn. The purple blade caught him between the helmet and shoulder, cutting deep, so deep.

Too deep, in fact…

There were yells of confusion from the stands as the Lancer's weapon, too, passed through her opponent. Then Lennon's body spasmed in a disruption of light, then vanished, leaving only his two chain-swords to drift, suspended, in empty space. Ivanov—her halberd making none of the contact she had expected—was left rolling forward as her momentum carried her in a clean line across the field.

Carried her, and left her vulnerable to the streak of black and red that launched itself after her from the very hunk of broken ship she herself had planned her failed ambush from.

Echo, was all Rei had time to think before the match came to an abrupt—and brutal—end.

Lennon's timing was impeccable. As he hurtled by his floating chains their handles snapped towards him, bringing themselves into his grip as though magnetically attracted to his waiting fingers. The black-and-red segments dragged along at his back like twin fiery tails of some wicked meteor. Ahead of him Ivanov slammed hard into the upper limit of the top of the wall, not far from the apex of the field. Only a blink later he was on her, with violent slashes of both arms he brought the chain-swords down at mirrored angles in a blur of razored steel.

They caught Ivanov—the *real* Ivanov, this time—in each shoulder, striking with a newfound force so terrible that the segments shred into her damaged armor and all the way through skin, flesh, and bone.

With the cracks and shrieking of shattering metal plating, the Lancer jerked once, her halberd spasming in her hand as her body was neurologically dissected into four parts.

"Fatal Damage Accrued," the Arena announced. "Winner: Christopher Lennon."

Rei and Aria left the screaming and shouting to Viv and Catcher, preferring to cover their ears just in time to spare themselves most of the apocalyptic roar of the stands as nearly every single attendee in the stadium leapt to their feet. Below them the field had already begun to fade, Lennon and Ivanov both dropping faster than usual since their fight had taken them some 20 yards into the air. As the black void of space faded away with the broken husk of the ship and scattered wreckage, the projection disk reappeared in full on the far side of the zone, and Rei realized that the colonel was obviously trying to speak over the noise.

He dropped a hand, straining to make out if his suspicions would be confirmed.

"What an end! What an *END*!" Guest was bellowing, his fervor as genuine as anyone else's in the Arena. "An *incredible* play by Ivanov *disrupted*! *Never* have I seen Echo used in such a manner! Never! One of the rarest Abilities currently in the ISCM database, it allows a User to temporally replicate any other Ability triggered within a sensory range of their CAD! Not only did Christopher Lennon beat

Cadet Ivanov at her own game, he did so with Abilities he likely has *never had the opportunity to practice with!*"

The announcement brought with it another tidal wave of cheering just as Lennon and Ivanov touched down on the projection plating, he coming to a graceful stand and recalling his Device in a blur of black-and-red, she collapsing immediately to her knees, then face-first, still in her armor.

"And it looks like Cadet Ivanov may have been KO'ed!" Guest continued his commentary. "Can't blame her with a final hit like that! Unless I'm mistaken, the Lasher was employing his Invisible Hand to add some extra power behind those chains! Another atypical use of Ability, and applied to great effect!"

"He did?!" Viv shouted as this did nothing to quell the gusto of the crowd. "You can use Invisible Hand that way?!"

"Apparently!" Catcher called back as Rei and Aria nodded.

It *was* atypical, but not unheard of. Invisible Hand—Lennon's other Ability, along with Break Step—had to have been triggered in tandem with his Echoed Mirage and Cloak. Those had been his *real* chain-swords the doppelgänger had swung—or seemed to swing, at least—since they'd broken Ivanov's own illusion. From there he had to have kept the Ability engaged even after using it to pull the weapons back to himself, manipulating the segments mentally to layer Invisible Hand's force into his own substantial physical strength.

The result had been a pair of blows powerful enough to cleave clean through even the thick layers of Ivanov's heavy armor.

Brilliant, Rei couldn't help but admit, not even realizing he was shaking his head in disbelief while he looked down on Christopher Lennon, who was standing impassively by while several officers tended to his opponent. *Absolutely brilliant.*

"Six days of training suddenly seems like even less time all of a sudden, doesn't it?" Aria asked him as quietly as she could in the noise.

Rei nodded at once.

"Seems like hardly anything," he answered as Ivanov got helped to her feet with a resounding cheer of support and relief from the crowd.

His eyes, though, never left the Lasher's slight form.

CHAPTER 42

"Despite the extensive and rigorous selection process that goes into the as-signment of a Combat Assistance Device, no exam in the world—nor intel-ligence or system allegedly involved in such an exam—can be absolute in its distinction of character. It is an important factor to be noted by any academ-ic making a study of CADs that there is a very good reason the ISCM has a disciplinary team designed specifically for dealing with rogue or corrupted wield-ers. In the more than 200 years humankind has proven capable of mastering De-vices, so too has it proven just as able of abusing them. The serial killer Holly Keeling, the famed 'Mercury's Butcher', viciously murdered nearly 65 people be-tween 2315 and 2317 before being apprehended. More recently, there is the case of Connor Galt, the major who fled his position on Sirius-12 against orders, aban-doning the majority half of contingent to an assault by the archons, providing the enemy with a planetary landing point. The resulting conflict lasted months, and in total resulted in the deaths of nearly 100,000 civilian casualties alone the military estimates would not have been lost had the major held his assigned post.

All this is to say, more succinctly: one should not confuse the bearing of a CAD with the bearing of heart and mind absent evil, jealousy, or fear..."

A History of the Intersystem Collective Military
K.S. Villaseno
Distributed by Central Command, Earth

Camilla was going to lose.

Logan Grant chewed on his tongue as he finally admitted it to himself, not quite sure how he felt about this understanding. On the one hand Reidon Ward was an upstart prick with an assignment Rank that should never have seen him admitted to the Institute in the first place.

On the other... Reidon Ward was an upstart prick who had clawed his way up from an assignment Rank that should never have seen him admitted to the Institute in the first place.

Logan's tongue chewing turned into teeth grinding as he faced once more the fact that he had—at some unfortunate point along the way—developed a begrudging respect for the A-Type that had started at the bottom of the first year class. He didn't deserve it. Ward didn't deserve it. Sure, he'd worked hard, but so had everyone else in the first year class, and no other student had climbed more than *fifteen ranks* on their own since the start of term. Not one. It should have been flat-out impossible, regardless of an amount of outside intervention.

And yet there was the User Rank—suspended before Logan's eyes while he'd only been half-watching the others spar while he took a brief break from training—hanging under Ward's name in the asshole's portfolio.

C0… He's only two ranks lower than me, Logan thought, taking a quick swig from a bottle of water he'd called from the West Center's service system.

Again: it should have been impossible, but there it was. There *had* to be a reason. This, in fact, was the very problem Logan had been turning over for over a month, now, ever since Ward had hit the Ds in record time. Was it the Iron Bishop? That Valera Dent had taken a personal interest in the scarred bastard was an open secret at the school, but why not? He was an A-Type, like her, and the captain was rumored to have also recently brought Christopher Lennon under her wing. But was that enough to explain Ward's meteoric rise out of the Fs?

No.

Logan frowned, the water bottle still hanging absently from his lips. There had to be more. There *had* to be. He might not like it, but there must have been some reason Ward had been allowed into the school, some portent of his potential matching that of the other cadets. No… No. *Surpassing* that potential. Otherwise why would the admissions board have taken the risk?

And if Logan's suspicions were correct, then not only had Ward ascended by climbing over the backs of his classmates for the last 11 weeks, but he'd been thrown a rope there was no way he could have earned…

Logan didn't feel his lip curl in annoyance. For the moment there was nothing to be done about it, and he had a more imminent disappointment on the horizon than being unsure of Ward's secret.

No matter how he cut the variables, Camilla was going to lose.

"Dammit."

Logan didn't realize he'd cursed out loud until he saw Mateus stir and look around at him, eyes wary.

"What's up?" the Saber asked in a light, friendly tone that ground Logan's gears nearly as much as anything else going on in his head.

Fake. So fake.

Fortunately, he managed to keep *that* thought silent.

"She's screwed," he said simply, a line of sweat dropping off his nose as he nodded towards where Camilla was sparing with Tad. They usually cycled—having every standard Type present in the group between the seven of them—but Logan didn't miss that the girl had spent most of the last week finding ways to pair up with her fellow Brawler. "She's screwed, and she knows it."

Mateus shrugged beside him. Whereas Logan had stayed standing, the blond Saber had taken to sitting and lounging back on one hand, the other resting across a bent knee. He cut a handsome figure, sure, but it was the kind of posturing that looked posed, as though Mateus needed to impress even when there was no one around *to* impress.

So fake.

"You're not giving Warren enough credit," the boy said. "She's good. Not Sectionals good, sure, but she's still good."

"And you're not giving *Ward* enough credit," Logan growled back. "The guy's got two ranks on her, now. Plus—" he stopped himself, finding that the words he'd been about to say aloud tasted too bad on his tongue to voice.

Plus he's a better fighter, he thought instead.

Mateus gave him a puzzled look, clearly waiting for Logan to finish what he'd been saying, but found himself ignored.

After a moment he shrugged again. "Warren's been training with Ward since the start of the term. He's in her group. She knows him, which means she already has all the tools she needs." He made a face. "Of course, personally I think the major should have just pit him against *you* and gotten it all done with. You or Khatri. You're the only two summer-group members in the loser's bracket right now."

Logan decided he would ignore the not-so-subtle jab at his loss to Aria Laurent earlier in the week. He had nothing to prove to Mateus Selleck, after all.

He'd kicked the boy's teeth in once already, along with every other person's in the very training chamber they stood in now.

"It would have looked too suspicious," he muttered instead. "As it is it's pretty blatant Reese's has a bone to pick with him."

"Sure. But you won't hear me complain about it. That's exactly why Warren is the best fit for him. She knows him, knows how he fights. She might be a lower rank, but you saw his match against Jiang. She's still got Strength on him, at the very least. Probably Endurance, too, judging by how conservatively he was fighting…"

It was Logan's turn to shrug. Doing so and swigging from his water again was preferable to caving in to his desire to put his knee in the Saber's smug face. Yes, it *was* obvious the major was out to get Ward, and yes, it *was* true Camilla was the best match to achieve that end without Reese blatantly announcing his intentions by matching Ward up with another top first year, like Mateus suggested.

And it was all exactly why Logan was annoyed at the world—including himself.

After all, he too wished he'd been the one matched up against Reidon Ward, but not for the reason Mateus and the major would have liked to line up with their irritating agenda. It was all so underhanded, so deceptive. As with the occasion the Saber had taken it on himself to try and "teach Ward a lesson", Logan felt like he needed a shower after doing nothing more than talking about it all.

No. He had his own reason. Ward had spent a quarter of the year wasting the time of the Institute and its cadets. He'd made himself the center of attention during the Commencement Ceremony, then passed 10 weeks lagging behind and drafting off the hard work and sweat of their 1-A classmates as he'd climbed through the CAD Ranks like it was nothing. Sure, he'd made some friends along the way—and even brought one in Logan still couldn't wrap his head around, no matter how often they argued about it—but that only proved the boy was as plastic and scheming as Mateus Selleck and all the rest of them.

Indeed, whenever Logan thought of Reidon Ward, all he could see was the back of the A-Type's combat suit as he'd fled from him during the one real match they'd ever had.

The image made his blood boil, bringing to mind a different older face.

"Cowards," he snarled under his breath, ignoring Mateus this time when the Saber cocked a curious eyebrow at him.

Fortunately for everyone in the room, that was the moment Logan's NOED blinked, a notification flashing in the corner of the screen atop the edge of the ISCM profile he still had pulled up. Seeing who it was from, Logan felt the anger ease from his shoulders, knotted muscle he hadn't even realized he'd tensed relaxing all at once. With a flick of his eyes he exited the database, then opened the message.

Reading it, he just managed to hide his smile with another drink of water, the text below several animated images of a crying emote.

Tell me I can take on the best Brawler in our class. Tell me I've got this. Then stop grinning like an idiot, jackass.

CHAPTER 43

"It's not uncommon for the best of us to come from nowhere. Tradition. Blood. History. All that only means so much when it comes to being selected as a User. In the end, what our Devices and duty demand the most of from us is heart.

Heart, and the willingness to sacrifice what we must to become as strong as we can possibly be..."

Colonel Rama Guest
Funeral of Brigadier General Blake Horne

Viv was in less trouble than she could have been, but in a lot more than was ideal. From the lowest row of the central view section today, Rei and Aria watched with bated breath as she retreated back up the grassy hill of the windswept slope she was fighting on. Around her arms and legs Gemela flashed purple-and-yellow in the sun, blades bright with silver light while they danced in front of her. Barreling up the incline in pursuit, the hulking form of her opponent dipped and ducked with an obscene level of grace for his size, dodging the testing slashes of sword and dagger both as he jabbed a solid piston of green-gold steel at her chest.

Viv managed to avoid the strike by a hair, twisting away, but was again left retreating, laterally along the hill this time.

"He's got her backpedaling," Rei groaned. "*Backpedaling*! Her!"

"Are you really surprised?" Aria asked, trying for a smirk but failing as Viv ducked under a haymaker and threw herself forward to roll by the large boy, slashing at his legs as she did only for Gemela to ring harmlessly off his armored thigh. "He's a Rank higher *and* was part of the summer training group."

Rei grunted, conceding the point. "I guess... This is probably the first time she's been pitched up against someone better than her, isn't it?" He paused, then glanced sidelong at Aria. "Uh... In an official match, I mean. Obviously."

"Obviously," Aria said with a laugh, waving the comment aside. "But don't put words in my mouth. I don't think you're right."

"Oh?" Rei asked, looking at her full-on.

"No," Aria confirmed, having not taken her eyes from the fight. "Benaly's good—*really* good, even… But I don't think he's better than her."

Rei—loathing the fact that he wasn't sure he agreed, for once—returned his attention to the field below them with a frown.

Jack Benaly moved like no human his size should have been capable of. Without his Device he might have been an inch or two shorter than most of the other first years, but his CAD had proven to be developing extended, clawed toes, much like Annika Ivanov had shown off on Saturday, 3 days prior. It was an uncommon adaptation Rei had found out was dubbed a "lupine foot" by CAD scientists, and they brought the Brawler up to over 6 feet in height, after which his naturally mountainous frame gave Benaly the look of some ancient hero from Earth's Grecian histories.

Add that to the gleaming, green-over-gold-and-yellow of his Device—encasing both arms and legs completely—and the C1-Ranked Brawler indeed could have cut the form of a titanous demigod.

"Oh!" Aria yelped suddenly, and Rei was brought back from his study of Jack Benaly to the fight itself. Viv had managed to sidestep a kick from the Brawler and had taken advantage of the opening to drive her dagger down at his leading knee. Benaly twisted away in time to avoid what would undoubtedly have been some awful limitations, but the point of the blade still caught the side of his leg, the stabbing tip doing what Viv's earlier slash had failed to against the thick shielding. It cut through, punching into the metal, and Rei was pretty sure Viv had managed to stick the Brawler with a solid inch or two of vysetrium-lined steel before he hurled himself clear, diving into a roll down the hill that brought him up facing her as she chased after him along the incline. Viv cut with her sword, but Benaly sidestepped with no visible loss in speed and threw a punch at her open side that fortunately only caught her a glancing blow as she managed to parry it away from a direct hit.

"Damn." Rei cursed aloud. "No limitations? That guy's Defense spec is *ridiculous.*"

At his right, Aria grunted an agreement, leaning over her knees so far to watch that her face was practically sticking out into the walkway.

Seeing the fight from up close like this was a different experience, Rei had to admit, and he regretted not having pushed the others to fight for better seats the week before. Still, it made no difference now, because with regular classes having resumed with the conclusion of the Intra-School's opening week, the spectator presence at the matches had plummeted. Most—like Catcher, today—were limited by their school schedule, but there was also the fact that Rei had felt like the students—all the students, across every class—had been in a bit of a fervor since the weekend. Like those first days of fighting had lit a real fire under the already-driven cadets, Rei hadn't seen anyone from their class not cheering on a specific friend or suitemate the day before, and not a *single* second- or third year had been present to speak of. Even their own little group had packed up and made for the East Center the moment Aria and Catcher had wrapped their matches for the day—both managing unsurprising victories—leaving the remaining combatants with a sparse scattering of spectators and applause.

It was unfortunate, too, because some of yesterday's losses had been second defeats, marking those luckless cadets as the first in the class to lose their shot at qualifying for Sectionals.

Nope. Not dwelling on that. Rei forced down the knot of worry in his gut that started to form at the thought. All the same, he couldn't help but glance away from Viv and Benaly's fight for a moment to look over his shoulder, up into the stands. There, Camilla Warren sat—ironically not too far from where Rei and the others *usually* spectated from—accompanied by the usual entourage. Mateus Selleck and Tad Emble were both present, as were Giano Perez, Gathers—whose first name Rei had learned was Jeffrey, the week before—and Leda Truant.

Only Logan Grant was conspicuously absent from the gang, for once…

Warren didn't look down at him, but Rei *did* catch Selleck's eye, and the Saber graced him with a sneer before giving him the finger. Rei returned the gesture with a smile, then turned back as Selleck's face shifted into a furious scowl, satisfied with that small victory.

Not dwelling on that, he told himself again.

As though on cue, however, his NOED pinged him at that very moment with a notice that made pressing the worry from his mind much, much harder.

Rei took a steadying breath before speaking. "I'm up."

At his right, Aria stilled, then looked around at him carefully.

"How do you feel?"

"Good," Rei lied with a nod, avoiding her eyes by reaching to pull his combat uniform out of his bag, which had been tucked between his feet.

"Rei… You've *got* this. I've been telling you all week—"

"I know."

He said it too quickly, he knew. Definitely unconvincingly, at the very least. He *did* know, in fact. Despite his lower specs, despite the fact he was aware Warren would be stepping into the field below them with a chip on her shoulder. He *did* know. He was probably just as fast as the girl, and definitely the superior fighter on a level field. She would be stronger—and likely better defended—but Rei knew Warren's combat style as well as he knew every line of Shido's black-and-white CAD bands with their layered blue. He'd spent two-and-a-half months training within 10 feet of her, and every spare moment of the previous week not conditioning had been used to review the recorded footage of her lost match the previous week, sometimes even under the desk during class. He knew, even just standing there, that Warren would open the fight with either a roundhouse at his temple or a cross-jab at his leading shoulder, and he knew how he'd respond to both.

He knew he had the fight. Honestly he did.

But what if…? Just… What *if*…?

Rei grimaced. This was exactly what he'd been trying *not* to do: let the fear get in his head.

There was a loud series a screaming *clangs,* and both Rei and Aria looked up to find Viv in the middle of a violent exchange of blades and fists, doing a fair job of holding her own against the barrage of strikes as she managed to sneak in a few herself.

He decided to try and take advantage of the distraction.

"Wish me luck," he said quickly, pushing himself to his feet and turning east along the walkway in an attempt to escape before Aria could try for more encouragement.

He barely made it a step when her hand caught his sleeve.

"Rei…" she started when he looked around at her, hoping his face didn't betray any of his uncertainty.

After a moment, though, she let her hold of his uniform slacken, her hand falling again.

But not before they brushed the side of his palm ever-so-slightly, lingering there for brief, warm instant.

"Good luck," she finally settled on, giving him a smile that might have outshined the sun had the Arena roof not been shut to the autumn winds. Rei grinned back, feeling a sliver of his shaken confidence piece itself together again.

Then he turned, and—with a surer stride than he'd sported a moment ago—made for the stadium underworks.

The tunnels swallowed him, claiming much of the sound of Viv and Benaly's match. Rei regretted that he wouldn't be able to see the end of the fight, but he was honestly more relieved to find that Warren didn't share the hall he descended into, having either lingered a bit longer with her "friends" or more likely taken another stairwell down. Thinking it best they *not* run into each other if it could be helped, Rei turned left instead of right, heading north up the tunnel as the smart-glass panes along the walls flickered and faded in and out of life when he passed.

As he walked, he fought back the worry.

Mateus Selleck had gotten through both his first *and* second matches. They'd been advantageous pairings for him, but the fact remained that he was now in the top thirty-two fighters in the winner's bracket, halfway to qualifying for Sectionals undefeated. Logan Grant, meanwhile, had performed as expected the day before, following up Catcher's win with an utter domination of poor Casey Foreman, who couldn't seem to get a break. Grant might have lost his first match against Aria— and even that not without an impressive fight—but there was little doubt he would be ripping through the losers bracket to qualify. Tad Emble had lost his match the previous day, knocking him into the losers, but even this Rei knew would only be a small comfort until he stood victorious over Warren.

If he fell now, he suspected he would never have the same chance to impress on Grant or Selleck, or any of his other doubters, that he deserved his place within the walls of Galens, and had deserved it from the very start.

The first of the eastern professional locker rooms came into view as the tunnel straightened out from its bend out of the south end of the stands. Ordinarily kept barred from access by the cadets, the chambers had been set to unlock for use from noon to 1700 every day while the Intra-Schools were going on. Most students, funny enough, had still preferred the longer trek down to the subbasement to change in more familiar settings before they fought. Rei had been one of them the week before, but he was curious, and decided not wanting to run into Warren made a perfect excuse for a change of scenery. The pros had to have it better than the student's subterranean locker rooms, right?

As soon as he stepped under the sensor, letting the single steel door slide open for him with a *hiss*, Rei knew he wasn't likely to be disappointed.

The chamber was smaller than the subbasement's—a *lot* smaller—but that made sense. There were a good number of such upper-level locker rooms built for the pros who visited on the not-infrequent occasions Galens hosted a major tournament, and had been designed so that squads prepping for Team Battle and Wargame matches could do any last-minute prep and pepping separate from the other groups. What was more, Rei got the impression that each of the rooms was probably individually decorated.

It was hard to imagine a dozen such identical spaces lining the underbelly of the stands.

The theme looked to be Victorian red and black, complete with a pair of wide, burgundy sofas taking up the middle of the chamber. On either side of this handsome seating arrangement a row of lockers gleamed crimson under several ornate solar lights that each hung with dark crystal, like small, gothic chandeliers. The back wall of the room looked to be entirely comprised of smart-glass, displaying the image of a massive fish-tank painted black. This might have been odd, except it made it easier to show off the rippling, incandescent forms of several long, glow-in-the-dark inhabitants awash with blueish light along slow-moving fins and tails.

Then Rei made out the gentle *blub-blub-blub* of air circulating through water, and realized abruptly that the "image" was no image at all.

He decided then that saying the pros "had it better" was something of an understatement.

A notification blinked into Rei's vision, the courtesy reminder that 5 minutes of his allotted 15 had passed since his summoning to the Arena floor. With a curse he hurried to the nearest row of lockers to pull open the first he reached. In quick order he'd stripped out of his uniform, hanging everything in the anti-grav compartment, then slipped into his combat suit. As it zipped itself up for him automatically, he realized the fabric was starting to feel a little tight around his thighs, shoulders, and other—more concerning—places. He made a note for himself to talk to the quartermaster about getting resized again soon. According to his checkups he'd gained nearly an additional half-inch, and in another couple weeks he was probably going to push over the 5'7" mark.

The thought made Rei pause, and as his suit sealed close behind the nape of his neck he brought his arms up to take them in. A black hair tie—borrowed from Viv—ringed one wrist above Shido's band, but aside from that…

No new scars.

It was strange to think about, strange to consider. It wasn't something he was used to. Shido had gotten control of his fibrodysplasia faster than any of them—even the optimistic Lieutenant Colonel Mayd—had been willing to hope. The old markings were still there, pocking and lining his skin like the healed battle wounds of an old life.

An old life…

Rei smirked at himself, then snorted out loud as he let his arms drop. What was he worried about, in the long run? So what if he fell? So what if Warren managed to take him down today? Had he started down this path—this strange, wonderful, *excruciatingly* difficult path the MIND had offered him—to prove himself to a bunch of ISCM *cadets*? Of course not. Rei was after bigger game. He was aware of that, now. Ever since he'd hit C0, he'd been aware of that. Seventeen ranks, he climbed. Seventeen, from the day he'd stepped within the borders of the Institute. Shido had slowed down a bit when he'd hit the Ds—and he had no doubt the CAD would do the same as he pressed into the Cs—but it all made no difference. His trajectory was higher, *much* higher.

So what if he fell?

Rei's smirk turned into a grin. He knew he'd kick himself for a fool later if he *actually* lost, but in the moment coming to terms with the reality of his situation was exactly what he needed. If he fell, he'd probably spend the next couple of months hot around the collar and unable to meet Logan Grant's black-red eyes for disappointed embarrassment.

But then the day would come where Rei would pass the Mauler's Rank, and he was pretty sure a slip-up of the past would be pretty quickly forgotten.

The weight of concern lifting of his chest, Rei stood straight, closing the locker he'd claimed to move with purpose out of the chamber and once more down the south hall. As he did he tugged the borrowed hair tie from his wrist to bind the top and back of his white locks—which had grown long in the months since school started—into a tail behind his head. Fortunately he'd be called to report to the east side of the field, just like during his match with Jiang, so there was no risk of meeting Warren until they faced each other now.

But then again… What did it matter?

Still grinning, Rei finished gathering his hair up as he reached the ramp he was looking for. Pulling the tail once to make sure no loose strands would fall into his eyes during the match, he turned right, and a few seconds later emerged from the underworks onto the Arena's main field.

The fight happening now was no longer Viv and Benaly's. With guilty disappointment Rei peered up at the suspended field to make out none other than Kay taking on a Duelist from 1-C he was pretty sure was called Ashely Renton. Kay had won her opening week's match, Rei recalled, which made this fight a battle for who would claim the second of the four wins the two girls would need to qualify right out of the gate.

Unfortunately for Ashley Renton, however, the fight looked already largely well-decided.

While he'd only ever had minimal opportunity to see Kay fight during cross-training days, what Rei *had* witnessed had been more than enough to call her out as a likely shoo-in for Sectionals. One of the summer training group, she'd consistently demonstrated a scary aptitude for the long-spear that formed the weapon of her Lancer-Type Device. The CAD—funny enough—was a blue-and-purple lined with red vysetrium, almost perfectly matched Kay's own hair. At the moment, she was streaking through a Woodlands variation on armored legs, chasing the green-and-grey retreating form of Renton, spear slashing left and right. The weapon had a long, wide crimson blade, trailing bright arcs through the canopy-shaded air with every swing. Where it made contact with a tree there was always an explosion of splintered wood, and judging by the respectable amount of kindling that littered the field—and not a few felled saplings—Kay had been doing everything she could to clear her vicinity of obstructions everywhere she went, refusing to allow her reach to be limited. Renton, it appeared, wasn't willing to play her game, and kept withdrawing into a new part of the forest, denying any engagement as she did her best to force Kay into an advantageous position. It was entertaining for a minute.

After two, Rei was more bored than impressed.

"Warning: Match Violation."

The Arena's voice chimed in, and immediately everything within the boundary of the field froze like time itself had come to a standstill. There was a flickering of the projection, then the whole thing turned transparent, leaving barely the ghost of the forest's outline suspended in the air around the two girls, who were less statuesque than the rest of the area only in the fact that they appeared still-able to turn their heads.

And turn them they did, facing as one the north end of the ring, where Dyrk Reese and John Marcus—the day's commentator—stood atop the observation platform.

"Cadet Renton, I find you in violation of combat etiquette." Major Reese's voice rumbled, amplified, and his tone was one that had no one mistaking him for any sort of pleased. "I assign you a penalty for excessive flight. Should you suffer a second penalty, I will assign you a match loss. Is that clear?"

With her head turned away from him, Rei couldn't tell the kind of expression Renton was making. Her sullen answer, however, was enough to tell she wasn't thrilled with the situation.

"Yes, sir. It won't happen again, sir."

"No. It won't."

And then, on that threatening note, Reese's eye flared, and the field blinked into opacity once more. Almost at once Rei made out a floating red number 5—the same markers they used in their parameter testing days—appear before both Kay and Renton as the two faced each other again.

"Combat resumption initiated," the Arena announced calmly. "Countdown begins... now."

The 5 flicked to a 4, then a 3.

When it hit 0, the projected field resumed all motion without arrest, like no interruption had occurred. Both Kay and Renton stumbled a little as momentum that had only been temporarily suspended reclaimed their bodies. Kay was the first to recover, but she'd chased the Duelist into a thick knot of young maples, and so her priority became opening the area for herself to keep from getting her spear stuck against a tree when she tried to close in for the killing blow. Narrow trunks exploded around her with every step she took, the Lancer chopping at everything and anything that came into range. Splinters and bark sprayed across the air, serving a dual purpose now. For one, it wasn't more than a few breaths before Kay had managed to cut herself a miniature sort of clearing for herself within the copse.

Second, the timber shrapnel made it hard for Renton, who had finally halted in her flight, to close the distance between the two of them without covering her eyes for fear of being blinded.

Rei found himself disappointed, when the real fighting finally began. The Duelist was no match for Kay—that had been obvious from the go—but she was hardly unskilled, and put up an excellent show for herself once the pair of them finally engaged. She was never allowed within range to strike with either of her blades, but nor did she provide Kay with anything like an easy target, slipping and sliding between the Lancer's thrusts and slashes with a fluidity that was nearly as impressive as Viv's grace. Had she been willing to engage from the start, Rei was pretty sure no one would have had cause to think less of the girl.

Instead, he wasn't the only one to sport a frown along the east wall of the Arena floor, shared with the other first years who were preparing for their own fights.

In the end, Kay resorted to playing dirty, turning the tables so fast on the Duelist the end of the match came in a flash. The volleying of strikes were one-sided, the Lancer's longer weapon a snaking blur as she whirled it expertly through both hands, about her body, and even around her neck and waist on several separate occasions. Her movement was without pause, the red vysetrium of her spear a constant streak in the shadows of the greater trees at the edge of the space the pair were battling it out in. It screamed through the air, joining in the clanging and shrieks of steel on steel. A trio of movements slammed at Renton from both sides, then down in a ripping chop at the girl's head. She caught the blade in both her own, shoving it up and away. Kay went with the momentum, tucking the weapon close and making to lance the blunt end of it at the Duelist's gut. Renton dodged back, blades ready to parry a follow-up slash.

Unfortunately for her, that was the exact moment she stepped into the trap set by the feint.

Instead of driving forward with the butt of the spear, Kay swung down and let the blade tear into the earth beneath the trampled grass and shattered wood at her feet. The ground erupted in a small explosion of dirt and splinters, spraying Renton full in the face before the Duelist could think to shield herself. She reeled, hacking at what must have been a mouthful of earth, rubbing at her eyes with the back of one hand in an attempt to clear her vision. For Kay, it was more than enough time to lunge, spear thrust forward to its fullest extent.

The vysetrium blade vanished into the grey of Renton's tunic, running her through the sternum with almost impeccable precision as the Duelist went stiff in a spasm of pain and confusion.

"Fatal Damage Accrued. Winner: Kay Sandree."

The scattered cheering from the limited spectators that had been in the stands was a little muffled from his lower place against the wall, but Rei himself made sure to clap as loud as he dared when the Lancer and her defeated opponent drifted down to the projection plating. Kay gave him a smile when she caught sight of him. Once she touched down and turned her back to him—recalling her Device to see about helping a prone Ashley Renton to her feet—Rei finally took a moment to pull up his NOED, crafting out a quick message to Aria.

Viv?

He didn't have to wait too long for a reply.

I'll tell you after the match. Focus.

Rei snorted, supposing he shouldn't have been surprised.

What was more, Aria was right. He *did* need to focus.

After Kay took her leave of the floor—passing with a quick thumbs up to him for good luck—the three matches before his own went by in a flash. He was pleased to see Sense take down a Mauler from 1-D named Emanuel Ramir, but the bald Brawler had come in from the west side of the stadium, and didn't notice Rei before or after the match. After that it was a winner's bout between Conrad Fae and Misha Fethers—with the Brawler Fethers taking out the Lancer in rather quick order—followed by Gillian North against one of the 1-B Phalanxes, Oscar Colt. After North finally walked away from the match the victor—leaving Colt trembling on unsteady legs after having been cut in two by the girl's massive axe—Rei felt his mouth start to go dry.

"A solid fight with a satisfying end," John Marcus—in a rather unenthusiastic voice for an announcer—intoned. "Congratulations to Cadet North as she moves on to the next round. Next up, we've got Reidon Ward versus Camilla Warren. Cadets, approach the field."

Rei might have imagined it, but it felt like an unusual number of eyes followed him as he stepped away from the wall and made for the east edge of the Dueling area. Reese's glare he could have sensed from a mile away, he was sure, and Marcus' eyes moved from him to where he knew Warren would be paralleling him on the other side of the floor, but just those two wouldn't have made the hairs on the back of his neck stand on end like they were now. If he'd looked around, Rei would have bet anything almost every face in the stands would have been turned on him, rather than his opponent.

It seemed the school as a whole, too, felt like there was something for him to lose in this match.

Feeling a little of that earlier resolve not to care crack a bit, Rei focused all his energy on holding his confidence together as he made the edge of the field, turning inward. Across from him Warren looked to have reached her waiting spot a second before, because she was already glaring over the plating when he met her orange eyes. She wasn't smirking, though. She wasn't even leering. Indeed, she seemed like she was anything but keen on the position she'd found herself in, as though she would have rather been anywhere else in that moment than standing opposite him on the field of battle.

For some reason, this—more than anything else—turned out to be what Rei's shaking self-assurance was in need of, because with the warmth of satisfaction at the sight of her glowering face he found himself able to smile at the girl with ease.

He thought he heard more than one laugh from the stands as Warren's expression darkened.

"Combatants, take position."

Dyrk Reese, as ever, was nothing other than professionally clean-cut when he gave the command, as though nothing in particular was out of the ordinary regarding this specific fight. Rei and Warren together did as they were told, moving as one towards the mirrored circles of red that had appeared at the officer's words.

"This is as an official Duel." The major—infuriatingly—had returned to his full rendition of the combat consent as soon as the first years had started their second week. "It will therefore be subject to regulation ruling. Once the field is formed, you will be ordered to call, then engage. Premature Device manifestation will result in a penalty. Premature approach, attack, or the like will result in a match loss. Is that understood?"

Rei nodded. Warren nodded. Neither of them had looked away from the other the entire time they'd closed in on their starting circles.

For that reason, they didn't see Reese's NOED flare before the field began to change beneath them.

Rei knew the zone almost the moment the projection started up, noting first the spreading blue overhead, then the grass rising up under their feet. Compared to a lot of other fields it was a simple hologram, and so he and Warren were standing in a yawning, open plain of endless green long before they reached the apex of the 10-foot climb. Above them the sky could have been a calm ocean, an infinite azure ceiling obscured only by scattered patches of clouds as a warm breeze danced around them, setting the short grass to shifting this way and that about their ankles. In the distance there was nothing, the vastness of the zone surreal in its expanse, like the open plain extended beyond the flat horizon, absent even the curvature of a planet. For Rei's part, he couldn't have been more pleased with their lot of fields.

With no obstacles or obstructions to be found within the 30-yard diameter of the fighting area, no one would be able to complain about tricks and schemes.

"Field: Grassland."

The Arena's announcement of the obvious was amusing to Rei, for some reason, and he had to hold back a laugh. He was feeling good. It wasn't great, actually. He had to keep it together. Warren was likely to open with either a roundhouse or a cross-jab at his leading shoulder. He had to keep it together, to focus.

But the scowl that only got uglier and uglier across the girl's face across from him gave Rei no reason to really want to stop grinning.

"Cadet Reidon Ward versus Cadet Camilla Warren. Combatants… Call."

"Call," Rei said, hearing the word echoed by the girl. In a heartbeat Shido was about his arms and legs, the new mirroring of claws shining bright in the projected sunlight. On the other side of the field he didn't miss Warren cast a nervous gaze at his most recent evolution, one she'd only seen twice now in combat training. In comparison, her own punch daggers—grey over green with orange vysetrium—looked bulky and crude, down even to the thicker plating about her legs. Unable to help himself, Rei bounced up and down on his toes a couple of times, taunting the girl with one last smile, then settled into a ready stance with hands up.

He was feeling good.

"Combatants… Fight."

For the first time since Shido had been assigned to him, Rei met his opponent in the middle of the field. He wasn't outpaced, this time, wasn't outmatched for agility. Even if he was marked two ranks higher than Warren, Rei knew his specs would overall be lower. Despite this, his D8 Speed turned out to be a match for her, because it was with the wind of their passing rippling through the grass behind them that the two hurtled towards each other, neither closing an inch faster. Rei felt his D6 Cognition light up his neuroline even as he rocketed forward. They were going too fast for the kick. Warren would open with the punch.

There.

The swing came as expected, the brief flash of red across Rei's frame an unnecessary warning. He saw Warren's right arm draw back in careful time with her gait, measured to impact with the greatest momentum possible. He saw the lithe muscles of her shoulders contract in preparation.

What he didn't see, however, was the swing itself, because Rei was already ducking low by the time it came, shifting his direction ever so slightly with a push leftward, so that he passed *by* Warren—under the arm—rather than colliding into her. As he did, he let the momentum of his run carry the claws of both his fists through the Brawler's undefended right side, exposed for only the blink it took to make the opening strike. He was surprised when he felt the resistance through his left hand when steel sliced through ribs just under the Warren's armpit, every inch of the black metal ripping into what he knew with astonishment had to be lung.

It was his right, though, that truly shocked him. His right, cutting lower to cleave into her hip, deep enough to sever the femoral artery where it rested along the inside of where the femur met pelvis.

The silence that settled across Rei as he came to a stumbling halt several yards beyond Warren was strange. There was a pause, a stunned moment in which the two of them stood with their backs to each other, both unmoving.

Then the Brawler's knees *thudded* to the ground, and she collapsed face-first into the grass.

"Fatal Damage Accrued. Winner: Reidon Ward."

The field was already fading as Rei turned to stare at the twitching form of his fallen opponent. Despite this, not a single sound could be heard, not a clap or a cheer or even a jeer. Rei started to drop, the earth beneath his feet dematerializing all of seconds after the fight had begun, his graceful lowering to the ground eerie in the quiet. Only after he'd touched down on the projection plating did he jolt to his senses a bit, the *clink* of his heels against the steel waking him to his disbelief.

He turned, slowly, to look south and up, needing no time at all to find the two figures gaping at him from the stands, both having taken to their feet and rushed forward from their front-row seats to lean over the guardrail of the lower walkway.

And then Viv, still in her combat suit, smiled so wide her face looked like it could have split in two only a second before screaming at the top of her lungs.

"HELL YEAH, REI!"

The sound rolled through the empty Arena like a storm, waking the other score or so of first years from their astonishment in one fell swoop. Almost together nearly every student scattered about the stands started cheering, the sparseness of their number made up for by the enthusiasm of their applause. Rei saw Sense positively jumping up and down in excitement from higher in the seating, with Kay at his side standing more politely, but nonetheless yelling with her hands around her mouth. He saw Emily Gisham punching the air, and even Jack Benaly, alone in an upper corner of the section, clapping from his seat. Only Selleck and his friends weren't moving, glowering down at him and Warren both.

And then, slowly, he met Aria's eyes.

She was staring at him like he was something simultaneously mesmerizing and terrifying, like she wasn't sure what to make of what she'd just seen. That was fine by him, because of everyone standing in that Arena Rei was pretty positive *he* was the one who was the most at a loss, unable to comprehend what was going on. Aria's eyes, though, grounded him, shook him with their crystalline green.

Finally, he managed to mouth up to her.

What happened?

All he got in answer was a slow, uncertain shake of her head.

"Cadet Arada, control yourself!" came the snarling voice of Major Reese, and at last Rei returned to himself completely. Quickly he turned around, the metal of Shido's heels barely keeping purchase on the smooth plating, but he ignored the precarious footing in favor of staring up at the projection disk that still hovered some 4 or 5 yards above his head. The major wasn't looking at him, however. Indeed, he seemed distinctly intent on looking *anywhere* but directly at Rei, his ire currently transfixed on Viv. "Return to your seat! The rest of you as well!" His eyes lifted to scan the other first years, causing the commotion to cut off abruptly at Rei's back.

"Oh they're only cheering for our victor!" John Markus seemed to have finally found his voice, and for the first time all afternoon sounded genuinely enthusiastic in his commentary. "What a win! Congratulations, Cadet Ward! That may have been our quickest match of the tournament yet!"

Rei was so dumbfounded by this that he could only nod, his gaze falling down to where Camilla Warren was struggling to get to her feet, her right arm and leg both looking like they were still recovering from the neural interruption. He didn't understand. Couldn't comprehend. Had she thrown the match? Had she tossed in the towel before the fight had begun?

But no. No way. The rage on the Brawler's face as she finally managed to stand—if unsteadily—spoke of anything but resigned defeat. She looked incensed, her Device still around her limbs as they shook.

"Again!" she growled, teeth bared at Rei. "Take me on again! That was a cheap trick!"

Rei—still at a loss for words even if he *hadn't* been thrown by this ludicrous proposition—only stared at her in confusion.

"What's this?" Markus asked energetically. "Cadet Warren has challenged the victor to another fight! Well we can't have that, arbiter, can we?"

In answer there was a silence, and Rei looked up again. This time he found Reese had swallowed his irritation enough to look him in the eye, one cheek twitching in what could only have been anger. The quiet hung for several uncomfortable seconds.

"Again!" Warren demanded once more, starting to advance on Rei, her left side looking to have finally recovered its function. "In a straight fight, I would have—!"

"*Enough*, cadet."

The major's voice was a low, dangerous growl, reverberating through the Arena like a thunderstorm. Glancing up, Rei saw that Reese's gaze hadn't left him, but his face was dark, still and resigned.

Warren whirled. "Sir! You had to see it! It had to be a trick! In a straight fight—!"

"*ENOUGH!*" Reese snarled, and Rei wasn't sure if he'd imagined the projection plating under his feet vibrating. "To imply this fight wasn't 'straight' is to imply that I am incapable of moderating something as basic as a match between two *first year Users*! You've had your chance. Grasslands. Nothing in sight for miles. Cadet Ward beat you—" for the first time, the major betrayed just the slightest hint of annoyance as he spoke the words "—and did so fairly in full meeting with combat regulations. You are disqualified from this tournament as per the understood parameters, and you will take your leave of the field *before you cause either of us further embarrassment.*"

Warren looked stricken, her whole body going rigid at the reprimand. Once more the Arena was silent, every eye in the stadium on the two of them. Rei couldn't have been sure, watching her from behind, but he thought the Brawler might have been ready to say more, might have been willing to risk greater ire to insist again on a second fight.

In the end, however, she looked to think better of it, seeming to cave in on herself as she hesitated, then turned—deliberately not looking at Rei—to walk slowly off the field with a blank look on her face, heels *clinking* against the plating.

She'd just reached the edge of the perimeter when a form blurred into being before her, taking the shape of Michael Bretz standing with his hands behind his back.

"Your Device, Warren," he said in a warning tone, glaring from beneath his cap. He was dressed in his regulars, the black-and-gold uniform snug about his broad frame. "You'll recall it before stepping out of bounds."

The girl blinked at the sight of her sub-instructor, then nodded. With a mumbled word her CAD retracted from her limbs, and she was allowed to pass the chief warrant officer with no further exchange, though he did watch her go by with a disappointed frown marring his handsome features.

After she was well on her way to the west exit from the Arena floor, Bretz looked back around to Rei.

"You too, Ward. Recall, and clear the field for the next match."

"Y-Yes, sir," Rei stammered, still in shock. He'd won? He'd *won*? All right, maybe that *particular* fact wasn't a complete surprise, but for it to have happened so quickly…

"Recall," he muttered, and Shido returned to its bands in a blur, dropping him down so that the coolness of the projection plating sent a shiver through his feet and up his back. At once he turned and hurried across the silver boundary, making for the east tunnels with his head bowed, not even paying attention as Marcus—returned to his unenthusiastic drone now that the entertainment had ended—announced the next combatants.

Taking the ramp down, he turned left and made it to the professionals locker room at double pace. Stepping into the darker chamber, he felt the red-and-black of the place settle on him, and he allowed himself a few deep breaths, leaning against the door of as it slid shut at his back. For a while he just stood there, quieting himself in the somber glow of crystalline lights overhead and the bubbling of the tank set into the back wall.

What had happened…?

His first clue, oddly enough, came not in the form of any new information, but rather in the *lack* of it. After more than a minute had gone by without a hint of his NOED coming to life, Rei was just short of sure Shido wasn't going to be presenting any notification of improved specs. That was… surreal, in a way. The CAD hardly lit up for him after bouts with Aria or Viv or Catcher anymore, but every major fight he'd ever been in had been followed up by *some* notice of upgrade, as well as most of the minor ones aside from class sparring. For Shido not to inform him of *any* change after a sanction match—not to mention one against a User with specs likely several ranks higher than his on average...

Had it been the speed of the fight? Had it been the rapidity with which it had started and ended?

No, Rei thought, knowing himself correct. *Not exactly.*

It was because Warren hadn't been a challenge.

That was what Shido was telling him, in its silence. *That* was the message he suspected he was meant to understand. For all his concern, for all his fear, it turned out Aria had been right.

Rei *had* had the match from the start, and from a much larger margin than he could have believed.

Oddly, the image of Lena Jiang's face, resigned to playing dirty for her win, swam across Rei's mind, and he suddenly wondered if he hadn't *yet again* been selling himself short on just where in the curve of the Galens first years he stood, spec ranks be damned.

The hiss of compressed air startled Rei, then, and he jumped away from the locker room door just in time to keep from being pulled along with it as the heavy steel slid open. On the other side of the entryway, Aria and Viv both stood, breathing so heavily they might have run a mile flat out.

"Found you!" Viv shrieked, leaping on Rei to wrap her arms about his neck in excitement. "You son of bitch! You *son of a bitch*!"

Despite his recent growth, Viv was still a *solid* 4 inches taller than him, and a little heavier. Rei was knocked backwards by her enthusiastic hug, and fortunately caught himself on the edge of one of the seating area couches before he actually toppled over.

"H-hey!" he exclaimed, surprised, returning the embrace automatically and looking at Aria over Viv's shoulders. "How did you guys find me?"

"Aria," Viv answered at once, pulling away to hold him at arm's length, taking him in top to bottom. "We ran to the SB2 locker room, but when we only found Warren there we came back upstairs. Aria was the one who figured out where you'd be."

"You make it sound like rocket science," Aria herself interrupted with a raised eyebrow. "Pretty sure all I said was 'closest locker room *not* where Warren was'."

Rei chuckled. "Yeah, that's about right. Figured it was probably a good idea the two of us didn't risk butting heads. And that was *before* that fight."

"And what a *fight*!" Viv squealed, bouncing up and down so that her brown curls— as always in perfect, inexplicable order—leapt about on her shoulders. "Holy *hell*, Rei!

Marcus was right! That was the fastest win of any match so far! We looked it up!"

This news only sent Rei reeling again, and he allowed himself to sit down on the back of the couch, staring at the ground in disbelief.

"I... I don't get it," he said after a moment. "It shouldn't have been that easy. There's *no way* it was that easy..."

"It was."

It was Aria who said it, stepping closer to stand before him with her arms crossed. Of the three of them she was the only one in regulars, and a few strands of her red hair had fallen out of her braid in the run to spill about her face from under her cap. If she noticed she couldn't be bothered, however, staring him down as she was.

"It *was*, Rei," she repeated when he said nothing. "I get it. Whatever your CAD-Rank says, she was supposed to be better, stronger."

"She *was*," Rei insisted. "No, she *is*. My average is closer to a D5. She was an *8*. That discrepancy—"

"Means jack if you fight better." It was Viv's turn, and she cut him off with a much more sober expression than she'd born a moment before. "What do you think happened with Jiang, Rei? I told you last week: you almost *had* her, and she was part of the summer group. But you didn't almost have her because you were stronger, or faster. You almost had her because you were better."

"And Warren is nothing compared to Jiang," Aria agreed with a nod. "Face it, Rei. You *earned* this win."

Rei looked between the pair of them for a moment, struck by the ferocious air the two girls cut like this, both looming well over a foot taller than him, seated as he was.

"You guys are scary when you're serious, you know that?"

Viv smirked. "If you think this is serious, you must not have been paying attention when we've been on the same squad-format team."

"Oh, I paid attention." Rei gave a mock shiver, earning himself a small laugh from Aria.

Her face was set again almost at once.

"Rei. You had it. From the start. Do you get that now?"

His one shot at changing the subject having failed, Rei took a breath, considering their words. Was it so simple? Was it as easy as that? Was he just that much *better* that Camilla Warren?

No. No, it was more complicated than that. Had his opening counterattack failed, Rei would probably have been in a much more precarious position. In a way, Warren herself had been right. In a truly straight fight and on a field like that Grasslands variation, he would have been at a much greater disadvantage than the Volcanic Slopes had granted him against Jiang. That had been part of the plan, though, right? Part of the reason he'd spent every spare moment not sleeping or eating or on the field training with the others and studying Warren's technique. He had *known* she was going to open that way, and had been ready for it.

By definition… wasn't that *exactly* what it meant to be "better"?

Feeling a little more sure of himself, Rei looked up from where he realized he'd been staring at the floor again.

"How'd your fight go?" he asked of Viv.

"Rei—" Aria started, sounding exasperated, but he held her up with a raised hand.

"No. Don't worry. I get it. I think… I just need some time to process, that's all." He looked at Viv again. "So? How'd your fight go? Had to get ready before it wrapped, and *someone*—" he tilted his head in comical indication of Aria "—refused to let me know how you made out before my own match."

Almost at once Viv's face fell, her shoulders dropping a little as she repressed what might have been a frown.

At once Rei regretted his humor. "Ah, dammit. I'm sorry, Viv. I didn't mean to—"

"I won."

He paused. She'd spoken so quietly, gaze down on her feet in what he thought had been disappointment as she'd spoke.

"You—Wait—What?"

And then Viv looked up at him again, her expression replaced with a grin of glee that had Rei knowing he'd been fooled.

"I WON!"

Rei stared at her, mouth agape.

Then, as he felt the smile start to build on his face again, he looked at Aria. "I really need to start listening to you more often…"

Aria cocked her head at him. "You're genuinely *just* figuring that out now, aren't you?"

CHAPTER 44

"Hundreds of times in the last 500 years has humanity pushed beyond its limits. Endlessly we seem to be able to do more, to be able to press ourselves further. First to Earth's moon in the 20th century, Mars in the 21st, then into the stars not 50 years after that.

And yet, as far and wide as our ships may take us, the one thing we seem unable to leave behind is the tedium and rigor of governmental bureaucracy..."

ISCM Acquisitions Chair Kennedy Shwant
Central Command, Earth
c. 2450

Yes, ma'am... Yes, ma'am... I assure you we're well aware of the circumstances, ma'am... Yes. Yes, of course..."

From her place near the back of the room by the closed door, Maddie Kent watched with feigned impassion as Rama Guest stood at ease on the far side of his desk, facing the window and the night sky beyond it. In the reflection of the glass she could just make out the flickering image in the man's frame, the indication of the video call she'd interrupted his last meeting of the day with.

Standing at attention in front of the desk, the subject of said meeting waited with rigid impatience, clearly understanding he was not at leave to depart the room just yet, and disliking that fact very much.

It was another 2 or 3 minutes before the colonel wrapped his call, and one more after it had ended that he stood looking unblinkingly up at the heavens overhead, watching the traffic of the sky-lanes play out against an overcast blackness lit to grey by the city light all around them. Maddie had to bite her lip to keep from smiling, having seen the man employ this very tactic a hundred times over with subordinates in need of rebuking.

Silence, after all, could be just as weighty of a tool as a raised voice.

At last Rama turned to face the room again, his eyes falling on the subject of his ire that evening. Major Dyrk Reese didn't so much as wince as his superior took him in with tempered irritation, the man's own gaze set somewhere above the colonel's donned military cap.

"That—serendipitously enough—was General Abel," Rama said after a second, his tone even. "In the entirety of the first quarter of the term, I received four calls from Central, major. All regarding the same topic, and all ending with my assurances that we are addressing the situation as well as any other school in the ISC would be able to." He paused, and when he spoke again, his words were cooler. "In the two weeks since the start of the Intra-Schools, I have taken *twice* that many."

His emphasis seemed not to phase Reese, who kept looking over the man's head without flinching.

"You need to understand that I do not *enjoy* these calls, major," the colonel continued after a few seconds of silence. "I do not *enjoy* being questioned a dozen different ways by just as many generals and lieutenant generals. It makes me feel like a cadet again, and—as much as I enjoyed my younger years—I have worked *very* hard not to ever feel like a cadet again. Do you understand that?"

"Yes, sir," the answer came, prompt and expected.

The bastard had always been a good actor.

"I'm not so sure you do." Rama started to walk around the desk, his eyes never leaving Reese's, who continued to stare straight ahead. "*Your* job, major, is to the students of this school, is it not?"

A silence, this time. The colonel raised an eyebrow, coming to stand before Reese with his hands behind his back. The major had removed his cap and tucked it under one arm—as was expected in the formal presence of a superior in their offices—and Rama Guest had always been a tall man. The result was like seeing a mountain stare down a hill.

"I asked you a question, major," Rama growled.

This time, the answer came.

"All due respect, sir, but I believe that's an incorrect summary of my assignment."

Both eyebrows rose up, now.

"Oh? Enlighten me."

Reese took that as leave to speak freely. "My first and foremost responsibility is to this Institute and its reputation, sir. While I can usually best serve that purpose by attending to the students, there will be exceptions when—"

"*No.*" The colonel's interruption was harsh, as close as he'd come yet to truly displaying his displeasure, in Maddie's opinion. "Don't try to feed me excuses, Reese. You are the principal arbiter of our sanctioned tournaments, which is *particularly* important when those tournaments involve our cadets. You are a guiding voice for young Users, and you have been allowed a great deal of power on the grounds of this school to aid you in that endeavor. Outside of professional SCTs, your entire *function* within these walls is to nurture and direct. Your responsibility to this Institute is carried out through our students, and *only* through our students."

"Exactly, sir. So if I deem one of my instructees to be of negative bearing to Galens' legacy and reputation, then I—"

"You bring it to *me.*"

The rumbled command felt like it vibrated, and Maddie might have imagined a flash of grey light piercing Rama's dark eyes.

"You bring it to *me*, major," the colonel said again. "You do not set about your own agenda, disrupting training and events and discipline. *Especially* for the likes of a *single* student."

For the first time, Maddie thought Reese looked a little nervous.

"Sir, Cadet Ward isn't just any—"

"No, he's not," Rama interrupted again, taking half a step closer so that only a foot of space separated the two men. "As it turns out, Ward is very, *very* special, major. Even more so than Valera Dent expected when she fought for his admission, I suspect. If you're so interested in the 'legacy and reputation' of this school, then I'm of the opinion you should be doing everything in your power to *support* Reidon Ward, rather than play your games from the shadows in some childish effort to tear him down."

"I'm not sure what you—"

"No," Rama hissed again, cutting of Reese's attempt at denial. "You do not get to *lie to me*, major. Of every instructor Cadet Ward currently has, *you* are the only one left whose feedback reports are consistently critical of the boy. Even the other sub-instructors have started to make note of his work ethic and obvious improvement. Compliments given despite their suspicions regarding his CAD's progress."

From what little of the man's face she could make out, Maddie was sure the major scowled then. "I'm entitled to a dissenting opinion, sir. I've stated from the beginning that Cadet Ward has no place at this—"

"You *also*—" Rama spoke over the man as easily as a train might rumble over a pebble left on its tracks "—saw fit to insert yourself as the Team Battle and Wargames instructor for the first year class."

"Valera Dent is a new staffer, and there were requests for her to participate in one-on-one training courses with our most accomplished students in the second and third—"

"Valera Dent is an S-Ranked Knight-Class User, Major Reese." Maddie found that she couldn't keep her mouth shut anymore, out of line as it was. "If you're of the opinion that you have more to teach the cadets than her, you should have applied for the position of chief combat instructor yourself."

Reese took advantage of this interruption to turn and glare at her.

"Sir, this is hardly correct." He spoke to the colonel even as his eyes never left Maddie's. "I resent Ms. Kent's presence in this meeting, and certainly won't allow a civilian to speak to me in this—"

"You'll *allow* what I say *you'll allow*, major," Rama thundered, drawing Reese's alarmed attention back to him. "And Maddison only makes my point for me."

Still, just the same, the colonel glanced her way once, briefly, the message coming clear in the slight narrowing of his eyes.

Stay out of this, he warned.

Maddie dipped her head in acknowledgment, though she could hardly bring herself to regret the words.

"I apologize if I overstepped the rights of my office, sir," Reese said through gritted teeth. "If you so like, I will resign the instruction of the first years' squad-formats back to Captain Dent."

Rama snorted. "I do not. That would only cause confusion and suspicion among the students, not to mention have them question your ability as instructor. Believe it or not, Reese, I'm not looking to embarrass you tonight."

The assurance seemed to do nothing to placate the major. "I'm sorry to say you've failed in that endeavor, sir. I resent these accusations. I state it for the record."

"'Accusations'?" The colonel echoed the word with an *actual* laugh, this time. "Consider for a moment nothing I've said yet has been an accusation, Reese. If you want an accusation—" his face grew stony "—explain to me how it is that Reidon Ward was pit first against one of the top sixteen Users in the class, and then a student he has had a suspected incident with? A student with superior specs to him in every class aside from one, despite his CAD-Rank, and a student in the same class-block *and* Type-group as him, giving them a significant edge on knowing his fighting style."

Reese, for once, paused for a moment before answering, licking his lips nervously.

"By now, sir, there are more first years Cadet Ward *has* had 'an incident with' than *hasn't*. In fact, that's part of my point. I hardly think it's appropriate to heap praise and expectation on a student—"

"I don't care what you think right now, major. I asked you a question. Answer it."

This time Reese was quicker on the draw, having earned himself the few seconds of time he'd likely been playing for to deliberate.

"The Intra-School pairings are constructed by lot, sir. I have no say in them, else I certainly wouldn't have paired Logan Ward against your n—" the major caught himself as Rama's eyes widened in angry warning "—against Aria Laurent." He blinked, looking like he'd been struck by a sudden thought. "That Ward was paired with two individuals he might have had some sort of disadvantage against is hardly unusual, but—I don't know if you saw—he *won* his match, today, sir."

"I did see." The colonel nodded slowly. "And in record time."

Reese did his best to keep a neutral face, but Maddie couldn't help but wonder if she imagined the hint of irritation that pulled at the corners of the man's lips.

"Here's the problem I have with your explanation, major." As he spoke, Rama stepped back and half-turned to reach down and tapped the surface of his desk with two fingers. "If you don't mind, could you explain what this is to me?"

At his words a tall image flickered into place above the lacquered wood, the projection device well-hidden within the carved contours of the detailing. Along the left side of the hologram, 128 names were lined up in no particular order, linked in pairs by lines that continued to come together until only eight remained. Beneath this, another sixty-four names repeated themselves, pairing in a similar way, but with dangling lines left for new names to be added in each column.

Though Maddie had known it was coming, it was still impressive to take in the extent of the double-elimination bracket.

"This is the matchmaking of the first year Intra-Schools," Reese said, his voice so steady it was almost forced as he pointed to the right of the initial line of names. "Given that the second column is filled, it looks like the results of last week's fights."

"Precisely," Rama said with a curt nod, gesturing towards the first line of the bottom bracket—the losers pairings—which had also been filled in. "At this point, the matchings we saw over the last two days had already been decided. Now—" he swiped two fingers along the surface of the desk, and a wall of text replaced the pairings, scrolling down the screen "—do you know what this is?"

Reese's voice was *definitely* too calm, now, as he answered.

"It appears to be the metadata of the brackets, sir."

"It is. Now I admit to having very little expertise in software engineering, but a very pleasant lieutenant from Major Hadish's office—one in possession of a *much* greater eye for these things than anyone currently standing in this room—tells me that there is something odd about this coding. According to you, these matches were to be decided by lot. Randomized. Is that correct?"

"It is, sir."

"Excellent. Then can you explain why—" Rama waved at the projection, and it stopped to light up a single line of the text in a blinking highlight "—there is a record of access to this data, logged for the evening of last Tuesday?" He turned his head slowly to look Reese full in the face again. "A record of access from *your* NOED, major."

To his credit, Reese was quick on his answer. "That would have been the input of the match losers into the secondary bracket, sir."

"Of course. Of course." The colonel nodded along for a moment before continuing. "That was what the lieutenant and I though as well."

Maddie thought she could *see* the effort Reese put into not sagging in relief in that moment.

Unfortunately for him, Rama wasn't done speaking yet.

"That is until we decided to take a look at the brackets you put together for the Intra-School in previous years."

Another wave of the colonel's big hand, and the projection appeared to replicate a score of times in a blur, the copies shimmering out and up until more than 20 years' worth of metadata was projected in several even rows all the way to the ceiling.

"Could you explain to me, major, why it was identified that this year is the only bracket that required manual input of the loser's names?"

Reese froze up, then. If he'd thought they'd ever look into things, he obviously hadn't expected them to look *this* deep.

"In fact—" the colonel's voice was dangerous again, calm but edged with warning "—every other assignment system for *any* SCT you've arbitrated for this Institute ran off automatic allocation. *Every* one. No manual input. No secondary access."

"I was trying something new this year, sir," Reese said, swallowing as he did. "In the past we've had top students being disqualified early in the tournament due to bad luck. I wanted to ensure—"

"You wanted to ensure Reidon Ward was knocked out of the running in the first two rounds," Rama snarled, suddenly inches from the major's face with a quickness only an S-Ranked User would have been able to achieve. "You wanted to *embarrass* him, to drive him a little closer to the edge. To what end? To grow the wedge between him and his class? To push for more 'incidents'? Why?"

Reese, at last, was starting to look pale as he obviously fought not to lean away from his superior's proximity.

"I don't know what you're talking about, sir. It's no secret I have my reservations about Ward, but—"

"Oh, you do," Rama cut him off. "You do know what I'm talking about. You don't just have 'reservations', major. You're trying to wage a war. A war. Against an eighteen-year-old who's just been handed a chance at real success for the first time in his life. No." He raised a hand to stop the man when Reese tried to speak. "*Do not interrupt.* I've also fielded a complaint of mistreatment from another instructor, spelling out in no uncertain terms that you deliberately ignored the initiating actions of a different student to reprimand Cadet Ward following his first fight, and Ward alone. This after more than one rumor that your interactions with him thus far in class have bordered on neglect and abuse. Enough. I've had enough."

He didn't ask if the man understood, instead stepping back to take Reese in with a frown.

"You're a smart man, major. You've no doubt identified that nothing I've brought to your attention tonight is grounds for dismissal—or even formal punishment beyond this reprimand, in fact. You're also probably aware that I have no actual evidence of deliberate tampering with the first years bracket. Lucky you." The colonel smiled then, a cold, icy thing. "However, the next time I receive a call from Central, I will be forwarding it to you. Perhaps *you'll* have an answer for the next general who comes demanding to know why what appears to be a developing pattern of mishandling of Reidon Ward—a User with *S-Ranked Growth potential*—has been allowed to fester in my school. What do you think?"

Reese's mouth dropped half-an-inch before he caught himself.

"Central has taken that much of an interest in—?"

"OF COURSE THEY HAVE!"

At long last Rama Guest exploded. He didn't approach the smaller man, this time, but Maddie thought she could *feel* the anger the colonel radiated from across the room.

"OF COURSE THEY HAVE!" he bellowed again. "DID YOU THINK HE WOULD GO UNNOTICED?! *HIM?*! THE BOY WHO HAS CLIMBED MORE THAN *TWO TIERS* IN LESS THAN SIX MONTHS SINCE HIS ASSIGNMENT?!"

Reese blanched. His shift in expression—genuinely alarmed—was enough to bring Rama back to a more level head. He took several deep breaths, steadying himself.

When he spoke again, he was informal, and in a quieter, almost gentle tone.

"Dyrk, you know I've had—*still have*—my own reservations. Ward is a wild card. He's been a wild card from the moment he was granted his CAD, and probably a long time before that. But Valera had the right of it. She saw it, and we didn't. If he continues on the trajectory he's following right now, the Central analysts think Reidon Ward will be at *least* a B-Ranked User by the time he graduates his first year of school, possibly an A. That's incredible. You have to see that…"

Reese didn't appear to have gotten over his shock, though, and said nothing. After a few seconds, Rama sighed, easing down to perch himself on the edge of his desk before crossing his arms.

"I'm not absent some sympathy towards your logic, major." He returned to titles smoothly. "You're concerned about Ward's character. His fiber."

There was a pause, but this time Reese managed to find his voice eventually.

"Yes, sir."

"You're worried he'll be a stain on this Institution's history."

"It's present too, sir." Reese hesitated. "All he's ever done on the field is run. Run and hide, or wall up and let the others come to him. He picks fights, and half his class wants nothing more than to see him dead, while the other half seems to eat out of the palm of his hand."

Rama's jaw clenched.

"Are you implying that my niece is 'eating out of the palm of his hand', major?"

Reese corrected with record speed, some color finally returning to his cheeks. "No, sir. Of course not. My apologies. I only meant that Ward clearly has a skill for worming his way into many of the student's graces, all while alienating most of the others."

"It's called 'making friends'," Maddie muttered under her breath.

Rama's gaze flicking to her a second time, lingering there in more substantial warning, letting her know she'd most certainly been overheard.

"As far as I can tell, Ward's relationships with the remainder of his class are nothing out of the ordinary." The colonel was frowning as he looked back to Reese. "He may be polarizing, but that's a self-fulfilling prophecy. His potential—and the starting place he was positioned in—made him either unworthy or sympathetic, depending on your point of view. As he progresses, those two camps will naturally evolve into jealous and vindicated respectively. But such is the way of children, major."

"And his fighting, sir? His cowardice?"

In answer, Rama reached back to tap on the desk again, his NOED flashing briefly. All together the still-hovering projections of the SCT metadata displays collapsed inward, transitioning into a single moving image that portrayed the same clip over and over again on repeat.

Two cadets hurtling towards each other, then meeting head-on only for one to come up short, stiffen, and collapse to the ground a second later.

"Tell me, major… does that *really* look like cowardice to you?"

Reese's lips were a thin line as he watched Reidon Ward cut down Camilla Warren several more times, eyes following the boy again and again and again.

When he finally opened his mouth to speak once more, however, his words were not what Maddie had expected.

"He's dangerous, sir."

Across from him, Rama's frown deepened, and he looked to be considering his subordinate—his *friend*—with a careful intensity Maddie hadn't seen all night.

"… Is that what this is really about, Dyrk?" The colonel finally asked. "Fear? For what? The Institute?"

The major shook his head slowly, not removing his gaze from Ward's flashing form.

"No, sir. Not the Institute…"

"What, then?"

"Everything."

It wasn't long after that that the colonel dismissed Dyrk Reese, though not before extracting assurances that the major would reformulate the remainder of the first year bracket—with automated randomization, this time—and present them for approval. With no hard cause to detain or punish the man further, Reese had been allowed to leave, looking shaken as he departed the room without so much as glancing at Maddie when he passed. It was alarming to see, in a way. For one thing it was strange to witness the hard, unbending officer brought low.

For another, though, she couldn't tell if this unmaking was the result of Rama's reprimand, or the concerns which had been forcibly dragged into the light…

When the door shut behind the major with a *click*, Maddie looked immediately to the colonel. She found him staring at nothing, not having risen from his place seated at the edge of the desk, his gaze distant and his arms still crossed over his broad chest.

She gave him a full 15 seconds before deciding to interrupt.

"Rama?"

The man blinked and came to, turning his attention on her with brow furrowed under the black brim of his cap.

"What do you think of that?" he asked without preamble, like they'd already been in conversation.

"Of what, sir?" Maddie replied, stepping away from the wall and giving herself leave to take a seat on one of the couches set opposite the man's desk. She'd only meant to poke her head in to inform him of the call from General Shira Abel, and as such hadn't been carrying her pad or any other materials when he'd waved her in a quarter-hour before, now. Unsure of what to do with her hands, she decided to rest her arms across the back of the couch, making herself comfortable by crossing one ankle over a knee.

The colonel smirked at this casualness, but instead of saying anything contrary stood up off the desk with a grunt to move to the seat opposite her, waving at the place Dyrk Reese had been as he did.

"That," he repeated before dropping down onto the cushions and assuming much the same position as Maddie, though he started drumming the fingers of one hand upon his knee almost immediately.

"What the major said?"

A nod.

"Which part?"

"Maddison…" the colonel growled impatiently.

Maddie managed a brief grin.

Then she felt it slide off her face as she contemplated.

"He's afraid of Ward," she said slowly. "He's afraid of him."

"Yes…" Rama agreed, just as evenly. His gaze had drifted again as he listened.

Maddie took in a breath through her nose, considering her next words carefully.

"Maybe he should be."

To her surprise, it was the colonel's turn to smile. "Indeed. I find myself of the same opinion…" He paused, chewing on his thoughts. "That doesn't make him any less in the wrong for his actions."

"*Alleged* actions, sir," Maddie corrected him with a raised eyebrow. "You said yourself we've got no proof."

Rama waved the comment away dismissively. "It doesn't matter. My point is that even the approach we know for sure he's taken is in the wrong. I'm of the opinion he's been making a play to drive Ward from the school of the boy's own volition. Central—" he pointed at his eye to indicate the call he'd taken "—happens to agree with me. And I say 'happens' because *I* sure as hell didn't appraise them of my concerns."

"They've got spies in the school."

Rama laughed dryly. "I'd hardly call them 'spies' given we *all* work for the military in the end. Even you."

Maddie nodded, but she was turning over something else as he'd been speaking. She smiled. "Well… I think we can confidently say the major's plan was anything but a success. According to Valera—uh, *Captain* Dent—" she corrected herself, feeling her cheeks redden "—according to her, the only students in the Institute to put *nearly* as many extra hours in are Lennon, Sidorov, and Cashe. Ward and his group—Aria included… If anything, it seems like Reese's games have only pushed them to work harder."

Rama nodded slowly, watching his fingers tapping at the black fabric of his pants atop his knee.

"All good things," he mumbled in agreement. "All good signs. And yet… He's not wrong…"

Maddie felt a shiver crawl up her arms, then. She didn't at all like where the colonel's head was going.

"If you really thought that—if you *really* worried Ward might be dangerous—you would have made sure to keep Aria away from him."

Rama grunted, but didn't say anything more for a moment. He looked to be mulling over the idea, eyes narrowing as he considered.

"It's not that I *don't* worry he's dangerous," he got out at last. "He *is*, Maddison, and if you ask Dent I can promise you she'll say the same thing. It's more…" he paused, taking a breath as he pieced together what he was trying to enunciate.

When he managed it, it was with the look of a gambler, wondering if keeping the dice rolling had *really* been the best idea.

"Do you refuse to pursue something—something so incredible—for fear of the *possibility* of failure? Do you not walk a path that will likely lead to greatness because it *might* take you to disaster?"

"No," Maddie said at once, firm in her belief on this. "You walk the path."

Rama chewed on his words a moment more.

"Ward has S-Ranked Growth. That's never been seen. Never, and much less *on assignment*. His potential could very well be limitless. He may not *have* a cap to how strong he can get." Finally, the colonel's eyes lifted to Maddie. "Think on that, and then tell me what failure could look like for us, in this case?"

CHAPTER 45

"It is surreal for me to look back and consider even my small, brief role in his ascension..."

Christopher "Lasher" Lennon, S-Rank Knight-Class

Despite a *life* of pain, despite long months of hard conditioning and Shido to help him with recovery, by the time the following Monday arrived Rei wasn't sure he'd ever completely recuperate from the beatdown that had been Friday night's training session. As he sat in class between Viv and Aria—the three of them struggling together to pay attention to Sarah Takeshi's lecture on "Height Dynamics in Self-Modifying Field Variations"—he could tell that they, too, still felt the weight of the time spent under Lennon's hand. 2 hours. 2 hours, partially divided among all four of them, including Catcher.

And it had still been more than enough to see every single one of them vomiting at least once before the end of the session.

The A-Ranked third year—it turned out—was a brutal, unforgiving teacher, and he cut none of them so much as an ounce of slack during their time together. What was more, for a second Friday in a row not once had the dark-skinned young man bothered to even partially-call his Device, working them into the ground with nothing but his ingrained Strength, Speed, and Endurance. Rei could still hear Lennon's snapping orders and feedback, coming quick and fast even as his bare hands had blurred in an infinite lashing of cuts and punches and chops that not even Aria's Third Eye had had a chance of keeping up with.

Still, whatever lingering soreness might be left over by the time his match came later that same day—he'd been paired up with Gillian North, the Mauler—Rei couldn't help but smile. Lennon had ended the lesson much in the same fashion he had the last. He'd taken the time, one by one, to point out their flaws, to point out the ways they could polish their techniques and style.

But he had also been careful to tell them how they had *already* improved in the week since they'd taken his last teachings to heart.

Yes, Rei felt comfortable smiling at that. He was getting stronger, after all.

He was *definitely* getting stronger.

"Is something amusing, cadet?"

Rei started and looked up from where he'd been staring at the desk to find Captain Takeshi watching him with an eyebrow raised, one hand on her hip while the other held a pad she'd been using to control the smart-glass wall display behind her. As he was called out, several muffled chuckles rose up from the back of the room, though they sounded more like Sense and Kay trying to hide their amusement than anyone having a laugh at his expense.

Ever since he'd taken down Warren, Grant's crew had been giving him a fairly wide berth, for which he wasn't going to complain.

"No, ma'am," Rei answered, sitting up straighter in his chair as Aria and Viv automatically did the same on his right and left respectively. "Apologies. I have a fight this afternoon. I let myself get distracted."

"You did," Takeshi agreed blankly. "You and a good portion of this class have a fight this afternoon, Ward, and more will have matches tomorrow. It's no excuse to be drifting off in lecture."

"No, ma'am. Of course."

"I'll give you a chance to redeem yourself. Give me three situations in which holding the *low* ground is better in a match."

Rei had to stop himself from grinning again. Ever since she'd witnessed Reese's asinine lecturing of him after his first fight, the captain had seemed to take a liking to him. It wasn't a handout, in this case, but it wasn't a question he thought she'd suspect he'd have any trouble answering.

He held up a finger. "Any Type with a reach advantage would be well-positioned on lower ground. A Brawler or Saber will have a harder time defending their knees and shins against a Lancer or Mauler, for example, and maintaining distance will help keep at bay potential attacks from above." He held up a second finger. "If you can get *under* them. It's probably easier in squad-formats since you can have someone acting as a distraction, but any field that allows you to actually get beneath your opponent can lead to advantage. We aren't accustomed to have to defend the bottoms of our feet."

"And a third?" Takeshi asked, looking unsurprised by his rapid-fire answering.

"If they're dropping down on you." Rei lowered his hand below the desk again. "It's a dangerous position to be in—and I'd say most of the advantage is usually on your opponent's side—but you do have *some* things working in your favor."

"Like what?" someone—maybe Adam Jax?—asked from behind Rei, higher in amphitheater.

"Like gravity." It was Viv who answered for him, half-turning in her seat to look up the incline of the lecture hall. "If you can escape whatever they're looking to hit you with from above, let them fall right on your sword."

"Or spear," Aria added, nodding along despite taking notes on her pad with quick scribbles of her stylus.

"Spear is preferable," Viv agreed with a snort, facing forward again and making a motion like she was planting a polearm to stick straight up into the air beside her. Then she winced at her own imagery. "Ooph… That would hurt."

"Yes, it would." Takeshi was giving the three of them the briefest hint of a smile. "Excellent. You can go back to daydreaming, now, Ward."

More laughter—from a wider range of classmates this time—and Rei resumed his own notetaking a little abashed.

His fight being later in the afternoon, he told Aria and Viv after class he'd join them for lunch and combat training. It was Monday, and while Dyrk Reese, too, had seemed less blatantly aggressive towards him since his victory the previous week, Rei was still eager to get any and all hours in he could under Valera Dent and Michael Bretz. Catcher had one of the early fights that day and couldn't join them, making the light meal of chicken and roasted vegetables a quieter-than-usual affair, though they all messaged back and forth with the Saber as they ate. It had been his turn to be paired with one of the top students in the class—the Duelist Laquita Martin, from 1-B—and though he'd done a good job of hiding it all week, it had been clear that he was nervous. Rei, Aria, and Viv all worked to bolster his confidence, and by the time they left the mess hall, Catcher's messages had been more cheerful, brimming a little bit more with his usual self. Upon reaching the Arena, though, the three of them deliberately ducked into one of the northern entrances to the underworks of the stadium, not wanting to distract him by catching his eye from where he would undoubtedly be seated in the south end of the stands, impatiently waiting his turn.

Some 10 minutes and a change of clothes later, they were walking towards the massive floor of the SB2 together among a scattering of 1-A classmates, chatting about Catcher's chances in the fight. Rei and Aria were of the opinion that he had a good shot of matching up against Martin despite the fact that the C1 Duelist was two ranks higher than him, but Viv had her concerns.

"She's fast. *Really* fast. Her Offense never seemed great, but Catcher's Defense is one of his weakest specs, so that cancels out a bit. I think she's going to be too quick for him."

"Catcher's fast too, though." Rei pointed out. "I'm pretty sure he's C1 in Speed?"

"That's *Saber* fast, yeah," Viv agreed with a grimace. "But that's not *Duelist* fast. I'm a C4 Speed at a C0 CAD-Rank, Rei. Martin is a level higher than me."

"Which puts her Speed at C5, and maybe higher." Aria groaned as they reached the massive entrance to the combat floor. "Damn... That's a gap for sure..."

"He's got other things going for him," Rei shrugged off the concerns, hoping he didn't let the blow to his confidence at Catcher having a fighting chance show through. "He's got better reach and perfect technique. If he fight's smart, he'll have the chance to—"

He stopped, then, though, Catcher's upcoming match slipping from his mind like water off glass. The three of them had just turned the corner into the subbasement's main chamber, and had found themselves greeted with the usual sight of the captain conferring the day's training schedule with her sub-instructors on a raised platform above Field 3. There, was, however, something different about the view, and for a moment Rei frowned in the direction of the officers, not sure what was strange.

It was Aria who worded it first.

"Uh... The Bishop's in a combat suit..." she breathed.

And so she was. It qualified, certainly, as a strange sight, and Rei understood at once why the buzz of noise that he hadn't initially noticed was louder than usual, coming from the already-gathering bodies of 1-A. It wasn't like it was the first time he'd ever seen Dent in a suit, of course. He'd caught plenty of her matches during her time on the circuits, and watched the records of those fights probably more frequently than any other User. Still, it *was* the first time she'd dressed for a fight *in class*, and this fact came with a tingle of anticipation up Rei's arms as he realized it.

"Oooh..." Viv crooned giddily. "It's about to be a *really* good day, isn't it?"

"Looks like it..." Rei and Aria said together, grinning at each other before moving with Viv to join the rest of the class.

Their anticipation was very clearly shared by the other students of 1-A, the regular groups clumped here and there around the usual gathering area just outside the east quarter of Field 3's silver perimeter line. Sense and Leron Joy caught sight of the three of them before they'd crossed half of the floor, with the bald Brawler waving them over excitedly, a broad grin splitting his face.

"Kay got a fight?" Viv asked once she and Rei and Aria had joined the duo.

"Yeah," Sense nodded, though he waved the question away as he did. "Another Lancer I don't know, from 1-D. We're not worried about her. More importantly..." He leaned in to whisper eagerly to the lot of them. "Did you notice?"

"Dent's suit?" Aria asked equally quietly, her voice barely audible over the buzz of conversation from the others all around. "We did. Anyone know what's going on?"

"Nope," Leron Joy grunted. He appeared to be trying to hide his own excitement, frowning at Rei in what was a clear attempt to make it known his was a dissenting opinion when it came to their gathering up.

Sense rolled his eyes. "No, we don't," he answered a little more fully. "We asked around, but no one knows what's up. Selleck sounded pretty confident we're going to be having matches against the instructors." The Brawler jerked his head towards the south end of the gathered class. "Seems to think we're gonna have it demonstrated to us how best to take on a stronger opponent as a group."

Rei exchanged a glance with Aria and Viv, suspecting they were probably thinking the same thing he was.

If they could glean any sort of coordinated advantage on how to take on Christopher Lennon when next they saw him...

Then again, Rei had his doubts. As much as Valera Dent stressed the importance of preparing them for the front lines as opposed to the SCTs, they were still in their first year, still learning the ropes. Finding themselves in a match where an enemy squad had a member that would be multiple tiers higher in ability than your own wasn't a likely occurrence in the standard fighting formats, and Rei was pretty sure the captain was still more concerned with making sure they got their baseline down before broaching any theoretical combat against the varying strengths of the archons they'd only made a passing study of so far. Indeed, it seemed the broader point of their entire first year: to get them up to speed on their CADs before anything else.

Rei looked around, in the direction Sense had just indicated, and it only took a moment for him to find the blond head of Mateus Selleck, turned with his back to them. In Rei's opinion it was more likely Dent was planning to start working in-person with the individual Type-groups, and had just dressed for the part. More exciting, of course, was the possibility that the captain was going to show off for them a bit, maybe with a study of her CAD, Kestrel, or with a couple exhibition matches against—

Rei blinked, losing his train of thought as he found his attention drifting from the back of Selleck's head to a pair of darker, red-tinged eyes he hadn't noticed until that moment were looking his way. As his gaze locked with Logan Grant's, he was surprised to find the massive boy frowning at him. The two of them hadn't really butted heads for weeks—not since Warren and Emble's backstabbing in the elevator lobby—but all the same the few times they'd caught each other's eyes the Mauler's expression had never failed to translate his usual sentiments. Annoyance. Disgust. Anger.

And yet, now…

Then, though, Grant, looked away, resuming a conversation he looked to have been having with the Phalanx Leda Truant. Rei continued to watch the boy for a while longer, not paying attention as Viv and Sense kept on with their discussion until Aria stepped to stand beside him and whisper in his ear.

"What's up?"

Rei shook his head slowly, unsure of how to answer.

"Don't know," he said after a moment. "Grant was just looking at me."

Aria started to make a sound of annoyance, but Rei brought her up short.

"No. No, it was nothing like that. It was weird. He looked… confused?"

"Confused?" Aria repeated, sounding like she didn't understand.

Which was fine, since Rei didn't either.

Before he could say as much, however, there was motion on the elevated Field 3, and as one every 1-A cadet turned inward to watch Valera Dent approach the edge of the platform, the sub-instructors right on her heels. The tall woman smirked as she came to a stop to look them over, obviously amused by the sudden silence that had fallen on the class despite any lack of instruction to settle down. Her short brown hair had been set tight about her head with flat pins, and her eyes were bright as they swept across the eager faces of her students. Her combat suit—the red-on-white of all the staffers'—bared her arms and much of her legs for observation, and though no wound Rei had ever seen would match the black line of the prosthetic that made up most of her face, the numerous scars that marred her pale skin were not lost on him. They lined her limbs in crossing patterns, maybe some twenty in all, marking her lithe figure like a battle-worn statue that had only barely survived a warzone. A few exceptionally brutal ones stood out in particular, including a thick line that practically bisected her right leg, and a circular band of healed tissue above her left elbow that was unmistakably the remnant of a surgically reattached limb.

"Holy hell…" Sense could be heard to mutter, and Rei had to agree.

All of a sudden, his own scars felt like nothing more than the unfortunate reminders of a moderately-tedious childhood.

"Yes, take it in," Valera Dent said with a nod, spreading her arms out for them in a motion that said she wasn't the least-bit surprised by their fascination. "If you think the rearrangement of my face was the only wound I walked away with, then you should educate yourself on the reality of war, cadets. I was an S-Ranked User in a fight that has too-few fighters of my caliber even now. I was sent to the parts of the front line where the blood spilled was the thickest. You have been provided great power, all of you. It comes with great responsibility."

She smiled then, looking around at them as though she'd just shared some grand joke.

When no one laughed, the woman sighed and dropped her arms with a shake of her head. "Kids these days…" she grumbled. "No interest in the classics when there's CAD-fights to watch."

There came a polite cough from behind her—Claire de Soto's—and Dent mumbled in unintelligible annoyance before continuing.

"It's come to the attention of the Institute that in the last two weeks, extracurricular attendance by first year students of the East and West Centers has gone up nearly sixty percent. I don't know whether to praise you all for your newfound enthusiasm, or point out that perhaps a good number of you might have been well-served with a few more extra hours of training a week than you were previously partaking in."

This time a light roll of laughter came from the class—as well as a sharing of sheepish glances from several cadets whose cheeks were brightening to red—but the captain kept on before anyone got too embarrassed at the call out.

"Regardless, it doesn't matter. The only conditions you are *required* to meet are those you partake in class. If you've elected to prioritize other activities outside that time, I can only hope it is in study, or at the very least something of such exquisite delight it will be worth your own future potentially covered in scars." She made a small gesture with both hands to indicate her body, the red-and-blue steel of her CAD-bands gleaming with white as they shifted about her wrists.

That cut off all amusement, and the class went quiet once again.

"While every one of your instructors is pleased with this uptick in taking advantage of the resources the Institute has provided you, we also have our concerns. Training is good. Conditioning is good. Pushing yourself and your bodies and your Devices is good. *However…* Without direction, there can also be consequences." She looked around at them all for a moment before settling on a face. "Cadet Hinks, can you tell me why—before you arrived at this school—individuals undergoing solo-training had access only to basic combat simulations and protocols?"

Rei felt his ears going a little hot, recalling the weeks he had spent stealing into the classrooms of the Grandcrest gym to use the projection tech to face off against just such holographic opponents. Before he could wonder too long on how few of his fellow students had been limited to such meager opportunities to train with, Emily Hinks' nervous voice spoke up from somewhere to his left.

"To avoid the development of bad habits, ma'am."

"Correct, but elaborate, if you please."

Hink's words came stronger now that she knew she was on the right track. "It's discouraged for new CAD-assignees without a sanctioned instructor to attempt to teach themselves. It's too easy to develop bad form, poor technique, and improper instincts that would then have to be stripped away before proper combat education could be applied."

"Yes. Exactly." Dent turned her attention back to the class as a whole. "You have spent months, now, within the walls of the Institute. For most of you, your basics are solid, and the rest of you are well on their way. You are trusted to know the essentials of right from wrong on the field, trusted to know how far you can push yourselves, and how best to do so. This is why you are allowed to train on your own. However, with this spike in Center usage it was decided by myself and your Type-instructors that some small additional direction might be best. A little light on the path to help guide the way. For that reason, rather than live combat we will be focusing this week on technique review. Combat suits will not be required Wednesday or Friday, though I believe Major Reese still intends to hold regular conditioning during your squad-based training days."

The sound of the excitement draining from the 1-A cadets was quite literally audible. Many students—including both Viv and Sense—let out groans of disappointment that were quickly stifled, but not before the combined dissatisfaction of the class rang loud.

The captain, though, wasn't finished speaking.

"Oh? Do you *not* want to see me put the beatdown on your Type-instructors, then?"

Immediately the enthusiasm returned as gasps of surprise and anticipation, and Rei knew he couldn't have been the only one to feel a thrill tingle up his spine.

Exhibition matches? Were they about to witness exhibition matches between the Iron Bishop and some of the strongest officers on the Galens Institute staff?

Dent might have been the only S-Ranked fighter in the room, but not a single among her sub-instructors was a pushover by any means. Every one of them was an A-Ranked fighter, and Michael Bretz—according to a recent ISCM profile update Emily Gisham had shared with Rei and Sense not a week past—had joined the Phalanx-instructor Catori Imala as an A9 fighter, only a single level from being Ss themselves.

"It's about to be a really, *really* good day," Aria mumbled in awe, repeating Viv's earlier words.

"Now then—" there was a flash in Dent's eyes, and the raised floor vanished to plain projection plating, dropping her and the other officers to the steel gently "—if you would all spread out around the field, we'll get started."

Rei, Aria, Viv, Sense, and Joy had happened to be standing near the center of the gathered class, so they largely had only to wait as the other students swiftly began moving to scatter in pockets along the perimeter. So eager was everyone for the demonstration to start that it wasn't more than 15 seconds before Grant's group finally settled on the west side of the field, opposite Rei and the others.

"Good. Sit."

Everyone took a seat, Rei at the end of their gathered five, and as he eased himself down he realized that his hands were shaking. Christopher Lennon had been impressive enough. The awesomeness of the Lasher's demonstrated ability in the first week of the Intra-Schools had been matched only with the disappointment that none of them but Catcher had been able to catch his fight the previous Friday, with Rei, Aria, and Viv prevented by classes.

But this… This would be the first time Rei would have the opportunity to watch an *S*-Ranked fight from up close…

"Today we will be reviewing high-level Brawler and Saber combat." As Valera Dent started speaking again, she indicated Field 1 and 2, then 3 and 4. "Wednesday will be Lancer and Duelist, and Friday—" she pointed to 5 and 6 "—we'll wrap with Phalanx and Maulers. I will be making commentary as the fighting takes place, but if you have any questions over the course of the combat, raise your hand and one of the other instructors will see you get an answer." With that, she gave a dismissing flick of her wrist, and Claire de Soto, Allison Lake, Liam Gross, Imala Catori, and Kayla Johnson all made their way swiftly out of bounds, spreading out as they did.

In the end, only Michael Bretz was left standing as he'd been, at ease a pace behind the captain, chin held high and gaze on the far wall at Rei's and the others' backs.

"Everyone all set?" When no one answered to the contrary, Dent nodded. "Good. Then let's give you a better view, shall we?"

Once more her NOAD blazed, and at once a 5-yard band of plating all around the field began to glow the same white as the combat zone, extending into the buffer between the perimeter and the west entrance behind Grant and the others. Dent and Bretz began to rise, as usual, but not faster than the class did, the ring that was their seating area lifting until they were a good 9 or 10 feet above the two officers. As they did, the captain and chief warrant officer moved swiftly to the twin red starting circles that had appeared for them, gaining their positions just as Rei felt the ring slow to a seamless stop.

In the end, the class was looking down from a perfect vantage as the S-Ranked Knight faced off against her A9 subordinate.

"Captain Valera Dent versus Chief Warrant Officer Michael Bretz," the Arena's smooth voice announced. "Combatants... Call."

Neither combatant, of course, required an oral command to summon their Device. With nothing more than a thought the paired CADs came into being, the bands dissolving from their Users wrists to take the forms of their phantom-calls. It was in that blink of time that Rei realized he had never actually seen Michael Bretz's Device. The sub-instructor had taken a hands-on approach to his Brawlers' training often enough, but he—like Christopher Lennon—had never actually called on his CAD during classes.

It was something of a pity, because it turned out to be a rare beauty to behold.

Bretz's Device was a pearlescent white that seemed to ripple in a mirage of colors in the subbasement lighting. Looking closer, Rei realized that instead of a true mother-of-pearl sheen, the armor was actually comprised of what looked to be hundreds of tiny steel plates, almost like scales, alternating ivory and purple to give the metal its deceptive shading. Broad at the shoulders and narrower at the waist, the entirety of the armor was accented with a stunning symmetrical pattern of black vysetrium centered around a small, solid circle of the stuff in the middle of Bretz's chest. From there the dark lines extended in all directions, even climbing up his plated neck to connect with a trio of black viewing lens set in a vertical line up the center of an angular faceplate, which formed the front of the man's curved helm.

His weapons, though, were even more impressive.

A Brawler-Type through and through, Bretz's Device had no hands to speak of. This might have been a disadvantage in more than one situation, but Rei suspected the pros outweighed the cons in many ways. Where fists and fingers should have been, a solid piston of white steel was capped with 6-inch point of smooth, black vysetrium. Further frightening still, these appendages were certainly more than they appeared at a glance, because as Bretz brought his arms up at the ready Rei realized that the vysetrium was actually shaped into a pair of curved hooks, their foot-long lengths nothing less than short scythes that flashed like sharpened onyx in the light. In any other situation, Rei would have found himself having a hard time breathing, then, so amazed would he have been by the impressive site.

Instead, he only found Bretz's incredible Device a brief distraction from the *real* star of the show.

Though he had seen it so many times before, Valera Dent's CAD was something altogether different to behold in person. Unlike the chief warrant officer's scaled, heavier armor, Kestrel was actually more blue under-layering than red steel, the protective plating it had limited to shielding the essential bulk of the captain's tall form. Fitted metal pieces layered her chest, thighs, and shoulders, with smaller partitions studding her abdomen, arms, and lower legs and feet. Her helmet was a slim, oblong thing not much larger than Dent's actual head, and the white of her vysetrium cut two bright viewing ports horizontally across the red of her faceplate, as well as shining in lines and pockets all about her body. In her hands the captain held two long, red sabers, blades edged with glowing ivory, and to the uninformed eye many would have been quick to call the woman a Duelist.

It was behind her back, however, that the portions of her Device that qualified her as an Atypical waited patiently.

In a graceful pattern of angular red-and-white, the steel of the captain's eight externals flared outward like paired wings beyond her shoulders. Light rippled from the flattened insides of the metal, pulsing with every slight movement of her body. So powerful was the anti-gravitational counterforce provided by these modules that Dent didn't actually touch the ground even as she waited for the fight to start. Her feet, instead, hung loose below her as she hovered nearly a full foot off the floor of the field. Like an armed angel of red-and-blue she lingered there, suspended before them all, and from around the ring Rei could make out echoing gasps of amazement.

It was a few second delay before he realized that one of them had been his own. And then the Arena spoke again.

"Combatants... Fight."

CRACK!

Instantly, Michael Bretz vanished in a spray of fractured flooring. The Break Step was so fast that even as high above them as they were Rei thought he could feel the wind of it after the chief warrant officer made his appearance once again directly in front of Valera Dent. A black hook flashed, but not at the captain. Instead, Bretz had angled his opening attack to go for the externals of the Bishop's right wing.

And still he was too slow.

With a grace that seemed impossible given the speed at which she moved, Dent slipped leftward, skating over ground she never touched, like a leaf blown by a smooth wind. Bretz's attack caught nothing but air, and by the time he turned to follow his opponent the captain was nearly a quarter of the way around the field.

And it had all taken about 2 seconds.

"Chief Warrant Officer Bretz is correct in triggering an early ability, here." Valera Dent's voice came through the Arena's system, magnified so they would hear over the sounds of the fight. "He knows I have superior Speed, so his prerogative *must be* to close the distance between us as quickly as possible, or be put at a disadvantage due to the better reach of my weapons."

Sure enough, Bretz approached her more cautiously now. He still moved with a terrifying agility—his armor shimmering purple and white like the skin of some hulking, jeweled serpent—but it was with less direct power as he closed the distance between them again.

Dent let him come as she continued to explain.

"The chief warrant officer—if you noticed—also elected not to attack *me* directly, but instead aim for my externals." Bretz reached her in a barrage of cutting blows, which she defended herself from with blurred blocks and deflections of both sabers while she kept talking. "This was advantageous for several reasons, namely that it can be a largely surprise attack, particularly from a Brawler. One expects their limited range to bring them very close, and if I had prepared only for a targeting of my person I would likely be suffering a severe reduction of Speed at the moment."

Which might have been as good as a match loss, Rei thought to himself, scooting closer to the edge of the elevated ring to get a better view.

Dent had disengaged sideways again, but this time brought herself around in a loose loop in an attempt to get behind Bretz. The Brawler, though, was too quick for her, spinning smoothly to keep pace with her circumvention even as he snapped up a thick arm to block a testing slash from the Bishop.

"If you wonder why we insist on teaching you physics, *that* right there is a simple enough example," Dent continued, retreating backwards as Bretz launched into and aggressive counterassault. "Despite my advantage in Speed, my attempt to flank the chief warrant officer failed because I went too far around, allowing him to stay with me. I *could* try for a tighter wrap, of course, but it comes with disadvantages."

Despite the statement, she did exactly that, and in a blink got behind Bretz successfully.

Or almost successfully.

Before the captain could bring her blade up to strike, her opponent was whirling, arms coming around in a cutting swing. Dent was forced to jerk away to keep from losing her head, but she turned the motion into a dancer's back-spring, both feet catching Bretz under the chin just as he finished his turn. He was sent flying, but tucked and rolled with such athletic precision that he landed in a crouch not a moment after the captain herself found her footing again.

"Against almost any other Type, such a flank can be incredibly effective." For once Dent initiated, lunging forward with a powerful pulse of her externals. "The length of their weapons does not allow for as quick or as close of a counterattack. Brawlers, however, can respond even faster than Duelists to surprise assaults, particularly ones from directly behind. It can make ambushing and flanking extremely difficult, not to mention dangerous."

Bretz met her aggression with his own, feigning a leading punch that he changed into a spinning kick. Dent blocked the blow with a blade—the white vysetrium digging only a little into the limb's thick scales—and Bretz shifted immediately into a whipping backflip that brought his other foot up at her face. She dodged it by an inch, but was again forced to bend away, giving Bretz enough time to land and launch forward again.

That was how the first quarter-hour of the lesson continued, with neither the captain nor the chief warrant officer showing any signs of fatigue over the course of the 15 minutes. It became clear very quickly that the match was rather one-sided, with Bretz being the only of the two of them actually intent on downing his opponent, but it was a fight worth drooling over all the same. Dent continued her live commentary all the while, and very occasionally would ask the man to repeat something he had just done, or perform a specific attack of defensive technique so she could demonstrate an appropriate response. Within 5 minutes Rei was regretting not having brought his pad to take notes, but when he'd muttered his disappointment out loud Aria had only laughed, then pointed to her NOED when he turned to look at her with a frown.

She was recording the fight, he realized, and with an exaggerated palm to the face in silent acknowledgement of what an idiot he was, he started to do the same.

After that quarter-hour, Dent called an end to the fight, bringing Bretz up short just as he'd looked to be preparing himself for another rush. Thanking him for his assistance, she dismissed the man, who saluted and recalled his CAD in the same moment before turning and in one go leaping the 12 feet or so to clear the head of a seated Biyu Yang. As he did, Claire de Soto took his place by dropping down from the other side of the ring, her pink pixie-cut a strange flash of color to Dent's clean red-and-blue.

The moment the Saber sub-instructor had taken her starting position in the red ring that had popped up on the floor for her, the Arena spoke.

"Lieutenant Claire de Soto versus Captain Valera Dent. Combatants... Call."

The lieutenant—as the only of the two not already clad in her Device—did as she was instructed, and at once Rei suspected he knew where she had gotten her hairstyle from. The woman's CAD was a dark shade of pink over grey, but whereas one might have found the color amusing in conjunction with the profession of an A-Ranked User, Rei wasn't sure he'd ever found pink so terrifying.

Like Bretz, de Soto's vysetrium was black, and it lined every piece of the solid plating that covered her body. The armor was angular, with sharp, jutting edges that looked like claws, and her faceplate was a rounded sheet of pure vysetrium framed in a pink helm by several triangular overlays along the top and bottom. It gave the impression that the headpiece had been formed in the shape of a beast's mouth, with this image only made stronger by the heavy wrap of shimmering black "hair" that looped about the sides and back of the woman's neck like a mane.

The only thing more impressive than de Soto's armor, however, was her sword. As a Saber, it was revealed that she was one of the two-handed variation. There was no black in the massive blade, its single 6-inch edge instead formed by solid grey steel along a heavy pink core, but for some reason this only made the weapon more intimidating. When the glow of vysetrium was what was swinging at your head, there was a part of the mind that made it a little easier to swallow, as though that especially fantastic nature of CAD technology could be acknowledged as just little less real.

On the other hand, Rei was pretty sure a solid sword like de Soto's cleaving at his face would leave him with an altogether different level of terror, phantom-call or not.

"Combatants… Fight."

Unlike in the match against Bretz, it was Dent who made the first approach. Lieutenant de Soto, in response, set her legs and stood her ground, bringing her great blade up flat before her. It accepted the impact of both of the captain's flashing sabers like a shield, the sound of the steel slamming against steel harsh even from above. At once Dent corrected, collapsing one arm to put the rest of her attacking momentum behind the shoulder she leveled into the defending sword.

De Soto took all of a half-step back.

"When fighting a Saber—" the captain's voice picked up as she disengaged for another assault "—one of the most important things you need to figure out is where their strengths and weaknesses are. With the other Types, it can usually be assumed that certain specs are at advantage." She sent of fury of slashes at the lieutenant, who continued to hunker down and defend with little more than the occasional twitches as a blade slipped passed the quick adjustments of her broad sword to ring against her reactive shielding. "Brawlers and Duelists share an affinity for Speed and Cognition. Lancers have their reach in addition to excellent Offense, which they share with Maulers, who also generally possess excellent Strength. Phalanxes have impeccable Defense, and usually the Endurance to back it up. With Sabers, however—" Dent leapt and planted a massive drop kick into de Soto's wall-like blade, sending her back another bare step "—their specs are much more balanced, with any favoring usually going in no more than one specific direction."

She paused as her opponent found her footing again, waiting until de Soto was set before continuing.

"Lieutenant, could you please share with the class what your field name was, when you competed in the Sol System's SCTs?"

"Stone Lily," came the answer at once.

Dent waited, looking up at her cadets as though expecting someone to laugh. When no one made a sound, she nodded in approval.

"Yes. You have good heads on your shoulders, all of you. As I suppose you can image, the lieutenant's style leans heavily into Def—"

CRACK!

With another shattering of projected light, de Soto lunged at the captain, massive blade arching in a diagonal cross-cut. She hadn't triggered any Break Step, but as close as the two of them were there was no need to. She was on top of the Iron Bishop in a heartbeat, weapon screaming down to—

WHA-BOOM!

A thrumming pulse of air and space, and an invisible force caught the lieutenant mid-stride. Incredibly, Dent's Repulsion didn't send the woman flying, but instead only staggering backwards, forcing her to slam her blade into the ground to keep from falling over. Rei knew, then, that not only did Claire de Soto have S-Ranked Defense, but the spec had to be S5 or higher to weather the captain's Ability so well.

"Stone Lily" didn't even *begin* to do the Saber justice as a name, he thought.

"An *excellent* example by the lieutenant on how to turn one's perceived weaknesses into advantages!" Dent called out in approval, having not moved from the place she'd triggered the Repulsion, though she had dropped her gaze from the students back to face de Soto ago. "I admit that I let my guard down for a moment, there, because it is easy to assume that a User with high Defense and Offense won't have the maneuverability necessary to make a quick attack like the one you just saw. If I hadn't had that Ability built up, that might very well have been FDA for me!"

"Liar," Rei muttered aloud before he could stop himself. Aria elbowed him in the ribs with a smirk, but even Viv on her other side nodded.

"That was deliberate, wasn't it?" she asked of them in a whisper. "What S-Rank would look away from an opponent in the middle of a fight like that?"

"None," Aria told her.

"Definitely none," Rei confirmed.

Then they shut up, because de Soto had lunged again, bringing her two-handed blade crashing down once more at the Iron Bishop, only for Dent to slip just beyond the range of the attack before launching into a countering barrage, calling feedback up all the while.

That was how the remainder of the class passed, in rotation every 15 minutes or so between Bretz and de Soto, with every match becoming a little more intense as the captain had less and less to point out of the sub-instructors' tricks and techniques with every passing fight. By the time the last of the rounds was wrapping, the final matches had been spent in near-silence, with the other teachers up on the ring with 1-A encouraging them to watch closely for examples of what Dent had been listing out for them all afternoon, as well as answering what few questions were asked. When the period came to an end, it was with more than a few groans of disappointment, which were met with a laugh by the captain.

"Don't worry, you've got plenty more to see over the next two classes!" She was inputting the command to dismiss the projection field even as she recalled Kestrel, and a moment later the class was being lowered gently to the ground again while de Soto called back her own Device behind her. "Remember that regulars will be allowed on Wednesday and Friday, and be prepared to answer questions next week from your sub-instructors on individual expectations for your evolutionary direction and developing combat style."

There was a collective "Yes, ma'am!" from the group, and as one the class got to their feet and started making for the east entrance. Before Rei and the others could take more than a couple steps to follow the flow of traffic, however, a call from Dent brought them all up short.

"Ward. Stay. Laurent, Arada, you as well."

They turned back to look in confusion towards where the woman still stood on Field 3, the instructors all having begun splitting up to attend to whatever post-training duties or break time they were allowed before the next session started. At her words, however, Bretz, Gross, and Imala all glanced around in interest, the others doing the same with a frown.

Dent dismissed the lot of them even as she motioned for Rei, Aria, and Viv to approach. "See to your reprieve, officers. This conversation isn't anything to concern yourselves with."

Most of the sub-instructors did as she ordered at once, with only Bretz lingering a little longer, looking torn between following his superior's command and wanting to know what sort of "conversation" would involve his most-prized student. Eventually, however, he gave in, and left the floor after the other teachers, speeding up to catch Gross and Imala, who seemed eager to confer with him on what might be going on.

It would have made Rei laugh, seeing the three adults put their heads together like children and casting furtive glances back at them until they were gone from the room, except he was too busy wondering himself what Dent wanted with him and the girls.

Once they were alone, the captain took them in, a knowing smile lingering on her prosthetic lips.

"Lennon tells me he may have overdone your training on Friday."

This statement brought a measure of relief to Rei, having expected something of much greater import to guide the conversation. Dent hadn't attended their second session with the Lasher, though, so he supposed it wasn't surprising she was curious about the special training given the lengths she'd gone to set it up for them.

"No, ma'am." he told her, feeling comfortable speaking for the group on this matter. "We'll just need to get accustomed to the intensity is all. We're incredibly grateful for the opportunity to learn from Cadet Lennon, even if the lessons are hard."

On either side of him, Aria and Viv both nodded their agreements.

"Good to hear." Dent sounded genuinely pleased as she reached up to wipe a line of sweat off one cheek with the back of her hand. "I told him much the same thing, but he was still worried. Apparently he expected at least *one* of the four of you to call for a break at some point."

Rei's mouth went slack at that, and it was a second before he looked around at the girls. They, too, appeared to have been taken by surprise, but as he considered it Rei indeed realized something.

None of them had bothered *asking* for a reprieve while they'd fought, had they?

Dent, for her part, laughed out loud. "By the looks on your faces, you're only just realizing it. Amusing. Lennon may be a third year, cadets, but he does not outrank you. He can't order you to do anything, and if you'd wanted a break in training, you could have taken one."

Rei almost let himself feel like a fool, but Aria saved him the chagrin.

"Thank you, ma'am, but I think we'll keep going as is. We only have two hours a week with the Lasher. Every second we can squeeze out of training will matter, at the end of our time together."

Dent cast her with a look that might have just been a little proud. "Fair enough. Still, don't expect another reprieve from me. This week worked out because the idea of exhibition matches to give you all some broader direction was actually one thrown out by Allison Lake, so I didn't look too bad putting it into motion. Next time, you'll be fighting your pairings tired."

Rei, for his part, stood there blinking at the captain for a moment before looking at his companions. Aria was staring at the tall woman as well, but Viv caught his eye, her expression just as surprised.

"Uh… Ma'am?" she managed to ask, turning her attention back on the captain. "Did you adjust the class trainings for… for us?"

"I did."

The answer was so blunt, so straightforward, that it took Rei a second of gathering himself before he could speak.

"Is that allowed?" he finally got out. "Won't you… Isn't that going a little heavy on the favoritism, ma'am?"

Dent graced him with an amused look. "Favoritism? Give me one way this demonstration wasn't equally valuable to everyone in your class, Ward. Or will be to the remainder of the first years."

Rei saw her point immediately, of course. 1-A had been energized as they'd left the subbasement space, much like they'd been energized after watching the first week of the Intra-School matches. And if they got an extra few afternoons to recover, what did it matter? It just so happened that Rei, Aria, Viv, and Catcher were probably the ones in most need of the rest, but that didn't mean there wouldn't be others who couldn't have used it.

But still… First Christopher Lennon, and now this?

The concern on his face must have shown, because the captain shook her head as she appeared to do her best not to roll her eyes.

"Ward, this Institute is not based on 'fair' treatment. You've been told that from the beginning. Instead of worrying about how my choice may or may not make me look in the eyes of the rest of the school staff, consider instead the fact that you might just have *earned* this assistance. Believe it or not the colonel and I—and several others among the higher officers—have high expectations for you. Setting that aside, consider too that Laurent is likely to be the backbone of your class' presence at Sectionals, and Arada and Catchwick both have an excellent shot of qualifying on their own as well." She smirked. "We support the cadets who reach for more than we offer them outright."

Rei felt a little better, at that. He'd been aware of this since the captain's speech at the Commencement Ceremony, of course, but it was still good to have it reiterated, to be made to feel like he—as well as the others—at least in some way *deserved* this extra attention they were receiving.

He had just opened his mouth, intending to thank Dent, when a message pinged his NOED. Beside him Aria and Viv both blinked in unison, telling him they'd gotten the same notification, and seeing who it was from Rei hurried through his gratitude.

"Your assistance is very much appreciated, ma'am. If we might be dismissed, I have a match coming up in an hour or so I need to prepare for."

"Of course," the captain answered, waving them all off. "Good luck, cadet. Fight well."

With mirrored salutes, Rei, Aria, and Viv all turned on their heels and jogged across the now-empty subbasement, making for the east hall. As soon as they made the corner, though, the three of them halted, every eye among them lighting up as they opened Catcher's message.

Reading it, Rei felt his heart sink.

"Dammit," Viv muttered. "Still… At least it sounds like it was a good match…"

Rei nodded with a grimace. Catcher had lost his pairing against Martin, unfortunately, but not without a fight. It had apparently taken nearly 6 minutes for the C1 Duelist to wear him down. His message was chatty as ever, but there also lacked a sincerity to it that that made it feel like Catcher was putting up a brave front. Who could blame him? Aria and Viv's matches the following day were against opponents neither were likely to have too much trouble taking on, and a single victory after that would have them qualifying as individuals for Sectionals. With this loss, Catcher was in the loser's bracket, meaning he'd have to win four more pairings in a row to make the team. Rei knew the feeling well, but he'd never really expected to start with anything more than a first-week loss given Dyrk Reese was at the helm of the tournament.

After hitting half of the 4-win streak, he supposed a lot of the wind would be sucked from Catcher's sails, at least for a few days.

"Whoa… *Whoa*."

Viv's sounds of disbelief had Rei glancing up and around at her through the text of the message, wondering what was going on.

"There's more," she answered his questioning look. "Keep reading."

Curious, now, Rei did so, finding indeed that there was an entire additional paragraph to the message as it scrolled up across his frame while he took it in line by line. Finally reaching the end, he stared at the final statement, then went back and reread the it all again to make sure he'd understood correctly.

"She lost?" Aria sounded utterly taken aback. "Kay lost? And to another Lancer? No way."

According to Catcher, though, it was true. Kay Sandree, considered the top User of her Type among the first years, had lost her match. But that wasn't the surprise, at least not for Rei and Viv. To Aria, the name of the victor probably didn't ring any bells given that the pair of them had only briefly met once, then in occasional passing when she came over to 304 to study or watch an SCT fight together. To Rei and Viv, however, the listed victor of the pairing was several times more shocking than Kay's actual loss.

But there, at the bottom of Catcher's message, was a cropped screenshot of the day's results so far, making the fact absolute. Kay Sandree had indeed lost.

To Chancery Cashe.

CHAPTER 46

ood, Ward! Now keep up that pace! Faster! *Faster*! Excellent! Now... switch!"

Rei disengaged from his brutal assault on Christopher Lennon's bare-handed—and yet impervious—defense, dropping and rolling sideways to let Catcher lunge into place after him, Arthus leading the way. Breathing hard, Rei watched the sword cleave in a flurry of sweeping arcs, driving the Lasher backwards one step at a time despite every blow being turned away by a snapping forearm or open palm like the vysetrium-lined steel was nothing more than a child's toy. Rei waited, trying to recover what energy he could while Lennon shouted out feedback and encouragement, holding for the call to come again. 10 seconds. 15...

"Switch!"

It was Catcher's turn to get out of the way, spinning sideways in a graceful off-step that offered a perfect opening for Rei to leap into. Shido cleaved through the air in a ripping punch, but Lennon stepped left and drove a knee upward at Rei's gut as he started to sail by. The blow came at what must have been less than half-speed for the Lasher, because Rei managed to get his free arm tucked in time to block, giving himself an opportunity to roll sideways, out of the way of the worst of the impact. He made to slash at the Lasher's other leg as he fell, but the third year turned the failed attack into a front kick that caught Rei in the chest before he so much as touched the ground. He went rocketing backwards, launched under the force of the almost-lazy strike by Lennon. He slammed hard into the flat wall that bisected their field, barely catching himself and lurching to his feet before he collapsed to the floor, seeing stars for a moment before Shido started to work his neuroline and clear his vision.

"Switch!" came the call again, and as he blinked away the brief bout of dizziness caused by the impact, Rei saw Catcher leap in once more.

It was their fifth week of training under the Lasher's guiding hand, and despite Lennon's apparent concern that second Friday that he'd been too hard on them, there had appeared no sign of letting up in the sessions since. He worked them bloody—often literally—and when it was only Rei and Catcher training against the third year the intensity of the conditioning seemed to double, and that despite the brief breaks in these alternating bouts. Even Aria and Viv—who now only worked with the Lasher for an hour each week—had learned not to eat before training, lest their dinner be lost to the floor of the training field.

Not like Rei cared. Christopher Lennon's training had been indispensable in the last half-month, for all of them.

Gillian North had proven a tougher opponent for him than Camilla Warren, having done Rei the courtesy of taking him seriously in their match the day after Catcher had lost his fight against Laquita Martin. She'd let him come to her, and theirs had been a fight of cat and mouse on the flat white of a standard Neutral Zone. He'd been faster than the Mauler—several ranks faster, in fact—but North had proven to sport an impressive Defensive spec in addition to the natural Strength and Offense of her Type. He'd had to dance around her, chipping away at the girl's reactive shielding and armored limbs for nearly 5 full minutes, all the while doing his best not to get caught in the direct arc of her axe's swing. He hadn't come out of the fight unscathed—a limp left arm had marked where he'd lost the limb just above the elbow in the last 30 seconds of the match—but he'd managed the win in the end, finally cleaving through the Mauler's shielding to hamstring her behind the right knee, bringing the back of her neck down low enough for an easy blow to the brainstem.

After North, the following week had proven easier, with Rei paired up against a poor D6 Lancer from 1-B named Austin Burrows. *That* fight had taken less than a minute, his opponent lacking not only in the Speed and Cognition he needed to keep Rei at bay with his longer weapon, but also in the Defense and Strength that might have saved him once the distance between them had closed. In the end, Rei had been left standing the victor as Burrows had tumbled off the ledge of the wide Cliffs variation they'd been fighting on, falling screaming after Shido had slashed through both his legs.

The match had been so short, in fact, that Rei had started to wonder if Dyrk Reese was trying to build up some false confidence in him, a suspicion not helped when his fifth pairing against Valentino Lewis—a Brawler from 1-C—had gone much the same way.

His own pairings weren't the only ones that had gone well, though. He and

Catcher were the only two facing off against the Lasher in that second hour of their Friday training because Aria and Viv had insisted it be so. The pair of them had dominated their third matches as expected, with fortune favoring them both a week later for their fourth wins. Viv had had the *distinct* pleasure of putting down Leda Truant with relative ease, while Aria had had herself a decent match against Amelia von Leef, a Saber from 1-D, and another attendee of the summer training group.

With those final victories, Aria and Viv both had earned themselves the nomination among the first eight to qualify for the Sectionals tournament that would be happening after the winter leave.

Along with them, Kastro Vademe, Laquita Martin, Lena Jiang, Zain Kadness, and Hannah Tethers had also claimed their four wins. Chancery Cashe ended up the surprising eighth and final no-loss qualifier after taking down a *second* top ranker name Xander Phillips, the only other summer group Phalanx aside from Aria. Rei had attempted to congratulate their silver-haired suitemate as soon as they'd seen her next, but the Lancer had only given him a quiet thanks before retreating—as was her fashion—to her room, red in the face at the attention.

Catcher, too, had done well for himself since his loss to Martin. He'd been down for the days following the match, but it had been the first Friday after that Aria and Viv had insisted Lennon spend half their session working with Catcher and Rei alone, and the Lasher hadn't tolerated the Saber's subdued enthusiasm for more than about 2 minutes.

"Did you think you were never going to lose?" he had demanded of Catcher after the third time he'd put the blond boy on his ass with even less effort than usual. "Did you think you were going to drift through life on talent and hard work? Get up. You're hardly a failure. You only get to think that of yourself when you *stop trying to win*."

It had, apparently, been what Catcher had needed to hear, because though he'd been quiet for the remainder of that training session, his usual energy was back by the following Tuesday night, returning after a decisive defeat against Sam Dorne. The next week, though, was the *true* victory, when Catcher took less than two 2 minutes to drop Mateus Selleck, who had also lost in the third round. That evening, the four of them had granted themselves a single day of rest, cobbling together a makeshift dinner party in Rei's room from food and drink smuggled out of the mess hall in their bags. They'd had ample cause to celebrate, after all. Not only had Aria and Viv qualified, but Rei and Catcher had both climbed one step closer to making it to the final rounds.

Almost more importantly, however, had been the fact that not a single one of them had been able to stop from relishing in the bitter expression on Selleck's face as he'd walked off the field for the last time, fallen from the year's Intra-Schools brackets for good.

WHAM!

Rei flinched and looked around. Viv had just slammed into the other side of the wall to his left, and he caught her eye only long enough to be shot a gleeful grin before she had to duck and roll under the driving thrust of Aria's spear. For a second or two he watched the girls going at it on their half of the field, Duelist-level Speed doing much to match Phalanx-level reach and Defense. It was nice, seeing the two of them having fun. Rei had always felt bad about hogging Aria as a training partner, and witnessing both of the girls enjoying themselves brought back memories of a time before the four of them had been a group. He recalled Aria's hesitation, her shyness around them even after they'd invited her to train with them. It made him happy, remembering the genuine excitement and—inexplicably—disbelief on her face.

It might have made his chest throb, too, watching Aria smile as she cut and slashed at a retreating Viv, except his own circumstances didn't leave much opportunity for feelings in the moment.

"Switch!"

The command brought him back in a flash, and Rei shoved off the wall to re-engage Lennon as Catcher leapt out of the way again. This time he didn't go in for the heavy lead, instead darting forward with a series of short, tight jabs, channeling a tempered version of the Gatecrasher's style as he tried to challenge the Lasher with Speed rather than pure force. His adjustment looked to be received favorably, because the A-Ranker was nodding even as he swatted the blows away like the annoying buzzing of a fly that wouldn't leave him alone.

"Good, Ward! Yes! Play to your strengths! When an opponent is quicker than you, closing up your attacks can help you keep a tight defense and fast offense."

They continued like that for almost a minute, Rei throwing his swift punches at a rate and speed he would have been amazed at had he been thinking of anything other than going faster, faster. When his shoulders began to burn he threw in a couple snapping kicks at Lennon's legs, which were blocked with the same ease as any other strike.

More nodding greeted this variation, though, which would have had Rei smiling had he had a moment to consider doing so.

"Switch!"

The call came again, then again, then again. For another 30 minutes it repeated over and over, ringing out in short order long after Rei and Catcher both were heaving in lungfuls of air, the reprieves between these intense bursts of assault no longer enough to keep up with exhaustion. At last the Lasher caught Arthus in an overextending slash, twisting to toss Catcher over narrow shoulders in a snapping pull that had the Saber flying across the floor some 10 yards, only barely holding onto his Device. The moment he'd bounced to his feet, though, Lennon held him up with a raised hand, doing the same to Rei as the third year looked between them.

"Hold. Take a breather."

For about 20 seconds they stood like that on either side of the Lasher, struggling to get enough oxygen while watching his lifted arms for the moment they knew was coming.

Then Lennon gestured them both forward with quick jerks inward of both hands.

"Together! Come!"

In a mirrored collapse, Rei and Catcher lanced in without a second's hesitation.

It was evidence not only of these special Friday lessons, but also of the weeks and long nights the two of them had been training in vicinity to one another. Not missing a beat Rei read Catcher's intended angle of attack in the slight crouch of his last few steps, and instantly he dropped to his knees. The steel plating of his greaves screamed across the projected floor as he slid forward the final yards, Shido slashing at Lennon's legs. Catcher, in the same moment, leapt, arching right over Rei's head while he cut at the third year's face with a passing slash.

They didn't so much as nick the Lasher.

One dark-skinned hand swatted Catcher's sword out of the way, while Lennon's right foot came up in a pair of snapping kicks to slam both sets of Shido's claws aside. Undeterred, Rei twisted and extended one leg in a sweep, hoping to catch Lennon behind the ankle. The third year leapt clear, but Catcher, too, had corrected his failed attack with record speed, and Arthus was thrusting at the red griffin stitched into blue fabric even as Lennon found himself in midair. For a heartbeat Rei thought they finally had the boy, but the Lasher simply smacked the sword downward as he threw his legs out into a split. Catcher tried to recover, but Lennon's other hand caught him a chop in the side of the head that had him tumbling sideways. Rei barely managed to miss being slammed into, and chose to rush forward with another volley of tight swings until Catcher could recover and rejoin.

For 5 more minutes or so they fought like that, the Lasher saying nothing now, trusting them to give everything they had to this final exchange. There were no breaks, this time, no rest or reprieve. It was just them, paired off against him like two sorry mortals charged with taking down a god of war. Every breath was agonizing, by the end, every motion coming in a burn of protesting muscle. Rei and Catcher fought on, refusing to slow down or give in even a little, but every movement was a push through pain and exhaustion.

Fortunately for all, the Lasher chose to put them out of their misery before their bodies could fail them completely.

WHAM-WHAM!

The two hits came without mercy, a quick coupling of punches at what looked to be Lennon's full baseline speed that caught Catcher in the stomach and Rei under the chin. The world went black for a moment, and Rei felt himself falling into a darkness with no beginning or end. The next thing he knew, he was looking up from his back at the solar lights suspended from the ceiling above, their brightness making it hard to read the lines of text that must have started spilling down the frame of his NOED while he'd been out.

...

Processing combat information.

...

Calculating.

...

Results:

Strength: Severely Lacking

Endurance: Severely Lacking

Speed: Lacking

Cognition: Lacking

Offense: Severely Lacking

Defense: Lacking

Growth: Not Applicable

...

Checking combat data acquisition.

...

Adequate data acquirement met.

Device initiating adjustments to:

Strength. Endurance. Offense.

...

Adjustment complete.
Strength has been upgraded from Rank D5 to D6.
Endurance has been upgraded from Rank D4 to D5.
Offense has been upgraded from Rank D6 to D7.

Rei let out a groan, shutting his eyes instinctively against the swimming script—which of course did nothing to hide the text. Gathering himself, he dismissed the upgrade notification, suspecting he would have been far more pleased with the night's results if he wasn't feeling nauseous from the blow that had obviously knocked him out for long enough to trigger Shido's post-combat analysis. When he opened his eyes again, a shape had appeared above him, and it took him a second to distinguish the distinct outline of Christopher Lennon's dreaded hair against the light. The boy was saying something, but it was a little while more before Rei could make out the words through the buzzing in his ears that had to have been his neuroline working over-time to rectify what would otherwise definitely have been some form of concussion.

"… getting faster!" Lennon's voice finally came into being from what seemed to be a very distant place.

"S-sorry, sir?" Rei asked blearily. Quickly the rest of the room's noises were coming into focus, and as he made to sit up he noted that Aria and Viv sounded to have stopped fighting too.

"You're getting faster!" the Lasher repeated approvingly, and when Rei blinked up at him against the lighting he thought he caught just the barest hint of a smile. "Both of you! Your teamwork is coming together well too!"

"Glad you think so," came Catcher's muffled groan, and Rei looked around to find the Saber doubled over on the ground nearby, speaking into the floor. "Would be nice… *urk*… if we could get fast enough to avoid the gut punches, though."

Lennon smirked. "Keep at it. We've got another couple weeks of lessons. By the time I'm through with you all you'll be avoiding a lot more than that, I'm sure."

A light hand came down on Rei's shoulder, then, and he looked around to find Aria crouching down beside him, looking worried. She'd recalled Hippolyta, and was tucking a few loose strands of red hair behind her ear as she took him in.

"You okay? I saw that hit…"

Rei gave her what might have been a bit of a lopsided smile. "Yeah." He raised a hand to tap at his temple. "D9 Cognition helps. Second best spec I have."

"C2 CAD-Rank, and he's proud of his D-level specs," Viv sniggered good-naturedly, popping into view from behind Aria. She too, had recalled Gemela, and looked highly pleased with how the evening's training had gone.

That, or she just took more sadistic pleasure in Rei's lagging stats than he'd realized.

"I'd leave him alone, Viv," Aria said with a sparkle in her eye, not looking away from Rei. "If I recall correctly you're a C0 and... Huh... Remind me what your Defense spec is? D5? D6?"

That shut Viv up, and she scowled at Aria's back as Rei managed a laugh, Catcher joining in a little more painfully after he'd finally started pushing himself up off his face.

The Lasher, meanwhile, had been watching them with an expression somewhere between entertained and bemused. "You're an odd bunch, you know that?"

The comment cut into their mirth, and together all four of them looked around at him.

"How so?" Rei asked. Lennon's gaze was moving back and forth between him and Aria with interest, blue eyes lingering on the girl's hand still on Rei's shoulder, taking them in like they were some fascinating curio.

"This is my third year here, and I don't think I know of a group like yours," he said with a shrug. His eyes flashed briefly, and from outside the hall the buzz of a drone started up. "I mean... I've got friends, but nothing like you lot."

"Blame the shrimp," Viv said with a snort, coming over and looking like she might give Rei's foot a kick. Eyeing the black of Shido's carbonized steel plating that still encased it, though, she seemed to think better of it. "He's been dragging me along like this since we were in nappies."

"We were *fourteen*," Rei said, exasperated. "Were you still in diapers at Grand-crest? I'm not judging, but if that's what you're into I want to be able to warn your future girlfriends."

"Or *boyfriends*," Viv corrected him pointedly. "As for what I'm into, that's rude to ask. You'll make Aria jealous."

Rei's face immediately felt about as hot as the sun. He gathered the courage to glance at Aria, whose mouth hung slack with an expression of paralyzed surprise, cheeks blooming an incandescent red.

Then her hand snatched away from him as she snapped to her feet before turning and, with a two quick steps, taking a grinning Viv by the arm to start dragging her towards the exit.

"Come here, you," Rei could hear Aria hissing sidelong. "We're gonna have a chat, just the two of us."

Viv didn't lose her smile, and instead looked back at him as she was hauled along, pointing at Aria's gripping hand about her bicep and mouthing "*This* is what I'm into."

Despite his embarrassment, Rei almost laughed out loud at the sight.

"Like I said, an interesting bunch…" the Lasher muttered, watching the two girls take their leave of the field with a raised eyebrow. After they were gone, though, he looked to Catcher. "Catchwick, go after them. Ward and I are going to have a chat on his way back to the first year dorms."

Rei looked around at these words, surprised. This being the first time *he'd* heard of this plan, it wasn't strange that Catcher's reply was a little hesitant.

"Oh… Uh… Yes, sir."

He glanced at Rei, who shrugged to indicate he had no clue what was going on, then pushed himself to his feet, recalling Arthus as he did. Hurrying after Aria and Viv, it wasn't long before he left Rei alone with Christopher Lennon.

"I have to admit to a bit of jealousy, Ward."

Rei frowned, unsure of what to make of this cryptic statement. Starting to stand himself, he massaged the bottom of his sore chin with the back of one gauntleted hand before answering. "Of what, sir? Of my friends?"

The Lasher chuckled, shaking his head so that his grey dreads shifted about his ears. "No, no. Well… Maybe a little, but that's not what I'm talking about." His cool gaze settled on Rei, and for the first time in a while they pierced him with that same predatory intensity that had graced their initial session, when Lennon had been getting the measure of them. "Correct me if I'm wrong, but you were a D9 when we first started these sessions, weren't you?"

Rei's mouth went dry, and he had to stop himself from taking a step back as he paused in his rubbing the tender spot under his jaw. He wasn't really surprised the topic was finally being broached—in all honesty he'd been wondering for a month when the Lasher would bring it up—but he wasn't any more ready to address it now than he had been at any time before. It was dangerous territory to wade into, especially when it had been made clear so many times—by Aria, by Viv, by Valera Dent, and Major Connelly well before any of them—that the fewer people who knew his secret, the better.

As expected, Shido's growth had slowed down dramatically once Rei had reached the C-Ranks. His individual specs had continued to rise steadily through the Ds—their average even catching up a little to his CAD-Rank—but his Speed had only moved from C0 to C1 after a couple of weeks of work, indicating he could expect the climb to get steeper across the board. Still, even with this increase in time between upgrades, Rei had gained more than two full Ranks in 4 weeks, an improvement rate that was still *several* times faster than the other Cs among the first years. By the end of November, Rei suspected he would be tied with Aria for the highest level in the class, or have caught up to the likes of Grant and Kastro Vademe at the very least…

With a pace like that, it was small wonder the likes of Christopher Lennon—star of the Galens cadets—had seized the strangeness of Rei's situation.

"To clarify, Ward, I'm not about to ask you *why* your CAD is upgrading at the rate it is."

Lennon's words caught Rei flatfooted, desperately trying as he had been to find a good way to escape the conversation. His astonishment must have shone clear, because the third year cocked his head as he brought his hands to rest on both hips.

"That's not to say I'm not curious, but I'm too keen on keeping my place in this school to hound you about it. You've been a bit of a conversation topic among the upper class for a while, ripping through the D-Ranks like you did after arriving as an *E*, but Captain Dent made it pretty clear to me I'd be out on my ass if I pressed the issue with you, so do me a favor and let her know I *didn't* when next you speak, would you?"

Rei nodded numbly. Dent again… One day, he would have to find out what it was she hoped to gain from all this assistance.

"Anyways, it's like I said: I'm a little jealous of you. CADs—especially one with a decent Growth spec like my Ouroboros—give back purely based on what you put into them in blood, sweat, and tears. You four are a rare group—outside of your peculiarity, I mean. For so many first years to be so driven… It's like seeing a front line combat team following on the heels of its squad-leader."

"Uh…" Rei wasn't sure what to say. "Is that… Is that a compliment, sir?"

"Definitely."

"Oh… Well… Thank you?"

Lennon nodded before pressing forward.

"You do know your growth rate is nothing short of alarming, don't you?"

Rei nodded again. "All too well, sir."

"I figured. I guess it's part of the reason Dent set these evenings up for you all. You're gonna have a lot of eyes on you soon, Ward. And not many of them likely to be friendly."

Rei almost laughed. If the Lasher knew just how late to the party he was, on that warning.

The third year's next question, though, brought him up short.

"Do you have any sense of the direction of the CAD's evolution?"

Rei, not sure he understood, paused. A sense of Shido's direction?

"Looks like you've got no idea what I'm talking about." The Lasher didn't sound the least bit surprised, his eyes lifting over Rei's head as the whirling of the drone he had triggered earlier sounded to be finally approaching. "Let's talk on the way back to your dorm. Otherwise you're gonna miss curfew. Sorry if it's awkward, but—" he motioned for Rei to turn around "—I didn't want us to be overheard, regarding this."

Looking over his shoulder, Rei was just in time to see the drone arrive, carrying with it two sets of military regulars.

C-Rank is around the time a lot of A-Types start to deviate. Were you aware of that?"

Fall was reaching a true chill with the arrival of November, and Rei's breath misted in thick fountains of fog in the dim light of Castalon's skyscrapers rising up all around them. After they'd changed, Lennon had insisted on waiting a few minutes longer, obviously intent on making sure Aria, Viv, or Catcher didn't linger in an attempt to walk with them.

Now, Rei understood why.

"*What?*" He looked around at the Lasher sharply, then caught himself. "I mean… No, sir."

"Calling me 'sir' in training is one thing, Ward. Out here, you and I are the same rank."

"Oh. Yes, s—I mean, yes. Okay."

Lennon nodded. "So you weren't aware… Not shocking. I didn't figure it out myself until most of the way through my first year, when Ouroboros started to change after I hit C3. They don't teach you much about Atypicals in class here, do they?" He looked a little annoyed, bringing one gloved hand up to push the brim of his cap back a little off his soft face.

"We're pretty rare," Rei offered, looking forward along the path again. "A-Types in general. Even more so those of us who are combat-functional."

"I suppose," the third year grunted. "There was another guy at my exam who got assigned an A-Type. Apparently it eventually developed into a sword that was half-again as tall as he was, but about two fingers thick. Totally useless. You gotta wonder about that…"

Variables, Rei thought, though he was careful not to say it out loud. If the MIND was willing to give him Shido, why wouldn't it distribute other extremes to see what happened?

"Regardless, the failures aren't what I'm talking about. A-Types like us—the successful assignments—tend to start to deviate in the Cs. When was the last time you evolved, Ward? After your fight with that Saber in Intra-Schools, first week?"

Rei was about to be impressed with the boy's information, right up until the moment he recalled that Lennon had no doubt been present—just like the rest of the school—at the match in question, where Lena Jiang had tricked him into eating lava.

He couldn't help but feel a bit embarrassed at the thought.

"Yes, sir," he answered at last, correcting himself when Lennon gave him a sidelong look. "I mean… Yeah. After the fight with Jiang."

"And that was when your CAD upgraded to D9, wasn't it?"

Rei thought about it a moment, then nodded.

"Did you notice anything odd, with that change?"

Rei frowned. "Like what?"

The Lasher shrugged as the pair of them took a bend in the path. "Anything means anything, Ward. You're lucky you've got Dent to guide you. I'd even say you're lucky to have *me*, if I didn't think it made me sound like a pompous ass. There weren't any other high-ranking A-Types on the Institute staff roster when I arrived, so I had to do all the research myself. You can probably guess what group I train with, in my class-block."

"Duelist," Rei answered at once.

"Yup," came the confirmation. "Before my Device started changing, I wasn't anything special. Just your standard Duelist, though my weapons were always a bit broader than what you'd expect. Made wielding them a hassle when you're trying to be the fastest on the field." Lennon grimaced and tilted his head to look up at the crossing sky-lanes high above them, like he was recalling an unpleasant memory. "My D-Rank evolution was only my second, but it was the first hint. A dozen angular vysetrium markings on the sword blades, which would eventually break up into the chains I have now. After they showed up—*definitely* not a typical development for a Duelist—I started digging into Atypicals, and learned I could expect the real changes to start soon after." He looked around at Rei. "So what about you? You evolved at D9, and if the rumors are true you're not far from another, right?"

Rei hesitated this time before nodding, wondering if they weren't getting a little too close to Shido's secret for his complete comfort.

Fortunately, Lennon brought them back on track at once, repeating his earlier question.

"So did you notice anything odd?"

Rei considered it more carefully this time, thinking back on the changes his Device had gone through following his loss that first week, more than a month ago, now. It had been the greatest adaptation Shido had yet demonstrated, the mirroring of its upper limb design combining with an overall polishing of the armor that had lent him a boost in Speed on top of improving both his Offensive and Defensive capabilities. It had been a big change, to be sure, but Rei had followed the careers of dozens of Users over the years, witnessing hundreds of evolutions of every Type of CAD as a result.

It had been a big change, but he wasn't comfortable calling it an abnormal one.

After a while, he shook his head. "No. Nothing like that. It was a pretty involved evolution—I don't know if you remember what my Device looked like during the fight against Jiang—but I can't say its outside any standard parameters *I'm* aware of…"

"Nothing? No markings? No hints at a direction?"

Again, Rei had to shake his head. "Sorry, but no. It was a jump, but Shido—my CAD—is still following the Brawler-path pretty tightly as far as I can tell…"

He had expected the Lasher to frown, or maybe even look disappointed.

What he *hadn't* expected was for the boy to grant him what might have been the first *true* smile he had seen part the third year's usually stoic face.

"I get the feeling you're in for a ride, Ward."

Rei didn't follow. "How so?"

"You'll figure that out on your own, if I'm right. If I'm not, I don't want to misguide your training direction." Still, the Lasher was yet smiling, which made Rei think he was rather confident in what assessment he was cryptically hinting at. "Let's just say I know of a few examples of the variation of A-Type you sound like you might be, and they all had a rare advantage even without your particularly… uh… interesting circumstances."

"*What* advantage?" Rei pressed, his curiosity piqued. In all honesty it had been some time since he'd really dwelled on the fact that Shido *wasn't*, actually, a Brawler-Type CAD. He'd become so accustomed to its design, so used to training under Michael Bretz with the rest of his sub-group, that it more often slipped his mind than not. He couldn't complain about the path he was walking, now that he'd finally largely caught up to the rest of the first years.

But here the Lasher was implying there was more to—

And then it clicked. The one advantage being an A-Type gave him a rare upper hand in attaining.

"Arsenal Shift?!" he hissed, nearly walking right off the path as it bent again. A patrol melted out of the dark, at that moment, and he and Lennon both had to pause and salute the two lesser officers as they passed, receiving a mirrored acknowledgement.

Only after the pair had vanished around the curve at their backs did the third year turn to look at Rei with an expression somewhere between impressed and surprised.

"Gotta say, you're a pretty well-informed guy, Ward…"

Rei could only stare, registering nothing more than the fact that Lennon's lack of disagreement likely meant this was *exactly* the direction his suspicions were taking him.

But… No. No way. Arsenal Shift? As a C-Ranked User? That had to be unheard of…

"That can't be right," Rei muttered. "Arsenal Shift is a high-level Ability. A- and S-Rank almost exclusively."

"Ordinarily, sure." Lennon seemed unperturbed by Rei's denial, motioning that they should get moving again. "But given you're the only User I've ever heard of to climb two-and-half tiers in less than six months, Ward, I'm not willing to classify you as any sort of 'ordinary'."

Rei didn't miss the math.

"You checked my baseline too."

"Too?" Lennon glanced at him with interest.

"Aria did the same thing, apparently. I think she was the first to catch on."

"Laurent? I guess that makes sense. She noticed after your match at the first year Commencement Ceremony, I'm assuming?"

Rei made a face. "You heard about that?"

"Oh definitely. We might be in a different world of power than you all are right now, Ward, but hearing that an *E*-Ranked User had been accepted to Galens, only to challenge the reigning queen of the class? You bet the third years heard. The seconds, too, undoubtedly."

Rei sighed, but shoved back another pang of embarrassment at the thought. He'd gone into that fight knowing he was going to lose. There was no sense in dwelling on it nearly 4 months later.

Not when Lennon was implying he might be on track to develop one of the most potent Abilities in the ISCM registry...

Arsenal Shift. The physical manipulation of the weapon-manifestation of one's CAD into a secondary form, maybe even a tertiary. It was true it was what high-ranking A-Types were best known for, but the reality was that *structural* Atypicals—like Lennon and Valera Dent—were significantly more common than Shift wielders. Rei recalled, suddenly, the day they'd met Catcher for the first time, how he and the Saber—newly acquainted—had bonded over excitedly discussing the Ability, and Rei's hope he'd one day count himself among its owners. It wasn't that he'd abandoned that desire. Not in the least.

But how could hoping to develop it so early be anything but a pipe dream?

"I see why you didn't want to tell me," he allowed as Kanes came into view, most of its smart-glass windows lit up while his classmates studied into the late hours of the evening. "That's a hell of a carrot to snatch away if it doesn't work out."

Lasher shrugged again. "According to what I've been able to find out, you've evolved four times since your assignment. Most User don't evolve that many times in *twelve* months, much less six. Judging by the climb of your CAD-Rank, your specs are likely rocketing along just as well. So why should your Ability development be any less accelerated?"

Rei had to admit, he'd never considered that particular point. Maybe it was the balls he was already juggling when it came to Shido, or maybe he'd always just been more focused on the CAD's stats than anything else. Regardless of the reason, Lennon's words had him halting mid-step, staring after the third year, who continued walking a second or two more before realizing Rei had stopped.

"You're serious?" Rei had to ask, the question fogging before him in the cold. "You think that's the direction Shido is headed?"

"I wouldn't bet my credits on it or anything, but it doesn't seem the likeliest course to you?" The Lasher half-turned to look Rei in the eye, sliding his gloved hands into the pockets of his black slacks. "You and your Device are moving on a trajectory unlike anything I've ever seen, Ward. Unlike anything I've ever *heard* of, actually, and I'm lucky enough to be privy to most of the information on high-level Users around our age. They're my rivals." He nodded down at Shido's bands, glimmering blue diamonds across black-and-white steel around Rei's wrists, asking the question again. "Why would your Ability development be any less accelerated?"

Rei had no good answer for him, he discovered.

"And… And you think it would happen soon?"

"Manifesting Shift? No idea. But I ask again… Your last evolution was at D9, right?"

Rei nodded.

"You're C2, now. Three ranks higher. How long between evolutions do you typically go?"

Rei scowled. "You just admitted to asking around about me. You tell me."

Lennon gave him a lopsided smile. "Fair enough." He drew out one hand again to hold up all four fingers. "Four evolutions. Twenty-one ranks—F8 to D9. You average just over five ranks between evolutions." He pulled down a finger to leave a trio up. "You're at three, now. Law of probability states you're due for another sooner than later, doesn't it?"

"Maybe, but that also means I've had four evolutions with no manifestation of Abilities. Why would Arsenal Shift manifest *now*?"

"Don't know if it will. But the major sign is there: you're an Atypical with no indication of structural variability, having reached the C-ranks. Dent had her first externals at this point in her career, did you know?"

"I did… And?"

"And my chains first manifested at C4. Ordinarily I'd actually assume you were more likely to develop something else. Another Ability, more common. But—I say it again—you're anything by 'ordinary', aren't you, Ward?"

Again Rei didn't respond, meeting the Lasher's gaze evenly. It was a strange feeling, standing there before a User who could be ranked among the most powerful within the walls of the Institute. The boy's eyes betrayed nothing, now, gave no hint of interest or amusement or even that dangerous acuity they sometimes held. It was eerie, like Lennon was deliberately keeping his thoughts to himself, seeing how Rei would answer.

In the end, of course, there was no sense in denying that which was becoming a clear and obvious truth.

"No," Rei affirmed, putting his own hands in his pockets in an attempt to seem nonchalant. "I'm not ordinary."

There was a pause in which the third year took him in, then, that same, still blankness behind his gaze.

And then the smile returned, lifting with it the sense of foreboding Rei hadn't realized was starting to claw at his gut.

"Nice to hear it out loud," Lennon said, turning and starting to walk ahead. "It's important to know your advantages as a User, Ward. On *and* off the field. You're going to have to get used to it, if you want to be able to live any kind of normal life in the future."

Rei, shaking the last of that lingering chill, hurried to catch up, his boots *thudding* heavily over the frozen stone of the path.

"I'm not fighting till Tuesday," he breathed after he was side by side with Lennon again. "Three days. If I push it…"

"Don't," Lennon warned, a little sharply even. "There's a reason Dent gave you all those training days off, in your third week. The four of you were already exerting yourselves to the point of exhaustion, and then she threw *me* into the mix. If you force things, you'll just end up hamstringing yourself."

Rei bit back his answer to that, his retort that he'd dealt with a lot worse than fatigue and a few strained muscles in his life. He knew the Lasher was right, but it was a hard thing to hear immediately after being given the hope of harnessing Arsenal Shift in his next rank or two…

The comment, though, brought to mind another question he realized he'd never had an opportunity to ask.

"How *did* she get you 'in the mix'? Not gonna lie, it's been driving the four of us crazy for a month now. What the hell do you have to gain from working with us?"

"The pleasure of your company," Lennon answered dryly.

Rei stared at him blankly as they walked until the third year sighed.

"Dent makes it worth my time, Ward. Sparring with you all might not have a lick of value towards improving my own specs, but I'm compensated. No—" he cut the start of Rei's question off with a sharp shake of his head as they made the dim glow of Kane's myriad of lit windows "—I'm not going to tell you how. Another condition of our agreement. Besides, I'm of the opinion you have bigger things to worry about right now then whether or not I'm wasting my Friday nights on a bunch of first years."

"You just said I shouldn't push myself more than—"

"And I meant it, but Arsenal Shift—or whatever Ability I'm expecting you might develop in the next few weeks—isn't what I'm talking about. You can't depend on something like that happening." Reaching the dorm, Lennon paused just before the double doors to the building would open for them, bringing Rei up short as the boy turned to look at him directly. "Who are you matched up with, this coming week?"

"Ashley Renton," Rei was able to answer at once. They'd gotten their pairing Wednesday afternoon, like they always did, and he was well into his due diligence or researching the girl's skill and style. "She's a Duelist from 1-C. Lost to Kay Sandree in her second week."

The Lasher gave him a flat look. "Am I supposed to know who 'Kay Sandree' is?"

"Ha… I guess not, huh?"

Lennon snorted. The gold detailing of his black uniform gleamed in the glow of the windows above them. Maybe due to the amount of time he'd spent trying and failing to land so much as a blow on the boy, Rei realized then that he could no longer see the slighter, softer figure the third year had cut when they'd first met, over a month past. He still *looked* the same, with his cheeks a little rounder and his shoulders a good bit narrower than most Users, but the deception was gone, now. Rei found himself unable to see anything other than "the Lasher" standing before him, eyes bright in the light, exuding an air of icy, steady confidence.

"Is she strong?" Lennon asked.

It took Rei a second to realize who he was referring to. "Renton?"

A nod.

"Strong enough. She's fast, and she plays dirty. As far as I know she's the only combatant in the tournament to have been handed a penalty for excessive flight."

Lennon's lip curled in disappointment. "If that's the kind of fighter she is, then I'm not worried about your match with her. What about the week after?"

Rei had to stop himself from standing a little straighter, feeling a swell of pride at the Lasher's subtle compliment.

Even if his question made no sense.

"The week after? We won't get our pairings for that until—"

Lennon waved his confusion away impatiently. "I'm aware how the Intra-School works, Ward. This is my *third*, I'll remind you. What I meant was are you ready? Are you prepared?"

Still Rei didn't follow. "As best as I can be, if that's what you're—"

"You're probably going to be facing one of top students in your class," Lennon interrupted. "You're aware of that, aren't you?"

Rei stuttered to a stop, feeling an excited tingling in his hands as he did. Yes. He *had* realized that. He'd even been looking forward to it ever since his loss to Jiang in the first week. Of the original top sixteen students who'd attended the summer training course, only six—including Aria and Jiang herself—had qualified for Sectionals undefeated. Two others—the Mauler Aadhik Khatri and Xander Phillips from 1-B—had fallen off in the last 2 weeks, suffering defeats in their four and fifth matches respectively to get themselves dropped from the losers bracket. That still left eight in the running, including the likes of Benaly and Kay.

Benaly, Kay... and Logan Grant.

"I'm aware," Rei eventually answered tightly, wondering if a User of Lennon's ability could detect the quickening of his heartbeat in his chest.

"And what are you doing to get ready?"

"Taking things one step at a time? I'm not sure what answer you're looking for, here. I can't be stressing about the fight I *might* qualify for before I worry about getting through Renton and—"

But Lennon cut him off again.

"Wrong, Ward. You're wrong. Setting aside the fact that it sounds like someone of Renton's mettle should be target practice for a fighter with your ability, let's pretend it's going to be a tough fight. It doesn't matter. You don't train to strengthen yourself for the *next* fight. You train to strengthen yourself for *every* fight you're ever going to have in your life, whether that's on an SCT field or taking on the archons on the front lines. Prep work isn't any different. Sure, educate yourself on Renton. Get to the point where you know her like the back of your hand. That's all well and good. But your next match might not be against someone you can study up on in a week. What if it was Laurent you were fighting next, huh? Hell—" he took a quick step forward, bringing his face within inches of Rei's "—what if it was *me?*"

Despite his shorter stature compared to so many of his sizable peers, Christopher Lennon was still some 2 inches taller than Rei's still-correcting height. Couple that with the fact that the danger had returned to his now-frozen gaze, and all of a sudden it was like that god of war had returned in a flash, only dressed in a fancier uniform.

Rei, once again, had to fight not to take a step back from the third year.

"Yeah..." Lennon said slowly. "That fear. That hesitation. Right there... *That's* what you should be preparing for, Ward. Not some hack who's too afraid to meet her enemy head-on in a real fight. Study Renton. That's fine. But do yourself a favor and start looking into every possible opponent you might be faced with two weeks from now. When you're done with them, you start looking into the top students from other schools you might go head to head with at Sectionals. I don't know if you've realized this, Ward, but my time isn't something to be wasted, much less that of Valera Dent. You think she set these nights up for you all because she wanted you to give it your best? Well she didn't." The ice in his still, iron gaze flashed. "She set these nights up because she expects you to qualify, Ward. Every single one of you. And she expects you to be doing everything in your power to make sure that happens."

Rei hadn't noticed he'd gone rigid as the Lasher spoke, every muscle in his body tensing up like prey before a predator it knew it couldn't outrun. As the words rang clear through the evening quite, however, he felt himself start to breathe again.

Start to breathe, and start to think.

"... I'll get on researching the rest of the summer group that's left in the tournament," he promised quietly, not looking away from Lennon. "Benaly. Kay. All of them. I'll start tonight."

"Not just them, Ward. *Everyone. Everyone* you might get matched up against. I don't care if you already have your final pairing by this time next week. On Friday, when I give you a name, I want you to be able to tell me their greatest strengths, their biggest weaknesses, and three different ways you would take them down. *That's* how you become king in this world, Ward. *That's* how you rise to the top." Slowly, a third and final smile crept onto the boy's dark features. "That's what you want, isn't it? No one in the world works themselves like you do unless their goal is the very top."

"Yes, sir," Rei said deliberately, allowing himself to stand straighter now.

After a pause, Lennon nodded slowly, not bothering to comment on the formal address this time.

"Good. Then you've got your homework, and don't think for a second I won't test you on it, no matter who you're matched with."

With that, the Lasher turned and started walking away, leaving Rei to stand half-at-attention in front of the first year dorms.

Before the boy had slipped beyond the glow of the windows, though, Rei found himself calling after him.

"Lennon!"

The third year stopped and looked over his shoulder.

"Arsenal Shift..." Rei started tentatively. "Do you really think I might...?"

He couldn't get the words out, though, so unbelievable were they to say out loud.

In answer, Lennon shrugged. "We'll know soon enough, won't we?" Then he turned away, lifted a hand in farewell, and started walking away again. "Get inside, Ward. You've got studying to do."

CHAPTER 47

"They always call promotions part of 'the climb', but that metaphor never made sense to me. I mean… If the brass are the ones who bear the weight—the weight of their responsibilities, of their choices, of their failures—then isn't it more like digging down into the ground and shouldering all that unfortunate heaviness you've deliberately placed upon yourself…?"

Chief Warrant Officer Valera Dent

after a few too many drinks

c. 2460

M a'am, you can't expect me to—! These are *cadets*, ma'am! Not playthings of the military for us to shift around like pieces on a—! No, ma'am, I'm *not* refusing the directive, I'm just trying to make you understand that—!"

It was no use, however. No matter what he did or said, Rama Guest couldn't get more than a handful of words in edgewise before the woman on the other side of the call cut across him, making it infinitely clear his opinion was going to have little bearing on the outcome of the conversation no matter how heated he got about it. After another minute of back and forth, what patience had been held out in toleration of his defiance ran out, and the communication was ended abruptly following a very direct and explicit final instruction. As the line went dead, Rama found himself standing in his typical place in front of the large window behind his desk, looking at the sky. Whereas the pattern of traffic above usually tended to bring him a measure of solace—a sort of zen in the awareness of the world beyond the limiting walls of the Institute—this night the flashing lights bore with them nothing more than a building fury.

CRACK!

Rama jumped as the pad he'd been holding during the call shattered, crushed as he failed to check his strength in his anger. Broken glass spilled from his fingers, and he stepped quickly away from the mess, imbibing in a rare expletive as he did.

"Son of a *bitch*!"

Fortunately for his reputation, the only other soul in the room wasn't about to run off whispering about the slip up.

"Technically she's the *actual* bitch, colonel, rather than any related male offspring."

He half-turned to glare at his chief assistant, who was standing at the ready with a stylus over her own pad. Maddison's blonde hair was tied back into a ponytail behind her head, today, and she sported a carefully crafted expression of disinterest as she watched him, waiting for his word.

"I'm cursing the command, not General Abel. That would be insubordination."

"And what command was that?" Maddison asked innocently, tactfully sticking a toe into the game.

"The most egomaniacal backpedaling I've ever witnessed from the construct that is our proud military," he growled in answer, bending down to start picking up what pieces of the glass he could. "Get me Dyrk Reese. He'll love this."

Maddison hesitated, the mask falling into a look of sudden concern, giving up on the facade. "The major? Rama, what's going on?"

"Chief Assistant Kent, I am in *no mood* to be anything other than your direct superior, at the moment!" Rama thundered from where he was crouched behind the desk, looking around to level her with a warning glare. "Get me Dyrk Reese. *Now!*"

The woman—unaccustomed to being addressing in such a manner—flinched, expression changing once again into one of sudden alarm. To her credit, she only nodded briefly before hurrying for the door of the room.

By the time she reached it, Rama was already regretting his outburst.

"Maddison. Wait."

She paused, just about to reach for the handle. Standing up with his fistful of broken glass, Rama faced her with a frown.

"I'm sorry. I shouldn't have lost my temper. If you can get me the major, you have leave to sit in on the conversation. You should know anyway, on the chance I get calls when some parent or preparatory school starts worrying whether our tournament systems aren't up to snuff."

Though this surely could have done nothing for her confusion, the unease in Maddison's pretty features lessened. Her nod this time was more meaningful, conveying just as much that he was forgiven as it did her understanding of the situation.

Then she was gone, the door swinging open behind her in her hurry.

Dropping the shards onto the clean surface of his desk, Rama pulled his chair out to collapse into it, groaning in frustration as he did. Resting his elbows on the wood before him, he was glad for the momentary solitude as he tugged his cap off to toss it unceremoniously onto one of the couches that took up the other side of the room. Feeling a headache coming on, he started to rub at his temples, closing his eyes against the building throb of anger and disbelief behind them.

"Aria is going to have my head…" he muttered to no one but the silence.

CHAPTER 48

"It is in the nature of man to betray. Our very system of governance is based on the concept. Seeing to the many too often requires turning one's back on the few. Addressing the greater good so frequently involves the casting aside of lesser needs, and those in said need. There is no real choice in it.

Betrayal, in the end, is more often than not a body's greatest tool of survival..."

Dr. Everett Weaver, Ph.D.
23rd century philosopher, Mars

Aria—to her later chagrin—missed the one warning that might have prepared her for the disaster that would become the Tuesday of the sixth week of the Intra-School Tournament. More accurately, rather, while she did *see* the message which might have braced her for the day, she had no way of deciphering it in the moment.

Aria woke up, as she always did, at 0600, a good half hour earlier than any of her roommates, who she'd never managed to pull out of their quiet shells of jealousy and intimidation. Groggy from the alarm and intent on getting the morning going, she started the coffee, brushed her teeth, and was washing her hair in the shower when she finally noticed the blinking notification in the corner of her frame. A little heat warmed Aria's cheeks, seeing it. The only person who typically sent her any correspondences overnight was Rei, and usually even then normally to gush about some fascinating topic he'd stumbled across while studying for class, or else sharing a clip of an SCT fight—typically involving a Phalanx—that she might find interesting. Still, it was getting to the point where Aria could no longer deny that she didn't look at least a *little* bit forward to these more and more frequent morning hellos, so she allowed herself a measure of disappointment when she saw that it wasn't from Rei, but rather from Maddie.

Still, the message had been sent close to midnight the previous evening, which had Aria concerned enough to open it even as she started rinsing the conditioner from her hair.

He didn't have a choice.

Frowning, she reread the sentence, then again before being sure she was completely at a loss as to what the woman might have meant. Was it a mix-up? Maybe a message meant for someone else? If it *was* intended for her, Aria couldn't make heads or tails of it, and finishing with her hair she started to craft a reply expressing just that.

Before she could finish her request for clarification, though, another message pinged her NOED, and this time it *was* from Rei.

Headed to East Center before breakfast. Catcher and I want to warm up a bit for our matches this afternoon. Viv's coming, too. You in?

Feeling a little jump in her chest at the invite—a feeling Aria was amazed hadn't faded even after months of spending all her free time with the trio—she typed out a quick response with her left hand as she shut the shower off with a swipe at the wall commands to her right.

Meet you downstairs.

She got dressed in record time, almost forgetting all about the coffee waiting for her in the kitchen as she rushed out the door still pulling her jacket on. Her suite was on the second floor of the dorm, so she made for the stairs rather than the elevator, not bothering with the actual steps in favor of vaulting over the railing straight down the twin flights to drop easily to the ground-level landing.

By the time she joined up with the others—Rei and Viv bantering on one of the lobby couches while Catcher stifled a yawn in a seat beside them—the cryptic message which had brought Aria pause in the shower was utterly forgotten.

They didn't stay long in East Center, not wanting to risk missing breakfast before an early 0730 talk by a visiting lecturer in the Combat Theory building. Rei and Catcher didn't even bother changing into their combat suits, content with going through the motions half-speed in their shirts and slacks to limber up for the day. They were both all smiles while they sparred, leaving the girls to hang out chatting by the door, but instead of taking Viv up on an offer to call their own Devices, Aria asked rather if they could just observe the boys, claiming they might have some last-minute feedback to give since Rei was matched with Ashley Renton—a Duelist—and Catcher had been paired with Adam Jax—a Lancer from their own class. The truth of the matter, though, was that she simply wanted to watch the two have their fun, wanted to take in the laughs and grins and shouts of encouragement, right along with the taunts and jibes.

It felt good, sometimes, to remind herself that she'd found something so far removed from the rigid world her mother would have preferred she confine herself to...

Breakfast was a simple affair of eggs and toast in their favorite section of the mess hall, along the south wall among the pines of the arboretum. Most of the conversation revolved around Rei and Catcher's matches that afternoon, though Aria did have to duck a question or two from Viv regarding who she was planning to pick for her Sectionals team, avoiding giving any answers only by insisting she hadn't been elected as a squad-leader yet, so it wasn't worth thinking on anytime soon. From there, they split with Catcher, wishing him good luck since he was scheduled for one of the earliest fights of the afternoon, and likely wouldn't be able to meet them for lunch if he was going to make it to the Arena on time.

Together, Aria, Rei, and Viv trekked their way across the shaded grounds of the brightening dawn to the Combat Theory Department, where the first half of the morning was spent with them privy to an *astoundingly* listless lecture on water-based combat zones delivered by a visiting ISCM Colonel who looked and sounded like he might have done better to have retired some 2 or 3 decades prior. Aria did her best to pay attention for the first half hour or so, even volunteering the only question in the class when the brief opportunity came to interrupt the man's dreary monologue, but her desk-mates proved bad influences on her in the end. Viv—two seats to her left—had given up 5 minutes in and was now absently doodling what looked like battling stick figures on her pad, while Rei had been studying up on Kastro Vademe from the moment they'd sat down a little higher in the auditorium than usual so as not to get caught. He'd already explained to her about Christopher Lennon's directive from the Friday before, so she let him be, only allowing herself a little envy that he was probably still going to get better exam grades despite having zoned out of *literally* every lecture since Saturday morning.

After Combat Theory, it was time for Tactical Studies, which mercifully passed a good deal faster when Sarah Takeshi had several of them selecting a recorded SCT fight they'd used before for personal review, involving the whole class in an open discussion on the involved Users' Devices, Abilities, and skills. Even Rei put his pad down now and again to watch with interest as some A- or S-Ranked fight got picked apart, and called out more than one answer when the captain asked follow-up questions after each examination. By the time the period ended, the three of them had ample topics to discuss on their way back to the mess hall, with Viv taking the lead almost the moment they were out the door of the room.

"*Gah!*" she groaned as soon as they were beyond Takeshi's earshot. "I *get* that it's just a matter of time, but can't I just fast forward to when Gemela has evolved into a full suit? Did you *see* how some of those guys moved?!"

"I'm definitely a little jealous," Aria had to admit over her shoulder, walking just ahead through the milling of the packed halls while she led them towards the stairs. "Hippolyta's got her tricks, but that speed you Duelists end up with… It's incredible."

"You *could* lean more into agility training," Rei offered from the rear. "Quicksliver was a Phalanx with a high Speed spec, wasn't he?"

"Yeah, but he was also a sword-wielding variant." It was Viv who answered for Aria as they reached the steps and started heading down. "Spear-users would have a harder time taking advantage of moving that fast, if they want to maintain their reach."

Rei's laugh echoed against the walls of the stairwell.

"What?!" Viv demanded as they took the turn in the steps. "What's so funny?!"

"He's laughing because you've turned into the right-little SCT enthusiast, Viv," Aria explained, glad she didn't have to hide her own smile, facing forward with a hand on the railing as she was. "You're starting to pull Rei and Catcher-level factoids out of nowhere."

"Oh…" Viv said, catching on. Then Aria could tell she'd turned on her best friend as she continued. "You shut up! There's no winning! Either you're making fun of me for not caring enough about the tournaments, or you're teasing me for knowing too much about them!"

"Nah," Rei assured her as they made the ground floor and started for the Department doors. "Well… Okay, yeah. But it won't last forever. Only long enough to make up for all the times you've made fun of me for fanboying."

"And how much longer is *that* gonna be?"

"By my count? You're about six weeks into a four-year sentence."

It was Aria's turn to laugh at that, Viv cursing at Rei as the entrance to the building hissed open ahead, allowing them to step out into a pleasant fall day. The dim morning had turned into a bright afternoon, with even a nice breeze complimenting the warmth of the sun set almost directly overhead, its light gleaming in a fractured halo against the ring of the city buildings all around them in the distance. Astra's vegetation—designed like all terraforming organisms to be a little heartier than their genetic parents on Earth—had only just started to change color despite the lateness of the season, and so it was between hedges and under hanging trees detailed in red and orange that the three of them passed as they made their way to lunch, enjoying the shadows that played across the path while they walked and talked. The day was so pleasant that the student body as a whole seemed livelier, with people calling out to each other and friends laughing together while they moved this way and that across the campus. At one point as they approached the mess, Aria let Rei and Viv go at it on the topic of Brawler versus Duelist dexterity, turning her face up and pushing her cap back to let the sun shine on her cheeks for a little bit.

It was the reason she didn't see Catcher until Viv called out to him in surprise.

"Hey! What are you doing here?"

Aria looked down from the sky, surprised to indeed find the Saber waiting for them, seated on a bench not far from the hall entrance. He looked a bit annoyed, hands thrust into his pockets and a small frown tugging at his lips, but brightened when he caught sight of them.

"Hey!" he echoed, pushing himself to his feet as they reached him. "Sorry, I would have messaged you guys, but I only just heard on my way to the Arena. Apparently a couple people got injured training yesterday evening and had to be hospitalized. Forced Reese to move some matches around."

"Oh," Aria breathed, concerned. An injury that couldn't be dealt with overnight? It must have been bad. "Any idea who?"

"None." Catcher shook his head. "My fight against Jax got shoved back, though."

"That's weird. *I* don't have anything about a time change…"

Aria, Viv, and Catcher looked at Rei, who'd pulled up his NOED and was reading what was likely his message log with a furrowed brow.

"Maybe you got lucky?" Catcher offered, stepping a little closer to them to let a chatting trio of second year girls slip by behind him. "Or maybe I'm just one of the few who got pushed?"

"Maybe," Rei shrugged, closing his neuro-optic and indicating that they should follow the group as they headed into the mess hall. "When's your new estimated time?"

"1645."

"Nice!" Viv exclaimed, looping an arm around Catcher's neck to jerk him close and starting to lead the way inside. "That's right before Rei's! Aria and I are gonna be able to cheer you both on!"

Her enthusiasm appeared to do away with the mild irritation the Saber looked to have been holding onto at the change, because he finally grinned.

"Already thought of that. I've made you guys signs to hold. 'I love you, Catcher!', and stuff like that."

"Gross." Viv made a face, shoving him away again as Aria and Rei both snorted.

All together again—and with a squad-based training session of the combined class-blocks after lunch—no one was in a rush to eat. It transpired that Catcher, too, had suffered the emaciating lecture in Combat Theory, and—after they'd traded a few good jokes about the visiting Colonel and the possibility of his birth before humanity had even left the Earth—the Saber could do nothing but groan with jealousy when he heard what they'd gotten to do in Tactical Studies.

"1-C doesn't have Takeshi until tomorrow," he grumbled, handing the remains of his salad off to a passing service bot. "On the other hand, at least I have something to look forward to. The Device Evolution lecture Alphonse is gonna treat you guys to in the morning is only *slightly* less dry than usual."

Aria was the only one who managed to suppress a sigh, with Rei and Aria both slumping back in their chairs at the news.

"I get it's important to study, but whole classes on CAD progress can be hard to swallow between lectures on fight theory and *actual* combat training," Viv grumbled at the ceiling.

"Weren't you the one who was *just* saying you couldn't wait for Gemela to evolve?" Rei sniggered. "Might be useful to understand the basics before you end up in a full suit of—*owe!*"

Viv had smacked him in the arm without so much as looking down, earning another laugh from the table.

After lunch it was off to the squad-training, and following a second pleasant walk under the autumn sun they arrived within earshot of the Arena in time to hear the sound of Hadish Barnes—the apparent announcer of the day—shouting at the top of his lungs with excitement. Exchanging a quick look, the four of them started running, happily risking an earful by any potentially passing staffer if it meant the possibility of catching a glimpse of whatever had the chief of campus security so riled up. Reaching the mouth of the stadium, they took the steps four and five at a time, attaining the top and rushing to the railing of the walkway just in time for Major Barnes to shout again.

"OH, and *that's* how you use the environment, cadets! Ranjha might have survived the kick, but she's falling now! She hits! Into the water with her! And Benaly is coming down after her without a moment to lose!"

There was the *wham* of a heavy impact, coupled with an eruptive splash, and what few onlookers were gathered in the stands all bellowed with excitement.

As many times as they'd seen a projected field before, Aria knew she wasn't the only one of her friends to stare with glee up at the transparent, towering hologram they were taking in from the back. A variation of what had to be "Cliffs", the zone was a two-level fighting space bisected by a narrow river. The flow rushed across a flat, upper plateau for 15 yards before spilling off into a waterfall, which collected in a shallow stone pool almost 50 feet below.

And it was from this pool that Jack Benaly was fighting to get to his feet, wrenching the steel of his green-gold fist from the still, submerged form of the Mauler Jasmine Ranjha to hold it aloft.

"Fatal Damaged Accrued," said the Arena on cue. "Victor: Jack Benaly."

"Well that's another top sixteener down!" Despite the sparsity of spectators, Catcher still had to raise his voice over the echoing of the cheers at this announcement. "Only a good thing for us!"

Aria nodded, not looking to see if Rei and Viv agreed as she watched the field begin to dematerialize, bringing Benaly and Ranjha—who had indeed been another of the summer group—down to the projection plating below.

Seven more to go, she thought to herself, ticking off the names she knew Rei and Catcher might have to face off against once they made it through the day.

She didn't bother letting herself consider the fact that they might *not*, in fact, make it through the day.

"We'll have to remember to congratulate Benaly tonight, if we catch him," Rei said, and Aria felt the brushing of his hand against her shoulder. "Come on. I've got *no* doubt whoever Reese has instructing squad-training is on orders to brig the lot of us if we're so much as two seconds tardy."

The place he had touched her tingled a little under her jacket even after she'd turned around to see him pass, making for the nearest entrance to the underworks.

Catcher was right on his heels, but Viv slipped an arm under hers to pull her along be-hind the boys, giving Aria a knowing smile but—for once—saying nothing untoward.

With Reese's consistent absence from their squad-training afternoons second to his arbiter responsibilities, the environment of the sessions had rapidly grown much less stressful with the rotating staff of instructors and observers. Even Captain Dent had taken over a class or two—though undoubtedly not at the major's request, based on what Aria had gleaned of the man's opinion of her—with those days being particularly enjoyable. This afternoon, Liam Gross had been put on duty, and she thought it was a testament to Rei's improving performance in class that the sergeant major had only seen fit to glare at him once or twice by the time training wrapped, ending with a final exciting Team Battle that had come down to Kastro Vademe and Logan Grant as the last Users standing among their squads.

It was Grant, unfortunately, who'd come out the winner.

Given that the main floor of the Arena had been claimed by the Intra-Schools nearly every afternoon since the start of the quarter, *all* of the Institute's post-noon training sessions were held in the subbasement, and so it was to the regular locker rooms that everyone retired to once Gross had dismissed them for the day. Rei and Catcher stretched and stayed loose in their combat suits while Aria and Viv show-ered and changed back into their regulars. After that, it was with a good portion of their joint class-blocks that they returned to the Arena proper together, climbing the steps out of the underworks right on time to see Kay take down poor Candice Brett in what must have been the first minute of their fight, impaling the Duelist against the crumbling brick wall of their Deserted Settlement variation. As Major Barnes congratulated the Lancer on her wholly unsurprising victory, Aria followed Rei's lead up the steps into the southernmost section of the stands, finding their usual seats. Since the entirety of the first year class was done with lectures and training for the day, the rows were abruptly filling up quickly, most everyone choosing to linger either to cheer on a friend who was fighting soon, or merely wanting to watch the upcoming matches.

Unfortunately for their group, they'd all barely sat down before Aria saw Catcher blink at a flash of his NOED.

"Oh, they want me downstairs." His eyes lifted to the corner of his frame, a look of surprise crossing this face when he caught what must have been the time. "Whoa.

Yeah, I should get going."

"I'll come with," Rei said, standing up with him. "I'm probably the fight right after you anyway. Are you east or west entrance?"

"East."

"Nice. Me too." Rei turned to Aria and Viv. "Wish us luck."

"I'll save that for next week," Aria answered instead, giving them both a smile matched by Viv's double thumbs-up.

When the boys were gone, heading down the stairs again quickly, Viv leaned in close. Aria was afraid she was about to be drilled with some *very* uncomfortable questions about Rei, but the girl chose instead to keep the conversation more immediate.

"You're positive they're both gonna make it through today?"

Unsure if she felt more relieved or disappointed, Aria nodded. "Yeah. Catcher can take Jax any day of the week, so long as he doesn't try anything stupid."

"And Rei? You're that confident in him taking on Renton."

Aria smiled. "Even more so."

"She's faster than him."

"She's also a coward."

"But she's faster."

Aria shrugged. "So was Camilla Warren, probably, and look how that ended up. Honestly, you could tell me Renton had C5-Ranked specs across the board and I'd still put Rei down as having a fighting chance against her. He's just... better."

Viv gave her a sidelong glance. "And you're not at *all* biased on that subject, are you?"

There it was. And Aria had walked right into it.

"Sneak," she muttered while Viv grinned.

"Well it's not like you're gonna talk about it outright, is it? I've got to pry it out of you."

"There's nothing to talk about," Aria lied as firmly as she could, trying to channel her mother's impassive face for once as Dyrk Reese started up the field for the combatants she hadn't even heard Major Barnes announce.

"Uh-huh," Viv said sarcastically. "Either you're in denial, or you're full of it."

Aria decided to change tactics. "What about you? Are you worried about them?"

Viv frowned a little. "Ordinarily? I'd say no. I agree that Catcher could take Jax with Arthus tied behind his back. Rei, I'm a tad bit more concerned about, but that's just me, I think. I'm kinda used to having his back. It's been... weird, not having to stand up for him as much."

"I have a hard time imagining him ever needing you to fight his battles," Aria muttered, trying to conjure up the image and failing.

"Oh, he never really did, and he always grumbled about it. But that's what friends do."

Aria nodded. Below them, the fight started—a pair of Sabers she didn't recognize, and whose names she hadn't caught. They were duking it out in one of the ship-bay variations of Zero-Grav, but after seeing the Lasher's bout on a similar field, the two first years' clashing looked nothing more than sluggish and unrefined.

"I just feel like the other shoe is gonna drop."

Viv's muttered words reached Aria over the slamming sound of carbonized steel. Concerned, she looked around to find Viv chewing on the inside of her cheek, arms in her lap and chin tucked to stare at the ground between her legs while she leaned against the projected seat back behind her.

"The other shoe…?" Aria asked tentatively.

"Yeah…" After a second Viv looked up to meet her eye. "You don't think things have been going too smoothly lately? For Rei, I mean. Galens hasn't been the easiest time for him from the start, but ever since he took down Warren…" She lifted a hand to gesture over the field, where the elevated disc that held Dyrk Reese and Hadish Barnes was hidden from view by the projected steel wall of the holographic bay. "Even Reese seems to have let up on him, hasn't he?"

Aria glanced away quickly. She had it straight from the horse's mouth that there was a *very* good reason Rei's last four pairings—including Renton—had been fairer, but that was information she was definitely *not* supposed to have. What was more, despite having confided her secret in Rei, Aria had never quite found the right moment to tell either Viv or Catcher about Rama Guest. She knew it was a stupid fear, born from the heart of a girl who'd never before had anything she would have called a "real" friend, but a part of her was afraid of how they would react, whether they would judge her for the fact that her uncle was the commanding officer of the very school she'd elected—or been made—to attended.

"It's not just Reese, though." Viv kept on, apparently not having noticed Aria's avoidance of the topic. "Michael Bretz has loved Rei since the first parameter test, but the other sub-instructors have recently been coming around too. His fibro has been in remission for months. He's winning matches. Selleck is leaving him alone."

At this, Aria couldn't help but give her a look. "You mean Grant."

Viv's mouth shut with an almost audible *snap*, and she refused to so much as glance at Aria, who couldn't help but laugh despite the conversation.

"Viv, when are you going to give up and tell us what's going on? I've *seen* the way you two have been sneaking looks at each other during training."

Still, Viv said nothing.

"Viv, if you're worried about what Rei will think, I don't—"

"I'm not."

The words came out as an uncharacteristic squeak, and Viv blushed as soon as she heard the blatant lie in her own voice. Clearly trying to save herself, she forged on.

"Rei thinks Log—*Grant*—has a thing for you. He thinks he's been picking fights because of a jealousy complex."

Aria almost laughed again, but stopped herself just in time. "Honestly, Viv, if Rei *did* think that at some point, I don't know if he still—"

"He doesn't."

Aria blinked. "Rei doesn't think that? I'm confused."

Viv's cheeks went even redder. "No. Grant doesn't have a thing for you."

Aria gave her an amused smile. "Yeah... That much I figured out on my own. He's got a thing for *you.*"

Viv didn't answer, but this time it might just have been because the fight they were supposed to be watching ended rather abruptly, with one of the Sabers cleverly using everything she had to rocket a heavy steel container at a port window near her opponent. The undoubtedly "impact proof" glass proved unable to handle a User's Strength, and the window shattered, pulling the other Saber out into the void. The Arena appeared to count this as a loss, because the announcement came only a second later.

"Fatal Damage Accrued. Victor: Amelia von Leef"

Aria felt a little ashamed of herself for being distracted enough to not have recognized the victor, given von Leef had been her opponent in the fourth and final week of the winner's bracket. She clapped as loudly as she dared to make up for it, keeping her applause going until Amelia had taken leave of the field, along with the disqualified loser.

The whole time, Viv hadn't said a word.

Her silence lasted through the next match, too, and Aria didn't press, wondering if maybe she'd poked a little too far. It didn't really seem fair given the girl's tendency to tease *her* about Rei, but she supposed the circumstances *were* a bit different. For one thing she'd always expected Viv more likely to go for some older girl in the second- and third year, based on several of the more private conversations they'd had when Rei and Catcher were around. For another... Well...

This *was* Logan Grant, they were talking about...

It wasn't until after that second fight and well into the next, nearing the moment of Catcher's match, that Viv finally spoke again.

"When I say I'm afraid of the other shoe dropping. Logan's not who I'm talking about."

Aria felt the knot of concern loosen in her gut, and she looked around. Viv was watching the fight—Leron Joy, who'd made it surprisingly far for being a prick, versus the Saber Clement Easton. For another couple minutes, though, she went quiet once more, not saying anything more until Joy lost his head to Easton's blade.

As Major Barnes began to congratulate the winner, Viv started up again, even raising her voice to be heard over the announcement.

"We've... been talking. For a while."

Aria didn't miss a beat, understanding now that this really wasn't an easy topic for Viv to discuss. "Since when?"

"Since the night Selleck jumped Rei with Warren and the others."

Aria tried not to show her surprise. That event had been more than 8 weeks ago. She was somewhat impressed Viv had been able to keep this a secret—if badly—for so long.

"He just..." Viv squirmed uncomfortably, still not looking at Aria. "He changed my mind a little, that night. About him."

"When he put down Selleck."

"When he put down all of them, Aria." Viv shook her head, leaning forward now to rest her elbows on her knees. "It was... shocking. I mean don't get me wrong, it was *hot*, too." She smiled slightly, and seemed to gain a bit more confidence in her words as she kept on. "But it was mostly shocking. Not in a bad way," she added quickly, finally turning to look Aria in the face. "Maybe it was a little scary, yeah, but it was more of a wakeup call. He's *still* an ass, but there's more to him. A lot more to him..." She shook her head, her gaze drifting off again. "You should have seen his face. I don't think I've ever seen anyone so *angry*. Like what they'd done made him want to tear them apart with his bare hands."

ions to be manually corrected by ISCM oversight."

Bullshit, Aria thought, something very much like fear crawling up her throat.

"Everything has now been properly implemented, though, and the rest of the day's fighters will shortly be notified of their modified pairings. For the time being, however, please give a cheer for our next combatants. Layton Catchwick…!"

Bullshit, Aria thought again, knowing what was about to happen.

"… versus Reidon Ward!"

At once their section of the stands erupted as the first years—who to a one undoubtedly knew that the two boys were close friends—suddenly smelled blood in the water. Several people were on their feet, some cheering while others hurled catcalls, and after an elongated pause a pair of figures both appeared from under the eastern edge of the walkway, awkwardly making their way towards the field side by side.

"What is this?" Viv snarled, half-rising in her fury. "*What is this?*"

Aria barely grabbed her by the sleeve of her jacket, pulling her back to sit again before the girl thought to leap down to the floor herself.

"Viv, calm down. There has to be an explanation."

"There's no explanation!" Viv snapped, yanking her arm loose as her brown eye lifted to the focus of her ire. Reese. "He did this! I'll bet you anything *he* did this."

"You don't know that," Aria insisted, though she could hear the disbelief in her own words. "You don't know what's going on. It could be anything. It could be—"

And then Aria stopped, a thought cutting her short mid-sentence. She tensed, going rigid so abruptly it was enough to have Viv take pause, turning to look at her with a hint of alarm punctuating her anger.

"Aria…?" she asked uncertainty.

Aria, though, didn't answer her, having already pulled up her contact log on her NOED, scrolling through until she was about halfway down, all while a single sentence reverberated in her mind.

He didn't have a choice.

She was afraid, suddenly. So afraid. Finding the name she was looking for, she dialed at once, ignoring a second press from Viv as she did.

He didn't have a choice.

For some reason, she wasn't surprised when the line only rang once before a tense, feminine voice picked up.

"Aria, listen to me—" the woman began, but Aria had no intention of letting her finish.

This reminded Aria of something suddenly. As Clement Easton helped his feet below them so they could walk together off the field, she recalled som Rei had once described.

"Like the time Grant went after him in cross-training? After the mat already been called?"

Viv's immediate nod said this was *exactly* what she was talking about.

"Then what's his deal?" Aria asked, feeling herself getting a little impat she recalled the story of how the Mauler had nearly beaten Rei bloody desp fight having ended. "As far as I know, Grant's had a bone to pick with you tw day one, hasn't he?"

"Not me." Viv shook her head. "Just Rei."

"That doesn't answer my question."

Viv took a breath, looking to the field again. On the observation disk, Rei Barnes looked to be conferring about something while the first years around all started murmuring in anticipation of the next match.

Finally, she started to talk in a gush, like the words had been held back many weeks to keep at bay any longer.

"Logan's got a history, Aria. Or his family does, at least. There's a rea hates Rei. Or did. Or does. I'm not really sure anymore, since we've been talki why he beat Selleck and the rest to a pulp, and has laid off us all ever since. H

Before she could finish her thought, however, Hadish Barnes started sp again, and what he had to say snatched away every ounce of her and Aria's tion both.

"Uh…" The large man looked a little uncomfortable as he addressed the s "Due to an incident that occurred last night involving multiple injured stu there has had to be some unplanned reshuffling."

Aria felt every hair on her body stand on end, and beside her Viv snapp to sit as rigid as stone in her seat, eyes suddenly narrow. Around them, there whispers from the rest of the class.

"Incident? What incident?"

"I heard someone from 1-C got hurt. Anyone know who?"

"I heard 1-B. Was anyone missing for squad-training?"

Major Barnes continued over the noise, looking down now to where Aria the upcoming fighters were waiting their turn along the wall of the Arena flo

"We apologize for the last-minute notice, but it's taken a little time for co

"Maddie, what did he do?" she half-yelled, realizing as she did that her hands were shaking as she watched Barnes direct Catcher around to the west side of the field below them. "What the *hell* did he do?!"

CHAPTER 49

"The questions evaluators field following the end of an exam are widespread, but consistent, no matter if they are received from assignees or those that left empty-handed. 'What was the answer to this part of the written test?' 'What does that spec rank mean for my future?' They come pouring in like clockwork the moment every CAD exam ends each year, but despite this fact there remains one which I always have trouble answering fully.

'What was the purpose of the third test?'

It's difficult, after all, to explain to the eager faces of hundreds of boys and girls—most of whom only months before wouldn't even have been considered adults—that not every mind is capable of bearing the brutal truths of war..."

Major Albert Connelly

It had been a long, *long* time since Rei had been this angry.

It was a boiling, churning thing, twisting and frothing in his gut until his entire body felt hot as he walked, forcing himself to take every step alongside Catcher. His eyes, meanwhile, never left Dyrk Reese, who had no qualms whatsoever meeting his gaze. Despite the stillness of the aging man's face, despite the composure of his features and the steadiness in his dark eyes, Rei thought he could detect a little—just a little—of something else in the major's bearing for once. It took him a moment to place it, a moment to understand the vague, unpleasant taste looking up at the man left his mouth.

Smug. Reese—behind the statuesque masque—looked smug.

"I'm gonna kill him."

Catcher's whisper, shivering with fury, brought Rei back, and he risked a quick look sideways to see that his friend, too, was staring up at the major with an intensity he'd never seen from the Saber. Catcher's yellow eyes were on fire, his handsome jaw clenched and his hands balled into fists at his sides.

"He's messing with us," he continued. "This is *bullshit*."

Yeah. Rei couldn't bring himself to say a word to the contrary. *That it definitely is.*

"Cadet Catchwick, please cross over to the western edge. We can't have you two starting next to each other, can we?"

Hadish Barnes's tense attempt at a joke drew a few laughs from the stands, but Rei got the feeling the chief of campus security was finding very little amusing about the situation himself. His big smile was tight, and there looked to be more space between the two majors now than there had been a minute before.

Barnes appeared to have preferred not to stand next to Reese once they'd finished their "conversation".

Catcher hesitated, he and Rei coming to a stop together. They looked at each other, neither exactly sure what to say.

In the end, it was the Saber who took control, knowing that Rei wouldn't be willing to.

"I'll go."

"Catcher—" Rei started as his friend began to turn away, but found himself promptly cut off.

"We don't give them a reason to claim we're ever *anything* less than our best." Catcher glanced back again. "We fight to win. This isn't any different than sparring. Got it?"

"Of *course* it's different," Rei hissed in answer. "Are you stupid? Do you not see what they're doing.?"

"I do. Believe me, I do." Catcher didn't look away. "We fight to win, Rei. Both of us. You understand?"

Still, Rei hesitated. There would be more to this matching than simply pitching two friends against each other.

But then again everyone—*especially* Catcher—was aware of that.

Finally, Rei nodded, and just as Hadish Barnes opened his mouth to repeat the order, the blond boy turned and crossed the field in quick, stiff strides. Watching him go, Rei could only grit his teeth. He hated this. *Hated* it. Until a minute ago the pair of them had both been set on making through this sixth round, been ready and prepared to rise to the final selection, whatever that would bring. Now, though…

Now, it had been a month since Rei had started being able to fight Catcher to a draw in training. A month since they had stood on even footing on the field.

A month for Shido to grow…

Sadness—a real, burdening sadness—grew like a stone in Rei's chest, then, seeing his friend reach the other side of the ring and turn around to face him. They locked eyes, yellow not looking away from grey, and Rei thought he could sense some echo of his own woe in the Saber's gaze, some measure of the same understanding.

Still, there was more, there, too, and as Dyrk Reese spoke the first opening command of the match, Rei was pleased to see determination hardening Catcher's expression, mixing with focus until the boy's face was nothing less than composed stone.

"Combatants, take position."

In mirrored approaches Rei and Catcher reached their red starting circle in four quick steps each.

"This is as an official Duel," the Major enunciated. "It will therefore be subject to regulation ruling. Once the field is formed you will be ordered to call, then engage. Premature Device manifestation will result in a penalty. Premature approach, attack, or the like will result in a match loss. Is that understood?"

Slowly, both of them nodded, still watching one another. They didn't see Reese's NOED light up, didn't see him make the field selection. Almost at once, though, they began to ascend, and the green, leafy undergrowth rising quickly from a grassy earth told Rei at once where they were headed.

The last thing he saw was Catcher offering him a small smile, then the boy was swallowed by the breadths of a hundred thick, heavy trees as they materialized into being.

"Field: Woodlands."

At once the noise of the Arena vanished around them, replaced by the quiet sounds of the deep forest, the trilling of insects joining the chirps and songs among the branches high above. Under Rei's feet a solid spread of moss and low-hanging ferns covered the floor, and overhead sunlight poured in handsome rays at an angle through the leaves, giving him the impression that the projection was meant to be placed in an evening pushing at dusk.

"Cadet Layton Catchwick versus Cadet Reidon Ward," the Arena spoke again, its voice ringing clear from everywhere all at once. "Combatants… Call."

"Call."

Shido blurred into place, snaking up and out in a flash of rushing steel and light to seal itself into place around his arms and legs. Though Rei couldn't see Catcher through the dense woods, he knew the Saber would be completing the same summoning. Arthus would be low in his right hand, the claws of his left outstretched and ready to meet a faster opponent.

A faster opponent like Rei.

Again, the sadness deepened. Again the weight of anger returned.

We don't give them a reason to claim we're ever anything less than our best.

The words seemed to echo in Rei's ears, and he took a slow, deep breath.

"If you say so, man."

Then the Arena spoke one last time.

"Combatants… Fight."

M addie was in the middle of delivering Rama his afternoon report on daily disciplinary actions within the Institute grounds when he got the call. The man didn't stay on for long, nor spoke for the greater duration of it as Maddie stepped respectfully back, waiting for him to finish. After less than 30 seconds of silent listening, the colonel sighed, then nodded.

"Yes. Thank you, captain. Your appraisal of the situation is appreciated."

Then, with a flicker of light, he closed the line, sitting for a little while more without saying anything, gazing at the bookshelves walling the far end of his office like they might host some reprieve to whatever frustration was simmering behind his calm exterior.

"That was Takeshi," he said at last. "It's done."

Maddie held her tongue, waiting for the man to elaborate, but after a time it was apparent she was going to have to wrestle the details out of him.

"And? Who won?"

Rama grimaced. "You know damn well who won. Central wanted to test Ward. Could he take down a friend? Someone who's been by his side basically from the moment he stepped onto the Institute ground? Well…" The colonel looked like he could have spit. "They got their answer, didn't they?"

CHAPTER 50

"We plan. God laughs."

-ancient Earth proverb

Rei and Catcher sat opposite each other in the red-and-black professional's locker room that had become a favorite of theirs over the recent weeks of combat. They didn't speak, Rei bent over his knees as he caught the last of his breath, watching sweat drip off his nose to dampen the dark carpet between his bare feet. Catcher, meanwhile, was leaning back with his head resting against the top of the mirroring couch, hands limp in his lap and face upturned towards the ceiling and the dark, crystal lights that hung from it. For a long time they stayed like that, using the excuse of regaining their wind to hide the fact that neither knew exactly what to say.

Eventually, it was Catcher who again took the lead.

"You know who they're gonna pit you up against next, don't you?" he asked quietly.

Rei tensed at the sudden question, then relaxed, giving himself a moment before answering.

"… Yeah."

"You ready for it?"

"Not yet."

Catcher brought his head forward just enough at that to look at Rei down the length of his nose.

"… But you will be?"

"But I will be," Rei promised.

Catcher nodded slowly, then let himself take to staring at the ceiling again.

It had been a brief, brutal fight. They'd sparred enough times before for Rei to have an excellent sense of Catcher's abilities, but it had been the days the Saber had spent helping him get ready for his bout with Lena Jiang which had spelled the final outcome, which had solidified Rei's read of his friend. On top of that, the 5 weeks of growth Shido had absorbed since that first week of the SCTs had raised him from D9 to C2, arguably placing him in a totally different class of fighter. Catcher's specs—aside from Speed—*had* been better, but Rei hadn't won any of his previous matches with overwhelming power or an impenetrable defense.

In the end, Catcher had fallen like the others who'd been "stronger", albeit not without a *lot* more of a fight.

And all of it for nothing, Rei thought, pulling up the last notification he'd received, shortly after the match had ended.

...

Processing combat information.

...

Calculating.

...

Results:
Strength: Lacking
Endurance: Lacking
Speed: Adequate
Cognition: Adequate
Offense: Adequate
Defense: Lacking
Growth: Not Applicable

...

Checking combat data acquisition.

...

Adequate data acquirement met.
Device initiating adjustments to:
Endurance. Defense.

...

Adjustment complete.
Endurance has been upgraded from Rank D5 to D6.
Defense has been upgraded from Rank D5 to D6.

...

Calculating.

...

CAD "Shido" has been upgraded from Rank C2 to C3.

Despite his earlier bravado, Rei felt his heart fall into his stomach yet again, coming to the end of the upgrade message. There at the bottom would have been the notice, he knew, the alert that Shido had evolved. He had to admit he suddenly understood why Christopher Lennon had been trying *not* to put the idea into his head, initially. He *had* hoped, he knew now. Dared to hope, dared to set his sights on what might come. There was nothing, though. No additional text. No telling script. No evolution alert.

And with it, the chance of Arsenal Shift—or any Ability whatsoever—developing just in time for his final Intra-School match.

The upgrade had come and gone, and had left him—for the first time ever—feeling hollow inside.

There was a *hiss* of the door opening, and Rei closed his frame to look around and find Aria and Viv entering the locker room, each carrying a set of regulars. They'd gone down to fetch the uniforms from the subbasement at his request, and their twin expressions of disgruntled fury hadn't faded in the 5 minutes since they'd all seen each other in the underworks after he and Catcher had limped off the main floor.

He didn't have the energy to decide if his own lack of anger now was due to him being tired from the match, or just tired of it all in general.

Crossing the room, Viv handed him his jacket, slacks, socks, and boots, Aria doing the same to Catcher across from him.

"Bullshit," Viv hissed as he accepted the clothes and got to his feet. "This is absolute, total *bullshit*."

Rei had to force himself not to sigh, moving around her to one of the rows of lockers behind the couch. Pulling a compartment open, he considered stripping out of his damp combat suit to go shower before deciding he didn't quiet have the enthusiasm for *that* either. Instead, he hung his jacket and slacks up, then dropped his boots down unceremoniously before taking a seat again, this time on the bench provided along the row.

"Is *no one* going to agree with me?!" Viv demanded, bringing her arms up and looking around at the three of them like she couldn't believe the lack of audible outrage.

"We *all* agree with you, Viv," Catcher grumbled without looking at her, having barely mustered the will to accept his own uniform from Aria with a small thanks. "We're just not in a mood to scream into the void right now."

"Who says it needs to be the void?!" Viv whirled on the beaten Saber. "There's another match going on *as we speak*! We could march out there and—!"

"Oh don't be ridiculous!" Catcher's head finally snapped up, and for once he appeared to be utterly lacking in his usually good humor. He glared at Viv, face contorted in frustration. "And do what, Viv? *What*? Yell at a superior officer in front of the entire first year class? Oh, *and* the chief of campus security? Yeah, that would go over *really* well with everyone, wouldn't it?"

"It's better than doing nothing at all!" Viv's voice was steadily increasing in volume, a tell-tale sign that she was reaching the point of her often-limited self-control. "It's better than sitting here and moping about—!"

"You'd mope too if you lost!" Catcher was on his feet, the regulars that had been piled in his lap spilling off onto the floor. "You'd mope too if you had your shot at qualifying basically *stolen*, Viv! But you didn't, did you? You made it straight through! Four wins! No trouble, no issues!"

"All the more reason to *do something*!" Viv was yelling outright now, her face going red with anger and—Rei suspected—a little embarrassment. "We know who did this! We know *why* he did this! This can't be something the school would just let continue if they knew about it! This is the *third time* Reese has manipulated the pairings to put Rei in a bad—"

"Reese had nothing to do with it."

Aria's hard, clear voice cut through the boiling tension like a sword, bringing Viv to a sudden halt and drawing every eye in the room.

Rei, abruptly, found a little of his energy again as he took her in, noting the clenching of her jaw and the tightness of her arms, crossed over her chest. Now that he thought about it, he didn't think he'd ever seen Aria angry, much less *this* angry.

Could it be that…?

"What do you mean?"

Viv's hissed demand was almost dangerous, doubly-so when she repeated it after Aria hesitated to answer.

"What do you *mean*, Aria?"

Still no response came for a second. Aria looked to be resolving herself, her arms suddenly a hugging presence about her torso, as though to brace for some coming impact.

Rei knew, then.

"Aria…" he started in warning, shaking his head when she looked at him. "You don't have to. Not yet."

She held his gaze for a moment, her eyes not leaving his, like she was trying to absorb something from their steadiness.

Courage.

"No. I do. It's past time."

She looked then between Viv and Catcher, who still stood unevenly on either side of her.

"Major Reese had nothing to do with the match change up," she started. "Not primarily, at least. It's likely he manipulated the brackets, just like early in the tournament, but this time he had orders to do so."

This news was followed by a ringing silence for 5 long seconds.

"Orders?" It was Catcher, surprisingly, who found his voice first. "Orders from who? And how do you know this?"

"Because my uncle is Rama Guest," the words came in a torrent, and Rei could *feel* how long Aria had been wanting to let them out, "and his chief assistant told me *he's* the one who gave the command."

This time the frozen pause was deeper still, like a quiet that swallowed even the shallow bubbling of the fish tank at the back of the room, but kept short when Viv opened her mouth to speak. Aria flinched, not meeting anyone's eye, waiting for the inevitable demand of explanation.

"Why the hell would the colonel order Reese to mess with Rei's pairings?"

The question had Aria blink, then frown, like she wasn't sure she'd heard correctly. After a moment she looked up and around at Viv.

"... What?"

"I said why *the hell* would Guest order Rei's pairing be messed with?"

"No, I know that's what you said, I just..." Aria peered at Viv like she wasn't sure if she was being toyed with. "Did you not hear me? I just told you I'm the command officer's niece."

It was Viv's turn to look perplexed, and she glanced from Aria to Catcher to Rei in confusion.

"Uh... Sorry... Was that supposed to be a secret?"

Aria's jaw dropped, and Rei almost laughed out loud, only partially managing to stifle it with a hand. From her other side, Catcher, too, was looking at her with confused amusement.

"Is *that* what you've been tiptoeing around for the last couple of months?" He chuckled when Aria's face snapped to him, her expression still one of utter shock.

"Girlfriend, people have seen you coming in and out of the administrative building since before school started. Same thing with you walking around with Maddison Kent, and having morning practice sessions with the colonel over the summer."

"Th-They did?" Aria stuttered, her face flushing.

Catcher snorted, eye blazing as he pulled up his NOED. "Yeah. Combine that with the fact that if you search the feeds for the names 'Laurent' and 'Guest', you get a bunch of articles about 'Comrades Carmen Laurent and Rama Guest' from their time on a SCT-squad together at Galens." It only took him a moment to find what he was looking for, then with a swipe of his hand he shared several screens with the group. Rei abruptly found himself looking at a number of pictures of two young men, one obviously a youthful colonel Guest, the other sporting a laughing expression and familiar green eyes.

Aria, seeing these, looked something between amazed and mortified.

"Oh, that's not even how I put it together," Viv said, a small smile breaking her anger as she shared her own frame. "Dig a little deeper and you find this."

Another screen popped into being in Rei's vision, and after a moment's perusal he did, actually, laugh this time.

It was an announcement piece from an Astra sector's local news, declaring the birth of one "Aria Meredith Laurent", complete with a list of her parents, her two siblings, and her godfather, Rama Guest.

In big, bold-ass letters.

Aria had apparently had enough. With a moan she brought her hands up to cover her face under the brim of her cap.

"Oh noooo…" she groaned. "No no no no…"

This time all *three* of the others laughed, but it was on Rei that her attention fell when she peered out through her fingers.

"Tell me you didn't know. If you knew and didn't say anything, Rei, I swear on the *MIND* I will stick Hippolyta so far up your—!"

"I didn't know!" Rei exclaimed at once, grinning as he brought his hands up placatingly. "I promise, I didn't know! Catcher has more friends than all of us put together, and Viv is nosy. Plus, you'd already told me before I got curious enough to start digging!"

"Hey!" Viv turned on him. "Rude!"

"But accurate," Catcher said under his breath, pretending to be fascinated with the ceiling fixtures when she whirled on him.

"Fine…" Aria said, though Rei wasn't sure if she was telling that to him or herself, given she still hadn't pulled her hands from her face. "Fine… But still…" She looked to Viv and Catcher. "It doesn't… It doesn't bother you?"

"What does?" the two asked together.

"Well… I got into Galens… And… Well… The commanding officer of the school is my uncle…"

The pair stared at her for a solid few seconds, then each other in the same way, then at her again.

"Aria…" Viv looked like she was trying to suppress a real grin, this time. "What was your score on the written part of the Assignment Exam?"

Aria finally pulled her fingers from her cheeks, though she kept them tucked under her chin like she expected to need to hide behind them again at any moment.

Cute as fu—

Rei had to pretend to cough to keep from staring, hoping no one noticed the heat in his own cheeks.

"Just under ninety-seven percent…" Aria answered. "Why?"

Catcher snorted. "And have you ever—*ever*—lost a fight here at school?"

"Yeah. Lots."

Not having expected this answer, even Rei looked around to gape at her again.

"Against *who*?" Viv demanded in disbelief.

"The colonel. When we had our morning practice sessions. He *always* managed to—*Why are you all laughing*?!"

Indeed, Rei, Viv, and Catcher had all burst into hysterics a second time, Catcher's guffaw so loud Rei thought it was a miracle no one from the stands above came running to see what the hell was going on.

"Let's try that again," Rei finally decided to join in, still chuckling. "Aria… Have you ever lost a fight here at school *against anyone not an S-Ranked User*?"

"Oh…" Aria immediately saw her mistake. In her embarrassment her voice looked to have abandoned her, because after a little bit she only shook her head.

"Exactly," Viv said, gesturing with her hands to indicate this settled the matter. "So consider you could wipe the floor with anyone who might want to throw a hissy-fit about it, and get over your *incredibly* over-anxious fears of being ousted for nepotism, Aria."

Another pause.

And finally a single, clear nod.

"Good," Viv said, still smiling. Then, though, the amusement slipped from her face a bit. "Still, though… You haven't answered my question."

It was a testament to them all, Rei thought, that the feeling in the room didn't slip right back into the over-boiling tension of a minute before. The laughter had cleared the air a bit, leaving them somewhat more even-headed to tackle the unfortunate reason they were all gathered together in the first place, there in the clean red-and-black of the professional's locker room. Aria, too, must have felt it, because it was with less apprehension now that she responded, finally dropping her hands to her sides again.

"It wasn't by choice."

"The order?" Catcher asked. "To redo the brackets?"

Aria nodded. "Yeah. It wasn't by choice. Maddie—Maddison Kent, sorry—told me he got a call. Last night."

"From *who*?" Viv asked, astonished. "Who the hell would order the colonel to do something like that?"

"Who the hell *could*, more like," Catcher mumbled, sounding equally astounded.

Rei, though, thought he was piecing together the puzzle.

There was, after all, only one place in the Intersystem Collective likely to take such interest in the minutia of the military academies, even one with a reputation like Galens. There were thousands of generals on the front lines—and another few hundred patrolling the systems and managing planetary security within them—but those men and women were unlikely to have had the time to divest in tracking the progress of a single CAD and its User.

There was only once place.

"Central Command," Aria answered.

Though he'd known it was coming, Rei discovered himself no more prepared to hear the words out loud than either Viv or Catcher. Together they gawked at Aria in shared bafflement, unable to speak.

"Central…" Viv finally managed to get out. "As in… *Earth's* Central?"

Aria just nodded, and Rei found himself in need of taking a deep, shaking breath as she, Viv, and Catcher all turned slowly to look at *him*, now.

He supposed he'd known it was coming. There was no way it wasn't right? Shido had now grown twenty-five ranks in just around 6 months. That wasn't just unheard of. It was unbelievable. Viv—who had above-average Growth—had climbed from D6 to C3 in the same amount of time. By the second quarter of next year, she would be in the high Bs, probably, and the year after that would be competing at this exact tournament as a User likely in the middle As. That was impressive enough.

Rei, though, might be an A by the end of his first two terms at Galens, if Shido continued on its current ascent…

"They have to have had their eye on me for a while," he told the others. "Probably from the very beginning, if I'm being honest."

He was sure of it, in fact, recalling the astonishment Albert Connelly had displayed upon seeing Shido's S-Ranked Growth. If some part of the exam system hadn't automatically flagged him on assignment, there was no way the major himself wouldn't have reported such an incredible occurrence…

Or the MIND itself…

Neither Aria, Viv, nor Catcher was fool enough to disagree with him.

"But why get involved now?" the latter asked them, looking around at the group. His yellow eyes were bright again, thankfully, no longer robbed of their usual energy by his loss. "They've been hands-off for months, haven't they? It's been half a year since assignment…."

"They haven't," Aria shook her head. "Not exactly. They're the reason Reese stopped skewing the fights against Rei in the first place."

This came as a surprise even to Rei. "They were? Why didn't you tell me?"

"I shouldn't be telling you *this*," Aria said, almost pleading. "None of this. You guys need to understand that half the stuff I know I'm not even sure *Maddie* is really supposed to be aware of. If it got out, the *best* outcome would be that she gets fired and my uncle gets dishonorably discharged."

"Are they crazy, then?" Viv asked, staring at Aria. "Why would they tell you these things?!"

"Because they trust me. Because they trust how I'll use the information." She allowed herself a small smirk. "Still sure I shouldn't be worried about nepotism?"

"Not so much, no," Viv said with a strained smile. "Then the question *that* bares: Why are you telling *us*?"

The answer came without pause.

"Because *I* trust *you*."

For the first time in a while, while watching Viv and Catcher look like something had caught in both their throats simultaneously, Rei was struck by Connelly's words to him, and he allowed himself a crooked smile.

Good friends can be hard to find.

"They were testing him."

Catcher had pressed on from the embarrassment of being so heartily touched by Aria's statement by returning to the issue at hand.

"They were testing him," he said again when he'd gained their collected attention once more. "To see if he had a killer instinct."

"Definitely," Aria agreed with a nod. "Maddie didn't hear the exact conversation, but it was obvious the general my uncle spoke to was pretty clear about that."

"After *stopping* Reese?" Viv asked. "Initially, I mean? Isn't that… well… backpedaling?"

"That's exactly how the colonel put it, apparently. He wasn't pleased with the order. Maddie wanted me—*us*, actually, I think—to know that."

Rei nodded on his bench. He had to admit, it made him feel a little better about the whole thing. Knowing *why* something was happening always helped, especially if that reason turned out to have a more concrete base than the unfortunate luck of having an officer on staff who'd happened to take a disliking to him. He wasn't as surprised as Viv, either, at the reversal. Shido's growth rate meant the CAD was a different beast now that it had been even 3 weeks ago. He could see the logic in the decision, understand the reasoning. Had he been disqualified from the tournament too early, then Central's ability to observe his developing strength would have been castrated. Now that he'd made it *this* far, though…

Now, just as Catcher had deduced, was the time to start testing him.

Well… he supposed he couldn't disappoint them, could he?

Aria, Catcher, and Viv were talking heatedly, debating what Central was about and discussing the military's interest in him. Leaving the three of them at it, Rei pulled up his upgrade notification again, staring at the last line for a while.

CAD "Shido" has been upgraded from Rank C2 to C3.

Just under 2 weeks. It had taken him just under 2 weeks to make that jump, to seize at what he'd thought was his last chance. It was Tuesday afternoon, though. *Only* Tuesday afternoon. Even if his final Intra-School match was scheduled for the following Monday, he had the better part of 6 days…

Rei grimaced, considering it. He and the others already pushed themselves to their limit, didn't they? Every opportunity they got they trained, didn't they? Every day, every spare moment.

But no… Not every spare moment.

Closing the upgrade notification, Rei watched Aria, Viv, and Catcher talking,

Viv gesturing animatedly with her hands as she continued to question Central's interference in the SCT. He wondered what they would say, if they could read his mind right now? If he told them of the insanity he was considering? Would they support him? Would they back him up?

He didn't know. He'd already been warned once in the last week that he shouldn't push himself too hard, in fact.

And yet…

It was Catcher Rei's eyes fell on. Catcher, who had just been disqualified from the tournament not by any fault or lack of effort on his part, but because of having the misfortunate of being Rei's only friend left in the pairings. It *was* bullshit. He agreed with both Viv and the Saber on that wholeheartedly. That his companions were the one's suffering the consequences of his circumstances now made him feel sick, and Logan Grant's sneering face, telling him he was dead weight, swam before his eyes for a moment.

What right did he have to let anyone down anymore?

Cursing under his breath, Rei pulled up the clock function of his NOED and adjusted his alarm, silently apologizing to Christopher Lennon as he did. There was no helping it, though. C3 had borne with it no answers. Catcher had just been sacrificed to the cause. Rei had 6 days. 6 days he could use if he started right now.

When the alarm woke him at 0400 the next morning, he would tell himself it was only his part of the price to get stronger, with the others in his life have already paid theirs.

His uniform forgotten, Rei stood up abruptly, the motion so sudden it caught the other three off guard. They paused, looking around at him with a little alarm, but he spoke before any of them could ask what was going on.

"Aria, do you still have access to the subbasement fields?"

Aria blinked, having clearly not expected the question.

After a second she nodded. "I do… Why?"

"Because I need to use one."

Aria frowned. "Rei, you just finished a match. You should take a break, recover a bit before you get your pairing for next—"

"No." Rei shook his head firmly. "I'll recover tonight. Right now I need to use a training field."

Aria was about to argue further, but Viv stopped her with a hand on her arm.

It was Rei, though, that his best friend was looking at.

"Did you hit C3?"

Like I was made of glass, Rei cursed silently.

Then he nodded.

Aria and Catcher's eyes widened a little, but before they could think to congratulate him Viv kept on.

"How long did it take?"

"Eleven days," he answered honestly.

She watched him for a moment more, ignoring the slow build of confusion in the faces of the others.

"… Are you planning what I think you're planning?" she finally asked.

Rei hesitated, seeing an argument coming at him at full speed.

Still, he nodded again.

Viv chewed on her tongue for another few seconds, refusing to look away from him while she considered.

Eventually her face broke into a pained kind of smile. "And you're not going to get talked out of it, are you?"

"You'd have to drag me off kicking and screaming," Rei confirmed, managing to return a weak grin.

Viv nodded slowly, then sighed. "Well I guess that's that, then." She looked to check her own time in her frame. "It's almost 1800. I'll smuggle some dinner out of the mess hall for you. You *will* eat, you understand me?" She paused. "And shower, on occasion."

Rei nodded. Seemingly satisfied, Viv immediately turned and started for the door of the locker room again, but it was Aria's turn to stop her.

"Wait. Hold on. What's going on? Why are you having to smuggle food for him?"

"'Cause he's not planning to leave the training fields until the last possible minute tonight." It was Catcher who responded, his eyes on Rei, his expression a mix of exasperated and impressed. "And the same for every other night until the fight. Isn't that right, Rei?"

"Mornings too," Rei answered carefully.

Catcher grimaced, then, but to Rei's surprise moved to collect his uniform from where he'd dropped it to the floor. Once he'd gathered up the various articles, boots in one hand and clothes over the other arm, he jerked his head at the door Viv was now standing by expectantly. "I'm not at your level anymore, but I'll be a better partner than the simulations I bet you were planning on using. Besides," he lifted an eyebrow at Rei, "you owe me a damn rematch."

Something very much like relief—mixed with a healthy dose of gratitude—washed through Rei, and for a second he couldn't speak. When he did, he was embarrassed to hear the hoarseness in his own voice.

"Thanks, man."

"Wait." Aria, it seemed, was the only one who hadn't caught on yet. "*Wait*. What's going on here? What the hell are you guys about?"

"Catcher's volunteering to be the punching bag, and I'm gonna be the meal delivery service!" Viv called over her shoulder, already halfway out of the room as Rei and Catcher both started following her. "Do your part, Aria! Go get them a field!"

"But *why?*" Aria looked completely befuddled. "What is going on?!"

"Oh, nothing too serious," Catcher assured her, glancing back to give her a tense wink before stepping through the door. "This crazy bastard is just going to try to get to C4 in six days or so."

CHAPTER 51

"I ask you to judge me by the enemies I have made."

Franklin D. Roosevelt

20th century ruler, Earth

Logan was in the middle of taking on Leda Truant and Tad Emble together when the notification pinged his NOED. He ignored it, bringing Honoris' haft across his body to smash Truant's testing spear out of the way so hard that she actually staggered sideways, opening her right flank up to him. He would have liked to take advantage of the chance, but needed to instead bring the axe around and keep Tad at bay as the Brawler closed in on his left. Leda recovered, and the spear slashed at Logan's legs, now. He stepped *into* the arc of the strike, letting the haft of the weapon—rather than the blade—smack him along the back of his newly armored foreleg and *ping* off harmlessly, all while swinging Honoris around at the Phalanx's head. Leda ducked, but it wasn't her who was the actual target of the move. Tad, seeing his chance, darted in once more, punch-daggers driving forward.

Logan's steel-clad fist—the one he'd released from the massive axe's shaft once the momentum of his swing had been enough to carry it through—took the smaller boy in the side of the head before he could land a hit.

Tad went flying, the blow taking him so hard he spun twice like a disk before slamming to the plain white of the Neutral Zone. Finding herself suddenly without support, Leda cursed and retreated two steps to assume a defensive stance behind her shield.

Logan followed right after her, uncaring of the heavy steel barrier between them while he drove Honoris down at the girl.

One. Two. Three massive swings was all it took before the Phalanx's Strength failed her. Her shield fell as the axe cleaved into the top of the metal, driving it down until the blue-and-white blade bit through her shoulder too, splitting the vulnerable flesh and bone between her neck and left arm. At once the plexus of nerves controlling the limb failed, and the shield dipped limply while Leda screamed in simulated pain. Logan didn't elongate her suffering.

Wrenching Honoris free, he took her head off with one last, clean blow.

"All Red Team combatants eliminated. Winner: Blue Team."

As soon as the Arena made the announcement, the blue glow of his CAD's normally-red vysetrium faded, the change back like an odd weight off Logan's shoulders. Honoris had become a part of him in the 6 months since his assignment. He'd had trouble at first, he could admit in retrospect. The fact that he had been assigned as a User of a common Type with his father had been unsettling, even infuriating in the first few weeks.

Now, though… Now it was as much one with his body as any of his limbs.

A slow, echoing clap from behind him caught Logan's attention, and he looked back to see Mateus Selleck providing the half-hearted—or sarcastic?—applause. On either side of him Camilla and Giano Perez sat with their mouths hanging open, though they shut them quickly when they caught Logan's eye. Of Jeffrey Gathers, none of them had seen much of the boy in several weeks, with the Lancer having long-since avoided sitting with their little group during class.

Logan didn't mind. He wasn't surprised Gathers was distancing himself from them. Giano was on the brink of doing the same, he could tell, and the only reason Tad hadn't already fled was because he was in the same Type-group as Camilla and Ward, which would only have made things doubly-awkward for the Brawler.

That fight—that *one* fight—had changed a lot of things, it seemed.

"Give it a rest, Mateus," Logan growled, turning to face the blond Saber while Leda and Tad recovered from their neural interruption enough to start staggering to their feet. "If you clap every time you see someone better than you fight, you'll end up with stubs for hands."

Mateus froze mid-motion, his bored face flashing briefly into one of annoyance. In an instant the facade was back, though, and he smiled before shrugging. "Just complimenting you on a good match, man. No need to get all up in arms about it."

"Uh-huh," Logan said, making sure the disbelief dripped from his voice. How the *hell* had he let himself get mixed up with a tool like this? "In that case, maybe you're looking for a lesson." He leveled Honoris' blade—still called—at the boy. "Come on up. We can do a one-on-one."

Smooth as silk, Mateus shook his head and raised both hands. "Nah. That wouldn't help you much, would it? There's no top-ranked Sabers left in the tournament. Whoever you get matched up with won't be my Type."

"Then let's just say it'll be a nice change of pace."

Mateus' mask cracked again for a moment, stiffening as he thought quickly. In the end, though, he just stuck to his guns.

"I don't think it's a good idea." He gestured to Giano Perez, sitting on the projection steel at his right. "How about swapping out Truant for Perez? Pits you against a Brawler *and* a Duelist? You might not be able to handle the speed…"

Logan felt his face twitch, and he fought not to rise to the bait. The coward knew how to push his buttons, that much was for certain.

"Maybe," he said through gritted teeth, "but Ashley Renton is the only Duelist left in the losers bracket, and I could take her on holding my breath with my ankles tied together. So I'm good."

"You never know. She's fast. She might—"

"Shut up."

Logan stopped listening to the Saber, because he had only just noticed the blinking notification in the corner of his vision. Recalling the alert he'd gotten mid-fight, he felt his pulse quicken a bit when he saw the subject line of the missive.

Pairings were up.

Without a moment's hesitation Logan selected the icon, and at once his view was mostly obscured by a single tall screen. Whereas every other such notice had required a scrolling to see all the participants, the fact was that there were only sixteen cadets left in the tournament. As a result, Logan found his name almost immediately.

And that of his opponent.

At once the pulse that had been speeding up settled, a cool, calm sort of focus grabbing hold of Logan so absolutely that he didn't hear Mateus asking him what was up, what he was looking at. He reread the name beside his several more times, taking it in, making sure he wasn't mistaken. On the one hand, there was no doubt left in his mind that the Intra-Schools were being rigged. What was more, there was no way Dyrk Reese could be alone in the plot, if he was allowed to get away with *this* after that questionable fight the week before had already raised so many eyebrows among the student body.

But on the other… Logan was suddenly very much looking forward to the coming Tuesday, more so than he could have imagined.

His anticipation was… strange, though. Had anyone asked him even just 2 months ago what he would have been thinking in this moment, he'd have said he couldn't wait to put an asshole and a leech in his proper place. There was still a measure of that in his expectations, he knew—a healthy measure of it—but there was more, now, too.

There had been more since Lena Jiang—the school's top Saber—had been forced to resort to dirty tricks to win that first fight in the opening week of the tournament.

Logan became aware, then, that his hand not holding onto Honoris' haft was shaking slightly. Closing the pairings screen, he brought it up to his face, watching his strong fingers shiver. He tried to make it stop, tried to press back the excitement, but to no avail. He breathed easy. His heart was steady.

And yet every fiber of his mind screamed for the week to pass and for the fight to come.

Finally, he made a fist, then looked past his hand to offer Mateus a simpering smile before turning his gaze on Giano. "On second thought, maybe I *could* use a little speed training. Switch in for Leda, Giano. Give me everything you've got."

As the Duelist got to his feet nervously, Logan turned his back on them both, resetting the field and motioning to Leda that she could go sit down with a jerk of his head. The red circles showed up—two on one side of the zone, with the third on the other—and Logan headed for the lone ring while Tad and Giano jogged for the pair. As soon as they were set and Leda was clear of the perimeter, he triggered the match.

"Let's see what you're *really* made of, Ward," he muttered under his breath, settling down into a ready position as his Device glowed blue again and the Arena started to speak.

CHAPTER 52

"Never seen anything like it. Not before, and not since. It wasn't passion that drove the kid. Passion is too insubstantial a word. It was more like... fire. Yeah. Fire.

It was like his every fiber burned for more, to become more, growing stronger and hotter with every breath he took..."

Lieutenant Michael Bretz, S-Rank Pawn-Class
concerning the Stormweaver

By the time Friday evening came around, for Rei to say that he was dead on his feet would have been the understatement of a lifetime. They were *all* tired, to be fair—he, Aria, Viv, Catcher—all of them, but his friends had only been rotating the morning trainings, each taking their turn getting up at 0400 with him to knock out an extra 3 hours or so of sparring before breakfast and the days' classes. Rei, on the other hand, had been getting barely 5 hours of sleep a night, and felt the weight of his decisions in every second he spent fighting not to doze off in lecture, not to mention the long, sluggish walks between buildings as the weather grew steadily colder and the days greyer.

Still, he'd thought sparring itself had always woken him up, so Rei was surprised when barely 20 minutes into the last training session with Christopher Lennon, the third year called a halt to their bout.

"All right, *stop.*"

Rei, having no way to pause in the massive punch he'd just thrown at the young man's face, nearly choked as the blow ripped towards Lennon's eyes. At the last possible moment, though, a dark hand snapped up, sliding fingers between Shido's claws with impossible precision, taking hold and stopping the fist as absolutely as might a stone wall. The impact was jarring, and Rei actually grunted as the force transferred into the bones of his arm, making them throb. Standing up straight, he pulled the

Device away carefully from Lennon's hand, shaking his wrist out in an attempt to dissipate the lingering ache.

"What's up?" he asked, doing his best to come off nonchalant.

Lennon, though, was frowning at him, ice-blue eyes burning into his own like they were trying to read his soul. They were alone on their half of the field, just the pair of them. Aria, Viv, and Catcher had all insisted Rei take these last 2 hours to himself to try to eke out every advantage he could from the session, and—when the Lasher hadn't said a word to the contrary—Rei had accepted gratefully, deciding it was all right to be a little selfish for once.

In hindsight, though, he was wondering if this one-on-one training hadn't been exactly what he should have been trying to *avoid*...

"Attack me."

Lennon's command caught Rei by surprise, and he hesitated, fearing what the trick was. After a moment of silence in which the Lasher said nothing else, though, Rei shrugged internally, and did as he was told, lunging forward to swipe at the third year's arm, hoping to catch his instructor unawares.

Of course, he hit only air, Lennon stepping back in a blur of motion.

"Stop," he said again, and Rei halted once again. The Lasher approached once more. "Okay. Again."

With a frown, Rei stepped forward to go for a kick at Lennon's side, this time. Another whiff.

"Again," came the command, and Rei followed through.

"Again," it came for a third time, then twice more after that, Rei stopping and starting in silence as he did as he was told.

"All right," Lennon finally said, clearly having made some decision or discovery Rei wasn't to be privy to just yet. "Let's try one more time." He took a step to stand in front of Rei.

Then he closed his eyes.

"Again."

Rei didn't budge, suddenly nervous. He might have always wanted to land a hit on the A-Ranked Atypical, but *this* was hardly the way he would have liked to go about it.

"Uhh, sir...?" he started, unsure.

Lennon didn't so much as crack an eye.

"I said 'again', Ward. Come at me."

"But how are you going to—?"

"*Again.*"

The Lasher didn't raise his voice, but the order was firm. In the corner of his vision, Rei became aware that the other three had all paused in their own training to peer through the dividing wall between them at what was happening.

Deciding there wasn't anything for it, Rei braced himself, crouching low in preparation. Lennon didn't budge as Shido's boots ground into the field. There was a pause, Rei trying to deduce what trap was coming, but he got nothing. No hints, no alarms, no red highlights in his NOED. It looked like a free and clear shot.

In the end, he took it, rocketing forward with as fast and powerful a thrusting punch as he could muster right at the red-on-blue griffin in the center of the third year's chest.

He was on the ground almost immediately.

WHAM!

Still with his eyes closed, Lennon had reacted to the sound of Shido's steel armor. In a deliberate movement that couldn't have been any faster than Rei's own C2 Speed, the Lasher kicked a foot out to hook the back of his leading ankle, lifting it up and inward. The result had been Rei toppling sideways under impetus, right side hitting the field floor hard under his own weight with no way to break his fall himself, and sending him sliding several feet along the smooth projection.

"Owe…" he groaned, more out of habit than anything else after he'd come to a stop and rolled onto his back. His Defense was tied with Endurance as his lowest spec, but well into the Ds as it was his reactive shielding had been more than enough to weather the minor impact of the fall.

Just the same, Rei felt almost naked when Christopher Lennon's shadow slid across him as he lay there, the older boy's form looming over him, silhouetted black against the overhead lights.

"You didn't listen to me, did you Ward?"

Rei swallowed, his worst fear realized. Scrambling for an out, he decided to try a redirect.

"I did! I studied up on every User I might have been matched up against for the fight next week. Even after I got my pairing, just like you said." He tried at a smile. "Give me any name. I'll wow you."

It wasn't untrue, to be fair. In fact, studying the other fifteen first years left in the final of their Intra-School losers bracket had very often been the only thing that kept him awake in class for the last 3 days. Reviewing his potential opponents—well, *theoretical* opponents, now that he knew for a fact who he was up against—had been a hundred times more stimulating than a majority of the week's lecture topics, and stimulating turned out to be exactly what he needed while running off 5 hours of sleep a night with more than twice that many spent training every day.

"Don't be cute," came the answering growl. "I told you you need to pace yourself." Rei cut the act.

"I know." He pushed himself into a sitting position, squinting up at his instructor. "I'm sorry, I just…"

He trailed off, not sure how exactly to explain himself.

"Just what, Ward?" Lennon pressed him, sounding like he was bordering on legitimate anger. "Just decided you would go-go-go until you keeled over?"

"I'm fine," Rei started to say, moving to stand, now. "All I need is a little bit more time, and I'll—"

Thud.

For the second time in less than a minute he hit the ground, this time landing on his ass. Lennon had shoved him down again, stepping in and around to hook him behind the knee, this time.

"You're *not* fine," the Lasher growled, lip curling in irritation to reveal white teeth. "You don't even realize it, do you?"

"Realize *what*?" Rei demanded, starting to get near snapping himself. He was too tired for a ribbing like this.

"You don't even realize I can read you like a book right now."

This brought Rei pause, and he frowned. "What are you talking about? You can *always* read me like a—"

"No, Ward. No I can't." Some of the anger left Lennon's face, and he crouched to be level with Rei. "The reason I can wipe the floor with you any time of any day is because I have A-Ranked Speed and S-Ranked Cognition. I *react* to you. I don't *read* you. I told you when we started this: you're unpredictable. Almost too unpredictable, sometimes, but on the whole it works in your favor. Usually you're a storm, the embodiment of chaos theory on the field. It's good. Really good." He cocked his head at Rei, then. "But you didn't realize every *single* one of those opening attacks just now led with your right foot, did you? Every. Single. One."

Rei stared at the young man, registering his words with disbelief and alarm. Could that be true? No way, right? There was no way he would do something so amateurish.

And yet…

"Shit," Rei breathed, thinking back on the repetitions and realized Lennon was, in fact, correct. "That's how you hooked me. That's how you took me down."

"With my eyes *literally* closed, Ward."

Rei nodded, at a loss for words. He replayed every attack in his head, every opening lunge, every first step.

Every *right-footed* first step…

"Shiiiiiit," he repeated, letting the curse linger as his disbelief and irritation grew.

They stayed like that, quiet for a bit, Lennon seeming to want to let his criticism sink in. Rei could say nothing, as mad at himself as he was frustrated by the catch-22 of the situation. More than 30 hours of training he'd put in, since Tuesday. 30 hours, and his last match had been scheduled for the next *Tuesday*, giving him more time than he could have hoped for. He could do it, he thought. He could push and make it to C4, snagging himself one more chance to snatch at the carrot the very person before him had teased him with.

But at what cost?

"You hit C3 after your fight with Catchwick."

Lennon's words came as a statement, not a question. Rei—realizing he was too tired to be excited by the fact that the *Lasher* was keeping tabs on his rank—only nodded.

"And nothing happened."

Again a statement, and again a nod.

"Is that what's going on? Is that what you're doing? Trying to hit C4 before your next match?"

This time, Rei answered aloud, feeling like his voice sounded small as he spoke. "Yeah."

"And you think it's going to make a difference?"

Rei hadn't noticed that, at some point, his gaze had drifted down to rest on the floor between his knees. He blinked and lifted his face to look up at Lennon again. "Yeah," he repeated. "It will be my fifth rank since my last evolution. If Shido could adapt one more time. If I could develop an Ability like you—"

"Ward, I told you *not* to bet on that."

The harshness was back in the third year's tone, now, and Rei actually winced. He deserved the reprimand, he knew. He was, in a way, grasping at straws.

"I know it's unlikely," he said. "But you don't understand who I'm up against. If

I can develop an Ability and gain that kind of edge over him, I might—"

"Rei. You don't get it. I'm not telling you I don't think you're going to develop an Ability."

A shot of electricity lanced up Rei's spine, waking him up completely. Christopher Lennon—the very Christopher Lennon who had competed as a second year in the last Collegiate Intersystem Championships—had just addressed him by his first name.

Lennon seemed to mistake his gaping in that moment for incomprehension, because the young man sighed and dropped back to sit opposite him, arms on his knees.

"I *do* think you're going to develop an Ability," he clarified. "It's common enough for all Types to have one by the middle Cs, A-Types like us in particular. On top of that, you're *not* a regular A-Type." He pursed his lips, scrutinizing Rei for a moment. "What I mean when I say you can't bet on an Ability is that even if you *do* get one, it's not as simple as flipping a switch and being the master of your own destiny. Some are a bit like that—Overclock, for example, or Repulsion—but even those require time and a *lot* of practice before they can be used with greatest efficiency. Others require all that time and practice before they can be used *at all*."

There was a whirling of black steel and red light, and all of sudden Lennon was holding one of his segmented chain-swords in his right hand. Before Rei could get anything more than a close-up glimpse of the weapon, though, the Lasher sent it flying over his shoulder with a flick of his wrist. The limp thing spun a few times in the air, dropping toward the ground again.

Before it clattered to the floor, however, it froze, suspended, to float some 2 or 3 yards above the surface of the field.

"What if you developed Invisible Hand?" Lennon continued. He had two fingers up, and with a twitch of one of them the chain-sword began to swim point-first in graceful arcs towards them, like some black-and-red serpent through water. "Do you think you could just do this overnight? Mirage is the same. Magnetic Hunt is only slightly less complicated. Puppeteer is *twice* this hard to master." With a small motion of the other finger, the weapon snapped back into Lennon's raised hand, then returned to its original form of the ring about his wrist as he recalled it with a thought. "Have you considered that, Ward? Have you considered that you might be chasing something useless?"

Rei licked his lips, registering the words as an echo in a chamber of worry in his own mind. Yes, he had thought of that, but not in such terms. For his part he had been more worried that he would see this grind to the end, work himself ragged until he was a puddle on the floor of the tournament field, and all for nothing. Either he wouldn't make C4, or he *would*, and find himself disappointed with the result again.

Now, though… Now he had another fear to add to the weight of those concerns.

Still… It didn't change anything.

"I have to try."

He was surprised by the certainty in those words, as he said them. He had thought they would come out quavering, or at least tired, but he was sure in that fact, and managed to make the statement sound as much.

"I have to try," he said again before the Lasher could respond. "I don't have a choice, Lennon. You don't understand. This fight… *This* fight, I need to win."

"Why? Why does this fight matter so much? What's suddenly making you push yourself like this the week after I *specifically* tell you not to?"

"Do you have plans to sleep tonight?" Rei grumbled. "Cause filling you in would take that long."

The third year made a face. "Fine. I don't want to know that bad. Not sure I really want to know the first year drama at all, actually." Still, he studied Rei a little more carefully, after that. "It's that important?"

Rei nodded, and there was another few seconds of silence as Lennon looked to consider something.

When he spoke, though, it wasn't an expected question.

"How many hours?" he asked. "Of training, I mean. Since you hit C3."

Rei grimaced. "Ten? Maybe eleven?"

Lennon frowned, looking unpleasantly surprised. "Since Tuesday? That's barely what I thought you were doing before you—"

"A day," Rei clarified.

It was strange, witnessing the Lasher gawk at him like he'd suddenly grown three heads. It was an altogether different expression than Rei had ever expected to witness from the A-Rank. For the first time—and only for a moment—he saw Lennon for the student he was, a simple cadet of the military, likely only 2 years older than him.

And then the shock was gone, replaced once more by the mask as Lasher got to his feet in a flash.

"We're done for the night," he said, looking down at Rei. "You're to go home and sleep. I also want you taking tomorrow off, aside from your regular course training."

"*What?*" Rei demanded, taken completely aback by this sudden command as he, too, scrambled to his feet. "No! I'm halfway there already! I can do it, I know I can—!"

"Sunday morning." Lennon interrupted him, turning his back to walk away. "0600. You'll meet me here. Pack your meals beforehand."

Rei stuttered to a stop, gaping after his instructor, who obviously had no intention of fighting anymore that night.

"W-What?" he eventually stammered out. "What… What do you mean?"

"I mean meet me here at 0600 on Sunday." Lennon stopped, half-turning to look at Rey again. "I mean bring food because we won't be leaving this room until you either hit C4, or we hit curfew." Again he appeared to be examining Rei, but there was something new there once more. Maybe… Pride? "You're going to do this. I get that, now. I can't brig you, so unless I pin you to the floor for the next three days I have no way of stopping you. So… If you're going to do it anyway, you're going to do it right, and you're going to do it with someone who will challenge that scary-ass CAD of yours in a way that will compress all the hours you still need into the fifteen I'm going to give you."

"Wait…" Rei breathed. "You're not…? Does that mean you're going to—?"

"Bed, Ward," Lennon said, interrupting him as he turned around and made for the door again. "And tomorrow off. I *will* ask Dent if you followed my instructions, and if she tells me you came within a hundred feet of either training center, you and I will be done for good."

And then, with that final promising threat, Lennon was gone.

Rei stood there alone, staring out the open door of the training chamber the young man had just departed through, uncomprehending. With the Lasher's departure, the field reset, fading to nothing and dropping Rei down the 2 feet as the solid white light gave to black projection plating.

He was awoken from his daze almost at once, however, when he found himself immediately accosted by three figures who surrounded him in a heartbeat.

"Rei. Rei! What the hell happened?!" Viv demanded, bending down slightly to look him in the face.

"Where's Lennon going?" Catcher followed this up with, face pale. "Is he pissed? What did you say?"

It was Aria's voice, though, that managed to best cut through the fog.

"Rei…" she said quietly, and he felt several of her fingers coming up to touch his shoulder lightly. "Are you okay?"

Taking in a shaking breath—a breath that might have been his first since watching the Lasher leave, he realized—Rei looked around at them each in turn, settling on Aria.

"I need to get back to Kanes," he said weakly. His heart felt like it was hammering out a thousand beats a minute, and he couldn't help but doubt he would get any sleep no matter how tired he was. "I need to get to bed."

This, clearly, was an odd answer to his friends' concerns, because they exchanged a worried look amongst themselves, like they feared the stress of the last few days had finally knocked a screw loose.

It was Viv—Viv, who knew him best—who put his desires above whatever consequences she thought he might be suffering.

"But, Rei... What about training? You've been working so hard..."

Rei turned to her unsteadily, not sure if he could believe the words he was about to say.

"I think that's taken care of..."

"What?" Catcher asked, clearly not understanding. "How?"

Rei shook his head in slow, uneven disbelief.

"I think... I think a potential Intersystem Champion just set aside his entire Sunday to put me through boot camp..."

CHAPTER 53

As it turned out, Rei had no trouble sleeping that night, his excitement—and that of the others—not holding a candle to his exhaustion in the end. He had the sense, fortunately, to turn off even his regular morning alarm, and for the first time since arriving at Galens was very nearly late for their starting classes the next day, getting up only when Viv and Catcher came pounding on his door. After a rushed breakfast Aria had cobbled together for all of them, they made it to lecture by the skin of their teeth, where Rei found out that a single decent night's rest wasn't about to make up for the abuse he'd put himself through since Tuesday. Making it to lunch proved a difficult affair, and Rei just barely managed to keep himself awake by studying up on more of the other Users left in the losers bracket with him.

Arriving at combat training after the mid-day meal, Rei discovered that Valera Dent was only willing to pull so many strings for him, because there was no reprieve in the afternoon's conditioning. Cross-training with the Lancers, Bretz and Allison Lake soon had Rei—and the rest of their two groups—building up such a sweat in the sparring matches that he wondered if Lennon wouldn't find cause to cut him off even if he kept his promise otherwise. Still, Rei got through the day, and—with no small amount of willpower—avoided East Center before and after dinner in favor of studying with Aria, Viv, and Catcher in 304, the three of them as much there to make sure he didn't give in to the itch to train as they were to help each other understand the complexities of quantum theory as related to carbon steel compression in CAD bands.

At around 2000, Rei's eyes started to droop, his body demanding more rest from him than he'd granted it the previous evening. Giving up not even 15 minutes later, he put away his pad and bid the others all a good night, saying he was going to catch a little extra sleep before his early morning. Changing out of his regulars at last, he slipped into bed, set his alarm for 0530, and turned out the light.

That night, however, despite his fatigue, Rei barely slept, tossing and turning with anticipation.

You're late."

Rei froze upon entering the training chamber, looking at a stern-faced Christopher Lennon standing inside the edge of the field closest to the door. After a moment he finished the bite of the bagel he'd already been in the process of shoving into his mouth, checking the time while he chewed and swallowed.

"I still have five minutes!" he protested as soon as he could.

"You're still in uniform," Lennon countered without hesitation. "We also haven't warmed up. 0600 means we should be *fighting* by 0600. Not getting ready to."

Rei thought about muttering something in opposition of this as he pulled his bag over his head to hang it off one of the hooks by the door, carefully to do so gently so as not to squash the sandwiches he'd put together for himself in a hurry from what he'd had access to at breakfast. Thinking better of testing the third year who would likely be throwing him around like a doll all day, though, he instead stuffed the bagel between his teeth before retrieving his combat suit from where it was tucked among the meals.

Making use of the other hanging hooks for his uniform, he was dressed and ready with 2 minutes to spare when he stepped into the ring with Lennon.

"Made it," he said with a grin at Lennon, rolling his shoulders to start to loosen his arms up.

WHAM!

The hit took him in the gut, his reactive shielding doing shit-all against his attacker's superior Strength and Offensive specs, even bare-handed as the Lasher was. Rei felt himself lifted clear off his feet by the force of the impact, and he fell heavily out of the air to nearly slam his face against the steel of the floor. He gagged, coughing and hacking, and it was an absolute miracle he didn't vomit up his very recent breakfast as his stomach throbbed with pain and nausea.

"Get up, Ward."

Lennon's voice wasn't cold. It wasn't malicious. It was merely firm, without pity for the position Rei found himself in, nor remorse from the surprise assault.

Fighting being sick every inch of the way, Rei did as he was told, trembling to get first onto one knee, then up on his feet. From there, it was several seconds before Shido got ahold of the pain enough for him to stand straight.

"I'm going to hit you again. Try blocking, this time."

"W-What—?" Rei started, still reeling from the *first* blow.

He didn't finish before the third year's fist indeed hit him again, a little higher now.

This time, Rei *did* vomit, sick splattering the floor of the field as he struggled to breath, lungs paralyzed by the strike to his solar plexus.

"That's twice I landed a blow." Rei couldn't look up, but knew Lennon was standing over him to the side while he spoke. There was a whirring sound from outside the chamber, marking the approach of a service drone summoned for clean-up. "I even warned you the second time. So *why is your CAD still not called?*"

Gut throbbing and head a struggling mess of incomprehension, it took Rei longer than he would have liked to register the suggestion for what it was.

"C-Call," he fought to get out between labored breaths, bringing one hand up to clutch at his abdomen.

Nothing.

Fear—a suddenly, terrible fear—clutched at Rei, and he felt every muscle in his body tense up. What had happened? What had happened? Why wasn't Shido—?!

"Breathe, Ward." Lennon interrupted his panic, his voice a little gentler now that his charge was taking the right steps. "Breathe. You're forgetting to focus. You're letting what I've done distract you. Remember the basics."

The basics. Right.

As he heard the door of the room open automatically for the incoming drone, Rei turned his thoughts from his pain to his CAD.

"C-Call," he said again, no less unsteadily.

But this time, Shido answered.

The moment his Device was in place, Rei felt his head start to clear, his neuroline engaged with the CAD's summoning. He shoved himself to his feet and leapt away from Lennon, hands up and at the ready, waiting for a third descending blow.

It didn't come.

"Good," the Lasher said in approval, stepping aside as the service bot went about its duty. In 30 seconds or so the field floor would be shiny as new. "Good. *That's* the response I wanted to see. Maybe next time you'll be faster about it."

"What the hell, Lennon?!" Rei demanded, not for a moment considering dropping his guard. "What was that for?!"

The Lasher frowned. "I'm sorry, did you think today was going to be an average day for you?"

"I *thought* I could at least get my bearings before you put me on my ass!"

"Why?"

ace halfway up the hill. Almost in
back, and he was suddenly hurtling
end he caved in, diving forward and
feet at the ready. This time he held his

ontward kick, catching him in his defending
im reeling back once again.
m displeased.
adjustment! When someone is faster, you don't
try to escape. You stand and fight. Forcing yourself
lend itself to a faster loss."
ppening, now, Rei went with his gut, dropping the next
him below the neck. He rolled backwards before shoving
hands in a modified spring to land deliberately hard, digging
es into the dirt for purchase as he dipped into a half-crouch,
w. Another blow came at his shoulders, but this time Rei went
a single tucked step back that didn't allow Lennon to throw him
n.
re talking!" the young man shouted, and Rei thought he saw the flash
th that might have been a smile, accompanying a pulse of the Lasher's
Let's see how well you keep up, shall we?"
d then the field began to change, and the Lasher became a blur.
Cliffs variation lifted them into the air, and for an untold count Rei hunkered
n, blocking where he could but always giving to the direction of whatever attack
me, absorbing most of the impact with a step or two back and never allowing himself to be robbed of his footing. He barely saw his instructor in those long minutes,
barely made out more than a streaking shape of black skin mixed with the red-on-
blue of his combat suit. He didn't need to *see* Lennon, though, to take in the lesson.

One had to be able to adapt, but there were times when standing firm was the
only decision to be made.

After two more field changes and maybe 10 more minutes—in which Rei's leg's
started to burn from the constant adjustment—the barrage of shoves and pokes and
prods finally ceased. He was left reeling a little across the dusty road of a Deserted
Settlement, breathing in gasps of air that still made his chest hurt from the initial

Rei pause

was the pl?

"Be

year

own thoughts.

Rei blinked and the boy was gone from his p

the same instant he felt a hand shove into his

down the slope, fighting not to fall. In the

tucking, twisting to snap him back onto hi

ground, waiting for the attack.

It came head-on in the form of a fr

forearms with enough force to send

Despite this, Lennon didn't se

"Good!" he said again. "Goo

try to outpace them. You don't

to stay on the move will only

Picking up what was h

time an open palm struck

off the ground with his

Shido's clawed steel

keeping his body l

with it, giving in

off balance aga

"Now w

of white te

NOED.

An

do

an

to stop

"When .

continued to press

pause when they see an

a fight is on even ground aga

A finger shoved at Rei's right s

pushed on his chest, keeping him stum

"I looked up who you're fighting, Ward

outclassed in five out of six specs, and most of th

opponent isn't just strong, either. He's talented, and he

put in. If you want a *prayer* of taking him on, then you'll ne

need to adapt to the fact that you're facing a guy who has every

as you are right now."

There was a flash of light in the Lasher's eyes, and abruptly the field too.

It wasn't the usual Neutral Zone though, and Rei felt a foot catch in a sudden swe

of grass as it materialized under his backpedaling foot. With a yelp he spilled back-

wards, but managed to tuck into a roll that had him landing in a crouch. Taking the

opportunity, he tried to spring sideways as the sloping incline of a Grasslands varia-

tion bloomed into being around him, swallowing the chamber they'd been standing

in with the bright blue sky of the zone.

Trying to escape Christopher Lennon, though, was like trying to outrun your blows Lennon had delivered. The Lasher himself was standing some 10 feet up the way, watching with an approving air, arms crossed.

"All right," he said after a moment. "Now let's see how you do against strength."

Then he took a step forward.

Rei's arms snapped up, expecting the shredding wind of a second Break Step, but Lennon just approached at near-normal pace, like he was doing nothing more than taking a casual stroll through the buildings projected all around them. When he reached Rei, he stopped, looking at him flatly for a moment before bringing up one hand slowly.

Rei was so confused he didn't even move when that hand took him about the wrist of one guarding arm.

And then he was literally flying.

10 yards into the air Lennon sent him with what looked to have been a casual, pulling throw. Rei yelled as he spun, trying to deduce which way was up and which was down. In seconds gravity took hold of him, and he felt a pull in his gut as he started to plummet.

As it turned out, hitting the ground from a 3-story drop was a quick way to recoup one's bearing.

Even if one left said ground as cracked asphalt and dirt, only to return to find it had turned to solid stone.

THUD.

Had he been any regular person, Rei was pretty sure he would have broken most of the bones on the left side of his body, his shoulder and hip being the two parts of him that struck first. Instead—while the landing certainly wasn't painless—he was turning himself over and shoving up to his feet with nothing more than a couple grunted curses, blinking around. The last of the dirty grey sky of the Deserted Settlement was fading, the final hint of color vanishing from the edge of the field. Dark smoke swirled through the air to join a smoke-choked sky, and only a few feet away a wide river of bubbling magma flowed by at a terrifyingly languid pace. Lennon had sent them to the Volcanic Slopes.

Lennon.

Rei whirled, intent to search the choking smoke of the zone for his opponent. He didn't have to look around long, because the minute he turned he found a hand splayed wide as it came at him, reaching for his face. With a thrill of alarm Rei felt his neuroline going into overdrive again, and the fragile rock cracked under his feet as he lanced sideways, away from the Lasher and out of his dangerous reach. Lennon didn't pause, following him with surgical precision, but he'd slowed his movements down substantially.

In favor of going full-bore on the power, Rei realized, finally sure of what was happening. Lennon wasn't training him on how to fight just any opponent, today. He was training him on how to fight a *stronger* opponent, one that could potentially outclass him in every way.

Despite the reduction in his speed, the Lasher wasn't moving at an easy pace. 5 more minutes of dodging and dancing past, then 10, then 15, the field changing again and again and again around them. Despite his best effort, Rei got caught no less than thrice more, and sent sailing just as high and far every time. It was a terrifying experience with every repetition, and a solid reminder that a single mistake was all it could take to end a fight against an enemy with the right amount of power behind their blows.

Plus, when the actual flight didn't nail that awareness in for Rei, the landings—consecutively suspiciously close to lava, broken brick walls, and the long drop of snow-swept ledges—certainly did.

"Okay! Break!"

Rei was so taken aback when the Lasher called for a pause that kept dodging backwards for a full 2 seconds before he realized the boy wasn't following. Coming to a sharp halt that ripped carpet up from the battle-torn hall of the Hostel variation they'd ended up in, Rei kept Shido up before him warily at first, suspecting another surprise attack as he fought to catch his breath.

"Recall your CAD, Ward," Lennon assured him with a snort, his NOED live. "We're taking a rest."

Sure enough, the field was already vanishing under their feet, the walls and floor of the hotel fading to drop them down to black plating as the training chamber reappeared around them.

"Al-Already?" Rei wheezed, dropping his hands. Not that he wasn't grateful for the reprieve after a half hour of high-intensity action, but he also didn't understand.

A half hour gone meant a half hour less of the precious day Lennon was offering him.

The Lasher, on the other hand, gave him a strange look, like Rei had said something weird. From out in the hall there came the buzzing of another drone, and this time a bot zipped into the room carrying several chilled bottles of water.

as he lanced sideways, away from the Lasher and out of his dangerous reach. Lennon didn't pause, following him with surgical precision, but he'd slowed his movements down substantially.

In favor of going full-bore on the power, Rei realized, finally sure of what was happening. Lennon wasn't training him on how to fight just any opponent, today. He was training him on how to fight a *stronger* opponent, one that could potentially outclass him in every way.

Despite the reduction in his speed, the Lasher wasn't moving at an easy pace. 5 more minutes of dodging and dancing past, then 10, then 15, the field changing again and again and again around them. Despite his best effort, Rei got caught no less than thrice more, and sent sailing just as high and far every time. It was a terrifying experience with every repetition, and a solid reminder that a single mistake was all it could take to end a fight against an enemy with the right amount of power behind their blows.

Plus, when the actual flight didn't nail that awareness in for Rei, the landings—consecutively suspiciously close to lava, broken brick walls, and the long drop of snow-swept ledges—certainly did.

"Okay! Break!"

Rei was so taken aback when the Lasher called for a pause that kept dodging backwards for a full 2 seconds before he realized the boy wasn't following. Coming to a sharp halt that ripped carpet up from the battle-torn hall of the Hostel variation they'd ended up in, Rei kept Shido up before him warily at first, suspecting another surprise attack as he fought to catch his breath.

"Recall your CAD, Ward," Lennon assured him with a snort, his NOED live. "We're taking a rest."

Sure enough, the field was already vanishing under their feet, the walls and floor of the hotel fading to drop them down to black plating as the training chamber reappeared around them.

"Al-Already?" Rei wheezed, dropping his hands. Not that he wasn't grateful for the reprieve after a half hour of high-intensity action, but he also didn't understand.

A half hour gone meant a half hour less of the precious day Lennon was offering him.

The Lasher, on the other hand, gave him a strange look, like Rei had said something weird. From out in the hall there came the buzzing of another drone, and this time a bot zipped into the room carrying several chilled bottles of water.

blows Lennon had delivered. The Lasher himself was standing some 10 feet up the way, watching with an approving air, arms crossed.

"All right," he said after a moment. "Now let's see how you do against strength."

Then he took a step forward.

Rei's arms snapped up, expecting the shredding wind of a second Break Step, but Lennon just approached at near-normal pace, like he was doing nothing more than taking a casual stroll through the buildings projected all around them. When he reached Rei, he stopped, looking at him flatly for a moment before bringing up one hand slowly.

Rei was so confused he didn't even move when that hand took him about the wrist of one guarding arm.

And then he was literally flying.

10 yards into the air Lennon sent him with what looked to have been a casual, pulling throw. Rei yelled as he spun, trying to deduce which way was up and which was down. In seconds gravity took hold of him, and he felt a pull in his gut as he started to plummet.

As it turned out, hitting the ground from a 3-story drop was a quick way to recoup one's bearing.

Even if one left said ground as cracked asphalt and dirt, only to return to find it had turned to solid stone.

THUD.

Had he been any regular person, Rei was pretty sure he would have broken most of the bones on the left side of his body, his shoulder and hip being the two parts of him that struck first. Instead—while the landing certainly wasn't painless—he was turning himself over and shoving up to his feet with nothing more than a couple grunted curses, blinking around. The last of the dirty grey sky of the Deserted Settlement was fading, the final hint of color vanishing from the edge of the field. Dark smoke swirled through the air to join a smoke-choked sky, and only a few feet away a wide river of bubbling magma flowed by at a terrifyingly languid pace. Lennon had sent them to the Volcanic Slopes.

Lennon.

Rei whirled, intent to search the choking smoke of the zone for his opponent. He didn't have to look around long, because the minute he turned he found a hand splayed wide as it came at him, reaching for his face. With a thrill of alarm Rei felt his neuroline going into overdrive again, and the fragile rock cracked under his feet own thoughts.

Rei blinked and the boy was gone from his place halfway up the hill. Almost in the same instant he felt a hand shove into his back, and he was suddenly hurtling down the slope, fighting not to fall. In the end he caved in, diving forward and tucking, twisting to snap him back onto his feet at the ready. This time he held his ground, waiting for the attack.

It came head-on in the form of a frontward kick, catching him in his defending forearms with enough force to send him reeling back once again.

Despite this, Lennon didn't seem displeased.

"Good!" he said again. "Good adjustment! When someone is faster, you don't try to outpace them. You don't try to escape. You stand and fight. Forcing yourself to stay on the move will only lend itself to a faster loss."

Picking up what was happening, now, Rei went with his gut, dropping the next time an open palm struck him below the neck. He rolled backwards before shoving off the ground with his hands in a modified spring to land deliberately hard, digging Shido's clawed steel toes into the dirt for purchase as he dipped into a half-crouch, keeping his body low. Another blow came at his shoulders, but this time Rei went with it, giving in a single tucked step back that didn't allow Lennon to throw him off balance again.

"Now we're talking!" the young man shouted, and Rei thought he saw the flash of white teeth that might have been a smile, accompanying a pulse of the Lasher's NOED. "Let's see how well you keep up, shall we?"

And then the field began to change, and the Lasher became a blur.

A Cliffs variation lifted them into the air, and for an untold count Rei hunkered down, blocking where he could but always giving to the direction of whatever attack came, absorbing most of the impact with a step or two back and never allowing himself to be robbed of his footing. He barely saw his instructor in those long minutes, barely made out more than a streaking shape of black skin mixed with the red-on-blue of his combat suit. He didn't need to *see* Lennon, though, to take in the lesson.

One had to be able to adapt, but there were times when standing firm was the only decision to be made.

After two more field changes and maybe 10 more minutes—in which Rei's leg's started to burn from the constant adjustment—the barrage of shoves and pokes and prods finally ceased. He was left reeling a little across the dusty road of a Deserted Settlement, breathing in gasps of air that still made his chest hurt from the initial

Rei paused, then. The way Lennon had asked the question, it seemed that *this* was the place he had been meant to get to.

"Because it's considerate?" he said after a moment, not sure where the third year was going.

"And when has your opponent on the field ever been considerate, Ward?"

In a flash Lennon was gone from his place some yards away, appearing before Rei so fast he might have teleported were it not for the rippling blast of air that accompanied the Break Step. The A-Ranker didn't hit him, this time, but he did take hold of Rei's two arms and pull them apart with such ease they might have been stalks of wheat.

Then he put a foot into Rei's chest with deft agility, and shoved.

There was only enough force to send him stumbling back several feet, but Rei still couldn't keep up his defense while his arms wind-milled to try to keep his balance. Lennon followed him like a shadow, pushing and prodding every second or so to stop him from finding his footing.

"When has your opponent ever been considerate?" he asked again even as he continued to press Rei. "Do you think the combatants you've watched on the feeds pause when they see an opening? Do you think pros are kind enough to wait until a fight is on even ground again?"

A finger shoved at Rei's right shoulder, sending him back two paces before a palm pushed on his chest, keeping him stumbling without so much as a chance to settle.

"I looked up who you're fighting, Ward. If I had to guess, I would say you're outclassed in five out of six specs, and most of them by head and shoulders. You're opponent isn't just strong, either. He's talented, and he adapts to whatever field he's put in. If you want a *prayer* of taking him on, then you'll need to adapt, too. You'll need to adapt to the fact that you're facing a guy who has every advantage on you as you are right now."

There was a flash of light in the Lasher's eyes, and abruptly the field took form. It wasn't the usual Neutral Zone though, and Rei felt a foot catch in a sudden swell of grass as it materialized under his backpedaling foot. With a yelp he spilled backwards, but managed to tuck into a roll that had him landing in a crouch. Taking the opportunity, he tried to spring sideways as the sloping incline of a Grasslands variation bloomed into being around him, swallowing the chamber they'd been standing in with the bright blue sky of the zone.

Trying to escape Christopher Lennon, though, was like trying to outrun your

"Already?" Lennon repeated, almost amused as he reached out to accept a drink. "30 minutes of non-stop anaerobic fighting, Ward. That's what we just did."

"Y-You usually keep us going non-stop..." Rei argued, still not having caught his wind when the drone floated over to him. Recalling Shido, he took his own water and cracked the bottle, immediately gulping half its contents down before speaking again.

"I guess—" he had to pause, gasping in a breath "—I guess I just thought you meant 'no breaks' when you said we wouldn't leave here till curfew."

He might have imagined it, but he suspected he caught Lennon rolling his eyes then, bringing his own drink down from his lips. "There's something to be said to endless perseverance, Ward, but there's a point at which it becomes being bullheaded. Pacing. Without pacing, training can become counterproductive, as you should damn well know. This isn't a 2 hour, once-weekly crash course. We're here all day. How do you think your fight Tuesday would have fared if I let you step into the ring in the same shape you were on Friday?"

Rei's ears went hot, recalling the way the Lasher had put him down with his eyes closed.

"Not great," he admitted, taking another swig.

"No, probably not," Lennon agreed, capping his bottle and tossing it beyond the edge of the ring. "Which is a polite way of me saying you would have made an embarrassment of yourself, even *if* you'd reached C4."

With no means by which to refute this, Rei could only nod silently as he imitated his instructor. His bottle landed with a *thunk* by the door to roll until it hit the wall below his hanging bag.

"I just... I didn't think I had the time," he said after a moment as the Lasher pulled first one arm across his body, then the other, loosening his shoulders and back as he looked to get ready to go for a second round. "I don't think you get it. This match—"

"No. I definitely *don't* get it," Lennon interrupted him, shaking his wrists out now. "I've never been in your position, Ward. No one has. We don't have the luxury of being able to time—even roughly—how close we are to ranking up." He paused, giving Rei a scrutinizing look. "But I *have* had matches I wanted to win more than anything in the world. Some of which I ended up losing, by the way. So if you have a fight that you're willing to train more than 10 hours a day to prepare for, I can get on that ride with you for a bit."

Rei grinned, and was about to voice his thanks when his frame popped up unbidden across his vision.

...

Processing combat information.

...

Calculating.

...

Results:

Strength: Lacking

Endurance: Severely Lacking

Speed: Severely Lacking

Cognition: Severely Lacking

Offense: Lacking

Defense: Severely Lacking

Growth: Not Applicable

...

Checking combat data acquisition.

...

Adequate data acquirement met.

Device initiating adjustments to:

Defense.

...

Processing.

...

Adjustment complete.

Defense has been upgraded from Rank D6 to D7.

...

Rei sucked in a breath, then let it out in a hiss.

"What?" Lennon asked, sounding almost interested. "What is it?"

"Defense upgrade," Rei told him. "D7."

Lennon frowned at that. "Only Defense? No Speed? Or Cognition?"

Rei shook his head. "Speed and Cognition are my best specs. They take more time than the others."

"Which tells me they're in a higher tier," the third year said with narrowed eyes. "You need to be more careful about saying stuff like that, Ward. You never know how people might piece things together over time."

Reprimanded, Rei averted his gaze and nodded. "Yes, sir. Sorry, sir."

After a moment more of watching him, Lennon relaxed, then gestured at the empty field.

"Ready to go again?"

Rei grinned, looking up again. "Yes, sir. Just say the—"

WHAM!

For the third time, the Lasher's fist took him in the gut, blindingly fast, and as Rei double over for the third time to retch, some sick part of his mind wondered why he had bothered packing lunch.

They weren't 4 hours into training before Rei understood why Lennon was so adamant about their frequent rests and recoveries. For the first 3 he hadn't been so much impatient as merely eager to absorb more, to take in all he could from the A-Ranker. He'd pressed for shorter breaks, asked if they could keep going a while longer. The Lasher hadn't indulged him a single time, to the point where Rei had finally stopped asking.

At the end of hour 4, he knew for a fact he wouldn't be doing so again.

"All right, break."

Rei staggered back, the sloshing of the Sunset Beach shallows about his shins fading with the dematerialization of the field. As soon as Shido's heels touched down on the projection plating he dropped to the ground, recalling the Device weakly to fall back and lay with his eyes closed against the coolness of the steel. It felt wonderful, biting through his sweat-dampened combat suit and soaked hair. For a time he just lay there, his heart hammering uncomfortably in his chest while the room felt to be spinning around him.

There was a light *thump* next to his ear, and Rei opened his eyes to find Lennon had deposited a fresh bottle of water beside him, the drone he hadn't even heard being summoned already zipping out of the chamber again.

"Drink," the third year commanded, his own forehead actually beaded with perspiration for once. "Then tell me if you get an upgrade."

Rei pushed himself up with a grunt onto his elbows, half-rolling to pick up the water. Cracking it, he guzzled most of it down once more in one go.

Unfortunately, even after pausing for a little while after that to wait, he had only bad news to report.

"Nothing," he got out between heavy breaths, fighting the urge to clench his teeth in frustration. "Nothing again."

He supposed he shouldn't have been completely surprised. He might have notched up his Defense in the first hour, but it had been a while since that particular spec had ranked, so there wasn't too much astonishing there. It was still disheartening, though, suffering the throbbing ache of effort in every muscle and bone in his body, but feeling like he had jack to show for it. They were already approaching noon, and he didn't sense he was that much closer to C4 than he had been that morning.

Was it all going to be for nothing, in the end?

"Too bad. No worries, though. We'll get there."

Lennon's nonchalant response took Rei aback, and he looked around at the third year, unsure if he'd made himself clear.

"I've only ranked a single spec," he stated more deliberately. "Tied for my lowest one. If this keeps up—"

"It won't," Lennon assured him, something like a knowing smile playing at this lips. "You spent half the week in training already. You've started the race. Our job now is just to push you as far and hard as we can in the hours we have left."

"You haven't been doing that?" Rei huffed.

He had intended the question to be rhetorical, even intended for it to be a little bit audacious, but Lennon looked at him with such pitying amusement in that moment that he immediately felt a fool for putting the idea out into the world.

"No, Ward," the boy said slowly. "Not even close." He pointed at the half-empty bottle of water. "Finish that up. We're starting again in a minute. We're going to try to get your Speed and Cognition up. Hopefully both."

Feeling some nervous excitement, Rei did as he was ordered, downing the rest of the drink before tossing it to join the other empty bottles by the wall. It was a testament to how much he was sweating that they'd only taken one bathroom break all morning, but that was the least of his worries as he shoved himself to his feet. He watched Lennon carefully, this time, always keeping one eye on his instructor's movements, particularly in the moments he might otherwise have been caught by surprise. The Lasher always moved too fast for him to dodge, but he *had* managed to block the last three or four ambushes, keeping himself from getting gut-punched again.

Lennon appeared to take note of his vigilance, because he offered a nod of approval while he pulled his NOED up. For the first time, he summoned the field *before* they got to fighting, and Rei was on high alert the moment ragged walls of jagged stone started to rise all around him, curving over his head as the ground beneath his feet became sandy and the ceiling above shifted into the grey, rumbling sky of a coming storm.

Sure enough, as the Arena made its announcement, Rei felt the first drops of rain against the bare skin of his scared shoulders.

"Field: Canyons."

"Call," Rei said at once, not waiting to be told anymore. In a second Shido was around his limbs again, and he was pleased to feel his heart settle into a normal rhythm. He'd been hoping to see a notch up in his Endurance already, but he couldn't pretend he wasn't happy with the difference in his ability to recover compared to the days when combat team practice would see him recovering on the bench afterwards for a half hour, usually with Viv pretending she needed a rest too, just so he wouldn't be sitting around on his own.

He smiled a little at the memory, but didn't take his eyes off the ravine in front of him. Canyons was a maze of a field—sometimes literally, depending on the variation. Only 6 feet across, the narrow gorge Rei stood in extended before and behind him before curving away to the right and left respectively, with a half-dozen turnoffs he could see cutting into the stone walls in every direction. He was going to have to be wary, especially since he didn't know what Lennon was planning to—

"Good," a voice from behind him said. "It pays to be watchful."

With a tingle of shock Rei dove into a forward roll. He wasn't sure what made him do it, but instinct took over, and rightfully so as something he didn't see screamed through the air exactly where his body would have been not a moment before. He came up sandy, the dirt and grit of the field sticking to him as the rain began to fall a little harder, wetting the ground. When he spun around, though, there was nothing.

Not even footprints in the earth.

"Oh f—!" Rei started to say, understanding dawning, but at that moment the cleaving sound of air rang from his left, and he lunged backwards, dodging desperately.

Dodging, and just in time to keep from being rent vertically in two by a coiling length of familiar black steel accented with red light.

"ARE YOU KIDDING ME?" Rei screamed to the air as the chain-sword—absent its owner—snaked away in a flash down another corridor, vanishing from sight again.

He might have been mistaken, but he thought he heard a laugh from above him, on top of the canyon cliffs.

For 2 hours the dexterity training continued like that, with Lennon only showing his face during breaks, and even then just long enough to toss Rei more water from the cliffs above, where he'd obviously set up camp. Had he had the mind for it, Rei might have been astounded by the A-Ranker's ability to keep Invisible Hand engaged for so long, even staggered between attacks.

As it was, all he personally had the mental energy for was keeping on his toes and fighting not to keel over from exhaustion every time he got a reprieve.

The first couple of attacks, it transpired, had been warm-ups. Warning shots across the bow. After that they'd come not only faster and harder, but more frequently, until Rei was simultaneously working to dodge the deadly steel *and* sprint through the labyrinth of the ravines, trying desperately not to get trapped *between* the two chain-swords. The weapons were slithering through the gorges like monsters guarding some grand treasure within its center depths, and as the rain came steadily harder it become more and more difficult to hear them or see them coming. In the beginning, avoiding the blades had required quick thinking and good reflexes.

By the time the 2 hours had passed, dodging demanded every ounce of focus, forethought, and prediction Rei could afford himself.

He didn't always succeed, and the explosive pain of being caught by either of the blades—wielded by a User with at *least* A-Rank Offense—had been enough to nearly send him spinning into the black on five different occasions. Still, Rei didn't complain. He had no right to complain. Hadn't he just been concerned about the first part of their training, had wanted more to be done as the race pressed on with the risk of leaving him in the dust? Lennon had certainly risen to his hopes, because every bout left him staggering and wincing, sometimes putting a shoulder into the nearest wall to help get himself to the ground without collapsing. Every time Rei thought he'd had enough, Shido was there to get him back on his feet, refreshing his limbs and steadying his breathing even in the brief 2 or 3 minutes of respite he was allowed. It reminded him of why he was there in the first place, reminded him of Valera Dent's words.

You need to get stronger.

In the end, he wasn't disappointed.

...

Processing combat information.

...

Calculating.

...

Results:
Strength: Lacking
Endurance: Severely Lacking
Speed: Severely Lacking
Cognition: Severely Lacking
Offense: Not Applicable
Defense: Severely Lacking
Growth: Not Applicable

...

Checking combat data acquisition.

...

Adequate data acquirement met.
Device initiating adjustments to:
Endurance. Cognition.

...

Processing.

...

Adjustment complete.
Endurance has been upgraded from Rank D6 to D7.
Cognition has been upgraded from Rank C1 to C2.

On his hands and knees in the now rained-soaked ground, Rei almost choked out a laugh reading "*Offense: Not Applicable*". It was true, he realized. Not a single time over the last couple of hours had he taken a swipe at anything, given there was no real enemy to strike at. He suspected he would find the image of himself running around like a rat in a deadly cage amusing later, but for the moment he could only be grateful.

Endurance and Cognition now. Three specs in 6 hours. They could do it. They *would* do it.

But would it be enough?

"Anything?"

With his hands still in the sandy mud Rei looked up and around, into the storm. He could barely make out Lennon squatting at the edge of the cliff atop the wall opposite him, the A-Ranker's expression inscrutable through the rain.

Rei nodded. "Endurance and Cognition," he called up as best he could, shoving himself over to sit with his back against the stone. Under the overhang, he was spared the worst of the downpour.

"Still no Speed, though?"

Rei frowned. "No. Why?"

Thump.

Lennon took the 30-foot drop like he wasn't doing more than hopping off the last step of a staircase, barely needing to crouch to absorb the impact of the fall. Kicking wet sand off his bare legs from where it had splashed up over his shin, the young man approached until he, too, was in the relative dryness of the outcropping.

"Speed is your strongest spec."

The words came as a statement, rather than any kind of question.

Still, Rei gave the third year a blank look. "You *just* warned me about giving away too much information."

Lennon made a face. "I'm not asking you to confirm, Ward. It's obvious to anyone who has any solid experience in CAD-fighting. You've been leaning into it in almost every fight you've won, including the one against Catchwick earlier this week."

Rei felt a twinge of guilt at being reminded. "Fine," he admitted. "Sure. Let's assume Speed is my strongest spec. All the more reason to up my others, isn't it? Speed will handle itself."

"Not if you don't make it," Lennon said with a shake of his head, rainwater dripping from his grey dreads. "As for upping the others, that's all well and good, but being a User with no weaknesses is the same as being a User with no strengths."

"I have strengths," Rei countered.

"Yes. You do. Which is precisely my point. Your Speed is your highest spec, closely followed by Cognition, I'm assuming. They've been key to you so far, haven't they?"

Rei thought to be dismissive—feeling like he was getting lectured a lot, lately— but suppressed the urge.

Honestly, getting lectured on improvement by *Christopher Lennon* was something he'd never dreamed of having the opportunity to experience.

"… Yeah," he admitted finally. "So you think I should lean into it, is what you're saying?"

"Until your Device decides otherwise, you're basically a Brawler, Ward. You've got no reach, you've got low Endurance, and your Defense is probably nothing impressive either. But what you *do* have is mobility. Agility… *Versatility*." He enunciated this last word deliberately, making sure Rei was following. "You've seen my Ouroboros. You think I leaned away from heavy defense plating because I enjoy getting skewered through the gut?" He shook his head. "My Device's maneuverability is its strength. I'd argue it's its *only* strength, down to the design of my weapons to my externals to my Abilities, Echo aside." He pointed a finger at Shido's bands around Rei's wrists. "Your CAD is high Speed, high Cognition, and damage dealing. You're unpredictable on the field, and talented, which makes you a lethal combo of adaptability. But you've got to embrace that to make it work."

"So more Speed?"

Lennon nodded. "More Speed."

As it turned out, the Canyons' conditions had *not* been the extent of what Lennon could put him through, once they decided on the focus of the next part of the training. After a quick lunch that Rei was pretty sure he was going to lose later anyway, the Lasher summoned up a flat, Neutral Zone for them.

Then he'd called on Ouroboros, and again set the twin chain-swords to swinging.

It was a different kind of conditioning now, though, Rei realized soon enough. Whereas among the ravines and ridges of the Canyons he had had to be constantly on edge and ever-vigilant, in the open air of the Neutral Zone he could allow himself to be less proactive in his assessment of where the strikes would come from, and more deliberately *reactive*. The segmented weapons rolled and roiled together through the air, a blinding mess of dark steel and burning vysetrium, but Rei could *see* them now, watch their movements and respond accordingly. His neuroline still whined in overdrive, a constant, uncomfortable buzzing in the back of his head and down his spine, arms, and legs, but his NOED, too, came into play now. Without an opponent with a body to read—Lennon circled the field opposite him, almost always more than 15 yards away from his CAD—Rei found himself absent much of his usual instinct and insight. The neuro-optical became a lifesaver quickly, its red highlights sometimes the only thing that forewarned of an incoming attack from the swirling Device.

Fortunately, it was more often than not all Rei needed.

In an avoiding dance with similarities to the agility-training Michael Bretz sometimes put them through, Rei never stopped moving during the repeated 30 minute bouts the Lasher kept him on. Had he paused for even a moment he knew he would have been caught by the segmented steel, and that would have been game over once again. As it was, he lost limbs more than once, a particularly unfortunate circumstance to find himself in when one leg or the other got cut off from his nervous system, bringing him crashing down to the floor at once.

When it was a hand or arm that got cleaved into, though, Rei shoved the agony away into the dark part of his mind and just kept dancing.

1 hour. Then 2. 3 came and went, closing in on 4. It was well into the afternoon, in fact, when Rei staggered to one knee after Lennon had called for yet another break, dropping down to the fading field even as he wondered if he would be able to get back up again.

Not 30 seconds later, while he crouched there struggling to overcome a bout of lightheadedness, commitment flooded back with the wave of text that claimed his vision.

...

Processing combat information.

...

Calculating.

...

Results:
Strength: Lacking
Endurance: Severely Lacking
Speed: Severely Lacking
Cognition: Severely Lacking
Offense: Not Applicable
Defense: Severely Lacking
Growth: Not Applicable

...

Checking combat data acquisition.

...

Adequate data acquirement met.

Device initiating adjustments to:

Speed.

...

Processing.

...

Adjustment complete.

Speed has been upgraded from Rank C2 to C3.

"Score," Rei wheezed at the projection plating beneath him, spotted with drops of sweat, as the upgrade notification faded away.

"What was that?"

Rei managed to lift his head, his grin probably more of a pained grimace when he found Lennon standing over him, ready to hand off the usual bottle of water.

"Speed," he answered simply, not trusting himself to say much more when he lifted an arm to accept the drink gratefully, the entire limb shaking with exhaustion. "Made it."

Lennon offered him a rare smile, then. "Nice. Were gonna take a longer rest now, then. Half-hour."

Rei started, the clenching of his hand at this statement almost blowing the cap of the water as he forgot to control his Strength.

"W-What? No!" He tried to stand as he protested, but only ended up staggering a step sideways before falling back down again. Just the same, he didn't look away from Lennon. "I-I'm close! I'm so, *so* close!"

"I know." Lennon's expression was strange as he answered, somewhere between impressed and sympathetic. "Four specs in ten hours. Unbelievable. I've got to say, Ward, you're definitely something special, and I don't just mean your CAD."

"But then why... why rest?" Rei actually had to blink several times as stars bloomed in his vision. "We're almost... there."

In answer, Lennon looked at him flatly for a moment.

Then, taking a step forward, he put a single finger on Rei's sweat-slicked forehead—the touch cool from having held the chilled water bottle—and shoved lazily.

Rei tried to get an arm out to catch himself, but his elbow and shoulder both gave rather than accept his weight. He crumpled backwards, reactive shielding absorbing what would have been a nasty bump on the head as he hit the floor. His vision spun and he groaned, but when he tried to roll back onto his side, intending to prop himself up, he found himself unable to move.

After a second of confusion, he realized that might have had something to do with the foot planted firmly on his chest, pinning him to the ground.

"Clearly you didn't hear me," Lennon said pleasantly, leaning over an elbow pressed into his raised knee, holding Rei down even more firmly. "You just ranked four specs *in ten hours*, Ward. Ten hours of straight training."

"Wasn't straight," Rei mumbled. "And I've been doing ten hours all week."

"Not with me, you haven't. Laurent is an impressive User, Ward, but are you really going to try to tell me she's as challenging a training partner as I am?"

Rei was pretty sure his silence gave voice to the obvious answer enough.

"Yeah," Lennon snorted. "Didn't think so." He let off Rei's chest. "You're going to lie there, and you're not going to bitch or moan for a half hour. Is that clear?"

Rei nodded, feeling his eyelids droop. With the Lasher's permission had come an overwhelming, staggering fatigue. "Don't think that'll be a problem," he muttered.

It wasn't more than a minute before he was out.

CHAPTER 54

When Rei came too, he knew instinctively that he'd been asleep for way, *way* more than the 30 minutes allotted to him. With a jolt he sat up straight, wincing as sore muscles and abused flesh protested the abrupt movement, but he didn't care as he checked the time.

1800.

Rei felt nauseous, and it had nothing to do with ripping out of sleep in a panic. 2 hours. 2 of the precious hours he'd already been struggling to take advantage of had slipped by him. He was angry, all of a sudden, angry at his stupidity, angry at his weakness.

Angry at the third year sitting by the door of the room far to his left, looking to be catching up on the day's messages on his NOED as he typed in the air with one hand.

In a flash Rei was on his feet. "Lennon, what the hell?!" he demanded. "Why didn't you wake me?!"

"Because you needed the rest," the Lasher answered simply, barely even glancing at him through his frame. "You passed out, and given you stayed that way on a *solid steel floor*, I decided you needed a little more of a break."

"But we only have four hours left!" Rei had to keep from raising his voice more than might have been forgivable. "What if we don't make it? What if *I* don't make it?!"

He couldn't believe it. He honestly couldn't believe it. It was true that his body felt largely recovered, but pain was nothing, fatigue was nothing. He could have pushed through those—*would* have pushed through those. Lennon, though, had left him to laze around, sleeping away the day.

"You're going to make it."

Once again the calmness of the answer took Rei aback, and the retort he'd had ready caught on his lips. Lennon was getting to his feet, having just closed his frame, using the wall at his back to leverage himself up. Once standing, he adjusted the seam of his combat suit around his neck while he approached Rei.

Approached, then passed him, heading for the other side of the field.

"How do you know?" Rei finally managed to get out between clenched teeth. "I cut my week's training hours short for this day, Lennon. If I'd known you were going to—"

"I suggest you not comment on who is more inconvenienced at the moment, Ward," the third year called back without looking around. "If you'd rather I not be here so you can get on with sparring with your friends until you keel over, be my guest."

That shut Rei up, and he suddenly felt less than gracious.

"Sorry," he muttered as loudly as he could. "I appreciate your help. More than you know. But if we aren't going to take advantage of—"

"You were ready to pass out. You were literally falling over, and—if you'll believe me—just short of going cross-eyed when you crashed. I told you we wouldn't leave here until you made it or we ran out of time. By that I meant I would do everything in my ability to get you there, *including* making the call on when you've had enough."

Lennon reached the other side of the field and turned around, taking Rei in critically with his arms by his sides.

"You're a monster, Ward. In more ways than one. But I don't care if you got gifted all the potential and drive of a *god*. Right now you're still a C3-Ranked User who just spent ten hours training under the wing of an A."

Rei sobered a little, not sure if he'd just been complimented for his pluck, and called out for being foolhardy.

Deciding it was probably a bit of both, he nodded apologetically. "Sorry," he said again. "I know you've given up your whole day for this. And I know you've done everything you can to help me. I genuinely can't thank you enough. I'm just—"

"No I haven't."

Rei fumbled to a stop.

"What?" he asked after a moment.

"I haven't done everything I can," Lennon clarified, like this should have been perfectly obvious. "I've been doing a lot, sure. I've been pushing you, shoving you to your limits and beyond them. But that's hardly all there is to do." He smiled, then, and for the first time all day the look was back in his eyes, the hungry, feral intelligence that had had Rei and the others take pause on more than one occasion during their training sessions. "Correct me if I'm wrong, Ward… You typically grow the most from direct combat. Is that right?"

Something clawed at Rei's gut at the question, a mix of feelings that took him a moment to parse out. There was excitement, there. Hope, too.

Excitement. Hope… and fear.

"Yes, sir," he answered slowly, carefully.

That predatory glint was still alive in Lennon's gaze. "Thought so. Tell me, then… Did you learn something today? About me? About my Device?"

Suspicion joined the cacophony of other feelings, the knot of anticipation in his stomach tightening.

Rei nodded. "A bit."

"How I move? How my weapons move?"

Rei was sure, then. All morning. All afternoon.

"Sir… Did we just spend ten hours warming up?" he asked.

Lennon's smile widened. "I wouldn't say 'warming up'? Seems benign… Maybe 'leveling the field a little'?" He raised an eyebrow at Rei. "So? What did you learn?"

This time Rei answered promptly. "That I might have a shot at hitting you if you were fighting at half-speed."

The Lasher snorted. "Ward, you couldn't touch me at *quarter*-speed."

"Will I be allowed to try?"

Rei let the hope rage, then, the excitement and desire burn away the fear and trepidation. He saw it, now. 2 hours of learning how the Lasher moved on open ground. 4 of seeing how he attacked when he held the element of surprise, and another 4 to take in how he applied his chain-swords in face-to-face combat. It had all been a warm-up.

A warm-up to *this*.

"Yes," Christopher Lennon, very possibly the strongest military cadet in the Astra System, said simply. "After some build up."

And then Lennon's eyes flared with light.

Rei's stomach did a flip as the field bloomed with shapes, pressing up under his bare feet to lift the yard or so the training chambers allowed for. The first thing to materialize were old, rusted structural beams, growing skyward and curving overhead as they did. Between them, heavy metal slats, worn by time and the elements, built themselves up until Rei and Lennon were standing in a sort of dome with eight arching walls, illuminated mostly only by a circular 4-foot opening at the apex above them. A rolling door to their left was askew, having fallen partially off its tracks, letting a few more rays of light in to cut through dust-choked air. Under Rei, the plain, flat concrete floor was caked with dirt and some kind of grainy residue.

Salt storage, he realized, just as the Arena spoke.

"Field: Abandoned Depot."

Rei swallowed, his original excitement getting weighed down a little bit as the voice solidified his understanding of what was about to happen. Across from him—apparently having to adjust the starting spaces to accommodate where Rei had already been standing—the Lasher waited, still with his arms lax at his sides, still with his white teeth cutting clear against the darker skin of his face as he smiled. There wasn't any anticipation there, per se, but there might have been interest.

And that interest was enough of a compliment to get Rei to steel himself as the next announcement made it all very, very real.

"Sparring bout," said the Arena. "Cadet Christopher Lennon versus Cadet Reidon Ward. Cadets... Call."

Rei forced himself not to hesitate.

"Call."

Shido came into being once more, the compressing weight of its steel comforting around his arms and legs. Rei's heartbeat quickened as he brought the Device's claws up to his face at the ready.

It redoubled again when he saw that Lennon, too, had called on his CAD.

There had been no holding back on the summoning, none of the restraint of a partial call. Where a slight, soft-looking third year cadet had been waiting before, a beast of black-and-grey lined in glimmering red now stood, the trio of glowing crimson strokes down the faceplate of his helmet like three vertical, hungry eyes. The armor of the Device might still have been wanting when it came to intimidation, but Ouroboros made up for it in the relative dark of the Abandoned Depot. Its light was nothing short of sinister among the shadows, especially where the red pulsed from the undersides of the three externals that hovered behind Lennon's back and shoulders.

And that wasn't even to mention where it shimmered between the razored segments of the two chain-swords the Lasher now held in either hand, their terrifying lengths coiled limply about the ground before him.

Rei decided, in that moment, that he wouldn't bother counting how many times he was about to die.

"Cadets... Fight."

Rei didn't let Lennon take control of the field. If he'd wanted to, the Lasher could have blitzed him in a blink and sent him flying into next year with his own natural speed. A fight like that would have been worthless, though—for *all* involved—so as he lunged forward Rei was a little relieved to see the third year standing his ground, waiting for him.

Pleased, that is, until he actually reached the Lasher.

Shing!

Rei had to go almost to his knees as a blinding flash from his opponent's right weapon cleaved through the air in a whipping horizontal arc. As soon as it passed overhead, though, the left was cutting down, forcing Rei to roll sideways out of the way. Shido's steel toes gave him purchase as he kept his feet, lancing forward even as the chain-sword struck the concrete ground right where he'd been standing, creating an eruption of fractured cement and a small cloud of dust.

Like a bomb going off, Rei thought as he closed in, supposing it was an apt-enough metaphor.

Shido shot forward, swiping at the Lasher's left arm, but the third year proved less than dependent on his usual agility as he twisted and dodged the blow gracefully only by millimeters, leaping laterally to put some space between the two of them. Rei felt his boots scrape roughly against ground as he shifted direction abruptly to follow, intent on keeping at better range. As he chased he found himself again in rhythm with the chain-swords, his Cognition and Speed pulling him just out of death's reach with every one of Ouroboros' strikes.

"That's it!" came Lennon's voice, mechanical through his visor. "Don't bother trying to block. Who knows if you'll be able to Tuesday? What do you lean into?"

"Speed," Rei muttered in answer, powering forward. He somersaulted under a low blow at his legs, landing in a crouch to avoid another that would have taken off his head. He cut at Lennon's own knees, but the young man kept careful pace with him, always staying just out of reach.

"Exactly. So keep up."

And with that, ever so subtly, the chain-swords began to move a little faster.

At first Rei felt a thrill of panic as he adjusted almost too slowly for the shift. What had been inches of clearance turned into *an* inch as he darted and weaved through the assault, ever pushing forward to try to get through. His eyes followed every blare of red in his NOED, reading every preemptive twitch of the Lasher's body. He was almost close enough to strike out again, almost to where he would be able to—

WHAM-CLANG!

The first impact precluded the second by so little time, they felt practically simultaneous. Rei had let himself get drawn in, let himself get so focused on Ouroboros' rolling song that he'd not kept an eye on the broader fight as a whole. The steel-clad leg had come up seemingly from nowhere, catching him a sweeping kick through the hips as he made to dodge sideways, rocketing him backwards.

Straight into the rusted metal slats of the slanted wall that he'd somehow missed being maneuvered against.

He fell to the ground with a *thump*, ears ringing from the impact that the reactive shielding hadn't completely been able to absorb. He tried to catch himself, but tumbled downward when he failed to get his hands out in time to brace himself. He landed on his side hard, his neuroline whirring to clear his mind.

"Get up, Ward."

The words were gentle, but unforgiving. Rei blinked once, coming back to, his vision clearing. With a grunt of effort he rolled onto his stomach and lurched to his feet, staggering for only a second before he found his balance.

Lennon stood 10 feet away, weapons calm on the floor again, waiting for him to regain the fight.

"Do you need a second to—?"

Rei, though, cut the A-Ranker off with a lunge at his throat.

He might have been mistaken, but he thought he heard a low "Ha" of laughter as Lennon dodged. Rei sailed by, turning the attack into a diving roll to keep from getting cut in half from behind as he made out the sharp sounds of clinking metal that told him the chain-swords were whirling into action at his back. Almost as soon as he hit the ground he was up, spinning and launching himself at Lennon again. This time he kept his assault tighter, depending on the short strikes and jabs they'd been working on so frequently over the last weeks.

"Excellent! Stay inside your range, but don't commit to over-extension! That's how you do it!"

Of course, not a single blow landed even with the Lasher going at a fraction of his usual speed, but the confirmation of improvement was welcome just the same. Rei redoubled his attacks, keeping low so as best to react to Ouroboros' unpredictability.

"Good adaptation! Good adjustment!"

Another kick came, testing him this time, and *this* blow Rei felt comfortable trying to block. He twisted and accepted impact on both forearms, then wrenched his claws down in an attempt to cut into the offending shin, but not fast enough before Lennon retracted the leg with a twist. Unwilling to be left disappointed, Rei bent low and swung his own kick at his opponent's knee. Lennon—deft as always—planted and shifted so that Rei's ankle took him in the front of the joint instead, sending a jarring shock from toes to hip as steel struck steel. He recovered by throwing an elbow at Lennon's face, but the third year jerked back.

That was when Rei knew he'd lost.

The twisting elbow brought him too far around, left him unable to defend himself. In such close proximity to a User who typically fought better at range, this might have been acceptable given Rei himself was basically a Brawler, might have been recoverable.

But then Lennon powered forward from his lean back, slamming his steel faceplate into the side of Rei's head.

Again Rei saw stars, staggering sideways, trying to catch himself. The filthy ground betrayed him, one foot slipping against dust and salt residue, bringing him to a knee. His vision cleared faster this time, steadying as he caught himself on a hand and made to twist around, looking to join the fight again. Lennon, though, seemed to have decided Rei only got *one* free pass in the match.

A free pass he'd already cashed in.

Shtunk-shtunk!

Pain bloomed through Rei's chest and abdomen, swallowing with it any breath he might have drawn to scream. With an "Urk!" his whole body spasmed, and he collapsed fully to his side again.

There was a wrenching pressure in his torso, echoed by a new bloom of agony, and he watched the twin chain-swords sliding across the ground away from him, recalled from where they'd taken him—point first—through lung and gut.

"Fatal Damage Accrued," the Arena announced. "Winner: Christopher Lennon."

At once the pain began to recede, and after a second Rei was able to gasp in a massive, aching breath. He twitched and jerked a while longer, but eventually his mind cleared enough to find himself looking at a pair of black steel boots.

"Not bad, Ward. Changing things up like that will be exactly how you win on Tuesday. Let me know when you're ready to go again."

Lennon's feet had only started to turn, likely aiming for the starting point again, when Rei choked out a word.

"Now."

The third year paused in his departure.

"Now?" he repeated.

The pain had receded enough for Rei to turn his head and look up, meeting the three vertical red lines of the monstrous face.

"Now," he said again, starting to push himself up on aching arms.

Sixteen times. In the end Rei wasn't able to stop himself from tracking his deaths. It became easier to do than trying to keep tabs on the time as he fought the Lasher, exchanging their breaks for the less-lengthy—but also more-frequent—reprieves the Arena forced him to take after every FDA. Sixteen times he fell, and sixteen times he crawled back up again. He didn't know how many hours had passed, didn't know how long they'd been facing off in the Abandoned Depot. The field was scarred, now, broken and battered by the passing storm of their fighting. Lennon had been opting not to reset it after every match, like he wanted Rei to have a visual representation of their efforts. The walls were dented and cleaved through, the ground a jagged mess of fractured cement and the occasional clawing slashes where Shido had cut into it in low swings. Rei was aware, distantly, that he had more than likely already hit C4. If he paused, if he just took long enough a break for his Device to register him as out of combat, he was almost positive he would get the upgrade notification.

He didn't pause, though.

Sixteen times. Sixteen times he died, but each one was a bit further apart, required a bit more effort from Lennon to achieve. They always restarted the match at a speed Rei supposed probably matched his own, but every minute or two the Lasher would accelerate just a fraction, just a little. Once, twice, three times. After his fifth death Rei managed to read the third year well enough to earn a fourth upping in the Ouroboros' terrifying whirling, and after his twelfth he reached a fifth. At that point, though, there was nothing much for him to do but survive the onslaught, dancing and dodging and twisting this way and that as he struggled to find his shot, fought for even the slimmest possibility of that elusive blow he so desired to land.

It was no good, of course.

He just didn't have the reach.

Shlunk!

With a retching nausea Rei felt himself get cut in half when a chain-sword caught him just above the waist, cleaving him into two. His entire body spasmed as the incomprehensible pain of the simulated death erupted upwards from the wound, lighting his every nerve on fire. He went down in a mess of spasming limbs, what little leg function he might have managed through the torment robbed by neural interruption as his spine was severed. He didn't even feel himself hitting the ground, landing with a heavy *thump* that kicked more dust and grit into the dimly lit air.

"Fatal Damage Accrued," the Arena announced. "Winner: Christopher Lennon."

Seventeen, Rei thought to himself, staring unseeing at the far wall as he gasped in air, feeling sensation slowly return to his lower limbs. *Seventeen deaths, and no closer.*

He just didn't have the reach.

"Keep going like this and I'm going to have to start going full-speed on you."

Lennon's legs appeared in his vision again, and with a groan Rei managed to roll onto his back to give the third year a lopsided smirk. "Bull." He winced as his abdominals—still suffering much of the simulated pain involved in being split wide—protested him speaking.

After allowing himself a couple seconds more, Rei tried again, ignoring the lessening discomfort this time.

"Bull," he repeated. "Forget full-speed. I haven't even matched you at *quarter* speed yet. Just like you said."

"How do you know?"

"It's obvious to anyone who has any solid experience in CAD-fighting," Rei threw the A-Ranker's words back at him with a snort, trying to sit up. Just barely managing it, he tested his legs out, bending his hips, knees, and ankles, pleased to find them all mostly working. "Plus, I've seen you fight."

Lennon shrugged. "If you know everything there is to about me, then why haven't you hit me yet?"

Rei's wince, this time, had nothing to do with pain.

"I can't," he grumbled, finally starting to climb to his feet when the tingling along his shins and toes started to fade. "I don't have the range."

"You've got claws. You've got more reach than most Brawlers."

"Being able to run faster than *most* people doesn't make me any more likely to outrun a horse, does it?"

Lennon's helmet dipped at that. "Point made. Still… You'll figure it out. You're a quick thinker."

"If I could think my way out of this, you expect that in the—" he checked the time at last, his heart sinking a bit "—*fifteen hours* we've been here, I would have come up with a way to lay a finger on you, don't you?"

Lennon shrugged again, the motion a little comical, clad in steel armor as he was with his face hidden and a chain-sword in each hand. "In that case I'd say not all problems can be overcome with brains alone. Isn't that why we're here in the first place?"

"Yeah," Rei grunted, looking down at Shido's claws somewhat wistfully. "If I evolve, I just want a little more reach. That's it. Just enough that I'm not so completely dependent on getting nose to nose with my opponents."

"You're probably there already," Lennon voiced the same assessment. "Want to wait and find out?"

Rei hesitated. He did want to, but…

"No." He shook his head. "Not yet. I've still got more to give. The last time I had a fight with this level of discrepancy in CADs was Commencement, against Aria. My Device Ranked in nearly every spec."

"And you want to eke out everything you can, while you can," the Lasher summarized.

"*Everything*, yeah," Rei echoed in agreement.

The black-and-red helmet tilted into a brief nod again. "Then get back to your starting ring. You've got one more hour of my time, Ward. Make it count."

Two times. In most of that last hour, Rei only allowed himself to be taken down a mere two times, and then only because exhaustion started to truly weigh at him. He was grateful, by that point, for the rest the Lasher had forced him to take. He saw again his own bullheadedness, his own foolish drive to run himself into the ground. As it was his arms and legs were screaming with every motion, every block and attack and step and dodge. Rei grit his teeth through it, unwilling to be brought down now, to fall in the final stretch. He didn't just want C4, anymore. He'd reached that, he was sure. 4 hours of live combat with Christopher Lennon would have put him over that edge and then some. But he wanted more, now. Rei was reminded of that every time he got just a little closer to putting a scratch into Ouroboros' dark armor, fighting there in the Abandoned Depot they were steadily destroying around them. He wanted what "the Lasher" had. He wanted what the most terrifying User he'd ever stepped onto the field with wielded. He wanted that, and more.

Then again, that was why Shido had been given to him, hadn't it?

Because he'd always wanted that.

In a blur that melted black with red the chain-sword in Lennon's right snapped at Rei's face. He sprung into a half-backflip to avoid the blow, pulling his legs off the ground in time to keep from having both ankles severed by a lower cut by the offending weapon's twin. Ignoring the protest of his elbows and shoulders, Rei accepted the weight of his body on his hands and twisted face-down, then shoved off again to drive both feet at Lennon's head. The third year dodged casually, having accelerated *six* times now, his speed once more no longer anything Rei had a chance of beating.

Didn't mean he wasn't going to try.

With a whipping of his arms and torso Rei turned the arching drop kick into a drill-like whirl of elbows and razored claws as he passed the Lasher. Again the blows were avoided with almost-serpentine fluidity, but Rei landed in a crouch on his opponent's far side even as he drove a fist into the already-broken cement beside him, sending an eruption of stone and dust into Lennon's face, who let the shrapnel pelt off his reactive shielding with a hundred tiny ripples of distortion, like rain drops on the surface of a still lake. Rei lanced forward all the same, hoping to have at least earned himself enough of a distraction to close the distance between the two of them.

Once again, however, he couldn't get close enough.

PING!

His lead-through ricocheted clean off the roiling shield of steel and vysetrium that came into being in a 2-foot radius around Lennon's body, the whipping chain-swords as absolute as a wall to Rei at the rate they were moving. With a curse he lunged sideways, hoping to get around his opponent's back, but the third year stepped in synch with him so that it felt less like he was running and more like the room was merely spinning about the two of them while they stood in place. There was a flash of shifting light in the dervish of sharpened metal, and Rei planted with a *crunch* of cracking cement underfoot, stopping himself just in time to keep from getting skewered by the chain-sword that broke formation to lance outwards, straight as a spear, exactly where he would have been had he kept moving. Seeing a chance with half of Ouroboros' weaponry suddenly separate from the whirling defensive barrier, Rei didn't hesitate, driving an arm into the storm of razored steel.

His claws were still 6 inches from Lennon's face when the limb got caught in the maelstrom, black steel cleaving through Shido's plating into flesh and bone just above his elbow, wrenching it up and back as the pain of the wound tore into Rei's shoulder, neck, and chest.

Then Ouroboros exploded outward, the paired weapons broadening in their circling sweeps just wide enough to catch Rei a dozen different ways from as many direction.

When he fell, this time, it was straight back, and even through the agony of the defeat Rei knew that—had the Lasher's blades been anything but phantom-called—he would have struck the ground to scatter into a hundred bloody pieces over the broken mess of the field.

"Fatal Damage Accrued," the Arena announced. "Winner: Christopher Lennon."

Twenty, Rei thought to himself as the pain faded little by little from what parts of his shoulders, chest, and head he could still feel at all. It seemed an appropriate number, somehow. 4 hours. Twenty deaths.

"All right, that's enough."

Lennon's voice was clear as he spoke, and when Rei managed to regain adequate control of the muscles of his neck to lift his head from the ground, he found the A-Ranker approaching him once again in his combat suit, Ouroboros having returned to its black-and-grey bands around his wrists, gleaming with the wicked red of their vysetrium jewels.

"That's time, Ward." The Lasher's assertion was almost gentle, like he was worried Rei wouldn't be able to accept the fact that they practically hadn't left their training chamber for 16 hours, now. "That's enough."

Rei, though, had no words left to fight with. He was so tired he was pretty sure he might have been able to fall asleep right then and there once again, atop the shattered remnants of what *had* been a clean concrete floor. He had nothing left, no energy remaining to protest with as he looked to the corner of his vision to see the time there.

2145.

He almost smiled. Lennon had let him fight to the very last. At this rate, he'd be lucky to make it back to Kanes before curfew.

It only added to the gratitude.

"Thank you," he managed to wheeze out, looking up at the ceiling of the Abandoned Depot that was still projected above them. "For this. For everything. I know you didn't have to."

Lennon's face appeared once more above him, then, framed against the light of the circular opening overhead like a ringing halo. "Maybe not, but I get the feeling it will be worth it, one day."

"How so?"

"Don't worry about it." The third years lips were a tight, flat line, and his icy eyes drifted down to Shido's black-and-blue over the white underlayer. "So... Now what? We just wait?"

"Think so," Rei said with a huffing laugh, wincing when the action lanced a spasm of pain through his abused torso. When the ache of it subsided, he wheezed out one word to mark a true end to the fight.

"Recall."

His arms and legs *thumped* in unison to the scarred cement as his Device retracted back into its rings, leaving him feeling somewhat naked after having kept it live for so long. Following his lead, Lennon's NOED flared briefly, and the Depot started to depixilate from the top down, the wall and support beams fading into nothing, revealing the stark-white of the training chamber ceiling once again, accented with its bright lines of solar lights. After a few seconds Rei felt the ground, too, dematerialize, and then he was settling down to the steel of the projection plating. It felt good, soothing and cool.

And yet it did nothing to quiet his anticipation.

His heart was refusing to calm. He tried breathing slowly, tried steadying himself as he lay there, not positive if he wasn't capable of sitting up or just unwilling. Nothing helped, and the lingering thrum of his pulse in his chest started to feel unpleasant. He was reminded of the moments before his larger surgeries, the seconds of shaking fear looking up into the light while doctors he didn't know leaned over him to place the mask about his face. In silence he lay with that, not sure of what to expect.

And then, just as Lennon started opening his mouth to ask if anything had happened, Rei's frame lit up with activity.

He read the scrolling text as it came, devouring the lines of script hungrily.

His moment of unpleasant memory was swept away as he took in the data, elation sweeping through him with every character. Strength, up. Endurance, up. Speed, Cognition, Defense, Offense. All up. His eyes continued to trace the information, growing wider and wider.

Until, that is, he reached the final lines of the notification, where a new alert was writing itself into being.

For a long, long time Rei could only stare, not comprehending. Whether due to fatigue or just genuine shock, his mind seemed to be refusing to understand, refusing to process. Slowly, still rereading those final sentences, Rei at last brought himself up to sit, not seeing anything but the alert before him.

"Rei, what is it?"

Rei was so engrossed, he didn't notice Lennon had once again slipped into using his first name. The third year had squatted down beside him, elbows on his knees, and if he'd had any attention for it Rei might have been fascinated at the genuine excitement that lit up the normally placid face.

As it was, there wasn't an ounce of focus for anything else, in that moment.

"I-I…" he started to try to explain, but found himself unable to manage it. "I can't… I don't…"

"Did you make it? C4? Did you evolve?"

Rei struggled to register the questions, still reeling. Eventually he managed to nod, and would later regret missing the moment of celebration on his behalf that was Christopher Lennon giving the air the smallest of fist-pumps.

"*And?*" the third year pressed immediately following this. "What else? You look like your CAD just jumped you straight to King-Class!"

Rei shook his head slowly, still staring.

After a few more seconds of shocked silence, however, he just barely got the words out.

"New Ability Assigned…" he read out loud.

"*Yes!*"

The Lasher's exclamation, so strangely unlike his usual composure, was at last enough to jolt Rei out of some of his stunned paralysis. He blinked and looked around unsteadily to find the A-Ranker peering at his eyes with a broad grin, like he was trying to read the miniscule script that would have been written backwards for him across Rei's iris.

"I told you. I *told* you!" He sounded ecstatic, about as excited for Rei as Rei supposed he should have been feeling for himself. "What is it? Arsenal Shift?! Tell me it's Arsenal Shift!"

For a little longer, Rei could only stare at Lennon, once again unsure of how to answer.

In the end, he decided his astonishment couldn't be expressed in words, and so he did the only thing left to him.

With a few slow eye commands Rei took a screenshot of the notification. He had the sense to crop the image down to just the lowest lines, those announcing the upgrade to C4 and evolution, along with the source of his disbelief. With a shaky swipe of one hand, he sent it over, and Lennon blinked as the picture popped onto his frame, his face lighting up once he realized what it was. Immediately he started reading, tracing the script swiftly.

And then he, too, reached the bottom lines, and the widening of his blue eyes told Rei he wouldn't get the answer he wanted even as he asked the question.

"Lennon... What the hell is that?"

It took a moment for the third year to respond, the astonishment marring his usually-steady expression. When he spoke, his voice was hoarse with shock.

"No idea. But I get the feeling you'll be needing to talk to your friend Catchwick again before Tuesday..."

CHAPTER 55

"As far as we are from the front lines, it had been a long, long time since anything riled up the top echelons of Earth's highest officers with half that amount of excitement and—to a certain extent—fear..."

General Shira Abel

Private Journals

In the years to come, Sergeant Major Cassidy Maran would wonder if she'd been blessed or cursed by the MIND to have been on duty that evening.

It was the graveyard shift, and even Central Command's main hub—usually a bustling hive of activity any time other than the two or three hours on either side of midnight—was empty and dead. Usually Cassidy didn't mind this, as it allowed her to catch up on work she might otherwise have neglected. The shift was a formality more than anything anyway, an assurance that a pair of eyes were on the outputs of the massive super computers that oversaw the million different facets of the ISCM's hundreds of branches across seven systems and the front lines beyond Sirius. She *was* a User—if a lowly C9—but this was by tradition more than anything else. There wasn't a force in the universe that would have tried fighting their way through the massive complex that was Central's main hub to reach where she sat now, amid a hundred flickering screens and dim lights which lined the multi-level seating of the large room.

Still, it was the very fact that she *was* a User that would have Cassidy waking up some of the most important officers in the world that night.

Blowing on her second mug of coffee of the evening, Cassidy was returning to her seat of choice when it happened. Intent as she was to file some paperwork for the warrant officer promotion she'd be angling towards for some months, now, she almost missed the blinking orange in a far section of the darkened room, the illumination that occurred when one of the monitors on the desks came alive to displaying a non-emergency high-priority notification. Catching sight of the light, though, Cassidy frowned and started towards it, squinting at the great letters in bronze that labeled the section against the shadowed white wall along the top of the three-tiered rows.

Astra.

That put a little pep in Cassidy's step, though she was careful not to spill her coffee as she hurried over.

While not as consistent about it as the Sol System itself, the Astra System was well known for producing a plethora of solid Users for the ISCM every year. It was small wonder, of course, with schools like the Galens Institute and Ellison Academy within its orbit. It was for this reason that Cassidy approached the screen in question with some expectancy, even ducking under the great hanging projection devices in the center of the room as opposed to going around them.

Despite the screens all being clear smart-glass, they still only displayed one way in order to keep information limited to the intended recipient. This forced Cassidy to climb the half-dozen steps to the higher row, then slip along behind the tucked-in chairs to the station in question. Reaching it, she leaned down with interest to read the few short lines of bright blue text, boxed in a large, blinking orange frame, her eye falling first on the bold words that topped the alert.

"Priority Case," she muttered to herself. "Ward, Reidon. C4."

Then her gaze dropped to the rest of the notification, and Cassidy didn't even notice as her mug of coffee slipped from her hand to shatter with a splash of hot liquid across the desk and screen.

She was gone in an instant, NOED already live to call the Central directory. She was halfway to the door of the room when the line picked up.

"Operator," a young man's voice on the other side answered. "State your identification and—"

"Sergeant Major Maran!" Cassidy was practically yelling as she took the steps up to the exit two at a time. It opened for her as she crested the stairs. "ID: Charlie-Charlie-Echo-77-89-0! I need you to wake up General Shira Abel! *Now!*"

She was out, then, the entrance closing behind her silently. As the doors to the central hub sealed shut, the automatic lights of the room dimmed at once, plunging the space into near total darkness.

Below the large bronze letters of the Astra observations section, though, the single screen still lit up with bright blue text inside the blinking orange alert frame.

Priority Case: Ward, Reidon. C4.
User-Unique Ability Assigned.

CHAPTER 56

"Do not be afraid; our fate

Cannot be taken from us; it is a gift."

Inferno
Dante Alighieri

From her seated place in the Arena stands beside Viv and Catcher, Aria only pretended to watch Jack Benaly prove himself once more as a terror on the field. She hadn't even registered who his opponent was, and in the state she was in had neither the interest nor the attention to spare to peer down and figure it out.

She, like Viv on her left, was waiting for the next match to start with disquiet trepidation.

It had been a bizarre last 36 hours, to say the least. All of Sunday she'd been on pins and needles, trying and failing to study between meals and the extra training the three of them had still put themselves through, even going to West Center for once to avoid the temptation to look in on how Rei's day with Lennon was going in East. As morning turned into afternoon, then into evening, they'd all watched Rei's profile on the ISCM database like hawks, waiting and hoping. It had been very nearly 2200 at night, approaching curfew, when they saw his CAD Rank tick up to C4, and the three of them had whooped with victory before gathering in the living area of Suite 304, ready to celebrate as soon as he got back.

When Rei did, though, it was bearing an expression akin to having been struck by lightning.

That's when things had started to get worrisome.

Hardly managing to offer Aria and Viv a smile, Rei had pulled Catcher into his room, where the two boys had stayed locked up for a good 20 minutes before the blond Saber stepped out again looking pale. He'd explained to the girls that Rei was beyond exhausted, and was sorry he couldn't say good night, which had stung, but been understandable. The next morning, however, neither of the boys had joined them for breakfast, with Rei also conspicuously absent from early classes. Not one of their instructors, though, had so much as blinked at his nonattendance, which had Aria suspecting something big was going on. Viv had been in agreement, and they'd messaged him, together and separately. When they received no answer, they did the same to Catcher, who replied only that everything was fine, and they would both understand soon enough.

Hardly appeased, Aria had sat quietly while Viv made lunch hell for the Saber when he joined them—without Rei once again—interrogating Catcher about everything from the confusion of the night before to the bags under his eyes.

"I'm sorry," he'd only said over and over again, sounding worn down. "I can't tell you more. Right now, I can't tell you more."

Needless to say, the meal had ended up being a sour affair, with the girl's paired farewells a little more venomous than might have been called for as they'd headed for the Arena.

Reached the subbasement, they'd been unsurprised to find Rei missing from their usual row of lockers. With a further exchange of worried looks, the two of them had decided they would head to the campus hospital after afternoon training, thinking maybe he'd had gotten himself injured, or that perhaps the intense Sunday of sparring had triggered some kind of aggressive relapse of his fibro he might be trying to hide from them. With a course of action set, Aria and Viv had felt a bit better as they'd made for the subbasement gym, ready to distract themselves—and maybe vent a little of their shared frustration—by pummeling whichever poor unfortunates they would be paired off with in the day's scheduled cross-training.

They'd been taken utterly aback, therefore, after entering the Wargames area only to find Rei already there, dressed in regulars as he stood off to one far side, speaking quietly with none other than Valera Dent.

It had become apparent to Aria, then and there, that something worthy of alarm was definitely—*definitely*—going on. Not only did Rei himself look hardly less pale than he had the day before, but the Iron Bishop was leaning in intently as she spoke. The exchange in fact, looked more like an interrogation than any sort of typical conversation, because Rei kept either nodding or shaking his head, only very occasionally opening his mouth to give a fuller answer to some question or another.

It was after nearly a minute more of this, when Dent had turned and started waving someone over from where 1-A had gathered as always around Field 3, that

Rei caught sight of Aria and Viv watching him intensely.

It was like he hadn't expected them to be there, as surprised as he seemed. He'd blinked and opened his mouth, clearly considering saying something, then shut it again as he thought better of it. The three of them had stared at each other for a time, at a loss as to how to interact in the moment, but then the person the captain had summoned broke from the crowd at a jog, and Aria's confusion had only redoubled.

Claire de Soto, the Saber sub-instructor.

Not sure what to think of this odd group, Aria and Viv had watched together as Dent pulled de Soto in close to whisper something in the lieutenant's ear. The more the Bishop had said, the more de Soto went rigid. Eventually the captain had pulled away again, and Aria might have imagined the unsteadiness in the nod and salute the Saber gave.

And then, with a word to Rei, de Soto had started leading him towards the exit of the subbasement gym.

That was when Aria hadn't been able to hold herself back anymore.

"Rei!" she'd called after the two of them, hating the hint of desperation and fear in her voice.

He'd paused, then, looking around at her at last. For a second they locked eyes, and she saw—strangely enough—those same emotions playing out across his feature, and much more. Desperation and fear, yes, but also confusion, excitement.

Hope.

It had taken her by such surprise that she only half saw him turn away to follow the lieutenant, who'd called out for him to attend her. Aria had stared after the pair as they disappeared, standing beside a muttering Viv, only left more at a loss.

A few seconds later, though, a message had pinged her NOED, and seeing Rei's name attached to it she'd opened it so quickly her whole head jerked in the direction of the icon.

Gag order.

The words had made Aria choke. Viv, too, had made a sound very much the same, making her realize the girl must have received the same message.

"*Gag* order?" Viv had barely managed to keep her voice to a low hiss of disbelief as the last of their class jogged into the gym around them from the hall. "Are you *shitting* me?"

Aria, though, had had no words to say to that, her mind awhirl once again. Rei hadn't been injured. He hadn't been sick. He'd hit C4 the night before, when he'd been hoping for Shido to evolve…

"Something happened," she'd whispered. "With Shido. Something had to have happened."

"You *think?*" Viv had grunted, then looked immediately sorry at her misplaced annoyance. Aria, though, hadn't noticed.

She'd been too busy staring as a second message pinged her.

If I told you anything, I'd end up telling you everything.

With a glance at Viv's lightless eyes Aria had realized that *these* words, this time, had been for her, and her alone. It had been a strange feeling, though not altogether unpleasant. It had quieted some of the fear, tempered it enough to let her tell Viv they should join the others. It had helped her sleep that night, assisted her in keeping the peace as Viv had once again ripped into Catcher about what was going on at breakfast and lunch the next day, and even allowed her to focus a little on her schoolwork even with Rei still absent from every class.

Now, though—as she, Viv, and Catcher all sat together in their typical seats in the stands of the Arena proper—even Rei's last message wasn't enough to keep her nervous anxiety at bay.

"Catcher," she started quietly, cutting across Viv's bad-tempered grumbling as below them Benaly won his match with a savage headlock and several driving punches straight into his opponent's skull, "you can't tell us anything? Anything at all?"

Two seats to her left, Catcher stiffened, then turned to glare at her. Gone was his usual pep and good humor. Gone was the amiable personality and energy. The boy looked exhausted, as he had for the better part of the last 2 days, his blond hair disheveled and his uniform less than crisp. This contrast was as alarming as anything else that had happened over the previous 36 hours, and Aria knew her concern had to be plain on her face when Catcher's own expression softened a little after he caught her eye.

"Nothing, Aria. I'm sorry. Just watch the match."

Hardly satisfied but knowing she wasn't going to get any other answer, Aria sat back again to look down at the Arena. The field Benaly had been fighting on—a variation of Flood Zone—was gone, and the Brawler was in the process of helping his opponent—Amelia von Leef, she realized now—to her feet. Since there were only sixteen fights to be had that day, the matches had started later, so it was from a relatively hearty crowd of spectators that the cheering arose as the pair walked off the field together, Benaly with a fist in the air, von Leef staggering a little while she recovered from the neural scrambling of simulated brain damage.

"Not bad, not *bad*!" It was Sarah Takeshi once again who stood on the observation platform today with Dyrk Reese, her commentary lively and energetic, in direct contrast to how Aria was feeling. "Congratulations to Cadet Benaly on his qualification as the fifteenth of Galens' sixteen individual Sectional combatants! Cadet von Leef, better luck next year!"

"Knew he'd make it," Viv mumbled, and Aria glanced left to see her watching the Brawler disappear beneath the lip of the walkway. "Still not sure how *I* beat him."

"By being better," Catcher answered bluntly. His lack of gusto, so truly unlike him, was genuinely distressing.

All the same, Viv only turned and snapped at the Saber. "You don't speak until you have something *useful* to tell us."

Catcher rolled his eyes. "Watch the match, Viv."

"What do you think it is we're waiting for, exact—?!"

"And now—!" Sarah Takeshi's voice rang out, cutting Viv off, and Aria was only barely aware of the deadening of almost all sound in the Arena as she snapped around to pay attention to the floor again "—our last and final match of the first year bracket of this Intra-School tournament! You know both these combatants well already! One, the lowest-Ranked User to ever set foot in a Galens Institute classroom, having slashed and clawed his way to this opportunity! From the left... Cadet Reidon Ward!"

There was a surprisingly enthusiastic boom of applause as Rei made his appearance, long white hair tied behind his head in a loose tail while he strode with chin held high towards the western edge of the field. Aria thought she made out fewer jeers than usual, and even heard clearly Sense and Kay's shouts of encouragement from somewhere above them. She herself only managed to clap, her throat clenched shut while she watched Rei make for the silver perimeter. Pulling up her NOED, she zoomed in, scrutinizing every inch of him, looking for anything, *anything* that would forewarn her of what she and Viv were being made to wait for. His scared arms and legs revealed nothing, unfortunately, and in the end Aria found her gaze lingering on his face as he came to stand at the expected point, eyes set and jaw clenched.

"He needs a haircut…" she muttered aloud before she could stop herself.

Even had Viv and Catcher *not* both turned slowly to look at her in confusion, then, Aria knew her face would have bloomed crimson at her slip. Fortunately, she was rescued from trying to save herself as Takeshi continued her announcement.

"And from the right, one of your strongest from the very beginning, and User who embodies the very meaning of 'power'… Cadet Logan Grant!"

The applause was louder this time, Aria could tell, but similarly of a mixed bag. As the hulking, black-haired form of the Mauler appeared, it wasn't just Catcher who managed to drum up enough energy to cup his hands about his mouth and boo. There were other catcalls, too, as well as a few shouts of instigation from the gathered first years. Grant, it seemed—whether by his own virtue or that of the unappealing entourage he'd managed to gather about himself—appeared to be growing steadily more popular for all the wrong reasons.

To his crediting, the massive boy didn't grace his hecklers with so much as a glance around at the stands, his eyes set straight ahead, his attention focused. The cheering and jeering alike had settled on its own by the time he'd reached the eastern point of the perimeter opposite Rei, and quiet descended even as Grant turned to face the field.

"They *both* need haircuts…"

As strained as it was, Aria couldn't help but smile hearing Viv's mumbled whisper, obviously intended for her alone. She didn't look around, but did reach out to seek her friends hand. Finding it between their seats, she slipped her fingers into Viv's, and felt the anxious pressure she gave them returned in trembling fashion.

There was more involved in this fight than even a smug bastard like Dyrk Reese probably knew…

It was as she considered this that the major himself stepped forward on the hovering platform, replacing Captain Takeshi at its head. In that steady, unflinching voice of a man well-versed in hiding satisfaction, Reese looked down on his two charges a moment before speaking.

"Combatants, take position."

Neither of the boys hesitated, stepping over the silver line before them to reach their red starting circles in near unison. Not once, still, had either looked away from the other.

"This is gonna be a bloodbath," someone hissed from off to Aria's right, but she couldn't be bothered to turn around and glare at the offending voice as the moment approached. Still clinging to Viv's hand, she waited.

"This is as an official Duel," came the arbiter's speech. "It will therefore be subject to regulation ruling. Once the field is formed you will be ordered to call, then engage. Premature Device manifestation will result in a penalty. Premature approach, attack, or the like will result in a match loss. Understood?"

The silence of the stands was so absolute, Aria could almost believe she could *hear* Rei and Grant nod in unison. There were another few seconds of nothing, and then finally Reese's eyes lit up.

At once, the field began to rise.

And rose white.

"Son of a *bitch*," Aria heard Viv curse. Catcher looked around at them in concern, not understanding the outburst of fury, but Aria's own anger bubbled as the starkness of a Neutral Zone variation took form. It started simply enough, the flat light of the ivory, hexagonally-patterned floor starting to lift the two boys from the ground, but as they climbed the distinct factors of the zone started to make themselves known. Some of the tiles ascended slower, and others faster. Uneven dips and rises in the floor began to show, though hardly as obvious as the multitude of plain pillars that took the form of a long, trailing set of stairs to arch around the south side of the field. At once muttering started up from some of the first years—their fellow 1-A classmates, Aria knew—and from below someone who might have been Mateus Selleck could be heard to give a sharp "Ha!" of laughter.

"Field: Neutral Zone," the Arena announced.

"Isn't that the Speed & Agility test field?" Catcher asked from two seats over. "What's up with that? And what's got everyone riled up?"

Viv—apparently forgetting her earlier vow of silence when it came to the boy—answered through gritted teeth. "It's the same field. The *same field*. Reese isn't even trying to hide the manipulation, anymore."

Catcher, understandably hardly enlightened by this, looked around the back of Viv's head to Aria.

"It's the field Grant attacked Rei on," she clarified, having a little trouble keeping her own voice steady. "After the match had ended, during the first quarter."

"Are you *kidding* me?" Catcher hissed, turning to look back to the main floor with fury in his eyes.

Before any of them could say anything else, though, the Arena spoke again, and Aria felt her heart skip a beat.

"Cadet Logan Grant versus Cadet Reidon Ward. Combatants… Call."

From either side of the field there came a whirling of metal and light. About Grant's body his CAD took form in a flash, and it looked to have evolved a second time since Aria had last taken careful note of it, after he'd developed Overclock. The white steel plating of his armor now encased not only both his arms, but also his lower legs, and his axe blade had broadened. It still extended half the length of the weapon's 6-foot haft, but the flat of it now was almost a foot-and-a-half wide, speaking to a truly massive Strength spec. Red vysetrium lined its keen edge, as well as the joints and layers of the armor, giving Grant the look of a standard-bearer holding his flag in both hands in defense of the ivory ground he stood upon. Overall, no one could claim the Mauler wasn't an intimidating presence.

The whispers and shouts of surprise that came at the call, though, weren't for Grant.

"Oh…" Aria heard herself whisper in awe.

In contrast to his opponent, Rei could hardly have stood out more against the colorless backdrop of the Neutral Zone. Shido—originally having covered only both arms and from his knees down—now rose as high as his waist, encasing his hips in black steel that bloomed with blue light. What was more, a black half-mask now shielded the lower part of his face, more vysetrium splitting the thing down the middle, and a loop of white fabric cut around Rei's head, centered with a single curved plate of steel above his eyes.

Despite the fact that he was still a good foot or so shorter than Logan Grant, he nevertheless cut an intimidating air that set more than one spectator to whispering.

Still… That was the measure of the change. As Rei settled into a ready stance, bringing his hands up at the ready, Aria saw the same metal-clad fists, the same black claws glinting in the light. Shido's adaptations were noteworthy, to be sure—what *C-Ranked* User had she ever heard of who sported even the beginnings of a helm?—but if this was the extent of it…

Fortunately for Aria's calmer temperament, Viv seemed to be of the same mind set.

"That's it?" she was already demanding, turning on Catcher with a slow, dangerous care. "I swear, Catcher, if the two of you have put us through the ringer for the last two days over an impressive evolution, I'm gonna—!"

"Viv." The Saber cut her off steadily, meeting first her eye, then Aria's over her shoulder. "Watch. The. Match."

Then there was no option left to them.

"Combatants," the Arena called out. "... Fight."

CHAPTER 57

"Now I am become Death, the destroyer of worlds."

Bhagavad Gita
ancient Hindu scripture, Earth

tanding there opposite Logan Grant on the Neutral Zone, Rei had to work to keep his breathing steady. Shido helped with that. His new mask had proven much more than just a decoration over the last day and half, demonstrating itself invaluable in boosting his body's endurance and recovery by—he assumed— adjusting the percentage of oxygen he took in with every inhalation. It had helped Rei keep his head clear, his thinking sharp and faculties focused as he trained, first with Catcher, then with Claire de Soto following Valera Dent's permission.

He needed all that assistance, now, as anger burned across every inch of his being.

He knew this field. Yes, of course he knew it. He'd been here before, and not just in the Speed & Agility parameter test. Dyrk Reese—or whoever was responsible for pulling the man's strings, now—had even gone through the pain of making sure Rei started on the same *side* of the Neutral Zone variation. To his left was open space, though the floor was uneven due to the offset settling of its hexagonal partitions. To his right, however, was the curving rise of the pillars he'd forced Grant to chase him up, the very ones he'd flung both himself and the Mauler from in an attempt to earn a shot at winning that long-finished fight. It was all meant to shake him, he knew. All meant to get in his head, to bang—loudly—at the walls of his focus.

Reese clearly didn't know him well.

Channeling the anger, Rei aimed it. Spreading his legs and settling down, he brought Shido's claws up before him at the ready, watching Grant do much the same 20 yards from him, on the other side of the field. There had been a few seconds when the CADs had first been called that the Mauler's black-red eyes had widened ever so slightly, speaking of measured surprise on taking in Shido's adaptation, but he hadn't looked away. Only now, for the first time, was Grant's gaze finally shifted to take in their battlefield, settling briefly on the looping steps.

For an instant—but only an instant—Rei was sure he saw the corner of one lip dip down. For that fraction of a second, it was almost like the larger boy was just as irritated by the choice of zones as Rei himself was.

Then, though, the flash of emotion was gone, Grant's eyes flicking instantly back to Rei's as the Arena gave its final command.

"Combatants… Fight."

WOOSH!

It was a testament to Shido's ever-growing speed that Rei could feel the wind through his tied hair as he launched himself forward, catapulting from his starting ring to reach the center of the field in five strides. No longer did he have to hang back and wait for the fight to come to him. No longer did he have to caution himself to patience, to settle for watching and waiting. His Speed was his strength, he knew. He was faster, now—*much* faster.

He was even faster than Logan Grant.

It was only by half a step, but Rei was the one who reached and crossed the midpoint of the field first. He took note of this fact, this confirmation of his superior agility, but kept his attention forward.

Forward, at the arching flash of the great, flat-edge axe that was screaming around at him in a massive horizontal swing.

Rei dropped under the blade, punching at Grant's right thigh. The Mauler twisted in time to avoid the blow and brought the butt of his axe sideways towards Rei's ribs. With a quick side-flip Rei dodged, slamming Shido's claws into the ground to give himself purchase as he landed, kicking out with both feet at a planted shin. Grant might have suffered lower Speed, but his Cognition was par for the fight, proven as he lifted the endangered leg, pulling it back even as he let the heavy blow land. The result was nothing more than a forced step back, which the Mauler made up for by bringing his axe down in the same movement. It was quick counterblow, though, lacking the usual weight behind it, and Rei wrenched his claws clear of the field to twist and fall onto his back, crossing them above his chest. He caught the axe in the guard, and didn't hesitate to kick up a second time, now at the hands, gauntleted in white-and-red, that held firm to the massive haft. Grant was forced to jerk the weapon back to avoid having his fingers broken, and Rei almost split his foot on the retracting blade before he turned the kick laterally, into the flat of the metal. The axe was wrenched sideways, and Grant made an audible grunt of sound as he fought to gain control of it.

It gave Rei the second he needed to pull his legs in sharply, rolling backwards to pop up on his feet again.

As expected, the next attack came without pause.

Rei accepted the kick on his forearms, but the force of it still knocked him back a step. The axe was next, sweeping up diagonally from below, and the leaning dodge he answered with had to be turned into a full sideways cartwheel as Grant followed it up with a spinning backhand at his face. Rei came up swinging, and Grant only barely managed to block the punch on the shaft of his Device, snapping one hand up only just in time to catch the wielding wrist of Rei's other claws as they came forward in response, aiming for his eyes. They strained like that for a moment, locked together as each tried to find the purchase to overpower the other.

Then Grant spoke, growling through gritted teeth.

"Nice mask, Ward. Is it to cover your face when your run away again?"

The question was unexpected, but didn't faze Rei. Ever since Lena Jiang he'd been on the lookout for opponents who might try to shake him with words. Even locked up as he and Grant were in the moment, all he did was smile, making sure it reached his eyes as the two of them glared at one another over their weapons, faces barely 6 inches from each other,

"No. No running today, man."

Then he wrenched his arm free of Grant's fingers, his D8 strength apparently just enough to break the Mauler's grip, and punched again.

It was hardly the same fight they'd had when they'd last met, on this very field. Then, Rei had been tossed around like a plaything, forced to lean on wiles and wit to earn himself even one meager shot at victory, a shot he'd still managed to let slip. Now, though, the months of training were proving themselves worth it, because that first minute of fighting turned soon into a second, then a third, all with little more than a few minor scratches earned by either side.

They were in their fourth minute, Rei suspected, when the tides of the battle started to show anyone any favor.

WHAM!

Grant landed a solid punch to Rei's left shoulder, but he accepted the impetus of the blow to twist with it, kicking up as he did. Rei's plated shin would have caught the Mauler clean in the side, but a quick flinch of Grant's axe sideways got the lower length of the haft partially in the way, absorbing most of the impact. The two of them were both left reeling, though, and it was a second before they came around to face off again, breathing equally heavily.

His Endurance might have made leaps and bounds, but even with the help of his new mask Rei could feel himself starting to tire. He hadn't completely recovered from Sunday's training, and while he'd intended to take the previous day off to recuperate, that had all been thrown out the window with Shido's evolution notification. He'd hardly slept, and what little he *had* managed had been interrupted multiple times each night to notify him that he was expected to meet this officer or that one the next day. Guest. Dent. John Markus. Even old Willem Mayd had requested a half hour with him so that he and Ameena Ashton could go over Shido's changes with a fine-toothed comb, looking for any sign that the shocking development had taken any kind of toll on his system or disease.

They let him leave the hospital with a clean bill of health, but with no more answers as to the incredible nature of the CAD's progress.

CRUNCH! CLANG!

Grant had lunged forward, bringing his axe down with both hands and all the speed he could muster. Rei only barely managed to smash the descending blade aside in time to keep from getting cleaved in two, but he still felt a slight burning in his left shoulder that said he'd gotten clipped by the edge. He returned the favor with a jerk forward of his whole body, smashing the steel plate of his headband into the side of Grant's face. The Mauler staggered only one step sideways, and this time his answering backhand took Rei full in the gut, blasting the wind from him and carrying him right off his feet. He might have been stronger and faster, but Rei couldn't have been more than some 7 or 8 pounds *heavier* then when last they'd faced off.

As a result, the blow sent him flying just as easily as it would have those weeks ago.

THUD!

The rippling sound of his body hitting the field's invisible perimeter was a dull one, the barrier warping slightly to accept him, then rebounding to jettison him back onto the floor. Rei rolled once, desperate to get his bearing back, and found himself finally looking up at the ceiling in time to see Grant's axe cleaving down on him from above once again. He twisted sideways, allowing the blade to *crunch* into the field, accidentally tumbling into a dip in the white floor as he did. Grant had wrenched the axe free by the time Rei got his feet under himself again, however, and the Mauler lanced after him with a horizontal slash that had him leaping backwards and out of the way.

Not good, he thought, seeing Grant's teeth bared in strained focus as the tall boy followed with another arching blow.

Rei could see his momentum leak away. In a flash he'd been pressed out of functional range for Shido's claws, and was now being steadily forced back as the axe came again and again in a blur of white steel and red light. He kept one eye on his footing as he retreated, not wanting to trip over the uneven ground, but mostly he watched for an opportunity to return the fight, to gain back his advantage. He was no good where he was, no good at range.

Unless…

But no. Rei shoved that idea aside. He might have a trick up his sleeve, but it was no ace. Hell, it was more of a joker, and surprise would be his only chance at using it effectively. He wouldn't waste it on the panicked hope of getting a foot back in the door of the match, particularly when Grant had his own trump card yet to tap. They both knew Rei was faster. It was the only reason the Mauler hadn't triggered Overclock from the very beginning. If Rei proved slippery enough to survive the onslaught of the Ability, Grant would have been a sitting duck following its terminus. No… Grant would wait. He would be patient, would work to whittle Rei's lesser Endurance down, just as he was now. With every dodge and parry Rei could feel his energy ebbing, could sense his limit approaching. They had to be almost 5 minutes into the fight, now. If he didn't find a way to finish it, he was going to end up defeated by his own lagging specs.

He needed to think. *Think.*

Easier said than done, when an axe that had to weigh several hundred pounds was cleaving at your head every few seconds.

The two of them managed a quarter circle around the field like that, Rei backpedaling while Grant chased. Every time an opportunity arrived to close the gap between them, it was gone in a blink as the Mauler corrected his stance and approach. After nearly 30 seconds of this Rei even realized that he hadn't yet gleaned a distinct pattern in the boy's assault, nothing he could work off of to adapt to. It almost made him smile.

Grant had clearly done his own studying up since his loss at Aria's hands…

"I thought you weren't running today, Ward!"

The snarled statement came between rolling cuts as the axe slashed down once, then twice with a heavy twist of Grant's body. Rei dodged left, then right, but before he could jump forward to go for an exposed flank Grant was sweeping the air with a steel-booted kick, giving himself the moment he needed to get his weapon back into place.

"There's a difference between running and retreating, Grant," Rei answered, unable to stop himself. "It's called 'tactics'."

"It's called being a coward," came the response, and Rei had to dart back yet again as the blade shrieked diagonally down from above. "And here I was hoping for more from you."

Rei forced himself to keep his trap shut, at that, even if it made it seem like he had no good answer to give. He was already very nearly winded, and talking would only bring on exhaustion faster. He needed to think, needed to focus. He *did* have the one trick, inefficient as it was. He just had to figure out how to apply it. On a neutral field, though, what did he have to use? No loose objects. Barely any variation in the terrain. Hardly any obstacles. All there was were the pillars that made up the steps.

The pillars… and Rei's own body.

With a grimace, an idea started to take shape, and the next chance he had Rei slipped to his right, southward, towards the arch of the stairway.

Grant, expectedly, followed him at once, pushing him across the uneven field in the direction of the pillars. It was to the Mauler's advantage, of course. In an open space like the Neutral Zone, Rei could run him around the perimeter until one of them collapsed. If Grant could pin him against the stairs, though, could trap him in the curve of the zone's one great obstacle, Rei would have nowhere left to go, no exit by which to escape.

The thought didn't shape any additional confidence in a plan Rei suspected was going to suck for him even if it worked to perfection.

Then again, the fact that he timed his first "mistake" exactly right felt like a good start.

As they crossed the midpoint of the field, Rei glanced over his shoulder. It wasn't the first time he'd done so as Grant had beaten him back, but this time he allowed his gaze to linger just a fraction too long on the pillars he was rapidly being forced towards, as though only just realizing his mistake. As expected the scraping sounds of the Mauler's following shifted accordingly, and Rei snapped his attention around again to see Grant launching himself forward with a grunt and a massive sweep of his axe.

"Eyes on the fight, Ward!"

Rei jerked back, lacking the time he needed to dodge the blow completely and absent the Strength and Defense specs he would have required to block the full weight of such an assault. He didn't have to pretend to hiss in pain as the very tip of the axe caught the upper left of his chest, the phantom-called edge slicing through suit and flesh like paper. At once Rei felt a little of the strength drain from his arm, and the notification he'd not been looking forward to flashed in the corner of his vision.

Skeletal muscle damage registered.
Left pectorals major laceration registered. Left pectorals minor severance registered.
Applying appropriate physiological restrictions.

Rei let himself curse out loud as he reeled backwards, only half-bluffing his scramble away from Grant. The Mauler followed with unbridled enthusiasm, knowing he'd landed the first real blow of the match. The win was as good as his to claim, now, and he took full advantage of the momentum gained by Rei's injury. Like the axe weighed no more than a lash Grant used it to drive Rei back and back and back. Another few, smaller blows landed—not all of which had been allowed deliberately— and by the time he stepped into the curve of the arching pillars the combat log along one side of Rei's frame was dense with minor limitations. A cut to the abdomen, to his right thigh, to his left shoulder. A kick to the outside of one hip and the blunt butt end of the axe full in the gut. Rei was well and truly staggering with every step now, only a few yards remaining between him and the stairway.

Come on, he begged silently of no one in particular. *Come on...*

Face skewed up against the pain, Rei struggled a little to follow Grant's assault. The blows came fast and thick, none any slower than the other. The Mauler's own face was slick with sweat, now, strands of his dark hair plastered to his forehead, jaw, and ears. The effort was there, Rei could see, the unwillingness to let this real, lasting chance to see him put down apparent in the strain. Grant still had Overclock up his sleeve, but he wouldn't use it now. Not if he didn't have to. This was the moment, this was the opportunity the Mauler had been looking for nearing 5 months. What sort of things would be said about the fight if he triggered his Ability in the close, when his opponent was already so thoroughly worn down?

At least, that was what Rei was banking on.

With Grant's eagerness, though, also came recklessness. No longer was his focus on his technique, on his form. No longer were his thoughts on doing everything he could to keep Rei from reading him. The win was there, right *there*, and it was time to take it.

It finally brought the patterns—those subtle repetitions in the Mauler's style that Aria had said she'd found—to the forefront of the fight.

There!

Rei saw the moment, saw the chance. As Grant brought his axe back for another massive horizontal sweep, Rei preemptively lunged backwards, sacrificing the last feet he had between him and solid white of the pillars. His back slammed hard against the projection, but he didn't notice as his thoughts screamed in success when Grant leapt after him, chasing his retreat. The axe descended just as intended, cutting from left to right, and it would very well have slashed Rei clean in two.

The jerk forward, though, the luring out of that last baited charge, had brought Grant closer than he'd anticipated to the pillars.

CRACK!

The great blade of the axe struck the physical hologram first, cutting a great, ripping gash out of the light. Rei braced himself, hoping he'd calculated right, but all the same he screamed as the red vysetrium bit deep into his left ribs, slicing a good 4 or 5 inches through his side before grinding to a halt. At once he felt the limitations applied, his left leg going mostly limp and one lung collapsing while pain spread like fire from the injury.

But pain was nothing. Pain, Rei could deal with.

And this fight wasn't done just yet.

With a scraping sound like steel on stone Rei felt Grant start to retract the blade from the solidified light, the shifting of the metal in his side a searing wrench. All the same, even as he hissed in renewed agony Rei brought his left arm up in a spasming jerk to grab hold of the furthest part of the axe's haft he could reach. There was nothing wrong with his grip, so he held on firmly. A little longer. He just needed a little longer. Grant's guard would still be up.

Just a little longer…

"Not a bad fight, Ward."

For the first time all match, Rei had to admit he was well and truly surprised. Through eyes squinted against the pain he looked up to find the Mauler standing with both hands at the very limit of his axe's hilt, smartly just out of reach of Shido's claws. Even with victory just short of a certainty, Grant wasn't taking any chances he didn't need to.

His eyes, though, were on Rei, steady and cool, and there was no smugness in the handsome lines of his face for once, no malingering dislike or disappointment.

If anything, the Mauler looked… satisfied.

"Weren't you—" Rei could only wheeze out a few words at a time with one functioning lung "—just telling me… that you expected… more?"

Grant smirked, then, but only a little as he pulled at the axe again. Rei hissed at the jolt of fire in his side, but held firm, fighting to keep the blade exactly where it was wedged between his ribs, tip still sunk in the stone at his back.

"Let's call it a step in the right direction," the Mauler grunted. "I still think you're a pain in the ass, but I didn't see your back today."

Rei chuckled weakly. "Thanks… for the approval."

A little more. Just a little more.

"Sure," Grant answered, his face growing serious again. "Let's end this now, though."

"Yeah," Rei gasped. "Let's."

And there it was. The moment, the blink in which his words confirmed for Grant what the larger cadet wanted to hear. For less than a breath he relaxed ever so slightly, the match already done in his mind.

That was when Rei lunged.

Despite his injuries—despite the pain and all his limitations—he still had enough speed left in him to get to where he needed to be. He didn't leap for Grant himself, of course. The Mauler's axe was still embedded in his side, preventing Rei from clearing the 4 or 5 feet that separated them. He didn't need to get that far, though. He only needed a foot or two. Just the distance from his left hand—still gripping the haft—to Grant's nearer the end. He made it, too. In a song of searing torment as he jerked his whole body up the length of the blade, he made it, catching the Mauler's right wrist in a grip through which he fed every ounce of strength left to him. Grant started back in surprise, but—instinctively unwilling to let go of the axe as he was, only end up pulling them both a little away from the wall.

It gave Rei the second he needed to voice the vocal command.

"Type Shift," he wheezed, not looking away from Grant's dark eyes. "Mode: Saber."

And with those words, Shido changed.

CHAPTER 58

The transformation was different than the whirling formation of metal and vysetrium that accompanied a standard call. Rather, the adjustments happened in an echoed, rippling wave along the Device's surface that drew first up Rei's limbs towards his heart, then back again. Electromagnetic energy released in shivering arcs of white lightning over his arms and legs as molecules of carbonized steel readjusted. Blue light flickered through the roll of the change. The claws protruding from Rei's knuckles retracted, absorbed into the CAD as it pulsed inward. When the wave came down again, the reclaimed materials reformed, adapted to fit his Ability's new call.

Rather than the close-combat weapons of a Brawler, however, in his right hand Rei was left clenching the hilt of a long, black sword, its curved blade lined with the azure glow of a pure vysetrium edge.

In his left, there was nothing, but each plated finger—still wrapped about Grant's wrist—was suddenly tipped with a wicked talon of the same vibrant blue.

A trio of short lines of script appeared in the combat log, white rather than red, and Rei didn't have to look at it to know what it said.

...

Ability [Type Shift] triggered.

...

CAD [Shido] has applied [Saber] Type-classification.

...

User and Device specifications adjusted.

...

Strength coursed through Rei's body. Over the last few days the first thing he'd always noticed about the transformation as he'd trained with Catcher and Claire de Soto had foremost been his reduction in Speed. Now—immobilized as he was by the axe that was practically cutting him half in two—that hardly struck him.

All he sensed was the power.

Redoubling his grip about Grant's arm, Rei felt the thinner plates of metal under his palm start to give under the pressure, the Mauler's Defense values suddenly no longer adequate to meet Rei's new peak specs of Strength and Offense. Grant's face—originally a white sheet of shock—spasmed in pain, the protest of his compressing bones appearing enough to draw him from his confused disbelief.

Expectedly, the boy didn't hesitate.

"OVERCLOCK!" he bellowed, and immediately ion flames of a crimson sheen bloomed into being along every line of his armor's red vysetrium.

Too late.

SH-SHLUNK!

With twin sickening sounds of metal carving into flesh Rei brought his sword up in a flash. Before Grant could take advantage of his temporary boost of agility and power, Shido had cleaved through both of his arms just below the elbow, severing their function from his body. The Mauler screamed in agony, his grip about the haft of his axe immediately going slack. He lurched back, and even Rei's newfound strength couldn't keep hold of the wrist he'd been clinging to. He let go, promptly falling to his knees under the weight of the massive axe embedded in his side not a few inches from his spine. Before him Grant staggered back several steps, doubling over atop his useless arms. His screaming lessened after a few seconds, first becoming a keening hiss, then sucking, angry huffs.

Then—as the Mauler raised his head again with teeth bared at Rei—something not unlike the savage growl of a wounded animal.

"WARD!"

Rei, in answer, grinned at the boy. With his left hand he held in place the body of the axe, pressing it into him so it wouldn't slip and send him into immediate FDA from blood loss.

With the right, he brought up Shido to point the length of the sword at Grant's face.

"Bring it," he wheezed through his smile.

To his credit, the Mauler did exactly that.

With a ripping lunge forward Grant closed the gap between them in a blink, ignoring his useless arms in favor of launching a spinning kick at the side of Rei's head. The red fire along his leg rippled in the air, and if Rei hadn't whipped Shido back to brace the flat of the sword blade against his shoulder he knew he would have been done for. As it was he barely managed to accept the tremendous force of the blow thanks to his new Strength, angling the sword so that the Mauler's steel boot screamed up its length to go wide over his head. Grant was hardly done, though, and despite his left leg still being midair he leapt up with his right to land the better half of a drop-kick in Rei's chest.

Kneeling as he was already, Rei was thrown back onto his ass, screaming as the impact jarred the massive blade of the axe he was having a hard enough time of holding onto as it was. A fresh wave of agony washed up from where the metal still held firm in his side, almost causing him to drop the weapon, but he pushed through it.

Pain. Pain he could handle.

Grant had managed to roll to his feet again, and his next attack came as a reckless knee straight at Rei's face. Seeing his chance, Rei slashed with Shido rather than trying to block, catching the Mauler in the exposed thigh of his leading leg. Already seeming to have lost all reason to rage, pain, and the boost of his Overclock, Grant didn't seem to notice as he lost this third limb, carrying through so that the steel of his knee ended up connecting with Rei's nose regardless. Reactive shielding could only do so much—this Saber form boasted no higher Defense than Shido's standard Brawler mode—and Rei's head snapped back from the impact, his vision going black for a second. Sheer willpower was all that kept him holding onto the axe in that moment, kept him from slipping and bleeding out, but he managed it, thinking he was lucky not to have been limited by a broken neck by the blow. He made out the sound of a body falling into a heavy heap at his side, could hear Grant's snarling curses while sight returned as a myriad collection of dancing, flashing stars.

Wham!

What felt like a steel-clad foot caught him in the temple in an explosion of light and pain. The power of the blow was almost negligible compared to the knee Rei had just taken to the face, but with no way to brace for it he fell sideways. He managed to keep from splitting himself open further only by giving up his hold on the axe and catching the ground with his left hand, feeling the talons there carve small divots into the floor. The weapon started to slip out of his side, but Rei allowed the bracing elbow to collapse, bringing himself halfway down until the haft rested against the hexagonal paneling, pressing the blade up and back in for him. The choice had his ribs screaming in protest, with more red text flashing in the combat log, but Rei ignored it all. For one thing, all he had to do was survive, no matter what it took.

For another he was still being rained down on with kicks that would rightfully have seen any normal man drilled into the floor.

Grant had lost both arms and his right leg, and yet *still* hadn't given up. He lay now on his side to Rei's right, where he'd collapsed, and was slamming his foot down again and again and again towards head and neck and shoulder—basically any part of Rei he could reach. Ion flames still washed across the Mauler's body—noticeably absent where his function had been severed—and he looked demented behind the sheet of black hair that now plastered his face. Stuck as he was, all Rei could do was bring Shido up again to block the worst of the kicks, accepting a sound four or five of them before finding his chance and slashing outward, catching Grant's one still-useful leg below the knee. Shido's blue-black blade bit deep into steel and flesh, but didn't sever the limb, and the Mauler only snarled louder when he wrenched himself free to attack again, foot now flopping with every strike. Another two blows and Rei struck again, then again, his hacks awkward given his mere 2 days of training with the sword and his unfortunate position half-fallen against the floor.

On that third slash, Shido cut clean, and Grant finally screamed as his body appeared to at last register the pain.

The Mauler rolled over onto his back, spasming and jerking, all four limbs now largely limp as he writhed. The fires danced and shimmered across his form, giving him the look of body in the process of immolation. Rei tried twice to lean back over, to gain enough reach to cut at Grant's neck or head and make a clean end of it, but couldn't manage it. The earlier damage to his chest had sapped the strength from his left arm, still bracing him against the ground, leaving him with no ability to do anything but watch while Grant thrashed.

Then, at long last, the Mauler's flailing subsided. The fire of is Overclock still burned, but it had only been 20 or 30 seconds since the massive cadet had triggered the Ability. It would be the simulated blood loss that got him first, that drained away his life long before those flames would die out.

Sure enough, after another 10 seconds or so, Grant's eye's rolled to the back of his head, and he went still. Rei suffered a few moments of ringing silence, hardly believing it.

Then the Arena spoke.

"Fatal Damage Accrued. Winner: Reidon Ward."

As soon as the announcement was made, the field began to fade way. The moment it did, sound returned to the world in a single deafening boom. As Rei felt himself start to drop—the pain in his ribs subsiding despite Grant's axe still being wedged between them—he managed to look around over his shoulder in time to see the pillars that had been at his back dematerialize in a flickering wash of fading light.

What he saw made his heart thud so hard in his chest it hurt.

Sarah Takeshi's distant attempt to commentate was being drowned out by the cacophony of nearly every single student in the stadium on their feet, hands coming together or waving above their heads as they cheered. Even what scattered second and third years had elected to show up for this final round of their underclassmen's matches were standing, with not a few whistles and shouts come from those cadets in particular. It only took Rei a few seconds to locate his friends, Aria's red hair a beacon to him even under her cap. Catcher looked to be cheering the hardest of all—leaping up and down and punching the air with both hands—while the two girls appeared to be hugging and crying on each other's shoulders, simultaneously dancing and shaking. He felt a pang of guilt, seeing this. He'd hated lying to them for the last 2 days, but it had hardly been his choice to make.

Hopefully they would understand better, now…

He reached the cool black steel of the projection plating, then, and like a breaking spell the exhaustion took over. Rei sagged. Dropping Shido's sword, he forced himself to twist around again and shove with both hands at the body of the axe in his side. The removal of it was painless, now that the fight was done, but the weapon would weigh no less until it was recalled. After several seconds of struggling he managed it, and the heavy *clang* of the massive blade hitting the floor was like music to his ears.

Then Rei, too, was on the ground, falling back only half-voluntarily to lie starring up at the closed roof of the Arena high, high above them.

"I won…"

He hadn't meant to say the words aloud, but the realization was too much to bear in silence. It swept away Captain Takeshi's second attempt to congratulate him, leaving his mind reeling.

"Yeah, you did…" a voice rasped from his right. "Wonder how long you'll be rubbing *that* in for…"

Rei only barely managed to lift his chin to his chest and look to where Logan Grant still lay beside him, head by his feet. The Mauler wasn't moving, his eyes closed and the back of his sweat-soaked hair resting against the floor as his breathing came heavy, the picture of a User trying to catch his wind after an intense fight.

Despite this, he still seemed willing enough to speak.

"Ward... What the *hell* was that Ability?"

Rei looked at the boy for a little while, still not hearing Takeshi's enthusiastic congratulations as the applause from the stands finally started to die.

Eventually, he brought his own head down again to rest once more against the coolness of the steel.

"You know about as much as I do," he answered. "What you saw... I don't have anything more to go on than that."

"It wasn't Arsenal Shift." It was a statement, not a question. "The change... Too complete. You got stronger... A *lot* stronger. Like you called a totally different Device..."

Rei nodded against the ground. "Yeah... It's an entire overhaul."

"And another trick."

Rei stiffened, but only for a moment.

"Tricks have their place," he answered, echoing Valera Dent's words to him from months ago.

There was brief silence before Grant responded.

"Yeah... Yeah, I suppose you've proven that much to me, at the very least."

The words, for some reason, felt like a gift, like the Mauler was releasing Rei of some weight he hadn't known he was carrying. Guilt, maybe? Or doubt? Whatever it was, even this tiny sliver of approval from the boy who'd been his greatest critic felt liberating, somehow.

Of course, Grant had to open his mouth again and ruin it.

"I still think you're a dick, though."

Rei snorted. "And I still think you're an ass."

"Fair enough," came the quiet answer.

For a little longer they stayed like that, allowing themselves the refreshing comfort of the plating beneath their bodies. Still Rei droned out the buzz of lingering applause and what sounded like an excited play-by-play rehash by Takeshi of the end of the fight. Rather, he focused on the single surreal reality, the single fact that trembled across his thoughts, so incredible it was hardly to be accepted.

He'd won. He'd won, and no one would be able to say he hadn't earned it, this time.

He was going to Sectionals.

"Ward... Can I ask you a question?"

Grant's request came low and hesitant, like a man very much unsure of the path he was walking. It surprised Rei, requiring a moment before he could give a tentative answer.

"... Sure?" he said slowly.

"You and Vi—You and Arada... You're not... You're not a thing, right?"

Rei couldn't help it, then.

He opened his eyes, accepted the brightness of the Arena lights and the lingering echoes of his name being cheered, and laughed.

CHAPTER 59

"With humanity's expansion into the stars came with it an explosion of industry and invention. A new age of Renaissance in its own right, what had once been the simple hopes of asteroid mining and the like turned—over the course of a single century—into more than half a million businesses devoted to everything from terraforming, to atmosphere-stripping, to intra-system transportation. No one desiring work couldn't find it, so long as they were willing to look. The concept of poverty faded, with those still in need suddenly being seen to by philanthropists and benefactors across every planet of every system.

After all, what else is one to do when one abruptly finds themselves in possession of more money than the entire GDP of some of the largest countries that had existed in the old world..."

A History of the Collective
Gilbert France, M.S., Ph.D.
Distributed by Central Command, Earth

Doctor Kamiya Hiroto was sitting at his desk, his back to the neon cityscape of a moonlit Tokyo through the great window behind him, when Abigail Smith—steward of the family estate—came rushing into the room with such fervor the hinged double doors slammed into the walls on either side of them as she entered. The young woman seemed not to notice, just as she hadn't appeared to notice the fact that she'd not traded her shoes for the slippers provided for workers and visitors in the genkan, the entrance of the building some hundred floors below. It mattered little, though.

For once, Hiroto didn't notice either.

"Doctor!" Abigail half-hissed, half-gasped, waving a small pad she was carrying in her right hand about. "I have something you need to see!"

"I am already watching it, Abigail," Hiroto said without looking up from the smart-glass panel that made up the top of his desk.

Indeed, as his steward hurried around to stand beside him, he replayed the recording for the fifteenth time since it had been sent to him by the Kamiya Corporation's information department. It was strange, watching the footage. For the first few years after he'd given the order to set a few of the company's servers to scour the feeds for him, Hiroto had felt some shame at the fact. He may well have been president of the conglomerate, but it had still felt wrong to repurpose even that minuscule fraction of their bandwidth towards a personal want—no, a personal *need*. Then, though, time had passed, time had healed, and it had to have been more than a decade since he'd thought of that order, since he'd given up on his search. Had it ever crossed his mind he might well have rescinded it on principle, eager to wipe even that small stain from a proud record.

Now, though… Now, Hiroto could not have been more pleased with the lapsing memory of his aging mind.

On the screen before him and Abigail he watched as the boy's lips moved, the words absent from the feed. The change in his CAD, however, was beautiful—breathtaking, even—and the brutal end to the match that followed would have been called worthy of praise by any half-decent SCT combatant on the part of both first year fighters. But it wasn't the match that Hiroto was studying. Not since his first playing of the recording had it *ever* been the match.

No. What Hiroto's eyes followed was the face of the white-haired boy, the features utterly unknown to him, and yet so familiar.

The face, and the name that hovered in one corner of the feed to label him.

Reidon Ward.

Hiroto drew a slow, calming breath, willing the terrible anger—the absolute all-consuming fury that had been simmering in his chest from the moment he'd laid eyes on the boy—to settle. It took some time, but he managed it, and at long last he reached out with a wrinkled hand to tap the desk's surface, pausing the recording on a still shot of Reidon Ward's set, focused features.

"Abigail," Hiroto said as evenly as he could manage. "Let Jasper know I need to see her. I'll be needing her services soon. And tell Keiji I want him in my office no later than tomorrow. Samantha, too. I don't care what protests she offers."

"Yes, sir," the steward answered at once, and in the corner of his eye Hiroto saw the woman pull up her NOED. "What about Sarah?"

"No," Hiroto shook his head slowly, not lifting his gaze from the image of Reidon Ward on the desk before him. "She only just finished her own Intra-Schools. We can leave her out of this for now. Just her parents." At his sides, he gripped the arms of his chair, willing himself not to crush the handsomely carved wood as Hyosube's grey-black vysetrium gems glinted in its bands around his wrists. "Don't tell them why, though. I don't want my fool son and his harpy of a wife readying more lies to feed me this time."

CHAPTER 60

"Never war for war's sake.

War for the peace that follows."

dying words of an unnamed User

Sirius System – front lines

Rei was puzzling over a particularly interesting block of script, displayed in blue on the semi-transparent smart-glass window before him, when he thought he made out a faint knocking of knuckles on wood. Seated at his desk, he looked around from his work with a slight frown, wondering if he'd imagined it. It was Sunday, just past lunch, and Viv and Catcher had elected to brave the snow he could see falling outside to make for East Center while he stayed behind.

Then the knocking came again, and he realized it was coming from the door of the suite, rather than his own room.

A brief moment of panic clutched at Rei's throat, and quick as lightning he closed out of the software examination tools and snatched the small disc of his NOED up from where it had been in the process of being scanned on his desk. He'd been careful, but was it possible Galens had caught wind of his poking around already? He'd only finally found the time to take a look at the coding in the last week or so, and it wasn't like he'd done anything wrong.

At least not yet…

Pressing the neuro-optic into the empty divot of its socket in his temple, Rei got up quickly and snatched up his jacket from the back of his chair, pulling it on as he hurried out of his room. Entering 304's common space, he heard the knocking a third time, more insistent now, and he called out as he jogged down the hall to the front door.

"Coming! I'm coming!"

Finishing with the buttons of the jacket just in time, Rei smoothed the black-and-gold fabric and grabbed his cap from where it hung on a hook in the wall to his right. His last check-in with Ameena Ashton had him topping out at just over 5'7", still not tall enough to feel great about walking around even Kanes without the 4 inches or so the hat gave him.

Tucking it on quick, Rei straightened his posture and finally took hold of the door handle, pulling it open firmly.

Instead of the representative of the school he had worried about, though, he found himself face to face with Aria.

"Oh!" he said, brightening at once. "Hey! What are you doing here?"

"Hey," she offered him one of her brilliant smiles. "I'm actually here to see—" Aria stopped, though, her gaze dropping and her head cocking to one side. "Rei... What are you wearing?"

"Don't worry about it," he said with a shrug. "I thought you might be one of the school staff." He lowered his voice. "I've finally had a chance to poke around in our NOED coding. It's pretty state-of-the-art, but there are a few places I think I could smooth things out to work better with Type Shift and—"

"You thought I was an officer..." Aria interrupted him with a bemused raising of one eyebrow. "And you decided to answer the door dressed like... that?"

"Yeah?" Rei asked, frowning as he looked down at himself. "What's wrong with how I'm—?"

He froze, mortified.

"Pants," he muttered. "Pants would be helpful."

"Very," Aria said with a laugh.

"Don't move," he said, starting to turn back for his room. "I'll be right back."

"No need. I'm not actually here to see you."

Rei paused, frowning. "You're not?" He hoped he didn't sound *too* disappointed. "Viv and Catcher aren't here either. They're off training."

Aria shook her head, the braid of her red hair swinging behind her neck a little. "Not here for them either. I've already invited them. Can I come in?"

Invited them? Rei repeated silently to himself.

At a loss, he moved dumbly aside to allow her entrance. Aria kept her smile as she stepped by him, striding down the hall past the kitchen and into the common room. To his surprise, she turned and made directly for the first door in the left wall, pausing only long enough to doublecheck the name on the plate in the center of it before lifting her head, straightening her shoulders, and reaching up to knock three times in quick succession.

There was a noise from inside the room, and Rei watched with confused interest as, after a little while, the door opened a crack for the occupant to peer out.

"Laurent?" Chancery Cashe sounded more than a little surprised as she widened the sliver further to reveal a baggy t-shirt and shorts, her silver hair in a loose bun behind her head.

"Cashe, can I talk to you for a minute?" Aria asked.

Cashe hesitated, then nodded, stepping out of the room looking utterly perplexed. She paused before shutting the door, though, catching sight of Rei and blinking.

"Ward... What are you wearing?"

Rei cursed, then turned and bolted into his own room, cap and jacket still on over his boxer briefs. By the time he'd stripped out of the regulars in favor of his own shirt and a pair of sweatpants, the two girls had taken a seat across from each other on the room's couches.

"Me?" Cashe was asking in disbelief. "You want *me?*"

"I do," Aria answered with a brief nod, and Rei realized he had missed some important part of the conversation.

"But... why?"

Aria smiled. "I want my squad to be balanced, Cashe. Right now there's me—a Phalanx—as well as a top-tier Saber and Duelist. I want your range. I need a Lancer who can hold their own in a fight."

It hit Rei like lightning.

"You got selected?!" he demanded excitedly from the doorway of his room.

Aria looked around at him, bemused. "Why do you sound so surprised?"

"No! I mean... I'm not. I just didn't realize they'd announced the squad-leaders."

Across from Aria, Cashe frowned at him. "How could you not know? They sent a class-wide notice over an hour ago."

Rei stared at her, not comprehending.

Then, at last, he saw the blinking notification in the corner of his frame he'd missed in the distraction of Aria's arrival and his wardrobe mishap.

Rei cursed. Of all the times he could have chosen to unplug... No. That didn't matter now. In a rush he selected the message, the frame of the alert opening in a short, square panel before his eyes.

ATTENTION ALL FIRST YEAR CADETS.

The following individual qualifiers have been selected as squad-leaders for the upcoming Collegiate Sectionals SCT:

Aria Laurent - Phalanx: C6 - 1-A

Laquita Martin - Duelist: C3 - 1-B

Kastro Vademe - Lancer: C4 - 1-B

"B-But if it's a Lancer you want, there's better than *me*." The girls had continued their conversation while Rei caught up, Aria having turned her back to him again to listen to Cashe trip over her protest. "There's Kay, for one. Kay Sandree."

"You beat Kay Sandree, Cashe," Aria reminded her gently.

"It was a fluke," the girl said at once, shaking her head aggressively as though to deny the very fact of the statement. "She wasn't at her best. I got lucky."

"No. You didn't." Aria reached up, swiping something over to Cashe that popped into her frame in a blaze of light. "I spoke to Valera Dent. She's been keeping tabs on the extra training hours the first years have been keeping. For extra logged hours in East and West, there's a leading pack of five people."

Five? Rei's brow furrowed, not having expected this.

"Rei is at the top," Aria continued. "I don't think that will surprise you anymore. After that, there's me, Viv, and Catcher—"

Makes sense, Rei thought with a short nod.

"—all basically tied for third."

Rei had to work to keep his jaw from dropping, not understanding for a moment. It wasn't until he caught sight of Cashe's averted gaze that it dawned on him, though.

All those days... All those times he had assumed the girl had just been in her room...

"Cashe... Do you mind telling me how old you are?" Aria asked gently.

It was an odd question, Rei thought with a frown, looking between the two girls. Cashe, though, jerked like she'd just been slapped, and some of the fire he'd seen in her on that very first day of school returned as she glared around at Aria.

"Did the captain tell you that, too?"

Aria shook her head. "No. This is all me. Rei and the others... They've mentioned you had a chip on your shoulder, when you first met."

"Aria!" Rei hissed in disbelief, but she ignored him with a wave, not looking away from Cashe.

Cashe's purple-green eyes, though, were on Rei, but the anger that had been burning there looked to have been abruptly replaced with regret.

"I still don't think I've apologized enough for—"

"He'll be fine," Aria interrupted, and this time she graced Rei with a glance back and the flash of a smile. "You're hardly the worst he's had to deal with." She turned back to Cashe. "But I'm right, aren't I? You're not our age, are you?"

There was a long, tense moment of silence, Rei looking on as suspicion scraped at him.

"No," the answer finally came. "I'm not. I'll be turning 20 in February."

It clicked, then.

"You're one of the exceptions," Rei said with awe, seeing Cashe in a whole new light. "You failed your CAD-Assignment Exam. The first time, I mean."

Cashe nodded unsteadily. It took her a while, as though the girl needed to build herself up, but when she finally spoke it with the breathless rush of someone who'd too long held onto a secret.

"In the final portion. The... uh... The psychological assessment." She looked around nervously, as though worried even this obtuse allusion to the brutal interview with the MIND might have agents of the AI popping up from behind the couches to drag her away. "It hurt. A lot, honestly. Being a User was all I wanted. All I ever wanted. It was so important to me." Her features grew harder. "But I learned. I was told, in that third part, where I was lacking. I spent a year training, a year conditioning. Non-stop. Every day."

"And you passed your second attempt," Aria finished for her with an appreciative nod. "Something that's almost unheard of."

"Only because people who've spent their whole life thinking they're owed everything can't stand back up when they're faced with the fact that they aren't," Cashe responded, sounding a little bitter. She caught herself, though, lifting a hand to her mouth as her eyes grew wide. "I'm sorry..." Her eyes drifted to Rei. "That sounded awful... I just meant that—"

"That people who've had things handed to them their whole life can't handle reality," Rei finished for her with a shrug. "I get it, Cashe. Don't worry. We're in the same boat, there." He offered her a crooked grin, crossing his arms to lean against the frame of his door. "Explains why you hated me when we first met, if you believed I'd been spoon-fed a spot in the first year class."

"I didn't hate you," Cashe mumbled, looking at her where her hands were fidgeting in her lap. "I just thought you didn't deserve it. That's all."

"And how am I doing now?" Rei asked with a chuckle.

Though she didn't look up, the Lancer managed a sliver of a smile. "Better."

Rei laughed at that, and Aria took advantage to redirect the conversation back to the purpose of her visit.

"You've just answered your own question, Cashe," she said kindly, scooting forward to lean over the table towards the girl. "You asked me why I want *you*? It's because if I've learned anything in the past couple months it's that potential and talent are rarely going to beat out will and work ethic. If you gave me the choice between someone who *is* good and someone *trying to be* great, I would pick the latter every time. Kay is incredible, and I consider her a friend, but she won't have any trouble finding a spot on either Vademe's or Martin's team. She *might* be able to be great… But when I look at your training log, Cashe, I know *for a fact* that your becoming one of the best Lancers on the planet—maybe the System—is only a matter of time and patience."

Cashe's fiddling had stopped. She was staring at Aria now, clearly overwhelmed as astonishment, gratitude, and doubt all flashed across her face. Her eyes looked a little wet, suddenly, and it was Rei's turn to avert his gaze.

"Yes."

The answer came so quietly, he wasn't surprised when Aria voiced her uncertainty.

"Yes?" she asked. "As in…?"

"Yes," Cashe repeated, more firmly this time, and Rei looked around to find her expression set again, even if one corner of her t-shirt sleeve was a little stretched from rubbing at reddened eyes. "I'll do it. I'm in."

Aira brought her hands together excitedly. "Oh! Great! I'm so glad! Do you already have plans over winter leave? The school wants squads to train for Team Battle and Wargame formats, but it's not technically mandatory. Viv, Catcher, and I are all staying, and maybe our Brawler and Mauler, depending on who I select."

"I can stay," Cashe confirmed slowly, but her eyes had once again drifted to Rei over Aria's shoulder. "But if you need a Brawler, wouldn't the obvious choice be—?"

"Great!" Aria said again, getting to her feet quickly and sliding around the couch. "I can't wait! We've got one more week of school, so I'll reach out in the next few days about coordinating training times." She graced Cashe with such a brilliant smile it almost made Rei jealous. "Thanks. I have a feeling that with a couple more strong picks, we're going to be unstoppable."

"Oh." Cashe looked confused, but pleased. "Yeah. Of course."

And with that, offering nothing more than a last wave goodbye and solemn nod to Rei, Aria was headed for the entrance of the suite again. He stared after her, dumbstruck, at a complete loss as she turned the handle and stepped out into the hall.

Then she was gone, leaving the door open behind her.

Leaving it open…?

"Ward!"

Rei started and looked around as Cashe hissed at him, her purple-green eyes wide as they stared him down.

"What are you doing?!" the Lancer demanded, like she couldn't believe what she was seeing. "Don't let her walk away! Go after her!"

Rei gaped at her a full 3 seconds, momentarily paralyzed by the snub, the abrupt departure, and Cashe's sudden energy in his presence.

And then he was running, bolting out of the room into the hall, catching sight of a trailing red braid vanishing around the corner at the west end of the corridor.

"Aria!" he shouted, engaging his Speed spec to chase after her. In barely a breath he'd reached the turn, skidding across the carpeted floor as he took it…

… and running right past where Aria had taken to leaning against the wall just around the bend, grinning at him as he nearly sprinted by.

"Took you long enough," she giggled as Rei stumbled to a halt before turning on her. "I was surprised you let me out of the room."

Rei glowered at her. "Not funny," he muttered. "You seriously made me think I wasn't invited onto the team…"

"Oh? And who says you are?"

Aria's mischievous smile sparkled so brightly, Rei had a hard time keeping his composure.

"Is this because I hid Type Shift from you?" he asked, narrowing his eyes at her. "How long are you and Viv going to punish me for that? I told you Colonel Guest put me under a gag order. The ISCM wanted a little time to get ahead of the news that a *C*-Ranker had developed a User-Unique Ability."

"Uh-huh," Aria said, the smile not even faltering. "And what part of those excuses makes you think Viv and I aren't going to run you into the ground about this until your dying days regardless?"

"You forgave *Catcher*!" Rei countered in exasperation. "He knew like… *fifteen minutes* after I did!"

Aria shrugged, pulling herself off the wall and heading down the corridor, towards the stairs at the far end. "Catcher got punished enough in the two days you avoided us. He's taken his licks."

Rei, thinking fast as Aria moved by him, considered his options. In the end he had only one card left to play. He'd been holding onto it, looking for the right time, but now seemed like as good an opportunity as was ever going to present itself.

"Fine," he said, effecting a casual air while half-turning to watch her walk away. "If you're not gonna invite me, then I'm not going to ask you the question I've been wanting to."

Aria froze almost mid-stride, and Rei had to compose his face to hide the glee of success as she looked over her shoulder at him.

"What question?"

"Well if I answered that, it would kinda defeat the purpose of my threat, right?"

Aria glared, staring him down as though willing him to break under the sheer power of her gaze. Rei didn't flinch, knowing her too well, and even when she shrugged and turned away again he said nothing more.

"Fine, keep your question," she told him with forced nonchalance, heading for the stairs again. "It's not like it's important to me."

"Of course, of course," he said solemnly, nodding along in mock agreement. All the while, he counted Aria's steps.

One, two, three…

She'd made it a solid ten paces before whirling around again, hands clenched at her sides.

"Ugh! Fine! You're on the team if you want to be! Now what's your stupid question?!"

Rei grinned from ear to ear, hoping Aria couldn't hear the frantic beating of his heart that he could feel in his hands.

"You're staying over leave, right?"

Aria frowned. "Yeah… I told you that last week I was planning to regardless…"

"Want to go into the city with me?"

Aria blinked. "The city? Castalon?"

"If there's a closer one, I'm not familiar with it."

Aria stuck her tongue out at him, then looked serious. "That might be fun. Viv said she's never been, and I don't think Catcher has either. Maybe we can—"

"I don't want to go with Viv and Catcher, Aria. I want to go with you. *Just* you."

Aria stared at him for a good long moment, mouth hanging open slightly. Then, slowly, in layered shades her face began to brighten, realization dawning on her as she blushed.

By the time she gave a single, unsteady nod, her entire face was nearing the color of her hair again.

"Is that a yes?" Rei asked, feeling his own ears growing hot despite his bravado.

Another shaky nod.

"Sorry. I need verbal confirmation."

A mumbled answer.

"Still not getting it."

"IT'S A YES, YOU JERK!"

Aria's yell had Rei laughing almost at once, which obviously didn't do anything to help her embarrassment.

"Shut up," she grumbled. "It's not smooth to make fun of a girl you just asked out..."

"Who says I asked you out?"

Aria's eyes went wide. "Wait... Did you not? You didn't mean...?"

"Oh, I totally did. I'm just saying you shouldn't assume things."

"Reidon Ward, if it wouldn't get me expelled, I would use Hippolyta to skewer you to the wall and leave you there until someone found you."

Rei only smiled broader, at that.

Then, though, he felt his humor slip ever so slightly.

"We still need one more, right?"

Aria blinked at him, confused. "One more what?"

"One more member. On your team."

"Oh," she frowned. "Smooth change to topic. But... Yeah."

"A Mauler, you said? You're sure?"

Aria hesitated, then nodded. "I think so. Cashe and I will form a solid defensive core, while you and Viv can provide speed and versatility. *Especially* versatility." She eyed Shido pointedly. "Catcher offers a good balance of everything, making him adaptable, but that leaves us without an aggressor. Without someone who won't have trouble charging right into a fight."

"That definitely sounds like a Mauler..."

"It does," Aria agreed with a grimace. "Problem is there aren't too many impressive options. I was thinking Easton. Or maybe Gillian North. Neither is a perfect candidate, but with the rest of our lineup we should be fine."

"Aria…" Rei said slowly. "There's one. There's one perfect candidate."

Aria hesitated, looking a little disconcerted. "Rei… You're not suggesting…"

"Yeah. I am. You want the all-star line-up, then that's what you build. No half-measures." He pointed to his temple to indicate his NOED. "Viv knows what suite number is his. If you tell her why you're asking, I'm sure she'll give it to you."

Aria looked unconvinced. "You're sure? You're *absolutely* sure?"

"Not even a little bit. But it's your team, not mine, and if you want to know one thing I *am* sure of, it's that if you don't get to him soon, someone else will beat you to it. He might not have qualified individually, but you and I—and everyone, really—knows he should have."

Aria took a breath, then nodded. "Okay. Then I'll ask him."

"Okay. Good."

"Good."

They stood there for a second, then, suddenly not sure what else there was to say, cheeks and ears still blushing.

Eventually, Rei decided to quit while he was ahead.

"I'm gonna get back to work," he said as casually as he could. "Don't forget: Castalon. It's a date."

Aria's redness redoubled, and her voice was just a little high when she answered. "Yeah. It's a date."

With a last smile, Rei turned away from her, looking forward to punching the air in silent success the moment he rounded the corner in the hall.

He didn't make it two steps before Aria called out to him again.

"Oh. Rei."

He glanced back at her. She was watching him with a bit more of her normal smile.

"I don't know if you heard. They released the recordings of the Intra-Schools to the public feeds a few days ago."

"Yeah, I did," Rei turned to face her fully. "Been watching a few, actually."

"Have you seen it, then?"

"Seen what?"

Aria looked suddenly unsure of herself. "In the forums. And the video comments. You haven't seen it?"

"I don't read them. Seen *what*, Aria?"

She paused, chewing on her tongue for a bit before seeming to give in. "Your name. What they're calling you. It's not an official field name, or anything, but that's how these things often start."

Rei stared at her, stunned.

"A name?" he asked quietly. "The viewers are giving me a name?"

"Yeah." she nodded. "And it's a good one, too."

Rei only hesitated a moment before asking. "What is it?"

Aria smiled. "Apparently there's rumors circulating that you're a favorite of Valera Dent. They say you're the 'heir apparent' to the strongest A-Type in the system." She brought a hand up to form a half-circle with thumb and fingers at an angle atop her head, like the start of a crown. "They're calling you 'the Iron Prince'."

THANK YOU! PLEASE READ!

After months of effort, back-and-forth, and editing, the first installment of this crazy collaboration that is the *Warformed Universe* has finally hit the shelves! We are so grateful to you—yes you, reading this right now—for making the investment in and taking the time for *Iron Prince*, joining us on this sci-fi cyberpunk adventure. It's your support that makes it possible for writers like the pair of us to practice our craft, and your involvement that makes this journey so enjoyable for us.

On that subject, a few notes:

First: **Please, please, consider rating and reviewing Iron Prince on Amazon, as well as any of your other favorite book sites.** Many people don't know that there are thousands of books published every day, most of those in the USA alone. Over the course of a year, a quarter of a million authors will vie for a small place in the massive world of print and publishing. We fight to get even the tiniest traction, fight to climb upward one inch at a time towards the bright light of bestsellers, publishing contracts, and busy book signings.

Thing is, we need all the help we can get, and that's where wonderful readers like you come in!

Second: If you want to join our growing community, be sure to join Wraithmarked Creative's private Reader's Group on Facebook! Both of us are active participants in the group, so tag us with any questions, check out all the other awesome books Wraithmarked is publishing in the coming months, and chat with those authors as well!

Regardless of whether or not you choose to review, reach out, or support us elsewhere, thank you again for taking the time to read *Iron Prince*, and we will see you in the sequel!

Your biggest fans,
Bryce O'Connor & Luke Chmilenko